VINCENT VALLANO[1]

CATAPULT SOUL

---

[1] Brian Celio[2]

[2] ???[22]

The following songs are listed in order of appearance. Each are owned and protected by their respective copyright claimants. They are used in *Catapult Soul* under non-exclusive rights.

The format for the songs is: "Song Title"; Artist; Album; Date of Publication; Authorship on Application (if available); Copyright Claimant(s); Registration Number; Registration Date

"Into the Flames"; Inhuman Clamour; Freeing the Old Artificer; 2001-11-09; J.A.A.J. Palindrome Records; SR0000338617; 2001-12-20

"Never Coming Back"; My Lonesome Exile; Take the Easy Way Out; 1993-06-04; Mitch Franzen, Brent Hall, Ryan Trump; Grunted Music Publishing, B.V.; AP0000699234; 1993-07-09

"At What Cost?"; Acronym of Pity; Help Me Help Yourself; 1998-09-17; Steven Hartline, Frances DeMilo, Nathan Miller, Robert Natz; Am-Scray, LLC; AP0001418860; 1998-10-30

"Fork It Over"; Pissant and the Pests: F.U.; 1996-06-14; Zach Huth, Justin McFarlane, Ryan McFarlane, Kris Royal; Playground Crew Records; AP0000119113; 1996-08-26

"Blacktop Shattered Dreams"; Sin Seizure; Obscure Mechanism; 1977-10-07; Chris Alvarado d.b.a. Primal Curse Music; AP0001622159; 1977-12-16

"Rot No More"; Crossed; Once a Believer, Always a Believer; 2000-03-10; Del Villavincencio Apple, Joshua Giddens, Matt Em, Kelsey Thurber; Hopewood Music; AP0001448641; 2000-05-12

"Options for the Optionless"; Yelp!; Poison Their Food with Thirst; 1981-02-09; Doug "Dirty Birdy" Bridges; Pubic Records; SR000192754; 1981-11-13

"Somnambulance"; Strung Out; Suburban Teenage Wasteland Blues; 1996-02-27; Jim Cherry, Jason Cruz, Jake Kiley, Jordan Lieberman, Robert Ramos; Unagi Music, Jim Cherry, Jason Cruz, Jake Kiley, Jordan Lieberman, Robert Ramos; PA0001010947; 2000-05-08

"Because You're Fake"; Backhand Brutality; Scratching the Surface of Something Strange; 1998-10-09; Jeannette Carnese, Tomaso Fontana, Mercedes Hoffman, Matthew Shellgren, Alfonse Yannuzzo; Scozio's Mafia, LLC; AP0000194954; 1998-11-06

"I Could've Sworn That Somebody Loved Me"; The Snippets; Curiosity as a Novelty; 1987-04-10; Elizabeth Michel; AP000014291; 1987-09-18

"Na Rosa senza Oduri"; Alessandro Abbate, featuring Laura MacNamara; Live at Teatro Massimo; 1996-11-22; Ericka Amor Rossani and Giuseppe Amato; Nciuria Musica; SC0000114460; 1997-12-12

"Down This Road"; Zero Down; Fat Music Vol. V: Live Fat, Die Young; 2001-03-06; Jim Cherry, Shawn Dewey, John McCree, Milo Todesco

"Hymnanthem"; Hyperocrisy; Better Dead than Read; 1984-04-13; George Bradley, Paul Hunter, Warren "Red" Kiefer, Xavier "X" Zielke; 1985-04-12

"Makes Me Sick"; The Blackhole Mothers; Excuse My Wrench: WHAP!; 1992-07-01; Sophia Akom, Lana Alley, Dalia Gracia, Karina Lambert, Jamie Morgan; Femalcontent Records; SR000340802; 1992-11-20

"Heroin of the Night"; The Dopest Kids on the Block; Grade-A Playground Meat; 1995-08-25; Jon "J-On" Alsippi, Carlos "Beans" Portilla, John "Stan" Tokarczyk, Von "Lil Whopper" Tumak; SR0000126885; 1999-06-11

"Dance Medicine"; Bree Brunette and the Blonde Hive; On a Moonlit Bridge; 1957-10-20; Justina Carlone, Lori Jean, Pauline Landeros, Shilene Norris, Liz Wilson; Honey Sweet Music Entertainment, Inc. (employer for hire); SR000203377; 2001-11-16

"Envision Your Reality"; B-Love; P.M.A.; 2001-05-25; In the Box Records, LLC (employer for hire); SR000229945; 2001-07-27

"Someone Called a Friend"; One Step Ahead; The Art of Coming to Terms; 1999-06-10; Thomas "T-Bone" Lawson, Mike "Shark" Markovic, Bryce "Knife" Stuiano; P.O.G.O. Records; SR00022122122; 1999-07-16

"Our Cultural Devolution"; Peeled Off Labels; Psychological Term Oil; 1977-06-04; Simon Fruehauf, Russ Jung, Steven Palaver; Them's Fightin' Songs, Ltd.; AP00002012982; 1978-05-26

"The Parade of Evil Persuasion"; Bare Knuckle Discussion; Tales from the Victim Vault; 2002-04-19; Matt Hewitt, Jason Ott, Mike Schlegel, Paul Schumacher; AP0000210523; 2002-08-23

"Marked"; Bad Religion; Stranger than Fiction; 1994-08-01; Brett Gurewitz; EMI Blackwood Music, Inc., Sick Muse Songs; PA0000744958; 1995-02-21

"Close Your Eyes, Child"; Hawa Halo; Our Cloud of Witnesses; 1981-09-11; United Sibling Records, Inc.; SR0000129401; 1981-12-11

"Hands of the Clan"; Chain 40; How to Be a Kid Again; 1995-04-21; James Blazowich, Nate Pietra, Ollie Zimmerman; Do Nothing Records; 1995-08-25

"My Past Ate Me Alive"; The Static Take; Nostalgic Rev; 1990-02-09; Holey Jeans Record Company (employer for hire); SR0000225787; 1990-04-20

"Insanity Deluxe Package"; Death to Hope; From Hell's Heart; 1998-12-04; Jesse Glamp, Tim Gordon, Adam Paletto, Jeremiah Rigoni; Plumb Sick Records; AP0000166163; 2001-08-24

"Covered in Grease"; C(A)S; Skinhead Alley; 1979-06-08; Colin Grymes; Melted Rubber Publication; AP0000947821; 1979-10-12

"Mouthin' off Again"; Zippy Zane; Folk Ballads for and by the Happily Mentally Deranged; 1968-04-12; Zippy Zane; RE0000727272; 1997-01-03

"Naked Echo of the Past"; Heartolins; In the Ashes of Our Wake; 1999-10-15; When I Make Power Music, Inc.; AP00002725922; 2000-12-17

* * *

Front and back covers: illustrated by ~~Brian Celio~~; formatted and designed by Laura Sheetz; pre-press development by Daniel Jason Decker

Spine: Does this book even have one?—

Make it past p. 418 to find out—

But don't look now—

You did it anyway >:)

IMPORTANT DISCLAIMER: Celebrities, illegal suggestions, and terroristic threats found within Catapult Soul are used ~~entirely~~ in a ~~fictional~~ context; otherwise, it would be dangerous to the status quo.

AN EVEN MORE IMPORTANT DISCLAIMER: Caveat lector.

THE MOST IMPORTANT DISCLAIMER EVER: Caviar collector, beware!

For more information, please visit:

www.facebook.com/~~briancelio~~fans
www.myspace.com/~~briancelio~~
www.goodreads.com/~~briancelio~~

LANGUAGE KEY

[ara]: Arabic

[deu]: German

[fre]: French

[grc]: Ancient Greek

[heb]: Hebrew

[inl]: Invisible Language

[ita]: Italian

[lat]: Latin

[pgh]: Pittsburghese

[scn]: Sicilian

[spa]: Spanish

[squ]: Squirrelese

[tha]: Thai

[unl]: Unused Language

[urd]: Urdu

DEADICATIONS

Political: Tresca, Sacco, Vanzetti

~~Art~~istic: Joyce, Nabokov, Nietzsche

Personal: Dad (WCH), Wimp-Wimp (ILY), God (SOS)

From different angles and for different reasons, these three
trinities set Catapult Soul in motion, forced me to endure it,
and challenged me to complete it with no regrets. May their
sacrifices seep into the he~~art~~ of every reader.

A special thanks to Steve Davis in San Diego for showing
me how to look at the other side of my hand. You solved my
"let it go" riddle, and for that, I'm forever grateful.

DIS CONTENTS

PART I

HOOFS OFF GOD

"Like a promise whispered from far away,
We lean in closer and fall into the flames,
That's where this story begins: in a clear blue hell,
With flames spun like clouds, we succeed to fail,
Laughing, without smiles; crying, without tears,
Watching years turn to ash in mirrors,
Into the flames (we will fall blindly)..." [1]

...History, lie of our lives, mire of our loins. Our sins, our souls. Hiss-tih-ree: the tip of the pen taking a trip of three steps (with one glide) down the chronicle to trap a slick, sibilant character. Hiss. (Ss.) Tih. Ree.

He was a pig, a plain pig, in the morning, standing five feet ten on one hoof. He was a pig in slacks. He was a pig in school. He was a pig on the dotted line. But in my eyes it's always the ones signing dotted lines that become pigs.

Did this pig have a precursor? He did, indeed he did. In point of fact, dating all the way back to the Biblical Age. Oh where? About everywhere you look there's pigs giving that fancy ol' snake a chase. Yeah, yeah, yeah, you can always count on a fuckin' pretentious sarcastican for a fancy prose style. Get over it and into this:

Ladies and gentlemen of my fury, Exhibit #1 is what the demons, the misinformed, simple, ignoble-winged demons, envy. Look at this tangle of thorns. As a matter of fact, why don't you stick your hands deep inside so I can have some blood for proof? Just kidding, ddikts.

Exhibit #1. It's 1857. The event: Henry Bessemer, a big fat pig from Charlton, England, purchases a lucrative patent from William Kelly. William Kelly wasn't a big fat pig like Henry Bessemer. Oh no, William Kelly was a tall muscular Pittsburgher of Irish descent. The transaction between the big fat pig and the tall muscular Pittsburgher concluded a series of events filled with fiery hearts and fiery metals. First things first: both were inventors, ambitious tube-tilters fond of the art of transformation. Second things second: neither knew they were working on the same metallurgic process at the same time. (This was 70 years before the first transatlantic phone call between New York City and London, therefore communication still traveled like rafts in a sea.) Henry Bessemer, the big fat pig, had been working in the rainy but opulent suburbs of London. Everything went rather well. But in the poor, immigrant-filled city of Pittsburgh, William Kelly's warehouse (where he did experiments while running a dry goods and commission company) mysteriously went up in flames. Some yinzers[2] considered it an unfortunate turn of events for the well-liked man. The religiously witty said

---

[1] Lyrics from "Into the Flames" by Inhuman Clamour, from the album *Freeing the Old Artificer*
[2] Pittsburghers who speak Pittsburghese and practice the local working-class culture

it must be an *ironic* sign from God, seeing as Kelly's steel-making process involved smelting pig iron in a blast furnace. And woah! what a combustion of flames he finally witnessed! Still, Kelly raised thankful eyes to the sky as he stepped through a curtain of smoke and took safety in a weed-choked meadow out back, which, despite being fully exposed to the sun of God, genuflected to the winds of fire. Sure, Kelly's business and lab had transformed into a pile of ashes. And with prior debts, he now had to declare bankruptcy. But when the smoke cleared, he still retained his burning vision (a brilliant idea in incubation), which he surmised would ultimately move us from the Iron Age into the Steel Age.

Not long after declaring bankruptcy, Kelly was sitting in front of a new fire finery (a small furnace to test his metal-melting) when the flames blew the solution right into his eyes: he now overstood how to perfect his brilliant idea! Wasting no time, Kelly rushed down to the Patent Office, which, at this point in time, was located in the Interior Department; in 1836, Blodgett's Hotel (the former location) burnt down, destroying over 7,000 patents along with Robert Fulton's full-color drawings. (It's like these historical retards didn't know the meaning of "flame-retardant," right?) Wait—that was ignorant. Fire is no laughing matter. In a drunken attempt to appear womanly, my neighbor tried to burn her pubes off when she was fifteen, but it hurt too much to get it completely smooth. My friend had sex with her two years later and said her clit looked like a chestnut. I've been pro-bush ever since. Anyway, once arriving at the Patent Office, William Kelly weaved like a hot wire through the queue. 'Excuse me...Pardon me...Gadda brilliant idea...Finally figured it out...Gonna change the world (just as long as nobody beats me to the punch).' And this is when Kelly became acquainted with Bessemer and his copypig work. Naturally, a fist-and-hoof fight for the rights ensued. But turns out Bessemer hadn't beaten Kelly to the punch, nor did Bessemer throw the best punches, for the Patent Judges awarded the match to the underdog. And the trophy? The patent! Oh yeah, muscle-man Kelly managed to ram that slow snub-snouted pig onto a spit—just above the flames of failure! Roasting, the pig squealed! *Oink! Eek! Oink! Errrrr!* It started getting piping hot between England and America! The foreign pig was on the ropes! on the spit! down for the count! broiling to a degree of desperation! And that's when the quicksilver swine decided to use his weight to reverse the situation: Bessemer took hold of Kelly's hardship and singed his nuts in the fire! Or as my Sicilian mother (a clean-mouthed Christian) would say, *'Chiddu arrusti u so pisci ntê sciammi r'incendiu!'* [3] Exactly, Ma. But here in America we don't explain things through proverbs. We're apt to say Nay to complexity, and Yea to complexes. So when Richpig Bessemer – purchased Poorboy Kelly's patent – it was what we Americans would call – "a mutually festive buyout." *Diu,*[4] what a delicious deal. *Mmm,* a marvelous makeshift meal. (*Sss,* such a sterling steal.) As a result, that filthy fuckin' swine took the American vanguard in the commercial production of steel via Kelly's brilliant idea: *air blow the impurities out of pig iron!*

---

[3] [scn] That one roasts his fish in the flames of the fire! [Meaning, someone who takes advantage of another's misfortune]
[4] [scn] God

~~(This Exhibit is to be scratched from the record. It's 1888. The event: W.K. dies in obscurity. In his lifetime, he earned less than 1/20 of Bessemer's profit from the patent, which, for the plumper pig, stuffed $10 MILL into his piggybank.)~~

Exhibit #2. It's 1889. The event: An agile architect named George "The Atlas Assassin" Fuller completes the six-story Tacoma Building in Chicago, a Bessemer-backed project. For the first time in architectural history, the building's outer layer isn't there to keep its weight in check but merely to keep the flies out of Bessemer's coffee-mud whenever he stopped by to shoot the breeze with other boss hogs like himself. But despite the warm coffee in his pot-belly, his 350 LBS of pork, and the freshly added weight of English knighthood, Sir Henry was always cold, for he now had 77 YRS crammed under his royal belt, which meant his thermoregulation was no longer working like it used to. Poor ol' pig had to wrap himself up in a blanket. *Zzzzzz...grunt, grunt...zzzzzz...grunt, gru—*

WAKE UP, LADIES AND GENTLEMEN OF MY FURY!—wake up and observe the final exhibit, Exhibit #3. It's 1902. The event: That same aerial architect, George "Eyes in the Sky" Fuller, now dead, but through earthly finances, sends the flames of the Industrial Revolution soaring even higher with the completion of the Flatiron Building in New York City. Shaped like a piece of pie, and infamous for lifting skirts—(gentlemen, please keep your eyes off the pies)—the Flatiron Building stretches 87 FT wide on East 23rd, 173 FT on 5th, 190 FT on Broadway, and above all, shoots up 285 FT closer to Heaven: nothing but Sir Bessemer Steel Beams. And right then, back then—*BANG!*—the starting-gun shot in the race to snag God by the ankle...

...But here it is, nearly a century later, and no hand has ever copped a feel. There's *some* good news however. See, when those ol' carious cutthroats started climbing ladders, while fast modes of communication were beginning to globalize, it put enough slits in the sky for a large slice of the world to lay eyes on my hometown: Pittsburgh, Pennsylvania. The smoky old town soon became known for its steel mills, although only three remain in operation; and its sad smoky skies, which, due to the decline of the mills, have gradually cheered up; and its 455 bridges, many painted Aztec-gold but varied by graffiti; and on a natural note, the three murky rivers, which converge at The Point: by the grate of God, the triplet rivers gave birth to a V-shaped plot of land on which a central business district (colloquially expressed as *dahntahn*) blossomed into clusters of sky-scraping stalks of steel. Yep, that's Pittsburgh, Pennsylvania: a traditional American city—a unique beautiful city—right in the heart, where three rivers converge and a large water fountain rockets out purities and invitations!

But like pigs in a poke, the precarious hills surrounding the city have remained virtually unknown to the world. Save for the affirmations of the hallow souls who subsist at the nadir of the dells, and thus can confirm a bottom, in my eyes (if you can still stand my eyes, for I'm observing under progression), from certain angles, the hills, fading and falling in green and gray decay, seem to drop into nowhere. Straight down into a Godforsaken nowhere! But hallelujah: throughout Pittsburgh's precarious hills, the County Belt System—a confusing, incomplete helix of colored-coded signs—

along with unkempt tunnels, bridges, inclines, lightrails, alleyways, and highways, provide ample ways for whomever to reach wherever.

Whenever looking through the eyes of Dahntahn Pittsburgh, facing southeast, the borough of Verna sits atop Mt. Brennan, a prominent hill with soiled houses dented into it. At the bottom, in the valley, there's a black truss bridge rusting above the Monongahela River that best connects the city to Verna, the first southeast borough outside the city proper. Once you cross the bridge...and make your way over to a secondary eastbound road (as opposed to the suburbia-bound Parkway East), you'll navigate through the faded neighborhoods of Avelwood, Dellwood, and Monport...then gradually ascend Mt. Brennan, passing through three leaning red lights...til you reach a looping exit ramp that merges onto Bullitt Avenue, which, from this view, runs due north into my neighborhood in Verna. By way of the road, the distance from dahntahn to my house is four miles. It's far enough away from the clickity-clanks and zippity-zips of the T (a lightrail subway that looks like a caterpillar crawling up and down hills)...the hungry growls of Greyhounds ever merging into the domain of cars whose engines both whimper like a puppy and ululate like a wolf...the thundering and beeping of construction curtailing every other block...the buzz and hum of electricity burning in too many spots to discriminate—all of which is accompanied by the daily grind of yinzers: bums jangling cans and playing guitars for suited hawks flying by...sidewalk roamers shilling and shrilling to anyone within earshot...aggravated drivers stuck in snail-speed traffic, beeping horns, blaring music, blurting curses: butting horns!...and lastly—(a deep breath: *huuuh!*)—the scores of lost souls, nondescript souls, wandering through The Steel City Labyrinth, silently calling out to anyone who knows the way out. HELLO!!!...Oh!...oh!...oh...(oh)...( )...*mum-mum phum-phum*—yes! Verna is far enough away from dahntahn that, at best, the cacophony sounds like a mild grumble.

Yet from several areas, where the crows only have to fly three miles to reach dahntahn, Verna is, in certain areas, close enough to view the upper portions of the skyscrapers. Behind them, up a bit higher, you can even see the fireworks set off for our beloved Buccos! Two things help this grand-slam view: at the bottom of Mt. Brennan, Monport's smoky business district hugs along the Mon snaking southbound, and Dellwood and Avelwood (neighbor 'woods holding each other's boughs) are flat residential areas. Altogether, it creates a brilliant twilight for Verna's frontside and hilltops. Pittsburgh's high-and-mighties reflect up into the sky, down into the rivers, and out towards the suburbs the most dazzling display of oranges, reds, greens, and whites. An opalescent nocturne worthy of a postcard! And in the day? So much more on display! From my front yard— out across Bullitt Avenue...down the slope of Mt. Brennan...into the valley of Monport...straight through the low boughs of the neighbor 'woods...then out across the slow-flowing green river...til it cashes into the banks of the city—the buildings look like clawing fingers trying to squeeze the life out of the sky! When I was about to turn ten, I told my father that I wanted to parachute off the tallest one for my birthday. I'd overheard a conversation about a man jumping from another building, and it sounded adventurous. Turns out the man had deliberately jumped without a parachute. Besides, my father's response was that he would push me off whatever building he could if I didn't go "redd up" my room like he'd been asking for the past week. Although it was my birthday wish, I didn't cry; I never did. I just went outside, looking at the edificial fingers from afar, and pictured myself jumping off the elevated palm of the city, diving freely into the cool air without a parachute too...

...Connecting at one point in Verna, there's two popular sections called East Square and South Square. Each encompasses two standard blocks. Both relatively flat. East Square mostly consists of corporate restaurants, while South Square is mostly corporate retail stores. What makes the squares unique are the openings throughout which lead to plazas within the interior, making the blocks "thick." True to their generic name, the entire layout has the austerity of a square: God could swipe His hand clean across the roofs. From His and the crows' eyes, it looks like a bunch of smaller squares within the large square that outlines the block. 'Stores within stores!' buyers crow. But if you look at, say, a fifteen-year-old photo, you'll see a *different* design in this area of Verna: jagged rows of stout, gray, Neo-Gothic and Renaissance buildings, complimented with Romanesque or Medieval features—buildings that had the "old-school" look and feel like the preserved areas of dahntahn, which were financed by the ol' American Robber Barons (namely, Carnegie, Frick, and Mellon). But the facades of Square East and Square South look so sleek, white, and plastic, while the "bellied" design was created in the early-90s by the ne' Japanese Architectural Pioneers who foresaw the need to economize the land in anticipation of future growth. And when the anticipated boom *did* occur, established entrepreneurs (who, unlike mom and pop, never show their faces) quickly filled the bellies of the squares. Now new stores only pop up when another fails to mother its shop, or when a foreign shop craves a local taste and gobbles one up, usually at any cost.

Because of the squares, the main streets in Verna are crowded during the day but drastically less by night; that's how it goes dahntahn too. But faced with less road alternatives in Verna, many impatient (or dense) outsiders try avoiding the chaos around the squares only to flood traffic into areas where congestion already exists due to narrow decrepit roads, cars butted into curbs, and idle DOT machinery. Here on the inside, outsiders roll up their windows, lock their doors, and enjoy the scenery. They can see (snaking along these rocky roads) gray, abraded, uneven sidewalks—and if they're lucky, clovers where the cement has fractured. (Some community-involved neighbors even voluntarily decorate the fringes of the sidewalks with empty beer bottles and potato chip bags. I always thought the profuse amount of salt 'n' vinegar added a lot of flavor to the scene.) Now if the outsiders can peel their eyes off the down-low splendor, and focus on the heart of the blocks, they'll find themselves absorbed by the sight of box-houses and box-stores: a third of which are boarded up, all closely wedged together, none too high, one after another, flyblown and forlorn. In the mix, there's still a few family-owned cafes, delis, and pizza shops: part of the original places to catch a bite before the fast-food joints in East Square popped up. Besides the distinction in surnames either stitched up on the awning or painted across the glass, they all have the same basic look: narrow boxes with large glass facades, where peaking in, past all the fliers taped to the window, you can see an abundance of green, white, and red, with the nooks done in dust. Each cafe, deli, and pizza shop (compared to another of its kind) even smells the same: all you have to do is breathe out on the sidewalks, anywhere on the same block, and you can smell the coffee, meat, and dough, respectively—*despite* the potato chip bags begging at your feet. Those baggers! I swear there's ten on every block! Every one salt 'n' vinegar! But truth is, it's not all monotony and chips in Verna: thin cuts between the box-houses and box-stores make way for crooked alleyways, and therein sewage-green dumpsters, shattered glass and wooden traps, little stray cats tiptoeing around both, and at night a calm darkness that breathes reservedly like a creature looming in the shadows; and *this,* if you're there, will paint many colorful pictures right before your eyes. Those little cats though! *Meow! Meow! Meow!*

The "non-square" blocks in Verna, aka the residential areas, are heavily populated with welfare-class Blacks and working-class Italians. There's also penny-picking Polaks and slog-squatting Irish folk who've found their niche in ditch. United, everyone conks their cots in the slobbering, burgundy Section-8s lining 3rd thru 7th, or in the whitewashed apartments between Division and Cassat, or in the drab box-houses that dominate residential Verna in the row-style found all around Pittsburgh. There's two streets, Bullitt and Scotch, where the box-houses, mostly bricked, only rise one story high. But the story is: despite the number of stories, residential Verna has a trashy feel to it. However—and I can't stress over this enough—in comparison to other places I've seen or heard about, Verna is certainly in no need of Mother Teresa, although she recently passed away anyway.

Anyway, I grew up in the Wop-West section of Verna where all the Italians reside, as opposed to Nigger-North where the majority of Blacks reside—Blacks who will venture to Wop-West just to "steal" Italian girls away from their families, so says my father. Now it's of utmost importance that it be said that, for some reason, despite heavy colloquial use, Wop-West and Nigger-North aren't found on any map. I really don't know why. All I know is that both Wop-West and Nigger-North, like America and the entire World, all share the same Sky, where for seventeen years I walked down below, often crooning, 'God bless Mitch 'n' Tess. God bless you 'n' me. God bless Rich 'n' Ness. 'N' God bless Poe, Bert, 'n' Tee.'

Now let me be frank here even though I'm Vincent and prefer to be called V: I don't really like hanging out dahntahn. It's not that Pittsburgh's overpopulated and thus claustrophobic: 325,000 live within the city proper (over 2.5 million in the metro), but only 3,300 live dahntahn. But see, the problem is the "visitors" dahntahn. Even if it's my ocular folly, they seem to be—ALIENS! Yes! I can never get a grasp on who they are, where they're from, or what they're about! Their skin: every line and curve determined yet accomplished; every hue and hair glowing yet unnatural. It always brings to mind hair-product commercials. What's stranger is they always move so fast in my reflections, like fleshy bullets. Even in the physical, there's a swiftness in their perfumed air: handsome aliens in unisex suits moving gracefully in and out of stores with several bags gripped up in one hand, some using the other hand to hold tiny phones up to their earless heads—then a moment of sibilance—phasing into a moment of static—a twisted momentary face as if caught by the paparazzi—then off to places I've never seen, as if fleeing for safety on—on MARS! Yes! MARS! But the yinzers found dahntahn (the homeless, the temptress, the apathetics, the shaky-bones who scream enough nonsense to cause headaches, the freaks, the geeks, the prowlers, and of course the lesser of two powers) always remain behind: a laaaaarge slooooow bluuuuur, like thousands of pennies dropped in water, or parts on a factory line that keep falling off and breaking, *li munzeddi râ genti, nostri piccati n pezzi:* [5] *chk chk – pshhhhh...chk chk – pshhhhh.* And they, the yinzers, herd together in my mind as the bovine.

Since the decline of the steel mills, Pittsburgh has taken extensive measures to clean up its image in the focal point; that is, dahntahn. Every year, roads are repaved blacker and stacked higher. Sidewalks are weeded and pressure-washed, nearly whitened to a point where it's blinding in the sun. Shining are new statues of dignitaries with large gawking eyes—new fountains blowing water further up than the last—new marble plazas sprinkled with silvery stars and dots, adorned with quaint wooden benches. So feel free to sit down and have a seat next to a star—but dot ju go chasin' doze waterfalls! See, weather wet or dry, location low or high, things dahntahn have learned how to lend a helping-elbow if room needs to be made. Sometimes Nature just seems to spawn new spaces out of thin air. But if the city simply can't find a way—that is, a space—then to the sprawl. To—the—sprawl.

Being one of the most overcast cities in America, Pittsburgh sees less of the sun and more of the artificial lights that recently took the lime: neon billboards and please-read-me signs now inhabiting the land like a second species. Sometimes they seem to read WAR IS PEACE, FREEDOM IS SLAVERY, IGNORANCE IS STRENGTH. Just kidding, ddikts. Many are actually auspicious and sometimes really witty. Colorful high-def displays all around: low in the windows, high in the sky, on the public transportation passing by, everywhere this great flashing technology! Some ads promote ways to be all that you can be, or how to be part of the action, go full speed ahead, and be among a few good men. Some, in long strings of competitiveness, display automobiles, furniture, toys, clothes, sporting goods, knickknacks, pattywacks, give-a-dog-a-bones—*woof!*—electronics, entertainment galore and more! Hey?! And MORE! Some ads reveal the newest foods for optimal pleasure, plastered with the lowest prices available. Others counter by highlighting the newest drugs for optimal strength and diet, of course at a higher price than the foods. Some go lite and promote only the business name and logo. (And some go subliminal and promote only the idea *behind* the business name and logo.) Nuances aside, dahntahn is becoming festooned, consumed, beleaguered even, with these magical signs everywhere: rolling! glowing! flashing! blinking!—BLINDING!

I began developing eye complications in kindergarten: astigmatism, followed by a bad case of myopia. I wore Roy Orbisons til I was twelve when I switched over to contacts. Things got worse at thirteen after a brutal fistfight. This little Irish lad swung a mighty right, and when he connected, his thumb dug deep into the lower part of my left eye, bursting the blood

---

[5] [scn] the piles of people, our sin in pieces

vessels. For the next month, my eye was a shiny puddle of blood, and thereafter my vision went to the wane. So despite the help of contacts, I never knew if I was seeing things right. Overstand?

Ehh, I just realized this is becoming a bit boring, confusing, and wordy. And if you want me to be honest about it, I can't stand holding your hands anymore...Oh real cute, ankle-biters! Fall down and cry about it! I really don't give a fuck! I was just trying to help yinz out before—well, I dunno; just good luck overstanding things *dahn 'ere* where people really do go chasing waterfalls around the murky rivers and precarious hills of Pittsburgh, Pennsylvania...

NUHGIHDOUDDADERE

"I went outside today: the city was burning bright,
The citizens shimmered in gold, slaves of the cold,
Living under a false light,
Come on hazy stars, drift into the night,
So I can wander off, without a word,
Wander off out of sight..." [1]

...Returning from the city, Pessi and I headed towards the front of the bus as it came to a stop. We were pushing each other all the way down the rubber-ribbed aisle. For some reason, several cocksuckers were acting like it was their God-given duty to mutter rude comments about how immature we were. The blubbery bus driver yelled out, 'Stop horsin' around or else yinzer gonna get banned for the rest of the year!' But after making it out the door and onto the pavement, I tried holding Pessi in place on the last step—the *steep* step. The bus driver had his right arm stretched out, with his hand resting on the lever for the accordion door. Pessi started juggernauting downward with his shoulder. Suppressing the laughter fluctuating in my gut, I was pushing upward with both hands as hard as I could. We battled and barged, punched and grappled, til reaching a deadlock—then we reluctantly let our hands fall. Pessi remained on the edge of the steep step, bent over and winded—but the stupid bus driver *still* refused to fold Pessi in with the accordion door! From his elevated seat, he stared at me with eyes that said, 'Scram, you little prick.' I thought about flipping him off but instead turned away. When I heard Pessi's shoe scuff the road, I swiftly turned back around and congratulated him on escaping the accordion of death by giving him a precise kidney-shot. Flexing courage to my thoughts, I flipped the bus driver off as a reminder to think twice about passing up another chance to fold Pessi in with the accordion door. In return, he flipped me off then levered the door shut. The growling bus pulled away, leaving behind a malodorous mist.

The stop was two blocks away from my house, Pessi's house one block in the other direction. Staying silent and looking around bashfully as if he didn't know me after nearly seventeen years, Pessi started rubbing his hand back and forth over his head. The friction against his short brown bristles was making a rough sandpaper sound. His hazel eyes sunk into a squint as he surveyed our blighted neighborhood. The severe humidity was making everything look fumy. With mischievous intentions still brewing in the air, we remained on the bank of the road.

'Man, you gadda beedda *stu*pidest faggot alive.'

"Oh yeah?' (He spit in the grass.) 'Why's 'at?'

'Why?' I repeated for effect. "Cause ya spell "cat" with a "k" 'n' penetrate male orifices: 'at's why. Now run home 'fore I beat dat *stu*pid look off yir face.'

---

[1] Lyrics from "Never Coming Back" by My Lonesome Exile, from the album *Taking the Easy Way Out*

As usual, Pessi smirked at my ruthless sarcasm. His ruggedly handsome face had tanned to a silvery-fawn, as it tended to do during the peak of summer. All year round it retained a solemn glare like one of James Dean's classic photos. (A mid-face spitting-image of the guy.) But whenever I could find a way to break his chiseled cast and bring out "the smirk"—that reluctant but approving smirk—I was content...for a moment.

'Don't make me fuckin' do it.'

'Keep wishin', V.'

'Wishin's for hippies; I *make* shit happen...' As I carried on with my mock machismo, I was doing everything in my power to get Pessi fired up again—but I couldn't make it happen. So I leaned in closer, a bit over his shoulder, and in a serious-like manner said, 'Well look: if you wanna do some yey[2] tonight, caw me after supper.'

'Mmm, we'll see, but prahblee not. Think I'm done hangin' out with midgets.'

That was my cue to uppercut his tough gut then push him back at the shoulder. Seeing that he didn't plan to punch or push back, I said, 'Fine 'en; I'll do it all myself—*you fuckin' faggot.*'

Pessi turned around indifferently, and with hands shoved in pocket, walked away like a rebel without a cause.

In the other direction, I headed down Bullitt Avenue, kicking along a golfball-sized rock. The sun was fully unmasked, burning with pernicious intentions; all the clouds were in hiding or gone to ashes. The weather had been the same for two weeks: the last time Mrs. Rain had visited; even Dr. Overcast was currently on vacation. In a matter of a few steps, my plain black t-shirt was drawing in extra waves of heat from which an ominous twinge began pricking a small spot in my chest. From that, I quit kicking along the rock; it was enough to keep having to wipe the sweat from my face. To my left, three little black girls dressed in all-white were enduring the heat much better as they took turns running underneath the umbrella spray of a sprinkler; they were singing a joyful song about "a silly fish," and the sound of the spray was giving the song a smooth and consistent melody. Next to them, the Hughes had a new sign posted in their front yard, almost right on the road. I took a closer look...a tax sign letting us neighbors know that if the Hughes didn't pay up soon we could buy their house at an auction. Since I was good friends with Mr. and Mrs. Hughes' son, Eddie, I thought maybe I should buy their house then give it to Eddie for his birthday; I could even put an oversized bowtie on the roof; that would be nice of me. Next block down—my block—a shirtless Mr. Klugman (like a hero in the heat) was cutting his small front lawn with a push-mower. Laboriously, he managed to wave, and I waved back.

When I came upon my house—a jaundiced one-story box in the middle of the block—Aunt Stella was rolling Uncle Alfonse out the front door. Hunched over in his wheelchair, Uncle Alfonse's mottled face was drooping down towards his lap; there didn't seem to be a set of legs wrapped up inside the floppy gray rayon. Up above, I noticed his umber liver spots were beginning to populate his jowls and dance up his bald head

---

[2] [spa] cocaine; short for "yeyo," correctly spelled "llello"

like a corybantic breakout. Wheeling around 76 years, Uncle Alfonse was my paternal great uncle and a second-generation Abruzzese.[3] I figured they must've been visiting Ma because Aunt Stella, like many others, didn't like my father. But no one really liked her either.

For whatever reason, Uncle Alfonse was yelling and complaining, mostly in English but also throwing in some Nonsense. Aunt Stella, a decade younger, was trying to appease him by slapping him friendly on the shoulder every time he swore. Moaning, he was swatting her and her synthetic-blond beehive away with that irascibility unique to disgruntled ol' gimps. No one really knew what was wrong with him. I think Aunt Stella had pressed the doctors to diagnose him with something juicy so she could legally dispose of him. But the doctors said most likely the early stages of natural amnesia—at worst, senile dementia. Based on the things he would blurt out, I assumed Tourette's. Perhaps even faking it as a last resort to express his discontent.

When he looked up at me (still some distance away on the sidewalk) he suddenly grabbed the left wheel with both hands and tried rocking himself out of the chair.

'Stop 'at, Alfonse!' yelled Aunt Stella, prying his hands from the wheel.

Struggling to turn around in his geri-generic wheelchair, he said, 'Stop inna name of love, woman!' (She ignored him.) Then he looked straight at me. 'Who's 'at?' he said with a rectal cough. 'Who's 'at?!'

'Whaddaya mean who's 'at? It's Vincent!'

Aunt Stella knew that I hated being called Vincent; therefore, just like every other time she struck a chord, I sung out *her* misnomer. '*Salutamu*,[4] Aunt Fella. (Uncle A.) Yinz headin' da the morgue today?'

'No, sm<u>art</u>ass. We're goin' home 'cause yir *faaah*der—' She flashed an exasperated rosy face; from the jerk of her flabby neck, I could taste the shaken mist of hairspray and cheap perfume. 'You know him! Bein' a drunk idiot again!'

'Awesome,' I whispered to myself. Surveying our small sere yard, I couldn't think of anything else to say. I didn't really like her, and he was too much to deal with in the heat, so I sidestepped them and headed towards the door.

'Who's 'at?' Uncle Alfonse asked again. 'Who's 'at?!' She rolled him down to the car as they continued quibbling over who I am or might be.

Then I walked inside, deep into the trenches...

'Taaay-yaaahh! Hello-oohh!'

He was marching around the dead room, drunk. Pungent vapors of bourbon were beating against the still musty air whenever he breathed, talked, moved: Mess-olini on another wasted prowl. I quickly shifted passed and hooked a right into the hallway between the kitchen and dead room.

'EH!'

I froze halfway down the hallway. *Don't retreat...never retreat.*

'Tell 'er da gihdoudda that fuckin' baffroom 'n' make some supper!'

---

[3] A resident of Abruzzo, a region in central Italy between Lazio and the Adriatic Sea
[4] [scn] Hello

Irritated, I squared up to the left and knocked on the bathroom door. 'Ma, ya gonna make some supper or wha'?...' (She failed to respond, so I knocked again.) *'Mà, chi cc'è? T'arripigghiasti?...'* [5] Again: no response. I put my ear closer to the door and heard sniffling and objects being knocked around in the cabinet. 'Well, I dunno; I'll be in my room if ya need any help.' Still facing the door, something struck the corner of my eye. I glanced left—down the hallway—and saw his shadow cross into the kitchen. I closed my eyes for a moment...saw a thick teal sea billowing towards me...and when I opened my eyes it seemed darker than before. (With no windows near the hallway, and the bedroom doors usually shut, the hall was fated to be of a darker nature.) After taking a few steps forward, I opened my bedroom door on the right. A distinct mustiness—different from the rest of the house—shot forward: stifling and melancholic, causing the familiar malady in my gut to awake from dormancy. I closed the door behind me. Sat down on my double-mattress of a bed. Fixated my eyes on my moppy caramel carpet. Then listened to the swirling sounds of darkness and mustiness pervading the thin wall.

'Tèa!—*Eh Tèa!!!...*' (A moment of silence transpired as the three of us remained attentive in our separated spaces.) 'Can't do 'iss; can't do 'at,' he resumed in a mumble. But returning to the frustrated, desperate tone, he screamed, 'For'ah'lass *fuckin'* time: I'm *fuckin'* hungry! Nuhgihdouddadere!'

Mumbling commenced in the kitchen. I was trying to decipher the words but the syllables sounded like slop being splattered inside a trough. Suddenly something fell to the floor and shattered; I felt the pieces spread across the linoleum as if tiny lyrate-shaped crystals were tearing through my veins. Then heavy movements in the hall. My door swung open. Sitting on the bed with my elbows resting on my thighs and my hands clasped together, I looked up. He latched onto the doorknob to keep his balance, leaning his hulking body against the door. His thinning black hair was sliding along the wood as he wavered. His eyes were dark and wet: the glaze from the booze. Underneath, dark and dry as stone: the incineration from the bitterness—the lifelong bitterness—this repose into our steel-cold ethos—his submission to soul-inertia...left so withered inside...all sensibilities now so weathered inside this shell of a man...which is why, while observing this shell, my senses told me that its deceptively rheumy eyes—so teary those mad eyes!—were searching for something not there, for it was only me before them: a something that was a nothing: a pile of ashes only needing the slightest blow to disappear. *Sooooo*...blow, father, blow!

And when finally he blew, his words blasted me in the face like a sciroccu[6]: 'Thought I tolja da redd up 'iss room! Huh?!'

'I did.'

'Den why dem books 'n' 'at all over da floor?'

'*Umm*—'cause I'm gettin' my shit together?'

'For wha'?'

I refused to answer. I rose from my bed—just two single mattresses stacked atop each other without a frame—and with my back to him, began sifting through a stack of poems I planned to take with me.

---

[5] [scn] What's the matter? You all right?
[6] Sicilian form of *sirocco*, a hot, humid wind in southern Italy and Sicily

'Where you think yir goin'?' he slurred. I thought he was about to fully enter, but like a doctored lunatic falling into relapse he punched at the door with a hammer-fist—then again, and again, and again: rhythmic thuds of frustration. 'Ya know, I fuckin' hate dishit!' he bellowed. 'No one knows howda cook! No one knows howda clean! No one knows where der goin'! No one knows *NUH'N'!...*' While he continued complaining to my battered door, I saw Ma sneaking past (having came from her bedroom, not the bathroom), edging against the wall with tremulous steps. But it was a botched effort, for her foot hit the basing. At the sound, he turned around with a new target in sight.

'Well look who could finely join us!' he declared, raising his hands up high; they fell abrupt and heavily like instant death. A gentle sway followed in which his tarpaulin eyelids (so close together) seemed to be his saving anchor...but then his eyes sprang open (so wide) as if he suddenly remembered what he'd been doing or had been struck with the greatest idea ever. The entire time, Ma (frozen in place) had been looking down at the ground, her long black hair snaking down the front of her nightgown, the buttercup-yellow one that she'd worn to the tatters.

'Tell me, *Tèa,*' he said belittlingly, 'whaddaya been doin' all day ditcha can't have supper riddy by da time I git home from work? I mean, is 'at too much da ask for? Hmm?—EH! I can't hear ya wichir face dahn!' He staggered a step towards her.

I stood up and maneuvered back behind his broad martial shoulder: I wasn't going to let him hit her. But Ma overstood the situation: she kept her mouth shut and dragged herself to the kitchen. He turned around to face me with a twisted grin demonstrating a job well done. Then he kinda nodded but without recognition, for his eyes were opening and shutting intermittently. His thick hairy neck was bobbing around, twitching a little, as if some proxy force inside him was trying to keep him conscious.

I slipped between him and the door frame, walked down the hallway, then froze on the golden fool's strip that divided the tan linoleum of the kitchen from the brown shag of the dead room. He followed but trailed off into the dead room, mumbling. In the kitchen, Ma was picking up the pieces of a white coffee mug; I still felt it shattering in my veins. Once giving the floor a quick sweep with a mini-broom, she pulled out two skillets from the cupboard above the stove, setting one on the back burner and one diagonally on the front. Without turning around, she called out several vegetables for me to retrieve from the fridge. It was for *la caponata ri mulinciani,* a side dish to go along with chicken cooked and seasoned in the healthy way. She was placing the raw chicken in the skillet strip by strip, telling me how much celery to slice when she got startled and jerked her head to the right.

'Wha' inna fuck is 'iss shit?!' he moaned; that's when Ma got startled and jerked her head to the right. 'Where's 'at fuckin' thing 'at...' He was stomping around the dead room, flipping up cushions, overturning magazines, looking for the remote. Then he stopped and pointed at the screen, I believe addressing me when he looked over at us and said, 'Dis is wha' she does while I'm at work.' He looked back at the screen as if in disbelief that a television was even there. 'Watches 'iss fuckin' Nazi coon blab away ah-day.'

After finding the remote, he plumped down in his wooden recliner, which placed his back towards us. He held the remote out like a wand and turned off what Ma couldn't have been watching all day, seeing as the program just started. Alwaysthemore, the magical power to banish a Nazi coon from his television pacified him. The bottle harmoniously tilted back with the recliner.

As my line of vision drew back to the kitchen, I looked at Ma cooking: a little sweat meandering down her temple...sneaking around her nervous mouth...the modest curve of her body weighed down, especially the slouch in her small rounded shoulders...her copper skin starting to look a bit yellowish...yet her hair still as full, thick, and black as mine, as if going gray, when the time came, would all happen in the course of one night. Whenever I used to look at her in years past, in prepubescent times, I would wonder what she was like as a *picciridda* in Catania[7]: I'd wanted to draw comparisons between us at the same age to see if I was "normal." With each passing year, my thoughts became more complex and polished but always retained the name nucleus with regard to her life in Catania: Did she sing? Did she dance? Did her skin shine darker? *U so accentu chiù duci iera?!*[8] Did she, as a little Sicilian girl, ever think about America, or being in America? Well, I guess it didn't really matter anymore, because, almost a man now, I overstood the futility of taking delight in little boy wonderings about little girl mommy, overstood how minds and eyes don't share the same canvases. Yet ever since the genesis of the pubescent being I hadn't stopped wanting to know what she looked like nude, and then once I could, explain to her why an artist, specifically a Greek-minded poet, gauging the cogitations and sensibilities both inside and outside the realm of sexuality would ever think of such a thing.

Outside, Razzle started barking: a nearby train was tooting its horn. *Choo-chooooo!* Standing at the sink, I looked out the smudgy kitchen window where I could see in our backyard our little gray dog standing on all fours, foaming at the mouth, digging his front paws down into the circle of dirt around his oak tree. Looked like something of a bull ready to charge into the bricks and buck us all.

After slicing all the celery and onion needed, I asked Ma if we had any dog food. Focused on the chicken food, she shook her head no and whispered a suggestion of bread and water. *Bread 'n' wudder? What, is my dog a fuckin' inmate or sum'n? My widdle Razzle prahblee starvin' out there! 'N' 'at stupid fuckin' chain around his neck! Ahhh!* To be sure, I wanted to feed Razzle, even more, *free* Razzle, but for now I was more concerned with *pacifying* Razzle just so Rick (who now had his head drawn back on the recliner, breathing stertorously like a worn horse) would remain pacified.

I walked outside, back into the severe heat, with a gallon of tap water and two pieces of bread. Rapidly shaking his curled tail, Razzle tugged his chain towards me. The little gray terrier then spread down on his belly and nuzzled his white-whisker schnozz between his filthy paws.

---

[7] [scn] A girl between the ages of three and six. Catania is a major port-city on the eastern coast of Sicily.

[8] [scn] Was her accent sweeter back then?

Although old, his eyes were young and tender, but his whimpering quashed any chance for his eyes to evoke delicate feelings in me. The more I observed what seemed a state of inconsolable misery, the more it felt like a loaf of bread was being worked up and down my throat like a saw. I squatted down—took a deep breath—and in a cartoonish voice, said, *'Ere ya go, widdle buddy.'* While petting his head with one hand, I used my other hand to nudge a piece of bread towards him...til it was sitting atop his paws. Uninterested, he used his schnozz to flip it off to the side; an army of black ants were quick to invade the crust. I stood up and dumped the gallon of water into his large metal bowl by the tree. But he wouldn't drink either. He rolled over on his back, panting, wanting me to scratch the scaling areas of his belly. As I touched down, reverberations from inside the house blasted through the bricks and glass. Razzle jumped up and, tugging his chain towards the house, started barking again. The train was gone by now.

After being provoked out of his repose, I could hear Rick saying something about not wanting *that* to eat. Through the rectangular kitchen window, it looked like he was puffing himself up and moving around frantically like a criminal trying to get their ransom at the last desperate moment. And poor Ma, she was trying to make everything all right (so to speak, pay the ransom) by making the food all right. But she didn't know that what is sweet to one may be sour to another.

I gave Razzle one last scratch behind the ear before walking back inside, deeper into the trenches than I should've gone.

No surprise that when I swung in the backdoor Ma had disappeared from the kitchen, most likely having gone to bed, despite having a meal in-progress; wouldn't have been the first time. I think in one of my blindspots—when I was heading towards the house and couldn't see them through the window—he'd steamrolled her to the ground or called her a bad name. So knowing the drill, I washed my hands and transferred the celery from the tawny countertop into the skillet where two eggplants were simmering in olive oil. I heaved a sigh and tried to let the sizzle soothe my nerves...*ststststs*...but it was useless—too overpowered by the sizzle in the dead room; once a "living" room til the reign of King Richard—(just a puerile name I called him in my head, substituted with Musso)—swept over the diminutive land and it became the dead room for a million and two reasons.

'Eh! I 'on't wan' dat shit she'z makin'!' he projected backwards from the recliner.

Fanning the steam, I was about to turn off the stove and let it at that but he shot up and came wobbling into the kitchen, slurring what he wanted *me* to cook. Knowing more about stratagems than cooking, I just wanted to leave the kitchen: get away without being blindsided by an attack or duped into playing one of his non-zero-sum games, namely, a lose-lose. Yet after some circling, twisting, and turning, while a fierce tussle was going on between my head and gut, I found myself stuck in the middle, in the fray between colliding worlds.

'Ya gidda 'nother job yet?' he asked as he crossed the threshold.
He forget? or can't he comprehend da fact dittum leavin' soon?

'I know whachir tryin'ah do,' he hiccupped. 'Think yir gonna sit arounda house ah-day now ahchir oudda school. Wanna suck my blood dry like 'em Klugman kids dahn'ah street do. *"Mommy, Daddy, gimmie! gimmie! gimmie!"* HA!'

HA! I silently laughed back. Such silliness! Besides having a basement, the Klugman kids didn't have anything special. And *suck his blood dry?* Not unless I wanted alcohol poisoning!

Scratching at his mean box-jaw where grizzled sprouts poorly hid the draconian monster lurking behind, my father walked passed, squaring up with the window, quietly musing as if sober. Behind Razzle's oak tree sat a line of twiggy bushes, followed by out-of-commission railroad tracks, then a glass factory that had gone under in the mid-80s. Good chance he was thinking about job security since the factories and mills that once sustained Greater Pittsburgh were drowning in the soup piecemeal. When he turned around, he surprisingly turned the stove off. Unsurprisingly he pushed the vegetable skillet back, causing a few pieces to fly out. Then he burped long and absurdly. Sick of it all, I skipped over the golden fool's strip (so as not to get stuck in the fray) and started walking towards my bedroom.

'Eh, come back 'ere.'

I kept walking deaf. *Don't retreat...never retreat.*

'I sa'cahmir!' he shouted in a voice loud enough to make the walls tremble.

Turning around, I saw that he'd nearly fallen forward with his words. His body (impressive in his military pictures before he gave up on physical patriotism) was beginning to give into the natural slack of middle age. Even so, he was still as strong as Atlas. Fairly compact besides his gut; he'd grown one of those rubber bellies suggestive of a once-athletic youth: not solid muscle but certainly not fat either: a belly you think you could take a swing at and knock the wind out of him but you would only hurt your wrist. Despite his rapid aging and his modicum of territory to rule over, he was still general of the house. He always made sure I knew that. In a sense too prolix for copper, he made sure I knew *everything.*[9]

'Fahder Carr tol' me boucher mouff in class,' he spat, launching spit missiles down the hall. 'Says you been givin' 'im lip. "Da congregation's gonna be castigated by God." Z'at whachu said, tough-guy?'

Once close enough, he started poking at my chest. Then he slapped the back of my head, sternly gripped the back of my neck, and guided me back into the fray between the kitchen and the dead room.

'Why ya gadda say shit like 'at in chirch? Huh?'

Facing him, I closed my eyes and raised my pointy black eyebrows towards the rust-flecked ceiling, shaking my head as if I knew nothing of the church situation. And I didn't...at least not til I browsed through my gospel recollections and realized that he was referring to something from when I was fourteen: approximately 1,200 days ago! Is it seriously possible to be that far out-of-touch?! Had Uncle Alfonse been wheeling him around?!

---

[9] A compound pun: *prolix* meaning "too much," as in a prolonged use of words; *copper,* as in a penny (or a cent), becoming both a play on in a sense and ironic of "too much"; pieced together, *in a sense too prolix for copper* means "too much explanation to be put into one line."

Guess it's time to change things up a bit. Gotta go to my bedroom and put on my Fourteen-Year-Old Vinny costume.........Okay, I'm back! Look at me now! I'm fourteen again! Go on Daddy Dear! Blow on!

'He tol' me 'atchu'er mockin' 'im 'n' pretendin' like yuzza preacher, sayin', "Whadda beaudiful castigation iddle be, my brudders 'n' sissers! Whadda beaudiful castigation iddle be!"...' Hallelujah! For once Father Vallano was dead-on with his mockery! He was even doing a little befuddled dance to boost his thespian virtuosity! While acting out the comical scene, he slung his boots off by kicking each leg up in the air. The boots—those filthy clodhoppers!—flew across the dead room one after another...towards the door...smacking off the wall. THUD!—THUD!

Meanwhile, I couldn't wipe the smile off my face! And apparently he thought I still had pride in mocking Father Carr 1,200 days ago because after he finished the scene, he froze and violently glared down at me. With help from the light above, his eyes looked so silver and rheumy, his body so drunk but clinched so tightly in defense of all that held him together down to the cell of his heart.

'Oh is 'iss funny da ya? Huh? Well lemme tell ya sum'n, kid—' He stopped to catch his balance by grabbing the sink counter. He tottered sideways over to our algae-green fridge and swung the freezer door open. He pulled out an ice tray, preparing to make a formal drink. 'One:' he decreed sharply as he smacked the tray off the counter to break the ice, 'you don't even know wha' "castigate" even means—'

'Don't cast the gate open?'

He turned around and twisted up his face, about to condemn me, but I interjected:

'Look, yir so wasted right now dit—'

'Nah'm not! Yir, umm—uhh...' He began stammering because he was dropping ice cubes into a rocks glass, with care, as if heeding to a recipe. But in a spasm of impetuosity he dumped the whiskey in, splashing some on the counter. He turned around and held the glass outward as if I was about to receive a toast. 'Ya know, yir fuckin' worthless. Yir juss out da make e'eryone's life miserable. Know who you are?' He paused to shoot the whiskey down—then slung the glass behind him in the sink, the ice ringing around the metal: more broken glass. 'Da devil in the flesh. I know. You know. She knows!' he projected viciously towards the back of the house. As it echoed, air slowly evacuated his nose. Then he groaned, 'Uhh-rrm...Juss git da fuck oudda my face 'n' godda yir room.' Since my only movement was a smirk, he zigzagged over to me...til coming toe-to-toe, towering six inches above me. His bourbon breath was stirring near my eyes, the acridity making them a bit watery...

...And that was it: he won: he'd found a way to dupe me into playing one of his lose-lose games where nobody wins. Not only had I dismorphed from a seventeen-year-old into a fourteen-year-old, but he also made sure I played the role of Mephistopheles, since I was "da devil in the flesh" and all. (Yes, Da Devil does take many forms.) Alwaysthemore, his mouth had finally fired me up again. Sparked my tongue again. So, hell, I fired back again: 'Why dohnchu gih da fuck oudda my face 'n' godda yir room?' He didn't; he only backed up a step and waited for my elaboration. 'I mean, fuck, if only I could be as articulate as you 'n' Father Carr. Such experts in language 'n' elocution. Yir like M-L-K—'

'Dohnchu *ever* caw me a fuckin' nigger.'

'Of course not, Uncle Tom; that would be against the law in 'iss cabin.' Waggling my little tongue in check, I could feel the friction mounting, ready to show him who's King of Wordplay. But before I could show him he suddenly folded over—a temporary collapse?—banging his knee hard off the linoleum. I laughed. "Ere ya go. Wanna 'nother drink, Uncle T? Or how bout Mr. T? *Ya piddy dat fool, G?*'

'Fuck you,' he mumbled down on bended knee.

I took a step closer, clinching my teeth together but unable to bite down on my little fiery tongue. A gigantic breath of air! *(Huuuuuuuuuh!)* 'No: *fuck – you.*' The acerbic tone, together with the paused measure, sounded like I was trying to cut through glass, as I pointed my finger down at him as if to keep him fastened to the ground. Face to the floor, he was breathing hard, looking and sounding like a wounded bear. *Roar?* No—no roarjoinder this time. So declaring myself the victorious dark hero, I stepped around him, anxious to change my clothes and leap forward three years to the true me, the one who was no longer a little devil. But before taking those critical steps, I still felt the need to add the finishing tongue to the matter. To his back, a step away, I said, 'I can't wait til you die.'

As always, I immediately (as if by instinct) felt so horrible and full of sin. But I was just trying to feel something other than the anger burning inside by spouting out—well, anger. Seemed to make sense: if you don't like what's inside you, then you get it out any way you can, at any cost. But alas, here comes the check:

'*Come 'ere.*' He quickly rose up from the floor, reaching out for my leg with desperate strength, sizzling, overloading, his body gnarling, his face wincing, his white shirt coming at my face in a great big blur, his calloused hands thrown into my black shirt, jerking me off-balance, jerking! jerking! jerking! His face flared up into a big red ball. The greasy black comb-over on his head seemed to stiffen. His gut sucked inward but with little avail. He had a firm grip on my black shirt, pushing and pinning me back against the wall, keeping me cornered with his weight. He was wheezing, coughing, spitting, sweating, reeking of booze, odor, smoke, grease. I held my breath—wished him a heart attack or more strength for me. But it was too late. Everything happened so fast that I only had enough time to close my eyes and clinch my jaw as one fell swoop rocked across my face, knocking my imaginary costume straight to the floor...

...Ya know, hard work hardly overcomes hard luck. But luckily, after having that hard dose of discipline shot into my jaw, I retreated to my room and overcame my conscience by convincing myself that leaving and never looking back would be the right thing to do. I even expounded my reasoning in my essay *On Filial Liberation*. The essay: a past forte of mine when my mind was feeble and desperate for any method of expression, when my whymeness hung all over me like cobwebs needing swabbed.

After writing for a bit, I turned up my stereo as loud as I could without enticing my father; it didn't take much with Punk Rock: what he called "that satanic crap"; what I called "the music of the rugged angels."

Then I sat down on my mattresses and hung my head like a Whooping crane. My mother's sullen face appeared before my internal eyes, and from that, the solemn face of The Blessed Virgin Mary, and from that, I began mentally bullet-listing my blessings. When finished, I pretended that I went through and rearranged them in a ranked order, and the blessing at the top (bold and underscored) was that I'd grown up with a father who worked lots of overtime, which meant the blessing was that, in a more unfortunate scheme of things, those extra hours at work could've been spent at home.

Since and before I was born, my father worked at a steel mill eleven miles southeast of Pittsburgh, one of the three remaining mills. But I was only concerned with *when* he worked: the shift and a half Monday thru Thursday, when he came home around 7 p.m., making his presence immediately known by getting drunk. After the half-shift on Friday, he usually went down the block to the dives, returning home in the same ol' condition. Whenever he worked Saturdays it was another half-shift; afterward, he usually visited family by himself—(his parents, two brothers, and sister)—or he went fishing/hunting with one or two of his buddies from work; he had no "real" friends. And on Sunday, "family day," we went to church: the only thing we ever did together. Before we left, he would shave his face clean, comb over what was left of his hair, and put on the same ol' black suit and red tie: must've been twenty-years-old but the best he had. At church, we always sat in the same pew, three from the back wall. Whenever the time came, Ma would croon the hymns and responses; Rick would hold the Psalms out in his palms but either keep his lips sealed or murmur with a scowl of discomfort; and I would observe, on both sides, up above the tall arcaded bays of the clerestory, the hallowed panes of glass, thinking about God knows what. After the collection of voices sobered, it was time for the Eucharist, followed by saying our last prayers and rites, at which point Father Carr—a carapacean sedevacantist,[10] attired in a mint-green cope thrown over an alb as white as his hair—would impart his blessings, even on Rick. (Thanks be to God, Father Carr remained unaware that Rick made Tartuffe look like Turibius.[11]) Then Father Carr would do a brief but heartfelt obeisance to an icon of the Lord nailed in the high sanctuary, held within a calculated shade, golden architecture glimmering all around. Finally, the organ would strike up the grand finale and Father Carr would slowly disappear into the hind recesses of the church: the cue for the congregation to exit the polished pews...file down the Romanesque nave...creep through the dimmed narthex...then burst out two ultra-thick doors upon which hundreds of silhouetted angels swirled in congested circles. Then we, the Vallanos, would quietly drive home where, reigning in the dead room, my father, presently absolved, would finish off the blood of Christ. Amen.

---

[10] A sedevacantist is a traditional Catholic who believes the Church hasn't had a true pope in a long time, usually dating the last one before the commencement of the Second Vatican Council.
[11] Tartuffe is a religious hypocrite in Molière's eponymous play. Turibius of Mogroveio founded the first seminary in the Western Hemisphere in 1591 and fought for the rights of Indians in America; consequently, Pope Innocent XI beatified Turibius in 1679, becoming a patron saint for native rights.

Eh men. Eh women. Listen up: sum'n's rotten in the stated mark of our den. Heaven will direct us. Nay, rest up, for we got a long road ahead of us, if we're to survive...

YOU SELLOUT

"What do you expect me to do?
Live in poverty to prove to you
That I'm a man of dignity?
That I will never sell my soul?
Even though I've stood the test of time,
Even though I paid for your crime,
With the tears held back deep inside of me,
I can't sell out something forever free..." [1]

Some people around town found it hard to believe that I got accepted into Aristod, a small laudable college about three hours southeast of Pittsburgh. (Once you cross the Mason-Dixon line and pass the M-crownstone, Aristod is right next to the town of LaSalle.) Despite all the chaos in the house and out on the streets, I upheld my dedication to education, although I took a deviant approach beginning in 9th grade when I turned away from the standard material and started seeking outside sources. Some of my "private" teachers from freshmen year had "funny" names and taught "funny" subjects, like Vladdy Nabby for Punology; Joey Hell for Catchology; Karl M. (and his T.A., Freddy E.) for Classology; and ol' Chompy Chomsky for Linguistics 'n' 'at! I was really overloaded that year, but the lessons were free thanks to Pessi and his black-'n'-bored antics.[2] Not to sound all arrogant but my private teachers helped me become pretty smart—even though my public teachers never realized it; with *certain* students (like me!) they were only concerned with abusing us with their paltry authority, instead of amusing us with the waltz of empathy.

During graduation (right before my principal *had to* hand over my diploma) the redheaded tyrant Ms. Charlton paused and seemed to be scanning through a mental file cabinet, looking for pending detentions for me to serve so she wouldn't *have to* hand it over. She didn't want me to succeed. She really didn't! Several times she privately told me in her office that I never would, and by charlatan,[3] she meant it! Well, after my name boomed through the auditorium, and I walked up to the podium, and she hesitated, I presented her with the biggest fuck-you smirk I ever gave anyone! She responded with a look of disgust and imminent revenge—then carelessly dropped the scroll in my hand. Ma had been somewhere out in the crowd, watching me with humble pride; the other one somewhere unknown—well, likely on the stumble after drinking himself out of his mind.

---

[1] Lyrics from "At What Cost?" by Acronym of Pity, from the album *Help Me Help Yourself*

[2] "Black-'n'-bored antics" is both a play on the word *blackboard* and a neological idiom meaning "to steal something out of *dark* humor and/or *bored*om."

[3] As if saying "By golly!" Also a play on the principal's last name, Charlton.

When I left high school with my diploma, it felt like I was holding a key that would unlock the door to a better world. Every teacher I passed on my way down to the parking lot—the ones who suspended me for questioning them both earnestly and in jest, suspended me for using a contumacious hip-shake as my hallway gait, suspended me for me being *me*—the ones who would roll their eyes if my behavior was, on the whole, unpatriotic, unjustified, and immature—well, on the way down that long black declivity, their faces seemed so contorted as if lurking shadows had vice grips locked on their kidneys, wrenching it every time a teacher didn't want to remain upright and respectful. Yes, they didn't want to me to succeed either! I pledge allegiance to the flag that united every authority in that indefensible school looked at me, even *treated* me, as if I was a terrorist, or at the very least, unpatriotic. But God—didn't the red blood, white skin, and blue balls that flagged my physical existence suffice for me to have a little liberty and justice?

...The summer was winding down. I was leaving on Sunday and it was already Friday: my last life-before-college weekend. Ma was asleep, Rick at work, the house in one of its rare tranquil moments. In my room, the sun was shining brilliantly through the window where several strips of the blinds had broken off, causing serrated gleams to cut across the center of the room. I was expecting a knock on the window from Pessi. In the meantime, I was prostrated on the mattresses—stripped down to a black t-shirt and plaid boxers—trying, in the afternoon heat, to keep up on my reading: just started *Things Fall Apart* by Achebe. In a fortified circle called home, it's the Powerful vs. the Powerless: and when the circle breaks, Civilization vs. Nature: which side are you on?—what colors do you see: back? white? or shades of gray? To be sure, I either groomed the goutweed or gilded the lily. But like in those flowery, clichéd movies, I had this resolute flame burning inside that I was going to walk into Aristod and turn it upside-down with what I knew from reading like an Ivy Leaguer, while having what no Ivy Leaguer could ever acquire: the street smarts from growing up in Verna. Oh yeah, I was going to be the next rags to riches! the genius from nothing! straight out of poverty and into the limelight like no other! so to speak, set the world afire with the Vallanic Revolution—no, the Vallanic ERUPTION! But the reality was: soggy thoughts of my friends were blanketing the fire inside. It suddenly blew into mind that none would be going to college. None had the means or desire to. Eddie Hughes wanted to be a DJ; he did the occasional party. Jeremiah O'Malley dropped out of high school and did plumbing with his two uncles; he was two years older than Eddie, Pessi, and me. Three years older than us youngins, Dante Zielinski was a full-time potato sacker who recently started budding herpes; evidently, from the way he picked jobs and lovers, Dante had a serious death-wish. And Pessi...ahhh! The thought of Pessi was scrambling, twisting, and blowing away Achebe's words like a hazy harmattan!

A triple knock on the window.

I rose with a yawn and slugged over, peaking through the hole in the blinds. On the other side, Pessi was hunched down to level himself to where he could see in. His sun-doused hazel eyes were staring back mockingly: eyes as unfathomable and brilliant as Hawthorne's. *'I seeeee youuuu!'* I sang out. 'But'—(I grabbed the blinds and gave 'em a violent shake)—'now I'm blind 'n' can't find the lock!' Smirking, Pessi shook his head and headed over towards the front door. I casually dove back on the bed as if he wasn't about to join me, but we were best friends and things were always casual between us, so I didn't need to greet him, be nice, look at him, or put on pants.

Pessi walked in holding a paper bag by the neck of the 40 inside. I'd asked him to stop by Dante's and tell him that I needed to "borrow one from his fridge." Pessi had nothing for himself because he didn't drink, ever. He had on army cargos, a wrinkled hunter-green t-shirt, and black Doc Martins. On his left forearm: a white gauze covering his newest tattoo. He handed over the 40, and then, without instruction to do so, peeled back the gauze. It was a traditional mermaid: generic facial features, swirling blonde hair, and a teal tail that curled sensuously around splashes of water. Every tattoo Pessi had (predominately green and black obscured on his bronze arms, chest, and back) had been done by our friend Anson, a basement tattoo artist who used Pessi as his manikin. Anson had inked an abstract Japanese dragon on the back of my neck, but I became cautious of getting any more from him after he messed up one across Pessi's upper back. On a banner flowing through thick bright flowers, it was supposed to say in black cursive lettering *Struck by the Fuck.* (No significant meaning besides Pessi thinking it sounded cool.) But freestyling while intoxicated, Anson began inking an extra line on the *F* causing it to look like a half-assed *E*. We always made fun of Pessi for it because if you read it as Eu- (as in Europe) it becomes "Struck by the Yuck."

'Man, yir still readin' those fuckin' books,' he said incredulously, handing me the 40.

'Gadda get my mind right for cawidge.'

'More like: gadda get da shit kicked oudda ya for bein' such a fuckin' yuppie.' As he moved passed, he punched the back of my calf.

'I'll 'member that when I'm rollin' in the dough.' I rolled over on my side with my head tilted and eyebrows raised as if to say, 'So idd be best if you juss keptchir mouth shut 'n' stuck by me.' Sitting up, I situated myself on the edge of the bed and twisted open the 40. As usual, Pessi was quick to knee it in front of my small television, which sat generically atop a foldout stand better suited for glassware and magazines. He started up a video game, the console placed between the open legs of the stand. With his back to me, he said, 'Da only thing yir gonna be rollin' around in is debt.'

'Nah, I gadda scholarship thit's gonna help a bit. Plus, when I'm done, I'll be makin' decent money, so it won't even madder da debt I'm in.'

Waiting for the video game to load, Pessi set down the controller and pulled from his pocket an orange prescription bottle. With an intent focus, he rotated it around as if looking for directions in fine print.

'Catch a summer flu?' I joked after taking my first bitter gulp. Whatever Pessi had I knew it wasn't prescription medicine. He turned half-around on his knees as if wanting me to watch. He carefully tilted the orange bottle into his palm...til three yellow horse pills fell out. 'What's 'ose?' I asked. I was astonished by their size; I didn't keep up with the latest trend of pills because I'd quit eating 'em junior year of high school.

'Umm, they're like Gorilla Biscuits. Big ludes for big dudes. But since I ain't all that big a dude maybe dill put me under for gude.' A quip that straddled the line between morbid humor and dead seriousness. Maternally Russian with paternal quarters on Irish and Italian, Pessi was christened Zachary Alan Pessini, and as Life worked its wonders, he zapped right into the name: the most pessimistic person I knew! But that aside, if you subtracted my self-motivated erudition from the equation, we were basically the same person. Then again, I hadn't imbibed my equilibrium of Sicilian fluids from Archimedes, so my math isn't to be trusted.

'Need a drink for deez puppies,' Pessi noted with a devious smirk. He went out into the kitchen to quaff down the horse pills...and when he returned, wide-eyed, he exhaled as if he'd just swallowed three elephants, or gorillas.

'So yuppie boy,' he resumed. 'Cominna fair tanight?'

'I guess. Ju talk da anyone?'

'Yeah, everybody wansta go. Anthony's sposta come too.'

'I hate that *stup*id fuckin' whore.'

'Well Zielinski's da one thit cawed 'im, 'n' ya know how der all buddy-buddy now.'

'Yeah, well he's in for a rough night.' Shaking my head, I grunted like a little *fear dearg* at what I had in store for our "friend" Anthony Durkin. Pessi didn't bother responding; he kneed back down on the floor and picked up the controller.

'Eh I wanna play too. But let's get high first.'

'Spark it up, bro. Spark it up like uhhh, uhhh—' Pessi couldn't finish the simile.

I set the 40 down on the three-door dresser next to my mattresses, reached inside the top drawer, and retrieved half a blunt from an old cigar box. Putting the blunt to my nose, I took in a deep inhalation. Ahh! what a pleasant scent flooding my nasal! Nature's antediluvian redolence! *'Even as the green herb have I given you all things!'*[4] Thank You! After searching around for and finding my lighter, we stepped over to the window. I drew the blinds up halfway and lifted the window the same. Then we got high, blowing the smoke outside, even though it hardly mattered. Ma had already caught us ten thousand times. Her typical reaction was to tell Pessi: *'You need to teach him good sense!'* Meanwhile, looking right at her, Pessi would be taking in a hit, gagging back heavy coughs, and, with his boyish smirk shining in all its grandeur, saying, 'I will, Ma; I will.' Then Ma would walk away as if she'd heard exactly what she wanted to hear.

Already feeling good (the world upon my shoulders provisionally removed), I shut the window and sat back down on the edge of the mattresses. Pessi kneed back down in front of me, and we began playing a video game. It was a football game and whenever I wanted or needed Pessi to mess up I would kick him in the back; he would gripe and threaten to restart the game. About thirty minutes in (not long after I finished the 40) Ma woke up. Peeking in through my cracked door, she said, 'Ciau, Pipi! And

---

[4] The words of God in Genesis 9:3

youuu, Tappiceddu,[5] spray some fragrance in here! I can smell it! Your fauter comes home soon!'—(I just smiled.)— 'Don't smile! Do it! I'll close-ah door; you keep it closed!' So she closed the door and I kept it closed. I also sprayed fragrance and lit a cigarette to normalize the smell of my room. Meanwhile, Pipi was carelessly wrapping up the controllers after losing 35-7. He was dispirited because he'd been Da Stillers, and to lose with them on a video game induced the same feelings as if it had been a game for the books: that's how deep Stiller Spirit runs in Pittsburgh: very intoxicating!

'So when you leavin' again? Sunday?'

'Yeah, prahblee Sunday afternoon. You gonna come over 'n' eat?'

'Yeah, if ya get Ma da cook up summa that Skeddi B.'

A nondescript but vicious thought suddenly capsized my mind. I let out a prolonged noise of distress: *'Uuuuuggh!'*

'Wha'?'

'—I dunno; juss gonna be a whole new life at cawidge, ya know.'

'*Yeaaah*, prahblee.' He set the controllers atop the console, then pushed it back. 'So how's yir major thing work? Jardee pick it out? or ya decide that wancha get dere?'

'Undecided for now. But iddle prahblee be English. Might even double it with—*Fffuck!*' Unknowingly, I was burning a hole in my boxers. I put the cigarette out and began picking at the hole, trying to rip out the blackened frays.

Pessi stood up and, yawning, stretched his muscular arms up and outward, allowing a myriad of reflections from the window to seep into the spaces between his ink. 'Ya know what you should, V—go inda Law or Business. 'At's where da *rill* money is. See, if ya rilly wanna get "dough da roll in," ya juss gadda putchirself where da dough *is*,' Pessi concluded sententiously, cracking his knuckles fist-to-fist.

'No chance of me doin' either.'

'Why? 'Cauzshir stupid?'

'No, 'cause I'm goin' da cawidge da akshly learn sum'n,' I replied with an air of conceit. 'I don't give a fuck about money; I'm gonna do whad *I* wanna do.'

Pessi turned away and began scratching his pipi, digging deep, hard and fast, back and forth, through the dark almond-brown peppered across his all too circular head. He'd never had his hair cut or colored any other way; our old-school barber, Zippi, loved Pessi's reliable simplicity and made fun of my requests for fades and thinning-scissors to enhance my little spikes. After the scratching ceased, Pessi stuck his finger in his ear and rocked it back and forth like a wobbly ship. With his back to me, mocking my voice, he said, '*I don't give a fuck about money; I'm gonna do whad I*

---

[5] *Pipi* is Sicilian for "pepper" and refers to Pessi's hair. Ma nicknamed Pessi "Pepper" because she said that his natural hairstyle looks like he'd been peppered on the scalp. As young kids, Pessi and V found it funny because it's pronounced the same as "pee-pee." *Tappiceddu* roughly translates as "sweet little wine cork" and refers to V's short and stout stature. It's pronounced tah-pih-CHEH-doo.

wanna do.' He let out a short grunt of laughter. 'Man, you rilly are stupid for someone goin' da cawidge.'

Taking no offense, I didn't bother responding. Instead, I fell straight back on the mattresses, scooted up towards the wall, and locked my hands behind my pillow-resting head. On the television, a fat loquacious cowboy was rambling off once-in-a-lifetime deals going on at his car lot this weekend. Next, a bald attorney with petite glasses was assuring no fees! absolutely no fees! unless he gets money for YOU! Then the scheduled program came on: dramatized court cases, small claims. Not knowing where the remote was, and not wanting to move, I watched it unenthusiastically. Meanwhile, Pessi was pacing around, flipping through a magazine he'd found on the floor. Minutes passed before he carelessly tossed it. He walked over to the window, peered through the blinds, turned around, then went into a staring contest with Darby Crash: a poster hung to the right of the television. As I looked Pessi on from the side, his face turned strange and inquisitive; straight on, Darby's remained young and feral. They eyed each other...til Pessi gave up and snatched another magazine off the dresser, the one I bought because it had the newest college reports and statistics. He flipped through it attentively, perhaps looking for information on Aristod, but suddenly stopped, laid it back down, turned around, and, unprovoked, bitterly said, 'Sercly, V: fuck cawidge.'

'Yeah: fuck 'at bitch.'

Just then, someone came in the front door; Razzle was barking out back. Pessi promptly said, 'Well I'm out. I'll caw ya in a bit.' He left out the door, although I'm surprised he didn't crawl out the window; nobody liked to face my father.

Lying there motionless, looking up at an old orange rain stain, I found myself absorbed in what I had just said: 'Yeah: fuck 'at bitch,' meaning college. Some days—well, in *past* days, I would've said the same thing in all seriousness. Although I was usually sarcastic with just about everybody, Pessi loved whenever I was serious and inflamed. He loved provoking me into preaching my "revolutionary discourses," no matter how pubertal and unpolished. He enjoyed that kind of thing: listening to tales of utopian battles, intensified by the drugs, experiences, and vendettas burning inside us. And I liked to make him smile, comfort him in my own twisted way. But it was starting to feel old. Touting this, by criticizing that. Hoping for this, by battling against that. I thought about how I would be leaving for college in two days, and no matter what, Aristod *had to* be a haven compared to Verna. I felt that I had finally reached the age of retirement from rebellion, criticism, and despair. In the amiability of my imagination, life at Aristod would be like an affluent retirement home; in other words, the environment (like how it's shown in brochures and on commercials) is such a scenic, peaceful place where any problem is promised to be a trivial one. One problem: you still get beat there.

...We were laughing boisterously. Taking random shots at each other. Yelling over yells. Jeremiah, Eddie, and Dante seated on a couch embroidered with swirling garbage flowers; Pessi and I were in metal foldout chairs, one on each side of the couch but closer to the television. We were watching a Buccos game. Cheering for homeruns, acrobatic catches, and the mad-eyed batter who just got hit in the shoulder with a wild fastball. Meanwhile, throwing curveball chips at each other. Getting up just to tag-out the person furthest away. Umping nonsensical rules. Swinging around an olive-green blunt. Coughing and laughing. Everyone but Pessi taking shots of whiskey and gin. United once again: Da Hoolies—a simple name for our crew but fitting of our collective disposition as hooligans.

Although our spirits were bright, the lighting was dim. In front of us sat a bulky old television, flush against the wall, with the corners of the screen besmirched with indelible grime; it couldn't help but emit a dull, listless light. Precariously fastened to the ceiling was a dual socket holding one naked bulb. Behind us, shoulder left, a tangerine haze filled the kitchen. The place had the feel of sitting in an alleyway except in lieu of bricks were gator-green walls, so obscure that it was hard to tell they were even there. By nature, Dante Zielinksi's first-floor Section-8 smelled like dewy cardboard. By habit, Da Hoolies smelled like dual intoxication: three innings in.

Eddie stood up from the couch to take a shot of whiskey. He perched one leg on the carved-up coffee table before him. Holding his smile, he waited for our attention so he could imitate how the jocks from our high school partied in their swaggering way. Eddie was of a deep brown color, and at 5'8", three inches taller than me. He had a square head sporting a high-fade flattop (we all made fun of it for being old-school), and below, long smooth checks with high cheekbones, broad shoulders and pecs, and chicken legs: all upper body, but a strong, fast, athletic kid who wasn't an athlete. All smiles, we turned our attention to him, ready for his imitation. He tackled the shot then roared like a linebacker, shaking his head with his long tongue hanging out in mocking fashion. After rolling it up, he dumped the residue from the shot glass on Dante's skinned head. We all laughed and began throwing chips 'n' 'at towards Veteran Zielinski as compliments from the rest of the team.

'I'm about da kick yinz assholes out if ya don't stop throwin' shit.' Since we didn't stop throwin' shit, Dante settled with grabbing Eddie's white tanktop to shine his head dry. After the buff-job, Eddie slapped Dante's dried head and attempted to sit back down between him and Jeremiah. But he had to push...throw 'bows...and squeeeeeeeze in because Dante was being difficult in making room. Once situated, Eddie looked like a helpless black kid stuck between two skinheads: Dante's head was skinned to the bone, and although Jeremiah's wasn't quite to the bone, his hair was a faint blonde. To boot, both had muscular bodies covered in ink, and regularly wore Ben Shermans, straight-legged blue jeans, and black Docs. Neither were skinheads, but back in the day both had ridden that train for a few stops, from which we made (and still had) older friends who were traditional working-class skins; that is, the non-racist kind.

I was sitting in the metal foldout chair closest to the door, close to being drunk. I was usually a loquacious drunk. Jeremiah was a quiet and poised drunk; you could hardly tell he was even intoxicated. Eddie was a buzzer, never getting wasted on booze; he liked to smoke more than drink. Herpes-infected Dante had a serious death-wish, as I already explained, and drinking himself into blindness, as he frequently did, only brought his dream that much closer to reality. Of course, once Dante acquired, we required him to keep his lips off the bottle, and I think everybody kept a conscious eye on the matter. Although I wasn't there, one time Dante had been drinking at a bar in West Eaton, a rough suburban neighborhood. (He was eighteen at the time, presently twenty-one.) Anyway, he got wasted, went out on the street, beat up the first person he saw, pulled his dick out, then pissed on the guy. Instead of zipping up, Dante took off his pants and began running down the street, taunting everybody in the vicinity, til he was arrested and sentenced to thirty days in jail, two years of probation, and fines out the dick. That's Dante's drunkenness. Finally, Pessi: although he didn't drink, his reckless synergism with everything else he did sometimes caused his intoxications to be far worse than our drunkenness: a tense, cold-eyed, jaw-clinched look that suggested someone was "really gonna get it" but no one would ever find out about it.

As I was about to suggest that we head to The Square Fair, Anthony Durkin walked in. Dante sprang up from the couch to greet him with enthusiasm, which only heightened my disgust for Anthony. He said what's up to everyone, and to me he said it very timidly; he overstood my feelings for him. Then he moved into the room like a timid turtle. Even the way he walked bothered me: so effeminate and cowardly! He was anorexic-looking with owlish eyes and an unshaven face; not fully bearded but it looked absurd paired with his scrawny frame; he recently grew the scruff in an attempt to hide his womanliness. Anthony had always been the kind to dress according to whoever he's around just to fit in; his closet probably looked a microcosm of the mall. And whatever Dante said, Anthony said. Whatever Dante wanted to do, Anthony wanted to do. Whenever Dante had to shit, Anthony had to shit. If Dante got herpes, then Anthony had to get herpes, which he hadn't been able to do yet—unless he'd been making out with Dante behind our backs which I'm sure he was burning to do, and not out of homosexuality but because he so desperately wanted to be somebody's little bitch. That's Anthony's sobriety.

He grabbed the fifth of whiskey on the table and asked whose it was. I said mine; it wasn't. He asked if he could take a couple shots; I said sure. He took a shot and glanced at me timorously—I nodded approvingly—then he sat down on the couch where Dante had been sitting. Yeah, I forgot: wherever Dante sat, Anthony had to sit.

'Well yinz about riddy?' I asked.
'Been riddy,' replied Eddie.
'Whadever,' said Pessi.
Jeremiah nodded.

Dante was in the kitchen but hearing me yelled, 'Yeah! Hold up a minute! Dere's sum'n leakin' in the fridge!' Since we have a minute, one last exposition if I may: In Da Burgh, the use of *there/dere/'ere* (like *the/da/'ah, that/dat/'at/dit/thit*, and the singular *you/ya/ju/ja/chu/cha*) depends on the tempo, tone, and preceding word. Yinzers tend to compound words; overemphasize the beginning of a sentence while underemphasizing the ending; and replace dental Ts with cacuminal Ds. Based on my observations, the generation of yinzers before mine are among the last to speak in the staccato flow unique to traditional Pittsburghese[6]; us youngins aren't as crisp and choppy: our flow has become more dismissive and slurry.

I slid my eyes left towards my avian anathema and noted that he was the only one wearing shorts. He probably felt so uncomfortable because he couldn't stand to stand out, couldn't handle the concept of individuality even in its most pathetic and provisional forms. He had the fifth resting on his shaking thigh, with a firm grip around the neck of the bottle. He was looking deep into rocking copper ocean as if making an internal decision whether or not to throw back a bunch of shots before we left. In the meantime, he decided to take another one, leaving his face to wince with a red glow.

'Bedder hurry up if ya wanna get drunk,' I advised, trying not to let my smirk be seen by rubbing my face in a fake yawn.

Without looking over, he weakly replied, 'Yeah, I know. I'm tryin'.'

'Juss start firin' 'em dahn,' suggested Eddie. 'Come on, Ant; do it!' Suddenly the red piss-ant laughed as if to say, 'Great idea, Eddie! I'll do whatever anybody tells me to!' And so SycophAnt put back *nùmmiru tri*.[7] Pressing into him, with bulged eyes, Eddie was egging him on for his own entertainment. 'Another one!' he yelled. *'Do iiiiiit!'*

'H-ukk, ughh, hold on,' hacked Anthony. He was already so splotchy in the face, trying so hard to hold back his grimace—but his owl eyes were about to capsize! HA! 'Hey, V. Can I bring 'iss with me? I'll give ya ten bucks for it.' About two-thirds down, the eleven-dollar bottle was actually brought by Jeremiah, who didn't care to speak up, probably just content I was about to con the stupid whore out of ten bucks.

'Ar'ight, you stupid whore. Juss keep it dahn 'cause 'ere's gonna be pleece everywhere.'

'Stupid whore?' he repeated.

'I fuckin' studder, you *dumb* owl-lookin' prostitute? Why dohncha go home 'n' shave 'at fuckin' shit off yir face? You *stu*pid fuckin' whore.'

Everyone laughed besides Dante because Anthony was seriously his stupid little whore...

...Outside we began walking towards the squares: about a ten-minute walk from Dante's, but with the way we were staggering and bantering, it was bound to take longer. The sky was swirled with vibrant pinks and blues...opulent with tender clouds...an hour and a half before nightfall. A cool, gusty air had supplanted the afternoon heat. It felt and smelled unusually clean whenever it whipped against my face, as if the local sky was a freshly opened Band-Aid. In some of the stronger drafts, I could smell the nearby foods. That's what brought most people to the fair: restaurants 'n' 'at from the metro area, as well as traveling food hobbyists,

---

[6] In the late 19th century, the dialect evolved primarily from Scotch-Irish immigrants (emphatic staccato speakers), with contributions from Germans, East Slavicists (mainly Russians), South Slavicists (collectively Serbo-Croatians), Polish Jews, Southern Blacks, and Abruzzese Italians. The sound of Pittsburghese is often described as similar to the Chicago dialect.

[7] [scn] number three

set up booths offering their specials, some at reduced prices or with free coupons. Although we had good food in mind, our main objectives were picking up chicks and gambling alla carnevale.

Walking in threes, me, Pessi, and Jeremiah, were up front; Dante, Eddie, and Anthony in the rear. Surprisingly, Eddie was the only one being too loud, pushing Anthony to finish the bottle. He really had it out for Anthony but in a joking way. I didn't care if Anthony got caught or dropped to the ground vomiting because if the police should happen to appear *I* didn't know him and he wasn't with *us three;* I would keep on walking with a sincere smile, glad he'd been taken out of the picture by any means.

As we neared the midway point, the streets were becoming more crowded. Most bodies were moving in the same direction, which was good because it helped us blend in with all the flesh and noise. Only the elderly were working against the current as the bridge and canasta tournaments (held in tents set up in the inner squares) ended. Occasionally glancing downward, I saw the cracks in the sidewalk beginning to heal: the area of boxes and boxes was phasing into the sleek, white, plastic strips.

'Eh, V,' *(hiccup!)* 'ya know, I can sercly see you joinin' a frat dahn 'ere,' remarked Dante, laughing and hiccupping simultaneously. Without hesitation, everyone laughed at the idea and began discussing it casually, but progressively the conversation escalated til, suddenly, like a riotous burst of debate, everyone began sharing hypotheticals of me at college as a fratboy. Our pace slowed as the conversation prevailed with a maddening gaiety. Into my ear, everyone seemed to be speaking so fast and loud now! Their tones sounded reproachful as if they were intentionally trying to make me pose questions to myself and come up with the answers right away or else there would be hell to pay! I—I—I—*izzer rilly a chance I'm gonna become wha' der sayin'?*...at the thought my head began spinning in a frenzy of delusion and intoxication...scores of people were suddenly enclosing in on me, melting twisting, breathing on me, staring, laughing...laughing, laughing, laughing...*ha-ha-ha! why won't dey stop laughin'? ha-ha-ha! who said that? who juss said I's tuwa sum'n? dey know sum'n about my existence I don't? wha' did Pessi juss say he could see? why'd he juss slap the back of my head?*...a flash of heat began sweeping over me in rhythmic waves of nausea, tingling, and a fatal trepidation so severe that I knew Death had arrived to take me away...and although the sweat was pouring out freely, the stinging heaviness pushing at my skin from underneath couldn't quite make it through—it hurt—I locked my left hand akimbo, kept thumbing at my jaw with the other hand, trying to figure things out, or save myself, or conceal my imminent death...with each second I was becoming hotter, the air thicker, the light blurrier, as more ponderous thoughts, some in alien languages, assailed my consciousness with no remorse...suddenly another heavy thought of another me somewhere else, a me I couldn't control or overstand, was indefatigably prodding the inner side of my face, trying to push outward through the back of my eye sockets...but I could still see it eyes open, that *other* me...then everything was—*why's someone behin' me screamin' sellout! sellout! sellout! is 'at Zielinski? Anthony? everyone?—yes! it's everyone!—everyone's after me!*...

For the rest of the walk, their vindictive judgment exploded throughout my head like tossed grenades: *SELLOUT! SELLOUT! YOU SELLOOOOOOOUT!!!*

'Wagers closed! Hands back! *Haaaaands* back!' shouted Gary the dice-thrower. Under a blue canopy, he rolled two oversized dice out across a wooden board decked with months and numbers. ("Die Trying": a rather complicated game for a fair, but I already conned it out of ten bucks. Luckily, once the anxiety attack ended, I was in a position to indulge in food and festivities since Dante finally paid back the hundred bucks he owed. He actually owed two hundred but I told him to give half to Anson who had a fake ID made for me so that I could drink at college, *alone.*) With a clunk, the dice banked off the wooden side and rolled back haphazardly like two jagged rocks...til stalling on their respective squares. 'Twelves! Sixes! and March!' announced Gary the dice-thrower. A collective moan rang out. He went around to all three sides, scooping everyone's change into a metal bucket besides Jeremiah and a fat furrball leaning over three spots down...

...After playing for half an hour, I stepped back a few feet to have a smoke. As I turned the leaf into a cherry, the thought of tainting the fresh balmy air with smoke passed through my mind disagreeably...til I inhaled again and it mildly restimulated my buzz. Meanwhile, I was taking in observations of the festive street: Fleeing from their parents, children were flying past with disheveled hair and cotton-candy faces twined with the sky. Flying all around, so free, so breathful while breathless, everything around them, which was rather mundane to me, must've seemed like the magical wonderland they fantasized about during the day or dreamt of at night because they were screaming with such excitement and curiosity that it brought to their small virginal faces a strong incandescent blush. The sounds of innocence and euphoria—(I believe it was the sounds)—flushed me with the sensation of *déjà vu* although I couldn't recall having had such experiences. Perhaps it was anamnesis mistakenly gapped together by paramnesia caused by unconscious disingenuousness? Or perhaps the primitive energy of my id buried too far within to allow conscious accessibility yet striving upward to bring about "the satisfaction of instinctive needs"?[8] Or perhaps, on a similar thrust, the complexity of a wistful reflection of a younger reflection: a nostalgic void (although not void of the sensation itself) creeping back up on me demanding some kind of fruition? But as the great wistful sensation dissipated and frustration set in from not being able to isolate and soothe the cry of the former sensation,

---

[8] Freud's psychoanalytical terms: *anamnesis* - a recollection of a memory; *paramnesia* – a false memory because it's blended with an actual experience and fantasy, the fantasy usually "filling in the gaps" because of "unconscious disingenuousness" which is the repression of the truth of the memory (both terms discussed in *Dora*); *id* - the "dark, inaccessible part of our personality...striving to bring about the satisfaction of instinctive needs" (discussed in *On Narcissism*)

I surrendered to the most hopeless conclusion: *ignotum per ignotius!* [9] I felt drained, sobered—rejected. Taking in a deep drag, I focused my attention elsewhere with a renewed breeziness. I observed better-disciplined families strolling closer together—much closer than the feral ones—taking time to enjoy their food and the musical neon atmosphere. And middle-schoolers hanging around in private groups, doing immature things like spitting pop at each other and giving each other sudden wedgies from behind. And high-schoolers (with that extra strand of maturity) walking in large defensive packs, eying others their age with spite as if no else belonged there besides them. All this absurdness brought a tender laugh. Then a larger nasal laugh came as I extinguished my smoke and spotted one of those imbeciles who'd won a gigantic stuffed animal—a pink unicorn in white boots?—just so he could haul it around with a proud struggle as if someone else actually gave a shit he won it.

I blinked. Passing before my internal eyes: a loose-lipped Anthony Durkin devouring his second Italian roast beef sandwich because Dante Zielinski was also devouring his second. That was almost an hour ago, before Eddie, Dante, and Anthony went off to scout chicks. Anthony was supposedly drunk, but you never knew with a slimy fake like him. I was looking forward to harassing him, but also glad he wasn't around. Besides, it was still early, so I had all night to treat him like a masochistic whore. But hold be blown, here comes Eddie, Dante, and the masochistic whore trotting towards the better half standing at the "Die Trying" tent, having, as Dante explained, "a liddle problem."

'What's 'at?' was Jeremiah's response.

With his large bald head, Dante directed our attention to five kids standing arms-crossed and cocky-eyed in front of a closed clothing store twenty yards away. Already knowing the situation, I rolled my eyes. In a quick simulated conversation in my head, I was saying to Dante, 'Lemme guess: one of 'em bumped inda ya 'n' started sayin' shit.'

'Fuckin' me 'n' Anthony were waitin' for Eddie takamaudda da baffroom,' Dante began fervently, his attention focused mostly on Jeremiah, "n'ah one widda red hat walks by 'n' kicks my boot—'cause we were sittin' dahn on a bench. So I stan' up da say sum'n. 'N' he comes 'n' gets up in my face. So I'm like, "Gih da fuck oudda my face, kid." 'N' 'en Eddie comes out, standin' 'ere not sayin' a word. 'N'—'

"'N'ah one kid says sum'n like, "Oh, I thouchinz two were on a liddle date together,"' Anthony chimed in.

'Yeah. So I told 'em if 'ey wanna run 'er fuckin' mouffs let's take a walk. All a sudden da one wearin'ah blue shirt lashes at me like he's gonna hit me, but dey grab 'im back, ya know. But I'm like is 'iss kid fuckin' seris?—'

'Fuck 'iss,' I interjected. 'I'm not tryin'ah get in trouble two days before I leave.' Aware of how loud we were being, I guided us away from the tent to prevent Gary the dice-thrower from hearing anything else. Da Hoolies, plus the whore, formed a circle in the middle of the crowded street; our potential enemies stayed put.

---

[9] [lat] A thing unknown by a thing more unknown. [Meant here to undermine the prospects of psychoanalysis.]

'Look,' Dante addressed everyone, 'I didn't start *shit.* But der gonna come inda our neighborhood 'n' run 'er mouths? 'N' fuck—*der* da wunzit kept followin' us, basically provokin' us.'

'They *did* follow us here,' affirmed Eddie, "n' were sayin' shit da entire time.'

'Yeah, bahchu overstand how many cops are out tanight? I'm sercly not tryin'ah get arrested righ' before I leave. 'N' *you* wanna go back on probation?' That was directed towards Dante Zielinski.

'Fuck it. We'll go over da the ball field. Iddle be dead around 'ere anyway, 'n' ya can't rilly see it fromma road, know whadda mean. Wha', you scared or sum'n?' Dante's big-jawed face jutted then went sober. 'Come on, liddle Rocky; one lass time—' He stopped to observe the five confirmed enemies walking towards us. Right away, I realized they weren't the jocks, the necks, or the metalheads we'd fought with in high school. They kinda looked like us: all in rebel-logo t-shirts; three in rough blue jeans; two in baggy skater pants; piercings in their ears; tats on their arms; three muscular, tough-looking ones but two skinny ones. Anthony was the only one with us small in girth, but more so, the only one who couldn't and probably wouldn't fight on his own will.

As they approached with apathetic limbs and confident smiles, we broke from our circle and formed a rough line. All the fairgoers (who'd altogether left my attention) were passing by inattentively as if we were only street statues they had to sidestep. But it still felt like I was in a scene spotlighting us, melting me right into sobriety.

The big-chest kid with the red hat spoke directly to Dante: 'So yir boys dahn or wha'? See yinz even got one up on us. Yinz'll prahblee need it.'

'Don't worry; he's juss gonna watch what I do da all yunz,' Dante said with a smirk, tilting his head towards Anthony.

'Yeah okay, faggot,' said one of the skinny kids in the back.

'Look: I ain't gonna stand here 'n' talk shit all night. So why dohnchinz juss follow us do a ball field a couple blocks away 'n' 'en we'll see what's up.'

'Aww, yir local ball field? Dat's cool,' said the kid in the red hat, pretending to swing a bat, his soft blue eyes so provoking in the shimmer of his turn. 'You'll be up against some sluggas from Rockwell.' His friends found that amusing. So did Pessi, probably because he was thinking the same thing as me: how lame this kid is for thinking Rockwell (a middle-class housing plant) is hardcore. Then the kid in the red hat turned to a smirking Pessi and said, 'What the fuck you smilin' at, you liddle bitch?'

Like a Mitch William's fastball, I lost it and went straight at him; we interlocked and a mini-scuffle broke out for a few seconds...til Jeremiah pulled me back by the neck and the kid in the red hat got pulled back by two of his friends. But he kept acting crazy and running his mouth, causing a scene. It didn't faze me or suck me into a shit-talking contest; I was already calm again because I was cop-conscious.

'Jah'shuh'da fuck up 'n' let's go,' I said with a condescending huff. 'We'll see how tough you are once we're alone.' I pivoted around, ready to lead the way and release gallons of bottled anger. Departing from The Square Fair, we began beating against the grain of the main roads, heading north, fast. Da Rockwells were at a safe distance behind. One said, 'Don't worry! We ain't gonna hurtchinz til yir riddy!' Umm, not by the hair of my chinny, chin, chinz. Yes, *chinz:* an inflection of *yinz,* the infamous trademark of Pittsburghese. Anyway, Chinzer Rockwell's comment only further inflamed us!—only snapped our heads back like gumbands just to make sure they weren't up to anything, trying to make an early move...only to see them laughing and gesturing. But we were in high spirits too! Even if I had the biggest one on my plate, I wasn't "scared or sum'n": the fear of fighting subsides once you've done it enough to win a few confidence fights, as well as get roughed up a few times, from which you feel and consequently overstand the mental and physical pain of *victory* and *loss* in man's most primitive form, and thereby the enigma conventionalizes itself.

Despite its peach intensity, the sun was now waning inside a nebular shield of molten light. Shadows were sticking to the sidewalks and flitting from box to box. Enough natural light remained to see what we would be doing. I looked up deep into the heavens: aristocratic blues were gobbling up Caesarean pinks...the clouds were thick and shapely, passing one another at various speeds like fleets in a crowded sea...and peaking through in transparency (opposing the dying sun) was a full moon: what one would call a picturesque evening sky. I was staring back and forth between sun and moon, admiring the phenomenon. I could faintly hear everyone discussing whom they planned on going after, even though their plans could prove fickle depending on how things transpired. However, I thought it strange how *I* was the one billed in what seemed the title fight—the one who finalized the decision as if my own promoter. I was off to college in two days, wasn't I? Well this evening I was off in the sky.

Nearing the battlefield, we marched on with cool confident steps. Anthony though—he was now up front with me, probably afraid to be the closest to Da Rockwells, a role Jeremiah didn't mind taking on. Unlike me, Jeremiah had never lost a fight; a southpaw who'd knocked many out with one punch; the quiet one: the toughest one. We made the final right turn in cadence, in silence. Da Rockwells were still at the same distance behind us. From our vantage, a horizontally long gravel parking lot lay up ahead...then a small hill that hid the field except the far end of the outfield. There was only one nearby road, which followed right field and then cut left into a small ghetto which ended in a cul-de-sac lined up with center field.

'Inna outfield, fellas!' instructed Dante with summertime merriment.

Stopping in the shallow, we turned around and waited. With a backward glance I realized Anthony had returned to the back of the pack. I wasn't in the right mind to confront his typical ways. Better to let things remain quiet and tense as we focused on the five Rockwells passing by the foul-line fence with energetic limbs and confident smiles...but once in the infield, they slowed to a halt. The kid in the red hat was in the vanguard, so I moved a stepped forward. They were beckoning us to join.

'Come on, pussies! Come gitsim!...Yinz fags gonna stand 'ere holdin' hands or wha'!...Come on!...Come run yir fuckin' mouff now, ya short fuckin' greasy bitch!...'

I turned to Pessi. 'Sercly, fuck 'iss.'

'Whaddaya mean?'

'If 'ey rilly wan' their faces rubbed in'ah dirt, then let's fuckin' do it.'

'V!'

I was already marching forward, tired of the anxiousness that comes with waiting, tired of being called on. The kid in the red hat threw his hat off and quickly put his hands up and bent his legs into position. He looked like a flaxen frog trying to shit in a toilet. His large lips were moving, probably still calling me on, but I couldn't hear a thing besides the swollen deafness ringing in my head. When I got close enough, it was like the air in my head suddenly sucked straight out and everything began playing in fast-forward. Standing with my left shoulder in the vanguard, I balked my left elbow at him. It made him swing wide and hard. I easily dodged the haymaker and shot back with a jab to his jaw. It emitted a sickening *POP!* As he took that critical stagger-step backward, I finished knocking him to the ground with a hard tackle. I jumped on top and began vying for leverage. In the tussle, I dug my knee up deep into his gut. When he dropped his guard for a brief moment, I let one fly into his nose. Another grotesque *POP!* While trying to rearrange his face (he was already in a balled defensive position) I could hear the grunts, wails, smacks, and thuds of the fights going on around me. I didn't see who went after who once I engaged, but I did hear Dante shout: 'What's up now, you fuck?!' The kid without his hat took his forearms away from his face and tried to push me backwards. I grabbed the front of his t-shirt, but he turned with the snatch, and we rolled sideways in the dirt. The dirt was kicking into my face. I could taste it. But I was trying to push the dirt out of my mind with the hope it wouldn't get in my contacts because then I might be done for. I was having trouble controlling his weight—had a good thirty pounds on me—but I was telling myself there's *no way* I'm gonna lose...no way! Back in the grapple, he threw a few quick punches to the side of my head: enough to trigger the explosion of strength I needed. I arched back, pulled myself upward, still clutching his shirt, then delivered a decisive punch to his nose. Immediately blood squirted out in two streams. He grabbed his nose out of fear—out of the rational need for confirmation. Rocks-for-brains! Well, not to sound as if I'd usurped the Power of God, but Rocks-for-brains just sealed his fate and put the epistle in *my* hands, for I began delivering punches to his guarded face with relentless rapidity...til he whined: 'Okay! enough! I'm done! I'm done!' And despite my current advantage and anger, I only hit him two more times—then once more in the mouth. A two-minute job: sign, sealed, and delivered.

I stood up, wiping the dirt off while keeping an eye on him. My arms were bleeding a bit and stinging a lot. He stood up, holding his nose, picked up his red hat, then limped off towards the hillside, indifferent to the donnybrook going on around us. Amid the chaos, the first person I spotted was Eddie. He was fighting with one of the skinnier kids, rolling around second base, trading off ineffective punches. I couldn't tell who had the ups so I ran over and said, 'You cool?' He didn't answer. 'Come on, Eddie; hit 'im inna nose! Da nose!' He was punching the kid in the ribs, while the other kid thumped the back of his neck. They were rolling around too much to get in solid shots: this chocolate-and-vanilla pretzel trying to untangle its flavors. In an attempt to gain leverage on Eddie, for Eddie was on top, the other kid tried pulling himself upward by sticking his hand up the back of Eddie's shirt. In that moment, I could see Eddie's back was scratched up. 'Eddie, juss smash inna fuckin' nose, man!'

'Shudup—I...' As Eddie struggled to reply, the other kid gave him a solid punch in the ear. I was about to jump in but Eddie somehow shot straight up from the ground—his ferociousness sounding out—and ventrally kicked the kid in the stomach. Throwing his whole body into it, he then came down on the kid's face, once, twice, three times, all hard shots...the kid cried out for him to stop. Satisfied, Eddie spit on him and kicked him in the ribs once more, then backed away. As Eddie brushed the dirt off his clothes, we moved forward, surveying the field, ready to lend a fist, although Da Rockwells were proving no match for Da Hoolies.

'Yo, you see Pess anywhere?'

Eddie responded in the negative but was wiping dirt from his eyes.

I jogged up between first base and the pitcher's mound where Anthony was on the ground spooning a big kid while Dante forked his face. Out of the corner of my eye, out to the left, I could also see the kid I fought, the one Eddie fought, and another huffing and puffing back down the hill, offering no help to their two remaining friends. Then I spotted action going on behind the fence near the third-base dugout. Jeremiah was just coming into vision, pulling Pessi back by the shirt...but Pessi was tugging forward, swinging wildly. Eddie and I ran over. En route, Pessi's forward momentum ripped his shirt right off his body, leaving Jeremiah holding it like a porno mag: curious amazement written all over his face. Then my heart suddenly jumped: the face and body of both Pessi and the other kid were covered in blood.

'Wha' da fuck happened?' I asked Jeremiah.

'Kid hit 'im widda bawdle.' He pointed to a nearby pile of beer bottles. I walked over and stood before Pessi, nudging him to turn around, but he kicked his leg out around me and spat the blood accumulated in his mouth at the blonde-headed bottle-swinger now down in the fetal position. He was moaning horrible sounds, and unless my vision was tricking me, it appeared his face was grossly swelling up. He looked up languidly, ignominiously, with a face splattered with blood like he'd been shot repeatedly with a paintball gun. While holding back Pessi—the blood on him rubbing off on me—I casually observed this variegated thing, almost without a drop of sensibility. But:

'Someone help 'im up!' unexpectedly shot out of me. Still holding Pessi still, I tried brushing off the shards of glass stuck in his pants and arms; Jeremiah was also helping, but nobody was helping the other one. Eddie, Dante, and Anthony had gathered behind Jeremiah. Dante said something about how he wasn't helping that fuck out. Laughing, Anthony concurred. I look up and glared at the slinking snake! the amoebic invertebrate! the *sadistic* bitch! His smile became indecisive. But his eyes! If I looked at his large hooting eyes a second longer, I was going to run over and pry 'em out! I turned to ask Eddie to help the other up—but I was mistaken about Eddie being around. Who knows where he went.

'Hold 'im for a sec,' I said to Jeremiah; he took Pessi into custody, as I began creeping up on the other, keeping my focus on the blood methodically flowing from his nose like an IV drip, and—suddenly an unleashed Pessi pushed me aside, knocking me into a long blood-red lock-box behind the batter's cage. *Ding!*

'Motherfucker wansta hit me widda bir bawdle!' said Pessi. Like lightning, he bolted back on top of the other, hammering away: blood and sweat misting into the air.

'Guess he ain't done yet,' said Jeremiah.

I went back into the scuffle anyway, Jeremiah following. Pessi was flailing and swinging so violently that even four hands couldn't establish one firm grip. It was like trying to catch and hold down a greased bullfrog. He actually turned around at one point, pushed me back by the chest and yelled something incoherent, but by the wrathful tone, I could tell it was a threat. He did the same to Jeremiah, who, frustrated, said, 'Fine, Pess; do whacha want.' Jeremiah threw his arms up in the air and walked away to become a spectator. I was thinking Pessi *had to be* stuck in a blind rage.

To my left, Eddie appeared. I told him to go over to the hillside to see what Da Rockwells were doing, to get 'em to come carry him out, that none of us would touch 'em, that it was over. He looked at me with a smile, as if to say, 'Why you even care?' Still, he abided and walked around to the side—but making a quick pivot, said, 'I don't even see 'em, dude.'

I heard Dante and Anthony laughing.

'Whaddaya mean? Dey juss *left* 'im here?'

'Looks like it.'

'Mighta went 'n' cawdda pleece,' said Jeremiah.

'I dunno. But we gadda gihdoudda here juss in case.' I turned to Pessi, who, winded and momentarily pacified, was lying on top of the motionless body; his head was resting on the other's chest like the close embrace of two lovers breathing with the stars. 'Hear that, Pess? They went 'n' cawdda cops.' Like speaking to a child.

'Motherfucker wansta – hit me – widda bir bawdle,' he stammered with heavy breathes. Dante and Anthony, watching from the bench—standing on it for a "cool" view—laughed at this. But I found nothing funny. Neither did Jeremiah. Eddie was pacing back and forth in a straight line, lost in his own world. But fresh action on the ground pulled Eddie (and us) back into blood-gazing.

Irritated, I walked over to Dante and Anthony. 'Yinz two think 'iss is funny or sum'n?'

'Oh cahm the fuck dahn,' said Dante. 'He's juss pissed 'cuzza kid cheap-shotted 'im. I'd be doin'ah same fuckin' thing. Kid's juss lucky we ain't helpin'.'

'Oh yeah? Well, say when all's said 'n' done he ends up fucked up in the hospital 'n' somehow it comes back on *us?*'

'Dey don't even know who we are or where we're from exactly. Juss don't caw anybody by their last name: 'at's all—not dit he's gonna be 'memberin' much anyways.' Laughing, Dante jumped down from the bench. Then Anthony jumped down.

'Yeah, V,' slurred the whore, 'Nobody said who we are.' He raised his bony, dismissive shoulders upward as if to assure me.

'Whaddaya mean who *we* are?' I shot back. 'I don't give a fuck about you. 'N' if ya laugh one more time I'm gonna knock yir fuckin' teeth out.' I turned away; my blood was boiling.

'Whaddaya think we should do?' asked Eddie. 'I ain't tryin'ah get arrested. I say we roll juss in case.' Just then, everyone seemed to stop and put an ear to the wind for approaching sirens; we were still unsure what Da Rockwell Abandoners had gone off to do. 'Let's juss all jump in 'n' be rough wid 'im or sum'n.'

'Go 'head!' screamed Pessi, looking up at us with a crazed stare. 'I'll fuckin' kill all yunz faggots!' He added in something unintelligible before returning to his beastly work. Dante and Anthony laughed; but so did Eddie.

'Look:' I addressed the non-fighters quietly but authoritatively, 'juss go back da Dante's—ya know, juss in case 'ey *did* caw da cops or sum'n. I'll figure sum'n out, 'cause sum'n seris happens do 'im 'n' we're all fucked—'

'Dere's no way I'm leavin' yinz here,' said Jeremiah. 'I'll stay 'n figure out whaddado wid 'em.'

'No,' I insisted quietly. 'Ya know he's only gonna listen'ah me. Truss me, we'll be right behin' jinz. But stayin' here's only gonna provoke 'im inda not quitin'. Dere's sercly sum'n wrong with his head. I mean, juss listen'ah whaddeez sayin'. Juss go back: iddle lessen'ah crowd, 'n' we won't be walkin' back in a large pack, ya know. 'N' don't fuckin' do anything stupid onna way back either.' But everyone kept staring at me, dumbfounded. 'Sercly. Fuckin' go. I'll take care of it.' Inside, though, it felt like I was setting myself up to be stuck in a real-life Ponyboy-Johnny Cade situation.[10]

Just then, Dante walked up to Pessi and the other. They were wrestling around but without much energy. Dante pushed Pessi aside, bent down to the other, and said, 'Yir friends got rocked well. But *youuu* juss got struck by the *fuck.*' Then he punched his bloody mouth. I watched Dante look right into Pessi's eyes to see if Pessi would like that—he didn't; he pushed Dante out of the way then socked the other across the jaw. Smiling, Dante straightened up and came back towards us in a cocky strut; but at this point, no one cared to acknowledge his wit, his hit, or his shaking hips—besides Anthony, who hooked himself right back onto Dante's shaking hip. As if unaffected by the turns of events, Dante and his bitch began walking into the infield, talking—probably Bitch saying how cool it was that Dante said "rocked well" and "struck by the fuck." They kept glancing back, smiling. Before following them, Eddie said something to Pessi, who was now standing up, towering over the other, arms crossed. From the mouth and temple, blood was dribbling down his cheek and chin, meandering into complex veins on his bare chest. But he didn't care. His foe was flipped on his side, hand over his nose and mouth. By now, the sun's sea-like facade was barely peaking out over the pink-and-orange horizon, bidding us adieu as the curtains of the sky's stage drew closed. And thankfully, it *was* a pretty cloistered area, so the violent matinee had drawn no audience. But who was expecting a sell out?

Once Dante, Anthony, and Eddie disappeared into the alley, Jeremiah turned to me, shaking his head. 'I don't care whacha say; I'm not leavin' yinz here.' It made me feel a little better knowing Jeremiah refused to leave me stuck in a Ponyboy-Johnny Cade situation; deep-down I knew

---

[10] Main characters in S.E. Hinton's novel *The Outsiders.* The two Greasers run away together after Johnny is forced to kill a rival gang member because he was drowning Ponyboy.

he wasn't going to anyway. So I gave him a look that said, 'Well, whaddaya wanna do then?' He turned to Pessi. 'Ar'ight, Pe—' He stopped, aware that he almost said Pessi's name. 'Come on; we gadda get goin'. Look, everyone else is gone—'

'Motherfucker wansta hit me widda bir bawdle.' Must've been the fifth time he'd say the same thing in the same morbid tone. I just couldn't tell if he was saying it as a question or a statement. Sighing, Jeremiah went over and picked up Pessi's gutted shirt. He tried handing it to him like a ploy to occupy Pessi's hands and thus prevent him from hitting the other anymore. But Pessi refused to take it. Instead, he flashed Jeremiah a look of disgust, which, as senseless as it may seem, was his way of saying, 'Wha'? you think he's tougher den me or sum'n? You think I need *yir* help?' Then he took a few running steps towards the kid...reared back his boot...and with one solid *THUMP!* in the ribs the other seemed to enter a state of rigor mortis because he let out a ghastly moan, cringed his midsection, then froze all over. Capitalizing on the freed mark, Pugili Pessi, ol' Punchin' Pipi, jumped on top of Ugili Other and swung away.

'Come on; gidawffavim!' spat Jeremiah. He wrapped his flexing arms around Pessi's neck. Legs were kicking. Backs arching. Throats grunting. Instead of helping, I watched inquisitively, unable to move, absorbed in the taste of color: flowing magentas and auburns, mixed pearls pocked with foggy gray pupils, soft pastels in the horizon but vibrantly-tongued from something clairvoyant: sights in potent taste...and lunacy.

'—hit me widda bir bawdle.'

Shaking my head, things came back into vision; an acrid taste came over my palate. Still holding Pessi's shirt, Jeremiah had him in a bear-hug, dragging him into the infield. I was still standing on the *other* side of the fence, a few feet away from the lump. I didn't want to leave him lying there helpless like his friends did; I was still shocked by that. I concluded they *didn't* call the police or an ambulance because they didn't even see how bad his condition had become. Plus, judging from their character, they weren't ones to take any risk in getting in trouble; chances are, he, the other, was the Anthony Durkin of their crew, and thus dispensable. Alwaysthemore, deep-down I knew I should get help for him. Deep-down I knew it was the right thing to do. Which is why, when I looked over at Jeremiah (who was struggling to beckon me to follow), I turned back to the other and said, 'I suggest gettin' some new friends'—then jogged out to Jeremiah and Pessi, who were waiting at first base; I guess "safe at first" because, finally calmed, with his shirt held across his temple, Pessi had the look of stone-cold accomplishment. Smirking, he said, 'You think I won?' I said, 'I dunno; izza close one.' Jeremiah gave Pessi a nudge forward, and we treaded swiftly across the darkened field...crossed the street where we slipped into the same alley the others had...then at the other end, we turned right and ran discreetly for several blocks...til we made it safely back to Dante's...

...Inside, it was darker than before: only the television and kitchen light were on. Pessi rushed into the bathroom to tend to his head; Da Early Birds asked Da Bearers to fill them in on Da Grand Finale. Standing in the hall, observing Pessi, we did, but in my head I was wondering if we would have to take him to the hospital: seemed inevitable, although he would have to be dying, for he'd had really bad experiences at the hospital. I asked if he needed anything; he said ask Dante for a shirt to wear home; I did. I asked if he needing anything else; no—he seemed content to hold a wet washcloth tightly against his temple where the main laceration was.

'Well? Whaddaya thinkin'? Ya feel dizzy or sick or anything?'

Inspecting himself in the mirror, he said, 'Nah. It's not dat bad. Don't look deep. Bleedin's slowin' dahn a bit.' After washing himself off, he turned dead sober. I didn't overstand how he was still standing and moving around, let alone conscious, although he'd already proven his immunity to pain via other similar circumstances; once took a crowbar across the head, remained upright, and "won," meaning, no hospital visit.

'You sure, Pess?' asked Jeremiah, peeking in over my shoulder. 'I'll take ya over da the hospital da get stitched up if ya want.'

Shaking his head, Pessi came out of the bathroom, sat down in the chair that I'd sat in earlier, and said once the bleeding stopped he was going home. Sounded like a plan but Prognostication was trying to convince me that his head *wasn't* going to stop bleeding, that we *would* have to take him to the hospital. I stood there, playing it all out in my head: *Sure, he'll be ar'ight, but we'll hafta take 'im da get stitches, 'n' he'll hafta lie in a hospital bed which'll make 'im feel like he's livin' out that nightmare again... Wonder if he has insurance? I'm sure 'ey'd fix 'im up either way. But if we DO go da pieces might fall together for the pleece if sum'n was reported, if sum'n should happen ta da other... hmmmm...*

'It stopped,' I heard him say some time later. 'Tolja it wasn't deep.'

'Well ya bedder put some rubbin' alcohol in it,' advised Eddie. 'Eh, Dante Zielinski!' he screamed towards the back bedroom. 'Gahdinee rubbin' alcohol?!'

Dante and Anthony appeared, Dante saying, 'Nah, I don't think.'

'Don't worry 'bout it,' said Pessi. 'I got shit at home.'

He remained seated but no one pushed him to leave or seek further medical attention. Standing beside him, I looked around the room: Eddie and Jeremiah looked exhausted, Anthony and Dante didn't. After they'd came out of Dante's bedroom—evidently having blown coke—they sat down on the couch and embarked on a jittery conversation, sharing esoteric laughs. At what though? What's funny at this point? I don't know why my anger was only directed towards Anthony but I had a torrid urge to rip the dastard's veil off and rend apart his epic-sized retinas. But Pessi suddenly stood up, ready to go. In silence, I followed him out, letting one "See ya" suffice for everyone. It was a "one lass time" that we could brag about tomorrow, or something...

...The air was very cool now and gusting quietly from block to block. When we reached the road, we stopped and turned to each other. An unidentifiable sound was humming off in the distance. A nearby streetlight was shining on our faces like solemn actors on stage. Although dog-tired and fish-fried, I pried into his eyes as if to hash out the details of tonight's events. But moody and mummyish—his jeans ripped and spotted with blood, scratches on his face and arms, grayish eyes twitching a bit, while he dabbed a fresh washcloth on his temple—he assured me that he was fine and would call if he wasn't; he didn't want me to walk him home either. Decisively, he turned the other way—(one hand shoved in pocket, the other holding the weancloth)—and began walking home in a stride quicker than usual. And so, alone, I turned the other way and began walking home, reflective, worried, and nauseous, carrying along the malaise that I'd been carrying a long time...

ALL IN THE FRAME

"Everybody is so lovely: (You're lonely and we're lovely!),
Getting something for nothing: (But none of it is for you!),
I tried to mix in: (Got stares like 'You wouldn't dare!'),
I tried to fix it: (But you just don't belong here!)..." [1]

...As soon as I woke up I called Pessi. He said, 'Ehh, I'm ar'ight. Eye's all puffy 'n' bruised. I'm cut up everywhere. Where da bawdle hit swelled up but dry.' When I asked the reason for the blind rage, he soft-pedaled the situation with the tough-guy routine, claiming the other had it coming. Story goes: Pessi had punched the other in the infield but fell down while slinging him towards the fence...then Pessi went chasing after him...back behind the batter's cage...but the other, with a good lead, had time to pick up a beer bottle before Pessi caught up...at which point the other blindsided him with it, consequently breaking his mask of sanity. But now Pessi was acting like nothing had happened, that he hadn't turn someone into mush. Oh well, I was just glad to hear he was "ar'ight" both physically and mentally, because I wasn't. I too had abrasions and contusions, along with heartburn, muscle spasms, dizzy spells, and my back hurt so bad that I had to lie in bed all day. It gave me an excuse to spend my last Saturday inside, reading. I had to pause, however, whenever the thought of college and how tomorrow was *thee* day popped into mind. Certainly wasn't any family pressure on me to excel. Ma just said, *'Mè tappiceddu vâ fari comu tutti i ionna.'* [2] Her idea of college likely came from some cheesy 80s movie about a "beach college" based around volleyball games. After a friendly coed game—Bikinis vs. Speedos—it's time to study in the sand by reading romance and mystery novels...til the night brings half-assed promiscuities. But at least Ma was fancying *some* kind of future for me. Rick didn't seem to overstand the first part: that I was moving out! When I told him about my matriculation, he dismissively said, 'Well don't think *I'm* payin' for it,' then buried the matter in the sand.

　　　　Stupid question, but is it true that many people blame themselves for the negligence and abuse of their parents and/or spouse? posing questions to themselves like *why's this happening to me?* or *what's wrong with me?* I was always wondering *what happened to him?* and *what went wrong with him?* It's like a psychological power-game: who can get who to ask what questions will determine who thinks what. In psycho-metaphorical terms, people like my father are cruel shepherds on the hunt for sacrificial sheep. They want to transfer their misery and negativity to the sheep through nefarious methods of herding: they seek a guilt-free conscience for the things they do but only at another's cost, sometimes the whole herd! And when the cruel shepherd *does* succeed, the sheep (now pelted into a downtrodden *subthing)* is left alone to cry little sheep-tears, dealing with things they can't overstand: waah, waah, waah'ing, instead of saying, baa-

---

[1] Lyrics from "Fork It Over" by Pissant and the Pests, from the album *F.U.*
[2] [scn] My sweet little Vinny will continue to do good.

baa-baa, I don't think so dad! I'm not your feeble sheep for sacrifice! Now a *true* shepherd is a gentle hub who brings the family together centripetally, for she gathers the sheep in her arms and carries them close to her heart.[3] Hence, the construction of the word *shepherd:* "she"-"p"-"herd." It stands for "she pieces the herd"; meaning, it's the soft touch of a woman that brings the family together; not the cruel shepherd dressed in sheep's skin, hiding the wolf inside, who, once securing the flock inside his fence, rips off his gilded garb, reveals the wily wolf, then drives the flock outward with no way of escaping, for the wolf's incisors will dig deep into the sheep's pelt then throw them back in for more! And poor Ma, she'd been sacrificed just like that by the insidious shepherd who'd beguiled her just enough to get her into his flock, for—in literal terms—she'd shed tears for him: the ultimate snare. At a young age I promised myself that I would never shed tears for his cleansing. *Never.* I jumped the fence. Baa-baa!

...I woke up Sunday morning to the sound of the cruel shepherd beating on the door, bleating for me to get up and unlock the door. When I got up and unlocked it (he hated whenever I locked the door!) he asked why I wasn't ready for church and why Ma was cooking supper this early. He'd probably already asked her these questions, and knew himself, but wanted to hear it from my mouth. When I told him that I wasn't going to church and that I—he slammed the door in my face. Minutes later, he was heading out the door, yelling that he was never coming back, which meant he would be back around ten, drunk, because he had work in the morning. '*Good,*' I thought, '*I don't wan'im da be around taday—my LAST day.*'

After brushing and flossing my teeth, I called Pessi to tell him to come over in a bit. Then I grabbed and shook open an oversized garbage bag. Down on my hams, I began shoveling my haggard Ishmaels and Ragamuffins into the dark hole. Meanwhile, running through my head was an image of the typical college-bound go-getter, spending his final day home on his bed, filling himself with nostalgia: First, he pulls out from underneath his bed a little box containing the movie ticket stub from his first date, old concert tickets, pictures from the prom, spring breaks, family vacations, hundreds of receipts totaling elation: all hard evidence for his young paid-for adventures. My only comparable items were crumpled up citations and subpoenas. The typical college-bound go-getter pays for (or has paid for him) his ticket first, then enjoys the event; I'd always enjoyed the event first, then paid the price later.

After closing up the box of memories, the college-bound go-getter turns to his nightstand where, slanting but up firm, sits a family portrait within a gilded frame. Family history and spirit just exudes from the photo...*The photographer is cheerfully arranging bodies and says, if needed, he'll fine-tune things back at the post. The sturdy-chinned father is positioned in the upper-middle of the photo. He swells out his chest, revealing the upper portion of his Armani. His accomplished smile tells the*

---

[3] Slight rewording of Isaiah 40:11: "He (Jesus) shall feed his flock like a shepherd: he shall gather the lambs with his arms, and carry them in his bosom, and shall gently lead those that are with young."

photographer: 'Look at this great nuclear family. Stop! Now look at me, the nuclear engineer of this great nuclear family. Yes, what a fucking success I am!' His petite wife is aligned where her head sits at the center of his chest. The sparkle of her diamond studs is overpowering the lighting. In her head, she's reflecting on a past image of herself: 'Oh, so young and so new back then...' (a mental sigh) '...I want new! new! NEW!' But other than new clothes and new gobs of makeup, the only thing new is additional wrinkles: the reason for all the makeup. However, she smiles anyway because the sudden thought of plastic surgery consoles her. Her red lipstick-smile conveys to the photographer: 'Hey, loser, don't you wish you were my husband? He's gonna keep this face looking new! You never could, but he, my husband, is such a fucking success!' Then hovering in the left-hand corner is the little girl. In the back of spoiled brat's hair is a pink bow. Luxurious and vivacious, her blond ironed curls are moving around like thousands of slinkies dropping down a winding staircase. Soon, she hopes, she'll be just like her mother. She gives a cute-as-a-button smile that says: 'You know, Mr. Photographer, I model clothing for young girls at the mall. My agent says I have a face for the frame. So you should probably focus a little more my way. No, a little more. Just a wittle-bitty more. There you go! Success! Success! Sweet freakin' success!' Finally, the new man on the rise: the strapping big brother on the right: the college-bound go-getter. His face is ruddier than his father's. The most ravenous eyes in the family. With his arms locked and gauged downward, he thrusts out his chest with pride and accomplishment. He glares into the lens with a smile that would assure anyone of anything. And that confident, suave smile says to the photographer: 'Hey, bud, I'm off to a good college. Same one my father went to. And here's a little secret: (that sucker is gonna send me so much money to blow on booze, clothes, furniture, a new car—just anything that'll impress those college whores! HA! And when I graduate with a degree in Business, which I'll have done shit to get, he'll even hook me up with a job! What a fucking success I'll be!) Now seriously, bud: take the picture before I go get the supervisor. I got things to do.' So together, The Great Nuclear Family faces forward in strength. All smiles. All stars. Annnnnd—SNAP!!! The picture captures a moment of their indestructible bond, letting all who look upon it know that THIS family is far from weak. They'll never show otherwise. It's all in the frame.

While bitter-reminiscing over someone else's sweet reminisces, I managed to fill two hefty garbage bags with my orphan clothes, one for the colored kids and one for the white kids: the Ishmaels and the Ragamuffins. *Orphan clothes?* Well, see, my room lacked a closet; I only had a dresser, and they, the orphans, usually sat piled in the corner anyway. Maybe they were the most excited to leave since they would finally have a cool place to hangout: a closet!

I lugged the bags of orphans over to the wall where I was situating everything I was taking. I had most of the room taken care of except the posters on the walls. I realized that I would have to leave most hanging, but Darby was definitely coming. Unfortunately, I would also have to leave many books behind for the time being. I really didn't have much else to bring besides three binders of music, my stereo, television, the orphans, and all the small things.

Ma appeared in the doorway. On my knees, I did a double-take because she wasn't in her tattered nightgown! *S'allicchetta?* [4] Yes, all dressed up in a long black poplin skirt, with a matching blouse flowered with bronze swirls. The blouse had a wide V-space of flesh wherein small violet glass beads with golden links hung tightly against her clavicle, and downward from the sternum, a golden Cross: reverence for the Rosary but not the Rosary itself, for that would be sacrilegious. She had a faint amount of blush powered on her bubbly brown cheeks; a glossy pink painted across her lips; and a sharp black curled atip her vigorous eyelashes, drawing the copper out of her irises like newly polished gems. Her ebony hair was also glimmering and seemed extra wavy as if heat-enhanced. Naturally, her hair was rather straight from root to shoulder...becoming increasingly wavier...til flickering out at mid-back. Stylistically, she threw thick individual waves in front of her shoulders and breasts, like a Greek goddess.

Once the moment in which she let me look her over ended, she smiled as if to thank me. And stunned, I smiled back because Ma was looking hot! OWW!

'*Ciauuuu, Tappicedduuu!*'[5] she crooned.

'*Bon giornu.*'[6]

'Almost finished?'

'*Yeeeeah*, gih'n 'ere.'

'Well Uncle Alfonse and Aunt Stella izza coming now. Is Pipi still coming?'

'Yeah. He should be here soon.'

'*Va beni.*'[7] Soon as everybody comes, we eat. Everyting izza *rrr*eady now.' (Ma humbly rolled Rs; initial- and double-Rs sound closer to flapping Fs. To the unlearned ear, the sound of Sicilian might suggest desperation or sorrow in the speaker, for Sicilian isn't like the giddy and jolly Italian dialects. But no matter what tongue Ma used, her tone was very guttural but in seductive, soporific, God-it's-so-dreamy kind of way.) 'I make-ah Spaghetti Bellini, and Aunt Stella izza bringing *capicola panini* and dee choke-a-lot cassata you like. *Mi dispiaci, Tappiceddu, nun iè mancu tiramisu, ie nun sacciu se c'haiu i soddi pi gghiri a cattallu o—*'[8]

'Ehh, don't worry about it. 'At all sounds fine besides'ah capicola; she knows I don't eat dat shit.' I stood up and lit a cigarette.

'Filty abit!' Ma stood in the doorway emphatically shaking her head as if to help drop that horrid "h": one of *her* abits. 'You better stooop—'

'Hellooo-oh!' rang out Aunt Stella's voice from the dead room. 'Anyone heere-eere! Hellooo-oh!' Smiling, Ma rolled her eyes at the

---

[4] [scn] She's all dressed up?
[5] [scn] Hello. [Pronounced the same as the Italian *ciao:* CHOW.]
[6] [scn] Good morning.
[7] [scn] Okay; that's fine.
[8] [scn] I'm sorry but there's no more tiramisu, and I don't know if I have the money to go to the bakery or—. *Capicola panini* are sandwiches cut in small squares with thin slices of capicola, prosciutto, mortadella, pickles, hot pepper relish, and olive oil. V doesn't like it because it has red meat. In the Italian-American dialect *capicola* is sometimes called "gabbagool."

pertinacity of *la pazza cu na vuccazza.*[9] Ma went to greet them because if you didn't right away both would stand (well, Uncle Alfonse would be sitting) there, confused, yelling and complaining...

...When Pessi arrived, I was still down on my knees, throwing the last of the small things into a box. Standing in the doorway, he braced his tatted arms out and high against the frame as if waiting for an introduction to enter. He was wearing a white tank-top with blue jeans that looked funny because they were way too tight. He was even smiling, in spite of the bruise beneath his right eye, which wasn't that bad after all. The scratches on his face and arms looked worse due to the abundance.

'Houzza head, Tyson?'

He walked in and bent over to show me the cut. It began near his right temple and went into his hardly-hiding-it hairline. About two inches long, black, crusted, and knotted: all things considered, a lucky break.

'Yeah, you'll live. But wonder if 'at other kid's ar'ight. I mean, you rilly fucked 'im up.'

'He'll live too.'

I grunted. 'Bedder hope so.'

He walked over to the television and turned it on. Then he plopped back-down on the mattresses, crossing his ankles over and using the remote at his waist. While he channel surfed, I finished taping up the last box. With a heave and ho, I hoisted it atop a larger box and slowly exhaled. I moved in front of a skinny floor fan and feigned a heavy sweat-wipe; the plastic blades of the fan were cutting the thick air into putrid slabs, while (like a phonic backdrop) providing our conversation with a methodical hum.

'So are you going to *meeeece* me?' I said satirically. Pessi didn't bother looking over at my silly eyelashing face.

'Nah. 'Member dat Teresa chick I yoosta bring out? Anson's cousin?'

'*Hmph.* Like I could ever forget a fuckin' mouth like 'at.'

'We'll ya know she lives like 5-10 minutes from Aristod. She akshly cawed me the other night. Stupid chick's still tryin'ah get with me—like 'fishly.' (Officially.) 'Figure might as well play along. Den I'd have a reason da come see ya.'

'Wha', you can't come dahn da see me on yir own?' I pushed him off the bed so I could lie down. He repositioned himself on the front edge, upright, turning from the television to me as we talked. Still a slight hum. Hmmm...

'Hmmm. So 'at's where Squawk lives,' I noted to myself. The thing that had remained in my memory about Teresa Cazzata was her loud, annoying, squawky voice.

'Yep. She'll be yir new neighbor.'

'Awesome; tell her da bake me a fuckin' welcome-da-the-neighborhood cake. But for rill, how you plan on gih'n dahn 'ere? Bedder get a license 'n' jack a car 'cause I ain't gonna be drivin' back 'n' forth every weekend juss da pick ya up. Too far for that shit.'

'Dude, there's a bus route thit goes dahn 'ere on the weekends.'

---

[9] [scn] the crazy woman with a loud ugly mouth

'Dude, don't be fuckin' stupid: there ain't no bus goin' dahn 'ere from here.'

'I'm tellin' ya, there is. Teresa told me on the weekends a bus goes from the campus upda Colbyville, 'n' 'en 'ere's 'at one 'uts always runnin' back 'n' forth between Colbyville 'n' Marian Heights.'

'Doubt it. (*Stupidest fuckin' thing I ever heard.*)' Not sure why I was being so skeptical about it—well, mostly likely because it had come from her mouth. Plus, Cobyville—a small city based around two colleges and some shopping centers, almost the exact distance between LaSalle and Pittsburgh—just seemed too insignificant for distant bus routes. But if true, then all the better: Pessi could visit with ease and a bunch of quarters.

'Well help me carry dishit out 'fore we eat. I wanna get it done 'n' over with.'

'You takin'ah TV too?' He pointed at it as if it once belonged to him.

'Yeah. I haven't even talk da my roommate yet, so who knows whadee's bringin'.'

"N' all these books?' He pointed at the three large stacks of books flush against the wall, left of the television.

'Nah, not dis trip. Dey'd take up da whole fuckin' car.'

Pessi walked over to my white-trash exhibit of high-class books. 'Man, ya know I sercly stole about half 'eez fuckin' books for you.'

'Yeah, 'n' ya coulda got me more if ya woulda taken'ah fuckin' metal oudda *Da Great Gatsby* 'n' not had da take off runnin'.' That's what happened. Pessi used to come with me to the local library whenever I wanted to add a book to my collection because the librarians knew me, liked me, and I went there too often to take the chance myself. So I would have Pessi cut out the metal strips that made the detectors go off. The last time he did it, he was shooting for three books, which he stuffed around his waist, but somehow didn't fully deactivate *The Great Gatsby*. I was watching from a distance—(I would never associate with him while there to avoid suspicions)—and when the alarm went off, he froze in disbelief for a second—before taking off quicker than Gatsby and Daisy in their own fictional hit-and-run.

'Yeah, I fucked 'at one up,' he admitted. 'Bahdiz like a sign you shouldn't be readin' so much. Izzer a word for someone thit has sexual fantasies over books?' He stylishly (and fittingly) picked up *Lolita,* holding it out for me to observe him pinching lil Lo's boob on the cover; yeah, he actually knew the gist of the book.

'I dunno; *uhh*—a bibliophile maybe?'

Pessi huffed. 'I 'on't fuckin' know. Yir the fuckin' cawidge nerd...Ya know wha': screw bibliophile. I'll juss caw ya a book-fucker. Yeah, I betcha fuck 'eez books when no one's around.' He held Lo up to the light to see if his forensic insight could catch any sexual foul play. 'I see sum'n. Look!...'

'Pipi, when did you-ah—*huuuh!*' A sudden and dramatic gasp from Ma the instant Pessi turned and she saw the black eye. *'Bedda matri, puvireddu! Chi succiriu a tò facci? Veni, veni ccà! Fammilla viriri!'* [10] She

---

[10] [scn] Dear God, poor child! What happened to your face? Get over here and let me see it! [*Bedda matri* (beautiful mother) refers to Mother Mary.]

rushed over to Pessi, grabbing his forearms to hold him still while she examined his eye...til spotting the knot. She gently brushed her hand over it, asking what happened. Although honest about getting into a fight, Pessi was sparing her the horrid details. At one point, she offered to embrocate his wounds with ointment, but since he denied with resolve, she continued to nurse him *verbally,* as if it had all been unprovoked, as if he was so innocent. She kept interjecting with *Caspiterina!* which is along the lines of "Wow!" or "Good Heavens!" And thank Heaven (as I had a time or two) that Ma taught me both Sicilian and English when I was young, even though at the time she was just learning English herself. She never got around to socializing, so most of her grammar remained back-at-the-boat. Since I ventured out into the Yinzer Jungle, I'd come back to the coast and feed her a line or two, but usually to no avail. Be that as it may, I assumed Ma had taught me Sicilian just so she could talk to someone in her native tongue and thus "feel at home." But Rick hated it because he didn't overstand Sicilian and thus thought we were "conspiring in the house."

Sitting on the edge of the bed, I watched her pampering with a dreamy smile. Once healed with a hug and a kiss on the cheek, Pessi started telling Ma how beautiful she looks; in parodic English, she told him to stop it, but I could tell she loved the flattery. He said that he'd never seen her so dressed up. Pinching out her skirt, with a bit of twist in her hips, she replied, 'What, *deece* ol' ting?'

Yeah, it was good to see Ma in a good mood, and a nice skirt.

'Can ya believe it, Ma,' Pessi began, already with an air of facetiousness, 'a cawidge boy now. Our liddle smartass goin' off da make millions for us.'

Moving behind him, Ma wrapped her bronze arms around his neck and rested her head on his shoulder, allowing her hair to snake down his chest. 'Ahh, you two grow up too fast. Yesterday you two-ah stand at my knees. And now look—' She backed away from Pessi and measured the top of her head to his neck. 'All grown up!'

'Taaay-yaaah!' bellowed out Pazza's vuccazza; Aunt Stella was probably deathly afraid (for whatever irrational reason) to come to my room to see what Ma was doing. Ma told her that she was coming, but first, in a whisper, she told me that she wanted to give me something before she forgot, and not in front of *chiddi vecchi.*[11] She stealthily slipped out and into her bedroom...then returned with an envelope.

'Ear, Tappiceddu.' As soon as I stood up, she pushed it into my hand. I opened it to find ten crisp fifty-dollar bills.

'*Nooo,* I'm not takin' 'iss. I got some money saved up.'

'Well you need-ah more. I try to help-ah you much as I can—my little baby boy.' May lee-tul bay-bee boi(yee). 'Ahh, look at him!' she glowed in light of my bewilderment. '*Tappiceddu miu: omu si sta facennu! Talia, Pipi!*[12] He is finally becoming a man!'

'If ya ask me, I think ol' Tapp's finally becomin' a book-humpin' beast—'n' 'at's a sin, Ma—a sin,' Pipi said inside-jokingly, perhaps with a touch of envy, and perhaps straight-up ironically since *he* was the one with

---

[11] [scn] the old ones
[12] [scn] My sweet little Vinny: he's becoming a man. Look, Zach!

the Devil's greasy grin and the Rebel's fight face. Ma moved back behind his shoulder, peaking out like that girl who stirs up unnecessary fights just to get off on the anticipation and hopefully the execution of masculine protection. She was smiling, Pessi smirking, both analyzing me as if I was behind a television screen a million miles away. I wanted to ask how she got the money but for some reason I felt uncomfortable asking with Pessi there. She probably thought it customary to give money, as a *rigalu,* in front of anyone who mattered, which is why it was just us three.

'Well soon as I get dahn' 'ere, I'm gih'n a job. So don't be worrin' about givin' me any more money; I'll be fine.'

She moved back in front of Pessi. 'Oh I know you'll be fine. But I still send-ah money wh—*Nu nu, pigghiatillu!*' (Just as I opened my mouth to retort and sneak the envelope back in her hands, she insisted that I take it.) *'Ie nun sfragari tutti i soddi ddaiusu, ie pi l'amuri ri Diu unn ti mentiri nna sti centu missi!*'[13]

'I won't, Ma—' All of a sudden she rushed towards me and embraced me with unforeseen strength: liberation from the subtle awkwardness and timidity we long shared. With her head buried in my neck, she let the tears flow, squeezing me tighter than I could ever remember. I didn't want to squeeze back too hard, but I also didn't want to fail to express myself. "Ahh! Sweet Embrace," I thought, "please don't end: all the impurities relinquished by this moment will flood back in—twice as harsh in revenge!" At the thought, I grabbed her harder, uncontrollably harder, then even harder til we became one. As her tears continued wetting my shoulder, I could feel her quivers transferring into my Cross-stamped chest, trying to shake something loose...to tear asunder the concreted darkness where, within, monsters reside, which the little boy had feared but not without curiosity, which is why he'd augmented to those walls the weight of solitude and transgression, while silently screaming for peace! and purity!...the same lair the maturing man still feared yet had a premonition of further augmentation from all the sanctities he'd hitherto questioned because of this certain inherent intuition he just couldn't ignore: *the paradox of taming and protecting the inner monsters from the ones trying to get in...*

She pulled her head back, smiled, and petted my checks. I smiled, and being a simple matter of inevitability, that old dark feeling flooded back into me as she let go, making my smile feel superficial and twisted. She said, 'Let's eat!' then walked away because Aunt Stella was about to call a federal search team. Uncle Alfonse was telling Aunt Stella to shudup! shudup!

'I sercly think I'm gonna marry her one day,' Pessi fancied. 'But ar'ight, book-fucker, let's take yir shit out rill quick.'

I nodded and watched his hazel eyes quietly wander around the musty room like when a family takes that long last-look at their house from the front yard before hopping in the car and moving far away. And a part of Pessi was moving away when I left. Unlike me, he had mostly pleasant memories in my room: it was *his* safe haven—his home away from hell.

---

[13] [scn] No, take it! And don't waste it all down there, and for the love of God, stay out of trouble! [Literally, "don't get into these hundred masses"]

We each grabbed a box, leaving behind three others, the television, stereo, three binders of music, several rolled up posters, a skateboard, and the two hefty bags of the racially profiled. In the end, not much would remain. Despite Aristod informing me that my dorm room came equipped with a dresser, a closet, a large sturdy desk, and a fully clothed bed, I decided to bring along my "winter blanket." It was a fuzzy cream-and-brown blanket with a large lion on it. The fuzz was frayed with one seam ripped two-feet and dwindling away. I'd had it as long as I could remember, and since it had kept me as warm as possible during winters that crept through the walls like an unstoppable thief, I decided it was time to set the lion free— so to speak, release it back into the jungle by taking it out of *this* one.

Exiting the hall and making a left, I could see over my box Uncle Alfonse in his wheelchair, watching television in the dead room. Pessi was already out the front door. But Aunt Stella stopped me for questioning. Grunting, I set the box down. She *had to* inform me that we needed to eat right away! because Uncle Alfonse was being impatient! and they had to be somewhere in an hour! Annoyed, I picked the box back up and marched off, while she continued complaining about my insolence and sloth.

'Okay, Aunt Fella! We'll be done in a three da nine months!'

...Outside, after finishing the final haul, Pessi and I stopped to rest, talk, and enjoy the breeze, which was carrying faint smells of the nearby moribund fair. A true Sunday ambiance (like a pastoral scene mistakenly painted behind a ghetto) was casting down from the sky wide rays of blues, whites, and golds. The clouds looked whipped, spun, fresh, close enough to taste their sweetened gobs. The lucidness dancing across the sky had not a bit of oppressiveness. The physical neighborhood was active with adults at work and kids at play, none sweating or sluggish. In nearby yards I could hear a rare geniality, nearly in accord, as if everyone knew I was leaving, and expressing their support, were soaring their spirits like unfallen sparrows.

Another rarity: Pessi and I began talking about my future at college—without any sarcastic or sour remarks! He was standing out in the yard, and I was leaning against my light-brown car. (My Uncle Jim gave me the beater, and for the past six months [ever since Pessi and I quit our job as potato sackers] I'd been driving it without insurance.) Anyway, just as our conversation was budding, Father Carr's sedan appeared, white and freshly washed. A compliment to the Holy Sunday. He braked to a stop right before my car, lining up his front bumper next to mine with each pointing in opposite directions. I moved over and waited for his tinted window to drop down electronically...*bzzzzzzz*...til his turtle head shone, just barely coming up out of his black shirt, the one with the peek-a-boo collar—so to speak, his shell. That's what Father Carr reminded me of: a turtle. He was a short man in his late sixties with a head that edged at you no matter the position of his body. But a healthy ol' *scuzzària*.[14] Still had heaps of glossy white hair left on top. He had this funny quirk, too, where he would always widen his eyes whenever you talked to him. It gave the sophisticated old man a touch of childishness. Even his voice was suggestive of a man half his age.

---

[14] [scn] Old Sicilian for "turtle," as opposed to the newer Italian-influenced use of *tartuca*. Thus, *scuzzària* alludes to Father Carr being behind-the-times.

'Hello, Vincent. You're not sick, are you?'

'No, I'm ar'ight. Why?'

Eyes widening: 'Oh. Just haven't seen you in church for a while. Today, though, we had a one of the highest non-holiday attendances of the year.'

'Oh, 'at's good.'

'You're leaving for college soon, right?'

'Taday akshly.'

Eyes fully popped out! 'Good God! Today! So what's it gonna be, Vincent: the next JKF? or the next Bill Gates?' He'd suddenly broke into his chumminess, apparently still heaven-bent on showing me how funny and cool an ol' turtle could be: but now it sounded real desperate, trying so hard to get me across the finish line on his back.

'Who knows?'

'Well like I told you before: Aristod has a Religious Studies program. Laudable, too, for a non-ecclesiastical school. *Of course nothing like a true seminary*,' he mumbled reminiscently. After a moment passed, he gave me a look that said, 'So how about it?' But not wanting to affirm a sure disappointment with words, I put my faith in Air to whisper the answer into his ear; that is, if turtles even have ears. 'Hey, you know what?' he resumed. 'Now that I think about it, I know a professor at Aristod. Dr. William Brody. You should look him up. Take a course of his. Or just talk with him. He can help you continue down the right road—if you know what I mean.' He winked and nodded once.

'Cool. Will do.' I was trying to keep my responses concise with the hope that he would leave quicker. I had things to get done rapidly—but turtles aren't rabbits, see.

'Nevertheless, you should still give serious thought to their Religious Studies program. It wouldn't even be hard for you. You really knew—and I'm not trying to flatter you here, Vincent—but you really knew Scripture like no other I've taught. I remember you were the only one—'

'Akshly I have no choice,' I interrupted. 'I gadda scholarship specifically for English.' An unholy lie because with my scholarship I could pick *anything* within the Arts and Literature field, which includes the Religious Studies program. Alwaysthemore, I wasn't as well-versed as he claimed: what seemed to be an extension of his desperation.

'Oh, then maybe you could pick it up as a minor. See, what you should do is...'

Stuck where I was, it felt like when I was in church, he in the middle of a sermon, and I had to go to the bathroom: if I got up, it would be (for no apparent reason) a rude disturbance. Even during studies, when it was a more "relaxed" environment, there was an implicit overstanding that thou wert to hold thy bowels til thou knowest thy vows. But at least I'd been blessed with The *Good* Water in a baptismal font and thus allowed to move beyond the prohibitive narthex. Pessi, too, had been baptized in the same church but he never went. Hence why Father Carr refused to glance in his direction where he was standing with his arms crossed a few feet behind me, scuffing at the grass, obviously annoyed. Whenever Pessi and Father Carr crossed paths, Pessi seemed to mutate right into the anti-Christ. It was like: *Tu autem effugare, diabole!'* (Something Father Carr would say while exercising Latin Scripture.) And to you, devil, begone!

'...So English?' said Carr the Chelonian in a low-key as if finally acquiescing to my future plans, but not without despair written on his face. I was waiting for him to get out of his car and shell then turtle himself in the yard. 'You'd like to teach then?'

'Nah.'

'Write?'

'Yeah, I wouldn't mind bein' a part-time model durin' the day 'n' a full-time poet at night.' (Sarcasm he didn't pick up on.)

Alwaysthemore, his eyes widened slowly with beams of pride. 'Well I'll be. *Vincent Vallano the poet.* Has a nice ring to it, doesn't it? I didn't even know you liked to write.'

'Yep. I do.'

'Well you're in good company in the world of literature. There's St. Ambrose, Augustine, Aquinas, Bonaventure, Jerome, and of course poets like Dante and Sacchetti. Heck, you could even say Mathew, Mark, Luke, and John were all great hands in literature. But with the direct help of you know who?' While preaching the amen, he pointed up through the black velvety roof of his sedan at the heavens, chuckling. Over what? Only God knew. But I think Pessi the anti-Christ began summoning his powers to make Father Carr's collar constrict because, despite the comfortableness of the weather, he began sweating in the silence that transpired. He pulled out a white handkerchief and dabbed at his garneted green face. Like statues, Pessi and I waited out the silence...(you could hardly hear Father Carr's car idling)...as the sweat continued pouring out like gunshots. But he didn't appear to be too bothered by it. In large quantities, the sweat was dripping down his turtle waxy face...flooding down into and resting inside the two big wrinkles on his lower cheeks that formed at the slightest movement. He sighed, pushing the fresh sweat on his forehead up into his white heavens.

'Okay,' he coughed, 'I must go spread the word at my brother-in-law's.' Again, he chuckled as if a witty joke had been told. 'Now, you keep your nose in those books. And I'll pray that you succeed and resist the many temptations at college that may cause one to stray one from the course of enlightenment and the worship of our Heavenly Father. I want you to call me anytime you need to talk; I'm always here for you, Vincent. Oh! and tell your mother and father I said hello and that I hope to see 'em in church next Sunday. Bye now. And God bless you.'

'Ar'ight. Thanks.'

He buzzed the window back up...*bzzzz*...then drove away. Pessi—and I was bothered by him doing it because *I*, not necessarily Pessi, would have to face Father Carr again—well, uncontrollably, driven by the Greater Forces, Pessi *had to* flip him off in the most flamboyant fashion. Jumping up and down, he was waving the provoking hand as if calling for Father Carr to stop because he forgot something. The effectiveness of the gesture depended on whether Father Carr glanced in the rear view mirror...and he did, for the car swerved a bit. Content, the anti-Christ smirked and waved a phony goodbye.

'Man, 'at guy,' Pessi griped. 'Why'd he juss sit dere when izz obvious we had nuh'n'ah say?'

'I think he'z waitin' for ya da join the congregation. 'N' look whachu juss did, you fuckin' sinner. Maybe it's time you should.'

Just then, Aunt Stella opened the door and screamed, 'Yinz guys come 'n' eat! For God's sake, Vincent, we gadda leave soon!'

'Okay, Aunt Fella! We'll be in in a few hours!'

Angered, she slammed the door shut.

'Ar'ight, let's go eat 'fore she has a fuckin' heart attack.'

'Ehh, akshly I'm gonna get goin'. I forgot I gadda go pick up some shit 'fore Anson leaves for Florida. I'm not rilly hungry anyways.'

'You seris?' I shook my head in disappointment. 'Man, Ma's gonna be fuckin' pissed. Ya know she made Skeddi B juss for you, right?'

'I dunno; juss tell her I'm sorry 'n' I'll stop by da eat some later. Tell her I got sick so she don't get all offended. No, tell her it's my head.'

'We'll see. But what's 'iss "some shit" you gadda get?'

'Nuh'n rilly—nuh'n you'd wanna do.'

'Oh, ya mean some dope.' But the real question was: what kind of dope, seeing as it was something I wouldn't wanna do. Probably some stupid pills. 'Well, whadever then. Guess I'll get aholda ya once I gidda phone hooked up in my room.'

'How long ya think 'addle be?' He was now looking at me with his hand saluted on his forehead, for the clouds behind me had just parted from the sun.

'I dunno; once'ah school gives me a number. Dey give students a free number. Juss gadda pay for long-distance calls. How 'bout that shit?'

'Cool. Well I'll be waitin' for da caw, Pluto.' (He probably meant Plato.) He lowered his salute, for a new swarm of clouds eclipsed the sun. 'So den, uhh, I dunno...Wha' da fuck you lookin' at me like 'at for, you stupid book-fucker. Fuckin' yuppie faggot.' (Standing stiff, I was intentionally smiling in a tenacious, provoking way just to make him paranoid.) 'Don't think I'm kissin' ya goodbye or sum'n weird like 'at,' he joked amid his awkwardness. 'Sercly, it's not like yir goin' do another country. Juss another county. 'N' I'm glad. I'm so sick-ah always bein' 'round here.'

'Yeah, I know watcha mean,' I sighed quietly, now feeling comically destitute. The guilt of knowing that I was leaving and he wasn't begat a struggle to look at him. But Pessi was right: this wasn't the final farewell, so, yes, emotional overkill was unnecessary. In a mutual initiation, we executed our signature see-ya-later: knuckles to knuckles to form the unified fist then taking an informal step inward. As we bumped shoulders, our hearts drew close together. But the shadow of us on the grass looked more intimate, like we were hugging or sum'n.

'Ar'ight, V. Drive safe.'

'Nah, I'm gonna try da get a few speedin' tickets on the way dahn. Maybe get maced 'n' clubbed for comin' straight oudda Verna and sayin', "Fuck da po-leece."' (He smirked, turned, and started walking away. About ten steps in, I heyed him. He turned around with furrowed eyebrows.) 'Make sure ya don't get struck by da yuck while I'm gone. Ar'ight?' Relaxing his brows, he smirked once more—paused—then turned back around. Hands shoved in pocket, he began strutting down Bullitt Avenue...then cut left on 12th, never looking back. After watching the traces of his shadow slip away,

I just *had to* wait for a squirrel in the neighbor's yard to finish entertaining me with its acorn magic tricks and trill tailwags.

When I walked back in the house, the overpowering scent of sauce smacked my nose. That would be Ma's Spaghetti Bellini, more commonly known as Pasta alla Norma; the operatic dish is composed of spaghetti enriched with sun-ripened plum tomato sauce, eggplant, olive oil, basil, pepper, and *ricotta salata.* I saw the large silver pan of it sitting atop the counter, steaming. Wafts of fresh dough were also floating through the air. That would be the *pani rimacinatu:* coarse yellow bread, broken not sliced, and by my request, bloody with olive oil and hairy with sesame seeds. I saw the basket of it on the table where everyone was talking while waiting for the rude sloth. As I slugged forward, I saw next to the breadbasket a silver plate heaped with capicola finger-sandwiches: gobs of goo Aunt Stella brought just out of spite.

Our kitchen—horizontally long for a small house—also served as our dining room. The table was on the left side, with the long side flush against the faded yellow wall. Ma had dressed the wooden table with a fancy fruit-embroidered tablecloth: silk-white with red and pink fruits strung along gold vines. She was seated at the head of the table near the back door. Aunt Stella was next to her on the open long side. Next to her, Uncle Alfonse was rolled in too close. Which left me to sit at the other head seat, right along the golden fool's strip that divided the kitchen from the dead room. It's where Rick would've sat (with me where Uncle Alfonse was sitting, and Ma unmoved) if we ate together as a family. Memory would say that it happened that way a few times when I was younger, before I was courageous enough to eat alone in my room.

When no one followed me in, Ma stood up with an exaggerated look of alarm. *'Ma Pipi unni iu? Câ panza vacanti si nni iu?'*

'Â ntrasatta si sintiu mali—mali ri testa.' [15] (I pointed to my temple as if it was Pessi's.) Said he needed da go home da sleep it off. But I'm sure he'll stop by sometime soon.'

'Dat boy made us wait 'n' he's not even eatin'!' griped Aunt Stella. She shot up, causing her chair to scrape violently against the linoleum. While she filled four plates with pasta, Ma filled the four wine glasses on the table with Nero d'Avola, a sweet red wine, with velvety tinges of violet, made from *calaurisi.* [16] 'Dat's not right, Teodora! I awwdda go after 'im 'n' drag his behin' back here 'n' make him eat til he's sick!'

I nasally huffed out some mockery at her griping and moralizing—her gigantic platinum-blonde perm—her fat bubbly ass *squeeeeezed* into a pair of black leotards cut at the calf. I sat down next to the man who somehow tolerated it, ol' Uncle Alfonse, whose head looked larger, more splotched, and more wrinkled since their last visit.

'How's it hangin', Uncle A? Like a horny horse? or a shriveled stallion?' (That's what he used to say when I was younger and he saner.)

---

[15] [scn] Where did Zach go? He left with an empty stomach? – He suddenly felt sick—headache.
[16] [scn] the grapes of Avola, Siracusa

'Huh? Oh, I'm good.' He turned sideways in his wheelchair and yelled, 'Stella!' When he spotted her, he turned back around and mumbled something incoherent.

Aunt Stella set the plates down, mine with carelessness. Treating Uncle Alfonse like a two year old, she stuck the fork down in his partially-receptive hand. Once she sat down, Ma said grace. By the time the Amen came, the two year old in a wheelchair was already eating like one in a highchair. Uncle Baby Alfonse had orangish-red sauce all over his little wrinkly mouth, down his wrinkly white shirt, and somehow a dot on his large floppy ear. But his ravenous manners were warranted because once I took a bite I too fell sweet surrender to the pasta. And Aunt Stella made sure I acknowledged Ma several times for making it; Ma would just look up obligingly, reply obligingly, then, when she saw her eyes were safe from theirs, give me a quick flash that said, 'Yeah, I know, Vinny: she's crazier than him!'

To punish me for not eating her capicola, Aunt Stella forced me to have two heaping plates of Ma's Spaghetti Bellini. Meanwhile, the conversation was lame. Aunt Stella was doing most of the talking, mostly about her old friends, most of which I couldn't have cared less about. But things changed when she served her cassata. *Her* cassata (for they vary) was filled with ricotta and fudge, with a layer of green marzipan on the sides, topped with cherries and almonds. At first, I thought about trying to decline Aunt Stella's cassata just to make her madder—and because I was so stuffed! *mi cafuddài na cona!*—but trying to decline Aunt Stella's cassata would be fruitless.

'Ya know, my nanna passed this recipe dahn da me,' she boasted. 'She's the one thit invented this kinda cassata in Calabria.' The latter statement was true; the former a homemade exaggeration she often fudged. Like Uncle Alfonse, Aunt Stella wasn't from Italy, but unlike him, she wasn't a two-boot progenitor; she had fifty on Italian, and quarters on Slovak and Polish, with an unutterable eleven-letter Polish maiden name. But the real bloody point about Aunt Stella is she was loud, easily offended, and dissatisfied with everyone but herself and *her* family. Before I could even enjoy the first bite of her nanna's world-renowned creation, she had to say, 'Now, Vincent, who do ya think'll cook for ya at cawidge? Ju even think about dat?'

You bedder believe I did. 'At's why I rounded up a team of highly-trained meal advisors, 'n' after hours of deliberation we came to a unanimous decision thit I should hire a personal chef.'

'Why you gadda be such a smartass about everything?'

"Cause I wanna git good grades in cawidge, Aunt Fella.' Childishly, I lowered my head and started jamming the cake in my mouth like a smartass pig.

'Ju hear whadee juss cawed me, Tèa! He keeps sayin' it! I wouldn't even let 'im godda cawidge if I's you! Der gonna kick 'im out! Dey will!'

'Oh, Vinny knows what to do at college.' Ma turned to me with a smile. 'So do you know where to go for all-ah your classes?'

'Uhh, I don't rilly know where anything's at yet.'

'You don't know where anyting is,' she said incredulously. 'You didn't take dee tour? I thought dey took you on a tour.'

'Yeah, bahdiz kinda brief. But don't worry: they got maps 'n' 'at all over the place.'

Satisfied, Ma lifted a fork of fudge up to her glossy lips; some fell to the floor. After chewing on the piece in a slow, unsicilianlike manner, she said, *Tisu si?*[17]

Concerned with a fly that had flown into my cake and stuck for a second, I didn't answer right away. 'Nah. I been readin'ah stuff 'ey do in cawidge for years. I mean, I didn't gidda scholarship for nuh'n, ya know.'

'I know, I know. But if college is-ah too much, you call me. Or Fauter Carr. I see him outside talking to you and Zach. He went to a *veeery* good university, so he-ah knows what to say. See, I don't even know dee first ting about university—'

'Goddamn seddes! Shoo! Shoo, seddes! Go git dat dog!' (Uncle Alfonse was warring to the death with the flies.)

'I'm not even a high school graduate.'

'Yeah. Never rilly said much about it either. Time da spill the beans maybe?' While taking a bite, I glanced up surreptitiously to gauge her reaction because I wasn't sure what the situation entailed. As she turned to Aunt Stella—who looked back sternly as if she was offering no sympathy or help in explaining the unexplained—Ma's day-long polished and happy look vanquished. The sudden quietness and somber mood told me that sum'n was being kept from me, and had been for a long time: a sensation that my intuition and curiosity had long been toying with anyway.

'Well? Was it 'cuzza money or sum'n? *Nun ieni pi chistu ca tu vinisti ccà: pô travagghiu picchì ddocu nun cc'è nenti a chi fari?*[18]

'Let's go!' interjected Uncle Alfonse, pushing his cake away.

'Well?'

"*Ca cettu, mi nni vinni ccà picchì vuleva ca mi facissi quacchi soddu, ca mi facissi na vita ri lustru. Capisci, pê mischini râ sicilia, l'amèrica na cosa bedda ieni. Tutti crirunu ca ccà si campa chiassài megghiu! Ora, i picciriddi mpàranu u ngrisi pi bbèniri un ionnu ccà. A nuddu cci ntaressa chiù u sicilianu. Â nova ginirazzioni mancu cci ntaressa maritàrisi cu n'autru ri sancu sicilianu o talianu. Iddi si maritàssiru macari cu quacchi miricanu!*[19]

'Yeah, okay, way da deviate from the point. I mean, you juss don't drop oudda high school 'n' immigrate withouchir family 'cause yir "seventeen 'n' wanna live in American so bad." Dere's obviously a missin' chapter in the story, so tell it.'

'No, no, I don't go into deez tings today. Anyway, it's not a big deal. Really.'

---

[17] [scn] Are you nervous?
[18] [scn] Isn't that why you came here in the first place: to work because there's no opportunities over there?
[19] [scn] Yes, I came over here because I wanted to make some money, to experience something new and exciting. See, to the poor in Sicily, America is like a dreamland. Everybody thinks life here is so much better! Nowadays, many children learn to speak fluent English in case they end up in America. They couldn't care less about keeping Sicilianu alive. The new generation doesn't even care about marrying another Sicilian or Italian. They would rather have an American boyfriend or girlfriend!

Bound by curiosity, I gave her gritty you-*will*-tell-me stare, while holding my fork upright like a mini pitchfork...til she conceded, her eyes rolling in either trepidation or preparation. 'Vinny, when I was-ah sixteen I-ah, uhh—what do dey say?' She squeezed her eyes shut as if trying to force the missing words out of the corner of her eyes.

'Yir mudder got knocked up,' Aunt Stella said forthrightly.

Whaaat?! Ma got knocked up and never told *meeeee?* Absurd! She was a reserved type of woman. (Then again, she'd been drummed into that tune.) Still, she never told me! No one did! Knocked up! *Nooooo!*

'Yes, I have a son before you,' she admitted with a tone of regret. 'But I would not-ah say "knocked up." Dee fauter Milvio went to Perugia to be a *gar-dzooh-nee: jee, ah, ehrrie, dzetah, ooh, ehnnie, ee: garzuni:* an apprentice.' (It was in that manner she taught me a new word, or reminded me of one we hadn't used in a while.) 'Anyway, after dee baby, I become-ah very sick, and we have nooo money. So Milvio's fauter says if he comes-ah home and learns dee family trade he can manage dee business wit his brahters. *Nun iera cosa fàcili travagghiari a catania picchi cc'era u pizzu. Ie u pizzu ancura cc'è. I cosi vecchi ie i tradizzioni, u capisti?'* [20]

'Yeah, I akshly juss read an <u>art</u>icle at da library about da pizzo in Palermo.'

'Mmhmm, mmhmm. It's common in Sicilia. But in Perugia your business eece safer and you can make-ah more money—'

'Whawuzzer business?'

'Fanu i ruggiara. Prima facèvunu—' [21]

'I sold dose things!' Uncle Alfonse screamed at Aunt Stella, sparking up his own conversation. 'Wha' were dose metal things I sold!' (Apparently, Aunt Stella had no idea what he used to sell, which only riled him up more.) 'Dose clicker things! When me 'n' Giuseppe were boys! We sold 'em over in Bloomfield! 'Member Beppo?' Apparently, Aunt Stella didn't know who this Giuseppe/Beppo character was either, which riled him up into a fuckin' frenzy. While they quibbled over what he and Giuseppe used to sell in Pittsburgh's Little Italy, Ma and I continued (amid our cassata-picking) talking about her adolescence in Catania, Sicilia.

'So den wha' happened?'

'Well-ah Milvio, he goes to Perugia, learns to make and fix watches, and sends me some money. But I have-ah bad chest pains and dee flu and—and some "woman problems," and dee baby needs care, so dee money was just not enough. I even wanted to work a job—*anyting*—but I just couldn't do it: just too sick, you know. *Ahhh...*' She sighed as if her explanation was reviving every prickly sensation of the pain she once had. 'Anyway, once I feel-ah better, *I* want to move to Perugia—'

'Fuckin' Beppo! He lived on Minerva, coglione!'

I couldn't help from laughing at *that* testicular outburst from Uncle Alfonse because I caught his slobber flying through the air and onto Aunt

---

[20] [scn] At the time, it was hard to have a profitable business in the <u>part</u> of Catania that we lived in because you had to pay the *pizzo*. Many people still do. The old ways and traditions, understand?

[21] [scn] They're watchmakers. First they make—

Stella's cheek. But Ma looked as if she was becoming frustrated; I motioned for her to continue anyway.

'Milvio, he says it's better for me to go to America because maybe we can make a *looot*-ah more money here. And then we have-ah good healt care for me and dee baby. He says once he's in a good position wit dee business, he brings it *here*. So I tell Papa, me and Filomena want to come to America. He says, *"Ma chi si foddi? Siti tutti ie dui troppu babbi ie carusi! Nun vâ pimmettu ri gghiriccî!"* [22] But *weeeee* don't listen.' (She smiled briefly.) 'So Milvio says him and his mamma will take care of dee baby til I'm situated here. See, Vinny, his *mamma* says it's *baaad* to take dee baby over*seeeas.* It's like dey didn't want *meee* in dee peekchur. I really didn't like it. *Nope.* But I also want dee best life for, uhh—*Gennaro.'* After mentioning the baby's name breathily, her eyes began to water. The fervent noise of Aunt Stella and Uncle Alfonse's conversation had to be making it even harder for her to talk. But as if trapped into telling me the rest, she went on, becoming emotional.

'Yes, Milvio says dey must take care of Gennaro til dee right time comes. He says, *"Ni viremu n'amèrica quannu i cosi megghiu sunu."* [23] What else could I do? Wait in Catania ah-sick and poor wit dee baby? And *myyy* family? *Spatti filumena mè frati ie soru avèvunu i sò figghi ri appuntiddari, ie nanna scandurra, uhh, ieni na fimmina ri raggia, cussì stunata, cu tuttu ca ciccava ri spiacari...'* [24] (Even though she began talking to herself, I still caught the drift that Ma—the youngest of six—having sex out of wedlock, especially at sixteen, didn't go over well with one of Sicily's remaining *famigghi ri na vota.* [25] Pains me to admit that, according to her, but not held as her own belief, our family deemed Gennaro of the bastard breed. She added that traditional Sicilians love family above all things, but if you disgrace the family then you're easily forgotten. Although my ears overstood her words, and my eyes her gestures of implication, and although I'd pictured her a thousand ways before, including her as a sexual being, my mind just couldn't paint clearly the story that she was telling: too surreal.) '...Nobody else to help. Nobody to-ah, *huuh*—' She sucked in her exasperation then released it: *'Cetti voti a vita iè cussi amara!'* [26] After sighing, she signed herself with the Cross and bowed her head to repent.

From across the table, I gave the top of her head a sad parting look. When she looked up, it was clear that her eyes were crying to cry, but staying American-strong, she pretended she just had a bothersome hangnail to mend before continuing. 'Finally I agree dat Gennariddu will have a better life wit Milvio's family for dee time being. So I tell myself me and Filomena must come here and do what we can til—' Again she paused because Aunt Stella stood up to refill Uncle Alfonse's wine; them two were

---

[22] [scn] Are you two crazy? You're both too young and stupid! I forbid you to go!

[23] [scn] We'll reunite in America under better circumstances.

[24] [scn] Besides Filomena, my brothers and sisters had their own children to take care of. And your Nanna Scandurra is a raging woman, so far out-of-touch, even though I tried to explain...

[25] [scn] families of the old days

[26] [scn] Sometimes Life is so unfair! [Literally, "bitter"]

still exchanging fervent nonsense. 'So Milvio tells me to come to-ah Peetsburgh because he has a cousin here from Abruzzi. He tells him it's-ah "cheaper den New York but still Italian-friendly." But he says we can't *live* witum because he has a wife, but me and Filomena can stay in a free shelter til we find apartment. So when we-ah come here, his cousin gets us work at Sole's, cleaning fish. And we save as much money as we can to buy apartment. But what is-ah left after dee rent only helps us for dee day. I couldn't save *any* money; I didn't plan for *deece* either! But den—*poof!*—I meet your fauter. And well, we fall in love so quick and everyting is wonderful! But he insists I don't work; he says he will take care of me. I thought, "Okay!" And I love-ah your fauter *sooo* much, you know. *(Mi rissi ca mi rava u munnu.)*[27] So, sure, I quit dee job for him, but den Filomena has to go back to Catania because he doesn't like her!

'But now I have Milvio calling every day. He would say tings like: *"Ma chi fai ddocu?"* And I would say, *"Sempri a travagghiari sugnu!"* Weeks later he calls very, uhh, anxious and *puuushy: "Ma dimmi unni stai! Vogghiu vèniri ddocu ie puttari u picciriddu macari cussì semu na famigghia comu chiddi ri na vota! Pozzu travagghiari facennu chiddu ca fa mè patri ie si ammurru fazzu n'autra cosa! Ma ti vogghiu!"*[28] But I don't know what to say; I's-ah—very confused about what to do. Den when your fauter buys deece house, he says I can move in too. And remember, Vinny, I'm now eighteen. I speak-ah *little* English. He takes care-ah *every*ting for me. But see, he gets *sooo* jealous when Milvio calls. He even threatened to kill him!' (That made me laugh.) 'So I call Milvio when your fauter goes to work. But now Milvio is mad too 'cause I live wit anutter man. I try to tell him he's only a friend helping me 'cause I have *nooo* money. But he don't believe me. Den—den he just moves away! witout even telling me!' Abruptly dropping into a somber tone, with her head hung and eyes to the plate: *'Sè, abbannunàrunu mpruvisamenti, ie ancura non sacciu unni stanu.'*[29]

'For rill? His family didn't give ya a heads up or anything?'

'Ô tilèfunu a famigghia d'iddu mi spàrranu a mia. Iddi mi pigghiàvunu a mali paroli...' (In sum, Milvio's family was cruel to the point where she couldn't take it anymore, but one day she called anyway to check on Gennaro and the phone number no longer worked.) 'So I sit in dee apartment. I tink about everyting. Cry about everyting. And I dunno, Vinny—' She looked up, so solemn her face, as she shifted into a sober tone: 'I just-ah give up and pray dit Gennaro has a better life wit his fauter.' (The bleakest wine-sipping moments pass by...) 'Ah maybe my nannu was right. He used to say to Papa: *"Acqua passata nun macina chiù."* Water gone no longer grinds. It means, don't hold onto dee past because it won't do you any good.'

"At's true,' avowed Aunt Stella, rejoining our conversation. She was still panting a bit from her argy-bargy with Uncle Alfonse. She turned to me

---

[27] [scn] He promised me the world.
[28] [scn] What have you been doing over there? – I'm at work all the time. – Just tell me where you live! I want to move there with you and bring the baby so we can finally have a real family. I can start my father's business there, and if that fails, I'll try something else! But I love you!
[29] Yep, they suddenly moved away, and I still don't know where they live.

with fiery cheeks: 'Even me 'n' Alfonse had trouble lettin' yir cousin Amanda move dahn da Georgia. Bahdiz best for everyone. Isn't 'at right, Alfonse?' 'Huh? Yeah, Donna was a tired loaf. She hated Beppo.'

Leaving my cake unfinished, I stood up and flashed a glance at Ma in her pensive, seemingly isolated state. I don't know what compelled me to the kitchen sink but that's where I went...peering out the window at Razzle in the backyard. His chain was shortened because he'd wrapped it around the tree several times, probably hoping that one time around he would fortuitously run into the portal of freedom.

'Hey, Ma?' With both hands cupped on the tawny counter ledge, I kept my focus straight ahead. 'You feed Razzle taday?'

'Yes, I give Razzu lots a food and water deece morning.' (When I was six, a neighbor gave us Razzle as a pup, and the name came with him, but trilling the R, Ma never failed to pronounce it *RRRAH-tsooh*. So yeah, even Razzle had been Sicilianized.)

After spotting me in the window, Razzu began tugging his chain towards me. His long dirty face looked so anxious. His paws, as they dug forward, were kicking up little clouds of dirt. He tugged harder and harder...til the chain jerked his head sideways. In an awkward, twisted neck position, he started barking to the sky. Quick little yelps. Poor Razzu: he was still trying to get in; and there I was: still trying to get out.

'Ya know, Ma: you should start lettin' Razzle in the house, like while Rick's at work. Iddle keep ya company.' Something I'd suggested before, and knew why it never happened, but still said it as if it was a novel idea.

'Oh no, it's not allowed in here. Your fauter says it makes dee house smell bad.'

'Well, ya know wha'? Fuck him 'n' whaddee says.'

'*Fallu pi mia, veni a finisci a tò cassata!*'[30] fretted Ma.

'He's gadda foul mouff *just* like his fahder!' carped Aunt Stella.

"At dog wants a bone! 'At dog wants a bone!' swaned Uncle Alfonse, hearing the ardent barks of Razzle. When I looked over, Uncle Alfonse was trying to rock himself out of his wheelchair, screaming, "At dog wants a bone! 'At dog wants a bone!'

'Ar'ight, Alfonse. We're leavin'. Vincent'll feed 'im. *Shhhh. Shhhh...*'

Aunt Stella stood up and wheeled him out from the table. When he wanted to he could wheel himself, but *not* to seemed part of his decline into infancy, or another expression of his discontent. Ma stood up and gave them kisses. I didn't. Aunt Stella told me to take her cake with me, which wasn't happening, and when she saw that I had no desire to kiss her, she gave me a perfunctory peck on the cheek. Then, wagging her finger, she had to remind me to "watchir mouff at cawidge!" because there they don't put up with "liddle smartasses" like me. Saying goodbye to Uncle Alfonse was futile but I did anyway. I walked to the door and opened it with a goodbye snarl. As Aunt Stella rolled the gimp out, he was still yelling something about Razzle wanting a bone.

Bones buried, I walked into the kitchen and helped Ma clear the table. To lighten the mood I tried joking around about Aunt Stella's humorlessness and Uncle Alfonse's delusion. Then—feeling as if I had to say

---

[30] [scn] Will you please just come and finish your cassata?!

something about the ghost that had been let out of the closet and seemed to be watching us from the dead room—I said, 'Ya know, I'm a liddle shocked about da whole Gennaro thing, but not rilly. I always had a strange feelin' sum'n was up. I juss wish you woulda told me sooner.' (I stopped to see if she would vocally agree, but with a sad look laying heavy on her face, she withheld any response or explanation.) 'Ya know, once I graduate 'n' get a good job, I'm gonna senja over da Catania. You can find Gennaro. Maybe even Milvio. Maybe I'll come too 'cause I dunno whaddle be waitin' for me after cawidge. But don't worry; I'll at least get *you* oudda here.'

Sweeping and keeping her focus on the linoleum crumbs around the table, she again withheld a response. Bones burning, I went outside and brought Razzle in. *Fuck him.*

Not much was said after promising that her much obliged second-son would one day send her over to Catania to regain her lost life. Standing at the door, I assured her that I would call once I arrived—regularly thereafter—and eventually make my way back home to visit. She cried, I comforted, we hugged, we kissed, I petted, he panted, I kissed, he licked, door opened, door closed, and I was gone. *Ciauuu!*

Torn between a quick getaway or a trip down memory lane, I decided to drive the scenic route to the highway, like a decision to retrace the steps I'd walked and stumbled, kept swift pace and stumbled, sometimes ran for my life and stumbled, crashing to the ground, not always able to get back up right away. First, I drove a few blocks down to the ball field where, only two nights prior, Da Rockwell Abandoners had lost a tooth-and-nail game to Da Verna Hoolies. But seeing it, another memory surfaced, one where I hit a homerun in a neighborhood pickup game. Chipped-ham-fisted Pessi hung me a high slider, and as I rounded the bases, I taunted him...til he threw his glove at me. Then he and Eddie tackled me before I could touch home plate. Jeremiah, Anson, Matty, Dubo, Conner, Samskin, and others piled on. Dante jumped in to take my side. He dug down to the bottom and started licking Pessi's face because that was one of his idiosyncratic taunts before he got herpes. After we all stood up, Pessi walked up to Dante and punched him square in the face. Dante took a step back, laughed, then tried bitch-slapping him, but Pessi kept dodging. Finally, Dante got a hold of him, hip-tossed him to the ground, then boxed him into claustrophobia. Since Pessi was claustrophobic and embarrassed by it, he went home pouting once Dante let him go, while we threw rocks at him. He was so pissed at me, and only me, for a couple weeks. I told him it would've never happened if he'd just kept his slider down...Looking through the rear view mirror, I spotted three teenagers—two white, one black—slugging 40s and passing around what looked to be a blunt. They were sitting on the bench where Dante and Anthony had watched the glassy fight and mirrored cold laughter. I drove down to the cul-de-sac and circled around...On the way back, now facing the smoking trinity, a hearty gust kicked up dirt from the infield...and as it swept through the tiny diamonds of the metal fence, the teenagers set their 40s down between their shoes, lowered their heads, and kept passing the blunt around with careful attention in the exchange. Go, team, go...

...At 6th, I turned left at the 4-way and crossed over to 5th. Passing between rows of two-level public housing, blacks were lounging around on interminable porches, some smoking cigarettes, many vocal and lively. For half a minute, three on bikes rode alongside my car, staring me down. Up the road, I came upon a now vacant orange-and-white gas station that we'd turned into a place for practicing graffiti. Anson, the tat artist, tagged some amazing pictures on the back and side walls. Even Pessi, as lousy of an artist as he was a pitcher, managed to tag a set of lopsided tits lactating profusely all the way to the ground. And wrapped around the weeded lot, and extended elsewhere, were the waxed metal railings and curbs that we used to grind our skateboards on...

...Crawling into the snail traffic from the fair, I observed with pensiveness the familiar but strange houses, stores, peoples, lands, and the fruited pastels coloring everything in. Millions of memories started pouring into me like a great internal rain...flooding my senses with thousands of droplets of laughter and sadness and anger and mystery, theirs and mine...flooding my senses with tiny, swirling pieces of reminiscences and adamantine substances which were somehow me and yet somehow them, somehow everything I *am* and yet somehow everything I am *not*...driving past, a light suddenly turned red, and about to drift into the intersection, I slammed the breaks, unable to do it in my head. A blue bullet zipping into the intersection beep-beeped at me. Sitting there like a frozen sigh, I posed to myself the choice to turn left and see a little more of Verna just to relive the half-broken memories, or to turn right down towards Pittsburgh and the southbound highway. When the light turned green I made a right.

Driving down oak-lined Mt. Brennan, making this turn and that turn, Pittsburgh gradually became larger and different angles of the city opened up. The Mon was shimmering its cleanest green of the year; even the Gateway Clipper was afloat, but I couldn't keep my eyes off the engorged eminence of dahntahn. The high-and-mighties still looked like they were trying to squeeze the life out of the sky, especially the tallest one: a solid black steel monster with hundreds of eyes, all homogenous: a monolithic powerhouse, scraping my thoughts like a Brillo Pad...*off the palm...diving freely into the cool air...diving freely...without a parachute...*

...Traveling down the southbound highway, the landscape was predominantly wooded hills with occasional yellow fields squeezed in; here and there sat farms and farmhouses, highway exits, gas stations—small towns too small to recall. At one point, I spotted a doe and two fawns darting through a field, but other than that, the only noticeable movements around me were shadow-driven cars and headless tractor-trailers. But my good ol' friend Music was keeping me company. CD-crazed, I was in a deep reverie in which I was the singer of a Rock 'n' Roll band performing to a soldout crowd. I cranked up the volume loud enough to bring the scene alive. Outside the reverie, the fast, hard music was secreting adrenaline from my glands, making me unaware that I had the pedal to the metal. But up there on the stage, I had the microphone cord wrapped around my wrist and forearm, my leg perched up on a PA speaker, wearing my infamous plain black t-shirt, my biceps bulging more than they actually did, down into the crowd whaling out in tremolo voice: *The devil lies in highway signs...the devil hides in broken lines...going faster than speed signs...the devil's gonna get me right...but not without a fuckin' fight...oh, with the highway in my mirrors...there's a shattered dreams everywhere...oh, there's shattered dreams everywhere...'* [31]

...Drenched in sweat and about to make an encore to thousands of screaming punk rockers, I snapped out of the dangerous reverie—nearly three hours later. I found myself sweating much like Father Carr had earlier in the day. And from that, his persistence controlled my thoughts til, low and behold, right before my hungry hazel-brown eyes my long-awaited haven appeared! From afar, Aristod glimmered like the Land of Oz! I was a driving Dorothy who sadly had to leave behind her little Toto.

I began maneuvering through the bricked streets, pretending to impress outside bodies with my sense of direction—but I didn't know where the fuck I was going! (I *had* taken an assessment test in a building on the edge of campus like I'd told Ma, but the "brief tour" was a lie. I'd cut out of the orientation [sure to be a thorough one] to come back home and attend a crazy party.) So the campus was a mystery land. After driving around in circles like a fool, not able to read the signs correctly, I finally broke down and asked a power-walker where I could find Philemon Hall. 'West Halls,' he answered hardly winded, pointing far out beyond my car, suggesting it was closer to the distant horizon than where we were. So I kept driving along the pastoral outskirts til I finally came upon West Halls where Philemon Hall—a large red brick dormitory in the shape of an upside-down T—rested in the mix of things.

Now prepare my room 'cause I need restored deep in the bowels. [32]

As I expected, there weren't many students moving in; most had moved in Friday and Saturday instead of waiting til the day before classes. I parked my car in front of the dorm...took a deep breath...then walked inside. I went straight to the front desk (a brightly lit cubicle) and asked for instructions. A pretty lil Asian chick said that she needed some information first. I was required to fill out a few forms, while she made copies of my social security card and driver's license. Then she instructed me to go to an orientation starting in five minutes—just for our dorm—and I figured I *had to* in order to get the key. Although a bit confused about things, I carried my confusion across the street...and into another building where I sat in an auditorium, half full with Philemonians...(blah blah blah)...After thirty tedious minutes of history, pride, and boasting, I walked back to Philemon. In the lobby I called Ma to let her know that I made it; it was a brief conversation; Rick was home. Then back at the front desk the pretty lil Asian chick kindly handed me the key. I thanked her, while squeezing the key so hard it left a print in my palm.

So I was off, walking down a blinding white hallway, wondering about my future roommate whom I hadn't received any information about nor had I bothered contacting the school to find out, and he, as far as I knew, never tried contacting me. I didn't know what to expect! I was suddenly bothered by the idea of being boxed in with a stranger who I couldn't avoid and would be sleeping six-feet away. And he could have one

---

[31] Lyrics from "Blacktop Shattered Dreams" by Sin Seizure, from the album *Obscure Mechanism*

[32] Allusion to Paul's letter to Philemon in the book of Philemon, as well as suggesting that he needs to defecate badly

or maybe all of my pet peeves: when people sneeze more than twice; cough without covering their mouth; phonically retarded people who play shit like techno music; guys who wear sandals everywhere; people who gulp while drinking, especially when it's going down their throat and their Adam's Apple undulates convulsively; all those other weird grunting sounds people eject unwittingly; meatheads who have that swelled-chest, jutted-jaw, cocky strut like you better move out of the way for them. Fuck that; I'm not moving! Halfway down the hall, I concluded that my roommate better be quite the mime if he didn't want any of my, umm, bad stuff.

Like a piece of petrified wood, I stood rigid in front of room 122. The door was nothing fancy: just a slab of oak with the number on it. Since my focus remained straight ahead, I had no other observations to make, which is why I took another minute or two to dissect the minutiae of the door...til gathering up the courage to slide the golden key into the lock, readying myself for the first twist—but suddenly a pang of uncertainty swept over me in a hot-hot flash!!!—but I resolutely pushed it away and away, as I pushed the door open with poise, ready (so fucking ready!) to take the next step in life—even ready (to a certain extent) to masquerade an act of excitement as I introduced myself to my roommate. But no one was inside except Jesus Christ...

ALTER OF REPOSE

"When the land is quite and all battles fought,
When the poor rise up and refuse their lot,
When open wounds become painted clots,
Then the world will flower and no longer rot,
Yeah, the world will flower and no longer rot..." [1]

...The room was quiet. Rising up from a pale-champagne carpet: the scent of talcum, like shaken baby powder. An eerie wisp of the lonesomeness and circumscription of a closet was wrapping around my wrist as I inched left—keeping my focus straight ahead—feeling around blindly for the light...but I couldn't find it, and I couldn't move my eyes to look for it, but I needed light! even if the light of day peaking through the white lace behind burgundy curtains—(straight ahead the curtains were draped on two double-paned windows, wide with inner ledges but split by a panel of veneered pine)—was sufficient and would last for at least another hour! Eventually I found the switch *waaaaay* over there. I turned the light turned on. Yes, more light, but the room remained as quiet as a shadow. Seems I was expecting something else: a surprise greeting or a mocking applause. But nothing besides a steady humming silence. Circumspectly, with small steps, I moved into the middle of the room, unable to avert my attention from what I first saw upon opening the door: Christ—a modest-size but elegant painting of Jesus Christ hanging straight ahead on the space of panel between the windows. He was held inside a thick mahogany frame with thin expert waves of amber and cream dancing around the border. Painted on the granular canvas in thick dark tones: a worn, dejected Jesus draped in an ashen jeweled robe...standing at the three-planked door of a hay-colored cottage[2]: small and heavily guarded by glaucous shrubs and vines...his right arm frozen in a forward knocking-motion...his left hand holding up to his waist a dimly lit lantern of a scratchy bronze color...his face turned to where his left eye is fully visible but his right eye only half...far off in the upper right-hand side: a serene wooded landscape shaded by a hazy dusk and the incalculable distance between. Besides the pulsating sensation of irony that shot through me, my initial reaction was that it was too formal to be on an ordinary wall—perhaps even profane having it there instead of somewhere more wholesome, like in a museum behind an electric rope with a muscled guard to the side. It was certainly no *Piss Christ* or *Ecce Homo*—but possibly a Rembrandt replica? I didn't ponder the possibilities much longer because the irony and wonderment soon dissipated and was replaced by inquisitiveness as the long-awaited sense of *gioia ri viviri* [3] overwhelmed me from realizing that, yes, I was at college, in my new room, far away from Verna, and so much closer to *it.*

---

[1] Lyrics from "Rot No More" by Crossed, from the album *Once a Believer, Always a Believer*
[2] Fashioned like a bower
[3] [scn] the joy of living

Turning my attention to the rest of the room, I saw that Jesus had apparently invited Moses over because the room was ~~par~~ted right down the middle. Dressed in plush burgundy sheets, with big *A*-embroidered pillows, two low-lying beds sat in the same fashion alongside opposite walls. The back of each desk (with its raised comp~~art~~ment for books) made tall headboards for the beds. Down at the other end were mahogany dressers, flush against the side walls, back ne~~ar t~~he windows. I decided to test out my desk. Cuffing the bubbled edge above the utensil drawer, I gave it a good shake: pretty sturdy. I went over to the other desk and shook it: even sturdier. Then I went back to mine, realizing that not only was mine a bit less sturdy but mine also had a recommendation carved into it: *Visit 160 UC for a good fuck, Kristen Thompson.* I thought I'd better make a note of it, but the recommendation (whether or not still valid) wasn't going anywhere.

I turned around and back behind the desk, next to the door, the closet—*caspiterina! chi ripustigghiu!* [4]—had plenty of room for the orphans! Metal hangers and all! They were about to be the happiest former-orphans ever! Anxious to try it out, I ripped off my navy-blue CIA spoof jacket, tucked a metal hanger into the pits, straightened out the collar with a brisk jerk, then hooked the talon onto the perch. Taking a step back, I stared at it...and with the help of the sun beaming through windows behind me (which, to reiterate, were on each side of Christ) the golden letters C-I-A, and below, the patriotic emblem adorned with a face-forward eagle, twinkled in the closet like something brand new. But *here* things were to rest in luxury like an old veteran should. Therefore, officially retired from the force: the American eagle whose keen eyes were put to rest as I slid the closet door shut. ZZZZZZZZZZZZZZZZZZZZZZZZZZZZZZZZZZZZZZZZZZZZZZZZZZZZZZZZ...

Snooping around on my roommate's side (the right side upon entering) I noticed his name was Luke Adams; it was written on school-related papers lying on his desk. Also on his desk: a small framed picture of the Lord's Prayer. Behind the golden italic scripture: a watery rainbowed face of Jesus hiding in modesty. From that, the painting, the fastidiousness of his side—his bed made tight, nothing modish on the wall, nothing on the floor besides a black backpack in the corner and shoes ordered underneath the bed, with his text books neatly arranged on the desk shelf—I had a strong hunch as to who my roommate would be: the ecclesiastical prodigy Father Carr had sought in me. Even the clothes in his closet were suggestive of a young paragon: black, blue, and tan dress slacks; blue and white dress shirts; quiet pattern ties; an assortment of polos and sweaters. On the base of the closet: three stacked cases of bottled water and an occupied bowling-ball bag. Besides that, not much else: not even a television or stereo, which meant he was either poor or studious. Either way, I thought it good for the sake of peace. *My* peace. That long-awaited sense of peace...

...Peace I found myself pulling out of my pocket: a tiny bag, spun tight with snow...Peace I found myself lining up on my desk in two tiny rows...Ahhh! the peace I felt as I shot each right to the back of my nose!...

Moments later, when I decided to leave the room on a whim, I suddenly found myself to be in even higher spirits! *La gioia ri viviri!* The intense formication beneath my skin (like millions of tickling ants, together

---

[4] [scn] wow! what a closet!

with the high spirits and joy of living) had the promise of permanency: the transitoriness of the feeling still trillions of moments away! Whistling, I jaunted down the hall: destination unknown. As the front desk came into clear sight, I saw that the same cute lil Asian chick was working, now with another kinda-cute white chick. I asked myself if I had a reason to stop there. Sure I did, my high spirits assured me: to make new friends! Yes! Now run there! Instead I walked very quickly. At the counter, I, with taut shoulders and a grinding grin, inquired about, uhh—where to park my car?...*yes, my car: yinz chicks wanna go for a ride, vroom-vroom, haha...hmmm, I wonder if either've 'em thinks my voice is charmin': been told it's sexy before: snappoudduvit!: ar'ight: but maybe 'iss is why I stopped here: why?: not da make acquaintances or friends but lovers: yeah, alla craziness: peace is nice but chaos is beautiful: so if we make crazy chaotic love, 'n' 'at brings me a sense of peace, den when all's said 'n' done, consummated beauty should be mine: like a viviparous birth fallin' from the aesthetic womb: bzzz bzzz: my hands held out for everything I want 'n' need: bzzz: bzzz: okay! okay! shudup 'n' talk do 'em!*

'So yinz, uhh, live here in 'iss dorm?' Sniff, sniff.

The newly arrived chick in the chair—a blonde with a powdery-pale face and thin penciled eyebrows—gave me a smug cheek raise with one brisk nod that said, 'Yeah, I do. Anything else, Romeo?' The Asian key-dropper had her ass my way, rummaging through a file cabinet, but conjured up an affable, almost waughable, 'Yes, I wiv on the fwourf fwoor.' When she turned around she bore a face far more pleasant than Powder Face. The fluorescents highlighted the natural glitter in her long black hair without affecting her plain, yet piquant, face. Her limpid brown eyes and small frame made her appear too young for college. My educated guess was that she was nineteen and Thai. (Just something about her said, 'Hi! I'm Thai!') With her dark exotic features blended into her deliciously yumber skin, I couldn't even begin to guess the verve of her sexuality, her philosophy on love, and how she embraced the two. Through the window, smiling with her eyes and cheeks, she was about to hand me—*come on! let it be sum'n good!*—nothing but more forms to fill out regarding my car ☹ Disappointed, I sat down out in the large foyer and tried concentrating on the papers, while shooting sniffy glances at her...After finishing the forms—and my handwriting was absolutely atrocious!—I wanted to say something witty and charming, but I found myself heading out the front doors, flushed and jittery, holding a parking pass.

Outside, a flamingo-pink and canary-yellow sunset was in effect. You had to look up and crane to know because, from the way Philemon sat, the surrounding buildings, trees, and knolls cut off the western hemisphere. My car was still parked on the curb of a no-thu-traffic road. Between me and my car stood groups of students hanging out on Philemon's lavish brick plaza, which was lined with fancy wooden benches, white, red, and violet flowers, and to the right, in the yard, a large white gazebo. Judging from their leisurely countenances and voices, they seemed quite affectionate towards one another. Some were smoking cigarettes since you couldn't smoke in the dorms. Amid the plaza, I stopped and fired one up. I noticed several people looking at me weird. Maybe because without my jacket on they could see some of my tats, and from what I could discern, nobody else had any. Plus, I was dressed all ruggedly, and they were all dressed about the same: the guys in factory-faded jeans or unblemished cargo shorts, with unblemished designer shirts, all tagged with top-notch names; the dolls dressed alike but with tighter, more provocative shirts. I moved ahead with the smoke cuffed in my hand, unable to hear the particulars of any conversation, but still felt as if they, *en masse*, were giving off an air of fraternal and sororal unity, making me the outside intruder.

I passed through, over the curb, around the front of my car. I stopped for a moment to take in as much smoke as I could in one hit. Off in the distance, beyond the fortress of trees, where I could only see through here and there, pleasant, playground-like noises were bouncing around in the cool air. I wanted to know who or what was making them and why, but I had other things to take care of first. I began by sticking the parking decal on my back window. Then I stopped to finish my smoke, leaning against my car, facing away from them, trying to listen to the distant sounds. Once I began unloading, I was a bit reluctant because there's a sense of awkwardness unloading your things in front of a crowd, especially when you're doing it alone; but physically I was more than empowered to do it. Although some lanky clown offered to help with the labor, and I told him no thanks, he opened the door for me haul after haul: seven trips in total. Nearly half an hour had passed before I finished, and most of the original outsiders had disappeared as new ones appeared; still no roommate. Strangely it had been the fourteen times I passed the front desk (not through the crowd outside) that brought the most awkwardness which my countenance probably failed to bluff. But they, or at least the affable *chomechai,* [5] probably thought I was handsome anyway. Or that my voice was sexy. Either way, I'd sobered down, so I no longer cared.

Leaving the unpacking for later, I went back outside to park my car. The parking lot was directly in front of Philemon, on a slight slope down towards the dorm. I drove up to my slot: the second to last row, facing another car's front bumper, underneath the shade of a large maple. Because of the tree and being in the upper corner, it seemed like the most clandestine spot in the lot. And I was glad, for there were things I would have to do in my car which I wouldn't be able to do in my room. Before getting out, I opened the ashtray and decided to renew myself by hitting the green a few times. I'd been struck with melancholy after riding high on my spirits. Yet it was the kind of melancholy any great artist must consume in daily doses, and the kind of melancholy any great comedian can meticulously discover the humor within, like the ability of a bird to pluck from a yew the bright red arils without digesting the poisonous seed in the middle....*ahh, if only beauty was so much easier da digest without such nausea!...maybe an ugly injunction'll teach me a lesson?...yes! prohibit deez ugly demons 'n' face an uglier sober world! for it's much too beautiful for damaged eyes!...hmm, I wonder if a waterfall dropped blood or a yellowish poison over its crest if tha'd be considered beautiful...is it the simplicity of the diaphanous substance which streams 'n' screams 'I-AM-purity!' thit makes a waterfall beautiful? or is it da grandeur of the cascade itself whether it's cascadin' water, blood, poison, juice, or—or pudding?...I'd rilly*

[5] [tha] beautiful girl

like da fall off a chocolate puddingfall indua milkshake lake: tha' would be priddy beautiful barring I didn't become a glutinous mess, or for that madder, a gluttonous whale...but I suppose fatness can be beautiful too—or at least in its ugliness lies the same qualities in the beauty of thinness...still a fat chocolate puddingfall, with a high viscosity, would be bedder then a thin one: no one likes runny pudding—at least not I...eyes are beautiful—but mine are damaged...where's my puddinous cataract at? (a wistful sigh falling into a sustained simper)...

...The last of the smoke wafted out the window, dissipating into the evening air. I opened the door and stood up: a wonderful feeling of summertime lightness spread over my body: nothing like the hard uppity-uppness of blowing snow. As if I'd failed to pay attention in the act and was suddenly concerned, I surveyed the area to see if anyone was watching me—I was good. So I lit another cigarette and walked out the backend of the parking lot...through a short plot of grass...and up to a white pathway. There, I studied a glass map of the campus, wondering if there was somewhere specific I wanted to go, or did I just want to briefly admire the colorful abstract view of my new home: the mansion with a mind waiting to be titillated and a heart longing to be romanced.

I decided as homage to Pessi my destination would be the library, being a bibliophile and all, or in slang, a "book-fucker." The library was the largest icon on the map, too, and for that I was excited all over, but most intensely in the pelvic region. So filled with purpose and tingles, I began walking sunward down the coiling white pathway. Right away (and I'd eyed the peculiar scene as I approached it) I walked into a shroud of vegetation where a mess of bushes, some with red berries, some with large white and red flowers, hugged alongside the path, which, further ahead, was curving into a blind turn to the right. In the thicket, aged maples rose high above on each side, forming a large umbrella overhead, casting an intimate darkness down on the path. As I walked deeper into the tunnel of dark greenness a mystical sensation befell me. I slowed my pace to enjoy my smoke, the scene, and a multitude of agreeable sensations. Suddenly something rattled in the bushes to my right...trailing away from me in nippy anxious steps. A nest of birds began chirping somewhere high up in one of the trees. It sounded like the morning tweet of hatchlings. I looked up—but couldn't see anything through the leaves. Then, in a different spot, in the thicket down below: more rattling and movement: branches snapping...leaves whistling...a faint squeaking—more than one animal. Maybe I could see what was going on if I ventured into the thicket? I could join their hide-and-go-seek games. Probably some rascally squirrels or—just then I heard humans approaching from behind, speaking in an Asian tongue. I suddenly felt abashed for standing around on the pathway so leisurely, and though no one could tell, for wanting to play games with the animals. I moved on.

Coming out of the natural tunnel, I, in the middle of an inhalation, nearly choked to death after being struck with the same breathtaking feeling you get when you're driving around a bend and a large city pops into sight: so surreal, intimidating, and in-your-face; this time coming from a sudden view of the inner recesses of Aristod, which was populated with many sunny and vivacious bodies despite the near descent of the sun. But the glimmer and glow of the other lights—scores of room lights beaming through windows, wall lights on the buildings, lampposts aligned all along the walkway just now flickering on, a silver moon in gibbous taking precedence over the waning sun—all made the opened up and stretched out scene lighted just as well. After stutter-stepping and coughing out smoke, I continued walking down the coiling white pathway.

Descending a small hill, my eyes crossed from side to side, up and down, not sure what to gaze upon first. Like nude chicks lined up before me: do I try to take it all in at once? or study one at a time? Well, since taking it in all at once and leaving only "the big picture" in the mind is dull for the memory, yet no one every stays nude long enough to get *that* into "particulars," I compromised by taking a quick glance at everything and everybody. Out to my left, a bunch of guys were playing football down in an open velvet yard. The one with the ball had just gotten away from the defense and was making a clean break for the closest pathway; gratuitous shouts of encouragement resounded even after he'd quit running. To my right was a small glass-façade creamery: there was a line of people inside, through the door, and onto the side patio. The ones leaving were either licking ice cream or drinking what I assumed were milkshakes. So many flavorful chicks hanging out like free samples. Unfortunately, the main pathway curved away from them and the creamery, and went down towards the football players, where, next to them, sat an enormous building. It looked like a Gothic cathedral: a skeletal façade with stained glass and high pointed arches and spires. Rising high above from the sides of the base: two gray towers that tapered into a spray of pinnacles. The building had a cloistered air of strength, piety, and solitude—comprising such humanness, such anthropomorphic certitude—that behind the watery stained glass seemed to be the glow of a solemn ascetic soul kindling a spark of divine light amid the material darkness. I didn't, just couldn't, approach the skeletal building. But walking passed, I could see engraved above the wooden doors: OLD MAIN 1846. Must've been the original building of Aristod. The pathway then leveled off and merged into a circle-shaped parking lot. It led to a campus road: right at the elbow of a turn. There were two main walkways: left and straight, or right and uphill. I went left and straight. Every building on the street, which was Virgil (the main drag) looked like 19th century England. On both sides of the road sat large Gothic buildings of grayish tones—some of an aged copper—all skeletal stone and adorned with arches, spires, stained glass, sculptural details, some even guarded by gargoyles. The masterly façades amid the verdure of shady trees, snipped shrubbery, and candy-colored flowers was so philosophical and romantic, artistic inspiration began flooding over my soul. And the area was much quieter and less populated than back by my dorm. I liked the quietness, for it felt like I was here all alone.

I crossed the street and walked further ahead...til coming upon a street running left-right, uphill to the right where another set of dorms sat: North Halls: brown-bricked. I headed that way. Further up, on the left, between two buildings connected by a hanging enclosed walkway, a small plot of land was filled with marble chess tables. Outside chess tables: I couldn't believe Aristod had something like that! I hated chess but seeing it sent a pang of vanity through me. I said to myself, 'These opulent sculptures are *mine* 'n' I'll sit dahn 'n' play if I feel like it!' But I didn't. There wasn't anyone to play chess with anyway.

Anyway, I passed through the yard. The sun had all but vanished by now, but like I said, it was still bright if you kept your eyes out of the sky. As I walked under the suspended glass walkway, another magnificent sight appeared. Down below, for I was walking downhill now, I espied more buildings and bodies to the left...and straight ahead, in a valley well below me, the town of LaSalle fading clear into the horizon where I could also see (in the glow of town) a large purple mountain and its lower shoulders—but it was too dark and obscure *that* far away to know if it was a true mountain or just a large hill: a good ten miles out if I had to guess. Now, drawing my vision back to *my* locale, the buildings in this section looked newer and brighter than those on Virgil. I could see that many were made with either white limestone or flecked marble. Some had sections festooned with large glass walls. Some had massive columns out front. Many had, wherever tasteful, strips of burgundy: the school's color. They all varied in size but together were colossal. Such a surreal sensation looking out atop the hill and seeing so much at once. Kinda like seeing Pittsburgh from Verna. But here the buildings shot up no more than five stories, and there were only 5,000 students with an additional 10,000 in LaSalle, compared to the hundreds of thousands in, and millions around, Pittsburgh. Anyway, once I descended the panoramic hill it became all flatlands, so my scope became limited, as the breadth of the campus came in subtler doses.

Ovid Street (as it was called) was so crowded with hectic bodies coming and going out of the Hub that my attention to its layout was obstructed. Many were storming out with burgundy Aristod Bookstore bags. The bookstore: evidently one thing found inside the enormous futuristic building. The bags looked heavy, too, suggesting the price just for the literary side of a semester wasn't any lighter, which brought to mind that I hadn't bought any of my books yet. (I'd planned to wait til I received the refund from my loans, but with the money Ma had given me I could do it right after classes.) I debated whether or not to go inside the Hub. I'd yet to do anything besides look at façades and faces...*I'll have a smoke first...I should quit dis 'filty abit' like Ma said...hmm, now if I step inda the Hub I gadda make a note of it 'cause it's always important da remember my-firsts, 'n' it rilly would be my first cawidge buildin' entrance since I don't count my dorm 'n' 'at since it was by necessity...wonder wha' my first cawidge words'll be since opening 'n' closing remarks seem da madder the most in hindsight...how the fuck is 'Caw me Ishmael' wanna the most famous opening lines?: 'One mornin', upon awakenin' from agitated dreams, Gergor Samsa found himself, in his bed, transformed indua monstrous vermin'—so much bedder: Lolita's is lewd but ripe for parody 'n' play: but nuh'n trumps Catcher's: 'If ya rilly wanna hear aboudit, the first thing you'll prahblee wanna know is where I's born, 'n' wha' my lousy childhood was like, 'n' how my parents were occupied 'n' all before they had me, 'n' all that David Copperfield kind of crap, but I don't feel like goin' indo it, if ya wanna know the truth. In the first place, that stuff bores me': hahaha!*

Filled with mental laughter, I found myself being swept into the Hub, officially entering my first building at college by choice. The first thing I noticed inside was the massive white marble steps before me, leading up to the second level. The flow of motion each way was slow but nobody was being pushy. To my immediate left was a large L-shaped aquarium. I walked over to it. It had many tropical fish matched with an artificial tropical setting. Most of the fish were small but I spotted a few larger ones. Their entwined fluorescence was remarkable: red, opaline, blue, violet, yellow, pink. I flipped through a book on a podium that had descriptions of each fish: angels, barbs, danios, rainbows, bettas, mollies, gouramis, loaches—sharks! I wondered if they fed on each other to survive: even though that might be the so-called "way of nature," kinda cruel and unnatural if humans are setting up the conditions. No doubt, an attractive sight, but I hated to see any life in a cage or on a chain for someone's trivial amusement, especially for the future yuppies around me.

I figured I would check out downstairs first. So I began walking rightward upon entrance. On both sides sat long tables only divided by the wide white marble aisle I was heading down; there were smaller aisles along the walls. Despite the hustle and horde not even half of the tables were full. Although a few diligent ones were seated and somehow reading amid the noise, most were socializing and having a hard time staying seated as they fished around. Probably more of a socializing place anyway, seeing as there were several food joints in the area: a pizzeria, a coffee shop, a Chinese restaurant, and a few corporate fast-food joints. All closed besides the coffee shop. After passing through, and there came to be no more tables, food joints, or as many people, and thus less noise, I came upon a circumscribed building, diagonally right from the aisle: some kind of artifact museum. That's what the golden letters above the glass doors said: Hathaway's Artifact Museum. Within, an Asian chick sat behind a C-shaped ivory desk. She was looking at me looking back like a confused tourist in a strange country. I didn't plan on venturing in, and if I kept going straight I would have to descend another set of steps which I didn't want to do; but it *did* intrigue me that there were *three* levels, not two as I'd previously thought. So I turned around and walked back passed the tables and food joints...til I came to the steps that went to the upper level. The steps were steep and crowded...but I made it up all right. At the top, to my left, was a sign for the bookstore and a helpful arrow pointing down the hall. But looking down the hall, I could see that it actually went outside to a wide table-packed patio...*then* into the bookstore: still part of the building but with an open-air cut-through. With no reason to go *that* way, I kept walking straight. There wasn't much up ahead before I reached the doors. The upper level was relatively short by length but had interminable wings. To my immediate right were lots of sofas, again around half full, where people were watching televisions flush inside tan walls, and one 52-inch screen on the floor. As my head was turned to the side, striding past the sofas, a little girl (around five) bumped into my leg. She had gorgeous black hair, some of it secured in pigtails which weren't on the sides but up high in the back, with the rest flowing down freely. She looked up—up through her big strewn bangs, half-mischievous, half-discomfited. Smiling, I comically widened my eyes, with gave prominence to my arched eyebrows. In response, her auburn eyes lit up, as her little lips parted, bearing a bug gap between her front teeth. *Chi sciuriddu!* [6] You could already tell that daddy would have to keep an eye on her in her teens. Up ahead, her mother called out: 'Brittany, watch where you're going!' Before the nympha zipped back to her mother and bag-toting big brother, I surreptitiously fingered her silky black hair. As I passed by them as a unit, her mother apologized with a high-class smile; hiding on the other side, little Brittany *(dda fudditta prizziusa)* [7] took a playful peak at me and snickered. At that moment, a foreign sensation mixed with vertigo and a benign craving befell me; felt like I had fallen into a pile of pixie dust, rolling around so freely.

Before choosing one of five glass doors to pull open, I looked to my left, and in the corner sat a narrowly built bank: presently closed, but (to the side) people in line for the ATM-in-the-wall. Evidently, the Hub had it all, and I hadn't even seen half of it! Nor did I care to at this point. Judging from its size and multi-purpose facilities, I assumed no other building stood to challenge its modern masteries and array of scents.

Back outside, in the warm night air, I lit another cigarette. I realized I forgot about my initial destination, and I chided myself for not letting the library be my *first* college building entrance by choice. Although growing tired of walking, I thought I would check it out anyway. Finding myself lost again, I searched for another map, which had me crossing the Hub's decorative horse-and-buggy street, where, on the other side of the sidewalk, another large glass map sat directly in the middle of a circular red-bricked plaza. In the back-center stood a bulky street clock with Roman numerals. I looked up: VIII-something. Reevaluating my location, it appeared that all along I'd been going in the wrong direction! I must've read the first map backwards because the library was *behind* Philemon and *to the left*. But now I was cocksure that I would get it right. Exiting the plaza to the left, I found something funny: a waterfall! Yes, a large smooth piece of gray marble rising six-feet from a tan rocky base. Lit up and contradistinguished with plastic lights, the water dropped perfectly from the top: the crest had such a round curl. Even more interesting, some of the water flowed east-west, and behind the main fall, neon water flowed upward. Must've been the cascade of some crazy collegiate mind. I *suppose* it was "beautiful." But nothing compared to a puddingfall.

I began striding southbound...passing lots of broccoli bushes, umbrella trees, static umbrae, fluttering phantoms...all dimly lit besides the intervallic emergency posts with flashing neon-blue lights...the pathway began curving down a small hill, then rounded left...now to my right: a darkened courtyard rolling into the wild black yonder...a minute of seclusion...til it broke back open in another congested area. To my surprise, these buildings weren't Gothic like Old Main on Virgil, or futuristic like the Hub on Ovid, but rather plain: large and plain with red or tan brick. I kept trudging along the pathway, hoping the library would soon come into sight. Although bodies were few, I could sense the thousands of books shelved in the vicinity. I had to stop, though, when I came across two adjacent buildings that had a bit of flavor: on the entablature—the banner of concrete protruding right above the top level of windows—were the

---

[6] [scn] What a cute little flower!
[7] [scn] that lovely little sprite

names of famous painters, philosophers, poets, etc. engraved into the frieze. I walked around the buildings and found the eternal names ran all the way around, although some areas were too dark to make out the names. It was most likely p~~art~~ of the Liberal ~~Arts~~ Dep~~art~~ment. I was glad, too, because it was close to my dorm and I would be having a lot classes here.

After returning to the front, a troop of athletic bodies came jogging by. Their sweat-soaked panting and plopping echoed in my ears. I suddenly felt a headache coming on. My energy was rapidly depleting, but I *had to* see the library so I could sleep in peace. Moving forward, another troop came jogging by; this time I refused to step aside, forcing them to split. Even those who weren't jogging looked like they did earlier, took a shower, got fancied up, and were now strutting around their healthy bodies. It was like someone, somewhere, had opened up a bunch of fitness magazines, pealed the pictures from the pages, crafted them into animation, then the *papier mâché* figurines took up curriculum at Aristod. I certainly hadn't come across many uncomely ones; no yinzers. Rather, everyone was dressed formally or stylishly, and sculpted by effort underneath. But what really stomped me: they all seemed to have legs as tall as me. Ahhh!

I st~~art~~ed legging it out. I had to find another map...and I did, in a plaza outlined with large Stonehenge rocks turned horizontally. Spread across one, a girl was lying on her back, knees up. Her mouth p~~art~~ed, she appeared to be napping or relaxing or letting a specter-slave drop grapes into her mouth. Yep, it was like godly servants were feeding her ambrosia as she lay in the gentle palm of Aristod, looking up into the starry night, so serene and profound. I almost had the nerve to shake her out of her repose, but I didn't; I had a date with the library, and I was long overdue. But while I'm reevaluating the third map, someone accosts me from the side.

'Eh, ya kna' where da Wor'n buildin' is? Sposta be around here somewhere but I can't read 'eez freakin' tings for da life a me!' By the end, she'd moved in close, almost to the hip. Angling a look, I was revitalized by the energy beaming from her small rosy face. She had wild, choppy, blonde-streaked hair with potent astral-blue eyes, offset with little pale lips. The toothsome sugar was dressed down in a solferino sweatsuit. And her voice was as sharp as a razor! In all probability, a NYC chick—a *streety* NYC chick.

'Well—looks like it should be over dere somewhere.' Moving my finger from the abstract to the real, I pointed in the general direction. What she called Wor'n (a whaling *WOR* with a faint "t" but a strong "n") was Wh~~art~~on. 'Sounds like yir havin'ah same problem as me. I been all over da place tryin'ah fine'ah liberry, 'n' itsa biggest fuckin' buildin' on campus!'

She giggled. 'Well, hun, it's aboudda five minute wok adda way.'

'Awesome. Think I might juss caw it a night. I'm sure iddle still be there tamarra.'

Tilting her head a bit, she grinned with her right cheek and batted her astral-blue dewdrops. '*Aww*, don't give up. I'd wok ya myself if I didn't hafta go meet my roommate.'

'Hmm. 'At's too bad. I think I'd enjoy yir company.'

'Well I tell ya wha': why don't ya take my numba, 'n' maybe ya can "enjoy my company" inside somewhere—like maybe next weekend.'

'Ar'ight; sounds good; but I don't have anything da write it dahn on. No cell phone either.'

Undeterred, she went over to the girl lying on the rock and shook her out of her repose. Hey, that's what *I* wanted to do! I smiled out of respect for her buoyant valor. She asked the sleepy girl if she could hava peaca paypa anna pen. The sleepy girl rose...dug into her backpack...then handed over Paypa Anna Pen. After jotting her number down, she came back over and handed me Paypa. Paypa said her name was Andrea No-Last-Name. When I concurred with only a first, she said in a flirty, teasing way, *'Oooo, Vincent:* one of my favorite names.' (I actually said "Vinny" because I'd always been uncomfortable introducing myself: couldn't start off with just "V.") Andrea and I then embarked on all that what's-your-major, where-you-from crap: she was from Queens, here on a full scholarship for math. And it didn't require to calculus to know this was one spry girl, standing so inly, chatting so bitingly but affectionately. She kept twirling a piece of her wild, choppy, blonde-streaked hair around her finger: in her own buoyant, streety way: a modern sylph—and about a dick-size shorter than me! Niiiiice!

'...ar'ight, Andrea, I'll definitely be in touch. Good luck findin' *Wor'n.* (Fuckin' New Yorkers talkin' funny.)'

'HA! *You're* da one thit talks funny. But yeah, good luck findin' *liberry.* Like I said, all ya gadda do is skip right downa path ova dere. Can't miss it unless you're *blii-iind!'* Her smile widened as she squeezed her eyes shut tight in jest. She popped 'em back open. 'Well, nighty-night, Vinny-pie.'

I didn't skip right downa path ova dere, but I did feel a bit jaunty again. So for the fourth time I was—ofta da liberry! This time—besides Gothic masterpieces, ultra-modern buildings, or the minimalist designs in the area where I met Andrea—on the way I passed (or could see) an old-fashioned cottage...a greenhouse...a recreation hall...a basilican church...a white château called Baudelaire...a scholastic fraternity house that looked like a Colonial mansion...and a plank-bricked alumni house with a large pond out front, which was stocked, for I walked over and saw fish swimming near the surface: it was brilliantly lit up by multi-colored lights everywhere. When I walked back up to the path, I was held in awe by that which was before me: the library—a book heaven and nothing less! The map was right: it *was* the largest building on campus, and from where I was standing (at the bottom of three sets of very wide steps), I judged I was only looking at the head of the body. Its high walls were smooth tan blocks that showed no separation like an adobe. And written on the blocks near the ground: Latin scriptures, lighted by antique lamps. At the top of the steps: a large portico with four Doric columns bracing a concrete slab embossed with Roman reefs and esoteric symbols. Straight ahead from the portico: a massive two-part door with alternative side doors. At each side of the main doors, placed on the portico like greeters: life-size sculptures of robed saints kneeling down in profound thought. Suddenly I, too, found myself kneeling down in profound thought. After all that time and determination, I couldn't make it up the steps. Something was creeping up through my innards, making me very nauseous and dizzy. I whipped around and began walking blindly down a split courtyard...after twenty-some yards, I stopped, struggling to breathe, being asphyxiated by the perfection all around me: air too fresh, grass too green, lights too bright—this place wasn't for real! I wasn't really here! Death was after me again! approaching from the inside! trying to push outward! trying to divide me in half!

I tried shaking off the dizziness, bring my breathing under control, settle my nerves—(felt like they were at war with each other!)—but I couldn't seem to remember how to breathe right! Felt like a twine of grapes had been lodged inside my throat! The tour had reached its end: I couldn't bear to see anymore or walk any further! So I sped back to Philemon, trying to escape the cutting jaws of Death!...

...Still a bit dizzy when I returned, but breathing better, I opened the door languorously—only to see my roommate in the act of springing up from his bed; also startled, I took a step back. The pungent smell of cheap cologne rushed into my face, striking me dizzier. Disconcerted, all I saw was something wobbling towards me with a blurry face. I braced my right leg, unsure how this wobbling thing would hit me.

'Well, hello, Vincent! You surprised me there, although I saw by your stuff that you'd made it. I just wasn't sure when you'd be returning. Anyway, I'm Luke Adams. Nice to finally meet ya.' His voice was very cheery with a mid-range twang.

I gripped his extended hirsute paw and shook it; his hands were sweaty. 'Nice da meecha too. 'N' yeah, I's a liddle behin' gih'n dahn here.' As we went to release grips, his hand turned sticky. I took a deep breath to recuperate. 'So how ja know my name? I'm guessin' 'ey prahblee sencha my information 'n' 'at.'"

'Yeah, like last month. Why, you didn't get mine?'

'Akshly, no. But mail in my house sometimes goes from the mailbox straight ta da garbage can.'

'Oh, it's cool. It happens. But, heck, I wasn't even sure if you were still coming or not. I tried calling you at home twice to find out the situation. I thought we could make some arrangements beforehand...'

Luke went onto say that when he'd called the first time, he'd been told he had the wrong number, and the second time, some guy flipped on him, saying if he didn't quit calling, he was going to press harassment charges; wonder who that might've been? After my sight came into focus, and my nerves mellowed, I realized that Luke was a little grizzly cub. He was short, hairy, and stumpy. His gawky stance suggested that at any minute he might fall over and roll around in a pool of honey like Winnie. Even his hair looked like a patch cut from a Californian grizzly: it was trimmed up short but not shaved uniformly like Pessi's, light golden brown, and really didn't fall under any certain hairstyle: it was just there, like a bear: you just look at it and that's about it. He was in a white undershirt (you could see the bear's forest underneath), long gray shorts that looked like plastic, and sandals with no socks! Yuck! Despite already hitting upon a pet peeve, he bore a round benevolent face that said, 'Yeah, I'm dorky and cub-scoutish, nevertheless, a friendly mind-my-own-business kind of guy.'

While I did some unpacking, getting out things I would need in the morning, Luke and I exchanged background information. I was keeping mine as brief as I could. He said that he was from Duneville: a town two hours southwest into West Virginia where two thousand residents basically knew everyone's favorite color. He had four younger brothers and an older sister. His father was the mayor of Duneville, which I assumed wasn't a big deal. And his mother stayed at home to take care of his brothers but also made and sold (right out of their house) "knickknacks for the home," which, as he explained, were things like candleholders, potpourri ornaments, refrigerator magnets, coffee table junk, and other junk. He grew up on a farm too—well, he said he had a "normal country house" but there was a "barn out back." I asked if there were animals in it. He said that when he was younger they had a bunch but now just a few horses and sheep. SHEEP! That was seriously just too much for me! SHEEP! BAAA! BAAA!

Until I bought a stand for the television, I set it on the ground between the two beds, against the wall, underneath the painting. Observing it for the second time, I said, "At's a nice painting ya got dere,' giving it a serious finger-pointing like an ~~art~~ collector looking to make an ~~art~~ful bargain. 'Kinda almost extravagant for a dorm room. When I first saw it, I's like, "Wow, 'at looks like it belongs in a museum."'

'Oh, I'm sorry, man. If it bothers you I can take it down. I don't wanna be pushing my religion on you or anything.' He let out a nervous laugh.

'No, I wasn't sayin' it bothers me. Akshly gives the room some flare, ya know.' (Exaggerating to make him feel better.) 'We definitely need some things on da walls so it's not so dull in here.' Although not my ~~particular~~ ~~t~~aste in *style* since I was more into Romanticism and Surrealism, the painting *didn't* bother me. Just caught me a bit off guard. Guess you could say the painting thrown out in before me was very intimidating at first, like the library, and sometimes it just took me some time to adjust to things I'd never been exposed to. Not Christ *per se*, but just a new environment, knowing this is where I would now rest my head. First day at college: it's all nerves and anxiety!

'Yeah, that painting's as old as me. My dad's friend is a professional painter, and he painted it as a gift for my baptism.' Luke sat down on the bed, while I jumped up on mine to stick-tab a poster to the wall. 'But I'm really glad it's not a problem. I'd rather take it down now than come back one night to see a pentagram drawn on Jesus' forehead or alien antennas comin' outta his head.'

To the wall, I smiled at his hypothetical nightmare, surprised he would even conjure up such a thought. 'Well, I's akshly thinkin' a puttin' a *swastika* on his forehead.' Silence befell the room. Unable to stop myself from turning around to gauge his reaction, I saw his face was straight and pallid, assuring me that my sense of humor was a bit too much, especially since we barely (bearly?) knew each other. 'I'm just kiddin', dude. I'd never do anything like 'at.' I also felt the need to say that I wasn't racist or a Nazi, but that might've added more awkwardness to the moment, so I turned back towards the wall.

'Yeah, I wouldn't think you'd do somethin' like that. You seem cool. I'm sure we'll get along just fine.'

'Yeah, I's akshly brought up Catholic, so I seen Christ a few times in my day.'

He laughed. 'Oh yeah? I'm Baptist. But really, I find more value in the way you live than in titles, ya know.'

'Exactly.' I jumped down from my bed. There was now a poster on the wall: the heavily-inked guys from Agnostic Front: a NYC band known as the Godfathers of Hardcore and whom I'd hungout with after shows a couple times, thereby proving their wall-worthiness.

'So, Vincent. You nervous about tomorrow?'

'Nah, not rilly. Juss here da do my work 'n' get out. 'N' if ya want, ya can juss caw me Vinny, or Vin, or V. Alwada my friends juss caw me V.'

'Cool, cool. *Veeee.*' Snapping his fingers, he swung his tubby body around as if Revelation had bumped into his love-handles. At his desk, he began sorting through things. And just then, I felt ill-mannered, perhaps conceited, because I was dying to burst out in laughter. Luke Adams was just so fuckin' funny-looking! He was like a chubby bumbling silly grizzly bear, except you could see the sweat underneath his arms. Even bearer, from the way his big lips flopped, and his fuzzy head bounced around, it seemed as if he was trying so hard to be "cool." That's what he kept saying: 'Cool, cool.' Like: *Cool man, I dig that. I'm a cool kid in college too...Cool, man...cool, cool, cool...Kewl beeeaaans, homeboy.* Yeah he was certainly ass-backwards in his slang, particularly in the delivery, but it was as harmless as an abandoned cub needing mamma's suckle.

'So, Luke, whachir major?' Like I was in for a shocker.

'World Religions, but it's also like a cultures major too. You?'

'*Mmmm...*' To show I needed time to think it over, I began rocking my head left to right in slight movements towards my shoulders. 'I suppose sum'n dealin' with literature. I like da write 'n' 'at. But I'm still undecided on which exact degree I'm gonna go for. Might double English with Hisstree.'

'Cool, cool.' From his desk he wobbled over to his bed and wiped the sheet with one long motion. With his back to me, he said, 'When I moved in on Friday, both sides seemed the same to me, so I figured my first pick wouldn't be a big deal.'

'Yir right: it isn't. I'm a left-side-a-the-room kinda guy anyway.' After that lame remark, I grabbed Darby Crash and hoisted myself back up on my bed.

'Left-side-a-the-room kinda guy,' he repeated like I'd just given him a new "funny" catchphrase to memorize and try out.

I tacked Darby up on the wall. He seemed even more disgusted being at Aristod: I could almost hear him screaming into the microphone, 'SELLOUT! YOU FUCKIN' SELLOUT!' Ahh! my head was pounding! and I needed to go to sleep soon because my classes started at 9 a.m. and I'd been staying up late all summer, although I'd heard on the first day of classes you usually get the syllabus, the teacher goes over it, then you leave: not so bad. After classes I planned to buy my books and maybe get a few things for the room. I had to get my telephone number, too, which brought Andrea back to mind. I wondered what she thought of me: Is she always so extroverted with guys she just met? or is she one of those love-at-first-sight people and believes I'm the soulmate she's been waiting to bump into? Back in high school, I never had a girlfriend that lasted longer than two months. I'd told myself that if I ever took the notion to try out that serious stuff, I would wait til *after* college so that I can do what I need to do academically. And to be frank, or rather, V about my mentality going into college—as if a token taken from high school—I was only accepting applications from doxies. Andrea Doxy? Yeah, even gotta nice drug ring to it.

'Hey, you, uhh,' Luke stammered as he struggled to put on a chalky windbreaker, 'you wanna come to the commons with me? I wanna get a little snack before bed.'

I was stacking up boxes at the foot of my bed just to get them out of the way. With two posters hung, some orphans homed, the alarm clock plugged in and set, and the television repositioned, I was done unpacking for the night. 'Nah, I'm not rilly hungry. I'm priddy tired from the drive 'n' 'at. I'm prahblee gonna godda sleep soon.'

'Okay, cool. I'll try to be quiet when I come back. But I'm goin' to bed soon too.'

'Ar'ight. Sounds good.'

'Well, hope ya sleep well and have fun at classes tomorrow. I'll probably catch up with ya tomorrow evening.'

I thought about using the voice of Opie or Beaver to say: 'Kewl beans, Luke! That would be just swell!' But gee-wiz, I just couldn't bring myself to do it. So the unsung ursine pawed his keys off his desk, lowered his head like a rejected dog, then left the room like a hungry but inexperienced cub that failed to catch a fish in the stream.

With Luke Adams gone for food, Darby on the spot, the campus titillated and romanced as much as I could allow on the first date, my stomach growling and biting itself (I was actually hungry but didn't want to go with Luke), my eyes rolling back into my head, where, within, it felt like nonsense was being yelled into the ears of my capsizing eyes, it was finally time to sleep it all off! First, though, I went outside to have one last smoke...came back in, dressed down...went to the bathroom, brushed the fuck out of my teeth...returned to my room, shut off the light, then dropped down carelessly—so listlessly, as they like to say—on my new bed...and out in the dark I stared at the silhouetted painting...til I slipped into neurotic unconsciousness...

...(All around me an abyss of whiteness is pulsating like a throbbing heart. A young girl in a yellow dress approaches. Her glittery black hair is hanging down to her tiny waist. Her eyes look like her hair: black and glittery. There's a pink daisy tucked behind her left ear. She's barefoot. She comes very close to me.) Hey, do you know where I can find Love? – Huh? – Love. I'm looking for Love. – Love? Arnchu a liddle young da be lookin' for Love, liddle girl? – I'm not a "liddle girl." Will you kiss me? – No. I'm too old for you. – That's stupid! I'm not young! Please kiss me. (Suddenly, off in the distance a silhouette appears behind the little girl.) So will you kiss me? – No. Whachir name? – I'm not telling YOU! – Well then tell me who's 'at behinja? I can't see. Tell 'im da come forward. – Will you kiss me? – Yes. (I kiss her cheek. She starts crying.) What's wrong? You told me da kiss ya. – (Sobbing) I want you to kiss me like you mean it! – I can't do dat. But who's 'at back 'ere? – I'm not telling you. You're mean! But I still love you. Hey, will you paint my face red? – For wha'? – Please. I can make you happy if you do. – I don't have any red paint so how'm I sposta painchir face red? – Here. (She directs me to my knees. She grabs my hand and starts rubbing it over her face.) Do you like painting me? – It's ar'ight. – Do you think I'm beautiful? – Yir very priddy. – No, I mean beautiful! I want you to see me as beautiful! (She gently removes my hand from her face and keeps hold of it. With her other hand she pulls down the top part of her dress. She grabs the *back of my head and guides me into her breasts.) Do you think I'm beautiful? – Yes. – Will you kiss me for real? – Will ya tell me who's back behinja? – He's waiting for you. – (I pull my head away but remain on my knees.) For wha'? – Ca vussia si nn'addunassi rê mè biddizzi. [8] (Suddenly, my hand is between her legs, and she screams so piercingly that my ears start bleeding. But my hands remain stuck between her legs. As the echo pounds throughout my swelling head, I remain trembling against her naked body. Then everything goes black. I can still feel the sensation of warm genitalia. Like clockwork, a piano begins playing: slow, plangent, 19th century Europe, All Hallows Eve. Moments later silence sweeps over the haze, and I feel wet, then just as quick the piercing noises resume and I feel dry—I jerk up and open my eyes. The guilt flushes through my body as if that's all that fills my streams: guilt flowing through guiltstreams. I feel really sheepish...*

---

[8] [scn] For you to become aware of my beauty. [Note: she addresses him in formal Sicilian, as opposed to using the familiar use of "you."]

SO MALADJUSTED

"I got drunk, I got high,
I did what I did to get by,
I got stoned, I got rocked,
I woke up in a haze and couldn't talk,
I got stalked by the demons inside of me,
Wanting more, giving less,
Chasing me til I'm left breathless,
I got drunk, I got high,
I did what I did to get by..." [1]

...*Beep!* *BEEP!* *Beep!* *BEEP!** sounded two competitive voices within the alarm clock. I slammed my palm down and killed one bird with two tones. After a pugnacious night of stick-and-move sleep, I was now up and getting ready for my first day of college. Luke was already gone. His bed was made like no one had ever slept on it. I didn't have time to make mine, although I wouldn't anyway. I rushed through all the morning stuff...grabbed my black backpack, which held two notebooks and some writing utensils, then headed out the door in a state of absentmindedness.

The sky was hanging low and overcast, the air unexpectedly chilly; if I'd known I would've worn a hoodie instead of a t-shirt. Through my grogginess I could see faceless bodies traversing in all directions. Hear blasé morning voices. Shrill morning tweets. Eek! the dreadful hour of 9 a.m. just minutes away. Before exiting the plaza, I lit a cigarette, knowing I would have just enough time to finish it before I made it to Bloy Hall which was near where I had met Andrea: a three-minute walk. Nervously, I pulled out my schedule from my jeans to double-check; didn't want to screw things up on the first day. My first class was *English 112: Intro to World Literature*, taught by a Dr. Rosenbaum. Sounded interesting even if I wasn't expecting much I hadn't already read. But my precociousness (or cockiness, if you will) wasn't shaking off the anxiety. The confident feeling I brought to Aristod, the one in which I had this resolute flame burning inside where I was going to walk into Aristod and turn it upside-down with what I knew from reading like an Ivy Leaguer, while having what no Ivy Leaguer could ever acquire: the hardened street smarts bestowed upon me from growing up in Verna— well, that feeling was no longer sitting well with me: the Vallanic flame didn't seem so bright and hot anymore. Intuitively, I overstood that I'm to be a writer, not an orator. I would just sit back, have a nice quiet time at college, and leave everything up to my written word, because whenever people who don't know you hear you speak in person, there's a greater chance they'll turn against you or misinterpret who you are and what you're trying to convey, based on the fact that people, by nature, in an attempt to sculpt into immutable fibers the mystery before them in the physical, will make subjective judgments on body language and appearance, as well as

---

[1] Lyrics from "Options for the Optionless" by Yelp!, from the album *Poison Their Food with Thirst*

judge according to rhetoric and tone rather than context and substance. But in *meditated words* absent of time-constraints and, for the witness, your physical body, *you're* the crafter, and if you wish to be, an enigma out of the reach of the greedy sculptors. And if you're one of the *exceptional* writers who come along perhaps five times a century, you're also a bestower of both conspicuous enrichments and recondite phenomena, and if the reader doesn't overstand all that, you have upon you no formal imposition to answer or justify: if they simply have an honest sense of things—(particularly in the disparity in the ingenuity, wisdom, versatility, twist of linguistics, and sweeping visions between artist and audience)—then they, the audience, will find ways to become amenable to your mother wit and fathered intellect, and thereafter grow from your seeds—in a more ideal connection, become *one* with you. Of course being a hack won't work: you really do have to be phenomenal, and to boot, a few luminaries have to give you their respect and perhaps adulation so that it "hits the streets": that's how it works. But what I'm really trying to say is that the anxiety trembling my nerves to the bone on my way to class made me realize that my powers lie in words and personal talks, not in speeches and presentations to strangers. Yes, I would shut up and just keep quiet. *Shhhhh...*

...Oh Bloy dee! oh Bloy dah! lifeless body goes ooo-onn! oh how timidly into the hard-carpeted classroom I went on. Cleft-footed, I cut left and took a seat in the back: a good start to staying unseen and quiet. Up front: no professor present. The bright room, in which a burgundy carpeted material went $^1/_5$ of the way up the walls before whipping into hard papaya, was filled with twenty-some blah-blah-bloy students. The quieter ones were flipping through an encyclopedic book. I thought, at a dime a page, I would be broke from this class alone! I sat there making these worthless observations til Dr. Rosenbaum came in. He walked swiftly to the front, threw a sepia attaché case atop his desk, opened it up with a brisk jerk, pulled out a stack of papers, then turned around to focus on his scholarly neonates. Dr. Rosenbaum was a handsome middle-aged man. Clean. Thin. Tall—about two dick-sizes taller than me! But his hair!—such fluffy hair, combed to the sides in an indiscernible part. Like salt and pepper but with a dash more of the salt—although not exactly "salt" since it wasn't white but rather strands of luxurious silver, just like the hair in his wiry mustachio. Behind his glasses (nearly invisible on his sophisticated face) thick black eyebrows puffed out a bit as if taking gentle breaths. What beautiful breathing browstachios! While handing the syllabi to each person in the front row, he complained to himself about some problem with Aristod's printing services. Then he stepped back, clasped his freed hands into closed-steeple, and introduced himself as Dr. Rosenbaum but said he also answers to 'The-meany-who-gave-me-a-bad-grade-for-no-good-reason, The-lanky-Methuselah-who-makes-me-read-too-much, and occasionally He-who-acts-like-he's-hopped-up-on-speed. All depends on what my dealer's got for the week.' He was obviously joking, but I was wondering if everyone else overstood that. I wasn't expecting anything so informal from a professor, especially right from the start; to hear that in high school would've been grounds for a mass parental protest! Then he said, 'For those of you who have to run home to the elders and assure them they're getting their money's worth, you can tell them I graduated from The University of

Pennsylvania with a B.A. in English, a B.S. in Teacher Education, and I received my A.M. and Ph.D. in English here at Aristod. But to be honest I really don't remember much of what was said during those years because I mostly slept and drank.' Everyone laughed at this. He said that he'd been teaching at Aristod since he was twenty-eight. 'Twenty-two glorious years!' he said half-sarcastically, indirectly revealing his age. Sitting down on his desk, he shifted into a whimsical story about his nagging grandma who was ninety-four "but still as strong as a Hebraic horse, or what us Americans call camels." Every single week, he complained, he has to go grocery shopping for her. And just yesterday he'd unknowingly bought her a bad batch of grapes. She wouldn't stop graping about it. When he went to the bathroom, she dumped the grapes out on the kitchen floor and began stomping on 'em with her walker. Then—(and this takes the batch)—he said that when he came out, she wanted *him* to clean it up, but instead he was "about to take that damn walker away from her and pop her head like grape. Now *that* mess I would've gladly cleaned up for her." The entire class was stunned besides a clan of hyenas in the upper left corner that couldn't stop from laughing. Stationed in the back, I was bearing a silent smirk. Before going over the syllabus, Dr. Rosenbaum followed up with two more anecdotes about his crazy grapist grandma. For the rest of the class, I couldn't get that damn smirk off my face! I knew I was going to love this guy like a classy lush loves grapes! Yum!

Following Dr. Rosenbaum's class, I sat in a dark auditorium with about a hundred other freshmen for *Biological Science 110: Human Anatomy*. Inside the slanted dome, it was like being at a baseball park at night and looking down at the pitcher's mound: rows of burgundy seats shooting straight down to the rostrum. I didn't mind taking a seat in the nosebleed section: my typical Buccos seats anyway, but unlike back in Da Burgh, I wouldn't be sneaking down to the empty chairs. The tall heavyset lecturer, who was perched behind his box like an amorphous slob, left me with no distinct knowledge of his appearance, and his voice echoed in mechanical distortion through the PA system: 'Hello, everybody. I'm Dr. Steve Loren. This is *static* static*...Today we'll be *static* static*...the human anatomy is one of the most complex *static* static*...' After the class was over, I (under the assumption the material wouldn't be all that difficult) decided if I wanted to continue showing up to Dr. Loren's class I would busy myself with other school work or brush up on my poetry. And if I happened to miss anything important it wasn't a big deal because he posted his notes and a taped version of the lecture on his website, which I could access at the computer lab in the basement of Philemon.

My final class of the day was, solely because of the teacher, just as boring as the last: *History 218: Bonaparte and the French Revolution*. It was a small class with a dork-clad atmosphere: evidence that History *does* attract The Uncool. Even though I found the material very cool, the teacher talked so slowly and monotonously, and her face was so droopy and blah, that, throughout the class, I thought I was having a flashback from a bad trip I had when I was sixteen. (There'd been slow blah'ing sounds coming from a forest of "marijuana trees" in the dead room! Ahhh-cid!)

After I bonaparted from my last class, I wanted to take a nap but had to go to the bookstore, which was pretty far away. I was dragging from a restless night of sleep. But I did find some energy in realizing I'd made it through my first day unscathed: nothing too discouraging besides knowing the reading assignments were a lot heavier than in high school. And all the material was invested in three or four tests—well, for Dr. Rosenbaum, it was four papers, no tests. Dr. Rosenbaum was funny. Despite him being an ectomorph, and I a mesomorph, I saw a reflection of myself in him. He straight out told us—and mind you, most of my classmates came from the traditional upper echelon where finding a strong sense of humor among 'em would be like spotting Pynchon and Salinger on the same day—anyway, Dr. Rosenbaum just said what he wanted to say and acted how he wanted to act, dark humor and all. And like he said, if you don't like it, go tell your elder blood that I'm more than qualified for the job. And if they want to match wits: I'll blow 'em outta the water. And if they want to match money as a measure of success: then I'll match money. (I figured Aristod professors made a pretty penny.) Yet I hadn't even talked to him, and it was only one day, and I'm taking what he said and stretching it into other contexts, so who was I to lionize the man? No roar.

On my way down to the Hub to buy my books, it came to light that Aristod housed more animals than students. Must've been thousands of bushy-tailed squirrels running around. And most didn't seem the least bit timorous among the students. They were weaving in and out of the traffic as if they had just as much the right, or even the right-of-way. In the yards, they were mechanically searching around for food in whatever thicket, bush, or tree they wished. Squirrels had always been my favorite animal, followed by chipmunks and kangaroos. It's all about animals with the coolest tails, and *no* animal could outdo the fuzzy, sensuous, robotic, trill-and-thrill tail of the squirrel! If I had my way about it I would've turned into a squirrel a long time ago and enjoyed a life of acorns, fascinating nibbling habits, mechanical pretenses, and (after wooing 'em by chasing 'em all over God's green earth) screwing other pretty squirrels! Hmhmhmhmhm!

Besides the squirrels, there were other animals scaling up, sprinting through, and flying around Aristod's green paradise: Little ocher-fur chipmunks that could be seen but not approached. They would dart into the bushes if you got too close. Same with the silvery rabbits. There were also brawny black crows that would swoop to the ground and beak and strut around arrogantly; but the squirrels were hardly intimidated! I didn't know much about the other birds but there was a variety. Together they ravenously pecked at the ground as if a delectable buffet was spread across the land. Perhaps Aristod really did have ambrosia and nectar! Yuuuuum...

...I was just standing there shaking my head like I was about to change my mind when the cashier impersonally said, 'And your total comes to $489.25. Will that be cash or credit?' I opened Ma's envelope, gave the cashier all the green inside, then shoved the worthless white thing back in my pocket. The horrible feeling of guilt that had been vexing me for taking the money from Ma dissipated just like the fifties as the draw clanked shut; desperate times force that gratitude out of you like a confession that's been festering in the gut for too long. As I'd guessed from its size, the book for Dr. Rosenbaum's class cost a pretty penny, 11,000 of 'em; the biology book and packet: 12,000! And I still had two more books to buy! Now I *desperately* needed my loan refund to arrive so I could open up a checking account and buy all the small things for my room and keep up on my day-to-day needs, all of which adds up to astronomical amounts when you're on your own for the first time without any help. But I was used to doing what I had to do to get by. Plus, I would get a job as soon as I could. I really didn't want to work while I was in school, but I would get a job just to make it through. Yes, I would make it through just fine—as fine as aged wine. Mmhmm...

...She was fucking me so good, and despite usually having indefatigable stamina, I thought I was going to blow a hole out the top of her head within the first minute. But I didn't. I was in shock, intoxicated, and involved—so far up in her that I thought at any minute Beauty would fall out of the aesthetic womb, and when it did, I would swallow it whole so I could have a taste of what I'd wanted ever since I wrote my first poem. But nothing was coming yet, at least not much. The bedroom lights were off but through the window the moon was casting a divine light on us, delineating her small fit body in just the right places. I didn't quite know how long we'd been going at it but I think it was about twenty minutes in when she pointedly said, 'Bite my neck!' So I rose up and bit her neck...then harder...til she moaned in ecstasy. I could taste the metallic tinges of her perfume. When I bit her nipple—just the very tip of it—her eyes widened in a bonanza of delight. She violently pushed me back down and continued rocking back and forth, begging me to pull her hair. 'Pull my hair!' she cried. 'Hauda!...*Hauda!*' So I pulled her punkish hair hauda, *hauda*...til her neck bent over to her dewy shoulder. When I let go she started pounding on the wall behind me with her fists and short huffs of laughter: reverberations of insanity shaking the bed. I had a sauna of sweat pouring out but had yet to attempt to wipe it away even if the salt was burning my eyes to the point where the irritation was almost unbearable. And having my contacts in didn't help. But when I finally tried to wipe the sweat from my eyes, she quickly grabbed my wrists, pushed 'em down to the bed—holding 'em firmly while grinding a bit slower—then said, 'No, no.' Yes, yes, she licked the sweat from my eyes...all around the sockets...over my checks. When she was rehydrated, she thrust her tongue deep into my mouth but quickly pulled it out and swung herself back up like an inverted catapult. 'Spit on me,' she said. I hesitated. A sober conscience suddenly crept up on me. *Buh dat's rilly*—'Spit on me!' *But that's degradin'. I juss wanna*—'If ya don't spit on me, you hot mother*fuckin'* dago—' (She slapped me while laughing herself into dead seriousness) '—I'll stahp fuckin' you righ' nah.' She stopped—leaned down to give me a tender kiss—then whispered, 'And I fuck so good, don't I?' *Through the salt in my eyes, I think I can finely see thit if I'm gonna find IT I'm gonna hafta work a liddle harder for IT.* 'Ohhhhh yeah. Oh my gawd!...again!...mwahr!...mwahr!...MWAHR!...'
      ...The cigarette tasted like bitter cocaine. The dregs of the last line were dripping from my nasal cavity into the back of my throat. A horrible thing if you ask me. I had to keep doing air-snorts. Maybe all my nasal membranes and friendly filters had disintegrated by now. Maybe my insides were beginning to look like Uncle Alfonse's face: Time can catch up on the wasted youth too, right? Let's see: Started drinking at twelve, drinking hard since sixteen. Smoking cigarettes and weed since twelve. Blowing coke

since sixteen. Codeine, whippets, downers, speed, and rubber cement during a trice of utter stupidity. Ate acid like it came out of a PEZ dispenser for a while but wish I hadn't: stuff seriously sucks! (Never could stand people who thought they were "seeing a whole new side of life" or "finding the truth" by dropping acid. Puke!) Anyway, my insides couldn't have been too good, aesthetically speaking. But me, an addict? Me, need counseling? Don't think so! No need to get into all the psychoanalytical jive: it's futile for geniuses and artists, and certainly a futile attempt at overstanding this for those who've never walked in your shoes but think they know how to tie the loose ends of the strings. Sniff, sniff. Sniff, sniff.

After the last biff she gave me across the cheek, Andrea went to take a shower, giving me a chance to catch my breath, resalivate, and above all, heal. Lying in her bed, I could only smoke half the cigarette; the taste was making me nauseous, but it could've been the booze festering in my gut. Still naked, I stood up and walked over to the window: five floors up with a nice view of LaSalle and the mysterious mountain. Standing naked in front of a window has a half-assed liberated feel to it. Andrea had said that her roommate wouldn't be coming in because she was staying the night at her boyfriend's. Her roommate was a sophomore, and, like Dante but not from Dante, had gotten herpes her unfreshwoman year: that's what Andrea had told me at the party. Didn't know if that was Andrea's way of proving to me that *she* was clean, but I buckled up anyway just in case there was a case—just in case she was one of those people who liked to give medical profiles for everyone but themselves.

Thankfully, things had fallen into place on Monday when I returned from the bookstore $500 down. In my mailbox was a check from the school for $2,210. I went straight to the bank, deposited it into a checking account, and signed up for a debit card. Then, using the $400 I'd saved myself, I went to the store and bought a phone, some of the small things, and a mini-fridge not only for food and drink but also to serve as a stand for the television. The next day, after getting the phone hooked up, I called Ma to give her my new number. There was something peculiar and restrained in her voice like she was talking with a bomb strapped around her. When I asked what was wrong, she said nothing, that everything was fine, just very quiet and lonely without me around. The ol' it's-just-not-the-same-without-you, even if in my teenage years I'd tried keeping to myself and strove to be home only whenever I wanted to read, write, or sleep. I didn't ask about Rick but she said that he felt bad for not being there on my final day. She said, *'Ahh, u sò travagghiu û fa stancari.'* [2] Riiiiight, the ol' working-class clemency. When she started asking about my classes 'n' 'at, I became irritated and told her that I had to go. Then I called Pessi. He said that on Sunday night everyone had been hanging out at Dante's, and Anthony (that unwise owl with no vertebrate but now in need of wings) said something to the effect that "V thinks he's bedder then us now that's he's at Aristod. Yinz guys see how he tried da referee the fight, like he's some kinda peacemaker—" And before he could talk anymore shit on me, Pessi said he went over and punched him square in his bearded beak. Pessi might've broken his beak but I still planned on plucking his feathers out the next time I saw him. Yet people

---

[2] [scn] Work is stressing him out.

like Anthony will either be quick to kiss your ass, telling you *their* version and how they're so, so sorry and how they're just so psychologically unstable because of whatever lame reason that they—they just hate their self! all until you feel sorry for 'em and let it go—or, knowing what they said will leak back to you, they'll go into hiding til it blows over. Knowing Anthony, he would probably choose the latter, then employ the former whenever I caught him by the wing, because I didn't plan on letting it (or him) blow over or flap away from my memory. And excuse my windiness on this matter, but I must add that the incident proved nothing I hadn't already known about Anthony, and only reaffirmed Pessi's loyalty to me whether or not I was there to fend for myself. Pessi also told me that he planned to come down the upcoming weekend to see his new *official* girlfriend Teresa Cazzata, a squawking succubus who makes Anthony look like an honest parrot and Andrea a vegetarian nun.

The bedroom door crept opened, but I kept giving the moon the full-frontal.

'*Aww*, look at my liddle Vinny-pie—standin' naked at da window.'

I turned around and mooned the moon.

'*Aww*, look at my liddle Andrea-cake—all clean now, not even a trace a spit on her.'

'Ha-ha, you're *soooo* funny. Now get your liddle ass back in 'at bed!'

'Yes ma'am!'

On Tuesday I'd went to my other two classes: *English 015: Rhetoric and Composition* and *Math 110: Techniques of Calculus*. I had those classes on Tuesday and Thursday for an hour and fifteen minutes, whereas my three on Monday, Wednesday, and Friday were fifty minutes long. I had a feeling that my attendance for my Tuesday/Thursday classes would be sporadic; I'd already missed Thursday's classes because I was hungover from the night before with Andrea. Besides, my Tuesday/Thursday teachers didn't even take attendance, and if you paid attention to the syllabus you would know when you *had to* be there and when things *had to* be done: I liked that about college. Nothing about syntax and numbers could hold my attention anyway.

Anyway, on Friday I was feeling better, physically. The first reading assignment for Dr. Rosenbaum's class was *Candide, or Optimism*. Although I'd read it in high school on my own time, I couldn't recall the specifics, so I reread it just in case I was called on to talk. So far I hadn't said a word in any class, and I wanted it to stay that way. But Dr. Rosenbaum—well, he had a knack for knowing when someone didn't want to be called on, and seemed to thrive on that ability to target the unexpected and make the predominately freshmen class uncomfortable. His various idiosyncratic hand-gestures, which moved in accordance with his fiery elocution, only enhanced his powers.

He began class with a random story about Slobodan Milošević. Up front, he was pacing around and discovering new directions. It was as if his lanky body was trying to punish the room for standing in his way. Once contentious energies settled, he picked up the text off his desk and flipped to a marked section. After reading something secretively, he had a scholastic paroxysm.

'You! You!' he said, pointing at me, hitting right upon his knack. His silvery mustache danced in cadence with his walk as he came towards me. 'Yes. Tell me what Voltaire meant when he said, "We must cultivate our own garden."' Not sure if it was because Dr. Rosenbaum said the line philosophically, but I felt nervous about my first college words, but I was determined to make them memorable.

'Well, uhh, I suppose since Candide was continually misled by everyone, Voltaire's sayin' we need knowledge gained from our own experience. Candide eventually realizes his blind optimism throughout his journey only made him gullible.' Even though I thought that would suffice, Dr. Rosenbaum just stared at me with his arms crossed, expecting more. 'So, uhh, all things considered, when someone "cultivates der own garden," I'd say it means 'er learnin' things on 'er own.'

'And you are *Mister?*'

'Vallano,' I said halfheartedly, reluctant to introduce myself to him *and* the class.

'Oh yes! Vincent, right?'

'Yep.'

'I took note of you during Wednesday's attendance because one of the professors who reviewed your writing samples told me that it was impressive and I should keep an eye out for you. So here it is.' Taking a few more steps down my aisle, the tall silvery wit squeezed his left eye shut while trying to bulge his right eye out—enough to where I could see it was bright blue. All around me, I heard laughter, but I could feel the deep flush on my cheeks from the awkwardness and blinding limelight. 'How old are you, Mr. Vallano? Seventeen? Eighteen? Nineteen?'

'Eighteen.'

'Well keep your head on straight and your eyes locked in because you have to *uphold* that Hugo.' He was referring to my scholarship; it wasn't rude or prohibited for him to mention it aloud because it wasn't concealed information: Aristod annually published who received the main scholarships. 'The English Department is excited to see your work. Especially me.' Flexing his prominent dimples, he smiled a smile of camaraderie and anticipation. 'You know,' he spoke nostalgically into the high air of the room, as he turned around and headed towards the front, 'it's been a dream of mine to teach a student who goes on to make a name in the literary world. A familiar name flashing in the neon. On the cover of *Harper's.* Ranked on *Times.* None so far. But I can feel it coming. Will it be Mr. Vallano?' Spinning around, his bright blue eyes returned to me. 'Or will it be *you*, Ms. Crawford? Or how about you back there, Ms. Yurmani? Ms. Yurmani certainly has a great chance; I had her last semester and was blown away by her writing. (What's your name again?)—Or will it be Mr. Schlesinger? Well—' He took in the whole class in one broad survey. 'Any one of you penbleeders! Someone please let me live vicariously through you! And please be kind and share your royalties with me too.'

Amid the remote, broken clashes of voices and laughter, I saw Dr. Rosenbaum glancing around the classroom, making sure everyone took a moment to observe the *real* anticipated student at Aristod: Mr. Vincent

Vallano, recipient of the Hugo Scholarship. Until that moment, I didn't think it was a big-deal; it only covered $^1/_4$ of my tuition each semester I upheld it. But now its symbolic value seemed greater than receiving a large monetary reward. It felt like I'd been put on a pedestal, and that was the last thing I wanted: *an onerous position,* for the gains wouldn't equal the great expectations! You just wind up with a big lump on your back, feeling miserable! Then your vulturous classmates encircle you and commence the hen-pecking: *He thinks he's so much better than us! Yeah, what an asshole! A classic teacher's pet!* Oh yeah, I had one hell of a record being the teacher's pet: more like the teacher's pet monster! But those birdbrains didn't know that!

'Getting back on track, Mr. Vallano. Do you agree that we must cultivate our own garden? That sowing our garden with seeds will lead us to enlightenment and provide us with a sense of fulfillment? Self-gratification through individual will? Seems to me a pretty reasonable idea.'

'Somewhat, I guess.' *Minchia!*[3] *Shoulda juss agreed so I don't—*

'Why only somewhat?' he fired back but keeping his distance at the front.

With the question hanging in the air, I realized I had an allegorical bomb to drop, one I roughly outlined while reading but would've rather kept upstairs. Yet I was, so to speak, being forced to drop it. So I gathered up all the mockery in my molecules and prepared to speak slowly and seem philosophical. 'Well, cultivating yir own garden can only go so far because, first, most cultivators are given a small garden—ones full of weeds—'n' never rilly have the means da get any seeds. So what's the point when only a handful of cultivators ever get da chance da cultivate a nice *fruitful* garden? The rest (no madder how hard they try) get stuck with a *see*dy garden, 'n' like I said, first a garden needs seeds da feed. So it's basically a matter of weeds and seeds.' A moment of absorption passed before the class tittered some, and Dr. Rosenbaum, he nearly cachinnated himself backwards over the desk—but the desk upheld him; and perhaps I'd upheld my Hugo.

'*Weeds and seeds, weeds and seeds,*' Dr. Rosenbaum spoke in song. 'I like that, Vallano. Satirical and lyrical: such is Life!' Twisting his fingers around in a palsy, he headed up to the chalkboard to jot down a better agenda for *Candide* before continuing to harass unguarded students. At the end of class he sang his new song to us as we filed out in harmony: 'Be prepared to discuss *Tartuffe* on Monday. And remember: if Life gets you down, just sing a silly song, like: *Weeds and seeds! Weeds and seeds! Our seedy garden needs seeds to feed!...*'

...I was already jaded after two weeks of college. Despite having a relatively light workload, that, together with skipping classes, no job found (although there hadn't been a search yet), no friends made besides Andrea, and the infinite thoughts running through my head—well, together it was like the catalyst to increase my drinking. I was so fuckin' glad that I'd spent a hundred on the fake ID, which luckily scanned as Anson had promised. It was an out-of-state license and quality work: the physical description

---

[3] [scn] Literally "Dick!" but equivalent to saying "Damn!" or "Fuck!"

flawless. At the liquor store and six-pack shops I was Robert Louis Albini. I could now forgo making friends over twenty-one, or worse, resorting to frats whenever there were no "open" parties. I dreaded that thought: the frats! the mansion halls of the hollow! I knew *exactly* who those kids had been in high school. Some might say, 'How close-minded!' But I was thinking, 'How mindful!' I had no desire whatsoever to frequent or take residence at the mansion halls of the hollow! Da Hoolie's hypotheticals were just that: hypotheticals made up to rib me and allay their envy, an envy that I overstood all too well. I could only think, '*It coulda been me jokin' around yellin' 'SELLOUT!' at wunna them, while the tears of bidderness drown my insides.*'

Like most colleges, Aristod strictly prohibited alcohol on campus. Every block and building had a cautionary-yellow sign that read NO ALCOHOL ON CAMPUS NO MATTER YOUR AGE! VIOLATION WILL RESULT IN SOBERING CONSEQUENCES! SO THINK, DONT DRINK, SCHOLARS! Yeah, *The Aristod Scholars*. Our emblem: a muscular philosopher wearing a toga, crowned with a laurel. (At least the fraternal roots of Aristod hadn't been hollow.) Anyway, the copious amount of warnings couldn't deter me from drinking in my room. But Luke Adams could. Not that he would ever say anything; I just couldn't picture myself drinking in the room with him. Maybe a beer or two on Stiller Sundays might be acceptable. The only other exception would be whenever I knew he would be gone all day at class. Of course then I could skip class and drink in the room, perhaps skipping with the sole intention *to* drink.

After failing to make it down for my first college weekend, Pessi visited the following Friday. Teresa took us to her friend's off-campus apartment where we drank (besides Pessi) and smoked and blew late into the night. Teresa kept sticking her middle finger up in my face, and I kept swatting it away. But that's just Teresa Cazzata. Later on, after Pessi went back to her place to sleep, I called Andrea. She was sleeping but said I could come visit. So I did. On one side of the room, her roommate was passed out drunk. On the other, Andrea was waiting...to tear me wide-open. And she did—literally. She kept digging her long nails into my back...til we had to stop because I could feel the blood coming out. Once we patched up that little boo-boo, I got slapped, bit, my hair pulled, and kinda punched. But that's just Andrea No-Last-Name.

Saturday afternoon I took Pessi out to lunch at Ving's. He had no objections to me paying because he had the defense of throwing up in my face that stupid remark I made about rolling in the dough one day. He added, ''N' ya think buyin' me lunch is sum'n? Wait til yir puttin' my kids through school. Fuck, dey can even caw ya Dad. I don't give a fuck.' Laughing, I tried slapping his face from across the table—but he skillfully dodged it. So I decided to throw some of his fries on the floor. Then we went to the mall where, with my new debit card, I bought him *Young, Loud, and Snotty*, not only one of the greatest albums ever but also the soundtrack to Pessi's life. Although he insisted that I go out with him later, I stayed in to study, leaving him to deal with the tyranny of Squawk alone. He left sometime Sunday afternoon...

...Sunday night, underneath the blackest of skies, with nowhere else to go, I sat in my car and drank. And I drank hard. I kept asking myself, 'Why'd I even come here?' I knew just from posing the question that I'd gotten away from nothing. I hadn't taken one step closer to anything I was looking for, although I didn't even know what I was looking for anyway. Intuition just said that it wouldn't be found in a college degree, nor was it entirely about geographic proximity where just one more trip up the road, just a few more miles up ahead, and—BAM!—there *IT* is. Nope. Over the summer I'd read Kerouac's *On the Road,* and while hovering in the car, drinking beer, listening to music, and thinking about that question, I experienced a belated overstanding of the book. I was reminded of Dean's folly when he moaned to Sal, 'Think of it, we'll dig Denver together and see what everybody's doing, although that matters little to us, the point being that we know what IT is and we know TIME and we know that everything is really FINE.' Wrong, Dean! Sal finally realized there is no IT. But *my* overstanding came late only because I had to take that drive to know what it meant, albeit my drive was a lot shorter than Sal's. But I still caught the drift of his wind in my own. At the end of the drive, the misery of the known, and the longing for the unknown, was still festering inside. And I couldn't see how any good grade or high acclaim from my professors could ever change that. "But no matter, the road is life." And so you keep moving on...

...Sometime later in the night, I decided Monday's classes weren't happening. My conscience had something to do with it. It began earlier in the night...

...I was back in my room, lying on my bed, drinking and watching baseball. The beer was being kept chilled in the mini-fridge underneath the television. I wasn't drunk yet but I was begging it to kick me right where it hurts. When Luke walked in, he tossed his backpack in the corner and heaved out a heavy sigh that suggested a rigorous week was finally over. After two weeks I still knew as much about Luke as I did the day we met. Seemed he mistakenly thought I harbored animosity towards him; truth is, I just wanted left alone. The only things I ever said were things like asking if my music was bothering him, or whenever he went to sleep, did he want me to turn off the television. He never minded the television being on, and I was glad because I was used to watching something til I fell asleep; I just kept the volume down. But not much else was being said. Whenever fate caused our eyes to meet, he would give me a look of kind sympathy. Not an empty sympathy. Just something humble and kind billowing in his plump face, like, 'If you ever want to talk, I'm here. I might not have seen the life you lived but I still have the same kind of ears as you. But if you don't wanna talk, I won't bother you.'

He sat down on his bed, his body facing me but kept his face on the ballgame. I knew if he looked over and I did too, I was going to get that face, so I capriciously said, 'So howzhur week?'

His face curved surprised but indecisive, suggesting he wasn't sure whether to answer briefly or thoroughly detail his week. 'Well—been pretty busy, man. Two long papers wrote, two hundred pages read, and all on what seems like two hours of sleep a night.'

'Yeah, I hear ya.' In a supine state, I took a swig and nearly emptied the bottle.

'Gettin' your drink on, eh?' Like a silly cub, he used his rounded paw to point at the beer (bear?) bottle (bawdle?). His forced slang made me crack a smirk; it was hard to keep it veiled so I just let it unfold into a full smile. Seemed he was still bent on giving off that I-might-like-going-to-church-but-I'm-not-a-complete-loser attitude.

'If ya want one, go 'head 'n' take one ouddadda fridge.'

Yes, maybe we *could* communicate, possibly be friends, if he threw a few back. Maybe he'd gone crazy with the communion wine before and liked it. No, *loved* it.

'No thanks. I'm cool.'

'Well if ya ever want one, feel free.'

'I really don't drink much,' he forewarned with a blush. Suddenly, instead of licking himself clean like any good bear does, he gathered up his bathroom commodities and headed for the community showers to cleanse his body from the iniquitous vapors of my breath, the same breath I'd offered him temptation with....*I feel stupid: shouldnt've offered 'im a bir: poor kid looked uncomfortable: maybe I shouldn't drink in here anymore: 'n' for Christ's sake it IS Sunday: he prahblee thinks I'm satanic!...*

Popping the cap off my fifth beer, a righteous buzz finally hit me. About time too because I only had a little bit of the green and white left, and no way of getting anymore til I met someone in the area. Thankfully on Friday night (when Andrea had dug her nails into my back, pulled my hair, slapped, bit, and kinda punched me) she also found the time to tell me that she, through her roommate, knew someone and would ask for me. That was how it worked at college: some yuppie with money, not really connections *per se*, believing he's so high-profile and powerful that he needs liaisons.

Well, blow and bestoned, while I'm thinking about it, Andrea calls. She tells me everything is good to go and gives me his number. For the sake of my body, I was afraid she was going to ask me to come over, but she didn't. She started complaining about her roommate Ashley. She said that Ashley always leaves her panties lying on the floor. She was worried that somehow Ashley's *genital* herpes (as I just learned the specificity of it) would get on something of hers. Sounded like a legitimate fear. So I advised her to either start picking up Ashley's panties with tongs and throwing 'em away, or, if Ashley had no civility whatsoever, then every time she finds her panties on the floor or anywhere they shouldn't be, just spray 'em down with disinfectants, and do it right in front of her face: that would teach Ashley a thing or two about facing the nongeniality of her sickly nature. Andrea laughed into the receiver of the phone: it felt the same as it did when she was right next to me: warm and connected. Then she tried making plans for next weekend, but I said we'll see when the time comes. So we said our goodbyes and hung up.

Without getting up or off, I crawled down to the corner of the bed and grabbed another beer out of the mini-fridge. Nearing 9 p.m., the ballgame would be over within the hour, and Luke would be going to bed. I felt unsure about continuing to drink in the dark while he was sleeping close by. But I really had no other choice other than to quit drinking. Once supine again, I popped the cap and took a swig. While trying to think up a better plan, my eyes uncontrollably ventured up to the painting. It looked like Jesus didn't have anywhere to go either. Seemed we were in the same boat—a sinking ship. *(Moments of vacuous thoughts...til my eyes anchored into a gaze.)* For the first time, I found myself consciously and meticulously studying the painting: The façade of the quaint cottage was piebald: mostly hay-yellow but tinged with aged browns. To the left of the door: a four-paned window. Although its gouache thickness caused the layered glass to look reflective, it was too obscure to see anything inside besides an ashy abyss. Alongside the door, thick sprouts of stalagmitic ivy climbed upward so sinuously: fuzzy golden and jade leaves (spade-shaped with tiny violet buds throughout) bent over listlessly. Indefinitely suspended near his waist, the golden lantern in his left hand looked iron-heavy, as most antique things do. The way his right arm was halted in-motion towards the Danish door without connecting also looked tiresome. (Yet no one inside was answering: no offers of respite and ataraxia for The Father of Peace, The Son of Salvation. *"L'ossa arrusicati da càmula, a tonaca sfardata, a vucca sicca, e circava acqua...facia pietati a vidillu."*)[4] I craned my neck to see he wasn't wearing sandals: his bare feet were planted deeply in downy viridian bromegrass. However, like most analogous portraits, he *was* wearing that grubby swathed robe that hung to the ankles, the sleeves to the wrists. But this rendition had something I hadn't often seen: draped across his shoulders (falling to the feet in the back) was a velvet-red sacerdotal chasuble. Where it linked across the sternum it was bejeweled with opaline gems spaced between tiny, square, corroded gold lockets. These pieces of regalia were the only thing in the painting that boded Hope. The rest was dark and woeful. His visible skin—face, upper neck, hands, feet—was gaunt and bronzed like a penny. And his long sinewy hair and beard was matted and dusty-looking as if it needed shook like a worn rug. Fittingly, no crown-of-thorns on his head: some artists throw that in for effect, but that wasn't til the days before and during the Crucifixion. Instead, a yellow-white halo of light (positioned symbolically like a sun) elevated behind his head in a perfect arc. It could've been the Light of Optimism if it wasn't highlighting the desolation on his face. The solitary light only inflated the gloominess all around him, made his sullen face demarcated with heavy shadows and the emaciation of hunger. Seemed his right eye was only half-visible not just because his face was focused on the door, but because he'd been in the process of turning to look at you right before the artist had arrested him there indefinitely in a state of mortification. If you looked deeper into it and let your imagination paint a little more onto the canvas, which I was doing, you could see the deified hunger within his watery-gray eyes waiting for the Sepulchral End. But since no one is letting him in, he must wait suspended at the door of eternal darkness.

I broke out of the gaze, regaining consciousness of my intoxication. Holding my beer up to Jesus, I said, '*Saluti!*[5] Ta sinkin' ships 'n' gih'n out—or

---

[4] [scn] Bones chewed by worms, tunic worn, mouth dry, and looking for water...it pained me to see him. (From Gnaziu Buttitta's poem *Ncuntravu u Signuri* – "I Encountered the Lord")
[5] [scn] Cheers! [Literally, "Health!"]

in yir case, gih'n in.' Just then, Luke walked in, wrapped in a red bathrobe, returning from the showers.

'Were you talking to me?' he asked timidly. 'If you did, I'm sorry: I didn't hear you.' He tossed his dirty clothes into a feminine-blue hamper next to his dresser.

'No.' I took another swig, keeping my eyes in focus. 'Juss chattin' wit Jesus.'

'Oh. And He was chattin' *back?*' He asked the question carefully and with interest: either an insanity-check or curious to whether Jesus had actually been talking back: the jealously he would've felt if that turned out to be the case!

'*Suuuure,*' I slurred. 'Jesus talks da people all da time.'

'Yeah, I suppose you could say He talks to people in a *figurative* way.' There was a mild reproach in his tone (or so it seemed). So probably trying to save face he explained more delicately: 'I mean, most people just pray to Him or God, and that's what's meant by talkin' with Jesus. I guess you could consider it talking with the voice of the spirit and not the mouth.'

Something in my head was assuring me that Luke was talking down to me as if I'd lied about being brought up Catholic and was actually some heretical monster deprived of the teachings of Christ. And if Luke *had* been trying to save face, he failed. Now I felt it *my* obligation to save *everybody's* face. But I was also becoming drunk.

'No, no. I overstan' that. I yoosta godda church all da time. All da time since I's born 'n' stuff. Father Carr—ahh, now *that* guy's a character. He'd say da me, "*Hey, Vincent: you're making the kids upset.*" But I wasn't, Luke. I rilly wasn't. I juss wanna da tell 'ose liddle idiots about Yeats 'n' C.S. 'n' T.S. 'n' Tolstoy. 'At's Christian stuff. But dey don't teach 'at in church. But if *I's* a priest, I'd march in 'n' say, "EH, buckle up yir diapers 'cause taday we're gonna write poetry, 'n' if yinz don't like it, den yinz can go straight da Hell!"' (I laughed aloud.) 'But don't get me wrong, Luke: I know Jesus was a rilly good man.' I took another swig. 'See, Jesus was like an orator of workin'-class poetry. Had a he~~art~~ like a Romantic. Blessed with a universal language. A shackle of complexity binds mine. Won't lemme get out all the—all the fuckin' things festerin' inside!' I stopped there. The room was completely strange. Not silent because the ballgame was on the television, but that—(not the sound of the baseball game but the drifty loneliness of the noise)—only added to the atmosphere a nostalgic pastime feel as if I'd suddenly slipped back into the 19th century where I was a young man of a more simple time, although still the hopeless poet lying in the gutter looking up into the stars.[6]

The entire time I'd been fixated on the painting, and when I turned to look at Luke, the skin on his face looked like it wanted to run out the door and never return. He couldn't, so to speak, save (his) face. Apparently, utter confusion or pity had overtaken his emotions. He was pretending to be watching the ballgame, but even in my intoxication, I knew he was now completely uncomfortable; and I was kinda enjoying it.

---

[6] Allusion to "We are all in the gutter, but some of us are looking at the stars" from *Lady Windermere's Fan* by Oscar Wilde

'I dunno, Bear; I don't know wha' da fuck I'm even talkin' about anymore. I'm startin'ah get a liddle fucked up, know whadda mean.' I rolled over to the wall and into Darby's crotch let out an abrupt, absurd laugh. HA! 'Yeah, I can tell, man. It's cool though.'
I rolled back over, squirming. Luke had stood up, indecisively facing the door. Then, as if another revelation had struck, he half-turned to me and said, 'Did you just call me *Bear?*' (I smirked childishly; he chuckled humbly.) 'Interesting.' Yeah, he played it off like a real cool man, not about to become a Cool Hand Luke to whatever I had to say or wanted to do.

On the whim, I stood up, grabbed the remaining bottles in the mini-fridge, and stacked them back into the case. Not concerned with concealing the case itself, I headed out the door. 'Later there, *BEAR!*' I wasn't too concerned with shutting the door either. In the hall, I murmured, '*Care Bear.*' I found that deeply amusing.

As I was trying to switch my grip on the case, a couple bottles fell out and began rolling down the white tiled hall. None broke but it did make a commotion right outside my RA's door; he was a quiet one who didn't seem to care about the rules; having a double major, I think he only wanted his hall to be quiet: that's all. So I picked up the bottles quietly. Then I quietly moved on. When I reached the front desk and saw that the affable *chomechai* was working, I yelled, 'Night, hun! Don't wait up for me!' ><

Which leads back to me sitting in my car drinking and thinking underneath the darkest of skies. For a while, I sat and listened to music, while secretly watching students walking around. From what I could tell, they all looked so happy like they'd never made a wrong decision in their life and never would. They were just walking around, laughing. Although I laughed a lot, their laughter somehow looked different: these sick twisted grins mocking me and motherfucking the darkness. It made me hate them, even if they'd never done anything *to* me. But everything about them repulsed me: the way they walked, what they wore, what I thought they were talking about and how they were saying it. I desperately wanted to believe that it was all so superficial and forced; but this coming from someone who was sitting in his car, drinking and thinking, alone...

...Later in the night, after I'd had my belated Kerouacian epiphany, I saw an Asian couple walking hand-in-hand in front of Philemon. In a casual stroll they were passing by into the unknown. It looked as if both were under five-feet tall. They were dressed in light-colored two-piece pajamas superimposed with Asian art. The guy took a piece of the girl's hair and tucked it behind her ear. Strolling along, they continued talking (and you could tell it was in a whisper), while exchanging modest smiles. They appeared to be in love. In a state of repulsion, jealousy, and heavy intoxication, I think it was at that moment that I passed out. I'd had enough. ZZZZZZZZZZZZZZZZZZZZZZZZZZZZZZZZZZZZZZZZZZZZZZZZZZZZZZZZZZZZZZ...

...A rapping on my window woke me up in the cool early morn. The windows were fogged with dew. The car battery had gone dead from leaving the radio on all night. As my legs shuffled around on their own accord, beer bottles clanked around. It took a moment to realize I was in my car and had blacked out sometime during the night. Again: rapping on the driver's side window. I sluggishly peered out—(my head pounding like a bass drum!)—and made out what appeared to be a police officer. However, everything was too blurry from the dew and my bloodshot eyes, which were further irritated from leaving my contacts in. I wiped the window clear with my hand. The badged blur was looking down at me.

'Excuse me, sir. Can you step out of the car?' His teeth clinched together, forming the you're-busted cop smirk.

Like a zombie rising from the grave, I edged up closer to the window, and through the window, screamed, 'What?!'

'Can you please step out of the car, sir?'

I opened the door and steadied myself to my feet. The blur wasn't a cop; just a Scholar Security Guard. Looking in through the window, he made a quick inspection of the contents inside. Then he pulled out a yellow tablet and started writing.

'Can I please see your school ID, license, and registration for this car—if it is *your* car?'

'No. Now can ya please geddaway from *my* car?'

'Sir, I think it would be wise if you watched what you say,' he advised in a calm tone. His hands were gloved in black leather, and while he pondered for another moment, he ran one gloved hand through his puffed-up blonde hair: finely combed in waves like his mother had done it. 'Well, do I have to ask again?'

'No, 'cause I'm not tellin' ya or givin' ya shit.' I returned a cockier smirk, shaking my head defiantly to tell him: 'Yir paltry authority ain't gonna work with me, *pal.*' I had to look menacing, like a savage train conductor with bloodshot eyes, pasty skin, and crazed hair who'd just taken his train off the tracks, watched it blow up with emphatic joy, then started running away with locomotive delusions while making psychotic *choo! choo!* sounds. But I could already sense nothing was going to force him off his power-track. He wasn't even intimidating: just average all around with a silly-looking cleft chin. 'Look, Officer—' (I read the nametag on his coppish-blue shirt) '—*Kenneth:* I dunno whachir thinkin' about doin' here, but I ain't done nuh'n wrong. I godda school here 'n' pay da live here, 'n' 'at includes *this* parkin' spot. Dis car—which is *mine*—is in the spot *I* pay rent for. So if I wanna sleep here, I will.'

'That's fine, sir. The problem is the beer bottles on the floor. We have a strict no-alcohol policy on campus. Therefore, I have a duty to cite you for possession of alcohol. Besides, you're lucky it wasn't the police who found you because you would've received a U.A.D. You'll only receive a small fine from the school and probably school probation which they'll explain to you at your hearing—a *school* hearing. Now can I please have your school ID, license, and registration, sir?'

His robotic "sirs" and "pleases" were starting to incense me. Here Kenneth the Kid is, maybe a few years older, but with his little can of mace, and his little yellow violation pad, and his little campus-based walky-talky, he thought he had some kind of grand authority over me. No chance of me standing for it. None!

'Look, Officer, I don't think it's a crime da have bir bawdles on campus 'cause I've see 'em decorated in dorm windows. It's juss *alcohol* dit's prohibited, 'n' see, 'ere's no alcohol in my car. Wanna know why?—'Cause I drank it all lass night.' I ousted a sarcastic laugh for effect. 'Unfortunately for you, you didn't catch me inna act of *shit.* Now I'm gonna give ya two choices. One: you can go caw da pleece. But by the time dey get here, deez bawdles'll be disposed of 'n' yir evidence'll be nuh'n but yir word against mine. 'N' of course I'll be hidin' out for a while, so da proof in my blood'll be gone too. Or: you can suck in yir pride 'n' juss walk away while ya still can, know whadda mean.'

He didn't move a hair. Probably couldn't believe that I just said that to him. And since I could see that he was going to be frozen a bit longer, I continued:

'See, yir liddle blue uniform don't mean *shit* da me. A fuckin' yuppie like you wouldn't lass a fuckin' second where I'm from. 'N' let's juss say you *do* get me in trouble—I'll juss find out where you live, 'n' 'en 'ere'll be no one da save ya. So go ahead, Sarge, keep writin'. Go take dahn my license plate number. Go ahead.' I stepped right into his face, letting my rancid breath spit a few more things at him. With his head and torso stilled in ruse, he began inching for the can of mace.

Undeterred, I laughed: ''N' if you even think about pullin' 'at mace out, I'm gonna knock yir fuckin' teeth out. Truss me: juss be sm~~ar~~t 'n' get da fuck oudda my face 'n' away from my car. Don't win the battle, juss da lose the war, know whadda mean.'

Some grunting noise stirred in his throat. He almost had the audacity to squint contemptuously at me but didn't because I smirked him out of it. 'Come on; I think *Police Academy*'s on. I mean sercly, dude: you gidauff on 'iss shit or sum'n?...' Ahh, I just couldn't stop! Sure, I was still miserable, dazed, and kinda wasted, but besides that, something else inside wanted me to fight him. Not for the sake of fighting, but I think I wanted expelled, looking for an easy way out. But if I got expelled, then where? Certainly not back to Verna! The thought of returning to Verna was an assurance to be *sm~~ar~~t* (not a sm~~art~~ass) about this encounter—that stress was probably just getting the best of me—and, sure, there will be more stressful moments but nothing to waah-waah over. Alwaysthemore, I couldn't eradicate from my gut the deputy feeling imploring me to make his face look like the one who got rocked well by Pessi.

Luckily (perhaps unluckily) the situation escalated no further than a fierce staring contest, with punishing vocal jabs on my p~~ar~~t. His real fear came to outweigh his superficial duty, and we both knew it: the eyes *do* tell all, and his sunk down into his gut. Without another word, he turned away, defeated, wheeled on by his "willingness" to "let it go *this* time." Thanks, you fuckin' asshole.

As soon as he wheeled away, I began clearing my car of the evidence just in case there was a case. (Who knew if he was going to call the real police as a way to amend his pride.) After filling the case up with empty bottles, I grabbed it and began walking through the painful daylight. Heading down the lot, I kept taking furtive glances over my shoulder to see what he was doing: he was keeping a steady watch on me as he wheeled down the path at a slow pace. I thought to go into my dorm and take the chance of making a quick left into the recreation room without anyone at the desk seeing me...but instead, decided to remain outside and head off to the right...til I came upon a dumpster behind one of the other dorms. It was a good plan because if he *did* call the real police, and they came to my dorm, there would be no evidence around, and they weren't going to go looking for fingerprints in *every* dorm and dumpster! So feeling victorious, I went back to my room and began plugging away at a video game, hoping there wouldn't be an ominous knock at the door, while Luke did school work at his desk.

The real police never showed up at my door. Which was good and all. I just needed to find a new place to try to rest in peace...

SOMNAMBULANCE

"I lie awake again, no sleep tonight,
I find no peace in the quiet absence of light,
A million whispered thoughts floating through my head,
A million seconds has passed me by in my bed,
One, two, three, now it's four in the morning,
As the emptiness swallows me one more time,
I grow a little older with every second that passes,
I die a little every time I close my eyes,
No sanctuary in my dreams, no quiet place to hide,
Every night I swear it's the same,
And I don't know where I'll be tonight,
But I know sleep will come if I walk all night..." [1]

...By the end of the first month, my professors who took regular attendance weren't very happy with me. I'd only attended about half my classes so far. The one time, at the end of my French Revolution class, Dr. Devereux pulled out the syllabus and mathematically explained how my truancy was already taking a toll on my grade. But the indifferent, methodical way she explained it suggested she was only *pretending* to care a great deal. So to mollify her, I too pretended as if I cared, just so I could go back to my room and sleep. It was partially my fault for missing classes and partially not. Sometimes at night I would fall asleep but jerk up every so often from the most disturbing dreams. And sometimes I would lay there for hours, wondering about Verna: it already seemed like a life wholly detached from my present self. Something in my head was convincing me that I couldn't remember my memories, that I really hadn't lived whatever life I once had. And it was working because my memories seemed to be dying off. So instead of thinking about the past, I would turn to the present. *Wonder wha' da guys are upda? Wonder wha' dey do when I'm in class? Are their weekends boring without me? Have I been replaced by someone else?!* Although I didn't want that to happen, I couldn't do *too* much about it being away at college 'n' 'at, but I did call everyone to give 'em my new number. Yet Pessi was the only one I was talking to on a regular basis. When I called Jeremiah, I told him to come down sometime soon, but he'd just moved out of his parents' house and in with his uncle; he said that they, his uncles' plumbing crew, were working large commercial jobs all over the place, which meant overtime and weekends, so visiting wasn't feasible at this time. Eddie was frank and told me that he had no desire to come down, and instead tried convincing me to come home. He too was looking for a job til his repute as a deejay improved. And I didn't even bother with Dante; I figured him and Anthony were still clinging to each other in their sick conjugal way, laughing at other people's pain: ya down with OPP? Then there was *the family*. Fuck Rick. But was Ma really all right? I'd been calling

---

[1] Lyrics from "Somnambulance" by Strung Out, from the album *Suburban Teenage Wasteland Blues*

her three times a week, and she kept saying everything was "all right; just a little more quiet." But *something* wasn't all right: I could hear the sunken inflection in her voice and sense more moroseness in her bones. It was like she wanted me to know something else other than the Gennaro story, but also wanted me to come home so that she could see I was still in one piece. With gentle anxiousness, she kept asking when I would be coming home. So finally I told her that I would. And I did, the weekend after one month away at Aristod. It turned out to be one of the worst and greatest weekends I'd had up until that point in my life: a paradoxical quagmire I prefer to walk through backwards and haphazardly...

'Mr. Vallano, what the hell's goin' on? Ya know, I give you an *A* on your first paper—worth every bit of it too—but I wanted to discuss it in more detail. See, I wrote it right on the front page,' Dr. Rosenbaum insisted with perturbation written on his face, as I stood at his desk by his request. Class was about to begin, and with week five now underway, the students had loosened up (had basically become friends just through class association), and behind me they were talking loudly, so our conversation at the front desk was as good as private. 'But you don't come to class for—what's it been?—three classes now? Yeah, all last week—oh! you came in on Monday just to turn in your paper before sneakin' out. So what's goin' on?'

'Nuh'n rilly. Like I said, I hadda bad stomach flu lass weekend. 'N' I didn't feel any bedder by Wednesday. 'N' Friday I wasn't around 'cause I had some personal issues back home. But hey!' I blurted out cheerfully, trying to rub my façade off on him, 'no bedder day da be here than taday 'cause taday is the day we become men!'

'I'm just worried you're gonna get too far behind. The readings for this class are intense, and I *do* grade on how much you participate in class.'

'Don't worry; I'm stayin' up on all da readings—even more than ya assign. Ya know, it's funny: Rousseau wrote, "In a short time I acquired by *this* dangerous method"—' I paused to make sure he was heeding to my referential wit, '—"not only an extreme facility in readin' 'n' understandin' what I read, but also a knowledge of the passions that was unique in a child of my age." [2] 'N' as a consequence from readin' so much, I've juss become so confused with emotions, ya know.' I smirked, satisfied with my obscure reference and my ability to remember passages verbatim.

'Very nice, Jean-Jacques. Problem is, you haven't been assigned any works by Rousseau.' He leaned up on the desk a bit more. 'Mr. Vallano, you're not a *child* anymore; like you said: today is the day you become a man. And as far as your "confused emotions" go? Let me help clarify them with some direction: come to class.' He pointed to the seat he wanted me to sit in: right in the front. I'd never sat right in the front, but apparently he wanted to keep a close eye on me to make sure I didn't flee from another lecture. Besides the past Monday when I was "sick," I'd never done that before.

---

[2] Passage from Rousseau's *Confessions* [Book I], in which a young man attempts to express his natural impulses being "of powerful passions but confused ideas"

As Dr. Rosenbaum beginning stressing the differences between the Enlightenment and Romanticism, I began stressing over the things that had happened on Friday...

...I lay prostrated on my bed, trying to study Calculus. But my head was droning with denial, sorrow, odium—lunacy, with the voice of vengeance narrating: I didn't know which emotion or what voice to heed to...*dat couldnta rilly happened: muss be a nightmare or sum'n: yes, I'm still at Aristod: no, I'm here in Verna: wait, I don't hafta 'member my memories when I'm still livin' 'em: but if it IS true, why?!...hmm, I don't even think it's mathematically possible: he woulda had do've wrapped around at least twice: 'n' "na risgrazia" while "feeding him"?: highly doubt it...whad if it WASN'T an accident: nobody'll deliver justice...maybe I should be my own Raskolnikov 'n' do it myself...but Jesus also said, 'Ye have heard that it hath been said, "An eye for an eye, and a tooth for a tooth." But I say unto you, "That ye resist not evil: but whosoever shall smite thee on thy right cheek, turn to him the other also."'* [3] *...even Dostoevsky said, 'If he has a conscience he will suffer for his mistake. That will be his punishment, as well as the prison.'* [4] *...yeah, but HE doesn't HAVE a conscience!—*
A knock at the window.
'Yuzza front door, faggot! Window's locked 'n' I'm not gih'n up!'
In response, Pessi punched the window, which was his way of saying, 'Whadever, dickhead' without actually being mad. I concentrated on the sound of his movements til he entered my room, smirking, at which point I could feel the lines of confusion forming on my face. 'Wha' da fuck happened da you?!' I sprang from the bed and rushed to him standing in the doorway like a guilty little kid. With my fingers, I took pathetic touches at his right eye. It was bruised, swollen like a massive bee sting, the blood vessels popped and flooded into the white, underneath the red eye, an abscess percolating some puss, the entire area glinted with black and greenish scabs. 'Well?!'
'Fuck friends,' he calmly replied.
'Wha' da fuck's 'at saposta mean?'
'Take a guess.'
'I dunno—juss fuckin' tell me.'
He flashed a superior smirk: another example of how numb to physical pain Pessi was. He walked over to where the television used to be and appeared to be looking for something. I shut the door, hoping privacy would render answers.
'Well?'
'One word.' Still smirking, he seemed to be having fun with the guessing game.
'I'm not in the fuckin' mood for guessin' games.'
He turned around to face me sternly. The popped blood vessels looked sinister: I'd sported that look before: besides the tenderness of the bruise, you can't even feel the blood in your eye, but it looks extremely painful and morbid.

---

[3] St. Matthew (5: 38-39)
[4] Passage from Dostoevsky's novel *Crime and Punishment*

Finally, he said, 'Dante.'

'Wha'? You got in a fight with Dante?'

'No. Dante got me indua fight with Anson.'

Absorbed in an instant stream of fascinations, I sat down on my old double-mattress bed. Pessi wandered around the air-choked room while casually filling my in on the details:

'It all started 'cause I told Anson da have 'at dude make me a fake ID—'

'Wha' da fuck *you* need a fake ID for?'

'Well 'cause Eddie 'n' Anthony's gih'n one too. So I figured if everyone's gonna start drinkin' at da bars, I at least wanna be able da hangout, ya know. I mean wha' da fuck am I gonna do if 'at's all everyone's gonna do now: sit at home 'n' get high by myself?'

'I dunno, man.' Shaking my head slowly, I was giving Pessi a look that said he's walking right into trouble. 'So ya don't think yinz are gonna end up gih'n busted when 'ey see the same people "from outta state" comin' in all the time?'

'Nope. Deez ones are gonna have Pixburgh addresses. I guess 'at dude figured out howda make perfect PA ones 'cause he couldn't before, like when he tried makin' yours PA. But anyways, Anson said the dude'll make us three PA licenses for nine hundred bucks. We said cool, we're in. So I ask Dante da spot me the money til my grandma sends me my birthday money in a few weeks; he says ar'ight as long as I pay 'im back by the end da the month so his rent's covered. Well long story short: *Anthony* ended up havin'ah lend *him* money but nobody told me. So Anson caws me up sayin' he needs my money soon. I tell 'im Dante was sposta give it to 'im, 'n' that's when I found out nobody covered me. So I tell Anson I'm comin' over da work it out. I get there 'n' I'm alriddy pissed cuzza Dante, 'n' I guess I said sum'n cocky da Anson 'cause next thing I know—*BAM!*—I'm hih'n'ah grahn 'n' he kept punchin' me til I got the chance da throw 'im off 'n' cahm 'im dahn. Look—lost a fuckin' tooth too.' (Pessi showed me the missing gap: the first-bicuspid on the right side, three away from the central incisor. Then he pointed to his eye...then back to the missing tooth. 'I mean, yeah I gadda liddle fucked up, but considerin' izz Anson, I got lucky.'

'Umm, if that's what you consider lucky, I guess. Whad Dante say about all this?'

'I dunno. I think he gives me one story 'n' Anson another. He's actin' like he's all confused about why Anson was mad—thit somehow it's Anson's fault thit he came up $300 short. But I guess now I'm not gih'n one; juss Anthony 'n' Eddie. Fuckin' bullshit, man.'

'Oh well; you don't need one anyway. Yir dad prahblee thinks someone's out da fuckin' kill you.'

'Ehh, he hasn't even seen my eye yet. But I could care less what he hasta say about it.'

I sat on my bed, feeling bad for him without letting him know it. He'd barely healed from the last fight and like he said—*BAM!*—all twisted up again. Maybe he was destined to be a boxer. He had the numb body and killer skills to excel at it.

'So guess wha'?' resumed Black-Eyed Zach, starting up a new guessing game.

'You got the HIV?'

'Close. But I's talkin'ah Teresa earlier taday, 'n' she told me if I ever wanted to, I could move in with her. 'N" I think I might akshly do it.'

'Yir jokin', right?'

'Nope. I mean, what's 'ere for me here anyway? School's done. No job. No prospects. 'N' I'm juss fuckin' sick of dealin' with all this stupid fuckin' drama. I was thinkin' about goindua trade school, 'n' dose are all over da place. Juss need a liddle money da help me through. Teresa's family's priddy rich—'

'Oh, so yir sayin' yir gonna move in with her with the hope her family'll putcha through school?'

'Nooo. I'm juss sayin' she told me her dad wouldn't care if I moved in 'cause, one, she's nineteen, 'n' two, he's always overseas on business anyways. No one else lives 'ere anymore. Her mum left. Her bro's like thirty 'n' lives in New York. Sercly has nuh'n'a do with money; I'm juss tryin'ah be a good citizen 'n' protect da weak 'n' lonely. 'N' ya know,' he sunk into a low, serious tone, 'I think I might akshly like her.'

I laughed like a sparked firecracker. 'Yeah, right, you fuckin' liar. Ya juss wanna fuckin' yuzzer for her money.'

'She don't gahdinee money; her ol' man does. She cuts hair. 'N' I'd never ask her ol' man da support me anyway. I'd get a job 'n' do everything for myself. Even pay rent if he asked. I mean, juss think about it: we'd be able da hangout all da time again. All through cawidge like nuh'n's changed buh da scene.'

'Yeah, 'n' you'd prahblee get me kicked out within a month.'

'Fine then: fuck you. If I do move, I won't hangout with ya.'

'I dunno, Pess. When ya plan on makin' a decision about dis? 'Cause I think it's sum'n ya should rilly think through. Teresa—she don't seem like she's wrapped too tight, know whadda mean. 'N' you don't even rilly know her all that well.'

'Yeah I do,' he said defensively.

'Yeah, how many times you been out with her?'

'A lot. I mean, I've known her since lass June when I met her at Anson's party. But we been talkin' ever since, 'n' been out every time she's come up.'

''N' officially together how long now?'

'I dunno; close do a month.'

'Nice. Maybe if things keep goin' so good, yinz can get married by Christmas.'

''N' maybe if things keep goin' so good for you, you can get gangbanged in the ass by some frat boys by Halloween.'

'Been there, done that.'

'Wouldn't doubt it. Oh, 'n' listen'ah 'iss shit. 'Member RB?'

RB was the perfect acronym for Renee Baughman because she was Rich and a Bitch. Since Verna is part of one of the largest school districts in the state, I went to high school with a variety of kids, including the yuppies from Chesterfield, although many from there went to a private Catholic school; unfortunately, RB was from a WASP hive. Anyway, when I was in 9th grade and RB in 11th, she punched me right in the face, right in middle of the hallway! Why? Because she thought she was the greatest, coolest, and hottest thing in the world! She was friends with a former friend of mine, and he told her that I'd said stuff about her, which I had because I hated everything about her. So when she came storming up to me, calling me a stupid worthless greaseball, I told her that instead of caking herself with makeup she should get her ass sown to her face because it would be an improvement. Then she punched me. I guess I deserved it. And I guess she deserved her nickname. The sweet execution of adolescent justice.

With my teeth clinched, I mumbled, 'Whaddabout her?'

'She's havin' a party tamarra night. Teresa's takin'ah bus da come up. I mean, we weren't rilly invited or anything, but I thought we could show up, get fucked up, 'n' break some shit. 'N' 'eez pills I got—I'm tellin' ya, V, dey make ya fuckin' nuts. Iddle be a ball. You can finely get revenge on her for when she puntcha in the nose.' He took a moment to reflect and laugh. ''Azz sercly wunna da funniest things ever.'

'Yeah, my fondest teenage memory. But yeah, I guess I'll go. I gadda godda the bathroom.' I remained seated on my bed.

'Huh?'

'Perry Como say *whaa–ahhhh–aaat.*'

Again, Pessi laughed both at my crooning and whatever devious intentions he thought might be stewing in my head. Deep inside though: not so musical, not so happy: still burning over another matter.

'Oh, 'n' Teresa said she's bringin' wunna her friends. I think it's Ivy. 'N' if it is, she's priddy fuckin' hot, dude.'

'Yeah, well you should see 'iss girl I been fuckin' at school.'

'Dat Amy freak thit likes da bite 'n' drink blood?'

'It's Andrea. But yeah, she's a hot liddle Vampira. Izz love at first bite.'

Dismissing the played-out pun, Pessi sternly said, 'Well yir juss gonna hafta entertain someone else tamarra night. But if ya care about dis Amy brawd too much da fuck around on er, you can juss cuddle with 'iss other chick.' Dropping his sternness, he picked up a baby and began rocking it in his arms, which made no sense at all, but I still swiveled my head and smiled at his goofiness—well, since he looked more like Daffy Duck than Goofy, better to call it his *daffiness.* Watching him rock the air-baby so fluidly suggested that he might be quite the loving parent one day. He was rarely like this whenever we were with the rest of the crew. It imbued me with a sensation of pride that he was *my* best friend; and not the kind of pride that's like a hellish serpent gliding through the heart, or a suckerfish stuck on a ship,[5] but like a content bat in a cave in which there's no need for external projections or the desire to transfer the sensation to another; that is, if there would've been another around.

'I dunno,' I began in serious tone. 'Maybe I should akshly stay in tamarra night. Use my time more efficiently 'n' get some school work done.'

Pessi stopped rocking the baby—dropped it—glaring the blackened red eye at me. He was shaking his head as if deep-down he'd already known my real desire, and loathed it. 'See, I knew you'd start changin' 'n' actin' like yir all mature now. *Look, everyone, I'm the Great Vincent Vallano! I read big*

---

[5] From Sir Thomas More's novel *Utopia* [112]

books with big words at Aristod! I'd rather drink iced tea 'n' smoke candy cigarettes at home instea—' THUMP!

I quickly rose from the bed and punched down on his thigh. Then I laid back down and began contemplating what would be the better choice...getting out of the house surfaced as the better choice because I couldn't stand not to hear Razzle barking.

'...Ar'ight, V. I'm out. 'N' you sercly bedder come tamarra. Tonight my aunt's pickin' me up. Said if I paint her livin' room she'll gimme two hundred bucks. So I prahblee won't be out. But if I do, I'll caw ya.' He walked over to the window and began fidgeting around with the locks.

'Come on, you fuckin' jag-off; juss go out da front.'

'No. I don't want Ma da see my eye 'n' have her get all upset like lass time.'

'She's asleep.'

'Well maybe she woke up.'

'Whadever. Fuck you.'

'Bye-bye, frat boy.'

As Pessi had one leg hanging out the window and was lifting up the other, I said, 'Hey, Pess, whaju say 'at girl's name was?'

Disconcerted in the window, he turned around. 'Who? Teresa's friend?'

'Yeah.'

'Ivy. But she hates liddle frat-fuckin' faggots like you.'

I waited til he was almost out the window again. 'Hey, Pess.'

'Now what? Need meedda come tuck ya in so you can rejur big math book like a good liddle boy?'

'No thank you. Juss wanted da see whad a pussy's face looked like one more time. Now gih da fuck oudda my room.'

...The memory of the latter p~~art~~ of my first day back home ended as Dr. Rosenbaum finished class by announcing that we were having a change-of-plan group project. He handed the sign-up sheet directly to me. Looking it over, I decided to take a stab at a comparative essay on Molière and Goethe. I figured once I signed my name, the rest of the class would riot over the sheet to fill in the other four blanks for my group, like "if you can't beat him, join him," seeing as Dr. Rosenbaum had put me on the highest of pedestals, in my eyes. And how the ground can look so far away at times.

As I stood up, I could see through the surrounding bodies that Dr. Rosenbaum was giving me a concerned, questioning stare. I think we simultaneously realized how ineffective his seating arrangement had been. Sure, I'd sat front and center, but only in body. I couldn't get my mind off other things. I did do it: I got up and walked away from another lecture in a mental somnambulance...

...I'd woken up Friday morning with the proof on my neck: I'd clearly slept with a vampire last night. Thing is, when you're with a vampire when the break of day comes, you're forced to go elsewhere, which was why Andrea had kicked me out. Well, actually she had to go to class, so I got up and trudged back to my dorm. On the way, a little squirrel kept following me. I never thought they could be sanguinary, but the little thing seemed to smell the fresh wounds on me. Hankering for blood, it kept looking up at me with a chubby deviousness puffing from its cheeks. Somewhere along the way, I decided that class wasn't happening and that when I returned to my room I would round up a few orphans and head back to Verna early. And I did...

...When I butted my car into the curb, Rick's hazard of a car was nowhere to be seen, which was good because I had no desire to see him since he'd failed to see me off on my last day before college. It's cool though because more often than not what goes around doesn't come around.

Standing on the non-welcome mat, I put the key in and twisted the grimy doorknob, but for some reason it was preventing my entrance. Angered, I kicked the bottom of the door. It duly submitted, and I walked in. Startled by the kick, Ma had sprung from the couch. She rushed over and buried her head in my chest, crying how happy she was to see me after all these days. Instantly, I could feel that old subcutaneous feeling rushing back into me: the motherly deliverance from transgression: that simple feeling of being alive and well. I was wondering if she felt the same. Just in case she didn't, I was pretending to press numbers into her back, temporarily reprogramming what Musso had trained her to do. 4-3-6-3 was the code—her birthday; hence, the day one comes alive. *4-3-6-3-(doot-doot-doot-doot)—'4-3-6-3 ac-ti-va-ted.' Now come alive, Ma!—Talia! Tu movi! Si vivu! Si VIVU!...* [6]

'Eh Ma! Unni iè Razzu?!' I was in the kitchen, minutes after arriving; Ma was in the dead room, sitting on the couch, hidden behind the wall. She didn't answer. So I walked in and again asked where Razzle was. But she just sat there, looking scared as if I was the angered parent and she the child about to be scolded for letting the dog loose. She was in a long nightgown, not the buttercup-yellow one that she'd worn to the tatters, but one of metallic brown silk. It matched her eyes: precisely where I was staring with stern intensity, waiting for an answer. Looking into her eyes that way for too long had never done me any good: within her dark cavernous pupil there would seem to be something inching closer to the surface, reaching out for my throat to convince me through force that it wanted out. So I could only stare as long as I could withstand the imaginary asphyxiation. But looking at her eyes at a distance or without meditation had a different effect: you could get sensuous pleasure from it because her irises were more inviting and so soporific that it could send you straight into a dream: all from this vibrant brown enticement within two sleepy-eyed almonds, with thick black flickers fanning you softly.

My throat was tightening. Nearing the threshold. But I endured because I could see she was about to break: nascent tears were rippling, her lips parting.

'Vinny.'

'Yeah?'

'I don't know what to say. He—Iiii—' Like spontaneous combustion, she went into a hysterical cry. She buried her face in her hands and lowered

---

[6] [scn] Look! You're moving! You're alive! You're alive! [A play on the words of Dr. Frankenstein when his creation comes alive.]

her head down to her lap. She was shaking her head like someone who can't deal with the guilt of what they've done. Calmly, I began asking what's wrong. But the more I asked, the more she cried. Visions of my father dead began flashing before my eyes. But that couldn't be it: she wouldn't have waited for me to come home to tell me. Then I remembered it was about Razzle. That's what I'd asked about. He was missing. So visions of Razzle dead began flashing before my eyes: bloody gray patchwork in blinks. I sat down next to her and tried pushing the sinewy strands away from her face, while asking her to tell me what is it? what's wrong? just tell me! In between sobs, she was declaring, I didn't do it! I didn't do it! I kept asking, do what? what didn't you do? Gradually, the sobbing eased and was replaced with brisk sniffles and measured trembles. I went into the kitchen and brought back a glass of water. When I put it in her hands, she dropped it. It splashed all over her legs and feet. She began crying again. Again she swore, I didn't do it! I didn't do it! I said, what didn't you do? *'Nun ncurpari a mia!'* she declared, asking me not to blame her. I went to the kitchen; this time returning with paper towels. I dabbed at the floor pathetically. She dabbed at her legs pathetically. And all at once she stopped crying. Head hung, she quietly said, *'Vinny, Razzu mortu iè.'* Although prepared by inkling, it still stung like hell. Then it hit me: *wha'd she mean when she said don't blame her?*

'So whaju mean when you said don't blame you?'
' U giuru su me matri fu na risgrazzia!' [7]
'Look, I'm honestly not in the mood for fuckin' games. I ain't tryin'ah find out da truth eighteen years from now—ya know, like when you told thit I'm nawchir first 'n' only child.'
'It's not so easy da explain that!" she cried. 'I mean, is 'at-ah *my* fault 'cause I didn't want to-ah hurt you 'cause I love you?'
'Oh of course it's not *yir* fault! It's Rick's, right? I mean, how could anything ever be *yir* fault? Yir passivity is juss so fuckin' virtuous! How dare I question that! I mean, do you even overstand dit when you told me you had another son I's suddenly displaced somewhere else on the continuum? Dit it changed my existence forever? Dat I's suddenly not who or what I thought I once was? You overstand wha' dat feels like? Do you? No, you don't! Now yir gonna tell me right now wha' da fuck happened da Razzle! 'N' if you don't, I'm gonna go inda the kitchen 'n' break every fuckin' dish we have!'
Although I hated to talk to my mother like that, I knew had to be harsh and intimidating to get the truth now and not later. But when I asked again, she just kept crying, so I started stomping towards the kitchen to carry out my threat: to break every dish we had. Crossing the fray, I wildly swung a cabinet open: it smacked hard off the one next to it. She must've overstood how serious my commitment was because she yelled out in desperate Sicilian a promise to tell me. So I stomped back across the fray and into dead room—both impatient and sickened to hear the details of Razzle's death. She had her face focused into her dark, wet cleavage.
'Ar'ight. Spit it out. I ain't got all day.'
'Vinny, dee mill laid off your fauter last week.'
'Wha'?'

---

[7] [scn] I swear on my mother that it was an accident!

She lifted her head up; the silver trails of tears glistened from the light coming through the picture window behind me. 'Dey, umm, *outsource* his de~~part~~ment to a company in Germoney. I see it on-ah news too. Dey say, "Over two hundred Peetsburgh millers were laid off today. Find out which mill and how thousands more around dee country face-ah *saaame* fate because of company in Germoney." And-ah yesterday your fauter went to visit Uncle Dennis and Aunt Patty. And he hasn't even come back yet.'

I swallowed back an explosion of wrath and sickness to deliberate, wondering, first, if I really cared about him losing his job, and second, what this had to do with my original question about Razzle. But outsourced? I guess that's what twenty years of loyalty gets you. So much for the union! (A long strike in thought...) Ahh, sometimes (so it seems) Life im~~part~~s a capricious moment in which you're given a loophole to escape the confines of your accustomed personality: I fell into one and transformed into someone who was still me in the sense that I was thinking for myself, but with what could be called "a temporary affectation of madness":

'Well, please, *Mother*, tell me how Razzle dyin' has anything da do with him gih'n laid off? Did Razzle take da news hard 'n' kill over or sum'n? Or did King Richard have a liddle "accident" out inna killing fields. Come on; don't be afraida tell me. Like ya said, *you* didn't do anything. So juss wipe yir tears away 'n' tell me. I already know he killed 'im. But how'd he do it? He shoot 'im? Stab 'im?—'

'*Femmu!*'[8] She stood up to flee—but my hand halted her and directed her back down on the couch.

'Did he kick 'im da death? Beat 'im?'

'No! It was an accident! He goes outside to feed-ah Razzu, and-ah Razzu comes around him like deece—' She gestured how Razzle came up from behind Rick and placed himself directly in front of his legs. 'And your fauter falls over dee chain and crushes dee poor little ting wit his knee!'

''N' you saw 'iss happen?'

'No, I was in dee batroom and heard it.'

'Ya know, Ma—I bet it was more like 'iss:' Crunching my right hand into a fist, I gestured it up in the air as if something with weight was dangling below.

'*Ma chi dici! Mancu su to patri fussi 'mbriacu, nun cci facissi mali a Razzu u fici apposta!*'[9]

'Yeah, that's what you'd like da believe. So, uhh, who buried 'im 'n' where at?'

'Your Uncle Louie. In-ah, uhh—*unni vurricanu l'ammali n Dellwood.*'

When we were younger, Pessi and I used to venture down to that pet cemetery in Dellwood to visit Pessi's cat Garfield. We'd buried Garfield ourselves but never marked the grave because it had been a "sneak burial." The cemetery was on a hillside facing the Mon, and the ground was always swampy: played out in the colorful but confused thoughts of my youth, I'd never been sure if it was from the river or the sewage plant down the block, but now I had to convince myself that it was from the river, for Razzle's sake.

---

[8] [scn] Stop it!
[9] [scn] No way! Even if your father was drunk, he wouldn't harm Razzle on purpose!

'So when did this happen?'
'Tuesday.'
'Tuesday?! Fuckin' *Tuesday?!* 'N' you didn't caw me *why?*'
'*Mmm, addisiava fari chissu ma, ma—*'[10]
'Ma, ma, ma, but *what?!*'
'I didn't want to upset you at school!'
   'Oh that's a rill *fuckin'* good reason not da tell me da dog I've had since I's liddle died. Fuck yeah, Ma. Fuck yeah.'
'*Pi favuri, Vinny!*'
   'Oh I'm sorry; I don't wanna upset *you* anymore. I forgot *yir* the only one with feelings. I forgot I was standin' before da fuckin' Sensitive Sicilian Soul. Hold back your feelings, Vinny. Hold 'em back! I mean, sercly—wha' da *FUCK?!*'
   She started crying again but not as violently.
   'I bet he'z all drunk, right? Yeah, he's such a great guy when he's drunk. You like when he's drunk? Huh? Do you?!'
'*Femmu! Mi fai scantari accussi!*'
   'Oh I'm scarin' da Sensitive Sicilian Soul, am I?' I blurted a delusional laugh. 'See, me—I dunno a fuckin' thing about fear. Or even givin' sympathy da others who do. My heart's as black as yir hair. Ahh, bahchir hair—it should *never* be mentioned with the bad things! Ya know, I've always thought you had da most beautiful hair in the world.' I reached down and took a lock into my hand, stroking it as I continued: 'I juss never tolja 'cause it woulda been awkward. *I picciotti miricani nun sunu capaci r'amari cussi a cori apettu. Ma iù û pozzu fari: ai i capiddi comu na dia reca, cussi chiani ie fotti comu a sita r'aragna...Hmph,* I betcha *he* never tells ya things like 'at abouchir hair—or yir eyes. *I tò occhi beddi ie bureddi!*'[11] 'N', hmhm, ya know wha' funny name I caw yirs cuzza the shape? Do you? Fuckin' answer me!'
   'Noooaa-naaooh.'
   'Sleepy-eyed almonds!!!' I laughed beside myself; she didn't move or laugh at all. 'Ya know, for bein' brown, sometimes yir eyes are so fluorescent 'n' profound. Especially when I sense a strong sexual magnetism in 'em. 'Zat make you nervous? Yir son saying *sexual* in front of ya? I bet it does. Wanna know why? 'Cause yir so *fuckin'* abnegated 'n' conditioned thit you've become so powerless 'n' oblivious. Thus, everything can only make you *nervous.* Thus, everything can only *scare* you. Thus, everything *controls* you. See, yir tears aren't da tears of pain, for *the expression of pain* is also *an expression of liberation.* Yir tears are da tears of fear, 'n' *the expression of fear* is just *an expression of enslavement. Mmhmm...*
   '...God, juss thinkin' about yir sleepy-eyed almonds I wanna write a poem—or eat 'em! Look up. I wanna see 'em. Hey! I said SEE 'em, not eat 'em!' (Head hung, she just continued sobbing.) 'Hey, ju ever hear of the Oedipus Complex? 'At's wha' juss popped inda my head. See, the Oedipus Complex was made popular by Freud, but it originated from an old Greek myth. I read Sophocles' version called *Oedipus, the King.* See, 'ere's 'iss guy

---

[10] [scn] I wanted to but, but—
[11] [scn] American boys don't have the capacity to love so freely. But I can do it: you have hair like a Greek goddess, so smooth and strong like the silk of Arachne. – Your beautiful dark brown eyes!

named Lauis who rapes one of his students—a boy—'n' the boy's father finds out 'n' curses Lauis for it. Years later, King Lauis 'n' his wife Jocasta have a son Oedipus, 'n' the curse is passed on da him. Den a blind prophet tells Oedipus thit one day he's gonna kill his father 'n' marry his mother. Well, King Lauis becomes afraid thit Oedipus *will* come back da kill him, so he pierces Oedipus' foot 'n' leaves 'im in the woods da die. But after King Lauis leaves, a servant takes Oedipus to the king 'n' queen of another kingdom. Den one day, the prophet returns da remind Oedipus of his fate, so Oedipus flees da kingdom he grew up in 'cause he thinks *that* king 'n' queen are his *rill* parents 'n' he doesn't wanna hurt 'em. So one day he's juss roamin' around 'n' comes across his father, King Lauis. But, see, Oedipus dunno it's him 'n' 'ey end up gih'n indua argument 'n' Oedipus kills 'im; thus, *prophecy-one fulfilled*. Denee makes his way da Thebes where he'z born 'n' ends up savin' it by answerin' the riddle of the Sphinx, automatically makin' him da new king. 'N' guess who he marries? Guess!'

'*Pi favuri,*' she whimpered. '*Mi fai scantari.*'

'Exactly! He marries Queen Jocasta, his mother; thus, *prophecy-two fulfilled*. But guess wha' she ends up doin'? You won't get dis one, so I'll juss tell ya. She hangs herself! 'N' Oedipus (in my opinion) can't stand lookin' out indu'n ugly world anymore now thit his beautiful mother *and* lover is dead, so he stabs his fuckin' eyes out! But, see, it wasn't juss about him losin' the physical love or visual beauty. No, it's thit he'd once been able da *see* sum'n so beautiful *and then* transfer it inside himself by *fuckin'* her, whereupon he experienced a sublimated form of Beauty. By *feelin'* it inside 'im, he could, so to speak, *taste* Beauty. Yummy, huh? *La biddizza sapi cussi dilizziusa!* [12] But see, Ma, most people'll tell ya he did it 'cause he realizes his wisdom failed 'im, seeing as he was known for his intelligence but in the end da prophet was right. Buh dat's juss sum'n'ah lay audience can identify with. Truth is, he did it 'cause he lost his connection to sum'n so consummated. So his *rill* tragic fate is da be doomed to a world of darkness, literally; figuratively, a livin'-hell without da flames of passion. Dohncha think 'at's beautiful 'n' romantic?...Oh come on; don't cry like 'at. Don't worry; I don't wanna have sex with you or anything. I'm juss leh'n ya see who I *rilly* am. You been oblivious all deez years. Everyone has. I keep stuff like 'iss locked up, 'n' I put on this—dis *facci fausa.* [13] I know once 'iss moment ends, dis'll never happen again. But I wanted ja da see who I am at least once. I'm an artist. Nuh'n but a twisted artist tryin'ah unwind 'n' fly up inda the heavens. ('N' yet tryin'ah go deeeep Inside this strange dark place so I can paint it externally for others.) 'N' I'll never really be "successful." I'll never make alawda money, or have a normal job. 'N' when I finish cawidge, I'm prahblee gonna burn my degree 'n' laugh like a madman while bein' da sanest person in the world. But one day, I know, disappointment will finely catch up da me 'cause I'll realize (juss like every other great artist) thit I can never make da outer world like the one I have on the inside. I'm prahblee gonna die on the quietest of days in the loudest manner. Ya know—*finiri cûn bottu.* [14]

She shot up in a flood of tears and ran to her bedroom to hide...

---

[12] [scn] Beauty tastes so delicious!
[13] [scn] false face; façade
[14] [scn] to end with a bang

...Time passing by like a raft inching through a dead sea...
...Chain still tied to tree. Chain slung into bushes...
...Gray hair in mouth. Withered vestige of vicious weather...
...Water tastes like rust. Punching wood. Mad laughter...
...White lie: black lie: blue lie...
...No tears ever fall from my eyes. Freedom doesn't cry...
...Chair consumes me. I'm turning into a shadow...
...Feel like a numb pebble sinking in water. Goodbye...

...An hour later, in a different state of mind, I entered Ma's bedroom to check on her. The atmosphere was dark and serene, the sun rejected by the thick one-piece blind pulled down over the window. I kept the lights off because, from the door, I couldn't tell if she'd fallen asleep. After a few quiet steps, I could see that she had. I moved to the side of the bed, standing over her tiny reposing body. I surveyed my hands over the air above her head...carefully feeling around for the right part to touch more passionately. When I found it, I stroked her hair away from her face, and softly kissed her forehead; I'd never done anything like that, but it felt natural.

She opened her eyes: an entangled look of curiosity and consternation. Her lips parted with anticipation but also diffidence, like a shy girl awaiting her virgin kiss.

'Juss seein' if yir ar'ight.'

She answered with a vacuous gaze into the abyss above us...

'Sorry 'bout earlier,' I said blandly. 'Juss had some things I had da get off my chest. It's juss thit I was—well, still *am*—in complete shock Razzle's gone. Poor dog. Prahblee better off dead anyway. But when I see Rick I'm gonna—'

'*Vinnyyyy*,' she exhaled, her eyes closing for a second as if the sound of my voice pained her. 'It just makes tings worse. Please just try to-ah let it go this time—*for me.*'

I sucked into my diaphragm a deep vehement breath, ready to explain thoroughly why something like that should *never* be left go...but with the heavy breath dissipating into the dark air, I suddenly found myself overstanding something else: *her.*

'Well I dunno. Why don't we go out tanight so ya don't hafta lie around here? We can go out da eat. Iddle be on me. I got some money.'

'*Razzi—ma sugnu troppu stancu. Nun aiu dummutu assai sta simana.*'[15]

'Come on; you never go anywhere.'

'You go out wit-ah friends. You haven't seen 'em in weeks.'

'Ma—I'm not twelve anymore. I'm not embarrasedda be seen with my mother in public.'

'I know you're not-ah twelve anymore. You're a man. And I'm very, very proud of you. But I'm just so tired.' She snuggled tightly back into the sheets. 'You don't have to tell me when you leave. I'm-ah so tired I can sleep til tomorrow... *Tappu?*'

'Yeah?'

---

[15] [scn] Thanks but I'm so tired. I haven't slept much this week.

'No drinking a lot tonight. Okay?'

'I didn't plan on it. But I'll leave a note onna table where I'll be juss in case anything comes up. I think I'm gonna go over Jeremiah's for a bit.'

(True, I wouldn't end up going to Jeremiah's, but the note would say that I had. After Pessi made his stop two hours later, telling me the Anson/ID story and giving me Saturday's invitation...and the day languidly progressed into the night, I would actually drive around the city, alone, thinking about not thinking anymore...til returning to a dark tranquil house at 3 a.m., feeling as if I was somnambulating.)

'*Ti vogghiu beni,*'[16] she said sleepily.

Without hesitating, I leaned down and put a soft kiss to her listless lips; they were as dry as sand. But I felt *it*—so piercing—something that failed to calculate as anything speakable. '*Ti vogghiu beni macari iù.*'

As I crept out of the Master's room—the Master presently absent—I could sense and almost see the smile on her face, for a simulacrum of her inner-self was gracing the shadowy wall, blowing thousands of phantasmal kisses outward...before slipping backward into the tenebrous infinity like a grain of sand dropped into a vortex. Maybe there in the utter darkness where the darkness creates the illusion that you're suspended in a substanceless world, away from it all, not really on any side of the hallway, or stuck between any room, or among any world, thereby allowing the simulacrums of the heart and mind to converge into a phenomenal oneness—maybe there, alone and unconscious, eyelessly watching the internal somnambulance, she didn't fear, for the simulacrum of herself walks far away...

---

[16] [scn] I love you

SCRATCH THE SURFACE

*"You're so afraid of what you might find
That you lock yourself up inside your mind,
Chained to superficial chains,
Fuck you, you're fuckin' fake!..."* [1]

...The tendency of the malcontent (no matter what they vow) is to say "the worst" while always finding a way to leave out "the greatest." But shame on me if I should ever dismiss the bliss! "The greatest" only followed "the worst" with delay and division because that was the true order of things. But here it is: the big backend of Saturday: a starry, starry night that was begging for the attention of Van Gogh's ghost...

...Pessi's father was sitting at a cluttered kitchen table, sorting through bills. We were in Pessi's dead room. I was shadowboxing in front of the wooden panel walls. Pacing back and forth behind me, Pessi was on a cordless phone, talking to Teresa. Apparently, they, Teresa and Ivy, had arrived earlier than expected. We hadn't planned on leaving for another hour; it wasn't even 7 p.m. yet. As they continued chatting, I continued being nebby in between swings. Pessi's contention was they *couldn't have* arrived already. But again, *apparently* Teresa had told Pessi the wrong time the bus would be arriving, then decided not let him know til she *had to.* From what I could decipher, once arriving, they'd ventured (by bus) from Marian Heights to Chesterfield. Now Teresa, who knew Pittsburgh well enough from having family here, was trying to pry the exact directions out of Pessi so we could just meet 'em at the party. (The original plan was to meet 'em at the bus stop. But since they'd made their way further southeast of the city, or "back behind Verna," they were now sixty walking-minutes away instead of a twenty-minute walk or a five-minute bus ride if they'd stayed in Marian Heights.) But Teresa wasn't having it; she was having it her way or the highway no matter how long, backward, and complicated her way was. So not wanting to argue anymore, Pessi yielded and gave her the directions, adding that we're leaving now. 'I juss said we're fuckin' leavin' now. Fuck, man. Ar'ight.' *Click!* Instead of leaving now, Pessi and I went into his room to gas up on the white. Then—*the fun buuuuus riiiiide! whap! slap! whap! crack!* After fighting our way off the bus, we decided to step behind a forest of gumdrop shrubs to mellow out on the green. (We weren't going to wait to get to the party to party just to have cocksuckers we don't like hound us for a hit.) Then we continued into RB's private neighborhood, and Pessi—well, he put to use the bottle of water he brought to ease down an unspecified amount of Baby Blues: some new pill he'd come across. *GULP!*
RB's estate: a brown-bricked castle-style mansion amid Seclusion, where neighbors are far enough away that the brunt of noise is at best blunt. The castle mansion, which wasn't really a castle but just a rich-man's

---

[1] Lyrics from "Because You're Fake" by Backhand Brutality, from the album *Scratching the Surface of Something Strange*

version of one, sat precisely in the middle of the yard. Towards the back-left portion rose an eminent tower, cone-tipped with a little window. Across the façade of the castle were fancy-paned windows with red sills. At ground level: a smooth brown-bricked veranda with a stony gray base wrapping around the front and off towards the tower. (Girlish gangs were drinking here and there on the veranda, enjoying the tepid twilight air.) The lawn was trim and, before the veranda, decorated up front with a fury of flowers. In the left part of the yard sat the main eye candy: a large golden fountain lit up with revolving wet colors of white...yellow...orange...red...blue...pink...purple.../darkness for a second/...then back to White—cascading and shooting water all around its confines. From the sides, two naked boys were spitting water at each other in unbroken arcs amid the changing colored water. (Still nothing as impressive as a puddingfall.)

Walking up the lamp-lighted sidewalk, I could see through the windows that inside was filled to the brim. Pessi and I had to push our way through the front door and foyer to get into the first room where, atop a large dark marble floor, fancy furniture was arranged in a way as if there for decoration. I began seeing old faces from high school: hated most. Moreover, it was too loud, hot, and crowded. I'd always liked smaller get-togethers, but I was now stuck, with little recourse. Although crowded, you could still make out divisions of people and fill in the blanks of the situation like a Mad Lib. In some areas were **THE RING LEADERS** entertaining their **ENTOURAGES,** gloating nothing but **LIES** while everyone else remained too **AFRAID** to call 'em out on their **SHIT.** Inline to do **KEG-STANDS** were **THE THIRSTIES.** Whoever did the longest one would win **CHEST PAIN** and **EVERYONE'S WORTHLESS ADMIRATION.** Standing **ALOOF** in groups of **2 TO 3** were **THE EXTROVERTED OUTCASTS** who weren't there to **DRINK** but to **SMOKE WEED** all night til they could act like **THOSE KIDDY CHARACTERS IN THOSE MENDACIOUS DRUG COMMERCIALS** where **GUNS** suddenly go off, **CARS** suddenly wreck into **CHILDREN,** and **FIBERGLASS FISH REPLICAS** suddenly tell people to do **REALLY BAD THINGS.** Moving from here to there and everywhere were **THE SCATTERBREASTS** who, **LOOKING FOR A LITTLE SUM'N SUM'N,** forgot to **PUT CLOTHES ON** before leaving. And courting **THE SCATTERBREASTS** were **THE SCRAWNYWIGS:** imbecilic **WHITE BOYS** dressed like they would **SHOOT UP** the place if anyone **MESSED WITH THEM.** Oh yeah, nothing like coming home from college to party with the mad kids of my past! But I was already learning Aristod was hardly different: if anyone at *this* party wasn't in college, they would be soon, bringing along their rage to party hard til someone thinks they're the coolest person alive. That's what drugs and booze are all about *here.* So come on everyone: grab your vice, your cock, your tits, and let's show each other what we can do! Let's fuck with some minds, then shoot guns at each other, and if *anyone* survives, they gotta smash a car into the house and have promiscuous sex on the parents' bed til they come home and cry out: 'My goodness! What happened?!' And you either reply: 'Fuck you! I'm the coolest, hardest partier alive! And everyone finally knows it! *Yeeeeeaaaaa!'* Or in a calmer, more dazed tone, slur: 'I dunno; the fish told me to do it.'

'Yo, V, go gitchirself a bir,' advised Pessi while scanning over top of heads and hats. 'I'm gonna go find 'em.'

Parting ways, I went out to the patio and poured myself a beer in a red plastic cup. Then I returned to the first room and found a spot in the corner. I was about as far away from everyone as I could get, *inside*. There were several metal chairs around me as if earlier there'd been a circled congregation. I took a drink: the premium beer was cold and refreshing. I slipped into an embittered observation of everyone chatting and laughing and screaming and singing...til I finished the beer; it emptied fast. I walked back out to the keg and went straight to it, forgoing the line. I thought if anyone had a problem with it, they could let me know. No one did. This time I brought myself back two beers and again began drinking alone in the corner. I was telling myself not to think about *it*. And I know I would've thought about *it* and only *it* if Wes Parsons hadn't shouted, 'Hey, V!' as he approached with his hand prematurely thrown out for me to shake.

'Shit, haven't talked to you in a while. You been hidin' out or what?'

'Sum'n like 'at.'

'So how's life-after-high-school goin'? Workin' anywhere?'

I could've let *that* bother me but he didn't mean anything by it. Although he'd been an all-state golfer, Wes Parsons had the overriding distinction as a kid from a very wealthy family. Besides, he played the role of the urbane yuppie better than the dogged athlete. He sported thin and high lemon hair. His eyes were blue, small, and placed too close together, trailed by an effeminate nose and tiny mouth. None of his features seemed to account for his long flaxen face. Like always, there appeared to be a waxy film over his cleanly-shaved skin like he'd used skin-enhancing cream; probably had. And although not fat, he was awkwardly tall and husky. His grandparents founded Parson Petroleum: a petroleum products company. They became lifetime millionaires when they were bought out in the 70s, at which time they moved into one the richest areas in Pittsburgh: Chesterfield. I met his parents before: real down-to-earth. Sure, they spoiled the heaven out of him, but the fact that his parents had made him attend public high school because *they* and *their* parents had said a lot about the family's character: carried around hundreds in their wallets but never ashamed to let the change jingle in their pockets. Throughout high school Wesley drove a Vette. One day I told him how Vettes have been my favorite car since I was a little and I'd always wanted to know what it was like to drive one. Without asking, he invited me over and let me take it for a spin. Felt exactly how I'd imagined: like flying through space while getting head! So it's trouble-free on the mind to overstand why I wasn't bothered when Wes asked if I was working anywhere as if I had no other options waiting for me after high school.

'No, but I'm lookin' for sum'n.'

He sat down to my right and put his calfy khaki-covered leg up on the metal chair across from him. After taking a conservative sip of beer, he said, 'Just loungin' around home then?'

'Nah, I'm in cawidge.'

'*Really?*' Suddenly interested, he took his leg off the chair and turned to me with fervor. 'Wow! Way to go, V! I never knew you wanted to go to college—and I don't mean 'at in a bad way. But wow, what college?'

'Aristod.'

'Yeah right!'

'Right on. I'm a fuckin' Aristod Scholar now.'

'Wow. I applied there but didn't get accepted. Bucknell and Penn rejected me too. They didn't give a shit about my golf game. So now I'm stuck here, goin' to Allegheny. I mean, it's a good college 'n' 'at; but wow, V, you really go to Aristod? What did you get on your SATS?'

'Uhh, 1210.'

'What was your GPA?'

'3.5.'

'Man, I don't believe it! You weren't any in clubs either, huh?'

'Nope. My one professor told me I submitted good writing samples, which is prahblee why I gahdin 'cause I gadda scholarship for English.'

'A scholarship! Fuck! I'll tell you what, V, that's seriously awesome! So whaddaya wanna do after you graduate?'

'I dunno; prahblee write.'

'You mean like for a magazine or a newspaper?'

'Nah. Like novels 'n' 'at.'

'Holy shit! Well you know I'll be reading *all* of 'em! Fuck, man! This is crazy!'

Just then, someone called for his attention. He stood up and aggressively shook my hand, his white-blonde features gleaming modestly like alabaster. He assured me that he would come back to talk in a bit.

As I continued drinking in the corner with the empty metal chairs, I watched the reaction of his group when they heard the tragic news. At least that's what I imagined Wes was talking about in the room to my right. I might've known Wes from high school, but we didn't "grow up together." And I didn't know any of his current friends. Certainly weren't from *my* neighborhood. Perhaps not even from our large diverse school district— diverse insofar as it's class warfare, but not race warfare, for my high school turned predominantly White in the 80s when the Board mandered the Jheri Curls from Nig-North in with two other ebony 'woods holding boughs: the good and bad of the city of I love: the intricacies of a steel city with a small-town feel and big-time problems, outside of winning sports teams of course, of which Annie Dillard failed to scratch the surface.

Anyway, minutes later, Pessi came strutting in with his arm draped around two girls, beaming a superior smirk that conflicted with the black eye. Strut and smirk together, he was giving off an air that suggested he'd just used his rebel appeal to coax the two girls into a threesome. He'd been gone long enough! I knew the lanky skank on his right: Teresa "Squawk" Cazzata, one of The Scatterbrains who forgot to put clothes on. The girl on his left I assumed to be Ivy, my "cuddling partner" for the night (in the black eye of Pessi).

They halted in front of me. Pessi removed his arms from their shoulders. He began fidgeting around with a silly look plastered across his face. Having imbued a new personality into his veins, he was ready to "start shit," though in the spirit of *this* night, it was to be his good-tempered side, seeing as no bir-bawdle-swingin' enemies were around. But flying forward first was the reedy-framed, red-lipped, sandy-haired skank. So much attitude in her step; even more in her raspy, nails-on-glass voice: 'Hey, Va-llano. Hate to inter-rupt your lit-tle fa-king private party but I want you to meet—'

(Teresa forcefully drug Ivy forward) '—my beautiful friend, Ivy. Isn't she beautiful? Isn't she?'

'How's it goin'?' Seated, but leaning forward and upward, I shook Ivy's hand. Then she stepped back behind Teresa's wing. I didn't want to be rude, but my initial intentions were to come across as distant, like the four of us were about to engage in a strictly-business arrangement: the primary contracting to be done by Teresa and Pessi. While they spent the night working out whatever major deals, such as Pessi's future living arrangements, Ivy and I would pound out the small provisional details. Once the meeting (or the party) ended, the *ad hoc* business arrangement would expire. Thus, no need to scratch the surface.

Anyway, as Squawk started squawking, she kept nudging Ivy at the hip, but Ivy wouldn't budge; she seemed embarrassed by what Teresa was doing to her; and I couldn't blame her. And Pessi, he was staggering around both, talking nonsense. They were harassing the poor girl so much! Although I had yet to get the full look on Ivy, I wasn't blind to the fact Pessi and Teresa had schemed to hook us up; they probably thought it would make everything more feasible if we all joined together.

While Pessi stood in front of Ivy, harassing her, Teresa came and stood in front of me, harassing me with her eyes. Wide, squinted, piercing, red-blazing eyes directing me to talk to Ivy, like the consequences of disobedience would be dire, which in Cazzatan terms means you'll never hear the end of it: *Squawk! Squawk! Squawk!* She and Pessi were exaggerating the situation, making it uncomfortable. But I (with an unperturbed, nonchalant face) kept drinking, flashing an occasional smirk but giving no verbal responses. I was more concerned with the waning effects of the white and green, wanting to get more brown in me.

Once I successfully ignored Teresa, she switched places with Pessi, allowing her more harassing time with Ivy, and Pessi with me. Pessi—(and I had no clue where he got it from because he didn't smoke)—pulled out a cigar and lit it. He puffed it twice while smirking as if to say, 'Ha-ha. Now *yir* fucked. Maybe next time you'll think twice about sayin' ya juss wanted da see what a pussy's face looks like one more time.' But his cocky swagger only made me want to stand up and blacken his other eye!

'Well whaddaya think, bro?!' he yelled in secretive fashion, pointing over at the girls by pointing in the wrong direction.

'I dunno, man. Yinz two are sercly da fuckin' shit.'

Leaving the smoking cigar limp on his lips, he shoved his left thumb into his lower jawline, with the opposable gap just above his cheek and his pointer-finger on the lumped bridge of his nose, to mock The Big Secret: '(Hey, she told me she don't drink blood.)'

'(Fuck, 'at rilly sucks. Whaddum I gonna do now?)'

Again "secretly," he began making a sexual gesture with his uncupped but now capital-*O* hand held firm while a lower-case-*I* finger from the other hand slid in and out.

"At's rill cute, Pess. Know what else is cute? Da way yir lovely girlfriend forgot da get dressed tanight.' I nodded my headed towards an oblivious Teresa. 'Touchin' 'at shit must *rilly* be like gih'n struck by da yuck.'

He just kept smirking and bobbing his smoking head; evidently, whatever he'd put into his body prior to and since arriving was now in full effect. The blasted synergy!

'Okay! Come on Zachy! We're gonna leave 'eeze two lovebirds alone!' Squawk came over and stood before me, giving me the *malocchiu;* I countered with a sarcastic *manu cornuta.* [2] 'You better be nice to her, Vallano, or I'll break your fa-king neck. Come on, Zachy!'

'Peace be with you,' jibed Pessi, with that damn glowing smirk. Locked at the elbows, the two schemers smoked and strutted away into unknown territories like they owned the place and three others just like it.

To my right, Ivy sat down on a gray metal chair, the one next where Wes had sat, leaving the space of a chair between us.

'*Wow, them two got some issues,*' I exhaled, after finishing off one beer and picking up the other.

'Yeah, tell me about it,' she faintly replied.

I glanced to my right. Her eyes were fixated on the wooden floor. She was wearing black Mary-Janes that had a large bubbled tip and a thick elevated back-heel, tight faded blue jeans, and a vintage-style velour shirt (long-sleeve with belled-shaped cuffs) with a black, gold, and maroon floral pattern: overall, conservatively chic. But with her torso in half-turn, and her knees pointed away from me, she was keeping herself, as in the real fabric of her existence, shielded like a nun. I hid my face behind my drink, thinking: *Prahblee should say sum'n. Wha' dough? Mmm, houzza weather? Nice shoes, wanna talk? Wonder how long it's been since 'ey left us? Hurry! Say sum'n! Umm...minchia! How can a writer not be able da find words? I'm not even shy by nature. Well I don't gadda say anything; SHE can say sum'n'ah ME! Buh dat would be priddy peddy of me. Well then juss look at her 'n' sum'n'll come da mind—*(I looked at her. She looked up.)—*Oh my! Oh my wha'? Why'm I actin' like 'iss? I had no problem with Andrea. Whad if Andrea knew I's in 'iss situation? Would she be jealous? Fuck, I'm still lookin' at her! Say sum'n! Hurry!—Wow! Her hair! 'At's gadda beedda most bea—*'I rilly like yir hair.'

'What?'

'Yir hair: it's rilly, uhh, unique.' Yes, a *continuance* of my tongue's mishap, while further down my throat, my gut was suffering from horrible shock for my brain choosing "I rilly like yir hair" as my first words of the conversation. And "unique"?! Yuck!

'Really?'

'Yeah, it's so incredibly brown 'n'—'n' sinuous.'

'Sin-what?' she laughed.

I let out a nervous laugh too. *Hmph! Way da lay the poetry out dere, Byron! Migh'diz well've told her her hair "waves in every raven tress"! Ahhh! I'm so fuckin' lame! Why would I even say sum'n like 'at?!—But her hair rilly IS amazin'. The color of mocha. Ophidian in nature. Snakin' tresses of chocolate delight! Oh shit, how long's it been since she asked me whad I said? Tell her whachu said!!!* 'Sinuous. Means yir hair's curly but not like short curls: dey wind 'n' wave 'n' twist everywhere in long stands.' With my finger, I illustrated the nature of her hair.

---

[2] [scn] *malocchiu* – evil-eye; *manu cornuta* – sign of the horns

'Oh.'

Oh? Oh?! What's 'at mean?! Fuck! Stop doin' 'iss RIGHT NOW!

I quickly emptied my third beer. 'Hey, I'm gonna go refill my bir. I see ya don't gahd anything. Wanna a bir? A mixed drink? Uhh—'

'No thank you. But could you maybe get me some water—please?'

Sure I'll gitcha some wudder. Wait—wudder? Who the hell drinks wudder? Wudder! WUDDER! Okay, dis girl's gadda be mock pure! Faux-naïf! [3] *But deep-dahn rilly a—a SUM'N! But ar'ight, Ms. Faux Nïvy, I'll gitcha some WUDDER?*

'You got it.'

I stood up, and by design, passed by slowly, nearly touching her legs: she smelled like a garden of sweet alyssum, which, with one inhalation, could ameliorate a lifetime of woe and abjection. Ahh! but I *had to* keep walking! First, I went out to the patio where a bunch of kids were gathered around the keg. I cut straight to the front again, although the line was considerably shorter than before, but if anyone had anything to say about it, they could let me know. While filling the cup up, I forgot to tilt it. Half-full with foam, I dumped it on top the barrel and resquirted. Back inside, I cut down a short hall bedecked with family pictures and ornamental paintings which I didn't stop to spit on because I had to make haste in getting Ivy a glass of *wudder? Wudder? HA! HASTA be a façade! A trick of some sort!...*

...As soon as I enter a kitchen as large as my house—(it had a shiny island table, and above, a sky-lighted ceiling!)—the overpowering scent of bitch smacked my nose: RB and her Barbie-doll friends standing around the shiny, swirly, pearly sink.

'Umm, why are *you* in my house?' RB was quick to sneer.

Ehh, I always hated the fact that she was actually hot, and now I hated the fact that I *had to* be nice so as not to cause a scene. I felt so servile, so aware of where I grew up and who I hung around. 'Hurrja were havin' a party so I thought I'd stop by with Pessi da see some friends.'

'You have *friends* now?' The Gang of Barbies tittered.

'Well I saw Wes earlier 'n' he tol' meedda stop by.'

'Well, whatever. I don't care. Just stay away from me. I don't like you.'

Oh, you fuckin' cunt. Juss you wait 'n' see.

'Yeah; I know I yoosta be an asshole sometimes. Mind if I yuzza sink?'

'For what?'

So I can fill this fuckin' cup up 'n' splash it yir face, you fuckin' bitch.

'Needda glass of wudder.' Although the Gang of Barbies hardly parted, I made my way to the shiny, swirly, pearly sink. I turned the spigot and began filling up the cup. Meanwhile, I could feel I was flushed as all hell, and to make matters worse, the water seemed to be coming out in single droplets. *Drrrrrrrrr–IP. Drrrrrrrrrr–IP. Drrrrrrrrr—*

'So, Vallano,' began RB to my left, 'you ever graduate?'

'*Ehh*—no, I didn't.' Such a low, gloomy tone: forged but convincing. 'I's doin' good for a while but den my grades juss started droppin' too much,

---

[3] [fre] A false show of innocent simplicity

so I dropped out in 11th. But I'm gonna get my GED soon 'n' 'en gidda good job.' I looked down: my philter of water for Ivy was finally full. I walked away without another word, while the gang of barbies laughed at my dropout ass...

'How's come yir not drinkin'?' I handed Ivy the philter of water. 'Juss don't feel like it tanight? or donchu drink?'

'(Thank you.) Oh, I never do—I mean I *have*, but I don't do it on a regular basis. I've been *drunk* drunk maybe two times before; that's about it. I haven't drank in like a year. No drugs either.'

'Ahh, so you don't do nuh'n, huh? No weed? no cigarettes? no—'

'Nope. Not a thing.'

'*Hmm*. Well this is kinda awkward. I don't have much experience with people our age thit don't drink or do some kinda drug or have *some* kinda vice that makes for good conversation,' I half-joked with a smirk. 'Any specific reason why you abstain?' *Maybe her dad died drinkin'-'n'-drivin', or maybe her mum's a crack addict. How stupid of meedda press the issue! I know deez things!*

'I guess many reasons.' (She was still talking in a whisper as if unaware voice levels had to be raised at parties.) 'For one thing, I don't like the feeling of not being in control. Plus, it's an expensive habit. And it's definitely bad for your body. *Umm*—' She paused—readjusting herself—finally allowing me to observe the full physical Ivy: couldn't gather the appropriate words: but a few corporeal facts were in overture: She had lyrical green eyes, wide and bright, the black circle around the iris and every sliver within sharply defined. Her skin naturally tanned to the shade of wild thyme honey: definitely not white, but not exactly a hard brown either. It had a soft, calm feel to it which would likely cause most first-time onlookers to melt right into it; that is, fail to consciously analyze the exactitude of the color. Although we hadn't been aligned in a way for me to judge properly, she seemed a bit shorter than me. What I did know for sure is that she had a thin, tight body, as if she exercised regularly, and three natural protrusions of voluptuous treat: her bubble-gummed lips, modestly covered breasts, and wild rocking hips—altogether making her a singularly classic beauty with a touch of the exotic. While I was taking Ivy in on the aggregate, an epiphany rocked through my heart, almost swept out before my eyes, but it lacked a clear visual aspect, and although I had no control of my words within, it was like a simulated speech from me to the world: 'To those who don't believe in "love at first sight," let me say this: For the first time, I taste crème brûlée, and I love it. For the first time, I *touch* a squirrel's tail, and I love it. For the first time, I *smell* an Angel's Trumpet, and I love it. For the first time, I *hear* "In Dreams," and I love it. And now, for the first time, I *see* Ivy Pineda, and well—I love her. See?'

'Well this one time I smoked weed with Teresa,' she laughed, 'and was so paranoid once it hit me. I ended up runnin' home, cryin' to my mom that I was really high and scared. (My heart seriously felt like it was gonna burst through my chest.) But she just laughed and said she hoped I learned my lesson. But I kept runnin' all around the house, fannin' myself til it wore off.' I was finding the anecdote amusing til she countered. 'What about you? Why do you drink and stuff, Mr. Vincent Vallano from Verna? Yes, I'm well rehearsed on the Vs since Teresa has done nothin' but talk about you.'

'No surprise 'ere. 'At's *all* she does.'

'Yep, that's her thing. But tell me, Mr. V: what's *your* thing—your reasoning for doing what I don't?' Her tone rang out like a curious tease. Instead of answering, I was busy trying to decipher her accent and blood: a kinda Southern-twanged voice, with the look of a Latina, but like I said, not *too* dark. Maybe half-Latin, or a mestiza.

'Well come on; tell me,' she insisted with that same teasing tone.

'Ehh, juss sum'n'ah do onna weekends, I guess.' Sure, I felt bad about lying already, but I also felt inclined to clean myself up a bit because I was starting to acquiesce to the idea that she *wasn't* putting on a show; and for that reason, she was out of my league—perhaps part of the *true* Ivy League.

'I see, I see. Hey, do you mind if I sit here? It's kinda hard to hear what you're sayin'.'

'Yeah, sure.'

She moved to the seat next to me: still at a comfortable distance but made more intimate as she turned the chair inward to face me in a more appropriate manner.

'I's havin' a liddle trouble hearin' you too. 'N' forgive me if I'm way off here, budder you Mexican or, uhh, sum'n along 'oze lines?'

'Yep, I'm Mexican and Spanish on my dad's side. My great grandparents left Juárez, Mexico to part of the first international students at Aristod. After they graduated, they both ended up teachin' there. They had five kids and *they* all ended up goin' to Aristod,' she laughed, 'which is why it was fitting for *me* to go' there. But, see, what's funny is: Aristod is the tradition for my *dad's* side 'cause no one from my mom's family ever went there even though they're all from around LaSalle. My mom's not Mexican or Spanish either. She's just, uhh—plain white.'

'"Plain white,"' I laughed, '"at's funny.' (Since I was obligated to comment on the humorous ethnicizing of her mother, and she quickly followed up with a question, it consequently diverted me from talking about Aristod, for the time being.)

After a giggle, she quickly followed up with: 'Why, are you just *plain white?* You look pretty Italian to me.'

'Rill tough one da figure out, huh?'

'Yeah, I was really goin' out on a limb there. So are you a hundred percent Italian then?'

'Mmm, depends on how you look at it. My dad's grandparents came here from Abruzzi, Italy alriddy married. Dozzer obviously the Vallanos. 'N' my Ma's maiden name is Scandurra. She'uz born in Catania, Sicily, which is like straight across the Ionian Sea from Athens. She immigrated here with her sister when she'uz like seventeen.'

'No way! *Really?* Your mom was *born* in Sicily?' She seemed flabbergasted at this in her doe-eyed surprise. 'I mean, you *do* have dark features but your skin's not even as dark as mine. (And keep in mind, this isn't a tan either. *Au naturale.*)' She put her philter-holding arm next to mine: hard to tell whose brownishness was darker: hers had that Spanish pepper-red tinge, and mine the Sicilian olive-green tinge.

'Well my Ma, she's sercly about da color of yir hair—well, maybe not *that* dark but close. 'N' Rick—('at's my dad)—I guess he juss looks *"plain white"* but still got that strong "must-be-Italian" look to 'im, ya know.'

'I see. So is your family all cultural? Seems alotta Italian-American families are.'

'Ehh, in some ways. I mean, my mum is; Rick: not so much. Whaddabout yirs? Your dad all cultural with the Mexican 'n' Spanish stuff?'

'Not really. He's too busy with work to be cultural.'

'Well I know what that's like. I mean—'

'Stand up,' she said impulsively.

'Why?'

'I wanna see who's taller.'

'For rill?'

'Yes.'

'Do I *have to?*' I moaned.

'Yes!'

I stood up, and when she stood up, already smiling—a straight, perfect-teeth smile—she exclaimed, 'I'm taller than you!'

'Yep. You win.'

'What do I win?'

'Da prize of watchin' me sit back dahn.' And I did. Still standing, she styled a playful eye-squint. I was beginning to feel a little better, more comical. To keep it going, I quickly finished off the beer but held the cup to keep the nerves held back.

'So Ms. Ivy part-Mexican, part-Spaniard, part-Plain-White, whachir lassname?'

'*Pineda,*' she enunciated briskly with a feigned Spanish accent: *pih'NAY'duh.*

'¿Hablas español?'

'Just the basics. My dad's fluent though. He just never taught me much. You?'

'Yeah, I can speak the basics too. So tell me sum'n: how is it you gahdis Southern accent bahchir half Latin 'n' not rilly from the South?'

She shrugged her shoulders. Was I being too hard on her? Was I insinuating she's a fake? 'I dunno; I guess it comes from growin' up in LaSalle. A lot of people there talk the way I do—very soft and sweet—just not Teresa. But most of her family is from Pittsburgh anyway. Besides, *you're* the one with a funny accent.'

'You rilly think 'at?''

'*Mmhmm.* I do. So do you speak any Italian?'

'A liddle. *Ma pozzu parrari u sicilianu.* I can speak Sicilian—buh dat's nawdda dialect of Italian as most people assume. Sicilian has its own dialects, words, conjugations, hisstree—literary canon. It's akshly the oldest Romance language in the world.'

'Oh wow. Guess I learn somethin' everyday, even at parties.' She took a bashful drink of water then indiscreetly wiped a bead of sweat from her temple. 'I must admit: I always thought Sicilian was a dialect of Italian.'

'Nope; it's a language in its own right. Buh da problem is: Sicilian lacks orthography; meanin' 'ere's no established way da spell it, 'n' even speak it. Now they juss teach Sicilians standardized Italian—that's it—which means Sicilian's a dyin' language; only kept alive in conversations at home. It's not even used in local political institutions. I mean, even though I haven't been da Sicily yet, I'd rilly love da help keep Sicilian alive—see it become the *official* language *without* Italianisms. See, Sicilian's been influenced by like fifteen languages, all from when other countries controlled Sicily, Italy juss bein' the most recent one.'

'Well aren't you quite the history book,' she replied without condescension. 'So is Sicilian, like, what your family speaks at home?'

'Yeah—well me 'n' Ma usually talk in Sicilian. Rick doesn't know it; he can barely speak English wid us.' (Ivy naturally found this funny without knowing that I was alluding to his drunken babble. Although I didn't let any signs of discomfiture show, I felt awkward and stumped and consequently pulled out my smokes. 'Wanna join me outside for a smoke?'

'*Aww*, you smoke cigarettes *too?*' She sounded sincerely disappointed.

'Yeah, 'n' I'm not gonna lie 'n' tell ya I plan on quittin' soon 'cause I haven't considered it yet 'n' I don't think I'm ready da find out how soon is now.' I put the unlit the cigarette in my mouth. ' So ya wanna come outside with me while I smoke? It's priddy hot 'n' loud in here anyway.'

'Sure.'

So we walked outside where the air was sweet and tender. Caligula would have coveted the callipygous, hip-swaying figure I was following down the bricked veranda, weaving melodiously through several boozing groups, surprisingly none loud, wild, or rude. After going a ways (or so it seemed), we found a secluded spot where it began to curve around the side of the faux-castle; a rich rocky base beneath our feet; a small metal lamp hanging above us with a bronze burn. As I took to my smoke, Ivy pointed out the man in the moon, describing in scientific terms what made it look that way: maria, basalts, crust, regolith, highlands, anorthosite. I was finally able to hear her voice clearly: it did sound a bit Southern and old-fashioned, but above all, euphonic enough to give any small creature of the night heart palpitations. After she finished her discourse, I mentioned something trivial about the stars: millions were in view, opalescent and constellation-friendly, which I found more splendid and charming than the false stalker.

'Oh, I know whad I wannadda ask ya.'

'What?'

'You, uhh, mentioned Aristod.'

'That I did.'

For some reason, I suddenly felt devious: an empty deviousness cultivated by the fact that I too went to Aristod and *apparently* Teresa (as hard as it was to believe, though prone to be sleight) failed to mention it. But as a counterattack-thought arose, I wondering if it was perhaps *Ivy* being devious, stringing me along just for fun.

'Are you in college?' she asked, initiating a nocturnal standoff.

'Yep.'

'Around here?'

'Depends on whacha mean by "around here." Like in the state?'

'That, or just anywhere around here, like in Pittsburgh.'

'No.'

'No what? No you don't go to college?'

'No, I don't godda cawidge in Pixburgh.'

'So you go to college somewhere else?'

'Yes. 'N' I think you know where.'

She gave me a quizzical look. 'No, honestly I don't.'

'Yir tellin' me Teresa never said anything about where I godda school?'

'No, never. She just said you were Zach's best friend. And that you were eighteen. Everything else was about—' An abrupt stop.

'About wha'?'

She smiled deviously. 'You know, stuff girls talk about when they tell each other about guys?'

'No, I don't; I'm nawdda girl.'

'Well we're gettin' off the subject anyway. Tell me where you go to school.'

'I think yir juss playin' some kinda game with me.'

'Ha! Why would I wanna play a game over this?'

"Ca ya nah we gah ta da say skoo,' I mumbled in the lowest indiscernible voice, as I extinguished my cigarette in a fancy marble ashtray. When I playfully turned my back on her, she quickly grabbed my arm...casually letting go as I turned back to face her. I was being very nonchalant about everything because I realized that I'd managed to put the ball in my court over something so trivial. But perhaps she was playing along just to—well, play in the game.

'What did you say? You mumbled it on purpose.'

I hacked a laugh. 'On purpose? Right. 'At's whachu'd like da believe.'

'Oh I see: you're one of those people who likes to be difficult. Isn't that so, Mr. Vincent Vallano?'

'Yes, Ms. Naïvy Pineda.'

'What did you call me?' She reached out towards my chest, trying to give me titty-twisters; if only I could've countered likewise!

'Ahh, stop 'at...ahh...ya heard me: I said *Ivy*.'

'No, you said Naïvy Pineda or somethin'.'

'See, when you gadda add "sum'n" it basically means you got *nuh'n*—nuh'n on me!'

'You know what: you're just doin' this to divert attention from where you go to school. I mean, are you embarrassed or somethin'? Do you go to community college?'

'Well if ya think about it, I already said I don't godda cawidge around here or in Pixburgh, so why would I goddua different county ta attend community cawidge?'

'Touché.' Her face became serious, her body still. 'So just tell me.'

'Ooookaaaay.' A pause for a fake deep breath. 'I godda—guessa firss ledder.'

'Are you serious?'

'Always am.'

'Fine. *A*.'

'Thanks for playin', ma'am, but you've juss been *DIS*-qualifiiied!'

'Why?'

The ball was so in my court, and good thing I knew how to dribble and keep it there. 'You were juss gonna go straight dahn the alphabet. 'N' 'at's againsta rules.'

'Nuh-uh. I only said *A* because that's what *my* school starts with.'

'Me too.'

'Me too what? Your school starts with an *A*?'

'See ya on campus, Naïvy.' I began walking back inside. But beguiled, Naïvy froze for a moment—before pulling up next to me with steady elation in her green-gemmed eyes, like a wave that refused to fall back down to the surface. Crossing the threshold, the tip of her finger whimsically fashioned a loopy symbol on the nape of my neck: frissons within me, I could feel the philter of water was now in effect, within her...

...Strange things happened after we went back inside, sat down, and I acquiesced by telling her that I went to Aristod; she played out her astonishment by sticking to the claim that she hadn't known beforehand. Meanwhile, my brand of astonishment was right before me in the physical: this vessel of cordiality: her aura of allure. And perhaps clichés and sentimentality exist for a reason: the truth, because I truly felt secluded with her: there was no party, music, mad kids eyeing me in disbelief, RB and her snobbish RB Dolls—not even the house itself! Just us in a cloistered sphere of energy. Thanks to a deep, warm, fluid conversation, I found out more about Ivy than anyone else in any prior conversation. We talked about our potential majors: she was pre-med in Veterinarian Science. That led to us appealing to each other over who had the greater love for animals; she used her vegetarianism to her advantage. I told her that I (an Italian!) didn't eat red meat. She said, yes, a good start but hypocritical and inconsistent. I couldn't have agreed more! Then I asked if any of her clothes contained animal products while pointing down at her *leather* Mary Janes. I told her *that* was hypocritical and inconsistent. She couldn't have agreed more! Then she began elaborating on her family. Her only sibling, Holly, was fourteen and spoiled; they kept their distance. Her mother Sandy, the Plain-White, was a finicky stay-at-home mom but also a *bas bleu*.[4] Her father Edward, the Spanish-Mexican American, was a nuclear engineer and part-time braggart. And Ivy had been doing retail at a mall til recently securing a secretarial job at a veterinarian's office. She claimed to take as little as she could from her parents. Overall, the Pinedas seemed like a tightly-knit nuclear family. 'Very bourgeois, but way too close,' she disclosed, further complaining of parental suffocation and filial obedience. But perhaps that suffocation and obedience had created the air of refinement in her twang and posture. Whenever *I* had to respond for the sake of conversational duality, I kept my biography concise: very surfacial. The place where Rick no longer worked was named as the place where Rick worked, and Ma's oppressive fears were sugarcoated as kindness and sensitivity. Enough about the Vallanos and Scandurras! So we made our way back to our present lives. She informed me that she lived in North Halls (as did Andrea Doxy, but in different dormitories). Still, a strange sensation in which Coincidence seems to the one open eye of God, with the other closed for

---

[4] [fre] A woman with literary or intellectual interests

the wink. But perhaps the strangest thing was, when I opened *my* eyes, I realized I'd quit drinking after the third beer. After going back inside, I began slipping into an equal state of sobriety, almost feeling drunk by other means. Another sensation: Ivy had this distinct celebrious energy. *Of who?* would've came to me sooner if Ivy herself hadn't kept me from making the connection. But then she did this thing where she mimicked her father whenever he stuck out a Spanish tongue...for a second smiling the smile of the person eclipsed in my mind...before dropping her head down in coyness...allowing (in the slow motion of the effect) the chocolate waves of her hair to brush across her breasts like a velvet blanket unfurled in the wind...shadowing the flesh between her upper and lower neck like how a piece of land divides just at sunset—in that moment I realized Ivy reminded me of Elsa Aguirre[5][6] in *Algo Flota Sobre el Agua,* except Ivy had green eyes, darker skin, and obviously a different voice. But I wasn't about to tell her *that.* It would've been so anti-romantic, for it's one thing to have that uncontrollable picture brought to mind, but another to say it for the sake of a compliment, taking away from Ivy the individuality and celebrious nature she already possessed.

'...Dohncha think it's strange dey haven't checked up on us?'

'No; it was Teresa's plan to leave us alone to get "acquainted" with each other. And whenever she makes a plan, she sticks to it.'

'So how you rilly know her anyway? She don't seem like da kinda chick you'd hang out with.'

'Well she lives two streets over, and our parents used to be good friends.'

'Whaddaya mean *used to be?* Her parents take after her?'

Tittering, she said, 'Maybe a little. But see, her parents divorced a couple years ago. Rumor has it, her dad found out her mom was cheatin' on him while he was away on business. So he told her he wanted a divorce. Once it was finalized, her mom just took off to Indianapolis with the guy she was cheating with. Teresa and her mom never really got along, but she still took it hard. So it's like, Teresa will vent to me about her broken home, and I'll vent to her about my smothering home.'

'I see. So semi-related question, but why you live on campus when idd be a lot cheaper da commute, even if it's juss for yir parent's sake?'

'Umm, well I have a full scholarship, so it doesn't cost my parents anything extra whether or not I live on campus. But I really wanted the privacy and—Hey, speakin' of the devil, look who it is!' Before she finished explaining, The Devil and Pessi came stumbling back in. I couldn't tell who was holding up who: both looked straight from the depths of Hell. As they approached, Satana kept yelling, '*Aww,* Zachy, look at the lit-tle lovebirds! Look at the lit-tle lovebirds!'

Ivy and I stood up, and when they made it all the way, we broke into gender huddles.

---

[5] An actress of the Golden Age of Mexican Cinema, also considered one of the belle divas of the time

[6] Memory dispute: might have been a photo of Silvia Derbez

'Yeah, V, you'll get it. Donchu worry, bro.' Pessi was displaying one hellava incoherent face: black bloodshot eyes all over the place! He privately shouted, 'Yeah, you'll fuck her! You'll fuck Ivy Penson good 'n' hard! Then drink *AAAAALL* her blood from a fuckin' shot glass!'

Ivy Penson and Satana Cazzata looked over at this. Ivy was either appalled at the idea of her blood being drank or Pessi butchering her name, and not just in jest as I'd done. Meanwhile, Pessi was still shouting privately things about Ivy Penson and me.

'Sorry, Ivy. Juss ignore 'im. He says stupid stuff like 'iss da everyone.'

'Zach, quit say-ing stupid stuff,' Satana added in halfheartedly.

'Eh, Mudder Teresa—don't tell me wha' ta do,' Pessi answered in Slurese.

'Well what's goin' on?' I asked anyone who cared to answer.

Satana came walking over with clear intentions burning in her lurid snake eyes, obviously having told Ivy to stay put. With alcoholic vapors spraying into my face, she squawked, 'Well? Do ya like her? Huh? Huh?— Answer me!'

Annoyed, I responded by shaking my head and rolling my eyes dismissively. Suddenly Pessi came up from behind, put his arm around my neck—started choking me—and whispered loudly into my ear: 'DO – YOU – LIKE – HER?'

'Gih da fuck offa me!' I threw his arms offa me. 'Let's juss gihdoudda here 'n' go somewhere else. I'm sick of bein' here.'

'We can't go anywhere else now, you fa-king moron!' screamed Satana. 'Unless we're stayin' at Zach's, we gadda be at the bus stop by one or we're fucked.'

'Nobody's fuckin' stayin' at my place,' grunted Pessi.

'Where'zshur bus stop? Over in Marian Heights?'

'No, you fa-king moron! Right down the road from here!'

'Like I fuckin' know a bus route I never take! Pessi said—'

'Pessi said nuh-thing! We're lea-ving!' Satana went up to Ivy, grabbed her by the arm, then started for the door—but suddenly halted their inertia, turned around, then dragged Ivy back by the hand. 'Why don't *you*,' (she firmly poked her finger into my chest) 'and *you*,' (then poked into Ivy's) 'come stay at *my* place.'

'Maybe another time,' I yawned deceptively. 'I'm tired. Plus Ma's expectin' meedda stay for supper tomorrow before I head back.'

'What-ever!' squawked Squawk, spinning back around in anger and regrabbing Ivy by the arm as she made a beeline for the door. 'What-fa-king-ever!'

Pessi and I followed behind, Pessi temporarily silent. But the party, which had slipped from my consciousness til now, hadn't died down. Neither had the mad kids changed their ways: it was just verbally sloppier. Then, with an angled glance, I saw a random but familiar face (Patty Hertz?), and somehow she struck me with a reminder.

'Eh! Waydup a second.'

Everyone restlessly came to a halt.

'*Whyyy?!*' whined Teresa. 'We gadda *goooo!*'

'I gadda godda the bathroom rill quick.'

'Just fa-king go outside!'

'No. I'll be back in a minute.'

I had no idea where the bathroom was because I had yet to go. I could've just asked Ivy who *had* gone; that is, *if* I was even looking for the bathroom. First, I had to find Wes as quickly as possible...which I did, downstairs in the basement.

'VVVVVV!'

'Hey, Wes, look: I need a liddle favor.'

'Anything for you, King Aristod.' He was wasted. All the better, just in case.

'You been over here a lot, right?'

'Where?'

'Dis house.'

'Yeah. Man, I can't believe *youuuu* got *intoooo*—'

'Look. Don't ask why—'n' it's not da steal anything—but I neeja da tell me where Renee's room is?'

'Oh, gettin' some action?' he whispered with a wink.

'Yeah. But I'm tryin'ah get it on in Renee's room. 'N' no madder wha' happens ya can't say anything da anyone, know whadda mean?'

'My word's good as gold. I've always liked you, V. I really have. Umm, it's, ahh, up on the top floor, second room on the left. But it might be locked.'

'Well if it is, I'll go somewhere else. But I rilly gadda go, man.'

'Get 'er good, V,' he slopped. 'And good luck dahn at Aristod.'

'Thanks. You too.'

We shook hands longer than I had wanted.

''Member: nawdda word.'

'Good as gold,' he reiterated, zipping his lips like a tipsy mime.

I shot back up the stairs...moved down the hallway speedily, dodging several bodies...then ascended the next set of stairs...at the top, the hallway was dark but several rooms up ahead had lights on. I dropped into stealth mode and crept past the first set of doors. At the destination, no lights appeared to be on but the door was shut. I was desperately hoping that, first, the door was unlocked, and second, nobody was inside. Anxious, I paused to gauge nearby voices, making sure they were stationary, but I knew that could change any second, so I grabbed the door handle, and quietly, very gradually turned it—UNLOCKED! I slipped inside and shut the door. Pitch darkness, pure quietness. I thought to turn the light on to see what I was doing but it would've been too risky. So with small steps, and my hands held out, I felt around for the bed. When I found it, I patted at it to make sure no one was sleeping on it—NOT A SOUL! For the sake of requiting several incidents, I couldn't waste another second, so I flashed back to yesterday when Pessi said, 'Iddle be a ball. You can finely get revenge on her for when she puntcha in the nose. 'Azz sercly wunna da funniest things ever.' And I replied, 'Yeah, my fondest teenage memory. But yeah, I guess I'll go. I gadda godda the bathroom.' Well, I finally found the bathroom. *Psssssssssssssssssssssssssssssssssssssssssssssssssssssssssssssssssssssss...*

'What the fuck took so long?' complained Teresa as soon as I came back into sight. God, I was smiling so wide and unbroken that you would've thought I was getting paid millions just to smile.

'Uhh, couldn't find it.'

'It's at the end of that hallway,' pointed Ivy, thinking I had yet to go.
'Oh I know. But I had da wait in line.'
'We looked down the hall to check on you but we didn't see you.'
'Now's not the time da make fun of my height 'cause if we don't leave now yinzer gonna miss the bus...'

...Outside in the cool relief, we walked out of the private neighborhood...down into more suburban-looking streets...cutting through yards...then down another block where I decided to wait at the vacant bus stop with 'em. At a safe distance, Ivy and Teresa began conversing in private, I assumed about me. And Pessi began drooling in my ear, I assumed about nothing.

'Look here, Liddle V-Cup,' (he copped a feel on my little V-cups) 'I know dat girl over dere, actin' like she fuckin' owns you. I known her for years. 'N' lemme tell ya:' (he pointed over at Ivy like he was holding a gun but unable to keep a steady aim) 'I don't like *her*, 'n' she don't like *me*. Wanna know why, Liddle V-cup?'
'Why, Big Breast?'
''Cause I wouldn't fuck her.'
'Yeah, sometimes you can be a heartbreaker like 'at.'
''N' 'at fuckin' bitch Teresa hates her too.' He paused his prattle for a moment to suck in some air—then screamed at the top of his lungs: 'We all hate her!!!' He threw his arms up in the air, twirling around as if he had just broken Hank Aaron's homerun record. Fortunately, I don't think Ivy had a clue it was directed at her.
'Fuckin' bitch.'
'Come on; don't be sayin' shit like 'at. She's a priddy cool chick.'
'Teresa,' he said coldly.
'*Hmm*. Thoucha said ya rilly liked her.'
'I didn't caw her nuh'n, so shudup, bitch-tits.'
'Wha'? You sound like yir fuckin' drunk. How many a those pills ju eat?'
'I dunno; but dey make ya feel drunker den a bull.'
Now I was really stunned, not at the nonsensical metaphor, but at him considering himself to be feeling drunk. I knew he wasn't *really* drunk because I would've smelled it on his breath, but *something* wasn't right. All I could assume was that he was telling the truth: Baby Blues *do* put you in a drunken-like stupor. But so do many other things!
'Well here comes 'ah bus.'
A big hunter green bus was turning off the main road, heedlessly pulling into a large indented curb. The yellow digital-ticker above the flat spacious windshield said COBYVILLE 1:00 AM. It was three minutes early.
Ivy capered over and anxiously held out a piece of paper; I quickly took it before she lost the nerve and retracted. 'Here's my number at school. You can call me sometime if you want. Doesn't matter when...' As she elaborated, the wind gusted, causing a lock of mocha to stick against her sparkly bottom lip. I was trying to pay attention to what she was saying but I was too engulfed in the thought of removing the lock from her lip then immersing it in my mouth just to know the taste of epicurean delight. But with her neck turned to the side she removed it herself, smiling as if she

knew what kind of poetry was running through my mind. In an unforeseen *flash!* we leaned into each other and kissed on the lips. In the moment, I couldn't determine if it was one of those thanks-for-being-nice-and-passing-time-with-me kisses, or one of those I-hope-this-isn't-the-last-kiss kisses. After a slow separation of our lips, I found myself firmly holding both her hands down near my waist. I raised my left cheek up and into my characteristic half-smile, staring far off into the ebb-and-flow in her eyes...

'*Umm,* yeah—I'll, uhh, definitely caw ya. So, uhh, have fun with 'ose animals onna way back.'

'Oh I'll probably be sleepin' the whole time.'

'Well den have a nice nap.'

'I will. G'night, Mr. Vincent Vallano.'

Pessi was already aboard, sitting in the back with Teresa. Through the tint of translucent blue light, I watched him pound on the window. He stopped to flip me off, while screaming things I couldn't hear. When he attempted to moon me, Teresa started wrestling with him to stop because (with the bus door still open) I could hear the bus driving yelling, 'Sit dahn 'n' quit poundin' on the windows!' Ivy moved into view by sitting down in front of 'em. Still another minute or two before the bus would depart because the bus driver started chitchatting with another driver on the CB. Since I didn't feel like leaving yet, I lit a cigarette, enthralled by Pessi the Possessed. I figured there might even be a chance the bus driver would give him the boot, so best to stay just in case there was a case...but soon enough the bus driver cranked the bus into gear and began merging back onto the road. At the point of parallelism—when Ivy waved, and I smiled and nodded in response—I overstood that the surface had in fact been scratched...

...Back at the Vallano residence (after opting out of a bus ride for a reflective two-mile walk through the southeastern streets of Pittsburgh in memory of departed souls, and the welcoming of new ones) all was provisionally safe and calm. I went straight to bed...but couldn't sleep...finally nodded off...but soon awoke from a dream instantly slipping from memory; it felt like a piece of silk being pulled through the top of my head...knowing a solid night of sleep was futile, I lay in the dark, musing, while scratching up and down my body as if covered in ivy...

TO GO DEEP INSIDE

"In my dreams I'm loved,
I'm held, I'm safe, and it's real,
But why never out there?
Why am I left alone, unknown,
With the air as the only thing that won't leave me?
Oh I know: you've heard this all before,
But that doesn't really answer my questions, oh no, no, no..." [1]

...On Monday night, she was fucking me so good that I thought—well, I really wasn't thinking, but I was feeling all right. Just a bit surprised she wasn't saying much. But it didn't matter much: I'd learned a few things. I grabbed a handful of hair and aggressively directed her head from one shoulder...to the other...then down to my face so I could clean her gullet...then (her motions unvarying) I arched her flexible neck backwards...til the resistance reached a quivering threshold...on the surface: wrought domination like a sculptor beating his material around before giving it the final touches...an aggression delicately counterbalanced by a tenderness oscillating deep within my grip. I couldn't decide which one to stick with and how to stick it. But the consolation of whatever I was doing was her sweat of sanction, her gifts of gratification, dripping down on my chest like melting wax. The dale in my chest was filling up like a micro-puddle and I was a bit out of breath, even though (in the light of being a smoker) my cardio had been improving...I was so ready to demonstrate *my* spirited libido, whenever she wanted, or rather, *allowed* that to happen. But she seemed to be in love with me lying there able to remain steadfast around the waist and yet lively and dexterous with my hands and mouth. Perhaps from that alone, she, rolling her eyes around euphorically, began scratching my chest slowly—then a pause—then a hard thunderous thrust—then more red acrylic tips digging down into my wet chest but with longer, deeper, harder aggressions...Eventually, my libidinal turn came and she called out for a full-release crowned by the target to hit...
...She heaved a deep sigh from her naked chest. 'Well?'
'Well wha'?'
'How was your weekend? Have fun back home?'
'Yeah. Izz ar'ight.'
'Yeah? Wha'd—' So breathless! 'Wha'd ya end up doin'?'
'Juss hungout with friends 'n' drank. You?'
'Well, *Friii*day I went with my friend Anne da a party on Rolsen. *Saaaa*turday me, her, and a few of our friends went da the movies, den hungout at Anne's. And *yeeees*terday, I just studied all day.'
'Sounds like fun.'
'Tons.' (She rolled over.) "I meeced you, Vinny-pie. Meece meeee?'
'Mmhmm...'

---

[1] Lyrics from "I Could've Sworn That Somebody Cared" by The Snippets, from the album *Curiosity as a Novelty*

LA BIDDIZZA IE LA FESTA

"I watch the stars light up the sky,
And in my ~~heart~~ I wonder why
This man is in misery,
(Oh a man without love is like a song out of key),
I watch the sun rise in the sky,
And in my ~~heart~~ I wonder why
This woman is in lament,
(Oh a woman without love is like a rose without a scent)... "[1]

...With no hairy hangovers holding my eyelids down in the mornings, and no naughty nightmares waking me up in the middle of the night, I made it to all my cockcrow classes on Monday, Wednesday, and Friday. On Friday, Dr. Rosenbaum said, 'That's what I like to see!' taking keen observation of my perfect attendance for the week. Exploiting it, he hugged his arms around me, delicately set me up on my pedestal, then gave me a heap of attention, thinking it might've been a fluke week, and therefore he might not get another chance to harass my ass for a while. But I handled the burden with poise, discussing literary quandaries with a radiant ego beaming through a half-cocked smile. I could tell he was enjoying my energy too because his body was jerking around every which way like a wrestler bouncing off all the ropes before a match. He was ready to jump into a spandex jumpsuit, knock me off my pedestal, then wrestle me while we talked lit. But I wasn't that gay!

After decomposing in Dr. Loren's class of *static* static*, then again in Dr. Devereux's class of monotony, which was always putting me on the brink of an acid flashback, I walked down to a convenient store...just off the edge of campus where crampy stores and digital restaurants (specifically catered towards the students) vied for control over two streets. Since I'd been smoking more since college—a pack a day now—I decided to st~~art~~ buying by the c~~art~~on and walking to get it: lose some adipose tissue, regain some lung liters, and save a few bucks doing it. Reaching the corner of the block, I went inside what I imagined Edward Pineda might call a *bodega*. Dehydrated from the smoky walk, I grabbed a bottle of spring water from the cooler; I opened it and drank while I surfed the store. Strolling down an aromatic fruit isle, I came across sunflower seeds hung in a conspicuously brown display filled with other protein power products, all organic. But when I went to take the package off the metal hook, I knocked to the floor a package hanging below the sunflower seeds: *Hazelnuts? Hmm, I know who might like 'eez. Anything I gadda do taday? Mmm, not rilly.* So seizing the opportunity, I bought the bottle of water, the c~~art~~on of smokes, the

---

[1] Translated Sicilian lyrics from *"Na Rosa senza Oduri"* (A Rose without a Scent) by Alessandro Abbate, the live version performed with Laura MacNamara at Teatro Massimo in Palermo, Sicilia. *La Biddizza ie la Festa:* Beauty and the Feast

package of sunflower seeds, the package of hazelnuts, and then, instead of retreating to my room, I took my seeds to the weeds...

...In a humble area in the south-west corner of campus, back behind Philemon, down off the white pathway, and out of sight from most walking bodies, I sat down on a white lacquer bench shaded by an enceinte elm. Although its leaves had gone amber, it was still in full bloom: one long stubbled leg, its skirt hiked up, clearly pregnant—summertime shaggy because it had that extra weight to spare before its reserve cells started breaking down from the nocturnal chills now in effect. Within its realm lay wheat and keylime samaras: V-shaped like me. The O-shaped elm hung over us Vs like a big umbrella, shading the sun's autumnal rays which were bright but lacking heat. I opened the carton, packed a pack, pulled one out, then lit it. For flavor, I popped in a handful of sunflower seeds, tucking 'em into the side of my mouth. With the fresh air coming in through my nose, and the noxious air through my mouth, I closed my eyes and enjoyed both: *I should prahblee caw her taday...I don't feel too bad for da other night 'n' shouldn't...but dey say if ya feel yir hidin' sum'n den ya prahblee did sum'n ya shouldnt've...but den again 'at don't rilly apply da me in 'iss case...either way I obviously can't tell her*...When I finished the smoke and opened my eyes, I had company: the company I wanted! Out on the clipped yard three rambunctious squirrels were chasing each other around: around the tree...around the bench...around a bush...swatting tails, tumbling in circles, flipping up the spinning samaras, obviously having fun. After watching 'em frolic and search around for food—(frozen in enthrallment over their curious nature and how much I wished to be a squirrel)—I opened up the bag of hazelnuts. Cautiously, I squatted down in front of the bench so as not to intimidate the little russet creatures. Once they recognized my new lowered position, the squirrels, in a mechanical gesture, perched themselves up on their hind legs and looked me straight on. Then (not too positive if what I was trying to do was even feasible, or if I looked any different to them kneeling on the ground) I began talking to 'em in a genial, deferential tone.

    'Yinz guys hungry? Well look.' I gingerly opened my hand, revealing the nuts placed on my palm. *'Come on, ya screwy squirrels—POWER UP!!!'* And sure enough, they seemed to overstand that I wanted to feed 'em, except one that wagged its tail with infolded hands, while staring me down for saying *"POWER UP!!!"* in a quirky, energetic voice; that one scurried off.

    But what an unbelievable encounter followed! I hadn't known squirrels could be handfed: they seemed too quick and self-concerned, and when being approached and not doing the approaching themselves, too timid. Yet as I tossed nuts out on ground, they fearlessly zigzagged over to pick 'em up. But the nuts I laid *too* close to me, they wouldn't approach. I was *trying* to convince 'em that I had a bad throw, or that my stamina was wearing down, just so I could touch 'em, but the two remaining squirrels weren't falling for it. Seemed I would never get to touch 'em! But when all hope seemed lost—when the vicious through struck that I would *never* be able to touch the skin that *should've* been mine—a new recruit of three appeared! *Plus vair pour moi!* [2] And they were stupider, sassier, and

---

[2] [fre] More squirrel fur for me!

screwier, because, as I tried the short-throw approach again, they were easily duped and lured right into my reach. Sure, the first squirrel I tried to touch backed away. But with the next nut, I decided to hold on very tightly as the squirrel tried snatching it away with its tiny clawed hand, giving me just enough time to grace its fuzzy head! Same with the next one! I was melting—no, morphing! I really was! Ahh! Since I was finally able to touch 'em, making me *partially* satisfied, I didn't tease 'em anymore by greasing my palm. Instead, I started tossing the nuts out liberally. After picking 'em up, they would tip their walnut-sized heads towards me in comical gratitude, then carry 'em elsewhere for safekeeping.

Once the original two squirrels failed to come back, and the other three also had enough of me—nearly an hour of brown-loving bliss!—I stood up to leave. But our acquaintance, I hoped, would turn into future friendships, or a body swap. So after parentally seeing my three Screwy Squirrels safely off into an entangled mess of nature, I decided to take my seeds back to the room and smoke some weed. Weeds and Seeds! Weeds and seeds! HA! Rosenbaum, you nutty character! Hmhmhmhmhm!...

...Back at the room, Luke was gone, probably til late since he'd developed a routine of studying at the library til around ten, at which time he would come back, shower, then go straight to bed: few words between us. Growing less receptive of the school's regulations, I rolled a blunt and smoked it in the room, watchfully blowing the smoke out the window. Then I plopped down on my bed and began watching a Texas Hold 'em tournament....*well no bedder time den now: what's it been: five, six days?: izn'at wha' chicks do: wait a while da get back da ya juss da prove they coulda cared less if 'ey ever got back da ya?...but I bet Ivy wouldn't do that: she seems different...still I met enough people da know all about the deception of character found in the honeymoon stage of acquaintance: yes, then out come the TRUE COLORS...then again I dunno if I ever rilly seen 'em but I can taste their essence...hmm, I think cawidge is makin' me fuckin' stupid...good: daddle teach no one a lesson...*

'Hi. Is, uhh, Ivy dere?'

'*Umm*, this is her. Is this who I think it is?'

'Well if yir thinkin that awesome kid you juss met in Pixburgh, den I suppose idd is.'

'Wow. I seriously didn't think you were gonna call.'

'Yeah, I know, I juss been priddy busy. But I promised I'd caw.'

'Yeah. Well I'm glad you did. So how are you?'

Lying on my bed, I was fiddling around with the remote.

'I'm ar'ight. 'N' you?'

'Fine. Just a bit stressed over this biology test I have on Monday.'

'Yeah, I know whachu mean.' Trying to turn the television volume down so I could concentrate, I accidentally turned it up—up way too much—then the batteries in the remote suddenly died. The poker players broke their faces and started yelling while the sound of chips shuffling roared!

'Hello? What's that noise?'

'Hold on a sec...' I got up and turned the television down manually.

'Sorry. Badderies in my clicker juss died. So anyway, uhh, ya done with classes for da day?'

'Yep. Been done for a couple hours. I have all early classes. You?'

'Yeah, I'm done too. I'm juss lyin' around, watchin' poker.'

'I see...' (Silence ensued—but I was enjoying it because I had this sensation that she was feeling awkward and having a bout with herself to say something.) 'Soooo,' she finally resumed, 'what are ya up to this weekend?'

'Nuh'n rilly. Gadda write a paper. At's about it. Whaddabout you?'

'Well, besides studyin' for my biology test, I have to work tomorrow afternoon then I have a lunch date with my parents on Sunday. Other than that, nothin'.'

'Oh. Where you work at?'

'A veterinarian's office. Remember I told you how I just sit around, file papers, and watch the vet work on animals? Kinda like a pre-internship.'

'Oh yeah, you did tell me. Sorry, my mind's been out dere lately.'

'It's all right, I suppose.'

'Anyway, I, uhh, juss seeing if maybe, uhh, ya wannudda do sum'n.'

'Sure!' she answered with alacrity. 'That's why I gave you my number, silly. When were you thinkin'?'

'Well not da sound desperate for human interaction, but if yir not doin' anything tanight, you can, uhh, stop over here 'n' we can figure sum'n out.' For the two seconds it took her to respond, I waited anxiously for a while, wondering what she looked like whenever she talked on the phone: how *did* she hold the phone up to her ear?

'Sure, I'm up for some *human interaction*. Ya know, since I really don't have any friends and all.' A reiteration of an incredulous statement from the first night.

'Oh. What's Ms. Teresa Cazzata doin' tanight?' I asked sardonically.

'She's workin' til 9. And listen to this: she told me that Pessi's movin' in with her. Is that true?'

'Beats me. I haven't talk do 'im all week. He'z tellin' me about it before, 'n' I juss told 'im da rilly think about it 'fore he makes a decision. Could spell trouble, know whadda mean.'

'Yeah, that's definitely a big step, especially since they haven't been together all that long.'

'Well two great idiots think alike, so I dunno.' I deliberately coughed for redirection. 'So izzer anything in particular you wanna do?'

'Whatever is fine with me, Vinny. Or is it Vincent? Or Vin? Or Vince? You never did tell me what you prefer.'

'Vinny or V works for me. Bahwhaddabouchu? You like it shortened dahn da Iv orwha'?'

'Nooooo. Teresa and my mom call me Iv. Teresa, she says it like the name's all slimy. And my mom says it like it's high-class patois. Like, "*Heeey, Iv, let's go shopping*."' (Ivy was mocking her mother's "high-class" voice.) '"*Hey, Iv, do you think I'm gettin' fat? Please tell me if I am. Am I, Iv?*" And besides, why do you need to shorten a three-letter name?!'

'I dunno; maybe cause if ya ever had a talk-show idd be catchier da say *Live with Iv!* instead of *Liiiiv-UH with Iiiiveee*.' I exaggerated and manipulated the pronunciation of each version to make it look like I had a valid point. In response, she tittered but halted to tell her mom to get out of her room.

'Okay, sorry. My mom. Did you hear her just call me Iv?'
'Unh-uh.'
'Well she did. But anyway, here's the deal: I'll call you *Vinny* if you call me *Ivy.*'
'Ar'ight. It's a deal as long as it can be occasionally broken.'
'Deal. Now when do ya want me to come over?'
'I dunno; whenever ya want.'
'Well I have to get a shower and get ready. Is that okay?'
'Absolutely not; I like my chicks da be as filthy as possible.'
'What?'
'Huh?'
Again, silence ensued.
'*Weeeell,*' again, Ivy buckled. 'Where's your room—*Vinny?*'
'122 Philemon Hall—*Ivy.*'
'I'll be over soon—*Vinny.*'
'Ar'ight. See ya soon—*Ivy.*'
Click.

Knock! Knock! Knock!
Already styling a large fantastic smile, I opened the door, all dressed up and smelling good. "All dressed up" for me was putting on cargo jeans I hadn't worn since last washed, a plain black t-shirt that was a bit tighter than the others so my large biceps would look like they were ready to bust out, and black Doc Martins, which I polished. My hair (which took twenty minutes to get right!) was spiked up with messy precision. I was so sharp that I could cut a thousand wrists and not dull a bit!
'*Bommegna, Signura Pineda.*'[3]
Also smiling, Ivy walked in and scanned the room, probably to see if anyone else was present. She was wearing black Mary-Janes, blue jeans (light and tight), and a long-sleeve V-neck sweater of silver which sparkled like Christmas snow. Also sparkling: her ophidian mocha. How it snaked down her shoulders like diamond links hung from a grand chandelier! And how profound her green oceanic eyes! And how aromatic her wild thyme skin! Strangely—and the sensation was unforeseen—I'd missed her so much it hurt! She was sweet like sugar, and pure like water: and like sugar, she was addictive, and like water, she was essential. *Ahh! Diu aiutami!*[4]
'My roommate's gone,' I explained just so she would know for sure.
'I see, I see.' Like divine magnetism, she moved closer to the painting, eyeing it with a trace of confusion. 'Is that yours?'
'Nah. It's my roommate's.'
'Oh. It's really beautiful.'
'Mmhmm.'
'Just a little surprised to see somethin' like that in *your* room.'
'Why's 'at? I come across as satanic or sum'n?' No offense taken; just a smirk.

---

[3] [scn] Welcome, Ms. Pineda. [Note: written Sicilian would be *bon vegna*, but in the spoken language, when a word ends with an "n," and the following word begins with a "v," it elides as an m-sound.]
[4] [scn] God help me!

'No, silly. I didn't mean it like that. You come across as philosophical and independent—when you're not jokin' around and stuff. But you *do* believe in God then?'

We hadn't touched upon religion the first night, and now she was asking about it with an answer-now-and-be-serious tone. Be that as it may, sometimes you're put to the test, and you *have to* take it; sometimes you pass...sometimes you fail. 'Yeah. But I try da keep an open mind about things. I like da learn about all kinds a religions 'n' 'at.'

'Oh okay.'

Standing by my bed, to her lovely left side, I watched the corner of her lips kinda purse and gnarl up: she seemed disappointed with my simple "yeah" but attempted to cover it up with her insouciant "oh okay," while failing to look over, as is the way of taking pity on someone you don't know well enough to look in the eye.

Facing Jesus, she said, 'Well I guess you could say I'm a good little Catholic girl.'

'Oh yeah? So I take it ya know yir *Ave Maria?*'

Now she glanced over at me. '*Ave Maria? The Hail Mary?* So you're Catholic then?'

'"Hail Mary full of grace, the Lord is with thee, blessed ~~art~~ thou amongst women, and blessed is the fruit of thy womb, Jesus. Holy Mary, Mother of God, pray for us sinners now and at the hour of death. Amen." Yes, I's raised Catholic.'

Raised brows, widened eyes, iced ovals, Ivy was stunned by my recitation. When her amazement leveled, she emanated a new elated spirit, saying, 'Wow, I'm impressed, especially since people tend to say t-a-t-t-o-o-s spells t-r-o-u-b-l-e,' she joked, 'and here you are sayin' 'The Hail Mary' so fluently with scary tattoos on your arms.'

'Yep. Makes you wonder what's rilly skin-deep: the ink or those people you refer to?'

She slapped my shoulder on her way to sit down on my bed, replying, 'You say such silly things sometimes, ya know that?' She put her posture straight up, knees pressed together, to prove that she *is* "a good little Catholic girl." Then she began telling me how her parents had already persecuted her with a million questions about me because she'd told 'em— she paused—because she'd just told 'em about "meeting" me. She said that if her father knew she was with me in my room he wouldn't be mad but would want to meet me pronto, from which I began contemplating what kind of situation I was in if parents were already involved. But since I hadn't done anything yet, or made any kind of commitment, I just shrugged it off as nothing more than the early stage of a situation where a chick's parents are prematurely involved because they've yet to cut the umbilical. It's like some parents just won't ever cut it out, while others cut too soon—then try to strangle you with it!

Bored with my bed, Ivy stood up and went to the large window on my side, surveying the scene outside which showed, to the left, the tailbone of the dorm, and straight ahead, a line of red-bricked buildings about a hundred yards away.

'So,' she began with her fingertips tapping the sill, 'what do you have in mind?'

I sat down on my bed where she'd been sitting. 'I dunno. Wanna drink? Lass night I bawda bawdle of Southern Comfort with my fake ID.'

'HA!' she blurted out, turning around. 'I don't think I'm drinkin' tonight, hun.'

'Why, ya don't like the South? or is the comfort?'

She walked out to the middle of the room, squared up, and gave the most frustrated stare. 'You don't remember anything about me, do you? First my job. Now the drinkin'.' Ouch! Caught me off guard with such a stern reproach. But she quickly broke in with relief: she came over, grabbed me up by the arm, and assured me that she was just teasing; sometimes, she too forgets details about people she just met. Ohh!

'So tell me somethin': do you drink a lot? Be honest.'

'Nah, not rilly.'

'Okay. Good.'

'I'll be back—bathroom. 'N' keep in mind: I got my cameras turned on.' I pointed up to fake cameras hidden around the room. This one. That one. And this one.

'Okay,' she snickered.

...Well if it isn't neighbor Ralphie 'n' his nondescript face: the way he opens his door 'minds me of a spy: if I catch 'im spyin' on me his eyes are gonna espy my fist...fuck, I hate deez fuckin' bathrooms: I know I'm gonna get sick from bein' in here: ya worsh those germs off yir hands with germs!...yeah, Ivy, I honestly don't drink a lot juss like I honestly didn't juss worsh my hands with germs: I can see me dyin'ah germs one day...I'm rilly gih'n sick from seein' everything but whad I wanna see: maybe that's it: my eyes are infected with germs: the gametic copulation of germ cells fucking over my fuckin' pupils!...ugh, I prahblee wouldn't be a good spy...

'Back! So whaja steal? Hmm?'

Ivy was standing at my desk, flipping through a book. She'd failed to jump a heel or turn around when I shot in and announced my return and her alleged thievery. But as I moved forward I could see her peering out of the corner of her eye, looking to see if and how I was looking at her: part of her coquettish nature. In that moment of furtive glances and coy smiles being held under the veil, I noticed that she had very prominent eyelashes: long shiny slides shaped like the cusp of a crescent moon where someone tiny enough could start from the top...*sliiiiiiiiiide doooooown*...and pick up enough speed to launch off into space! Just like the first night, she wasn't wearing any gaudy makeup either: only sparkly clear gloss on her lips, along with a whitish-silvery eye-shadow which matched the sparkle of her sweater: a favorite feminine mesh of mine.

'Find any good passages?'

Ivy was flipping through *Naked Lunch:* probably a random pick-and-pull from my sundry stack. She stopped and pointed to the shelf above my desk where I had books piled up vertically atop the horizontal row. 'Are *all* these novels for class?'

'Nah; I brought most from home. Still gaddabout a million da bring.'

'For what?'

'I dunno; CDs, books, 'n' the pen have been my life since I's like ten, so I just like havin' 'em around. It's comforting.'

'I see. So would you rather be a poor writer who becomes famous *after* death, or a rich rock star livin' it up now but soon forgotten?'

'Makin' me pick my poison, huh. Well let's see...I guess the dead famous writer, for "fame after death is the noblest of goals." *Beowulf.*'

'Neat. I read *Beowulf* before.' She slid *Naked Lunch* back into the vertical row, then meticulously tinkered with the stack to restore it to its original position as if failure to do so would jeopardize the order of the world. Afterward, she moved back to my bed and dropped down weightlessly like falling ass-end into a pile of leaves. 'So do you have any of your poetry here? I wanna read some of it.'

I did—I had all my writings with me—but I just couldn't share any of it with her—at least not yet. 'No, sorry. All my poems are back home.'

'Oh.' Her dreary oh-of-disappointment seemed to be a euphemism for oh-he's-lying, or oh-he's-probably-too-embarrassed-to-show-me-because-he-sucks-at-writing—poor kid. Pretending to be unaffected by the ohs and blows of the silence, the poor kid focused in on a baseball game. Someone just hit a rocket of a homer. Standing back behind her right shoulder, I looked over to gauge her reaction: seemingly apathetic.

'You inda sports?'

'Ehh, not really. I like soccer though. I played a couple years when I was younger. What about you?'

'Well I'm from da Burgh, so, uhh, I was born with helmet 'n' pads.'

'Did you play growin' up?'

'I didn't play football for a team, but I played rec baseball a few years. 'N' I skateboarded for a long time. But hockey is my favorite sport. I never miss a Penz game. I can't...' All the while, I was wondering what to do with my body. I could either remain standing or pull out my desk chair, which would've been awkward but not as awkward as sitting down right next to her on my bed. Besides, she seemed to be the new ruling queen of my bed. She had her scintillating arms braced and splayed behind her as if to warn me: 'This is *my* domain now.' But something suddenly irritated her eye, for she jerked up and began pulling at her crescent-moon eyelashes near the canthus of her eye...and once pulling out the loose lash she began blinking her doe-eyes: *blinkity-blink-blink*. It made me smile a boyish smile.

When she recuperated, she looked up at me and authoritatively asked, 'Well did you decide what you wanna do?'

'J'eet yet? 'Cause we could go get sum'n'ah eat 'n' 'en go from 'ere.'

'Okay, that sounds fine. Wait, you have a car up here, right? 'Cause mine's back home; it needs new brakes and tires, and my dad won't let me drive it til it's fixed.'

'Yeah, my car's here,' I replied without letting my disappointment be heard. Deep-down, I was hoping that she had a sports car she would let me drive like Wes Parsons did. Even if she had one, which I failed to inquire about, we were presently doomed to take a ride in my embarrassing death-on-wheels, although I didn't overstand why we had to drive anywhere anyway since everything was within walking distance and the weather was comfortable. So I asked: 'Why, where ya wanna go thit requires drivin'?'

'Well there's this one diner I like to go to. It's about fifteen minutes from here. But we don't have to go that far away if you don't want. But!' she recovered sharply, 'if we *do* go there, I can show you where I live on the way. And maybe—*if* you're good—we can go to this other place.'

'Oh yeah? 'N' whad other place would that be?'

'It's a secret. You'll just have to take the risk if ya wanna find out.' She was smiling as if she knew something so wonderful that I didn't. And of course it was just eating me up inside! Alwaysthemore, instead of letting her get the ball in her court by giving her the pleasure of an emotional inquiry, I gave her the cool smirk of skepticism with a complementary eyebrow raise. 'Don't worry, Mr. Skeptical,' she added, perfectly reading my face, 'I'll try to make it as enjoyable as I can. And bein' a poet and all, you should really like this other place.'

'Ar'ight, Ms. Facialump; I guess let's go eat then trick-or-treat ...'

...Outside, dusk was settling in. The sky looked like an immense canvas covered with panicles of sea lavenders, spotted throughout with patches of marvelous teals and purples like a peacock's ocelli. Another evening destined to be a cobalt-blue night with a million 'choly stars. At the car, I opened the door for Ivy: a my-first. And by the time I rounded the back bumper, strutted up the side, and was about to stick the key in, she'd already unlocked my door—manually: another my-first, a surprising my-first. At the jerk of a knob, she just made me feel like a natural woah-man!

After driving through some red lights, and shooting down the long sloping hill that milked into LaSalle, Ivy began guiding me through several upper-middle-class streets...til she said, 'That's where I live. The—ut oh, don't slow down, Vinny! My dad's out in the yard!' She quickly ducked down. Laughing, I decided to drive by slowly. Her house was a large impeccable white Victorian, looking authentic as all hell. The shrubbery and lawn was well kept and decorated with ceramic scenes of regality. In a wide-brimmed straw hat, her father was down on his knees pulling weeds in front of an elaborate porch on which an antique-looking little metal table with two chairs sat to the left—just above where he was picking through the nectarous pedals so vaingloriously. I could already tell his ass was affected.

Snickering, I poked her in the back, and sung: '*It's safe da come oww-oout.*' (She pulled up and looked out to the window to see if it was true.) 'I don't think he woulda spodded us anyway. 'N' wha' wouldeeah done if he had? Jumped in his car 'n' chased us?'

'*Maybe,*' she joked. At least I was hoping that was a joking tone...

...About five miles past LaSalle—on a long barren road, closer to the purple mountain—we came upon Chow Down, the diner. The parking lot only had four cars; on the right side of the road there was a blacktop pull-off lined with three idle tractor-trailers. When we entered Chow Down, there was only one chower in sight, which meant the truck drivers were probably better off down in Dozer. Instructed by a WAIT TO BE SEATED sign, Ivy and I stood in the entry...til this fat gal—about two D-cups wider than me—approached. She told us to follow. As she turned, I caught (within the inflating lines in the plumpness of her rosy cheeks) a poorly-restrained smile; glancing right, I caught a similar contortion in Ivy's cheeks. Leading us down a white tiled floor, in which red-topped tables only sat on the left side, the sebaceous grinner stopped three tables away from the backwall restrooms. We sat down, Ivy facing Jane Walls, I John Stalls; in other Does, Ivy towards the front, and I the back. Ruby (as her nametag read) handed us homemade menus, then asked what we wanted to drink.

'Lemonade,' said Ivy.

'Iced-tea,' said I. But that wasn't good enough for Ruby; she also wanted to know if I wanted a lemon with it, sweetened or unsweetened, or even raspberry-flavored iced-tea. 'Sweetened with a lemon,' I clarified. Looking up at ma-lady of flesh, I didn't know if my appetite was going to hold up. The 40s-something gal kinda looked like a—well, a white-trash entrée: French-fry fingers, watermelon breasts, ketchup lipstick, a peach-fuzz mustache, and to top it off, graying spaghetti hair. Yum.

When she promptly returned with our drinks, she said, 'So how's college goin', Iv?' She flipped out her pale-pink notepad, waiting for answers and orders.

'I'm likin' it so far...Uhh, I'm just gonna have the usual, Rube.'

'You got it, dollface!' chirped Rube, lighting up her appetites.

Then she turned to me, her devious smile now looking ready to jump out and devour me; it felt like I was trapped inside some kind of rustic inside-joke—or a Rubik's Cube! 'And for you, you handsome devil?' She edged closer to the table, her aproned belly making a move on me. From the force-fed diner-line, and the secret wink that followed, I was wondering if she wanted my order or my number. 'Need some more time, babe?'

'Uhh, I'll have a grilled chicken salad. 'N' izzer any way ya can put fries on top a dat? If not, juss bring me a side of fries.'

'Oh I can put 'em on top for ya. What kinda dressing?'

'None.' *But that doesn't mean an undressing either.*

'Alrighty then. Be back soon.'

I watched her waddle over to the kitchen...impale the order through a metal spike, then give the carousel a wrist-flick. To make sure "Butch" in the back was being attentive, she yelled, 'Order, Butch!' before heading further west. So with Ruby and her carnivorous customs at a safe distance, I refocused my attention to Ivy.

'So whatsa "usual"?'

'Fettuccini Alfredo. It's really good—you handsome devil.'

'Yeah, rill funny. We can juss pretend azz never said.'

'Oh can we?'

'We can oh.'

'We'll just see about that. So tell me, you handsome devil, what else do you like to do for fun besides read, write, and listen to music?'

'Well bein' a handsome devil 'n' all, I tenda prostitute myself out da older ladies who caw me dat. Think Rube's willin' da spend her tips on me?'

'I can ask her if ya'd like.'

'Please do.'

'Okay. But for real: what do you like to do?'

'I dunno. Whacha named is priddy much whad I like to do. Da only other things I do, or rather *have* done, is nuh'n'ah talk about.'

'And what does *that* mean?'

'*Mmm*, juss like all da stupid shit I did growin' up, ya know.'

'Yeah mean like drugs?'

'Yeah, like drugs 'n' all that good stuff.'

'Yeah, and what's all that good stuff include?'

'Truss me: you don't wanna know too much about me.'

'Trust *me:* I do. But don't worry; I won't judge you by your past.'

'Well—let's juss say, aldough a *handsome* devil, I's a priddy *bad* devil growin' up. Like I gahdinah alawda fights, stole some shit, always in trouble at school, started drinkin' 'n' doin' drugs when I hit puberty (but not cuzza puberty,' I laughed. 'But here's sum'n funny about my past: me 'n' Pessi yoosta be in a band with our friends Jeremiah 'n' Dante.'

'Oh really? So then you *could* be a rich rock star?'

'Nah. We sucked. I's the singer. Jeremiah played drums. Dante played guitar. 'N' Pessi played bass, but I wrote all the music 'cause 'ey sucked at comin' up with shit. It's funny: at practice, we'd usually end up gih'n fucked up 'n' breakin' bir bawdles over our heads; 'ere's a certain way you can do it without gih'n hurt. Even Pessi'd do it, even'o he don't drink.'

'Yeah, why doesn't he? Teresa said it's cause he's allergic to wheat?'

(Another question I was wishing hadn't been put to me.)

'He's not allergic da wheat. I guess it's 'cause when he'z ten, his mom was, uhh, killed in a car wreck involvin' booze.'

'Oh that's so horrible,' she whispered, her face chagrining into a deep red. 'I guess that's why he and Teresa can relate to each other: not havin' a mother around.'

'Yeah. His dad's the one who wrecked the car. Dey were both drunk 'n' fightin' 'n'—'n' 'ere's juss a buncha hearsay about what rilly happened, but I'd rather not get indo it now.'

'Understandable.'

A long moment of reflection and lamentation transpired.

'So what's this music you guys played?' she resumed with interest— or maybe just drawing back to whatever she could in order to end the awkwardness she had brought on.

'Izz like da Hardcore Punk from the mid-80s: ya know, not so hard dit you can't overstand the lyrics but still priddy aggressive.'

'I see. So is that the only kind of music you listen to?'

'Well there's different kinds of Punk I like, like Oi!, Ska, Psychobilly— juss Rock 'n' Roll period. But I also like Jazz, Bluegrass, Reggae, Folk—even Rap as long as it has substance, like KRS-One, Public Enemy, Nas. I need music thit I can relate to lyrically, or music with an overwhelming energy, which is why Punk's the main one for me: it's a good combination of both. You know any Punk bands, old or new?'

Ivy took a moment to think about it, while I squeezed the lemon into my iced-tea, whirling the straw around. I loved talking about music but I didn't think talking about Punk Rock was going to happen with *her*—well, maybe she knew a few of the old famous bands like The Big Three: The Clash, Ramones, and Sex Pistols.

'You mean like Nervama, Lime Week, umm, Wink 281?'

Siphoning iced-tea from my straw, I jokingly spat some on the table.

'Okay, real funny. So I take it those aren't good enough examples for your high-standards of Punk?'

'You got it, babe. But it's cool. *What's punk?* is a *pons asinorum.* I grew up on the old shit, so it's easy for me da criticize MTV bands thit look 'n' sound punk. Nuh'n makes me madder din seein' my culture—'cause I rilly do consider it *my* culture, *my* way a life—but juss seein' it exploited by fakes punks like Lime Week or Hardcore wanna-bes like Floppy Nuggitz—'

'Eww, I hate them!' she scoffed with a funny gnarled face. 'They suck!'

'We're off on a good note then 'cause 'at shit's for fuckin' retards. I'll have ta put summa the good shit on for ya. I had it on in the car bahdiz turned dahn. 'N' I'll tell ya right now,' I smiled, 'iddle prahblee take a while da get yoosta da sound. 'N' sorry if I'm soundin' pushy or preachy. Music's juss sum'n I'm rilly passionate about it. Anyway...' Yes! I was off again! speaking so ardently that my heart was palpitating! my arms shaking! my mouth—someone tape my mouth shuuuuuuut!

'...Yeah. So name some of your favorite bands.'

'Well, see, I have a thing where I'm always makin' up lists in my head, so for music, I know my Top Twenty-five off by heart—(even'o it's always changin')—but I'll juss give ya my Top Five.'

'You have a Top Twenty-five?' she laughed; I nodded back with the face of a puppy dog that's proud of some inane accomplishment. 'Okay. Top Five: let's hear it.'

'Ramones, Sick of It All, Misfits, The Clash, 'n' The Smiths.'

'Well I've heard the Ramones and Clash, but who hasn't? But the other ones, *mmm*...' Meditation and Perplexity co-authored a few lines on her face. 'To be honest, I don't think I've even heard their names before.' She followed with a girlish sip of her lemonade.

'Me neither. But whad about Johnny Cash? He's one of my favorites. I'm sure ya heard his songs before, right?'

'I think a couple.'

'So whachir Top Five?'

'I don't have a Top Five. Besides, you'd probably just laugh.'

'Nah. You didn't laugh at mine so I won't laugh atchurs.'

'All right. Well first would definitely be Celine Dion—' (Instant burst of laughter on my part.) 'See! I *knew* you'd laugh!'

'I'm sorry. That was rude of me. Celine rocks. Please continue.'

Although squinting hard, Ivy's eyes had a glint of a good-natured greenness. And I loved it! I could *feel* her tolerance and easiness! Such energy in her stillness! Such rich greenness! But she likes Celine Dion? CELINE DION! 'Celine Dion, Whitney Houston, uhh, Mariah Carey, uhh, Sarah Brightman, and—let's throw a guy in the mix—Chris Isaak.'

'No way! Chris Isaak! I akshly gadda fewwa his albums.'

'Really? I think he has one of the sexiest voices.'

'Perhaps. But who's 'iss Sarah Brightman chick?'

'Oh you never heard of her?'

'Nope, don't think I have.'

'Oh she's so amazing. It's hard to describe what kind of music she sings, but it's like Pop Opera. She looks very exotic, too, like an Egyptian queen. And her voice is just so diverse and mesmerizing and—and you'll just have to hear it because I can't explain it,' she concluded breathlessly. How music creates such passion!

'Yeah, you'll hafta lemme borrow wunna her albums sometime...'

We continued talking about music: at first, more about Chris Isaak...til I zealously went back into the essence of Punk Rock, which led into a consciously gentle explanation of Rockabilly and Psychobilly: "consciously gentle" because I was conscious that, by the natural authoritativeness of my voice, I could come across as a know-it-all, so all I could do to balance it was to try to speak in a soft-smiling didactic manner, not an angry-eyed sermonic manner. I was just hoping that she found my passion enlightening and sincere—hoping that she didn't see me as some pathetic Ananias[5] or Anthony Durkin. But things *did* seem to be going good just by the way she was looking at me. And staring back into her emeralds—those wide, profound, oceanic, vibrant eyes!—it just filled me with the inspiration to say anything, and to say anything without thinking about anything but her overstanding eyes!

With the tray held right in front of her paunch, Ruby plodded over flatfootedly. She had her face contorted as if to serve as an equalizer for her unwieldy body. After setting the plates down, she asked if we needed refills; we said no. Then of course she had to call me another name. This time it was "cutie pie," but that didn't hold a dinner-candle to "handsome devil." She then bestowed upon us the typical diner blessings of have-a-nice-meal and let-me-know-if-you-need-anything-else before shambling to the other side where there sat a vagrant-looking old man who, every time I looked over, was gnawing on a piece of toast or sipping coffee.

After exchanging approving glances, Ivy and I began eating—at least *I* did. She was being slow and careful because most don't like to eat the way they usually do when they first meet someone. She had a fork in her right hand and a knife in her left. She was cutting up the saucy noodles with such gentle determination, like she just *had to* cut the poor things if she was to survive, but at the same time, it was making her feel so bad as if noodles had nerve-endings. It made me realize that I was eating *chicken* and she was a *vegetarian* and thus *she* loved animals more, although I was the one who wanted to free the tanked fish in the Hub and morph into a squirrel! Once she wrapped a bundle of noodles around the fork, she glanced up surreptitiously, then sent the fork into her mouth, sucking the noodles in like a quiet vacuum. WOW! By far the sexiest thing I ever SAW! EVER!

'So houzza "usual"?' I inquired prematurely.

She let the pasta slide down her throat, while I fancied the internal itinerary of the noodles. 'Really good, which is why I always order it. Do you like your *chicken* salad?'

'Yeah. Check out da cheese 'n' fries on top. It's a Burgh thing.'

'Yeah, and where's the dressing?'

'Didntcha hear me say nay on 'at'?'

'No. But who eats salad without dressing? You're like a rabbit.'

On cue, I did my best to imitate a rabbit by grabbing up a piece of lettuce and mechanically, so rapidly chewing on it while making musical-squeaky voices in my throat like I had for the Screwy Squirrels. Even if rabbits make no such noise, she still laughed. *Ahh, ie mancu i cunigghi sunu i scuiàttuli! Hmhmhmhmhm!*[6]

---

[5] An early Christian who, with his wife Sapphira, deceived other Christians about a piece of property he sold. Instantly, they dropped dead for lying not just to the community but also to God. From Acts 5:5.

[6] [scn] And rabbits aren't squirrels either!

'Well I think if things don't go work out with the writing, you could always be a comedian.'

'Nah; I'm too short da stand up. Plus, my humor's based on playin' off what people say; need the live interaction, know whadda mean. But now atchu mention it: who's yir favorite comedians?'

'*Umm.* Well I dunno if I really have any. But I still watch Roseanne reruns, if that counts,' she giggled as she sexily slipped in more noodles. Those slick creamy wits!

'Yeah, I guess 'at counts; she akshly yoosta do stand-up back in the day. My *Top Five Stand-up Comedians,*' I laughed, 'is Mitch Hedberg, Lenny Bruce, George Carlin, Richard Prior, 'n' Chris Rock.'

'Ooo, Chris Rock is super funny! But his bug-eyes creep me out!'

'Well they're not as bad as Rodney Dangerfield's. But not everybody is as blessed as you witchir perfect peepin' love-eyes,' I mumbled as I sloppily slid in more salad. Those dry crunchy lids!

'What?'

Chomp! Chomp! Chomp! 'Nuh'n.'

In harmony, we subdued our intensity to indulge in our meals. Halfway through Ruby came over to give complimentary refills. She further questioned Ivy about college-life, but I could tell that she was burning to ask what the deal is; that's to say, who am I? Meanwhile, I was sipping on my surprise that Ivy evidently came often enough to have relationships at Chow Down. Despite the chow being a bit tasty, the place itself was downright trashy, from the tawdry design, to Ruby the mannish floozy, to the ripped upholstery, to Butch the Chef who made me doubt eating his food ever again: he looked like he'd been swimming around in a dumpster. Following Ruby's chat, he stopped by to talk to Ivy about this and that. But I guess I was happy that Ivy didn't have a bit of conceit. Maybe I *was* in her league. Or maybe with her there was no league, or, at the very least, an egalitarian Ivy League, giving a fair chance to any fair taker.

After Ruby cleared our plates, she came shambling back over to ask if we wanted dessert. We imitated serious contemplation but said no. So again, Ruby exited. Truth is, I *was* still hungry—starving!—yet I couldn't see how any dessert at Chow Down would gratify this peculiar hunger pulsating within my senses: a cerebral, concupiscent, both-taken-to-the-soul hunger for something I'd never had in any prior attraction or infatuation, while intuitively attached to the ever-present *fami pri biddizza.*

'So I have a question,' chimed Ivy. First, she pulled her silvery sleeves back down to her wrists. 'Do you know anything about philosophy? I have a philosophy class—nothing *too* deep—but we're learnin' about Descartes right now, and I have to write a comparative paper on him and Hobbes, who we're starting next week. But I'm already lost with Descartes.'

'The ol' *cogito, ergo sum:* I think, therefore I exist.'

'Exactly. Do you know much about either of 'em?'

'Yeah, I've read 'em before.'

'Well tell me what you know. The instructions are vague as what to focus on besides drawin' on their general differences.'

'Well first, I'd discuss the obvious fact dit Descartes believed in free-will, 'n' Hobbes was a determinist. Accordin' da Hobbes, man in the state-of-nature is forced inda vyin' against everyone else in order da prevent death, 'n' since 'ere's only a finite amount of resources, man will ultimately engage in an all-out-war for 'em. See, Hobbes had a priddy pessimistic view on Life. He said sum'n like Life's "nasty, short, 'n' brutish." 'N' whad he meant is thit man must use his instincts da survive 'n' succeed within our place in Nature. Now Descartes focused more on rationalizin' questions involvin'ah Self in an attempt da overstand Reality; meanin', he thought external objects are trivial 'n' can't answer the questions: *Who am I? Why do I exist? Do I even exist at all?* So in sum, you could say Hobbes was more about man vs. man or man vs. Nature; whereas Descartes was more about man vs. himself.'

'Jeez, Vinny. It would've taken my all night to come up with that! So which one do you agree with? 'Cause at the end of the paper we have to make a convincing argument for which one we agree with more.' Titling her head, she smiled coyly. 'Well? Come on; don't be afraid to help me a little more; I don't mind.' A wider smile.

'Well it's been a while since I read either. But I dunno; Descartes is too mathematical for me, too certain of his own knowledge. His "Wax Argument" is garbage: melts the life right oudda Life. See, Descartes' philosophy completely dismisses our senses. He believed our senses are deceptive, yet he believed through consciousness *all of* Reality can be discerned, which is juss plain arrogant, 'cause reason is only one facet of man; man is only one facet of Life; 'n' Life is only one facet of All. So I think Descartes makes a mediocre, at best, quarter-completed argument. 'N' Hobbes believed in absolutism, or at least thought it's inevitable thit one man will *always* rise up da rule a society or a country, so he figured it's bedder da juss give up our freedoms to an absolute ruler 'n' hope it's a good-hearted one, or else we'll be subjected to the barbarian state-of-war— basically layman's anarchy. But I think 'at's juss paranoid-based theory. Now accordin' da Nietzsche, 'n' others like Marcuse, if we take back our creative freedoms, we, through individual-will, can use 'em da transcend beyond all systems of artifice. Marcuse cawed it da *aesthetic ethos:* the unification of reason 'n' sensibility in an environment of freedom. 'N' aldo he'z talkin' about a communal effort, my interpretation is *anyone* who can do that would be the personification of Nietzsche's *Übermensch,* which is like someone thit can continually transcend their present state. See, I been readin' alawda Nietzsche lately, 'n' despite his scruples with God, his criticism of man's denial-of-life is so true. But if you like him yir wha' dey caw "*a trendy intellectual,*"' this I said very mockingly. 'But wow, I've completely flown off the track. Sorry.' (Ivy only smiled as if not to disrupt.) 'Anyway, I'd juss argue thit both Descartes 'n' Hobbes are only half-productive with 'er philosophies since tendentious approaches are riddled with igno-arrogance. Life's far-too intricate da think headin' dahn one road will gitcha da every mark on the map. So juss focus in on 'er weaknesses 'n' gaps. Professors love when ya can find faults insteada juss agreein'. Isn'at wha' cawidge is saposta be about anyway: *critical thinkin'?*'

'Okay, that's it!' she declared with a smiling glow, 'you're helpin' me write my paper!'

'Oh am I?'

'Yes. You're seriously like the smartest person I've ever met.'

'Please. I already feed my ego three times a day; it doesn't need anyone else sneakin' it snacks on the side.'

'Very well then. But tell me, Professor Vallano—' She stopped to flash an inviting smile: a diversion for the surreptitious inching of her hands towards mine. 'If you have issues with all these philosophers, then what's *your* philosophy on Life?'

'Mmm, either live slow, die low; or live high, die fast.'

'No, seriously.'

'Yes, sercly. Da be honest, philosophy kinda makes me sick. When it comes da things like *determinism versus free-will*, it juss drives me insane 'cause I think both exist, both on the micro 'n' macro levels, both carryin' about the same weight, but certain circumstances can swing the balance one way or the other but never to a point where the scales completely tip, 'n' it's always too intricate 'n' ever-changin' da map out.'

'I see.' (She bent down to her straw and took another sip.)

'I juss say feel witchir he~~art~~, think witchir mind, 'n' open yir eyes da whatever you may find. Now can we godda the *ooother place?*'

'*Mmm*—I *suppooose*,' she replied with mock reluctance, batting her long Latina eyelashes twice and heavily. 'You've been good, so I guess I *have* to take ya.'

'Yir right: you do. But where exactly ya takin' me?'

'You'll see.'

'I know I will. But I gadda know beforehand. Ma always told me I'm not sposta godda strange places with strange people or strangers.'

'So you consider me strange or a stranger?'

'No. But I'm the one who's been doin' most of the talkin', so wherever we go ya gadda fill me in on the *Ivian Philosophy.*'

'Sorry to disappoint ya, hun, but I don't have an "Ivian Philosophy." But I really like yours.'

'"N' I rilly like you.'

'What?'

'I dunno; I didn't hear nuh'n. Did you?'

Saving just half of Old-Fashion and throwing the rest out, I insisted I pay for the meal, and, in turn, Ivy insisted she leave the tip. So that's what we did, all left on the table. Ivy was too busy bantering with me over the secrecy of the "other place" to give Ruby a formal goodbye. But as we rolled out the door, Ruby waved us off, and I think I caught her winking at me. And maybe—(I wasn't too sure because I needed to drop contact solution in my eyes)—but I think she held her hand up to her ear, making a telephone gesture, while mutely moving her lips as if to say, 'Now you call me, you handsome devil.' I checked my pockets to see if she'd slipped me her number—Ahh, thank God: nothing!...

...Following Ivy's directions, we were heading further down the long smooth road, further away from campus. Although the night was gripping up on the sky, I could still see the basic geography of the land. On both sides lay wide-open fields, which soon turned into dense plots of stalked corn...then into stunted wheat fields covered in lackluster gold, and in one plot, medium-sized pines positioned all too perfectly to be of natural development. Outlining each side, a ridge sat naked and unbroken, periodically dipping just enough to make hilltops, with (as Ivy informed me) a creek running along the hills to the right. Out before us, in the lower ~~part~~

of the horizon, sat a fortress of piney woods, forcing the hills to head east and west respectively. Even though the night was bright, I wanted to eye these pastoral lands during the day. Meanwhile, I was sampling my music for Ivy, praying she would like it. My first calculated choice was The Bouncing Souls because they're melodic, friendly, and vocally overstandable. After two songs, Ivy said, "Ehh, they're all right, I guess." Not a good enough response, so I ejected and resorted to Plan B: Good Riddance. She winced and said, 'Too hard and fast.' 'But juss listen'ah his voice!' I yelled. "'N' listen'ah whad he's singin' about! Animal rights!' Oh I wasn't screaming *at* her, just *over* the music, because it's a sin to listen to Rock 'n' Roll at a low volume or to interrupt a song for petty conversation. 'Animal rights!' I screamed again, with a devilish smile and a teasing fling of the hand. 'Ju hear 'im?! He said burn the slaughterhouses ta the grahn! Listen!' I locked both hands on the wheel and looked over—Ivy was just sitting there all cute and coy, and with her hand on her forehead in a shading fashion, playing the role of the innocent girl who's wondering how she got stuck with such a maniac. I believe inside we were both experiencing the kind of fun that tastes even better when reimbibed as a memory.

Minutes later, she turned the music down. 'See that barn up there?'

'"I see," said the barn man.'

'Well there's a little gravel road right past it. Turn in there.'

'Yes barn ma'am.'

Nearing the large weathered barn, I finessed the brakes and turned left down the said road: a rock-'n'-dirt road. The main road (now behind us) went into a hard right towards a rolling hill that made a mystery of everything beyond. In our current position, precipitous woods shot uphill to our left (the barn-side), and to our right, more woods but on level ground; here, Ivy picked an indiscriminate spot for me to ease the car halfway off the bank and park. Only one person lived on the road, she said, all the way up at the end: an old man who was a friend of the family. She added how friendly he was *if* he knew you (or rather knew that your car was on his road), but he didn't drive anywhere, and was surely asleep, and therefore my car would probably remain unnoticed.

'Well this is the other place!' she chirped. 'Let's go!'

'But I still don't get where we goin'.'

'Only way to find out is to get out.'

'Mmm, I dunno; I'm a liddlo nervous. Mind if I patcha dahn first?'

'Please. There's absolutely no reason to be nervous, just as long as you promise to be good.'

'Juss as long as I can break 'at promise,' I stipulated, popping in a piece of gum. When I opened the door and stepped out, the balmy October air slithered up my nose. Since I didn't know where we would end up or how long we would be staying, I grabbed my hoodie just in case it became cooler. When I stepped forward with Ivy, she halted my motion as if she had a job to do alone. (She whispered something about not wanting to walk all the way up the hill, by the house.) So I leaned back on the front bumper and crossed my hoodie-tangled arms, while my eyes tangoed with Ivy's curious and focused movements. She was walking alongside the bank in a measured skulk, scoping around and into the murky thicket. Reflexively, my observations moved upward with instant admiration. The sky was a profound cobalt-blue, and, as I also forecasted, impregnated with lively stars. The moon (as conspicuous as a moon can be) was incandescent like an immense pearl rounded precisely at three-quarters. It even seized a portion of the sky beyond its own niche—this circular chiaroscuro of indigo and chalk, a breathing force-field whose exhalations softly feathered into the cobalt-blue—which evinced, for the moon, respect and solitary, while retaining an air of majestic benevolence. For some reason, I was waiting for a thunderous sound to burst from the heavens, perhaps through the mouth of the moon. But the celestial intensity, from the nearest star to the furthest, remained suspended in a natal gasp of hush—while down below several sounds played in delicate improvisation: twigs and gravel crunching underfoot; cicadas drumming rapidly in spurts; katydids and katydonts bickering in chirps; frogs gulping in bass.

When I broke from the upward gaze, Ivy was walking back down the declivity of the rock-'n'-dirt road, incessantly glancing left with a dismayed posture. Hope seemed to be skittering away from us like a creature abashed by letting itself be seen despite uncaptured. Seemed we would be getting back in the car with quelled expectations—dreams reshelved for another night. But out of the cobalt-blue, Ivy, as if compelled by desperation, took a semi-plunge into the dark—paused within, before pulling back out—then turning towards me, whispered with suppressed authority: 'This is it. Follow me in.' From an irrational decision to have my hands free, I threw my hoodie on, and then, keeping quiet, followed her seductive lead, suddenly finding myself, as I moved forward with uncertainty, swallowed by an obsequious sensation wherein I knew nothing about, was oblivious to the ideas of, comedy and tragedy, conversation and inquiry—while fully conscious of the innate inadequacies of language: a lung-swell of crisp fragrant air; a tug from a phantasmal rope made of fawning fibers; swept into the strangest of woods...

...Through the darkness, we carefully navigated down a thin pathway of treaded grasses and parted trees; an owl hooted twice. Besides feeling obsequious to Ivy's command, I also felt myself slipping into that mortifying state in which I became vulnerable to facing new things, much like my first experience with the library, which I later discovered was truly a biblio-labyrinth but certainly nothing to run away from. Trying to exorcise an apprehensive monster in my gut, I was praying the dubious change of reality wouldn't induce a panic-attack. Slightly up ahead, Ivy was either talking to herself or talking herself through. I throat-gagged a *Huh?* and a *Wha'?*, but she didn't answer. With crunchy steps and stealthy swivels, we moved through the rest of the thicket as if engaged in a gut-stirring adventure reserved for ones of youth.

When we came out at other end, the sky and its brilliant blueness (even more oceanic in this quarter) opened back up into a panorama—a Cézanne demystified, yet still mystical within its natural frame—allowing us to behold a large orchard and that which went beyond. In a cadent amble, we headed towards a dense plot of apple trees spread out in asymmetrical perfection. I had a good view of the trees' horizontal landscape; they were about fifty yards away. I could see where they tailored off to the sides in a woolly, spherical fashion. Their shadowy leafiness suggested they were still in bloom. On the left side was a collection of crabapple trees copious with downy white blossoms which at a distance had a pinkish reflection: perhaps an illusion caused by the potent moonlight. Adjacent with the right margin of the orchard was a bald field descending into the darkness where the woods again rose, so daunting and dense, extending beyond sight. To the left margin of the orchard was a roll of vegetation short in height but interminably long; it had remarkable breadth and verdancy. Altogether, the orchard (with the help of the celestial pearl and the millions of scintillating stars) had a warm poetic glow where it was dark enough to cast out substantial shadows but also lit up enough to see the color of someone's eyes.

    To the left, along the outer set of trees, she led me by the hand into a white stilted arbor. The tunnel was long, wide, the top within reach, the lattice superimposed with bristly branches: shoots and slats of hazel. Weaving in and out of both woods were plump carmine grapes, knotted vines, and "long, dangling, intertwined green tendrils,"[8] and therein, coexisting in peace, thousands of fuchsia flameflowers and whimsical white cloudflowers. Sucking in the weight of my steps, the ground was soft and mossy—garlanded with fallen pedals, brittle stems, and tufted grasses full of natural emotion. Before waxing a body of words to exchange, if that was even possible—coherently possible—we looked up at the metallic moonlight peaking in through the overhead lattice: the angled, agile woodwork was eclipsing parts of the light, creating a myriad of penumbras all around us.

    'Whad is 'iss place?' I whispered in a tone suggesting we might've slipped into a third realm.

    'An orchard, silly!'

    'Obviously. But what's the story?'

    'Weeeell, I've been comin' here since I was little. It's been a while though.' She fingered a flower recoiled in a lattice hole. 'The guy who lives at the end the road we parked on, Jack McArdle—he owns all this. Before his wife Eleanor died they used to take real good care of everything. There used to be a bunch of flower gardens and vegetable gardens out yonder. Now he just prunes the apple trees.'

    'Are the apples ripe?'

    'I'm sure if you look around you'll find some that are.' She moved her face closer to the vine of flowers. As if tenants facing eviction with nowhere else to go, she whispered, 'These poor little flowers will be gone soon.'

    Ivy exited the arbor and went left where a mass of rose bushes flourished amid the long roll of vegetation. I walked out and went right, straight into the orchard. Once inside the shroud, the light dimmed. But under the guidance of a million slivers I could see a calculated design to the trees. In small sections, there were three to four grouped together...before a row of uncultivated land opened up...then crossed back into the next set of trees. Most were short: bushy dwarfs around 10 FT tall. I continued walking further in, looking for good fruit. I inspected several green apples by stretching 'em into a good sliver of light. I squeezed each one, and since all

---

[7] From Gustave Flaubert's novel *Madame Bovary* [I, vii]
[8] Forming a bower

were tender, probably not ripe, even though I didn't know much about farming, or even fruit-shopping. Not wanting to chance a sour bite, I turned around and went back to see if Ivy could assist me in finding edible apples before I poisoned myself or something...

'I wanna an apple. Find me a good one 'cause 'ose are all mushy.'

'Okay. But let's walk around first, then I'll show you *my* tree where all the *good* apples are.'

'*Your* tree? All the *good* apples?' I said with fake stupidity.

Locking hands again, Ivy and I began walking between the glowing verdancy of the vegetation and the apple trees. She was telling me how she knew Jack and Eleanor McArdle. When Ivy's parents were in their late 20s, they came across land for sale by The McArdles, who for whatever reason wanted to cut down on their property assets. Ivy's parents decided to acquire ten acres, nothing but woods and fields. They planned to build a big solitary house there, but when Ivy and Holly came along, the idea went into remission. Anyway, on the sale date, Jack had taken Edward, Sandy, and Little Ivy on a tour of his orchard. Ivy said that she begged Daddy to let her come here to play; and playing angel's advocate, Jack said that she certainly could, anytime she wanted to, and she didn't even have to ask! And so her and Daddy would frequent the orchard "just to play, take walks, eat apples, throw rocks into the creek." She went on to say that after getting her license she would go to the orchard alone whenever she needed to get away from everything. Being at the orchard alone, she claimed, was like no other experience. And besides her father, she'd never brought anyone else here, not even Teresa who wouldn't have been interested anyway.

After walking down the vertical span of the orchard, it opened into a field. It appeared uncultivated, undulating in small shadowy dells...til it reached a distant cliff, a wide mysterious plateau, which in some manner became the purple mountain seen from campus. Reeling the eyes back in a few miles, this new area of the orchard, the backside, was under the limelight of the moon. To our immediate left, the natural vegetation ended by running into the side of a large garden shed: blush with white trim and double doors, crowned with a solar lamp. To the right of the shed, incongruous trees separated the aforesaid field from the land *behind* the roll of vegetation. In this divisional plot, a cluster of magnolias were exfoliating yellow flowers: many withering on the ground like delicate little cradles.

Strolling along the horizontal backside of the orchard, we then passed, on our left, thorny honey locusts undergoing their seasonal change from mint-green to a yellow that buds flat fruit pods. Then—just before the field broke free—there stood two evenly planted rows of white pines with prominent banana-like cones. I went down, broke off a cone, then shot it up at Ivy—but missed. She grabbed a nearby apple and fired back—but missed, then re-fired. I intentionally stepped in the line-of-fire and let it smack off my leg. Uninjured, I ran back up and we continued walking between the field and the orchard...til coming upon another attraction off in the distance, out in the middle of the field: three weeping willows: still obscure from our vantage but easily distinguished by their moppish mammoth nature.

'Dozzer weepin' willows, huh?'

'Yep. My favorite tree.'

'Rilly? Mine too. Dere's a neighborhood near mine dit has some. I 'member goin' inside 'em when I's liddle 'n' thinkin' izza most amazin' thing ever. Wanna go dahn 'n' see 'em?'

'Sure.'

So we headed down into the dark bottomless field towards the trinity of weeping willows. They looked like apparitions of a godlike nature, ones with veiled secrets; so anxiousness to know what they were, I wanted to run down; yet it was impossible to let go of Ivy's hand—as impossible as growing roses with dandelion seeds! The only thing being let go, I realized, were past apprehensions; they skittered out into the ether like blown filaments of the dandy clock...

...As soon as we arrived at the willows, I picked the closest one, parted its sinewy leaves, then slipped inside. It was nearly pitch dark in the heart but still effloresced that surreal feeling of entering a new world, like stumbling into a child's fairytale through a painting chalked on the sidewalk. After a moment, Ivy followed with less enthusiasm but perhaps with more concentration.

'Where are you, Vinny?' she playfully called out.

I crept to the other side of tree and shook the flexible branches, one in each hand, like tolling swishy-sounding bells. *Swish, swash. Swish, swash.* Letting go, I slipped back outside, and, flitting, circled around the tree, following the same pattern of shake-and-move on the other side.

'Hey! Where'd ya go?!'

'*Oooveeer heeere!*' I yelled out in a slurry Mickey Mouse voice. From the right side, I slipped back inside and crouched down to minimize my shadow. Like a sylvan stalker, swiveling my head from side-to-side with a keen but nervous eye, I edged towards the trunk of the tree. Once there, I knelt down on one knee and tucked my elbows into my ribcage. Peaking around the trunk, I could see her out in front of me, her backside, standing perfectly still, trying to catch movements from me that weren't being made.

'Are you in here?' she asked with soft sincerity.

I didn't answer. I waited til she moved far enough towards the front of the tree so I could slip out the back. Once creeping around to the front—a thirty-second task of diligent stop-and-gos—I dropped to my knees and peaked underneath the limbs to see if I could determine her location. Ahh! Her shoes! Right in front of me! Busted! But either she didn't see me or she was just playing along. So I stood up and with both hands swung the curtain open like someone with the intent to expose two adulterous lovers showering together but only finding one.

'Ahh-HA!' I exclaimed. 'I knew you were hidin' in here!'

She came out and dove straight into my arms. I was knocked for six, seeing stars, imbued, as if by injection, with the good and woozy. Twined like two vines, I finally got to stroke—no, *thoroughly caress,* Ivy's ophidian mocha, and, ahh, how my hands turned to sand! as my internal language turned to turned to turned to turned to turned to...

'So I take it you really like the weepin' willows?'

'You know it, baby-loo. Goin' inside 'em is juss like I 'member.'

Untwined, I turned to look at the melancholic willow at the fore. Like the other two, it had about ten large fluffs of umbrellas dropping down in various degrees of protrusions and cascades; aggregately, an exotic triad of green waterfalls: *like flushing water...falling emotions, bedded in motion, deluging outward with perfect fluidity in imperfect repetition: green waterfalls, green sensations...it begins youthful, blind, vivacious, this growth aspiring for infinite fecundity...millions of infinitesimal parts consummated, made one and universal in the verdure far and wide...but what comes down must go up: into the airy nothingness, now ready to fly away like green stalks shooting into the solar plexus of the clouds...climb, climb, climb: the motions, the sensations, of liberation.*

'So you wanna go down to the crick and cove now?'

'Uhh, a *cove?'*

She tittered. 'Yeah, I dunno what else to call it. It's like a little bay before the crick heads out in the other direction. I've just always called it a cove since it cuts further into the land more than the main stream does.'

''Izz it got fish in it?' I asked with true stupidity.

'No, it's filled with hippos, silly.'

'Hey, how'm I sposta know?! Maybe it's manmade 'n' unstocked.'

'Nope. It's natural and has fish.'

'Well, umm, how 'boucha take me when it's light out so I can see da fish? I gadda sit dahn for a liddle anyway. Oh whaddabouchir tree? I wanna eat a *good* apple.'

'Okay. I guess since you're still bein' good I'll take you to *my* tree.'

In another hands-held amble, we headed up towards the orchard, talking about her knowledge of animals, which was very impressive. Of course, I asked for her Top Five Animals. With meditative pauses, she answered: 'Orcas. Koalas. Roo-roos. Bearcats. Sugar gliders.' Surprised to hear bearcats and sugar gliders, I complimented her on her worldly tastes and, like a kid, told her bearcats are neither bear nor cat but smell like popcorn! She laughed and stopped walking for a second to look right into my eyes as if amazed and curious how I knew all these things—but didn't dare to ask. Then she asked for my Top Five Animals. Because I was full of premeditated lists, I said without hesitation and in order: 'Squirrels, chipmunks, odders, raccoons, meerkats.' Ivy had tittered in harmony with my list. When I asked what was so funny, she said that it's just because all my animals are, of course, trouble-makers. When I told her about the time a raccoon seriously broke into my house and tried to rob me, fully masked and armed, that was even more to her delight.

Thanks to our mesmeric bantering, I was unaware that me and the sugar had glided clear into the hub of the orchard where all the other trees took a step back for *it*. Upon gaining cognizance of what stood before us, I too thought to take a respectful bow. Ivy's tree was the largest apple tree I'd ever seen! To take a good guess, twenty-five feet high, V-shaped, spread up-and-out like an albatross, branches raised in a boughs-in-the-air Baptist-hallelujah. From where we approached, we could walk straight under it, but on the other side thick twisty branches were dipping down to the ground. Even under the nighttime sky, the tree had such vigor, character, and predominance. It was a Red Delicious in bloom. Circling around the tree, just out of the reach of the branches, were ten or so river rocks large enough to sit on. Each one had vines wrapped around it. I had no idea what they were about but I was about to ask.

'What's with 'eez rocks? Why's 'ere vines tied around 'em?'

'Those are my magic rocks.' she laughed. 'You really wanna know why they're here?'

'For sure. 'N' I wanna know why they're "magic."'

'Well you're gonna think I'm crazy, but when I was little, me and Daddy were here one day, and I wanted to decorate this tree because I claimed this one as *mine*. So I made him carry up rocks from the crick—' (I laughed) '—Yeah, I know, I told you you're gonna think I'm crazy. Anyway, weeks later we came back and they were gone. Jack was workin' in the garden that day, so I went up to him, cryin', told him someone stole my rocks. He said swore it was probably some of the kids that live in the neighborhood up the road, takin' 'em somewhere else and makin' their own little fort with *my* rocks. So I was seriously, like, crushed seein' my fort destroyed. I cried and told Daddy to go get more rocks and figure out a way they won't get stolen anymore. So he hauled up the new rocks, which were much bigger than the old ones. Then he went over to the arbor and pulled out long strands of vines. Then we tied the vines around each rock and planted the ends in the ground. He told me the vines would grow into the ground and protect the rocks from bein' stolen again. Like a ball-and-chain deal. And guess what? These are the same rocks. And, jeez, that was probably ten years ago!'

'You bein' seris?'

'Yes. Why?'

''At's sercly the weirdest fuckin' story I ever heard. But what's 'iss?' I scuffed my shoe at a hole underneath the tree about two-feet deep.

'Oh that! Now you're *really* gonna think I'm crazy. *That*,' she pointed at it, 'is the apple cubbyhole.'

'Da what?'

'The apple cubbyhole. I dug it myself a long time ago, and whenever I eat an apple, I throw the cores in it. It's like a natural garbage can.'

'Okay. Maybe yir right: you rilly *are* crazy.'

'See, I told you.'

'Should I even truscha da lemme know if 'eez apples are ripe?'

'Taste one and find out yourself.'

'I don't wanna get worms.'

'You don't know much about the country, huh?'

'I know enough not da go bitin' inda things. Why dohn*chu* try it?'

'Fine, I will chicken!' She grabbed an apple with an impulsive but professional pluck as if she didn't need to inspect it first; she just intuitively knew which ones would be good. She polished it off on her jeans before taking a crunchy bite.

'Here, this one's good.'

I took it from her then took a cowardly bite. A little sour but juicy. I didn't want anymore. I'd actually been exaggerating about wanting to eat an apple. Just an empty ploy with no real meaning besides pretending to want something I didn't, like personality quirk. I asked if she wanted anymore or could I dispose of it in the apple cubbyhole. She said that I wasn't allowed to put it in the cubbyhole. With false fervor, I asked why not. She said (in what seemed to be a joking manner) that it would disturb the order of the orchard. So I hurried up and threw the twice-bitten apple down into the cubbyhole, and, in the process, she came at me trying to stop me, grabbing my wrists, her ophidian mocha swinging into my face. Trying to prevent her from taking the apple out of the apple cubbyhole, I bear-hugged her, lifted her from the ground—she let out a girly squeal!—then I moved her yards away, setting her down with virile, alpha-male power; huffing, she was winded, squirming with laughter.

'You jerk!'

'Ut-oh! The orchard's gonna be unner a spell now!'

'Probably will!' She marched over to the apple cubbyhole...retrieved the twice-bitten apple from the two-foot depths of her occulted fortification...then fired the apple off into the distant galaxy. 'There! What do you think about *that?'*

'Yeah? Well wha' wouja think abouchir liddle precious vine-tied rocks disappearin' again. 'Cause—'

She quickly came at me, poking, pinching, grabbing. 'Oh, if you even *think* about touching my magic rocks, mister—'

Suddenly I tripped backwards on an invisible root. As I was falling, I reached out and grabbed her hand, making sure with a careful precision to have her tumble on top of me. When she came flying back with me, and my back hit the ground painlessly, and she hit into my chest, in that decisive moment, with my mouth gaped, a lock of her hair slid into my mouth, and I slipped out of my mind:

'POWER UP!!!'

With her hands braced behind my head, her face lit up like a Christmas tree. Her hair was swaying down in my face, and I was still trying to chew on it.

'What was *that?!'*

'Wha' was wha'?'

'That noise you just made!'

'I dunno whachir talkin' about.'

'Yes you do! Now do it again!' From her spacey smile and elliptical green eyes, amazement and anticipation beamed down on me. So without hesitation I grabbed a thick lock of her hair and stuck it in my mouth. I began nibbling on it and was about to— 'Whaddaya think you're doin'?!'

With her hair in my mouth, I said, 'Well if ya want meedda do the voice again, I gadda chew on yir hair. Dat's how the voice gets the power da make the noise.'

Adjusting her hips to get into a more comfortable position, she made a subtle movement which caused too much of her hair to fall in front of her face, so I parted the snaking waves back, again letting her emeralds shine down on me, while her crescent-moon eyelashes warmly lulled my insides with each coquettish blink. Meanwhile, she was doing a bad job of maintaining a dubious squint...til she finally said, 'Go ahead if that's how it *really* works.'

Giving it all I had, I sucked in the cool salubrious air, along with the flowered-and-honey aroma of her skin, while chattering my teeth all over her silky wet hair...til the threshold of energy was ready to explode and sustain itself in the orchard like a natural amphitheater. So thunderously, so melodically, I echoed out the dynamic sound: *'POWER UP!!!'* And, wow, how it echoed out into the entrails of Night...and never faded...neither did the taste in my mouth. Pleased, she giggled, then comfortably rested her head down in the dale of my chest. We were just barely under the branches. Up and out beyond us was the opaline moon and the millions of scintillating stars in the rich cobalt-blue sky—but nothing seemed far beyond the reach of the starving imagination. We were looking up together, smitten with wonderment, while breathing in harmony with the ornery cricket chirps and the distant frog gulps and the drone of the fluorescent insects and the poetic glow of the verdancy and the historical peace of the trees and the *POWER UP!!!* that never faded.

'Hey.'

'Yes?'

I took a moment to catch my heart. 'So make up an "Ivian Philosophy" for me.'

She mused for a moment, then replied, 'To love and be loved in return. And to feel with my heart, think with my mind, and open my eyes to whatever I may find.'

I smiled with my cheeks. She snuggled deeper within the dale of my chest. And thus we lay, her head on my chest, my arms around her body, watching the sky watch us forever...

(If that forever was broken, it was with language...sometime later.)

'...So you definitely wanna be a veterinarian?'

'Yep. And I wanna work with exotic animals.'

'Nice. If I had da pick a "normal" job, I think 'at's what I'd do too. Animals are so amazin'. Speakin' of which: wanna know sum'n about me dit might make ya think *I'm* crazy?'

'Of course. We need to be on level ground here.'

'*Umm*. Well I sercly—'n' I mean *literally*—wanna be a squirrel.'

She briefly rose up from my chest to give me a quizzical look—then nestled back down. 'That doesn't really surprise me now that I'm gettin' to know you better. But why a squirrel?'

'Not rilly sure,' I exhaled. 'I juss love 'er tails. 'N' the way they eat. 'N' the way they play 'n' run around. I guess 'ey 'mind me of innocence, know whadda mean.'

'Yeah. Sometimes I wonder what it would be like to be an animal. Like, I know everyone says it, but that feeling of freedom if you were a bird soarin' through the air. Just bein' so far away from all the sad things in the world.'

'Yeah, but even birds gadda land sometimes. When it comes dahn do it, nuh'n, in the physical sense, can get away except through death.'

'What about all the things in the ocean?'

'I'd say good point if it wasn't for natural predators, which everything has, then of course unnatural oil spills, harpoons, nets, hooks—nuclear fuel rods. 'N' I'm sure as technology advances, humans'll find more extensive ways da exploit water, land, 'n' space—ya know, juss anything da keep pushin' outwards since we're destroyin' everything at ground-zero. Oh man,' I suddenly laughed, 'I'm startin'ah sound like a fuckin' hippie!'

'No, I think it's great you think about stuff like that. Most people don't because if it's good for 'em right now then they could care less.'

'True, but...'

'But what?'

'I dunno; juss loss my train of thought...So tell me more about you growin' up. With all yir orchard games, 'n' knowin' wise old men in the country, makes me think ya had some Huck Finn-Tom Sawyer adventures growin' up. Me 'n' Pessi were like da urban version of Huck 'n' Tom—'

'Yeah, that's just it: I didn't have a Pessi growin' up. Teresa grew boobs and an attitude at too young an age. She really should've grown up in the city; she was just always so out of place around here. But with her mom and all, and her dad always bein' away, I kinda understand. And my parents aren't even country like you might think.'

'Whaddaya mean?'

'They're just your typical middle-class—'

'You mean *upper*-middle class? I saw yir house.'

'Maybe. Do middle-class families go on vacation every year?'

'Depends. Where've you gone?'

'Well last year we went to San Diego. The year before, Madrid—'

'Yeah, middle-class people aren't takin' vacations like *that*. But, hey, 'at's awesome you gah ta go. I betcha have some priddy amazin' memories.'

'*Mmm,* I guess. But for me, it got to the point where I became spiteful of it. See, my dad worked so much durin' the week, so when the weekend came he'd overdo it; he desperately wanted to have money *and* a close family. And my mom, she'd say, "Iv, I know you wanna stay over Casey's this weekend but your father wants us all to go to the park. You can do stuff on the weekdays." But during the weekdays, she'd always be like, "Come on, Iv, let's go shopping! let's go to the spa! let's go out to eat!" or she'd tell me I couldn't go anywhere because I had homework. Then when I got old enough—I know you probably don't want to hear this—but whenever I had crushes, I really couldn't do anything about it because my dad said I wasn't allowed to date until I left the house, which is just overdoin' it. But now do you see the situation I was in? why I didn't care about all the vacations? And why I never had any Huck Finn-Tom Sawyer adventures besides my dad bringin' me here when I was little before I was of any material use to my mom?'

'Yeah. Wow. So would you say yir parents forced ya da godda cawidge?'

'I wouldn't say *forced*, but I bet if I hadn't, they would've been really disappointed since they both went to college, and notable ones at that. Why, did your parents *force* you to go to college?'

She shifted over on her right side, more inward towards me sprawled on my back. Her head inched towards my shoulder. Together, we began twirling around locks of her hair over top my chest.

'Yeah my parents *threatened* me if I didn't go 'cause 'ey were so fed up with me.'

'Really?'

I vaddled.[9] 'Nah. I kinda decided da godda cawidge on my own. See, neither of my parents went da cawidge. Nunna my close friends have

---

[9] [neologism] A type of laughter in which the mouth remains shut and vibrations from the throat exit the nose; usually a short "smirky" laugh

gone da cawidge. 'N' for rill, I'm prahblee wunna the few from my neighborhood da ever godda cawidge.'

'Why, what's wrong with your neighborhood?'

'You ever been da my neighborhood?' I said half-rhetorically.

'Nope. I've only been to Pittsburgh a few times. How far do you live from that house we were at?'

'A few miles,' I replied, unconcerned with elaboration; a large insect with a fluorescent purple belly was distracting me. It was buzzing loudly—flying around chaotically in front of the moon, with pestiferous intentions in its movements. I was intensely keeping my eyes on it because I was worried that it was poisonous and might swoop down and bite me. I'd never seen anything like it so I wasn't sure what to do. Once it flew out of sight, I returned to what we were talking about and suddenly realized we were edging into a conversation about my past: things I didn't want to think about, or share, or scratch the surface any further than I already had. Like, 'Hi. I'm V from Verna; juss southeast of Pixburgh. Got two parents. Dad's an O.G. still miller. Mum's a young chill Sicilian. I'm a lonely only child.' (Of course omitting the story about my half-brother, Gennaro.) And just leave it at that. But I realized at some point those pathetic excuses for a personal history wouldn't suffice. It's just that I was worried about showing her Past Me, especially when *I* hated to see Past Me and didn't overstand Past Me yet. But again, since I had to st̶a̶r̶t *somewhere,* I mustered up some courage with a deep breath, preparing myself to set a few basic things straight, and *then* see if umbel Ivy the resinous Pine would stick da me and our blossoming relationship.

'Ivy, I feel I should letcha know sum'n about me,' I began boldly but already feeling abashed and lowly, as if calling out for sympathetic attention I didn't want. 'See, the neighborhood you were in, 'n' even the ones we crossed through when we walked dahn da the bus stop, are nuh'n like where I'm from. I'm not rich at all. I'm a straight-up lower-class rat.'

'HA! So what? Do you actually think I'm *that* kinda person?'

'No, not at all. But I dunno; it's juss a tough thing da explain 'cause people tend da think yir wantin' some kinda praise or respect or sympathy or special attention for it.'

'Well how about I give you none of that? Ya know, Mr. Vincent—what's your middle name?'

'I akshly have *two* middle names...'

'Okay? So what they are?'

'Don't laugh buh da name on my birth certificate is—Vincent Ignazio Scandurra Vallano. Ignazio Scandurra is my grandpap's name on my mum's side. 'N' Vincent Vallano is my grandpap's name on my dad's side.'

She giggled. 'Okay, Mr. Vincent Ignazio Scandurra Vallano: I'm nothin' like that. Just because my family has money doesn't mean it's somethin' I go after or care about.'

'I know. I'm sorry. It's not dit I pre-judged you or anything; it's juss thit growin' up I was involved in alwada violence, crime, 'n' at times, poverty. Wasn't always priddy, da be honest.'

'Well you already told me you used to get into fights, and that's all right: lots of teenage boys get into fights; plus you're not in that situation anymore anyway. As for the poverty: there was nothin' you could do about that, and if you made it this far then that only shows how strong you must be. As for the crime part: you said you'd stolen stuff before and did drugs. Any *other* criminal activities you care to share with me?'

Like a swift checkmate, she put me right in my place with her impeccable memory and judicious rationalizations! Which was fine and all, but I could never explain in words what all that truly encompassed and the inner impact it had. She could never truly relate to it no matter how badly she wanted to overstand because she genuinely cared to overstand. Yet I must admit: no one could've handled it better than she had. She and her palliative retort just kinda made me laugh at myself and my whymeness.

Anyway, "yes" was my answer to having committed other criminal activities.

'We're not talkin' about anything serious, are we?' She lifted her head up a bit and looked over at me with a prayerlike, anxious, all-money-riding-on-one-hand face.

'Yeah, I'm afraid so. Like *rill* seris.' I felt the goose bumps rise up on her skin; my left hand was casually up under the back of her shirt. 'Well, izz when I's fifteen, sixteen, a liddle when I was seventeen.' (A deep breath.) "N' I've never told dis da anyone besides Pessi 'cause he helped me sometimes. But I, uhh, I yoosta do—contract murders. But don't worry: ever since I got accepted at Aristod, I've quit doin' 'em 'n' demoted myself da simple muggings 'n' grand theft auto.' Ahhh! A busted bluff right from the start! The half a man in the moon fully illuminated my pokerface, causing me to smile! So Ivy's all-in wager paid off, and she knew it: she let it show in the collective glow in her protrusive nubile lips...her tight pearly teeth...those long slender cheeks...that tiny bubbled nose...those large glittery emeralds...those long crescent eyelashes *(blinkity-blink-blink)*...and of course her ophidian mocha, which, after my false confession, had slipped back into my mouth like I was stealing candy, and no matter what mommy said about it, I was neither returning it, paying for it, nor apologizing for it.

'I see, I see. So thankfully I'm not gonna *die* tonight since that's old business, but I might be losin' my necklace and purse. And whenever you get the chance, my car—Mr. G-T-A.'

'Exactly.'

'Well—I think I can deal with that. But sorry, you're not gonna be risin' outta poverty tonight because I only have about twenty bucks on me.'

'Every penny helps, hun.' Just then, the wind kicked up a refreshing gust of air, causing her sinuous waves to dance over her face. I instantly lost sight of the eyes I'd been locked into from the side. She was about to pull the hair away, so without thinking about it, I turned a bit on my side and quickly pushed the hair to the side for her...but kept a lock grasped in my hand...tucking it behind her ear...wrapping it around her earlobe...giving it a little tug towards me, very tentatively, inch by inch by inch. Our eyes were now locked again. And so were our smiles.

'*Hmmm*. Well, Vincent – Ignazio – Scandurra – Vallano...' she began in a measured whisper. The breaths in her chest were deep and rhythmic, with the ebb of her breath in favor of asceticism, the flow for liberation, as if contemplating and struggling with the most important spiritual decision she would ever have to make. '...How about—' She paused again to take the final breath of sanction, followed by a tender gulp. 'How about since you've been very, very good tonight, *like I asked*—and honestly more than I expected—how about I give you somethin' worth a lot more than any amount of money in the world? somethin' you don't need to steal either because it's free?'

Suddenly, I could feel our hearts racing—our arms and legs shaking a bit—my teeth quietly chattering like a squirrel on the nut—a thick plum warmth running through my veins: everything overtaken by so much lack of language that language itself was falling into *ignotum per ignotius* then tumbling over and falling even deeper into AHHHHH!

'Wh(a)—' was all I could emit from my parched throat.

'*This...*' was all she needed to say.

...To exaggerate in words but not in sensations: in the hub of the cool orchard, I fell in to a burning ring of fire! I went down, down, down—but the flames went higher! No, seriously! The sudor from the verdure! the ashes from the trees! the embers from the stars! were coming down and rising up! bi-bi-bi-billowing out like massive waves in an ocean! twi-twi-twi-twining like pipefish! but unlike ocean emotion, it was all just so incendiary! phenomenal explosions of heat! an intense, esculent, powering-up feast of ophidian mocha delight! With the sky hanging over us like a snug blanket—then rolling up—and the great apple tree swallowing us alive—then rolling around—and Time turning itself over—then rolling away—there was just no doubt whatsoever in my heart, my mind, my eyes—in my everything and all!—that the present beatification ran far deeper, and more natural, than human libido...

S( )NDOWN

"Another day, another dollar, another bill-collecting caller,
Disillusioned, let down, all my heroes are junkies now,
I've been down this road, in the end it's all the same,
Another day I'm getting older, another day nothing's changed,
I've been down this road, I'm wrong when I know I'm right,
Hard pressed to make it better, but I've got no will to fight... " [1]

...The following night my leg got into a fight and got itself broken. I couldn't overstand why my leg would ever do such a thing, but it did, then refused to apologize for it. No surprise that Al Cohall had provoked things, and since I couldn't remember the particulars of the incident and take the blame myself, my leg was unquestionably at fault. After waking up Sunday in a hospital bed—visibly startled for several minutes—I was having trouble deciding whether to feel hungover from the booze, sedated from the meds, or pain from the black stirrup boot inserted on my lower left leg: mid-calf to foot. When the doctor came in she began informing me that an unidentified witness alleged that last night, at approximately 1:45 a.m., at Squirrel Terrance, an apartment complex on Wapiti Street, I'd been drinking with a horde of Scholars up on the roof. This unidentified witness also alleged that, for no apparent reason, I screamed, 'Fuck all yinz stupid motherfuckers!' staggered downstairs, then (with the roofers watching from above) fell off the side of the front patio, at which point my swaggering leg got into a fight with the ground and the ground shattered my leg's lateral malleolus. Well, not so much shatter as what the doctor called it: a first-degree external rotation. She said that once the swelling goes down, I'm to come back for a boot-cast: a fortunate option since it was only a spiral fracture and my Achilles tendon had remained intact. In the meantime, she advised me to walk sparingly and with aid of the crutches. 'Even after we put the boot-cast on, you need to make a serious effort to stay on your back for the next month.' 'A month!' I griped as if too ungrateful and stubborn to realize that it could've been much worse. Still, staying on my back for a month! More like being on my knees for a month! But to help reconcile the enmity between me and my leg, the doctor told me that there would be no legal implications, seeing as Al Cohall had been there. She then gave me a two-month prescription for painkillers. That's why, after taking a taxi back to my dorm, I lay conked out all day Sunday except when I woke up to take more medication, during which time I explained to Luke that I'd twisted my ankle coming down the steps. Shining his chubby artless face, he expressed his sympathies, adding in that my phone had been ringing off and on all day. I figured it was Ma since the hospital had called to inform her of the situation. So I called to inform her that I was all right but couldn't keep my eyes opened, thereby hanging up and falling back asleep til Monday morning...

---

[1] Lyrics from "Down This Road" by Zero Down, from the album *Fat Music Vol. V: Live Fat, Die Young*

...Monday morning I began trying to piece it all together. I could remember walking to the store to get sunflower seeds. Then taking a different route on the way back and coming upon Squirrel Terrace: the name of the apartment had caught my attention. Perhaps I'd been hoping squirrel enthusiasts or even real squirrels lived there? Yet for the life of me I couldn't figure out who actually invited me up, if anyone even had, and how social or unsocial I was being once I got drunk. I mean, the witness said that I screamed: 'Fuck all yinz stupid motherfuckers!' Yet I could only remember walking around on a pebbled roof...drinking from a yellow plastic cup...loud horrible music...a group of frat-like kids cooking kielbasa and hamburgers on a grill. I began wondering if maybe Andrea and I—but realized that couldn't have been the case because I wasn't with her prior, and if something *had* occurred between us, *by chance*, she would've been at the hospital, or at least stopped over since. Besides, I had no conscious desire to be with her anymore after Friday night: and that's the truth insofar as the consciousness tends to be truthful at times. So, yeah, it seemed I would never know how the fateful night transpired! But since the end-result is what I was actually stuck dealing with, it hardly mattered anyway.

Anyway, the day only became more frustrating when a lady from the hospital called to inform me that my health coverage was no longer valid. With the ghetto insurance company closed for the weekend, I must've tried to foot those busy hospital workers with an insurance card I could've sworn was valid. Must've! The hospital wasn't too concerned however; she said that I could call the insurance company, work it out, then report back to her with an updated policy number, which again the hospital would have to verify, and would have to predate the injury, or else I would be left ankling the entire bill myself. Still trying to foot the hospital—well, now I had a feeling that I was only footing myself—I told her that *this* was impossible, that my father had *just* been laid off, so I *have to* be covered through the current cycle printed right there on the card. Right? Hello? Right?—Nothing like talking to deaf ears! Accommodating the lady's handicap, I yelled, 'Yeah I'll caw ya back!—Ar'ight!' *Click!* Right away, I called Ma to find out why I didn't have insurance. She was also perplexed, saying that, yes, I should still have health insurance til the end of the current cycle when my coverage, she claimed, would transfer over to a subordinate policy for "unemployed fulltime workers." Her foreign rambling over domestic matters—her pathetic ignorance that I'd grown so sick of—only provoked me into chiding and questioning *her* for the green swamp that I was slipping into. I explained how wonderful it would be if the bill wasn't covered somehow because then all the money I'd received from school loans would be gone in a flash, or at least gone in monthly payments. Then how would I make it through?! (Of course I could get a job.) But still, how would I make it through?! She was about to resort to telephone-tears, which I couldn't handle, so I asked if Rick was home. She said yes. I told her to put him on. He was sober. Again, he was so-ber; no-beer.

'Yeah?'

'We got health insurance or not?'

'Nope.'

'Wha'? Why?'

"Cause I cancelled it a few months back. Da card's dead.'

'Dat's such bullshit. You gadda have health insurance for jobs like yirs.'

'Yeah, it's cawed workmen's comp. Family 'n' life insurance was my choice da have or not.'

'Well why wouju even cancel it?'

''Cause I been tight on money 'n' we never use it. The shit ain't cheap, ya know.'

I could only laugh, not out of comedy or rage or his stupidity—it wasn't even done out of stupidity!—but from a conscious effort to revive his draconian spirit as a little reminder of his great powers which were nowhere close to great; I was almost certain of it. 'Okay, Rick,' I shifted into a cool tone, trying so hard to selfishly push out of my head the thought of Razzle being crushed into the earth. 'I'm at cawidge now, dahn here in Maryland. It's almost thirty-thousand a year. But, hey, I gadda liddle scholarship da help me. 'N' I'm gih'n a job soon. But I still been left da take care a everything else *by myself.* 'N' 'iss was juss an unfortunate accident dit's gonna set me back a good bit if I gadda deal with *this* by myself too. 'N' whether or not ya believe me, dis ain't a fuckin' playground dahn here. It's a tough, challenging school where I'd *like* da not worry about workin'—'n' not oudda laziness, but because I wanna concentrate on my schoolwork so iddle pay off in'ah long run when the job I get in the future'll be a lot more valuable den "bein' responsible" now 'n' workin' 'at "liddle part-time job" da help me through cawidge.'

'Yeah, that sounds like you: wantin' sum'n for nuh'n.'

'Ya know, Rick—*Dad*—I've never asscue for much. 'N' I know we don't rilly get along. But all I'm askin' is for you da send me a liddle money every month so I can get by. I'll keep track a every penny, 'n' whenever I gidda rill job in a few years, I'll pay ya back 'n' 'en some. Ar'ight?...Hello?'

'I ain't got much comin' in, 'n' I still got da *saaame* bills da pay 'n' da *saaame* table da put food on for me 'n' yir—'

'So is 'at a no?' I interjected viciously, as Razzle started barking vociferously in my head.

'Look,' he yawned, 'all da money's gone from the unemployment check. I'll getchir mudder da senja sum next check.'

'Like how much?'

''*Eeeere's* yir mudder.'

'See, Vinny, we-ah send you money next—'

Click!

Ring! Ring! Ring!

'Yeah?'

'What's up, bitch?'

'Well if it ain't da liddle book-fucker. What's up?'

'Saturday night I broke my ankle all drunk: 'at's what's up.'

Pessi vaddled. 'Oh yeah? 'N' how dat happen?'

'Me 'n' Teresa bawda Karma Sutra book 'n' I insisted on perfectin' da Rusty Bike Pump.'

'Cool. So you takin' a fuckin' comedy class dahn 'ere or sum'n?'

'No, akshly after I fucked her I fell off da steps at some apartment. Only like a five-foot fall but enough da put me in a boot-cast for a month. Got me all fucked up on painkillers too.'

'Thoucha don't eat pills.'

'Yeah, not da get fucked up. Buh dis is for medicinal purposes.'

'Right. You'll be tryin'ah forge prescriptions after yir out. It's easy too if ya gadda boner-fide injury. Juss tell 'em yir pussy's still hurtin'. 'N' if ya don't wan' 'em, den I'll buy 'em from ya. I'm seris.'

'I dunno; we'll see. But guess whad else happened?'

'Wha'?'

'Me 'n' Ivy whistled Friday night.' (I blew out a two-noted whistle.)

'Yeah right, you fuckin' liar.'

"'I *lie 'er* down 'n' fuck her, boy,' I replied in a mock redneck voice.

'*Suuuure*—' (*cough*cough*) "—What, you been hangin' with her or sum'n?'

'Firss time we went out. But looks like 'ere's more da come.'

'I'll ask Teresa abouddit 'cause I think yir lyin'.'

'No, don't go sayin' anything da Teresa 'cause she'll run da Ivy 'n' fuck everything up. I know how she is. She'll say I tolja I *fucked* Ivy 'n' was braggin' abouddit. 'N' Ivy's a rill sensitive girl, ya know. Dat kinda thing would rilly hurt her. Like you said about Teresa: "*I think I akshly like her.*"'

'I dunno, V; I think 'ose painkillers are goin' straight da yir head. But look, I gadda run 'n' meet my boy. But guess rill quick what's happenin' on *my* end?'

'You came oudda the closet?'

'That, 'n' I decided I'm gonna move in with Teresa. She's usin' her uncle's truck da come get me 'n' we're gonna haul all my shit dahn 'ere next weekend—'

'HA! Who's the liar now?!'

'Yeah, well juss keep 'at fuckin' leg covered up 'cause when I come over da visit I'm takin' a fuckin' hammer to it, you book-fuckin' pussy.' *Click.*

Ring! Ring! Ring!

'Hello?'

'Hi. Is this Ms. Ivy Pineda?'

'Well if it isn't Mr. Vincent Ignazio Scandurra Vallano. Nice of you to call me.'

"Fore ya go gih'n all mad, I wancha da come over.'

'Why? Is there somethin' wrong?'

'Juss come over 'n' you'll see.'

'Well, I'm in the middle of paintin' my nails but I'll come right now if it's an emergency—'

'No, it's not an emergency. Juss come over when yir done. Ar'ight?'

'Okay. I guess I'll see ya soon then?'

'That's what I was shootin' for. Ciao, bella rosa.'

'Ciao, yellow bello.'

Click.

Ahh! How could this chick be as quick-with-it as me?! That's what I was thinking as I took down a double dose of medication along with a small snort of snow, which I'd purchased from Mike (Andrea's connection and my new collegial connection). I sprawled out on my bed, reading my favorite passage in *Animal Farm* for fun. I hadn't the desire to do schoolwork or attend class, and now I had a bona-frag excuse not to for a couple days. Luke, though, *was* at class. Poor Luke—each passing day his disposition towards me became more introverted: a result brought forth by my own introversion; in other words, he had no choice but to mirror my wall.

I stuck the little blue book closer to my face. The words were moving around in a slow pleasing eddy, inexplicably soothing my nausea...but suddenly everything burst into gut-wrenching anarchy! animalistic chaos running around like a menagerie of typography let loose! thousands of black words jumping off the page like frightened sheep lolloping over the fence! I couldn't regain focus! I couldn't—*no, fuck countin' sheep: I'm not a sheep, I'm a squirrel: hmhmhmhmhm!.........what's he lookin' at?: still tryin'ah knock: still strugglin'ah turn further towards me: his cheeks look like melted wax or wrinkled tattoos: a face showin' the consequences of frozen adversity: I wonder how long he traveled before reachin' 'at door?: like all wanderers he juss wants in...that unabashed desperation dit makes wanderers yearn for a door-opener, juss one greeter, one taker, in an attempt da assuage the tempestuous storm of pain found in the cold dew of words in the internal book?: one which can't be read by one's self, no less by another...it's funny how once we realize our shortcomings we always turn ta da next hopin' dill be the decipherer of our soul!: anything da not be an unequivocal nothingness!: maybe he'd been thinkin' if he coulda knocked once more it woulda been the one heard 'n' answered: in more ways den one!: yet all's frozen precisely at the moment when the paint spread across da canvas: colorin' over the phantasmal hope an everlasting despondency 'n' emptiness: but since he has nuh'n but time why quit—*
Knock! Knock! Knock!

The rapping on the door broke me from my esoteric and (more precisely) maudlin thoughts, given that I was buzzing, and they, the thoughts, had streamed swiftly with poetry that had already been, so to speak, written inside my mind. I was spread out on the bed like a cheap harlot, with watery eyes, a sniffy nose, and a twitchy jaw. But I was sober enough to converse with Ivy without her knowing. I'd always been able to handle and hide a buzz. Besides, the snow turns cold pretty quick.
Knock! Knock! Knock!

I hurried to cover my leg with the ol' fuzzy lion blanket. 'You may enteeeeer!'

At first, she paaaaartially entered, acrobatically bending around the door, secretly peaking in. When I looked back behind me and smiled—(her ophidian mocha dropping down like a chocolate weeping willow)—she turned her face away in diffidence. 'Don't be skurr'd,' I said in jest. Like a little kid being called upon to recite holiday poetry in front of everyone's mother, she timidly walked into the middle of the room.

Blushing: 'So what is it? What did you want to show me?'

'Dis...' Lying on my right side, I extended my left arm out to her like a crane, drawing her directly down to me. I was quick to give her a somersaulting-tongue kiss while stroking her glabrous cheek with my right hand and my lefthand fingers drawing tickle-hearts all over her lubricous limbs, also making sure to work into my mouth the tip of an epicurean lock (lick-lick the licorice!) before she withdrew. Downwardly, the squint-eyed angel angled an unconvinced, lippy smile. I resorted to fashioning funny faces for her...til her smile broadened with pearly assurances. Subtly—so slooooowly (as if she didn't want me to hear her air), she let out a breath that seemed to be of spiritual relief.

'So now ya wanna know why I haven't caw ju?'

'Of course. I just figured I got dealt the dumb-slut card and had to deal with it.'

Like giving her a licentious peak at something she shouldn't be seeing, I flipped up the blanket—flashed the black stirrup boot—then covered it back up.

'Oh my God!' she fretted, not hesitating to remove the blanket completely. 'What happened?!' She sat down on the bed with her ass my way. She was wearing a preppy pink hoodie with stonewashed jeans rolled up three inches from the ankle in one flap. Therapeutically, she combed her genteel hands over the boot. I could feel her thaumaturgic bestowal of euphoria and resurrection pervading the plastic filaments of the orthotic barrier and down into my deeper fibers. *Mmmmm!* But this inexplicable feeling might've been the meds: strangely, they were beginning to stimulate my nerves more than I'd expected.

'I'm ar'ight,' I muttered, with heavy blinks and facial tics to her pink-clad back. 'See, Saturday evenin', I's visitin' a friend 'n' on my way back dahn'ah steps, I twisted my ankle. It's a first-degree external rotation injury. A spiral fracture. I's plannin' on cawin' ya when I gahta the room. 'N' 'en I wanted da caw ya at da hospital but dey had me knocked out on 'eez meds, 'n' 'ey made me stay overnight. Prahblee juss wanted da run up my bill. Ended up sleepin' all day yesterday. I'm sorry, bella-loo.'

'No need to apologize,' she said distantly, turning around in slow motion. 'How long did they say it'll take to heal?'

A pause. 'Ehh, a month or so.'

She was vanishing. 'Well that's not too bad, I guess. Would you like me to help you to claaaaaasssssss ooooor geeeeet youuuu anythiiiiing frooooom theeeee stoooooore? IIIII dddooooonnnnn't mmmiiiiii—'

All of a sudden my eyelids began fluttering as the medicine collided with the snow, antagonistically swooping through the ducts in my brain, tingling and pinching my senses simultaneously. Trying to stay conscious, I focused on Ivy's effervescent eyes. The greenness was good! better! best! to the point of being unparallel, I thought, not able to think much else...good! better! best! good! better! best! good! better! best!...til the room, swirling around in a cyclone of static haziness, finally took a stronghold on my mind, and becoming ever so nauseous and dizzy, I passed out...

...(*All around me an abyss of whiteness is pulsating like a throbbing heart. A young girl in a yellow dress approaches. Her glittery black hair is hanging down to her tiny waist. Her eyes look like her hair: black and glittery. There's a pink daisy tucked behind her left ear. She's barefoot. She comes very close to me.) Hey, are you going to do it? – Do wha'? Why you talkin' like a bird? – Because I want to fly. – Where to? – Heaven. Hey, will you kiss me again? – Again? – Yes, again. (Suddenly, off in the distance a silhouette appears behind the little girl.) So will you kiss me? – No. Whachir name? – Angel Beautiful. – You mean Beautiful Angel? – I think I know my own name! Now kiss me so I can take you to him! – You mean take meedda that shadow over dere? – Tell her to quit screaming and leave us alone! – Who? Who's screamin'? – Look, my breasts are crying too. Like yours inside. – Yir not makin' any sense. (Instantly, her dress disappears. She grabs my hands and cups them over her prepubescent breasts. So soft. They begin crying on my naked legs. Melancholic whimpers are vibrating from her mouth. Her eyes are bleeding. With one hand crossed over mine so as to hold them against her breasts, she takes her other hand and grabs my dick. She continues to whimper and bleed from the eyes.) What's wrong, Angel Beautiful? Please tell me. I'm gonna start cryin' too. – (Whimpering and bleeding, she takes hold of my right hand, and leads me towards the shadow...but before we get there our steps keep repeating and repeating, going nowhere, still holding hands, repeating and repeating. Suddenly, everything pauses and the shrill clangorous sound of an injured bird rings through my head. But I can still feel her hands. Everything begins fading to gray. The sound of a piano begins playing mockingly. A monstrous deluge of guilt is flooding through my body as if that is all that fills my streams: guilt flowing through guiltstreams. I feel really sheepish and the desire to)— Vvvvviiiiiinnnnnnyyyyy—Vvvviiiinnnnyyyy—Vvviiinnnyyy—Vviinnyy—Vinny!'*

Ivy continued screaming my name like a clarion call to the World. She was violently shaking me by the shoulders.

'Ar'ight! Quit yellin'!' A hardcore tetchiness was pricking my bones. 'You hear 'em? They here?'

'Is who here?' she asked, baffled, looking down at me. 'No one's here besides you and me. God,' she gasped, 'you just scared me so bad.' She put her hand over her heart in an effort to calm herself. 'You were passed out for like thirty seconds. I dumped the rest of your bottled water on you but it didn't do anything. I was about to call for help.' She kept her hand over her heart, recuperating.

I felt disgusted with myself for yelling at her—so bothered by the possibility that the drugs were being disagreeable due to some unforeseen anomaly. Looking down on myself halfheartedly, I pealed the sopping shirt from my chest. I clenched the shirt, yawned, and in the process, foolishly squeezed more water out on my bed, but it was all wet anyway.

'Sorry for gettin' you and your bed all wet.' She hung her head down forlornly as if I could never know the real sensitiveness within her.

'No nee'dda be sorry. You did whacha had da do. Besides, it's juss wudder.'

'Are you seriously all right? Do you want me to get you anything?'

'No, I'm fine. It's juss 'eez painkillers I'm on. I think 'ey gave me too strong a prescription so the pharmacy could charge me more money.' I slowly rose up from the bed. Although she moved out of the way, Ivy looked me on like I was crazy for attempting such an endeavor, adding in that I should lie back down. But I carried on like a discontented old man in a nursing home who disobeys the nurses out of boredom and loneliness. I hobbled over to the closet, needing a dry shirt. She came over to observe my taste in fashion.

'Looks like *someone* needs a new wardrobe,' she noted professionally. 'All your clothes are black or blue.'

Pointing at a green hoodie didn't seem to change her mind; I needed a new wardrobe. With her standing next to me, I pulled my shirt off bashfully although my body was muscular, just not in top-cut form. But she didn't stick around to examine it; she went back to my bed, playing around with the sheets, talking to herself about what to do with 'em. After putting on a new black shirt and the green hoodie over top, I dropped contact solution into my eyes...til my face was soaking wet. Probably looked like I'd fallen into a severe state of bereavement. Looking like this—in bereavement, or in a more positive light, wildly child-eyed—I smiled at her, as she was asking me serious questions as what to do with the wet sheets. On a whim, (now feeling warm and comical), I said in a child's voice, 'Look, Mommy; I peed the bed again.'

Without diverging from the maternal role by laughing or cracking the slightest smile, she said, 'Seriously: you want the sheets just left here like this? They'll smell.'

'No.'

'Then what should I do with 'em?'

'Throw 'em out da window. I peed on 'em.'

'You did not pee on 'em,' she said mother-surely—but cracking a childlike smile.

'I know. *You* did.'

'No, I didn't pee on 'em either.'

'Well somebody did or they wouldn't have pee on 'em.'

'You're so weird. Maybe it *is* that medicine.'

'Or the pee I drank before ya came.'

'Okay; now you're just bein' disgusting.'

'Oh yeah? Well back in the day people yoosta drink 'er urine da cure ear infections,' I remarked educationally, my face straight and philosophical as if verifying my credibility; inside, I was giggling because, although the snow had gone cold, the painkillers were pleasantly humming my skin. 'So wouja caw someone who's juss tryin'ah alleviate the throbbin', excruciating, un*bear*able pain in 'er ears *disgusting?*'

'Oh please. Nobody used to drink pee to cure ear infections.'

'Well *I* sercly had to before 'cause we couldn't afford real meds. But my hearing has never been bedder.' I came across real defensive, contorting my face with a clenched mouth.

'Are you really bein' serious? You drank urine for an ear infection?'

'Wha'?'

I hobbled over to her like a rusty robot, snatched the sheets out of her hand, slung 'em to the floor with mock fury, then pecked a kiddish kiss on her large lips.

'Hey, I wanna get some fresh air. Can we godda the orchard again?'

'Did you forget you have a cast on your leg?'

'Yeah—but look!'' I sputtered gleefully, acting like an airhead just for fun, 'I have crutches! ' I hobbled over between my desk and closet and grabbed the crutches, flinging 'em out in front of me like makeshift machineguns ready to blow Luke's wall to smithereens. 'Got me some new walkin' legs, maw. So let's go. You'll even get da drive my sports car—oh wait, you prahblee dunno howda drive a stick, huh?'

'Actually, I do,' she answered brusquely, as if believing it was a chauvinistic remark. 'What, you don't think girls can drive sticks?'

'Ohh trust me, sister,' I quipped with a calculated tremble of overly supportive mirth, 'I know *aaall* about how chicks can drive sticks.' Funny thing is, I think she actually overstood my humor. And that might've been sexier than the way she sucked noodles into her mouth like a quiet vacuum, her green doe-eyes surveying up and around, with those blinkity-blink-blink crescent-moon eyelashes...

...To my surprise, the sunlight didn't unpoeticize the orchard one bit. The pastoral paradise still had rich, wavy, thick-stroked colors with dreamy depth; still proffered tactility through soon-to-be-fallen leaves and fruits hanging on tender limbs bent towards you by white-haired epimeliads, for your love and taking, as tufted flowers and wild grasses blew upward-kisses on your way; and aggregately, the sunlit orchard still encompassed a primordial serenity that sung nothing but breezy lullabies. After putting a better ear to the wind, I could still hear the *POWER UP!!!* echoing through the cool, waltzing air: this being the *ethereality* of the orchard: no tactility: just keep your hands to yourself—perhaps down in your pockets like an old-timer—while you listen to Memory singing old tunes as you stroll through Nature's phonograph.

The first thing Ivy wanted to do was show me the creek and its unstocked fish—"real fish," as she called 'em, as if she knew about those *other* kinds of fish made of fiberglass that tell people to do bad things whenever they take drugs. Anyway, we headed directly off to the right...down over a lime-green field. It was a slow journey because of my calculated crutch-steps; I'd never used crutches before, so naturally it was an awkward first experience, but nothing to run away from. She was on my left with a ready-hand just in case. On the way down, I finished my fabricated story: the cause and effect of the fall, the Aristod EMT who didn't exist but took me to the hospital, the poor hospital treatment which I exaggerated to hyperbolic extremes, and then, absentminded, I slipped into the insurance mix-up but said nothing about the outsourcing of Rick's job (which I found out via internet news was supposedly not due to wage cost but "the more intricate details involved in the technological infrastructure and logistics"), nor did I mention that Rick canceled our insurance because "we never use it" (which I found out via life lessons was undoubtedly due to wage cost).

'Well there it is!' chimed Ivy. 'Now help me look for fish...'

The creek was larger than I'd expected: about twenty yards across. The water was clean (a whitish-green), with a scent of high altitude. There were rocks throughout, rising above the surface: some long and flat enough to walk a few steps on. The current was flowing just enough to emit a steady gurgle, with some spots bubbling like *kalte ente;* [2] this from water hitting into submerged parts of rocks then breaking up- and outward— unless there were actually cold ducks farting deeper down than I could see. Either way, I took it all in, deep into my lungs: ahh! such reprieve from the uptightness of everyday life! I could've laid by the bank and listened to this

---

[2] German for "cold duck" which is champagne mixed with the dregs of unfinished wine bottles

meditative gurgle and watched these bubbles til life passed me by. Perhaps *that's* why Ivy drank water: if you like what's outside of you, then you get it inside you any way you can, at any cost.

'See the fish?!' she exclaimed, elated by the sight of a little furrow in the water.

'Where? I don't see nuh'n.'

'Well it's gone now!' she huffed, throwing her hands up and looking at me as if I'd just failed to witness the Loch Nest, leaving her with no one to vouch for her sanity whenever she tells everyone about it.

'I dunno, Ivy; I don't think dis crick is very fish-friendly. Da wudder's priddy clear 'n' I ain't seein' nuh'n.'

'It's not clear enough to see all the way down where they usually swim. But watch, they'll come near the surface. The water will ripple—See! look! look!' She pointed five-feet out where I briefly saw something reddish.

'Was 'at a lobster? It had a red face.'

She shook her head almost in serious frustration. 'Are you blind? It's face was green as grass!' She stepped to the brink of the bank and bent down, wading her hand in the water. 'I think it was a rainbow trout,' she murmured.

'Is 'at all dere is?—trout?'

'No, but that's probably the most common one. But I've seen catfish, bluegills, chubs, little minnows and daces, and I think I saw a few carps before.'

Fishing out was what presently swimming through my mind, I said, 'Hey ju ever see 'ose exotic fish 'ey goddat the Hub?'

'Yeah. Why?' (She was still down stirring circles in the water, not looking up.)

'Whachir thoughts on it?'

'I mean, they're beautiful and all. But no livin' being should be caged, leashed, *or* tanked for pure entertainment.'

'Exactly. I'm gonna find a way da free 'em.'

She stood back up, shaking her hands out, but now with an intent focus on me. 'Oh yeah? And how you plan on doin' that?'

'I dunno; I'll think a sum'n. Wanna help?'

'As long as it doesn't involve gettin' in trouble.'

'Guess 'at's juss'ah risk you'll hafta take in the name a liberation.'

'Mmm...' An inexplicable smile came over her face, half-devious, half-suggestive of an epiphany for something unrelated to the conversation. 'So you feel like walkin' down to the cove?'

'Wanna do me a favor firss?'

'What kinda favor?'

'Well since idd be too much of a project for meedda ben' dahn 'n' taste 'n' touch the wudder, can you juss throw some on my face?'

Her big eyelids sprang up as her green eyes sprang out like lottery balls. 'Are you serious, Vinny?'

'Yep. Juss use both hands, cup some wudder, 'n' throw it in my face.'

'Wow. You're seriously a nut job.'

'Well if you don't do it,' I stipulated, 'den I'm juss gonna jump in. *'N'* *nut jobs,'* I broke in with a low menacing voice, *'put in cramped boot-casts?—(They don't survive, Ivy...They rilly don't.)'*

'Fine, you asked for it.' Not taking the chance that I might drown myself, she carefully kneeled back down on the bank so as not to rub stains into her jeans. I wobbled over as close as I could get before my boot or crutches would sink into the tenuous ground where it quickly went from solid ground to mud to water. On her knees, she glanced up with an anticipatory tilt—*the reflection of the diaphanous creek rocking within her ocular green waves*—to give me one last chance to back out—but I stood strong. 'Okay, get ready.' She cupped her hands down in the water. Brought 'em up in open prayer. Held 'em steady at the surface. Rescooped one more time. Readied herself. Then quickly shot up, throwing the water in my face.

I swallowed a few drops, and through the watery blur I could see her shuffling off to the side in an odd lateral movement, laughing like a hyena, shaking her hands with childlike merriment. Standing motionless with the crutches locked under my pits, I let the cold water run down my face, neck, and chest like I'd just been hit with a pie in slapstick.

'Happy now?'

After a long pause, I stoically replied, 'Look, Ivy: I'm mel-ting.'

We walked down to the cove where not far off to the left, down in the vast billowy field, stood the weeping willows; they still looked like exotic green waterfalls. Ivy was telling me about her mother's recent legal dispute with a lady who'd wrecked into her mother's car while it was illegally parked, and how her mother didn't get full compensation from the insurance company, and according to her mother, *that's* why the country is going to hell in a handbasket. Meanwhile, I was examining the "cove." Rather small, the cove cut spherically into the orchard-side, about six feet at the apex. The water seemed murkier and deeper in the cove. It was like the creek's heart: a two-chambered vessel receiving water from its atria—(the end that streamed along the field bordering the orchard)—then pumping water from its ventricle down towards the interminable woods at a sixty-degree angle. I asked Ivy if you could swim in the cove. She said she didn't know about "swim in it" but you could go in and move around a little. The water, she explained, was only four-feet deep with one small area that went over her head by a foot. She said that when she was little she would get in and just hang by the bank. I asked if she'd gone in lately; she said no. I said that we should whenever it became warm again; she said, 'We'll see.'

I needed to sit down and rest, so we headed back up towards her big apple tree.

'How's the leg holdin' up?' (We were halfway up through the field.)

"Priddy good. I juss nee—" Suddenly my left clutch landed on top of a hidden jagged rock and slipped out from under me. I was stumbling around, while Ivy was doing all she could to hold me up by grabbing me around the torso. Thankfully, I rebalanced myself before falling to the ground. 'Yeah, okay. 'Azz alawda fun.'

Ivy laughed shamelessly as if I was clumsy by nature. 'Would you like me to carry you the rest of the way?'

'Please do.'

Well, she didn't carry me the rest of the way but she guided me as well as anyone could. Once back in the hub of the orchard—(in reverence, all the surrounding trees were still parted backed in monarchial fashion for her tree)—I sat down and leaned back on a flattened river rock. I stretched my legs out in the direction of the thick leathery trunk. I craned my neck back to look up into the pavonine sky with its scooting clouds and open but temperate sun, the late afternoon air a bit cooler than it had been several nights past. When I craned my neck forward, Ivy was inspecting the large red apples, picking out the rotten ones and piling 'em off to the side. Pulling the drawstrings on my hoodie back and forth, I watched (with heart-warming adoration) her groom the tree with familial affection and surgical precision, both manifest in the fastidiousness of her hands. She had layers of hair tucked behind her diamond-studded ears while several individual strands in the shape of repetitive *S*s graced the sides of her silky face...sinuous...sensuous...*sssssin*...for a moment I slipped away as if a reserve of drugs (stored within me) had suddenly broken open and deluged all through myself...

'Oh look!' I heard her chime. 'A caterpillar. *Aww*, aren't they so beautiful?'

I took a moment to ruminate—but couldn't concentrate: a paralyzing sense of nostalgia was hugging me—pulling me outside myself: I felt detached, as if immersed in a movie, as if there were two mes: and I could neither shake one nor get a grip on the other. Although perplexed and catatonic, I forcefully pulled my selves back together and replied: 'You consider caterpillars *beautiful?*'

'Sure: they turn into butterflies,' she said babyishly. 'Do you know the stages?'

'*Mmm.* Egg, larva, pupa, butterfly?'

'I'm impressed. Ya know, they only stay in the egg stage about a week. Then the larva for a month, which is this little guy,' she petted the back of the lime-green caterpillar edging up trunk, 'Then they go into the pupa for another week, which people usually think are cocoons, but that's what moths make; butterflies make a chrysalis. Did you know a butterfly doesn't even live long after all the time it takes to become one?'

'Oh yeah? How long?'

'Sometimes only a few days. A month or two at the most. There's a few species like the Monarch that can live about nine months.' She delicately petted its back again. 'But isn't it amazing how somethin' goes from an amorphous egg, to what people consider the ugly caterpillar, to somethin' that doesn't even seem alive anymore, and finally, when all is said and done, the beautiful butterfly emerges? What a process!'

'Hey, come sit dahn,' I said, looking down at my green hoodie mindlessly. Absorbed in whatever thought, Ivy, standing akimbo, continued to watch the lime-green caterpillar slowly but surely ascend into the fruitful abyss. 'Hey, come here.'

She turned around and whimsically shouted, 'Yes, sir!' saluting me like a general. She capered over to me reclined back on one of her vine-tied rocks. She then threw her hands on her shapely hips, looking down with a galvanizing stare to counter against, or trying to amend, the dour look on mine. I worked up a toothless smile. She settled down on the ground to my left, lying on her right side. She planted her right forearm firmly on the ground, while shifting her legs to where her knees were bent in towards mine. While she ripped out blades of grass and piled 'em atop my chest, we got to talking about our infamous school icon: a calfy-legged, glasses-wearing, middle-aged man known as the Bloy Preacher. At first, the only thing I knew about him was that he was *always* standing outside Bloy Hall, the building where I had Dr. Rosenbaum's class. I hadn't even known his nickname til Ivy told me, and the name was fitting: everyday, no matter the weather, the Bloy Preacher stood at the bottom of the steps of Bloy Hall, dressed casually, and preached without breathing as students came and went with deaf ears. I was usually in too much of a rush to stop and listen. But one day I had decided to since my next class had been cancelled. After leaving Dr. Rosenbaum's class that day, I sat up on the short brick wall running along the steps. I smoked cigarettes and ate snacks while listening to his homiletic litanies of pride, envy, gluttony, lust, wrath, sloth, greed, the carnal sins, the venial sins, the mortal sins, countless forms of blasphemy, countless disregards to the poor, countless capitalistic corruptions, countless communistic tendencies, the decline of family manifest in divorce statistics, the rise of hedonists manifest in the gays, pedophiles, pornographers, starlets, and college girls who go to parties believing "sex with popular fraternity brothers will boost their self-esteem and gain respect from their peers." Then he fulminated the "godless wealthy elite" whom he comically analogized with the Sybarites, quoting Strabo by saying they, America's plutocrats, "through luxury and insolence have in fact been deprived of their felicity." Then he outlined the decline of attendance at the local churches, and the national rise of traitors who unpatriotically speak against our leaders. And all these things were parts to the monstrous sum of what he believed had gone wrong with society. During the forty-five minutes I stayed, he never once made eye contact with me, even though there were only two other stationary students. For some reason, I felt it was because I was smoking cigarettes or sum'n.

     '...Yeah, that's what I kinda thought too. Talk about tellin' stories,' Ivy segued, 'you wanna hear a story about the orchard? It's kinda creepy.'
     'Sure.'
     First, she blew off the large pile of grass blades atop my chest like attempting to extinguish a hundred birthday candles all at once—but the endeavor proved too difficult; she used her hands in a broom-like motion to clear the remaining blades.
     'Well when I was little Jack used to tell me this myth about the orchard. He said it was once the home of some guy believed to be a madman. And this guy used to live here by himself and never left for anything—oh! and keep in mind, this is supposed to be a really long time ago. Anyway, one day his cottage and the entire orchard burned down to the ground along with the village that used to rest below those hills—' She turned around and pointed out back behind us, to the right some, towards the smalls valleys where the weeping willows stood but no longer a village. 'You wanna hear the whole story? It's kinda long.'
     'I wanna hear it beginnin' da end.'

'Okay. And I'm not gonna begin with callin' this guy the madman because it doesn't make sense to.' She looked straight into my eyes to see if that was fine by me.

'Tell me however ya wish.'

On her side, facing me on my back, she began the orchard myth.

'So there was this guy who lived here all alone in a tiny cottage which used to be over by the arbor. He had no job and nothin' of material value besides necessities. Everyone in the village believed he obtained this land from a forged inheritance, but they had no proof. He never ventured down to the village for *anything.* Not even for food. He ate from the trees and gardens, and bathed and drank from the creek. And back then the food here was so plentiful, more than he could've every consumed by himself. But no one from the village really knew that because they created the *original* myth about him bein' some madman murderer, and so they stayed as far away as they could. I guess they made that up because they didn't know any better and needed an explanation of why he hid away and never came to the village. In the beginning, everyone just called him The Madman. But then they started callin' him Antonio Dene—'

I broke in with laughter, saying, 'What, now he's some Italian asshole like me?'

'Noooo. But see, that's what this drunken bum in the village told people his *real* name was. The bum claimed to have been rich where he used to live—on the *other* side of the mountains—and there, the people knew the guy as Antonio Dene.'

'Ar'ight. This is priddy weird, but go on.'

'Well, one day, for the first time ever, the village decided to elect a mayor. No one knew how to be one, so they sent for the illustrious Luno Pestapelti—'

Again, I broke in with laughter.

'What's so funny now?!'

'Where the fuck you comin' up with 'eez names? *Italians Names for Crackheads?*'

'I'm not comin' up with 'em! Jack told me! Now keep quiet!'

'Yes ma'am!' I saluted her briskly as she'd done to me earlier.

'So Luno was this well-liked fatcat brought from far away to reconstruct the village because it was in ruins from a severe food shortage. And the people knew he'd know what to do because he'd built prosperous towns all over the place. So in his inauguration speech, Luno says, "Taxes, people, taxes is the way of the world now." But the people shouted back, "What's *taxes?*" because til then the village had been real simple and used a barter system. So Luno says, "Quite a complicated matter, my friends, so I won't trouble you with all the details. But hear me! And hear me well! I shall create a money system for you to buy all your food and commodities! And these taxes on the things you buy and sell is money for all! That's right: ALL! Soon this dirty little village will be prosperous beyond belief! Soon a marble library shall entertain students! and coffee shops shall host businessmen on their way to control the machines that will do the donkey-work of the town! That's right: I didn't say *village*, but a *town*—a great big TOWN! Oh yes! and soon all the women will spend their time reading and gossiping in lavish recreation centers, without a care in the world! It will be prosperity for all!"'

Ivy stopped for a breath and to share a quick laugh over her thespian energy. Her body had been squirming around. I was amused by her shift in tone for Luno. So adorably she would draw her shoulders back, scrunch her face up, and speak in a deep exaggerated voice, parodying the intellectual fat man from the 20s who wore a monocle. Whenever his words needed stressed, she would pound on the ground behind my head. For some reason, I was picturing Luno Pestapelti as Howard Taft, who fittingly, (thanks to his blitzkrieg 16th Amendment) helped "lay and collect taxes on incomes, from whatever source derived, without apportionment among the several States, and without regard to any census or enumeration."

Ivy continued: 'So the crowd bursts into jubilation. They're completely enthralled by Luno's speech. After they quiet down, he says, "First we must begin by recultivating the land. But we haven't the time to wait for this pitiful ground below us to rejuvenate. Look at it!"' (Ivy was pretending that the very ground below us was the same land Luno was referring to as she dramatically patted down on it.) '"So we must move outwards." So the crowd becomes attentive, waiting for further instruction. "There!" he yells out, "I see fertile land beyond with what looks to be a fresh stream of water! We'll begin tomorrow with no delay!" But now the crowd suddenly starts fretting and runnin' around in a frenzy—'

'Nice.'

'Well this little boy who was said to have more stories of Antonio Dene in his head than victuals in his belly—' Ivy stopped to giggle as if realizing she'd just adopted both vernacular and a joke from Jack's version. 'Well this little boy runs up to Luno and tugs at his shirt and warns him of Antonio Dene. He cries and begs him not to do it. But Luno just laughs. Then he calls back the attention of the scattering crowd. He says, "Would the parents of this imaginative young boy please come claim him? A nice little lad but seems to be lost in the crowd and thought, speaking of some madman who lives in that precious land beyond."

'But the crowd jeers back at him, sympathizing with the little boy. Everyone's yellin' out their fears of Antonio Dene. But once Luno understands what's goin' on, he still doesn't care. He says, "Nonsense, my friends! See, this Antonio Dene fellow is no better than any of us! Not only will he let us cultivate the land for the common good, but he will also help pay taxes!"—'

'Okay, Ivy, stop for a minute.'

'What?'

'I dunno; be honest: are you makin' 'iss shit up as you go along—ya know, juss fuckin' with me or sum'n?'

'No. Seriously.' (A skeptical stare on my part.) 'I'm not! I just know it so well because Jack used to tell it to me all the time.'

'Well I'm juss shocked. Bahchir an awesome *raconteur*. If I'm a writer one day, you'll hafta do my readings for me 'cause I suck at public speakin'.'

'What's a *raconteur*?'

'Someone good at tellin' anecdotes. But go on. I'm lovin' 'iss.'

'Okay. So the same day of the speech, Luno sends two boys out to the cottage to inform Antonio of his plans. The boys beg him not to make 'em go. But he says if they refuse they'll be publicly whipped til they can't walk. So the boys are obviously forced to go. So they walk up to the cottage. And when they get there, they begin watchin' the strange man through a cloudy window. He's sittin' at a big old desk with his back to 'em. So finally one of the boys gets up enough courage to tap on the window . He gets up from his desk and they quickly duck below the windowsill. Then they hear the door opening and jump up and run back to the village as fast as they can, too terrified to tell Antonio the message.

'Well, Luno *does* have the boys publicly whipped for runnin' away without givin' the message to Antonio. But as the crowd watches, they start cryin' and havin' second thoughts about their new mayor—you know, because they understand why the boys were so scared. But they stay silent because they also fear such a powerful man. So after the whipping, Luno explains how the entire village is gonna march to the orchard with him in the mornin' so that he can personally explain his plans—'

'Why doesn't he juss go alone? Is he scared too?'

'Just take it for whatever it's worth.'

On a whim, I turned on my side, craned upward, and kissed her, telling her I wouldn't interrupt anymore.

'So the next day everyone goes to the orchard. Luno goes to the door and knocks. Antonio swiftly opens the door as if he was already waitin' for him. (Antonio's thin and dark with unkempt hair.) Luno asks him if he's Antonio Dene, and the man says, "I am." Then Luno tells Antonio his plans and warns him he's gonna be put in jail if he doesn't cooperate and pay taxes. With everyone held in silence, Antonio says, "Do whatever you think you must, but this land will never respond kindly to your designs. It will revolt at your very first move." But Luno just laughs and says, "Now I see why these people think you're a madman! Not only are you a liar, but you've also been deceiving many hungry people! I mean, my God, look at this immense fruit around us! You should be ashamed of yourself! However, no fret, Mr. Dene: I've dealt with your kind in every town I've been sent to restore. And everyone has ended up paying their taxes. And the ones who refused were easily defeated by the good-will of the people." And to this, Antonio says, "You're only gonna create a hunger within these good people that can never be satisfied."

'So the next day the town returns to the orchard and starts building the foundations of the new town. To maintain their energy, they eat a lot of the food from the trees and gardens. But Antonio never comes out. And Luno doesn't even *try* to get him to come out. He just supervises the whole project—you know, never gettin' *his* hands dirty—but he ensures everyone that Antonio *will* be jailed.

'So all the way up til dusk the people work hard, tilling the fields. Then they return to the village to sleep. Then out of nowhere, in the middle of the night, the old drunken bum screams out, "New town afire! Fields afire! Food afire! Everything afire!" Every one runs out of their little huts, cryin' as they watch the fire burn everything they'd done. And they couldn't attempt to put the fire out because it was already past the cove and quickly heading towards the village. So someone goes up to the old drunken bum and asks him why he didn't warn 'em sooner, like before the fire had blocked off the water. And the bum says he was layin' down, lookin' up at the sky, just enjoyin' his drink, and then the entire orchard suddenly went up in flames. Just like that!

'So now the crowd's runnin' around in a panic. People are knockin' each other over. Some are looting. Some are tryin' to run away. But before the fire reaches the village, the people start scorning Luno and tellin' him *this* is why they'd always stayed away from the murderous madman *he* let loose. But Luno fires back, I guess trying to stay bold, and just then Antonio appears. Everything grows completely silent, even the crackling sound of the approaching fire. Everyone's waitin' for him to say somethin'. Then in a calm voice, he says, "I told you the land would revolt at your very first move." Luno steps forward in front of the people, like he was taking full responsibility, and mournfully says, "But why? Did you do this on purpose? Did you destroy out of spite?" And Antonio Dene declares—and I'm just usin' the words Jack used, so don't laugh.'

'I won't.'

'Okay. So Antonio Dene declares, "How great a forest is set ablaze by a small fire! And the tongue *is* a fire! The tongue can be placed among our members as a world of iniquity! It can stain the whole body! It can set the Cycle of Nature on fire! And can be, itself, set on fire by the flames of Hell! But it doesn't have to be as such! for the tongue is like a rudder: when it's in our possession, it can be used to steer us to towards the skies of freedom! But when our tongue is steered by another, we fall down into the shackles of slavery! And it's from your silence and docility that your master grew stronger and your chains tighter! Thus, never resign your tongue to false masters! All men are born of the same fiber! all born with an equal tongue! and all are but one tooth in the Mouth of Nature! and the Tongue of Nature, my brothers and sisters, has never spoken of taxes! Nature does not and shall never pay taxes! Nature is forever free!"

'And just then a great blaze shoots forward and burns everything to the ground. Everything instantly gone! And the people from the other towns around the area said that a flood washed over the ashes the very next day and the land was soon restored. But there was no one left to tell the story besides—guess who?—the old drunken bum, who was spotted up in the new orchard, mashin' an apple into pieces.'

'So den—'

'Wait. There's a little more. So the people who came to see what happened walk up to the bum. They ask him what happened. But he isn't very smart and can't talk very well, so all he's able to say is, "The tribulations of life took all my pearls, you see." (And he smiles an ugly smile.) But I can still taste the sweetness of this apple on my tongue."

She laughed, then girlishly said, '*Theeeee* end!'

I paused before releasing any reaction, then sitting up, exclaimed: 'Wow! 'Azz sercly fuckin' awesome!' I was partly stunned from the story itself, partly from her dynamic delivery; and to boot, the story had that classic hook-line-and-sinker! We kept looking at each other, smiling and jittering around in excitement, breathing in the spirit of the story. And how fresh and relieving it was! As magical as water into wine!

'I'm sure Jack would be proud you can recount his myth like 'at.'

'I would hope so.'

'Dere's obviously a great allegory to it, but my head's spinnin' too much da analyze it right now. But I wancha da tell me again sometime.'

'I will,' she promised with her soft doe eyes focused down on our joining hands. 'Hey, random question, but has Pessi said anything about movin' in with Teresa?'

'Oh, I haven't tolja the news, huh?'

'What news?'

'Teresa hasn't said anything da ya?'

'No. Why? What? Tell me! Tell me!'

'Pessi tol' me dis mornin' he's movin' in with her next weekend.'

'No way! Are you serious?'

'Yep; sad but true. I mean, don't take any offense, but I think Teresa's rill shady. Like, I get bad vibes from her. Da be honest, I juss flat-out don't trust her.'

Ivy only shrugged, either afraid to backbite Teresa out of loyalty or ignorant of the sadistic and malicious intentions I could see burning in Teresa's red beady eyes. Just earlier in the day, I'd been thinking about how Teresa and Pessi reminded me of another Sid Vicious and Nancy Spungen waiting to happen. Pessi even used to play the bass like Sid! And whenever Teresa would hang over his shoulders like a spread vulture, squawking all her squawk, and Pessi would just stand there like a rugged model, cocking up his smirk with his hands shoved down into his front pockets, the idea didn't seem much of an exaggeration. I had no trouble picturing Teresa—having just cropped her hair and dyed it blonde, with that reedy frame and ironic cuteness of her sunken cheekbones—pushing dope into Pessi's veins. Then years later, after she gets murdered, *he* would be wrongly blamed for it. That's how highly I thought of Squawk Cazzata. But of course I didn't quite express it to Ivy like *that*. Doubted she would even get the reference.

The cool air was whistling and rustling the brittle leaves still hanging on the boughs while scattering around the fallen ones. Ivy leaned in towards my chest, wanting affection. She sighed (like a whimper), gradually letting herself melt into me...*yeah, Ivy, I'll stop da world 'n' melt witchu: I see da difference 'n' it's gih'n bedder all da time...*There's nothing I would've rather been doing than what I was: stroking her hair in harmony with her shifts and cuddles to rest her head comfortably into the dale of my chest. I put a lock of her hair into my mouth, trying to do it discreetly. I started chewing on it. Then harder.

Quashing my discreetness, she said, 'You really like chewin' on my hair, huh?'

'Definitely. You hair's my aphrodisiac. Tastes so perfect.'

'What else do you like about me?'

After a moment, I tritely replied, 'Everything.' I was now chomping wildly on the epicurean lock, using my skilled tongue to guide it (and more of it) further into my mouth.

'You mean everything *so far*,' she noted sullenly.

'What makes you say 'at?' (I slithered the fill of hair out with my tongue so I could talk better.) 'You mean how people never seem the same in hindsight, like when ya learn more about 'em 'n' 'en look back 'n' izz all a façade?'

'Yeah, I guess somethin' like that. People just always put on a show in the beginning or just change for the worse in time.'

'Yir right, so says my experiences. But tell me sum'n: whad is it ya like about *me?* You haven't chewed on *my* hair.'

'Oh please. You know that I like everything about you too.'

'Everything *so far*, right?'

'Right.'

We began kissing passionately, twisting our tongues tighter than her ophidian mocha ever could! We were wiggling the tips of our tongues, forming smiles we could feel but not see...then slowed into soft, steady rolls like wheelwork done clockwork. Meanwhile, I was petting her face with one hand, and with the other, using my thumb and index finger to play with her ear. She was sweeping her pink fingernails up and down the side of my neck. I used my head to push hers to the side so I could kiss her neck...til it phased into a tender gnawing, gently pinching up her skin with my teeth. She did the same to me but not as long.

As the passion took rest, she playfully said, '*Soooo, my handsome devil.*'

'Yes, my plump Rube?'

'I dunno; just wonderin'.'

'About?'

'Stuff.'

'Well can ya stuff me with a liddle more detail?'

'No.'

'Ar'ight; den I'm gonna take a nap.' I curled up into a protective ball, carefully putting my booted leg on top of the other, pretending I was going to sleep on her. But before I could settle into slumber she quickly jumped across my torso and, laughing, started tickling me.

'Stop! I hate bein' tickled!' I really did too!

'Then quit bein' an ass!' she swore—accidentally!

'HA! I'm not bein' an ass!'

'Then wake up and tell me what's goin' on?'

'Where?'

'Here!'

'Well, here—in this mighty fine orchard—we have many trees sayin' goodbye da their fruit. 'N' the sun is fallin' dahn. 'N' as you can see, my ankle is in a ridiculous boot. 'N' to boot, *you*—yir on top of me even'o I'm tryin'ah take a liddle squirrel-nap, so now I'm mad atchu.'

'No! You know what I'm talkin' about!' Keeping her body along my side, she braced her arms just outside my shoulders, letting her sinuous hair sway down in my face; I slipped another lock into my mouth. 'And you're not allowed to be mad at me,' she warned. But the weight of her seriousness was ambivalent due to her childlike tone; I couldn't decide (and this had been in and out of my thoughts) whether I was with an adult-in-body who had the innocence of a child, or with an adult-in-body who was just now learning to give into the passion of an adult. Tipping the scales my way with the movement of an adult, she gave me a childish peck, keeping me mentally puckered! But one thing was certain: as I pulled Ivy back inly and gave her a deeper kiss, the tress secured in my mouth was now stuck in between our tongues, being wetted and commanded by cushy cycles, allowing us to taste together her inexplicable taste of *POWER UP!!!* Perhaps with that shared taste we transcended far above maturity, rationality, language, and overstanding.

And how these turning chaoses and tasty colors were all swirling through me in the sundown moment after she said, 'And you're not allowed to be mad at me!' then gave me that quick childish peck. Yet I couldn't control myself. I had to kiss her *heavily.* Had to taste it *together.* Had to say *something*—just anything!—to let her know how I felt! And so I said, 'Oh you know I'm juss fuckin' with you.'

And saving me—how she saved my poor misspoken words!—she replied, 'Oh—well maybe I want you to come fuck with me some more...'

CRUCIFIXION

"Give me pain or give me death,
Teach me how to be alive,
Take my joy or take my breath,
We all need crucified,
Nail me to a cross, yeah, let me hang all night,
Nail me to a cross, yeah, I won't even fight,
Nail me to a cross, yeah, you know that it's right—
Because it's Hymnerica! (Land of the loop!)
It's Hymnerica! (Home of the hung!)
Motherfuckin' Hymnerica!..." [1]

...Hark! the winter of my leg's content was approaching! made glorious by the sun of Orchard!—and the fact that it was now a week into November and three days away from getting my ankle reexamined and (hopefully) the walking boot-cast removed so I could navigate around the forthcoming wintry campus with less statistical chance of getting hurt while being hurt. The doctor had informed me that there was still a chance my ankle might not be healed, and that I might have to do physical therapy afterward, which, no matter the diagnosis, wasn't an option because without insurance I couldn't afford it. Like Rick had promised when he said he would send money when he got his next unemployment check, he didn't send money when he got his next unemployment check, because, as he stated during another telephone conversation, he had "bills, groshirees, day-da-day expenses, 'n' Christmas is right around the corner," which meant he needed to save a little extra for the presents he didn't buy anyone, unless I'd been checking under the wrong tree all these years. So, yeah, it looked like I *would* be footing the entire bill myself, and in costly monthly payments. But I didn't plan on setting up a payment plan til the hospital's dunning reached the threshold.

Ever since the day I told Ma about Oedipus, she quit asking me when I would be coming home next. She probably thought I'd finally lost my mind, and as a result she was now deathly afraid of me just like she was of everything else. But that's all right: I was thinking that she too had finally lost her mind, which would compliment her missing he~~art~~: and if anything, at least I still had a he~~art~~.

A few days after the second orchard visit, I decided to write about that chilling Oedipus incident using something of a stream-of-consciousness technique, hoping to capture and overstand something intriguing about my psyche. I streamed out five pages without pause or punctuation...reflected on it...then said to myself, 'Wonderful! Guess I won't ever do this again! It's all fuckin' shit!' Outside schoolwork, it was the first thing I'd written since

---

[1] Lyrics from "Hymnanthem" by Hyperocrisy, from the album *Better Dead than Read*

high school. After stuffing it inside a box with my other disappointments, I flipped through some old poems...and they were all fuckin' shit too! Although alone, I was so embarrassed—*manqué* over the prospect of becoming a writer. So to reject the idea of ~~Art~~ and all the other shit in my head, I told myself that I didn't even have *time* to be concerned with ~~Art~~, having Ivy Pineda, Ivy-Leaguish Aristod, financial issues, disobedient limbs, squirrels, fish, raccoons, and other animals, such as Pessi, to deal with.

And Pessi! That dim-witted wildebeest *did* move in with Teresa the next weekend! The day he moved in, he stopped by to visit. Right away, he hammered down on my boot-cast. Luke was there, and having witnessing it, fell into a state of shock. His mottled face was surreptitiously telling me, "Vinny, are you sure *this* is your best friend? Just wink if you want me to call for help." At first, I thought it was an urban-rural dichotomy where friends act "nicer" or "calmer" towards each other in laidback towns, but I realized that, no, we Da Hoolies were just plain ruthless towards each other even in comparison with other Yinzers. But at least Pessi was friendly with Luke, even if he thought he was being cute by telling Luke stupid stories about me, thinking it embarrassed me. Like the time in 9th grade when Billy "Gay" Bosco gave me a Valentine that had an invitation to get together some time; restraining a smirk, I politely thanked my shamelessly effeminate classmate for the self-esteem boost, but Pessi had celebrated the incident for the rest of February and annually thereafter. While Pessi was roasting me in front of his one-man audience—unaware that Luke wouldn't taunt me afterwards like he was obviously hoping would be the comical aftermath—I made the observation that Pessi was swearing a lot. Of course just like any other time. But it brought to mind how I rarely swore around Luke, and it kinda bothered me. It had nothing to do with Luke *per se*. It just dismayed me to think that my expressions, of any nature, even trivial ones, were being locked up or euphemized, in this case because of Luke's piety. Still felt like I had so much inside to get out. But what is "so much"? And where is "so much" supposed to go once it "gets out"?

...Friday morning I hobbled into Dr. Rosenbaum's class with the group paper on Molière and Goethe in my backpack. (I'd been making an effort to keep my backpack as light as I could since Ivy could only assist me at certain times during the day.) As a way of awarding me for having done most of the research, my thoughtful group members had let me finish typing up the ten-page group paper alone in the computer lab the night before. On the way up to Dr. Rosenbaum's desk, adroitly clanking myself forward, I looked left at my group members, sitting here and there. They were giving me utilitarian stares, hoping their minimal efforts would realize maximum measures of happiness in the form of an *A*. All the way up the aisle, I made sure to give each one a nice, superficial, assuring smile. I should've just typed up ten pages of repetitive *S*s so we would've received an automatic *F:* wouldn't have hurt *my* grade much—can't say the same for those other crutched motherfuckers.

'How's the leg?' inquired Dr. Rosenbaum.

'Feelin' priddy good. Hopin' da boot comes off Monday.' I took the transparent folder out of my backpack and handed it to him. Without looking at it, he set it atop the stack. 'Hey, quick question: you know of any jobs on campus?'

Leaning back, he began meditating...stroking downward his blue-and-yellow striped tie...til he fingered his silvery moustache with rapidity as if stricken with an excruciating itch. He quirkily popped his lips, emitting a loud *POP!* sound: it caused his distinct playboy dimples to disappear for a second. Then, leaning forward on the desk as if it was top-secret information he was about to give, he said, 'I'm not involved with the paper but I know a few people who are. I mean, it's competitive, and chances are you won't be doing many articles your first year. Plus, no matter how much time you put in, or your position, it only pays minimum wage with a maximum of 24 hours a week. It's basically a way for journalism and communication majors to build their résumé, not make yacht money.'

'Well it's not dit I'm lookin'ah make millions, but I dunno; not sure I'm interested in *The Scholar*. I read it 'n' it bores me. I mean, whaddum I gonna do: be a current-events writer 'n' reword the AP a day late each day?'

'Mmm, well if you're creative enough—let me rephrase myself—if you're *interesting* enough, you could write editorials and say whatever you wish. Bein' an editorialist could make *yooou – a local celebrity!*' he fired out in jest. He wasn't jesting about how it could make me a local celebrity, but by now we'd talked enough times for him to know my attitudes towards certain things. So the jest was: he knew that I wasn't trying to *becooome – a local celebrity!* Out of loyalty to myself, my pen, and my papers, I was adamant about always choosing Dignity over Experience-for-Experience's-Sake. I saw editorials and other political ramblings as topical and short-lived, even artistically mortifying because of the insular process in which puppeteers behind the curtain danced the strings, or in the larger outlets, "wagged the dog." Besides, I horsed myself on the idea of creating *only* timeless masterpieces, while foo dogging myself against *all* ephemera. I could *never* let my writing, my art, my not-yet-known reputation, grace the garden of snakes, whether big or small, whether throttlers or biters.

'*Staaaardooom!*' he sung out in high notes of spurious enticement.

'No, 'at's ar'ight,' I sighed. 'Journalism juss isn't the direction I'm lookin' da go in. But thanks anyway.'

'What, you got beef with journalists?' he spat paranoically, squaring up his lean frame in order to block out the rest of the class, while sharing an inviting, conspiratorial look suggesting that *he* might have "beef with journalists" but wanted to see what *I* would say first.

'What don't I got beef with?' I replied dryly. 'But sercly, think about it: newspapers, hisstree books, fortune cookies, adlibs, Mad Libs: izzer rilly a difference? It's *aaall* wishful blanks fit for arbitrary lit.'

Dr. Rosenbaum stared at me blankly then peaked around and yelled loud enough for everyone to hear, 'Hey, Michelle!' (Michelle was in the very last seat of the middle row. The class quieted.) 'Can you do me a favor and tell everyone to open up their books to *Death in Venice?* And make sure you tell everyone we'll be talkin' about it in two minutes. Would you mind doin' that for me?'

'No problem, Dr. Rosenbaum!' yelled Michelle, giggling, not about to tell anyone a mann-damn thing.

He refocused on me with a frozen, serious look as if dead-panners who hide their humor, even if vocally loud, are the most humorous. 'I'll tell you what, Double-V , I'll ask around at the writing center and see if there's any tutor positions open. Sound cool?'

'As cool as a *Scholar* editorialist!' I sung out with a frozen, serious look...

...Since I didn't have a reason to go to my other classes, I didn't. I frankensteined back to Philemon to rest and watch television. I'd become addicted to those dramatized small-claim cases that I once loathed. On one channel, two judges alternated shows from mid-morning to mid-afternoon. I particularly liked the black guy who'd risen up out of the streets of Detroit, overcame crime and drugs, went back and got his GED, then moved onto more prestigious institutions, while keeping his heart in the streets and maintaining a sense of humor. Quite a sarcastic fella too! I loved when he got a hold of suburbanites who hugged on extremes, like the ones who act like their life is so hard or that they're too above being subject to criminal activities.

I hobbled into Philemon. Straight ahead, within the two-window cubicle, I saw the pretty lil Thai chick playing with her hair. The only time we talked at length was when she first saw my cast and asked for the story; I gave it to her, fabricated and spun like your run-of-the-mill headline story. Other than that, we usually just said hi.

'Hi,' said I, unable to wave.

'Hello. Does your leg feel better yet?'

'Yeah, it's gih'n 'ere.' As I square-turned the corner, tall and burly Agent Ralphie appeared out of the wall. He was dressed slick, with a khaki hat pulled down over his head and heavily tinted glasses—spying on me again! *Oh, you slick-sly bastard. I know whachir up to. You were waitin' for me after class, 'n' when ya saw I wasn't goin' da my other classes you snuck in the back door da see if ya could catch me doin' sum'n I shouldn't'. Juss wait 'n' see wha' happens da ya for spyin' on me. Hey! Dohnchu DARE look at me like 'at under yir glasses! I can see you! I'm not blind, you fuckin' spy! 'At's whad I thought: you bedder keep walkin' 'fore I smash yir fat fuckin' mole face in with my Docs!*

Upon opening the door, and smelling the difference of the air in the hall, I noticed the room was developing a permanent cigarette smell. (I would occasionally smoke out the window, or when I was too messed up to care, in my bed.) Of course Luke hadn't said anything about it, but when alone, he was probably dealing with it like an unabsolved sin. Either way, I thought I'd better buy some air freshener before I got written up by the RA who didn't write people up.

After taking my meds—the *proper* dosage—I lay on my bed and turned the television on. I flipped to my timely court show. Some lady was suing her white-trash ex-husband over an unpaid loan. He was countersuing his white-trash ex-wife for emotional distress and medical bills from being bitten by her dog when he, according to the ex-wife, trespassed into her backyard, trying to spy on her because he had suspicions that she was cheating, but, again according to her, only because he was addicted to and hopped up on cocaine and didn't overstand it wasn't "cheating" if they were divorced, and, yes, when he was looking in she *was* having sex with her new boyfriend, and so when the ex-husband tried getting in to fight her new boyfriend, she released the dog and the dog bit him, but the real point, according to the ex-wife, was that she wanted her money back from three years ago when they made a pact to split the costs of a vacation he still hadn't paid back. *Ahh! Payback's a bitch! Literally!*

Ring! Ring! Ring!

Remaining supine, I reached behind me and grabbed the phone off my desk.

'Yeah?'

'*Vinnyyyy!*' wailed Ma on the other end.

I sprang up from the bed. 'What's wrong?!'

'*Vinnyyyy!*' she bawled again.

Instantly flushed and sweating, I asked her to speak more clearly because I couldn't overstand a word that followed. But she continued to answer with incoherent cries, scarfed breaths that ebbed back out in vibrato whimpers, and Sicilian fragments spoken so tempestuously that I couldn't decipher 'em.

'*Iddu muriu ie mi lassàu sula pi sempri! Nun cci pozzu cririri ca chistu mi sta succirennu...*'

'Ma! Stop cryin' 'n' speak clearly.'

'*Vinnyyyy!*' she sobbed, then sobbed some more. Everything was sounding like a cyclone of static and sobs and gabble. But then, in brisk declarations, she said, '*Oh signuruzzu! muriu tò patri! ie comu fu?! iddu iera ancura cussì carusu!*'

That time I heard her as clearly as I would a bomb hitting right outside my window: 'Oh God, your father's dead! How's this possible? He was still so young!'

'Wha'? Juss calm dahn 'n' speak slowly so I can overstan' ju!'

Fervently, she sucked air up through her nose, ready to struggle through the explanation of how my father was dead. 'Deece morning he-ah, he-ah—Vinny, he—I find him on dee ground in bathroom! And—' She paused, choking back tears. 'And I call ambulance! Dey pound on his chest and-ah breathe—and-ah breathe into—' Every word convulsing so violently, transferring directly into my gut. 'But he-ah wouldn't wake up! Den—den dey-ah rush him to hospital! And I ride with him but, but dey say he-ah—he was-ah, probably dead all night!' She erupted back into an explosion of irrepressible tears, denials-of-reality, and questions-to-a-Sicilian-God.

But me—I was smiling wider than a canyon, like I was getting paid billions to smile that way. 'Wow. So did he drink himself da death?' I asked straight from the shoulder, smiling so wide now that my face actually hurt. 'Or was it suicide?...Well?' No answer besides telephone-tears. I tried again. '*Hellooo-oooh?!* How'd he die?'

'*A iddu un coppu cci pigghiàu!*' she cried. He had a massive heart attack. '*Nun sacciu chi fari mancu unni hê gghiri! Mi scantu assài, Vinny!—*'[2]

---

[2] [scn] I don't know what to do or where to go! I'm really scared!

'Ar'ight, ar'ight,' I interjected coolly, composed on the edge of my bed. 'If he's rilly dead, den there's no reason da be scared anymore. My leg might still be in a boot, but I'm sercly about da get up 'n' dance. Looks like Christmas came a liddle early for us.' I vaddled. 'See, Ma, everything rilly *is* gonna be ar'ight. Now don't get all mad at me for sayin' 'iss, but now ya can go back da Catania 'n' be witchir *rill* family 'n' yir *first-born* son, 'n' maybe even 'at Milvio guy.' (At this point it sounded like she pulled the phone away to cry in a new position, perhaps the fetal.) 'EH!—EH! Put the phone back upduyir face! Jeez.' (She put the phone back up to her face because, jeez, her sniffling and sobs became louder again.) 'Look, Ma, I know yir rilly upset 'n' confused right now, so I'll wait da give ya my whole optimistic take on the situation; juss don't do anything stupid in the meantime. Now, I wancha da go stay with Aunt Stella. She'll take care of everything. 'N' juss da letcha know: I won't be comin' home for da funeral, so don't be expectin' me, 'n' don't bother askin' about it. If anyone has a problem with it you can tell 'em I said they can fuck off. Ar'ight?' She'd already hung up.

Hmmm...I couldn't decide what to do first. I wanted to yodel out in elation and dance in celebration...but it wasn't happening. I was telling myself to do it: express my long-awaited feelings of happiness and relief. But once I stood up I also felt obligated to feel sad and scared. But over what? What did I even lose?...I lost control of my body: icy brain, irregular heartbeat, quivering wrists, twitches in glutes, elbows, shoulders, rocks and sand in throat, cold skin, sweating—dry, calm eyes fixated on something not registering within my icy brain. I found myself hung up in a Gordian knot of indecisiveness, and though the handle of the sword was resting in my palm, the rope was like a million-pound chain wrapped around the same hand.[3] I couldn't swing. And even if I could, I couldn't aim. I could feel myself faltering, like how fickle people will lie about a deceased person they once despised: the all-too-human justification and absolution of the dead...*but whaddabout God 'n' the only Justice 'n' Absolution thit madders? is my father, the King of Nothing, presently before St. Peter, the Prince of the Apostles? will he try da use intimidation da make the Prince slide Heaven's Key inda the gate?...wonder if I'll be a part his particular judgment?...hmm, if it can be said that he had a thousand specks in his eyes, 'n' I but one large plank, will God still forgive us both? does God forgive ALL blindness? will he be forgiven for bein' another workin'-class zero? a reflection of his environment? a product of the times? will God overstand his soul on a level thit I can't?......HA! I can't believe it: my father's akshly DEAD, on his way da HELL!: I mean, where else could the destiny be for the man thit caused so much violence in my soul!...(a sustained moment of silence)...well, Rick, if you can hear me, I tol' myself I'd never shed a tear for yir cleansing, 'n' I*

---

[3] A Gordian knot is a complex problem that is unsolvable within the substance of the problem itself. Its origin comes from a knot tied by Gordius, the first king of Phrygia. According to an oracle, the only person who could untie the knot is the destined ruler of Asia. After failing to untie it, Alexander the Great cut the knot with one swing of his sword: "the Alexandrian solution." He went on to conquer Asia.

won't, 'n' never will, not in public, not in secrecy: not a drop for damnation, sensuality, sorrow, penance, or joy[4]: it's gonna be a long way dahn...

> *Ring! Ring! Ring!*
> 'Teresa, put Pessi on.'
> 'He's sleep-ing, and I'm busy get-ting ready for work. He'll—'
> 'No, go fuckin' wake 'im up right now!'
> 'Don't get fa-king smart with me, asshole!—Hey, Zach! Wake up! It's your asshole friend!—Of course!...'
> 'Yo.'
> 'I neejada come over pronto.'
> 'How's come?'
> 'I'm not gonna explain it over the phone but it's sum'n big, ar'ight?'
> 'Fine. I'll have her da drop me off on her way da work.'
> 'She's gotta car now?'
> 'Brand fuckin' new. She—'
> 'Look, I'm not too concerned with her fuckin' car right now. Juss come over. Peace.'
> *Click.*

...Without knocking, Pessi walked in. My sense of urgency over the phone must've sounded more positive than negative because, with the playboy smirk, he threw a punch at my boot-cast. After leg-dodging the swing, I stood up and told him to sit down. Instead, he jumped up on my bed and started bouncing up and down...his freshly-shaven head nearly hitting the ceiling with every jump...his black Docs unremorsefully twisting and grinding down into my burgundy sheets at the point of bounce-back. Yeah, Pess was having a grand 'ol time springing up and down like a four-year-old, doing twisty-turnies, and occasionally kicking his legs out at me, as I stood there watching indifferently...til I said, 'Rick's dead.' He jumped his last jump and fell straight down on his ass into a perfect edge-of-the-bed formation.

> 'Wha'?'

'Ya know, Richard Vallano, my dad: he died this mornin'. Had a massive heart attack. Ma found 'im rolled over in the bathroom. Said she didn't hear a sound from him. He finely learned da keep his mouth shut.'

At a loss for words, Pessi rubbed his hand down over his eyes very gradually...then his nose...then his mouth: a perfect course for disbelief. Although it was probably from being high, his hazel eyes were b-shot and bleary; his muscled jaw and chin atrophied into forlornness; his entire face and neck flushed into a disarray of mottles. I was wondering if I'd looked the same way; that is, before I sent Rick straight to the gallows.

> '*Well?*' I said gravely.
> 'I'm—I dunno—I'm juss in complete shock. I'm rill sorry, man—'
> 'HA! Gotcha!'
> 'Wha'? You mean he's not dead?'
> 'No, he's sercly dead. I juss don't give a fuck.'

---
[4] Reference to the five types of tears described in St. Catherine of Sienna's dialogue to God [Part III, "A Treatise of Prayer"]

Even Pessi, the one who knew me best, was dropped for six, evidenced by the sudden swell of his eyes, as the rest of his body fossilized on the edge of my bed. Once able to speak, he said, 'Wait, izzy dead or not? Don't fuck with me.'

'No, he's as dead as Larry, Moe, 'n' Curly, 'n' 'at's why it's such a great day for jokin' around. *Nyuck, nyuck, nyuck. However*,' I noted sharply, exaggerating the sullenness of the word, 'since people tendda get all fucked up over dishit, dere's sum'n we nee'dda work out.' I shouldn't have said the former p̲a̲r̲t̲ of the statement, but locked in a state of selfishness, I wasn't making the proper correlations. 'See, I gadda date with Ivy tanight, 'n' if she finds out, den I gadda deal with *her* tryin'ah deal with *me*, know whadda mean. So you can't say a fuckin' word da Squawk. I'm bein' dead – serious.' (Inside, I giggled over "dead serious," not because I fully sounded out "serious," but because it was a natural pun.)

'Ar'ight, V, but—'

'Don't worry; I'm gonna let Ivy know when the time's right. Prahblee after the funeral 'n' 'at, which I'm not goin' to.'

'Yir sercly not goin' da the funeral?'

'Nope. Why take my bidderness 'ere 'n' ruin everyone else's good time?'

'Damn, V. Not goin' da yir dad's funeral: dat's—I dunno—bold, I guess. I mean, I know ya hated 'im 'n' all, but people always say whenever you get older dat's the kinda thing you'll end up regrettin'.'

'Dohnchu overstand: now thit he's fuckin' dead dere can be *nooo* reconciliation for all the shit he put me 'n' Ma through. Fuck, he couldnt've reconciled if he woulda lived da be a hundred! It's like 'iss, Pess: ya never know when yir gonna go, but once yir gone, you can't expect everyone da forgive ya for shit you left hangin' in the air for f̲a̲r̲ ̲too long. Yeah, I could see if you fucked up one day 'n' didn't, so to speak, "redeem" yirself 'n' 'en died a week later. But with *him* we're talkin' years of—of—fuck! I don't even have da words for it right now. All I know is he fucked up his soul 'n' damaged mine. I can heal mine but never his. Z'at make sense?'

'Yeah, I guess. Never rilly thought of it dat way. But of course I don't goddua good cawidge like you.'

'Shuh da fuck up with 'at shit. It's got nuh'n'ah do with cawidge. I bet if I went around here 'n' surveyed da students, 99% of 'em would think I'm fuckin' demented. So fuck them too. Oh! here, maybe *dis'll* make my reasoning a liddle clearer. (Fuck, I can't believe I haven't shared dis nice liddle story with ya—prahblee 'cause I been tryin'ah block it oudda my fuckin' mind.) But anyway, lass time you were over my house—when I came home for da weekend—ju recognize anything different?'

'No. Why?'

'Well, ya know how Razzle was always the liddle barker?'

'Yeah.'

''Member hearin' 'im bark 'at day?'

'*Umm*, not rilly. But I dunno why I would even remember sum'n like 'at. Why?'

'Rick fuckin' killed 'im. Well Ma said he "accidentally" tripped over his chain 'n' fell on 'im, but I think he'z drunk 'n' pissed off about losin' his job, 'n' Razzle was barkin', so he went out 'n' strung 'im up by his chain. 'N' ya know, I hadn't seen 'im since 'en or I woulda straight out fuckin' *decked* 'im. In fact, I didn't seen 'im *once* since I been here. Talked over da phone about my insurance: but that's about it. So I mean, I don't think I need any more reasons not da feel da way I do. Right?'

'You rilly think he'd kill Razzle?' he asked, looking sadly into his lap.

'*Accident? Murder?* Who the fuck knows?! Who the fuck cares?! It's all the same in the end: no more Razzle! But for now, let's juss keep all this on the low so I can have a fun normal weekend. 'N' I'm serious, Pess: if you try givin' me any sympathy, whether directly or indirectly, I'm not gonna handle it well. I juss wancha da be *happy* with me. 'N' I'd think oudda all people you'd be da one thit would overstand where I'm comin' from.'

'No—I do,' he said distantly, probably running through his mind simulated images of Razzle's and Rick's last moments on earth. Then he looked up with the same childish sadness he bore when our friend Matty McCoo passed back in June. 'I juss feel bad for Ma. She's prahblee not in the best a shape.'

'No, she's not. 'N' ya know, on one hand, I overstand the emotional attachment 'n' 'at. But her pain isn't over his death *per se;* it's over her longin' for sum'n she so deeply wansta have. 'N' it's juss got ta da point where she was tryin'ah convince herself *it* was once 'ere, 'n' 'at she's gonna find her way back da *it.* But speakin' with eighteen years of experience, 'n' seein' what went dahn in *my* time, I'm guessin' 'ere's nuh'n for her da find, nuh'n'ah feel nostalgic over—no *it.* Da fact is, she was juss a young foreign girl who came over here, fell blindly in love with a monster, 'n' 'en was eventually beaten inda fear of ever leavin' 'im once she found out da monstrous truth, know whadda mean.'

'True...Hey, maybe now I can marry her,' he joked but not without hesitation as the mark of compunction quickly flushed into his face. But, no! I wouldn't have it!

'That's the spirit! Now come on, you punk-ass bitch.' I clawed the top of his beautiful fuzzed head. 'I'm takin' ya out da lunch. Bahcha gadda drive 'cause I gadda rest the 'ol leg for yir beatin' tamarra. See, nuh'n can stop me! Nuh'n!'

'Yir sercly fuckin' crazy, V.'

Perhaps he said that with double meaning? Just in case he had, I replied with double meaning: '*Lassalu friiri u tintu omu ntra u so stissu ogghiu.'*

'What's 'at mean?'

'"Let da wicked man fry in his own oil." It means, let bad people suffer the consequences of their deeds—alone. Why wastchir time strugglin' in vain for those who don't deserve it?'

Without another word, I grabbed my shit and we headed out the door. I had such a big smile on my face. But during my elated explanation of the proper etiquette for sackcloth and ashes, I'd forgotten to take into consideration that Pessi had gone through this before. The difference was: he'd been affected in the *traditional* way: he had cared...

...It had been about eight years since Pessi went swimming at the closest public pool to Verna, which was in Colt Hill: about a thirty-minute walk up and down the hills but only a five-minute drive. Although the tiled baby-blue pool-liner was usually grimy, and the water contaminated with fresh piss and bleach, it was refreshing when you had no air conditioner and the summer heat was unbearable. It had also been about eight years since Pessi's father drove him to the public pool in Colt Hill.

Outside the closed gates on that humid summer evening, Pessi just sat there on the curb, bored. He had his orange beach towel draped over his head, waiting for his father to pick him up as he did when Pessi went swimming and wanted to stay til closing time. (He'd asked me to come, but I had to go to my Aunt Gina's birthday party.) After waiting nearly an hour, Pessi desperately wanted to go home; the sun was now out of sight. The thought crossed his mind to walk home but when you're young everyone puts so much fear in you about walking home alone in the dark, especially since Colt Hill is filled with welfare-class Blacks. He was only ten so he didn't know any better and had to rely on parental guidance. No matter what neighborhood or town, the welfare-class Blacks were ever ready to shoot us working-class Italians either out of jealousy or the criminality borne within their wretched souls. 'Dem fuckin' niggers—' Rick once told me and Pessi when we wanted to walk to the store one night to buy candy cigarettes to smoke for the night '—will shoocha 'n' not think twice.' 'Deez fuckin' niggers around here—' Pessi's father once told us when we wanted to walk to the store one night to steal real cigarettes to smoke for the night '—want us all dead 'cuzza whad our ancestors did do 'em hundreds a years ago! I say chain 'em all back up!' (The little versions of Pessi and I tittered.) 'Yinz think I'm jokin'? Go turn on the news. 'At's all idd is: niggers robbin' 'n' killin' everyone. Why dohnchinz go walk over da Nig-North 'n' see wha' happens?' No, Pessi just couldn't walk home alone at night back then.

Finally, a ride came for him: two white wholesome police officers; he was saved from the darkness. They helped Little Pessi into the car, not speaking a meaningful word to him. He sat in the squeaky backseat with the dried orange towel still draped over his head, slightly dipping over his little flushed face. He didn't want to see what was coming anyway. I couldn't even imagine what it was like—(chlorine and confusion mixed with vendor food and fear?)—when they pulled into the emergency entrance at the hospital. Pessi wasn't sick or hurt. He just wanted his father to pick him up from swimming. Not sick. Not hurt. He just wanted to go home. He didn't overstand, and they didn't want to explain it. He would find out for himself.

Inside, his mother just bled. She didn't reach out to hold his hand. Didn't run her fingers through his short course hair. Didn't smile. Didn't cry. Didn't tell him everything will be all right. Didn't sing him a goodnight lullaby. Didn't say, 'Hey, it's my liddle Zachy,' as I'd heard her say many times whenever we walked in. No, his mother didn't say that nor did she look at him. But she didn't look anywhere else either. Her eyes were closed and her mouth opened with a tube. She didn't, just couldn't, say anything to him before slipping far away.

Sometime before all that, his father was up and limping around the eerie white halls of the hospital, trying to walk off a minor sprain. Maybe a little bruised up and worn out and hung over and of course a little late to pick up Little Pessi—but he was all right...he was all right...he was all right...he was *aaaaall* right...

At night Pessi could still hear two voices screaming and see three fists flailing...still hear the deafening sound of eight brakes locking and eight tires squealing...still see innumerable lights flashing and hear innumerable sirens screaming like vehicular armageddon...still see the Great Angel gently picking his mother up off the glass-covered road, some of her being carried into the ambulance, some taken higher above...still see his father's bloodshot eyes glared in the eerie florescence of hospital halls as he shook off an irritating sprain...yes, he could still vividly see all the flashing lights and sharply hear every deafening sound and acridly taste all the blood and water from that day...and he was never even there...she'd just bled herself dry while he was swimming at the public pool...but of course afterward he (and even I) had to piece together some kind of story for his memory of what it would've been like to watch his mother bleed to death in the hospital that he'd been driven to after all had been said and done.

...'Come *iii-iin!*' I sang from the belly of my bed, marking the page in *The House of Mirth,* my latest personal read. I gleefully tossed it up and over my other books; it slapped down on the desk like a brisk celebratory clap! What a day to be mirthful! Come on in and enjoy!

The door opened—swinging back like the cover of a classic book— and Ivy entered in her coy, peekish way. She seemed to be a habitual oscillator of shy-intros that nurtured into motherly-middles then culminated in sha-bam-endings.

'Hey, how's the leg feel today?'

'Not too bad. But wow! look atchu! You look fuckin' amazin'!'

She was wearing a cloud-white long-sleeve blouse with prominent cuffs yanked up just below her elbows; the blouse had shiny opal buttons running up the middle, all but the top two buttoned. Below the blouse, she had on an olive skirt made out of something thin and stretchy. On her feet were black pumps, adding uncalled-for inches over my black spikes. Her mocha curls were pulled back into a chignon with "flowers in her hair," as the Oldies song goes—well, actually just one little red flower tucked behind her left ear, but I knew that *"she could make me HAPPY!—HAPPY!—HAPPY! Oh I don't know why. She simply caught my eye. I loooove the flower girl."*[5]

'Aww, thank you. That's very sweet.' She gave me a chin-down-to-the-shoulder coy pose. 'You already know no matter what you wear I still think you're the hottest guy in the world.' She leaned down and kissed me on the lips; I wanted to grab her by the back of the neck and forcibly sling her down on the bed with me, then make love to her slowly but passionately like a budding grandiflora. Such a rosy, rosy day it was!

After I opened my eyes from the kiss, I said, 'Now that's a lie!'

'No it's not! I'm *sooo* attracted to you. I can't even control myself, and that's not good for a good little Catholic girl.'

'Well it can't be true only 'cause I'm number-2 on the Top Five Hottest Guys In The World.'

---

[5] Lyrics from "The Rain, the Park, and Other Things" by Cowsills

'Oh, I see,' she giggled. 'And who's number-1? Wait! It better not be *me* since it's the *guy's* list.' She pinched my shoulder. I sat up and she sat down next to me. I started running my fingers in all kinds of directions through her mocha curls.

'No, yir definitely number-1 on the Top Five Hottest Chicks. But for da guy's, number one *iiiiis*—' I bent down and began a drum roll on my boot-cast, '—the one, the only, *Alfredo Pacinooooo!*'

'*What?!* He's so old now! *Eww!—Eww!*' She scrunched up her face and shook the eww-no-not-him right out of her.

'Oh shudup. Pacino's not *eww! eww!* But if ya wanna dwell on his present age 'n' not his physical prime: chicks still love *Harrison Ford* 'n' *Mel Gibson* 'n' 'er old as fuck. Da only difference is Pacino can act. *HOO-AH! HOO-AH!*'

'*Awww!* You're so cute when you get all riled up. Wanna power up on my hair and do the voice?'

'Sure; I love you.'

'What?!'

'I said, "Sure; I'd love too."'

'No you didn't!'

'*Umm*, yes I did. I'm absolutely *positive* that's what I said, you crazy, hard-of-hearin', sexy scent-of-a-woman. Why, whaja think I said?'

'Nothin',' she replied coyly, letting herself fall against me.

At her request, I pulled a long thick strand from her chignon and wrapped it around her head and out over her check so I could look her directly in the eyes as I did it: '*POWER UP!!!*' Instantly, her emeralds exploded and her sorrel cheeks became ruddy. Then, for the first time, I decided to have *her* power up—on her hair, not mine; I explained how mine wasn't magical enough to power up on; besides, there was too much gel in my spikes. After persuading her to chomp down on her hair, I made her do it five times til she said *POWER UP!!!* in the right funny voice—a sound never known to the world of animation, but if ever, a surefire classic.

As we sat next to each other—the lock back in my mouth, looking into her tropical gems—seemed I finally knew (through two sensations) what *peace* meant: passion-in-the-heart coupled with attainability-in-the-mind. After some time, I slithered the lock out and stood up to get ready. We were going to the movies but hadn't decided what movie yet. While popping in my contacts, I was telling her humorous Dr. Rosenbaum-stories and how I thought he was coolest teacher ever and how we shared the same sense of humor and how he was looking into getting me a job at the writing center. I couldn't remember the last time that I'd smiled so much over basically nothing!

'Jeez, you seem like you're in a really good mood today.'

'Maybe 'cause I am.'

'How come?'

"Cause *yiiiiir* here. 'N' *Peeessi's* here. 'N' can't wait da whip his 'n' Squawk's ass tamarra night.' (I'd begun addressing Teresa as "Squawk" to everyone; Ivy and Pessi thought it was funny, and Squawk, embarrassed by it, was stilling thinking up a laudable comeback.) 'Ya bedder bring yir' A-game tamarra 'cause I refuse da lose—'

Just then, the door opened and an exhausted Luke walked in. He was dressed in wrinkled tan slacks and a plain white V-neck. Him and Ivy had encountered each other several times and would talk about the most boring things because there didn't seem to be much else you could talk about with Luke. We didn't do three-way talks either. If Ivy started talking to Luke, I would do my own thing til they were done with their boring confabulation. Sometimes I would catch a subdued hunger in Luke's blue-gray eyes; his belly wasn't grumbling either, know whadda mean.

After setting his books down, and two-hand gripping the back of his desk chair to get up the strength to speak, Luke, with an unctuous face, began telling me, by telling Ivy, how he was going home for the weekend since he'd yet to visit his family.

'Y'all on your way out?'

'Yep. Mr. Vallano is takin' me to a movie.'

'Cool, cool. What movie?'

'We haven't decided yet. He has picky tastes in movies. But I think I'm gonna make him watch a romantic comedy. And he'll just love it. Won't you, Vinny?'

I picked up one of the crutches that I no longer used and began smacking Ivy across the leg. She was arching and bending around like Gumby, trying to block the crutch's head from hitting her in the snatch, but it wasn't doing her any good. I was being too pokey.

'Hey! Come on now! Behave!'

'Hey! Come on now! Be got—before I pee myself!' I warned, randomly drawing on past memories, and speaking in plays, just to put Luke in confusion and Ivy in delight.

So Ivy told Luke goodbye, and good luck with weekend schoolwork, and good times with the family, and other good ol' boring bearshit. Then we headed out the door.

'All right, thanks, Ivy,' said Luke the bewildered bear, waving us a pawy goodbye. 'Have fun. See ya on Sunday, Vinny!'

Kewl, kewl. KEEEEEWL!!!

...'See, I told ya you'd like it!' declared Ivy, as she opened the car door for me. She placed her left hand on the middle of my back, and her right hand underneath the obedient leg, then tucked me into the seat. After wrapping both arms around my torso and half the seat, she kissed me.

'Wha'? You seris? I didn't fuckin' like 'at shit.'

'Please. I saw you tearin' up, my handsome sentimental devil. So quit your cryin' and face it: YOU – CRIED!' She shut the door in my face.

I seriously didn't drop one tear during *Runaway Bride*. If I would have teared up it would have been because I wanted to run away from the theater. But the one who had bride idea of picking the stupid flick wanted to stay and watch it. So I engaged in flicking popcorn 'n' 'at at the veiled idiots around me.

Unlike in my car, I didn't have to reach across the seat to unlock Ivy's door because she had—boot-cast drum roll!—a metallic-yellow Beemer! Her father bought her the sporty car as a $25K high school graduation present. And although she'd heard my Top Five Cars, which included

Beemers, she'd withheld her wheels from my knowledge, saying, at first, that she drove a Civic. When I asked the point of the white-lie, she said that she didn't want wheels to be a factor in me deciding whether I wanted to roll with her, to which I thanked her for thinking that I'm *that* shallow but when can I drive it, of course joking, but of course not joking because as soon as my leg healed I was fuckin' driving it.

'*Ummm.* Whaddaya doin'?'

'*Ummm,*' she mocked, 'taking out your CD and puttin' in mine.'

'Which is?'

'Celine Dion.'

I laughed just like I had at Chow Down when she'd sullied her Top Five Bands with the same name. 'Dat's ar'ight. I'll pass.'

'Sorry, hun: my car, my music. You got to listen to your CD on the way; now it's my turn. Plus, I'm drivin' so I need music that'll keep me calm and not make me wanna drive off a cliff.'

"Z'at so? Well I'm *not* drivin' which means whenever you ~~start~~ drivin'—focused on keepin' us *safe*—sum'n *else* is gonna end up in the CD player anyway.'

'*Grrr.* Why do have to be so difficult?!'

I snatched Celine from her hand and shoved it back into her CD case, hoping to scratch it up a bit. Then I stuck Ice Cube back in the tray. Without saying another word, she fired up the Beemer...jerked the clutch into reverse...cut the wheel hard to the left...backed out of the spot...then shot forward like someone ready to peel rubber and bust caps.

While Ivy finessed her Beemer through the weekend chaos of the surrounding shopping centers—this, about five miles from LaSalle—I smoked a fag; I had to con her into believing that if I rolled down the window it wouldn't leave an odor; she made me keep my hand hung out just in case.

'So you wanna go back to my place for a bit?'

'Sounds good da me,' I coughed. It was fortunate for us that she had a single room, which was a hard thing to get because of the limited availability, but not a problem for her given that the Pinedas had Aristod all mobbed up.

'Cool 'cause I told my parents I'd try to lure you back tonight so they can finally meet you.'

'Wait, you meant go back da yir *real* house?'

'*Mmhmm.* That's what I meant and that's what I just said.'

'Ehh, I dunno; I'm not tryin'ah meechir parents with my leg all busted up. Can't we juss wait til next week when it's off?'

'*Pleeeease!*' she blurted into plea, giving the Beemer more gas as we headed back down the dark bland highway. 'They won't care about your leg. All you have to do is say hello. They're super nice. My mom will like you for sure.'

'So z'at mean 'ere might be a problem witchir pop?'

'*Noooo.*' Keeping her eyes on the road, she fashioned a blatant ear-to-ear smile. I kept my face turned but drifted into thought about how I just lost my father, on this very day, and was already being forced into picking up a new one; God works in mysterious ways but rarely down the fast lane! But perhaps—to break it down here—I was about to receive a *better* father? one who would tell me that he's proud of me when I graduate college, since

I never had one proud of me when I graduated high school, no less against the odds, and moreover, matriculated at a laudable college?

'*Please, Vinny, pleeeeeease,*' Ivy continued to plead playfully.

'I dunno about dis liddle scheme a yirs,' I dramatized. 'Sounds like trouble up ahead.'

She looked over long at me enough to bat her long crescent-moon eyelashes, and say, '*For meeeee?*' Her hand moved down to my knee, inching ever so close to my—

'Ar'ight, fine: I'll go. But let's keep it brief.'

'Yeah—I was pretty sure you'd see it *my* way.'

Her way? *Riiiiight.* Shaking my head obstinately like a horny lil devil, I unfroze the Cube and we banged on down the road, heading towards—wait, her parents? *Ahhh shiiiiit. Her Nestside Connection! GULP!*...

'Daddy, this is Vincent Vallano. But most people just call him Vinny.'

'Nice to meet you, Vincent. I'm Edward.'

'Nice to meet you, too, Mr. Pineda,' I said clearly and politely, while matching the hard grip of his hand; he was a shade darker than Ivy.

'Hello, Vinny. I'm Sandy.'

'Nice to meet you, too, Mrs. Pineda,' I addressed her in the same waspy manner, while matching the delicate touch of her hand; her skin was three shades paler than Ivy's—just *plain white*.

'Ivy told us what happened to your leg,' said Sandy. 'Is it almost healed?'

'Yes, I believe so. I have an appointment on Monday to hopefully get it taken off.' *Ahhh shiiiiit! A split-infinitive! GU-uh-hu-uh-LP!*

'That's certainly good to hear,' chirped Sandy like a tiny thrush. 'Well come in. Tell us a little about yourself. We've already heard several good things from Ivy, so it's time for you to elaborate on your own behalf.' She winked at Ivy, who just rolled her eyes in return. As they took steps forward, I remained locked in the shining Douglas-Fir foyer. Not because of my leg: it was fine. But because not only did I feel nervous about another first-time experience, but I also found myself tied up in another Gordian knot of indecisiveness: how could I walk forward with a family that wasn't my own when I already had one? one that *needed me* (the strongest amongst 'em) more than ever?

Once the Pinedas realized that I hadn't taken a step, they turned around in harmony.

'Come on, Vincent,' Edward said brusquely.

'Don't worry; we don't bite' Sandy said brightly. She smiled, Edward glared, Ivy blushed, and I shook my head without shaking it and started walking forward with robotic steps. Edward was walking in the front with his arm around his little girl, while I followed slightly behind Sandy, checking her ass out: the ol' sexist, or rather, sexually-charged, find-out-what-your-girlfriend-will-look-like-in-thirty-years. And I was happy: Ivy had a real nice future ahead of her behind her.

'Sandy,' Edward began, releasing his hold on Ivy, 'will you run into the kitchen and bring out some *hors d'oeuvres?*'

Hors d'oeuvres? Hmmm, izzer a certain way yir sposta eat hors d'oeuvres? I don't wanna be made a spectacle of over that too. I seen 'at shit in movies: how some pauper doesn't know how da eat fine foods, 'n' everyone laughs at 'im but the pauper always woos 'em with his impeccable wit. But I'm not in the mood da be doin' 'at shit. I mean, hors d'oeuvres? Wha' da fuck happened'ah pop 'n' pretzels? I'd like da fuckin' throw some pretzels at Pop's head. Walkin' all stiff like 'at...

The Pineda's Victorian house smelled like vanilla candles, and from what I could observe from the foyer, which was a good bit, it was fastidiously decorated with idyllic paintings, nuclear family portraits, full but viable plants, and so many ornate antiques that I couldn't even begin to ramble 'em off or imagine what they paid for 'em; that is, if they hadn't been handed down. It was by far the most beautiful and sensual house I had ever entered. It was like walking backwards a hundred years to 1899. You could tell that it had been restored not out of love for the Queen but for the sake of wooing and wowing. I mean, you walked in through a wide wooden door with a colorful stained glass pane. The door so wide you could carry a coffin through it. The foyer was rather large too: had a redwood floor shooting straight ahead with a thin but long champagne rug thrown out. Immediately on the right: a winding grand staircase going up and disappearing into the area above me; at each turn, the balustrade had not regular bulb posts but large newels: a bronzed Adam (the first turn) and a bronzed Eve (the second turn) standing up with tiny lighted bulbs hovering around 'em. And directly above me was an opulent white ceiling medallion, a swirly diamond-shaped one, from which a golden gas lamp hung and held three cranberry-colored candle cups. To my left, still in the foyer, was a pristine grandfather clock that ding-donged as I stared at its prominent pendulum. To my right, about halfway up the foyer and cut into the staircase, sat a light-pink-dark-green settee next to a tall off-white statue of a naked boy covered in golden leaves and lit candle cups. The parlors, of course, had been replaced by a sitting room and a family room, both opened up more than the original Victorian architecture, if I had to guess. The walls started with a thick tongue-and-groove wainscot paneling, then above, all around, in every place I could see, the walls displayed an intricate millefiori pattern: shining golds and pinks slithering through spaces between russet wallflowers. A thin black "picture molding," as they called it back in the day, slightly jutted out about halfway up the walls, and at the top ran a fancy white frieze—this crown molding the home of dimensional figures of antiquity. Looking around, there seemed to be a Corinthian cornice in every corner, and silky cascade valances above the windows. As for the rooms, straight ahead, at the back end of the house, was the kitchen, mostly hidden to the right. Next to it, on the left, was the dining room—one of those million-dollar rooms, as I call 'em—which could be seen through the backend of the sitting room, which was up the aisle a bit, to the left. Inside there, on the hardwood floor, lay a large Persian rug decorated in red and gold. On the walls: Victorian paintings neatly ordered. All around: spider plants dropping down—down between a lavish furniture set of delicate cream with dark downy swirls. Atop little intricate metal stands: pink Asiatic lilies, African violets, Mexican Poinsettias. And in lieu of a television with a remote: a fireplace with tools, placed between double-hung color-stained windows. To the right side of the aisle was the family room, bejeweled in velvety Christmas colors so rich and deep; in the corner furthest away sat a large silver television angled towards me. Under Edward's lead, we were ordered to sit in the sitting room, not the lively family room with the television. Yes, he wanted to sit in the room with the fireplace to ensure warm person-to-person communication, making me a bit sweaty as the thought of talking with her parents over *hors d'oeuvres* swarmed through my head. But man, this Victorian manor was a wowzer!

'So Ivy tells me you go to Aristod,' noted Edward, looking like a stern Mexican dignitary. He'd sat down to my right in one of the euphoric chairs; Ivy and I had sat down on a matching sofa against the back wall, Ivy's knees near his.

'Yes, I do. But Ivy and I didn't know we both went to Aristod until Teresa 'n' my best friend introduced us in Pittsburgh. So it was all rather coincidental.'

Before replying, he stared me down with his black kingly eyes, and I knew not to look away, and at the same time, knew not stare back too defiantly. His brown face had intense taut skin and a rigid black moustache. The hair on his head was full and dull, combed up and back, but the style itself was insignificant: too common, too predictable, too necessary for his overall stature. Almost satirically, he was wearing a red expensive-looking robe, tied closed, with matching pants, and black slippers.

'Yes, *coincidental* seems like the right word,' he replied, crossing one leg over the other with cocksureness. 'Nevertheless, I'm glad to see you're in college, no less one of the finest in the nation. We're very proud of Ivy for getting in.' He shined at this as if no one else in their family had ever made it to Aristod. 'Ivy, did you tell your friend that you were the valedictorian in high school?'

'Oh who cares. Vinny is way smarter than me anyway.' Ivy smiled and winked at me because I'd obviously turned to look at her, biting my lip but burning to ask why she would say that! As I looked back at Edward— forming a modest countenance on my face—I saw that his boxed face had become perturbed at the thought of *me* being smarter than *his* daughter. Thankfully, Sandy came prancing in during the awkward moment with a fruit bowl, small plates, and forks. She was short and thin. On her small attractive face were blue-gray eyes with a copper ring around the pupil, tiny lips painted pastel-pink, the same color as her cheeks, which had faint freckles, and, at closer look, descended down her neck. Her sandy-blonde hair was cut straight around the collarbone, curled inward uniformly, with a quaint set of bangs. Ahh! didn't look a *bit* like Ivy! Probably from the present attention on food, I was thinking how she was like American pie: always sweet tasting and sweet smelling, but b-o-r-i-n-g!

'What would you like to drink?' asked Sandy (probably a former Smith) Pineda. 'Sprite, milk, juice, water—'

'Water will be fine. Thank you.'

'Iv?'

'Water.'

'Okay. You guys go ahead and dig in but I have more goodies comin'.' Sandy Smith pranced back to the kitchen like a little pale chic on the move, leaving the tanner skins to get back to business.

Not missing a beat, Edward struck back at Ivy, *while looking at me*, saying, 'Oh now is he? You're smarter than my daughter?'

'No, I wouldn't say that at all. Her knowledge on biology, animals, and science in general is really amazing. I love animals, too, but I don't know a thing about the complex science behind it all. And—'

'Well what *do* you know about?' he spat; I think I heard Ivy blurt a giggle. 'Ivy here wouldn't say such a thing unless she meant it. She's brilliant. The valedictorian.' Seemed he would've patted Ivy on the back and punched me square in the face if he hadn't decided to pick up a cup of hot tea from the glass coffee table in front of us. He took a snooty sip—without averting his gaze on me.

'Uhh, I guess literature,' I stammered, feeling edgy on the edge of the couch. 'I plan on being a writer of some kind. But for now I'm just trying to become well-read—'

'I usually read two books a month,' he calmly replied, leaving the vainglory to be read in his provoking eyes.

I'm sure ya do, you fuckin' liar. I betchu haven't read a fuckin' book all year. 'Wow, that's very impressive, especially when you work fulltime. Even if people have the time, not too many people read nowadays,' I spoke reminiscently as if suddenly a centenarian. 'Do you have any favorite authors?' Meanwhile, up in the noggin, I was thinking that Ivy was surely getting a kick out of my slow-talking, waspy façade because she wasn't doing anything to stop it, nor point out the change. Besides, it seemed necessary. 'Bahdif my workin'-class yinzers in Pixburgh cou' see me now,' I thought, 'dey'd prahblee be riddy da ram my ass with a fuckin' still girder!'

Just then, Sandy Smith came in and handed me and Ivy water. Still humming her b-o-r-i-n-g songs, she pranced back to the kitchen.

'Favorite authors?' Edward repeated incredulously as if the question was absurd or plain ignorant to ask. So he countered with: 'Who's yours?'

I thought that was pretty odd of him: to turn it around on me.

'Mine's Dr. Seuss!' Ivy quipped with a giggle. Now I knew *with certainty* that she was enjoying the battle beginning to heat up between her bragg~~art~~ boyfriend and her bragg~~art~~ father. But at least I could sense that she was also cheering for me to bust out at some point and outwit him.

'Well it's hard to say who my favorites are since I have favorites for each style, genre, and period. I guess—'

'American authors,' he demanded coolly, instantly dismissing all other authors, which sucked since most of my favorites weren't Americans, especially not those of the modern stock. Alwaysthemore, and more importantly, it finally struck me: what the fuck's seriously going on *here*, right *now*, in *this* house. I couldn't believe this kind of shit actually existed!

I sighed pensively, trying to collect my thoughts. 'American authors. Uhh, I like Faulkner, Fitzgerald, Melville, Baldwin, uhh...' (so far he wasn't looking very impressed) '...Salinger, Zuckerman—'

'Zuckerman!' he exclaimed, his face wincing into disgust. 'That man is a sick pig! I read that one book, oh, what's it called?—' He clutched his fist and turned his kingly head to the side. '—Ahh! *Portley's Objectives!*'

Hahaha! Whadda fuckin' moron! 'N' Porter's Objection is akshly a decent novel. Juss don't challenge 'im. Whadever ya do, do NOT correct or challenge 'im on ANYTHING. 'Oh, I never read that one. I've only read *Jersey Pastures* by him.' LIE!

'Well I tell you, he's a sick, sick man! I don't understand why they publish garbage like that!' He was visibly upset, disconcerted, indignant, ready to burn Zuckerman's oeuvre in the name of chainsmart.

'Oh, Daddy, you're gettin' crazy in your old age.'

'What are you complainin' about now, Edward?' asked Sandy Smith, prancing back in with a tray of crackers, cheeses, meats, tooth-picked melon cubes and avocado spread, which meant I *did* know how to eat *hors d'oeuvres*, although I couldn't eat the meat because it was red, and Ivy couldn't eat the meat because it was meat.

'Nothin'. Vincent here just likes perverted authors,' the meathead blatantly informed his meekwife while pointing at me.

And me flushed.

'Come on, Edward; now what did we teach the kids? "As long as there's no abuse or crime involved, you should at least respect what other people like even if *you* don't like it,"' Sandy Smith said sententiously. 'And I heard what you said about reading two books a month. Two books my ass!'

And he flushed.

And Ivy laughed.

And me was still flushed.

Glowing before us in front of the fireplace, Sandy Smith stood akimbo, like a tiny thrush trying to mock an albatross. 'Cripe, the last thing I saw you readin' was the *Sports Illustrated* swimsuit issue in the bathroom.'

And now his flush went redder than his red robe!

But I didn't dare look—at least not much!

Ivy put her legs up on the couch, rocking around in laughter!

'Nonsense!' he retaliated. Ahhh!

But Sandy Smith, still akimbo, just stared him down with her homespun features, unwavering, so glowingly serious.

'How in the hell would you know what and when I read when you're at the mall all the time?' he barked viciously. The beast is loose! Run, everyone! Run! 'Or when I come home from work and you're immersed in Oprah! And then more Oprah *after* Oprah!'

Edward Pineda was as dead serious as Richard Vallano was seriously dead. But just then, in the moment of it all—a miracle occurred! A miracle! I swear it was a miracle! Everyone started—*laughing?* I couldn't believe it. Laughing? The proud man had been called out, and he'd retaliated swiftly and intensely, and yet there had been a different result from what I'd experienced before. Edward had said the same thing Rick had to Ma, but this time it was funny. Everyone started laughing. He didn't say *coon*, points of accuracy were exchanged, then everyone laughed. We laughed! HA! She watches *Oprah* after *Oprah* and he reads *Sports Illustrated* on the shitter! HA! And Rick's dead! and will soon turn into a pile of shit! HAHAHA! I couldn't wipe the shitty smile off my face because there was just no way Life could get any better! I was living in a pipe dream!

Once the toilet-reading scandal was out in the open, airing itself out in the fresh-scented breezes swirling through the peaceful home, a proud—but comfortably proud—Edward Pineda eased up on me like a laxative. Oh yeah, it was going along real smooth, like fuckin' two-ply. We didn't even shit—excuse me, *sit* in the interrogation-room much longer. After we ate some *hors d'oeuvres*, we went into the more socially-stimulating family room where we watched television on a large flatscreen while conversing over petty things: the changing weather, college life, Hollywood, etc., etc. Edward continued to brag a lot, especially about his and Ivy's lifelong achievements, but most of the time, as if it was a learned habit in the house, we would just let the television drowned him out. Ivy and I sat at one end of an extremely long evergreen sofa, and on the other end, Sandy and Edward were much closer together, but I knew not to move *too* close to Ivy and challenge him on that one special authority of his. So Ivy and I sat side-by-side; whereas Sandy was cuddled into Edward's slender belly which would push her head outward whenever he would swell up with pride. But everyone knew deep-down he was the party's pushover, our personal rag doll, our—well, not mine—but their personal toilet. He didn't care though: he either laughed or let himself flush like a porcelain toilet. At one point, Ivy's younger sister Holly came home from wherever but went to straight up to her room before I could see her. I wasn't really concerned with meeting her anyway because, as Ivy had explained several times, she was a bratty little bitch. Only one other constipated situation arose before Ivy and I left. It was during the news, when Edward started inquiring about my parents.

'So what does your father do?'

'He's, uhh, a supervisor at a still mill right outside Pittsburgh.' I replied with as much false pride as I could muster; I'd previously told Ivy that Rick (of course, at the time, leading her to believe that he was still employed) was a laboring miller, but since he held seniority he was about to be promoted to a floor supervisor, which, if he *had* lived, would've taken another fifty years, or something like that.

'And your mother?'

'Well, she's more-or-less a homemaker. When she was my age, she emigrated here from Catania and—'

'Oh, now where's Catania at?' Sandy Smith chimed in.

'It's—'

'Sicily,' answered Edward, not me. 'Second largest city in Sicily next to Palermo, the capital,' he added, boasting geographic wisdom like a talking-map.

'That's exactly right,' I concurred, while punningly thinking what a *clod* he is: the talking "earth" *and* "oaf" who probably knows more about Gabon than his own clump of native land! I was burning to stand up and say, 'Shahchir fuckin' mouth 'n' lemme answer da—dat's right—DA questions directed towards *ME*, 'specially about *MY* family—WARDO! You know bout *yir* roots, WARDO? Or you like da typical Italian-American: memorize a few foreign swearwords, eat da food, watch American movies thit exploit 'n' misconceptualize yir ancestry, 'n' 'en touchir surname with such vainglory!'

'Well, Vincent, you better be back to visit,' said Wardo at the end of the night, putting his hand on my shoulder. 'And see that girl—' He pointed to Ivy who was waiting for me at the top of the steps. 'That's *my bambina* [6] if you wanna get Italian here. I know she's all grown up now, and I can't

---

[6] [ita] baby girl

always watch over her, but I'll surely be watching over whoever does. *Comprende?'*

'I overstand, Mr. Pineda. No need to worry when she's with me.'

'*Bueno. Ella puede cuidarse sola pero nunca la lastimes.*'[7] Oh man— oh man oh fuckin' man, how I wanted to knock him out right then and there! thinking he had an authoritative ploy to employ: deliberately speaking in a foreign tongue just to cast the unknowing into communicative servility! *Nun criru cussi, Wardo! A prupòsitu, cc'hâ fattu mali sulu u fattu ca si ntuppatu!* [8]

Out of the kitchen, Sandy Smith the songstress came prancing towards us with hum in her throat, pride in her eyes, and a plate in each hand. She'd told me that she had something to give me before we left: the reason why Edward and I were waiting in the foyer (with Ivy on the other side of the open front door). When pride-eyed Sandy handed me the plates, it was with donative humility: a breast-to-breast motion handled gently. 'Here, hun, I made you a plate. I don't know what all you like, but there's cheeses and crackers, some veggie rolls—éclairs, brownies, cookies.'

'Wow, you really didn't have to, but thank you very much.'

'Since you don't have a mother around to cook for you while you're away, you can consider me your college-mommy, if you like.'

'Sure thing. This is, uhh, very nice of you—*college-mommy*.'

With the door swung wide-open, and Ivy able to hear and see us, the four of us shared one last laugh. Then I kissed my new college-mommy on the cheek. Ivy came up, kindly took the plates, then guided beside me as we went down the steps.

'Remember what I said, son,' warned Edward with little authority, and thankfully no more mocking *español.* Without breaking my slow descending stride, I turned around and smiled. He waved and said another "bye, be careful, I love you" to his *bambina*, not me, which was just fine by me. Why would he tell someone who subtly outwitted him all night to be careful? then top it off with his love? I certainly wouldn't.

Ivy drove me back to Philemon Hall, and til she pulled in front of the quiescent dorm, she, yawning a few times, had listened to Celine Dion at a low volume, while I'd been forced to listen to and watch Ma bawling as Rick's heart kept exploding. I was there, too, laughing, as the macabre phenomenon kept replaying itself. Whenever Ma would cry, I would turn around and scream, 'Shudup! I'm tryin'ah enjoy this!'

Ivy turned her blinkers on. We started walking into Philemon.

'Seriously: thank you for meeting my parents. It's a must for them, no matter how old I am, ya know.'

'Yeah, it wasn't all that bad. 'N' at least now I can be *me* again, know whadda mean, my liddle queen.'

She giggled. 'Well I can tell my parents like you, and would no matter what.'

---

[7] [spa] Good. She can take care of herself but don't you ever hurt her.
[8] [scn] I don't think so, Wardo. By the way, the only thing that's hurt her has been your fuckin' constipation!

'You think? I mean, yir dad—he *tried* da be all macho at first but everyone knew da juss laugh it off 'n' so I played along. 'N' you were definitely right abouchir mum bein' so fuckin' upiddy-up 'n' 'at.'

'Seeeee. And now you have a college-mommy. But wow,' she laughed, 'I seriously thought I gonna *die* when...'

...At my door, I told Ivy that she should go park her car and spend the night, but she declined. So I gave her a long kiss goodnight...slowly licking her gums and enamel, while twirling her ribbony chocolate locks around...then, oops, one slipped inside my mouth—*POWER UP!!!*...kissed once more...then she started walking away but suddenly came back to kiss again...then again she walked away, wanting to run back just one – more – time—but didn't—so my Spanish angel waved goodbye with a smile, and I *gliiii*ded into my room with a bigger one.

I was really glad Luke was gone for the weekend. Since it was only Friday, I could get high all weekend without going outside somewhere. Going straight to work, for I was feigning and sore and trying so hard not to think about *it*, I sat down at my desk and pulled out a palette knife. Suddenly a sharp pain jolted through my leg, and from that, I reflexively stuck the tip of the blade deep into the desk, right across the scribbling that said *Visit 160 UC for a good fuck, Kristen Thompson*. I thought if Kristin Thompson could fuck the pain right out of me, I should. But of course, I stayed put because I had a real girlfriend now. I set the knife down...pulled out a blunt...licked it all around...slit it down the middle. After setting the knife down again, I pealed from the blunt the three thin olive-green leaves. Meanwhile, in my head, I was pretending that, together, the leaves constituted the material of the world, and the blunt was my back, so as I pealed the leaves off, it was concurrently lifting the world off my back. After using careful precision—(since pealing the leaves is the most delicate part)—I dumped the tobacco out in the small garbage can next to my desk. Next, I broke up the sticky green...then sprinkled it across the brown fold. Just in case there would be a case, I smashed up one of my painkillers and laced the green ridge. Finally, I rolled it up real tight into a perfected skill. But just in case there would be another case, I swallowed another painkiller before going to the window to smoke the blunt with constant vigilance, although probably unneeded so late at night.

Afterward, I turned on the television and laid down, hoping to fall asleep sooner than later. But the idea of Sleeping Well the night my father died was at war with Customary Custer because by custom such a thing should *never* happen; that is, if you have a civil heart. The stronger part of my conscience was telling me that I should stay up and do nothing but think about *it*, which, to my dismay, is what began happening, even after putting the time and effort into becoming comfortably numb but not becoming very comfortable or numb. I was trying to focus deep into the nostalgia of a classic black-and-white movie, as the power of the sedatives finally intensified. But coupled with and overridden by the all-mighty thoughts, it only made me toss and turn in itchiness, instead of being lulled straight to sweet sleep.

Finally, I got up and decided to pop another painkiller. Lying on my desk—by pure coincidence?—was a blank piece of paper. I sat down and stared at it. After meditating about myself and my strange life to the point that Rick seemed alive and well and completely severed from my present thoughts, while I (gradually being overtaken by a creeping, flushing, isolated sensation) became the one dead or dying, or stuck somewhere in between the two, yearning for one or the other—well, somewhere within that time a poetic epiphany blew through me like a foreboding wind. Taken out of body, and pressed between mind and heart like a curled fetus, I began writing, heedless to the niceties of the meter...

To Ascend and Descend: Nothing in Between

How torn am I, between these lines
To find what it is, which spears the light
Casts the shadows, with all its might
In the twilight, I begin to fly...

In the sky am I, between these spies
To find what it is, which hides my delight
See phantasmal walls; yes, I eye the sight
In the darkness, I deem my plight...

Through the sky I fall, farewell to the wall
Could not make it through, to the other side
Was not one hole or crack, in which to slide
Down by Law—I enjoy the fall...

I rhyme my way down, with chaotic laughter and verse
Nothing makes sense, since this plunge
Has beset my lungs, I mean my tongue
Rhyme I failed my way down to right: "Abjection: my curse!"

'Cause I've hit the ground, the same am I
I can walk and talk, laughter and verse chaotic worse
Further down I need to go, to the edge of the Earth
Into the abyss—now enjoying the flow...

Thewateriscoldbetweenthesewavesofquickspinningseconds
1. To swim is to fear
2. Exiled from up there
3. To the water I'm drowning in
3. Blend, blend, blend
4. Sucking lethean water in
5. Spin, spin, spin
6. To swim is to fear
7. The sky looks so far from here

Ring! Ring! Ring!
In bloody red digits, the alarming alarm clock read 3:36 a.m. Like luciferian eyes flipped vertical, the colon was blinking at me. (Yes, the Devil

does take many forms.) For seven hundred reasons, I was completely out of my mind. Beside me and myself, the phone rang seven hundred times. I picked it up somewhere in between. 'Yeah?'

'Viiiiinyyyyy!' (*sob*sob*sob*sob*) 'Viiiiinyyyyy!...' Yes, Ma angel, my dear little mother, was still wailing hysterically over our fresh bestowal of good fortune.

'What's wrong now?'

'He's duhh—eeeedddd. He's dee—dee—a-dd-duh-duh-dd.'

'So I heard.' (A dead silence of crying—for a while.) 'Hey, Ma, I'm priddy fucked up right now, but ju ever think about how sometimes da most beautiful things in life come from the ugliest?'

She replied by screaming the death right out of her. And I realized how much I loved the sound of it, so I started laughing with her. 'Hey, Ma— *guess whaaaaat? Oedipus is gonna giiiiitchuuu. Lauis is finely deeeaad...Hey—am I scarin'* you?' I let out an abrupt laugh then another then lit a cigarette. 'Don't worry; I'd never hurchu. Dohncha remember: dat's not how the story ends. You'll do it chirself. As for me—well, I'll—' But she'd already hung up.

Afterward, I finished my smoke then hurt myself with as much as I could get into my body.........completely wasted, I passed out.........

...(All around me an abyss of whiteness is pulsating like a throbbing heart. A young girl in a yellow dress approaches. Her glittery black hair is hanging down to her tiny waist. Her eyes look like her hair: black and glittery. There's a pink daisy tucked behind her left ear. She's barefoot. She comes very close to me.) Are you ready? – For wha'? – He's very mad at you. – Who is? – Hey, will you kiss me again? – Whachir name? You look kinda familiar? – Angel Beautiful. – You mean Beautiful Angel? (Instantly, we're naked and I'm on my knees, pulling at her legs. Her breasts are crying down on my head. She then pulls me up by the hair and kisses me. The feeling is beyond euphoria.) – Come. It's time. (We begin walking hand-in-hand towards a black apparition. It's vaguely delineated although sheer whiteness surrounds it. Each step on the way feels euphoric. My dick is erect. But from the waist up my body feels warm as if sheepish.) I have to go now. But will you kiss me one last time? (We kiss til she disappears. I turn towards the hazy apparition.) – Hello? (No answer, but it's not completely silent, for I can hear a methodical tapping off in the distance.) Whaddum I saposta do? This isn't makin' any sense. Dat liddle girl said yir mad at me but I don't even know who you are. Are you a person or juss a black shadow? Hello? Do you talk? Can I tou—(I'm snagged by the throat and thrown down on the ground being choked and choked: the air within me quickly dissipating: everything around me turning blacker and blacker but the apparition turning whiter and whiter: a piano now playing in slow mocking pagan fashion: shrills of a pained bird now resounding clangorously: methodical tapping now knocking loudly like gargantuan Hand of God knocking on gargantuan Gate of Heaven: suddenly my legs thrown straight back behind my head: suddenly wooden board back behind my head: suddenly my wrists forcefully held down to nothing: suddenly I'm being fucked and fucked and fucked: pain beyond pain: fucked and fucked and fucked: piano playing loud pagan songs: in chaotic keys but lugubriously inclined: inward: eclectic triumph: now cacophonic reinforcements:

somewhere metal birds crying clangorously: soft breasts and lowly voices crying desperately: shifty aliens laughing wholeheartedly: louder voices cursing dictatorially: but loudest sound is knocking of gargantuan drum being banged and banged and banged: wrists held down: head banging off wooden board with every fuck and fuck and fuck: pain and pain and pain: choke and choke and choke: knocking and banging, screaming and knocking, fucking and fucking and—'fuuuuuuuck!!!' i scream aloud, swinging my injured body up from the floor? and grabbing out for Jesus? taking a hold of the lower half the frame and ripping it off the wall? 'fuuuuuuucccccckkkk!!!' i scream again, tightly bracing the sides of the painting...smashing it off the wall...the television...the bed...the desk...the ground...smashing it with fury against anything and everything as the framing unravels too fast to notice of the process: but the mahogany pieces are flinging back up, stinging my bare legs like sparks from a welding-torch striking metal. *SMASH! SMASH! SMASH! AHHHH! SMAAAAASH!*...til i'm left with nothing to swing with brute force: just a piece of the lower frame, splintered and warm...

...bent over, i pant and wipe beads of sweat from my face...after catching wind, i feel a lot better...Life is in a natal gasp of hush ...feels like i just puked up gallons of acidic water swamped with stale afterbirth, all of which had been churning in my stomach ever since conception...then i turn on the light...survey the annihilated painting throughout the room...much of it has landed on luke's bed, making me realize the unpoetic reality of how i'm nothing but fucked...in quiet bewilderment and dejection, i began hobbling around, piling up the other pieces on his bed...at one point, i come across a part of the painting that prods me into a reflective moment: the part of the canvas where Jesus' rawboned face had once been: now torn violently at the neck in an upward husk, leaving only the upper-left half of his face: the mouth completely missing...as i stare at it, with a fitting tinge of a churchly nostalgia stirring in the air, seems he's looking up at me with that one diluted left eye, and with no mouth to speak, the eye is telling me in bleary-toned words, 'it wasn't me, my son. not me.'

...outside, underneath the night sky—the moon the only one to bear witness—i sling the garbage bag full of a shattered existence up and into the dumpster...

...inside, i want to go back outside. i can't sleep in the room. i know sleep will never come. the room is making me nauseous. i feel insane and suicidal and scared. it's too late and suspicious to call ivy. so i call teresa to talk to pessi. at first she sounds dead. then she sounds furious. pessi is up. he knows my father is dead. she doesn't. he grabs the phone. i tell him nothing but i tell him i want to sleep there for the rest of the weekend maybe forever because my room is trying to kill me. i tell him i just want to come and sleep and not talk to him. he says all right. i ask him what he'll tell teresa. he says he'll tell teresa that i'm wasted and at a payphone and can't make it back home so i need to come sleep there since i'm only a block down the road. then he says he'll tell her that he'll slit her throat if she tells ivy that i spent the night there. he's smarter than me and i got accepted at one of the best schools in the nation.

i can't walk there. if i walked from philemon to teresa's my leg would fall off or i would get there when it's time to get my cast taken off. i call a taxi. drops me off a few houses down to coincide with pessi's brilliant plan. i fuck up pessi's brilliant plan by bringing a teal-colored bookbag stuffed with clothes, deodorant, toothpaste, toothbrush, cigarettes, medication, money. i'm never going back. my room is trying to kill me.

pessi lets me in. i can't tell how wasted he is because i can't look him in the eyes. his eyes are funny looking. he says something about having just woken up an hour ago because he has a fucked up sleep schedule nowadays. i say, yeah, i'm all right. he walks upstairs to go to bed but he walks downstairs to give me a blanket and a pillow to sleep on the couch because he tells me i can sleep in a bedroom on a bed. i tells him beds are for lovers and i'm a hater. he laughs and jabs me in the shoulder. he leaves. on the couch i lie in a supine state, watching a colored movie on the blackened backdrop which is the ceiling: on the grass, we're encircled by steaming heaps of meat rising upward tens of feet. in the middle, luke and Jesus are kicking me in the ribs, while rick's he<u>art</u> keeps exploding all over my naked mother who's getting fucked from behind by a sphinx who's supposed to be oedipus. razzle is playing a piano with the grotesque hands of an old black man. in a gruffy, distorted, baritone voice razzle is singing the lines: '*feeeeeed*lot—dey sent some of us to the – *feeeeed*loooot. we been – bought 'n' bagged. – we been – priddy-FIED by the tag. – 'cause dey sent some of us to the *feeeeeedloooot*...(***piano solo****)...oh Lord, why can't they—' *(a deep dropping tone)* '—juuuuss – leeeet – uuuuus – RAW-OOOOOOOT?' razzle, with the grotesque hands of an old black man, is playing in slow downward scales but hits a shrill chord every time rick's he<u>art</u> explodes all over my naked mother who bears no emotion while getting fucked from behind by the sphinx who's supposed to be oedipus. this macabre saturnalia lasts til i plunge into a dark sleep of nothingness...

...besides our mouths, the three of us had gone to bed in the same fashion: i was lying on a couch with my mouth slightly open, hoping to let the water from the poetic plunge flood out of my lungs. rick was lying in the mortuary with his mouth completely closed, letting the embalming fluids flood into his lungs. and Jesus was lying in the dumpster with his mouth completely torn away, the trash seeping in through the lacerations, steadily flooding down into his lungs. all crucified by asphyxiation...

RESURRECTION

"They say we'll reunite in death,
They say there's no work of ~~art~~ like Heaven,
They say the gates are pearly and the clouds are white,
But you're going to Hell and it looks like it's about to rain..." [1]

...A bombardment of squawking was assailing my tympanic membranes, swiftly advancing towards the thalami. Teresa's army of timbre wolves were out to conquer each lobe on the trot. In the ominous undertones, all I could hear was Ivy this, Ivy that. But Pessi finally told her to shut up or else he'll fuckin' kill her. Thereafter she left me alone, from which I took the liberty to sleep clear into the evening on her couch. But it was a restless in-and-out-of-consciousness sleep, unlike the initial sleep I'd enjoyed after arriving in the dead of night, which, when it came, was a serene state of nothingness. But after Squawk had squawked at the crack of dawn, ~~start~~ling and threatening me, I began, in distorted cycles, nodding off—only to bounce right back up into a state of thinking. When thinking, primarily torn between thoughts thrice: Rick's death filling me with stubborn contentment, Ma's bereavement filling me with tense ire, and Luke's crucified Christ filling me with severe repentance. Every excuse I thought to tell him seemed damned. To be almost honest about the incident and say that I'd smashed the painting because of the synergistic drug war between the Prescriptionists and the anti-Prescriptionists, or Rick's dead death and Ma's living death, or the internal tempest that hadn't stopped storming since I decided to write my first poem when I was eleven, or simply the sudden onslaught of a vivid nightmare provoking me into blind action—so whichever or whatever it was, if not the combination of all, in addition to whatever else was trying to break free from my twisted subconscious, none seemed feasible excuses; they all seemed damned! So I was certain that I uncertain what I would tell Luke. God, if he'd once feared coming back to the room to find alien antennas or a swastika drawn on Jesus, wait til he discovered nothing but a dusty silhouette! But during my distorted time on the couch, I finally embarked on the makings of a solution: I could tell him that it was stolen. Yes, I could say that I'd spent the night at Ivy's and she would vouch for it, or that I'd spent the night at Teresa's and Pessi would vouch for it. (Hadn't decided which one yet.) Alwaysthemore, I could say that I'd returned to the room Saturday night, or Sunday morning—(hadn't decided which one yet)—and found the painting gone with the screen of the window busted out, which I'd have to do manually once I returned. (Hadn't decided if I would ever return anyway.)

But there was *one* place I was convinced I wouldn't be going: home for the funeral. I'd explained it as well as I could to myself, Pessi, and Ma: the only people who needed to overstand my reasoning. Regarding *that* decision, I was feeling quite justified; Pessi (although coming to agree with

---

[1] Lyrics from "Makes Me Sick" by The Blackhole Mothers, from the album *Excuse My Wrench: WHAP!*

me) was probably still unsure or concerned. And Ma was surely scared to death. I mean, she'd tried so desperately with that one last phone call to piece back together the broken pieces of a family that never once made a family. And when I resorted to referencing the family I knew best—literary characters—she (unable to choke back the tears) was forced to hang up on family like a sixteen-year-old tends to do when they suddenly find out they were adopted. Speaking of which, Gennaro crossed my mind for a minute or two while I was lying on the couch. I wondered who he called "Ma." Does he even *know* about *our* Ma?

Man, even with only one day of retrospection underway, it all seemed so quick, so strange, so intertrinecine[2]: Rick was in the mortuary, Ma was in tears, and I was in-sane!

When I finally woke up for good, it was 6 p.m. My body was comfortably depressed in the plush cream leather. Behind me, the sun was shining dimly through a large bay window. My head was near the front door where I could partially see straight ahead into the kitchen. Teresa was sitting at an oak table, smoking a cigarette. She was facing and talking to Pessi who was omitted from my view. She had on black stretch pants and a long-sleeve red shirt. Her cropped blonde hair looked like she'd just re-bleached it. For her, it was actually an attractive color and style: compatible with her straight, smooth body.

Feeling sheepish about the situation, I didn't want to be confronted by either. But knowing I had no other choice, I bent over the couch and reached out for my smokes. As soon as I retrieved and lit one, it sparked Teresa's attention.

'*Uggh,* look who's finally up,' she said phlegmatically. She was looking at me with her lax ruby eyes and lax ruby lips. Without averting her gaze, she took a long, seductive drag from her cigarette...letting the smoke roll out languidly. She remained stolid in her chair as if being weakly sexed by the cigarette. But Pessi came walking out. He was wearing baggy army pants and a black hoodie. His hazel eyes were rheumy but glossed over with happy-hangover, which meant he might've had a rough morning but was now starting to *feel* better, just not *look* it. As Sid and Nancy passed through my mind once again, I was worried Teresa would eventually seduce Pessi into something too hard, even if I had no knowledge of her doing anything he and I didn't already do or have done; it was just this malefic aura of hers whenever she slipped into one of her rare subtle dispositions.

Pessi flashed a smirk: exactly what I needed to see. He emphatically leaped over the arm of a green recliner chair placed on the other side of the room—but not far from me on the couch. With the remote control pointed out like a gun, he turned the television on; it was down near my feet, and as large as the Pinedas' flatscreen. Teresa's house was similar to Ivy's: a large Victorian, except Teresa's didn't have the "colors": it was completely

---

[2] Alteration of *internecine*, which means something marked by mutually destructive slaughter. In the Latin context—*internecinus*—"inter" was meant to add emphasis, as opposed to the modern interpretation of "between." So incorporating both, "tri" specifies the three parties being destroyed and is fittingly placed "between" the two subjects. The logical creation of a word.

modernized inside. According to Pessi, Teresa's father was a millionaire for two reasons: his prestigious job dealing with international contracting from which he spent extended periods of time in Europe; and he was also a middle-weight in the investment world, which is why, after the upshot of a recent bull market, he sent Teresa's aunt—(obviously not trusting Teresa with the entire lump sum)—30K to buy a new car of her choice, and any surplus she could pocket; after her purchase, she made about 3K in profit. Yeswithstanding, she still put forth the effort to support herself by cutting hair; she planned to open up a salon in the future. Pessi was explaining most of this (at least the parts I didn't already know) while we watched *The Simpsons.* Teresa had went upstairs to do whatever she did upstairs.

'So ya likin' it here or wha'?'

Reclined back, he answered, 'Yeah. It's fuckin' great. I'm havin' fun doin' nuh'n. But I been lookin' around for a job. But Teresa—she don't mind slidin' me bills til I find one. Man, dey sercly got everything here.' He exhaled freely, almost for effect. 'Dere's even a pool table dahnstairs. We'll hafta play sometime so I can school your ass. Hey 'member dat time when—'

'When we threw Kowal's pool balls over da hill?' I vaddled.

'Yeah. Daz funny as fuck. Tryin'ah hit rooftops dahn on Meade.'

Still satisfied by the results of our decision four years past, we grunted laughter like it just happened. Nate Kowalczyk had been an old friend we never liked: the Anthony Durkin of our crew before Dante divorced Nate and married Anthony. So in lieu of Nate Kowalczyk, and the friendship we once didn't share with him, we befriended by Anthony Durkin by egging his car at night and ordering (without his consent or our presence) an extravagant amount of food to be delivered to his house. That's the price Anthony had to pay for being a duplicitous, backboneless, chameleonic, amoebic, whatever-it-takes whore of a friend that wasn't our friend. Ol' Kowal had gotten his pool balls thrown over the hill just for being Dante's present whore, but he had nothing borne in his character as despicable, disreputable, or facile as Anthony's.

Teresa came plopping loudly down the wooden stairs; the stairwell dropped straight into the living room and served as a wall for the kitchen. Slinging herself on the arm of the chair where Pessi was reclined, she addressed me with a devious smile: 'Guess who I just talked to?'

'Ivy?'

'Yep. And she's been loo-king for you because she said you were sup*pose*d to call her, and she was sup*pose*d to come pick you up, and—'

'So whaja fuckin' say?!' I nearly squealed, as I finally positioned myself upright while sparking another cigarette like a nervous wreck.

'I fa-king told her you spent the night here! That's what I told her!'

Pessi pushed her off the arm of the chair, but she quickly explained that she was just kid-ding as she moved back up on the arm. 'Don't worry, asshole; I told her Zach came and picked you up this mor-ning to take you for a spin in my new car. And now she can just pick us all up together. Said she'll be here in like an hour or so.'

'Cool. So she didn't sound mad or anything?'

'How the fuck do I know?!' Apparently annoyed, she shot up with a wrothy scowl and a curled lip, looking like I'd just insulted her so severely that I inflicted within her an irretrievable pain. I was nearing the conclusion that she was either bipolar or literally psychotic. But since I couldn't berate her or be mean—presently stuck in a subordinate position with her—I answered her unwarranted bitchiness by licking the cherry of my cigarette. 'Gawd!' she bellowed, looking me on with hatred exploding from her pasty face bedecked in harlot-red. 'There's seriously some-thin' wrong with your fa-king head! Why don't you just eat the whole fa-king thing and choke on it?!' Dismissing Pessi's ass-slap, she marched back upstairs in groundless rage. But I was silently thankful to her for covering *my* ass, which no one, including me, seemed to know *what* was being covered up anyway.

Anyway, Rick was really dead, Ma figuratively, and Jesus Christ either both or somewhere in between: and I knew all of it would haunt me like the concept of inevitable death if I took the time to think about it, which is why I was glad I would be spending the night with Pessi *and* Teresa because they were boisterously rude together; at times, it could be comedic and relieving. They reminded me of two ticking time-bombs waiting to explode. Inside, they bore enigmatic atoms that danced around chaotically as if in an ancient bacchanalia, yet only today's greatest scientific minds could truly overstand how such infinitesimal things trapped within relatively small packages could (when they exploded centrifugally) produce such colossal effects. Teresa, as I saw it, was more like the unconcealed fission-bomb: continually breaking down and bursting out for all to see. And Pessi was more like the top-secret fusion-bomb: continually letting things build inside...til releasing everything in an unforeseen big bang. It made sense too because for the most part Teresa would never shut up, and so if there was something on her mind she didn't hesitate to let it out. And once someone or something was finally able to get Pessi's fuse lit, he would just fuck someone's or something's day up in one fell drop.

After watching *The Simpsons,* I went upstairs to take a shower, which Teresa had made me feel lowly about as if I was some *lordu dumanninu* [3] petitioning for more alms, or at least bartering on behalf of my aberrance, seeing as I no longer knew *where* or *what* to call "home." Rrrrr. Anyway, once I malimarged up a bit, I went back downstairs where we each got a little pick-me-up by shoveling a pile of snow; this, while we were waiting for Ivy to pick us up. The destination: the mall to play indoor miniature golf. When I first saw the course, I wanted to try it out; it looked adventurous; I never even heard of an *indoor* miniature golf course. And now, having stretched from the snow-shoveling, I was re-energized and ready to trounce Pessi and Teresa, even if I'd be slightly disadvantaged with the boot-cast. My only *real* worry—as all other vexing thoughts suddenly became foreign—was knowing that Ivy was athletically apathetic; thus, she'd surely think competitiveness in miniature golf is just plain silly.

Outside Ivy honked the horn twice: half an hour late. It was bad timing because, growing bored, Pessi had begun rolling another blunt (laced with snow) and just finished gyrating the lighter around the paper to dry it. We didn't have time to smoke it inside since we were running late, and with the time as late as it was, we needed to get to the mall and play before it closed. So Pessi suggested we smoke it on the way, manipulatively

---

[3] [scn] dirty panhandler

adding that he would get Ivy to smoke too. I told him not to pressure her, or even offer, and certainly not to spark it til I wheedled her.

As we pulled away, Ivy started explaining her tardiness—to deaf ears; I told her to floor it, also to deaf ears. So sitting up front I laid back in the black leather seat to enjoy therapeutic feelings, seeing as the seat had a built-in heat-massager. Pessi and Teresa were sitting in the backseat—Teresa behind Ivy, Pessi behind me—impatiently waiting for me to wheedle Ivy, but til I got up the nerve, which my nerves were now being tickled to death, Teresa passed the time with the latest salon gossip.

'Oh my gawd, Iv! Remember Cindy Ferguson?'

'Yeah. The nice, quiet girl with the bluest eyes ever. She sat next to me in 10th grade math. Why?'

Swooping up between Ivy and me as if from coach to first-class, Teresa *tissed* and closed her eyes in disgust over Cindy Ferguson being described as nice and quiet with the bluest eyes ever. She then returned to coach after I "accidentally" nudged her in the side of the head.

'Nice and quiet?! Yeah right! She's a lit-tle fa-king slut! My friend Chad—I cut his hair and shit, and he always leaves me big tips—well anyways, he told me some of his friends took her to Camp Muna and gang-banged her and—' She paused her breathless delivery to mutely communicate with Pessi. So far, Ivy seemed uninterested in Teresa's squawk and more focused on the nighttime road. Physically absorbed in tingles and mentally in her sexiness which sent tingles through me intoxicated or not, I looked over at her young eyeful body driving like a blind old lady. The way she pointed her legs out awkwardly while she drove drove me nuts! It was as if she wanted to drive faster (like I'd advised) but her feet were being too indecisive with the pedals to take a courageous trip down the dark fast lane; but like everything else: in time, in time.

'I'm tell-ing you,' Squawk yelped, 'she's a fa-king slut!'

'Yeah it's true, Ivy. I's 'ere, too, bangin'ah *shiiit* oudda that fuckin' slut,' Pessi added facetiously.

'Shut up, Zach. Anyways, I can't believe that lit-tle slut would even do that with three guys! THREE! I mean, gawd, can you at least close your fa-king legs one person in the world! And—this is the best part, Iv—oh gawd! this is seriously the best fa-king part!—guess who one of the guys that banged her was! Nevermind, you'll never guess so I'll just tell you. Eli. Yes, E-li fa-king Per-ez!'

'*What?!*' Ivy responded with enthusiasm, taking a sudden interest in Squawk's birdshit. '*Are you serious?!*'

'Swear da gawd.'

'Wow!'

'Wow what?' I interjected, also taking a sudden interest in Squawk's birdshit. Ivy was slipping into awe and shit right before me. And it was too late for her to explain herself before Squawk continued squawking, ready to drop shit bombs.

'Oh my gawd, Vinny! You're tell-ing me you and Dolly-Doll here have *never* talked about Eli Perez—her old *lover?*'

'Please. He was NOT my lover!' spat Dolly-Doll. 'I never loved that kid and I never slept with him! For that matter, I never did *anything* with him!'

'Liar!' Pessi casually joined in again, making a mockery of the shit bomb Teresa was trying to explode.

'Oh come on, Iv,' huffed Squawk, keeping her hawkish finger right above the big red button. 'I know you better than anyone in the world, and you mighta tried kee-ping everything all fa-king quiet and shit, but you can't *honestly* tell me you never sucked his dick before—'

Brakes pressed! Big red button pressed! And it began falling from the sky like a huge brown—well, *white* chunk of imminent hail!

'God, Teresa! Why would you even say somethin' like that?!' Ivy appeared appalled but defenseless against Squawk's warlike libel. 'I never did *anything* like that with him! I'm not a slut like Cindy or—'

'*Eli Perez*, huh?' I interjected, saving Teresa's ass from getting reamed since she'd saved mine earlier. 'What, was he some kinda Rico Suave, Bernardo-from-*West Side Story*-wannabe-badass.'

'No way!' Squawk laughed. 'He's SUCH a fa-king dork! Vinny, I honestly couldn't even stand this retard. Seriously, he was—' She stopped to finger the blunt from Pessi after he sparked it, hit it, then coughed violently; I'd obviously forgotten (or didn't have the time) to wheedle Ivy, so now things could only proceed in anarchy. Teresa hit it twice without exhaling then tried to resume talking while hacking out the thick pungent smoke. 'He was—' But more violent coughing ensued, echoing off the luxurious leather seats of Ivy's Beemer.

'What is that?' asked Ivy, as a cloud of smoke began engulfing the car. She tried looking in the rearview mirror—but talk about smoke-n-mirrors! She rolled down all the windows with the push of a button then looked at me as if she, lacking the gall, wanted me to make 'em put it out *right now!* But, hey, I wanted to hit it *too!*

'(Come on, bella;' I said privately by throwing my head down on her lap in an attempt to be cute and win over her approval. '(Don't be a mexican't about it.)'

'(This is seriously ridiculous. We're gonna have a talk later.) And this *isn't* gonna turn into a habit! You two hear me! If my parents—'

'(Cool.) Hey, Squawk, pass 'at shit up here!' I jolted up and turned towards the backseat, wanting to get higher and continue the Eli Perez talk. When I got the blunt, I took in two gargantuan hits...then passed it back to Pessi. 'Hey, Mother Teresa,' I quipped, copying Pessi's past wit, 'tell me more about Ivy's old lover. Somehow after five weeks she's failed da mention it.' I looked at Ivy, and when she glanced over, I winked with deep adoration.

'I don't—doubt it.' Teresa stopped to take another turn with the blunt, coughing as she talked. 'And I'll tell you how it is 'cause Ivy will probably just lie about it 'cause *some*-times—she likes to pretend she's all hoity-fa-king-toity. Ha! Just kid-ding, Dolly-Doll.' Teresa playfully squeezed on Dolly-Doll's shoulder like a chatter-box hand.

'Can we just change the subject?' Dolly-Doll asked politely.

'Can we juss change 'iss fuckin' CD?' Pessi-Pess asked rudely.

'Can you juss quit droppin' shit – takin' extra hits – 'n' pass 'at fuckin' blunt back up here – before I start da spit – on yir fuckin' beak, you yuck-yuck Squawk – with the face of a – of a fuck-up cock – yo, you go *caw! caw!* whenever ya drop – yir dirty bombs like a militant twat?' V da G rapped rhapsodically—trying to catch breath while hooting like a mad owl at his tonic, chaotic, moronic, simply right-on-it rhymes!

'*Bah! Vaffanculo!*'[4] squawked Squawky-Squawk.

'*Mi fai vutari i vuredda, figghia ri suca minchia!*'[5] Now gimme da fuckin' blunt back, you butanna babba—before I babba-abba-labba all over yir puke-smellin' face— BIAAATCH! Ahhhhh! I win! Ahhhhh! I wiiiin!...'

Ahhh! how swiftly things turned into vehicular anarchy! filled with banter! barbs! English cusses! Italian cusses! Sicilian cusses! entreaties! coughs! laughter! music! sibilance! thick clouds of herb-scented smoke polluting the once-fresh air of Ivy's Beemer with the much fresher air of Nature! ahhh! ahhh! ahhhhhhhhhhhhhhhhhh!

'Anyways,' Squawk resumed after things settled down, 'Eli Perez is this fa-king skinny half-Mexicano with a huge brown mark on his cheek. Seriously makes me wanna puke. It kinda looks like a big piece of chocolate stuck on his face with hair grow-ing out of it. Like—like a gawd-damn Mexican Milkdud!' Everyone in the car exploded into rapturous laughter, even Ivy, although she couldn't have been too happy with the smoking or the subject. For the first time I was finding Teresa to be an all right chick. Somehow we'd turned into conversational partners without any real tension between us. 'Then, Vinny, I swear to gawd! in 6th grade this dork tried to get me to give him a handjob on the playground! On the fa-king playground! So I kicked him in the nuts!' (We all laughed again.) 'But *noooo!* the stupid retard just doesn't get it and starts bu-ying me all this gawd-damn shit! I'm like, "*Helloo-oh! Go get that gawd-damn thing surgically removed from your face!*" So after a while the stupid retard finally gets the point, but that's when he started li-king Ivy 'cause she wasn't mean to him like me. But see, Vinny, what you dunno is Ivy *always* had a thing for Eli. Since we were like twelve. I even remember her be-ing all pissed at me when Eli was stal-king me. But then she got her way. They were a thing for like a year—'

'Yeah right, Teresa! You lie so much!' Ivy turned towards me, momentarily unconcerned with the driving—*or* speaking in a persuasive tone. 'We dated for like five months when I was sixteen. And mind you, *behind* my parent's back. So yeah: I had a little crush on this kid, but it didn't work out. No big deal.'

'*Hmm.* I dunno; sounds like yir priddy sad it didn't work out.'

'But then I woulda never met the greatest guy in the world: Y-O-U!'

'I juss P-E—' (Self-interruptive burst of laugher over my tongue-tie.) 'I juss P-E-E-D'd—' (Another one!) '—my pants, Mommy...'

...Inside the mall, Pessi and I stood at the counter paying for eighteen condensed holes. When we'd walked into the lobby (the course was through another set of doors), Teresa had slapped a twenty down in Pessi's hand: that's how he was paying for his date. On the other hand, I was more of a man because I was paying for my date with leftover money from school loans, which Ivy knew little about in terms of hard figures. All she knew (thanks to my lies) was that, despite being from a poor family, I'd

---

[4] [ita] Fuck you!

[5] [scn] You make me wanna puke, you daughter of a cocksucker. [*Butanna babba:* stupid whore]

saved up a substantial amount of money coming into college: a cultural pressure hard to resist: everyone's indebted to the notion of appearing so self-reliant.

Pessi and I were waiting for this gorgeous high-school chick to ring us up; the cash register seemed a foreign apparatus to her. Meanwhile, Ivy and Teresa stood behind us at a distance, chatting: probably in a tiff over Eli Perez. They'd already picked out their putter and ball without putting any thought into their choice. Teresa was swinging her putter like a defective pendulum. From her feathery demeanor, up to her cold rheumy eyes, she was visibly intoxicated, even though she acted about the same when sober, and even *looked* intoxicated in sobriety; then again, she simply might've never been sober. As always, Ivy was standing up with good posture—her putter resting against her hip—teetotal to the bone.

I turned to Pessi: with curious facial shifts, he was looking over a putter with a fluorescent pink grip; it made me vaddle through my nose.

'Wha'?' he said coldly, although not failing to smirk.

'I dunno; but I'm fucked up, man.'

'Yeah, me too,' he concurred indifferently. Seemed he was more concerned with the fluorescent-pink-handle putter: the way he was giving it amorous observations, while caressing it like silk, was like love at first-stroke.

From the organized display atop the counter, I grabbed a putter with a florescent-yellow grip, then a matching florescent-yellow ball. 'Okay; quit mediatin' around, Rocco. Rock a ball 'n' let's roll.' (Beguiled by an invisible looking-glass flush in the ground, reflecting back up the illusive nature of the honeymoon phase, Pessi didn't seem to hear me, as he continued taking promising practice strokes with his new metal consort.) 'Sercly: come on; time for me 'n' my doll da take you 'n' yir bitch dahntahn.'

'Please.' He stroked her again—with a pause for the imaginary rolling ball; but the ball really *was* rolling between them! 'Witchir leg all busted up, I don't think yinz guys even stand a chance.'

'How bout dat:' I noted to myself, 'a liddle optimism from the King of Pessimism!'

'Plus, Ivy's gonna be all distracted, thinkin' about when she yoosta suck on Eli's Mexican wutchamacawit.'

Holding my putter by the handle—upside-down up in the air—I let it drop loosely through my grip, catching it by the club-face. I swiftly swung it around and smacked Pessi hard across the thigh with the grip-end. He grimaced but probably suffered none of the brunt, being high and all. 'There. 'At should even out da playin' field.' The tail behind the counter giggled. I winked at her, and while we were locked in a moment of flirtatious ogling, Pessi called for national attention—got it—then farted loudly with pride. Flushing, I quickly gimped over to our chicks.

In valiant steps, we headed through the doors like we were about to enter a soldout sports arena filled with high expectations. And the place *was* enormous inside. It had a high warehouse-like ceiling with too-bright florescent lights, and down below, a surreal-looking course with vivid greens and absurdly painted wooden contraptions, which were nothing impressive at a closer glance. There wasn't a soldout crowd either: only a few high schoolers who (as I surmised from their location towards the right side) were nearly finished. Fortunately, the place had a couple benches throughout, which meant I could rest the leg if needed.

To our immediate left: a flat practice green riddled with holes. As if to uphold a meaningless tradition, given that the entire course was flatter than Florida, we went over to it to polish up our putting-game. Since everyone fell silent and began practicing too seriously, I began using my ball to knock theirs off their line; Teresa flipped me off for it, Pessi swore at himself as if he didn't overstand what just happened, and Ivy, it just made her giggle. She came up, threw her arms around me, and kissed me, while Teresa told us to quit ma-king her fa-king sick. Then we ventured to hole-1. On the way, Pessi and I glared at each other, smirking, shaking our heads intently like cowboys about to dual to the death. I tapped my boot-cast with the putter and nodded my head, calling it on. It's on. My boot-cast is on.

'So whaddo me 'n' Ivy get when we win?'

Instead of answering, Pessi turned his head over his shoulder to acknowledge Teresa who was now holding onto his hips, swaying incongruously with his practice strokes on the rubber mat for hole-1. 'Come on, Teresa!' Pessi griped, trying to shake the jealous leech. 'I'm tryin'ah focus so we can win.' Then I heard Teresa whisper into his ear that she was horny. He let out an abrupt laugh and wiggled out of her grasp. 'Okay, V, I'll tell ya what. Whenever *we* win, Ivy gitsta play on *our* team tonight, if ya know whadda mean. Fuck, we can even caw Eli da come join; just not you. But Ivy can lick on Eli's Mexican wutchimacawit.' Teresa quickly corrected him: 'Milkdud! It's a fa-king Mexican Milkdud!' Both names were funny to me. But no longer finding the humor in it, Ivy began wandering away...til Teresa walked over, spun her around authoritatively, then seductively brushed her fingertips up and down Ivy's chest.

'*Ooooo!* I think I *would* like that. Me and Iv have never—'

Ivy jerked away, her face extinguished of its usual tolerance. '*Ooooo*, I don't think so, Teresa. You're sick!'

'Well I dunno; sounds like a priddy good idea da me as long as I can watch.' I was really enjoying the uncomfortable position Ivy was in.

'How about if *we* win,' began Ivy, 'you and Pessi have to get naked and make out while *I* watch? How's *that* sound?'

'Ehh, me 'n' Pess do that all the time anyway—'

'How 'bout whether we win or lose,' began Pessi, readying for his first shot, ''n' I'll prahblee lose with fuckin' Sally McCrack-Feign over dere—' He pointed to Teresa with his undersized fluorescent-pink-handle putter; in response, Teresa managed to flip him off as she sparked a cigarette.

'You can't smoke in here!' warned Ivy.

'The fuck I can't.'

(Pessi was still talking but no one was paying attention anymore.)

'You're gonna get us kicked out.'

'Dolly-Doll, how *have* we managed to stay friends for so long? Don't get me wrong, I love ya like a sister but you're always so gawd-damn worried about every-thing. I mean, look at us! We're all fucked up and we're actin' more sober than you. Gettin' all hostile and shit.'

'Teresa, it's not like I'm tellin' you to *quit* smoking; I just don't wa—'

'Hey, Squawk, lemme hit dat shit—wait, never mind: you prahblee got mouff herpes, you scrawny liddle whore.'

'Hey—' She showed me her long boney middle finger, lacking verbal repartee. She took another seductive hit, and with a jerk of her long pasty neck, tried throwing her short blonde hair back to no avail; it just stuck like a wig which is what it looked like.

'Eh! listen up!' Pessi edged back in. 'If me 'n' Teresa win, yinz two gadda go dahn on each other tonight while me 'n' V watch.'

'Yeah,' I played along, ''n' if me 'n' Ivy win, yinz two gadda go up on each other tonight while me 'n' Pessi watch.'

'I don't—'

'Nope! Shudup 'n' play ball, bitches!' Pessi shot the starting gun as he eyed his pink golf ball down on the rubber mat. After slowly pulling back his metal consort, he let it fly forward with too much velocity. His first shot shot down the green carpet erratically...banking off the white wooden trim at the end...settling two feet from the pin. He cheerfully slapped Teresa's boney ass as she placed her red golf ball down on the mat. And she did just as well. Without waiting for us, they walked down to the hole to watch from there. Then Ivy girlishly set her purple ball down. After putting no thought into the shot, she hit Pessi's ball. Of course an argument ensued because Pessi claimed that he should be able to place his ball back to where it was, and I said, no, that's just part of miniature golf. 'Look, balls are gonna get hit. 'N' if we gadda keep readjustin' knocked-balls, den we're gonna end up fightin' about where da ball *originally* was. I mean, does anyone akshly feel like markin' balls for fuckin' miniature golf? 'Cause I will if 'at's whachinz want. But it's gonna be extra work.' Since no one wanted extra work, knocked-balls would have to stay knocked.

Finally, yours truly limped up to the mat like an old golf legend. Ivy placed the ball down for me, whispering mellifluous goodlucks in my ear. I eyed up the shot: I could either edge the ball around the wooden house, or aim through one of its three small holes. I decided to be bold and go for the hole in the middle: the one if the ball made it through you would get an automatic hole-in-one. With buzzing finesse, I smacked the ball smoothly off the G-spot of the club...it rolled smoothly through the middle hole...then (as I peaked around the house to see its fate) the ball dropped out of sight. Pessi whispered, 'Fffuck.' Teresa blurted, '*You lucky asshole!*' Ivy smiled and clapped her hands like a flapping hummingbird. Before making my way up to retrieve the hole-in-one, I pretended to shoot Pessi and Teresa down with my putter. Then I flipped my putter down to the ground and turned it into a walking cane...

...At hole-5, Ivy and sat down on a bench to chat in private, while the other two took their shots. I realized that I'd been being a dick to Ivy by ostracizing her, and I had a strong conviction that one (within a group of intoxicated people) should *never* ostracize a sober person. The conviction had its roots back in Verna: I never wanted Pessi to feel excluded when we drank, even though he was just as intoxicated by other means.

'So you think your leg's gonna hold up?' Ivy was gently rubbing my thigh; the friction felt good and motherly.

'Yeah, iddle be fine. I'm priddy fuckin' lit anyway. If I'm irritating my leg, I won't feel it til tamarra.'

'That's not good.'

'Don't worry; it's not like I'm doin' anything strenuous, ya know.'

'No. I'm talkin' about you bein' all messed up.'

'I'm juss a liddle high, hun; not on the verge of an OD.' Amused by her concern, I vaddled as I stroked her face almost condescendingly. Then—glancing over at Pessi and Teresa—I catch 'em moving their balls closer to the hole with their shoes, little by little. Teresa was even pondering taking a surreptitious shot til she looked over at us. I don't think Ivy saw anything because she was staring right at me, but *I* saw it—and, *ehh,* I was willing to let it go, not just because I was positive they had no chance in winning, but it was also something that I'd start a serious fight over, and I couldn't chance *escalation.* So all-too conscious of my subordinate position with Teresa—the feeling just eating me up inside!—I said nothing.

Ivy stepped up to the mat; she was proving to be a horrible miniature golf player. After another rickety stoke, Ivy missed by ten yards because the blades of the spinning windmill angrily spat the ball back. Expressing frustration, she slouched and twisted her body into a pretzel like a pro who just missed a ten-foot putt for eagle.

'Almost, hun. *Fuckin' windmill.*' I pointed my putter at the rolling windmill as if to warn it to think twice about doing the same to me.

'I suck,' Ivy said apologetically with an effusive hug.

'It's cool; we're only behind one stroke. 'N' 'ere's plenny of holes left da play.'

Being the only trustworthy soul in the group, Ivy had been ordained the scorekeeper. After nine holes, she added it up and declared that we were ahead by two strokes. Pessi claimed stroke-shaving; Teresa seconded it; and I let it go. I'd seen more things but I let it go. Just like Rick's death: I let it go as if it was all just nothing...

'Hey, bella-loo.' I was gimping behind Ivy on our way to hole-14. (Everyone was getting bored and sober by now.) Ivy arched her neck straight back, to look at me upside-down like a silly girl with a silly smile.

''Yes, bello-boo?'

'Whad is it with 'ose jeans?' I pointed to the bottom of her jeans where they were folded upward three inches in a single flap. She often wore her jeans like that, if wearing the proper shoes, but I finally decided to inquire about it. Although a style I typically disliked, it looked so sexy on her that I had to reassess: a sexiness comparable to the way she ate noodles with Alfredo sauce speckled around her mouth as those blinkity-blink-blinks looked up and around so innocently.

'Nothin's with my jeans. I love these jeans.' Turning about, she was taking glances at her legs to see if there might be a stain, a tear, or even a big black spider crawling up 'em. 'Oh, you mean how they're rolled up?'

'Dat's whad I mean, holy-roller.'

'I dunno. It's a Walzy Cuff.'

'Wha' da fuck's a *Walzy Cuff?*' I laughed.

'Just some word I made up so I could explain why I cuff my jeans the way I do—like whenever you finally noticed and decided to ask about it.'

'Oh I'll give you some word for whenever I *finally* notice 'n' decide da ask about it. I've noticed every single time, thinkin' about how fuckin' sexy you look. So don't even gimme 'at *WALL-zee Cuff* attitude of yirs.' Put in check, she came wrapped her arms around my torso, as we gimped to hole-15 at which point I began talking to Ivy in a secretive strategic voice,

discussing the final holes; Pessi and Teresa watched from afar, giving me that you're-fucking-retarded look, but I paid no mind. '...So keep 'ose Walzy Cuffs rolled up 'n' let's focus on keepin' our lead 'n' beatin' 'eez motherfuckers! Do I make myself clear?!'
'Yes, sir! Let's beat these stupid suckers!'

We lost. On hole-18, Ivy and I were tripped up by the ankles, her by the Walzy Cuffs and me by the boot-cast, losing by one stroke. Pessi and Teresa taunted and screamed and squawked in joy. I used the leg as an excuse and whacked 'em both across the calf before turning my putter in.
'I can't believe we fuckin' came back 'n' won,' buzzed Pessi.
'Guess it depends on whachu consider "winning,"' I muttered under my breath; I was reexamining the scorecard just to make sure.
'Oh! *shhhut* – up!' squawked Teresa. 'Your leg wasn't even both-er-ing you! We just flat out beat you! And I wasn't even try-ing, you fa-king pathetic rat!'
'Z'at so?' Impulsively, I threw the scorecard in her face, but I was trying so hard to tell myself to just let it go. Besides, I felt so groggy and irritable and sore. I desperately needed my medication which, of course, was in my bookbag back at *her* place.
'Face it, loser: you lost fair and fa-king square!' She turned away with a supercilious spin, and in cadence, grabbed Pessi by the arm. 'Gawd, he's seriously such a fa-king crybaby about *every*-thing!'
'Gawd, yir seriously such a fa-king *cunt*-faced cheater!' I mocked.
'Vinny, don't ever say that again!' Ivy quickly reproached me, trying to mediate something I should've been doing myself so as not to risk Teresa blowing up another bomb.
'I fuckin' watched jinz cheat all game.' (Teresa and Pessi halted and turned back around in cadence, both bearing that whaddaya-talking-about stare.) 'Ya know, when me 'n' Ivy'd sit dahn 'n' yinz two kicked yir balls closer da the hole. Yeah 'at's right: I saw yinz doin' it. I juss didn't say nuh'n 'cause I thought we'd still win, which woulda been even funnier. So why donchinz two put-put hacks shuh da fuck up 'n' roll out da red carpet for the *rill* winners. *Fuckin' cheaters.*' I raised my arms outward and did a fake strut around the office like a self-proclaimed king. They stormed off without another word. True, no red carpet was rolled out, but I did throw something out that tripped those fucking cheaters up by the ankles too: the truth!

In the car, everyone's spirit had waned: no name-calling or score-disputing, and thankfully, Teresa kept her mouth shut about me spending the night at her place, which no one, including me, still overstood what the big deal was anyway. Halfway back, Teresa began imploring us to come back her place to hangout for a bit. We finally agreed, although Ivy was probably nervous because of the wager which was a no-win situation for her no matter who'd actually won: she either had to go down on Teresa or go up on Teresa, while Pessi and I watched.
But once inside in the house, Pessi and Teresa, without explanation, went straight upstairs, I assumed to have sex or get high without me since I'd confronted 'em with unleashed alacrity which (hopefully) had tweaked their pride into humiliation. '*Fuckin' cheaters,*' I

thought pluralistically, as I sat down on the couch and turned the television on. Upon entering, Ivy had gone off to the bathroom. Good thing too because sitting there I spotted my bookbag on the floor and quickly tossed it down at the other end of the couch where she wouldn't see it: it was *really* bothering me what the big deal was since no one had expressed what the big deal was. Still, the evidence was hidden just in case there was a case.

When Ivy came back out, she sat down next to me, and with her shoes removed, put her Walzy Cuffs up on me, across my thigh. I turned on *South Park*, quickly falling into state of unremitting laughter where nothing around me could neither effect nor pull me away. But Ivy sat opposed to the satire, yanking me by the arm to give *her* some attention. "Hold on a sec" and "come on; juss watch 'iss; it's so funny" wasn't working. She whimpered and purred into my ear and yanked at me some more...til I turned around, away from the television and gave her the full attention she wanted. Soon we were making out like Stan and Wendy except I wasn't throwing up on her. However, I think (as Pessi had harbingered the month before) I *had* become a little fond of the painkillers: I was already consuming my second month's prescription, and not having had a dose in a while, was feeling nauseous as I made out with Ivy. So making out like Stan and Wendy in the literal sense might not have been far away...

...After thirty minutes—cycles of laughing, yanking, kissing, unspoken nausea: nothing vile expelled in between—the two cheaters still hadn't returned, not even a sound from 'em upstairs. So I decided to go check on 'em to see if they'd fallen asleep, because, as my "situation" returned to my cerebral forefront, I realized that I didn't feel like sleeping alone in my room, mainly because of the haunting atmosphere I'd have to endure, but also because I didn't want to chance Ma calling and wailing into the phone, and all the affliction that would bring. Plus I had to go back with Ivy to campus without being able to bring my bookbag where my meds 'n' 'at were stashed, so I had to return anyway. Abruptly Ivy vocalized just what I was thinking: that it was strange how Teresa had begged us to come over but left us alone right from the ~~start~~. When I stood up, she said she'd come with me, but intuition told me to go alone. So I kissed her like a strong shot of passivity that would last for just the right amount of time...then made my way up the stairs...into a tenebrous, quiet hallway, where on the left was Teresa's bedroom door. I knocked.

'Yo, yinz asleep?' I waited a moment...gave a closer listen...but no answer. 'Hey!' I shook the handle but it was locked. Then someone whispered something. 'Umm, I juss fuckin' heard you. Open up for a sec.' I kept knocking softly...til Pessi, naked with a white bed sheet wrapped around his waist, slowly cracked the door open—peering out with a cold, vanquished, almost ghostly stare directed down at my mid-section.

'Huh?'

'Whaddiyinz doin'? Lemme in rill quick; I nee'dda talk da ya 'bout sum'n.'

Standing hunched over like he was suffering from a backache, his head dropped—then ascended back up in a quick nod of instability. 'Huh?'

In sudden concern and curiosity, I pushed the door open. He didn't resist and nearly fell over backwards when I did. He galumphed back to the bed then laid down next to Teresa who was stripped down to red panties, listlessly sprawled on her back. The lights were off but it wasn't sheer darkness due to the window straight ahead; it was casting a paned light across her naked breasts. Like a classic movie, there was a grayish tint to the room, likely from a smoldering cigarette in an ashtray atop the dresser next to Pessi's head. The reflection of the smoke in the lengthy mirror bolted to the dresser was like an ominous simulacrum of the scene. The air, stale from smoke, had a shivering desiccation to it like a prepped surgery room. Unaffected by my presence, they were lying next to each other like old lovers spending their last night on earth together, staring upward with unyielding satisfaction. It was obvious *something* wasn't right. It wasn't break time after exhausting sex, or natural sleepiness, or the typical reaction, all the way up to the sobered aftermath, from blowing coke or smoking weed or even eating those strange pills.

'Wha' da fuck's wrong with yinz?' I asked sternly, yet already feeling terrified.

'Huh?'

'Yinz fucked up or sum'n?'

'Yes. Go home.'

'No; I'm spendin' the night here. After Ivy drops me off, I'm gonna take a taxi back 'cause I need my meds, so I might as well stay 'n' save a few bucks.'

'Okay.'

Dead silence took the podium for a while. So standing in the middle of the room, I began contemplating...and nothing but one thing kept piercing my mind like a bad dream coming true right before eyes.

'Pess, you bedder not be on what I think yir on. You hear me?'

Teresa rolled over on her side, her back now to me. Pessi, in cadence, rolled over which put his drowsy pallid face *towards* me, although half buried in the pillow. I walked up to the dresser and extinguished the slow-burning cigarette. Then I knelt down in front of his face with a fatherly air: so close that it was uncomfortable. A burgeoning feeling of acidic seriousness was rising up in my gut. *Something* wasn't *right.*

'Pess, lemme see yir arms.' Without further deliberation I quickly wrenched back the sheet, exposing his naked body, and violently snatched up his arm into a tight rotating grasp, examining it as best as I could by the light of the window...then the other. He held no objection to the forceful examination...but I didn't see a thing.

'Whaddaya on, Pess? Hey, Teresa: whaddayinz on?' My voice was now quavering, my gut now feeling disemboweled. In the back of my mind, I was hoping that Ivy wouldn't come up and witness this sickening ashy scene. 'Pess, wha' – the – fuck – are – you – on? If ya don't fuckin' tell me, I'm gonna fuckin' dump wudder all over you.'

'*Whaaaa'?*' he moaned, tussling with the sheet, turning over, now resting on his other set of ribs, his naked back like a large emotional wall. Lacking recourse, I vacantly stared at 'em for long agonizing moments. Finally, he spoke again. 'Hey, V?'

'Yeah?'

'Yir sercly goin' crazy since Rick died.' Said so soberly that I almost believed I *was* crazy and they *were* sober (or only intoxicated by the normal means) til Teresa, with a harsh voice (mimicking Pessi's first comment) said, 'Hey, V?'

'What?'

She turned over languorously and braced herself up on Pessi's muscled flank like a perched feline: her breasts in full view, her nipples proportioned perfectly on her breasts. With her synthetic-blonde head swaying, and her arms slipping as she giggled, she in one angry-sounding breath said: 'Don't think I won't suck your dick." She unperched herself, then fidgeted and kicked as she repositioned herself on her back. Emitting a struggled whimper, she turned inly to face Pessi's unseen face. Both giggled tonelessly, as ashy shadows cast darkness on their faces...til their comically-molested giggling gagged back in their throats...phasing into a romantic hibernation of tranquility. Confused, I turned around and quietly shut the door.

Coming back down the wooden stairs, I saw that Ivy was still patiently waiting on the couch with her legs tucked underneath her, but facing the stairs, not the television. I had my smile feigned before hitting the last step. In stride, I beckoned her to get up because it was time to leave.

'What took so long? What are they doin'?'

'Nuh'n. Dey were sleepin'. But I woke Pessi up, 'n' we talked about how you 'n' me won tonight. 'N' I refused da leave til he agreed.'

'Oh, then I guess we really *are* the winners huh.' She gave me a congratulatory kiss and hug. She then slid her shoes on and headed out the door. I followed, but before crossing the threshold, I paused—nothing, just nothing. Confused, I turned around and quietly shut the door.

Trying to blanket all suspicions, I told Ivy (while we were driving) to park in her lot because I wanted to walk her to her dorm. She said don't be ridiculous, to which I asked how is it ridiculous to want to see the girl I care about safe in her dorm, and considering it was only a five-minute walk from her dorm to mine, and I'd been walking around all day anyway, my boot-cast shouldn't serve as a factor. So she agreed and parked in her lot. And I walked her to her dorm...kissed her goodnight...waited for her to disappear inside...then called a taxi to take me back to Teresa's.

Once inside, I wasted no time swallowing three painkillers. Then I went back upstairs: the same ghostly gray scene but they were apparently asleep now. Just to make sure, I took their pulses: Pessi was alive but lifelessly asleep; Teresa too was alive, fidgeting and resisting my touch but with sealed eyes. Both smelled like medicated skin or the inside of a refrigerator: I couldn't decided which one made more sense. I thought to turn on the light and look around for the evidence that I didn't want to find, but I didn't. I was so exhausted: my senses had plummeted down into both insensibility and senselessness.

Not much later, under heavy sedation but unable to sleep, I heard a loud thump upstairs like someone had just fallen off the bed. I shot up, about to go see what happened, but someone was already out in the hallway, slowly descending the steps. Teresa: still dressed in nothing but red panties. She didn't look over at me as she rounded into the kitchen. She opened the refrigerator door. Bent over, the light was shining brightly on the side of her thighs and breasts, as she sifted through and clanked things together. Emphatically, she grabbed a jar, then slammed the door shut. At the bottom of the steps, she stopped, flipped me off with a bad aim, and drowsily said, 'Fuck you.' She somnambulated back up the steps. I laid back down to watch television but suddenly the jar dropped to the ground with a loud thud and rolled and banged down the steps like a grenade headed my way. I got up to see if she'd collapsed. She hadn't. She'd just dropped it out of mental whatever. It was a thick jar of grape jelly, and somehow didn't break. I took it into the kitchen and set it on the table to serve as a symbolic reminder of her mental whatever whenever she saw it in the morning. Once lying back down on the couch, I gradually became drowsier—(a million nebulous stars and spectral diamonds dancing behind my eyes)—yet still had to deal with pushing images of the incoming dead away and away and away with cantankerous exigency...til I—

I woke up around noon on Sunday. Since I was running late, I went straight upstairs to Teresa's room. I knocked loud and persistently til Pessi opened. He looked pale and hungover. But no time to get into this new business with bothersome questions because I had old business to take care of, and I needed his help. I told him to convince Teresa to let him drive her new car because I needed a ride back. He turned around as if he was going to shout for permission, but Teresa was awake (lying on the bed, facing the other direction) and yelled, 'I don't care!' So without getting into the details of *my* business—(if I couldn't explain it to myself then how could I explain it to him?)—I told him let's go *now.* He moaned but started getting ready...

...During the yawny drive, I kept my focus on the evaporating fog on the windshield. Up in the soggy stew, I was trying to hammer out the details: how to craft the crime scene, and who shall bear witness to the bear in order to confirm my alibi. But all my hammerings seemed as unnailable as the situation itself. It all seemed damned. Then—*flash!*—Pessi pulled into Philemon territory and said, 'Look, 'ere's yir fat liddle boyfriend.'

'You gadda be *fuckin'* kiddin' me.'

'Wha'?'

'Nuh'n. I'll caw ya later.' As soon as the car came to a stop, I hopped out and slammed the door shut.

'Hey, Vinny!' Standing next to Murphy Law, Luke Adams was beckoning me by the side of his car, having just pulled out a navy-blue suitcase. 'What's up?'

'Nuh'—' My voice stuck. Filled with a sea of ineffable feelings, I watched him pull out a plastic grocery bag from the backseat, setting it down next to the suitcase. He then shut the door and locked it. Knowing that I'd already done him wrong, I wanted to begin restitution by carrying his things, but I could only stutter a step forward—so frozen—as he waddled, hands-full, down the slope of the parking lot.

'Stayed the night at your friend's, I see.'

He was approaching too quickly.

'Yeah. Azz Pessi in his girlfriend's car. Want meedda carry yir bag?'

'No, no. Not with your leg. But I'd appreciate it if you opened the doors.'

So I led the way robotically...and opened the first of the doors.

It's ar'ight: the informational evidence has been planted: I spent the night at Pessi's 'n' I'm juss comin' in. Pure coincidence we came in at da same time. He'll have no objections da that. I can even show 'im the clothes 'n' 'at in my backpack. We'll walk in. Da painting'll be gone. Buh da door'll be locked. Da window'll—am I replyin'ah whadever he's sayin'? Sum'n about whad he did this weekend with his family? Did I nod or say sum'n? Stop it. I gadda think 'iss out. Shit! already in the hall! Juss stay cool. No can't it's too much it's happenin' again juss calm dahn deep breaths deep breaths don't show signs of nervousness smile juss smile don't feel good yes you do I'm wrong he'll overstand why's everything gih'n so hot don't feel good spinnin' spinnin' spinnin' overwhelmin' guilt it's hot he knows I'm guilty he'll know he's not stupid I'm not stupid we'll both know I know wha' happened I'm not evil I can't live with 'at feeling like some juss calm dahn deep breaths deep breaths don't feel good tell 'im juss tell 'im can't lie no can't lie juss be a man say whacha did yir runnin' oudda time almost 'ere ya can't be like 'iss da rest a yir life he's a good person he doesn't deserve so hot gonna pass out deserve juss stay conscioutellhimtellhimtellhim—

'You have your key, right?'

Pause. Pause. 'Ya know wha'?—I akshly left 'em at Pessi's.' *Then* I patted at my jeans; so dysfunctional, so out of sync. 'I been 'ere all weekend 'n' musta left in a pair a jeans I wore lass night 'n' forgot da pack back up.'

'Oh. Well I have mine.'

Pause. Pause. *Gulp.* 'Luke, 'fore we go in, uhh,' *(gulp)* 'dere's sum'n' *(gulp)* 'I gadda tell ya.'

'Is everything okay?'

'Well, I dunno. I—it's rilly hard da explain. Uhh.' *Gulp.*

'Here, we can just talk about inside.'

NO! Stop 'im from puttin' 'at fuckin' key in! Wait, why'd he stop? It's Ralphie. He's talkin'ah Agent Ralphie behin' me. Don't show 'im yir face. But he knows anyway. He spied da whole incident. Yes, too coincidental. He set me up. I knew it—fuck, Luke juss went inside! I didn't move! Didn't stop 'im! Thinking has worked against me again! Wait—listen. Suitcase juss hit the floor. He juss found out. Turn 'n' run! Turn 'n' RUUUUUUUUUN!—

'So what did ya wanna tell me, man? I mean, we don't have to talk now if ya don't wanna. It's up to you...Vinny? You still out there?'

Huh? What's he talkin' about? He didn't notice yet? No it's impossible not da notice right away. Go in 'n' can't breathe again so hot can't make it ta da door juss breathe juss breathe...slow steps slow steps...there ya go...now raise yir head...do it...face yir deed.........no...no not happenin im insane ive akshly gone insane feel so sick gonna throw up dont like iss feeling run away run run run run run cant rationalize all too coincidental too symbolic for reality sometimes truth is stranger than fiction who said that no nuhns right dont feel right body mind soul not right anymore juss lost head gone mad hate myself hate bein alive why cant i be normal why cant normal things happen da me wanna stop thinkin wanna sleep for a long time den wake up n feel aright again been thinkin for too long need a break too much has happened cant stop cant deal with anymore whys luke carryin on like everythings fine whys he sittin on his bed he looked at me but hes too afraid da keep lookin at me or say anything but hes not afraid at all he has a destination he doesnt think da way i think he knows nuhn of da hell im burnin in why did i slip inda insanity am i yoosta it yet gonna throw up no way out now lost all control ill never be able da live a normal life dis is the end of my life wish i woulda been a bedder person n listena everything God said n didnt listena music n read books thit said da challenge everything der da ones thit made me insane dey werent my salvation dey only led me further inda hell dey only opened my eyes ta da misery even more now i juss wanna shut my eyes forever i wanna be luke n sit dahn on the bed n not feel da way i do i wanna godda church n pray n say i love God n everyone else n have no doubt in my mind i do i wanna know im goin da Heaven n everythings gonna be aright dont wanna criticize anything anymore dont wanna do drugs anymore ey rilly are bad der makin me insane i am insane but i cant be if im sayin iss whats wrong with me do i still exist i think derefore i exist keep sayin it keep sane yes it musta been pardda the nightmare i dunno iss is all too much da overstand eres no rationalization anymore i am gone am i insane either way hafta change right now for good hafta quit doin what i do n thinkina way i think its gihn me nowhere besides insanity juss wanna normal life wanna pure easy normal life with a normal family n normal job dont wanna have sex less its the right way cause it does make you evil it makes you desire things juss like a drug if only i hadnt listened da punk read literature watched comedians did drugs acted da way i have with my friends n tried thinkin about things so deeply i wanna change it all its no good only more misery it ruins yir life n head you dont become smarter but deres no way out anymore i hafta quit goin against the grain den maybe i wont go insane for real im here i i i i think derefore not insane maybe if i start bein like everyone else wait nuhn seems right anymore im still slippin inda insanity no no no no stop i juss wanna state of innocence i want all deez lights around me da quit lookin so surreal i want peace inside i juss want oh God ill change i promise juss gimme back my sanity ill do whadever it takes i wont do anything bad anymore i wont ever listen da that music or read doze books i wont yell at my mother or scare her anymore ill quit bein friends with everyone whos bad i wont have sex with ivy anymore i wont swear do drugs fight steal complain i wont do anything ill only pray n serve You juss make me feel aright make me feel happy knowin You love me n i love You im so scared whyd i go dahn iss deceitful path i didnt know dey were judases please God i promise ill change lemme be happy ill do good in school n get a job n marry ivy n raise a traditional family ill forgive my father i wont ever criticize anything else again ill pray n godda church all da time n be completely good juss take iss feelin oudda me make me feel normal again stop iss feelin please put me back in my body please please pleeeeease ill return to the Church forever n ever...i exorcise myself every unclean spirit in the name of God the Father Almighty and in the name of Jesus Christ, His Son, our Lord and Judge, and in the power of the Holy Spirit, that thou depart from this creature of God which our Lord hath designed to call unto His holy temple that it may be made the temple of the living God and that the Holy Spirit may dwell therein...through the same Christ our Lord who shall come to judge the living and the dead and the world by fire...devil begone devil begone devil begone devil begone—

'You all right, Vinny? You don't look so good. Want some water?'

Pause. Pause. 'No. I'm fine. I guess. Akshly, I don't even know wha' da say right now. Sorry.' I forced out a dismissive laugh so he could see that everything was actually all right. At some point I'd moved myself to the bed and sat down.

'Well, what was it you wanted to tell me? Is somethin' wrong? You look—'

'No, I'm fine—sercly. Thanks.' I stood back up and moved to the desk. The poem was there. I wrinkled it up and threw it away with conviction. 'Sum'n juss hit me all of sudden 'n' made me feel all weird,' I explained tonelessly as if to myself. 'I think it was cuzza my medication. My leg started hurtin' rill bad earlier so I thought idd be best da double up. 'N' sometimes iddle make ya a liddle wired up 'n' anxious, ya know. But I'm through takin' 'em anyway 'cause 'er takin'ah cast off tamarra.'

'Cool, cool.' He began unpacking his suitcase. 'So how was your weekend?'

Pause. Pause. 'Not bad. But, hey, I'm gonna go out for a liddle boot-cast walk. Maybe sit dahn 'n' watch the squirrels for a bit. I juss need some fresh air right now. Again, thanks, Luke. 'N' sorry for actin' all weird.'

'No, don't worry about it. No need to apologize. It's cool.'

Confused, I turned around and quietly shut the door...

PART II

A TWO-WAY FIGHT TO HEAVEN

"He needed a needle because there was a cause
For being the effect of affliction,
He wanted to wallow without your claws
Prying open the eyes of addiction,
There's freedom in deception,
And shame in getting caught,
There's humor in anger,
But naught in not, naught in not,
Knotted knight, nodding knight,
Prodding hero of the night..." [1]

...What did three-hundred and some-odd days later prove? That I had retained my sanity to be insane. That my *motus animi continuus* [2] was still in motion, just in descending and backward motions. That I was becoming b i d r. That Pessi and Teresa were blowing H via the modern, more-acceptable sniff-like-glue method. That Ivy and I were in love, expressed via the primordial, still-acceptable I-love-you method. That Ma was still scared to death. That was Rick rotting in death. That Jesus Christ had resurrected through magical transmogrification—pardon the blasphemy—through *divine transfiguration!* which I gathered from rationalizing the strange late-night happening; namely, by piecing together two hallucinogenic nightmares, I suppose. That if you give a bear a fish, the bear will eat it; but if you teach a bear to fish, it will still eat humans. That if you lie, your knob will grow longer. That if you swear, a thousand curses— pardon the pun—a thousand *spells* will be cast upon you by the boogieman who invented barred—pardon the pun and my blatant disregard to *mot juste* [3]—who invented *the bar* of soap: yes, that sounds so much cleaner! That hospitals like their bills to be paid punctually no matter who you think you are—pardon the ego—no matter who you are. That Dr. Rosenbaum was the coolest, funniest, smartest professor in the world—pardon all past pardons. That, in all seriousness, I (torn between two conflicting worlds) was weak, pathetic, and duplicitous: the aspiring artist who broke down and implored God with promises of devoutness and prayers forever...then turned his back on his word when insanity turned out to be a momentary

---

[1] Lyrics from "Heroin of the Night" by The Dopest Kids on the Block, from the album *Grade-A Playground Meat*

[2] [lat] continuous motion of the spirit [a term used by Roman orator Marcus Cicero]

[3] [fre] the right word or phrasing [attributed to Gustav Flaubert's quote: "This concern with external beauty that you reproach me for is a method for me. When I discover a disagreeable assonance or a repetition in one of my sentences, I can be sure that I'm floundering around in something false. By dint of searching, I find the right expression, which was the only one all along, and at the same time the harmonious one. The word is never lacking when one is in possession of the idea."]

miscalculation. What did nearly a year later prove? That I had retained the ability to repeat myself, repeat myself, when need be—be—and to do things my way because I had a strong conviction that there is no right way which might be the wrong way.

The winter had arrived late and stayed briefly. But that didn't stop Ivy and I from making an extravaganza out of Christmas because our first Christmas together could be nothing less. But to digress a bit: After my first semester ended in mid-December—(somehow I managed to pull off a 3.7 GPA)—I ventured back home for the first time since the Oedipus breakdown: two and a half months later. No surprise that Ma was quiet, sullen, and scared to death. While we were embraced in the initial hug, and dead air transpired, she, like a slow-talking zombiette pushing out dead weight from her throat, said that she'd missed me to death. During the week that I stayed prior to Christmas, every word, object, action, and scene was laden with death: the dead room had never been more fitting. Then, for the first time, I told her that I had a girlfriend, and that I planned to spend Christmas with her. Ma smiled a great broken-hearted smile, although she was probably relieved that I, as Oedipus, might not be trying to have sex with her after all. And she didn't once harass me about not going to the funeral—discussed nothing of the matter itself—but did explain some of the financial aftermath, which I *was* concerned about. Turns out that the government paid for Rick's funeral because he'd served in war for a few months: in total, a two-year military tenure in his late teens before he "retired," or whatever it's called when you just don't feel like being physically patriotic anymore. Because of Da Ice Burgh's frigid economy for the true working class, Ma said that he'd been pondering welfare for when the unemployment checks terminated; she dropped down on the kitchen table a pile of bills to emphasize what the unemployment checks hadn't been taking care of. It was beyond our comprehension as to what was going on, about to take place, and then what to do about it. That's why I (for Ma) hired an attorney to situate the mess. By my request, John Grane took the case. He was a forty-something black straight-shooter with the cheapest fees around. Since Ma refused to leave the house, he came over with his findings and counsel. (She didn't even want him to come over. '*Nun vogghiu n'avvucatu!*'[4] But I told her that it was imperative to deal with the situation a.s.a.p. or else she'd soon be out on the r.o.a.d.) Anyway, turns out that Rick had a 15K life insurance policy; that money went straight out the d.o.o.r. to help pay off t.h.i.s. and t.h.a.t. Also turns out he'd been keeping a separate bank account, unbeknownst to Ma. What he'd been doing (when he was still working) was having a deduction from his check deposited directly into a side account. Apparently it was his "life savings" he didn't care to share with anyone else in his life, which was f.i.n.e. because, after twenty-plus years, it didn't amount to m.u.c.h. Under legal statutes beyond my comprehension, upon his death, all that money that didn't amount to much was to be put towards liens on the property (he'd been having problems paying taxes) and the original mortgage and *its* liens which long preceded the layoff. According to Grane, if Rick had ever brought himself back to Financial Square-One, the money *would've* gone to Ma, even if Rick had spiffed up

---

[4] [scn] I don't want an attorney!

the side account with blank legal bars; meaning, although he never *intended* for the money to go to Ma, it automatically goes to the spouse anyway; again, if there's no outstanding debts. Grane said that it looked like "with a separate bank account set up for savings-only, Rick had perhaps been preparing, a long time ago, for a divorce, and didn't want to lose everything he had when—*if* the time came." Ma lost it and ran into the bathroom. Sucking back the urge to deck him, I told Grane that *my* father and *her* husband had *just* died so what's he trying to prove in saying something like *that*. 'The truth,' he replied stoically. He then explained that the bank had informed him that Rick had requested that all statements (and any phone calls concerning the side account) were to be put through the channels at the steel mill, and for over twenty years both the bank and the mill had complied. I asked him what Ma should do with all the monthly bills. He said that she'd be able to buy some time with her present situation, but after that she'd either have to work, go under the wing of government programs, get help from family and friends (not happening), or, her last option, apply for institutional loans she couldn't get. I asked if Rick's time in the military could help us: no, too long removed, and typically it requires twenty years of service to receive pension. Now onto the will: in that, Rick kindly left Ma the debt of the mortgage, liens, and credit cards. And if she wanted to keep the house, she'd have to pay off the house with the money she didn't have or the money Rick didn't leave behind. (By now, Viduva Lano[5] had returned with quiet tears on her face). So by the power invested in the will, the deed to the house, property, and car was bequeathed to her; that is, if she wanted to buy 'em. As for me, by the power invested in the will, I was left with a million dollars to continue dreaming about rolling around in. The rest of the crap that Grane explained he explained to Ma because I had to leave, but not before I, in a sudden vomit of emotion, threatened him, saying that if he didn't be a little more considerate in how he explained things, and I found out about it, I'd have a lawsuit on my hands because he'd be in the hospital recovering from something fierce. But I think he was disappointed that it was a terroristic threat not worth pursuing legally, seeing as he was well aware of the house he was sitting in. What was he gonna sue for: a small house, property, and car that wasn't ours? or my books and CDs? And pursuing punition for the sake of moral restitution, such as having me put on probation or ordered to pay a fine to the state, just isn't an attorney's business. (However, *if* executed, it might've been considered a "hate crime," or as they euphemistically call it in Pittsburgh, "ethnic intimidation." Fuckin' right it was "_____ intimidation.")

Before returning for the spring semester, I told Ma that her best bet was to just give the house up, then make a break for the sea-border. But she said that she was going to take any job she could. I told her that I couldn't stand to see my mother suffering the ignominy of governmental programs or toiling just to survive; the thought of my mother working under those conditions, never really getting anywhere, pierced my heart a million-fold, making me feel as if this was somehow all my fault; it had nothing to do with another man (me) keeping her (a woman) in the house because that

---

[5] [foreign wordplay] *Viduva* is Sicilian for "widower" and connected with "Lano" it spells her surname.

was just as bad: good 'ol catch-22[2] for Ma. Til she decided what to ultimately do, she moved in with Aunt Stella and Uncle Alfonse, who, during dinner one evening, again started screaming, "At dog wants a bone! 'At dog wants a bone!' At that time, I concluded that he'd finally fallen into the depths of senility, as his dotage exhibited the most morose aspects of the moribund life. I mean, what dog? what bone?—that was so long ago.

Anyway, back to Christmas time with the Pinedas: wow what a time! Turns out that Holly Pineda—a cute chick who resembled Ivy in the face but with *light* brown hair and *un*developed breasts—hated me for no other reason besides having a virgin-sister complex, seeing as she knew that I was balling Ivy and she wasn't getting any behind daddy's back yet. I bought her nothing for Christmas. As for Wardo, I bought him a pricey book containing (in Spanish) the collected essays of Octavio Paz. This time he was pleased with my literary tastes, although he didn't overstand the shot I just took at his façade: so subtle, as opposed to the blatant jab that would've came from my first idea: buying him a subscription to *Sports Illustrated*. As for Sandy Smith, I cheated and had Ivy pick out all that crap women like to douse their body in, along with a gift-card for a few massages. And what they bought me just blew my ear: a cell phone—with a built-in camera! fresh on the market! They also purchased a moderate calling-plan: I had to get it transferred in my name, but I was to send 'em the bill stub every month—for a year! By having it in *my* name, they weren't, as Sandy put it, prying into my business by looking at who and when I was calling. I was stunned! I mean, a whole year paid for! However, I surmised that Ivy was behind it just so she could throw the lasso of technology around my neck, nullifying all I-wasn't-around excuses. And that little trickster just bought me way too much: a whole new wardrobe of preppy shirts; but counterbalancing that, a new pair of Docs, which we pretended had nothing to do with animals; five punk CDs; *War and Peace* and a rare edition of *Finnegan's Wake* from the 40s: books I told her I wanted; fashionable cologne; hair products because she wanted my hair spiked "at all times!"; contact solution (???); a DVD player; and finally, *A Clockwork Orange, Annie Hall,* and *Scent of a Woman* on DVD. Tallying all my past Christmas presents would still fall short of what the Pinedas bought me in just one year! As for Ivy, I (with the help of my new crew, Da Creds) couldn't seem to buy her enough: a new Sarah Brightman CD; *Casablanca, Titanic,* and *The Bodyguard* on DVD; some of that crap women like to douse their body in; an acoustic guitar: in late November, she told me that she wanted me to teach her how to play one day: and although it was no Ovation, she was so ecstatic and nearly gave me a standing-O for my painstaking attention to detail and execution; I also bought her a five-hundred-dollar platinum-coated Bolivian watch bejeweled in Austrian crystals; and finally, an empty white box.

After feasting with my shamily, I asked Ivy if we could get away. She asked for how long. I said an hour would do. She told S&E that we were going to visit T&P. We weren't. After bundling up, I&V headed to the snow-covered orchard with the empty white box. On the way, she kept prying for an explanation. But like a composed foreigner, I kept saying, '*Pacenzia, bedda, pacenzia.*[6] Once inside the orchard, we (under my lead) walked to

---

[6] [scn] Patience, beautiful girl, patience.

the tree. With a light flurry sprinkling down, it was like being inside a shaken glitter-globe. Not a very cold day but cold enough to blow out fake cigarette smoke. I scuffed the snow around us, plowing a circle to stand inside. Then I told her to open the box. She did, and with such enthusiasm! 'Nothin'?' she sighed as if expecting a magic trick to occur. 'You sure?' - 'Umm—yeah. It's empty.' So I scooped my hands down in, then brought 'em back up slowly, steadily, carefully. 'See?' I said didactically. 'See what? I don't see anything!' Her smile was growing with unbearable anticipation. I said, 'It's right here. Touch it.' So she touched the air hovering over my hands. 'What is it?' she asked in a soft childish tone. 'This...' I blew the air hovering over my hands towards her lips, then said, 'It's my I-love-you. I'm no longer boxed up. I love you, Ivy.' - 'Oh my God, Vinny! I love you too! So much! I love you, I love you, I—' I cut in with a long, passionate kiss, as the wind blew cold gusts against the huddled warmth of our bodies. It was our first I-love-you. And I knew that she (in accordance with her beliefs) had been wanting to say it long before but wouldn't break down and say it til I did (most likely because of the women's tenet). For the few months prior to fruition I'd been contemplating the matter because I'd never said that to a chick and wanted to "be cautious" and "make sure." But it dawned on me how stupid it was to think about whether or not to express something that I was positively feeling: if you feel it then what else is there to do besides express it? It made no sense to conceal such a feeling no matter how "tough" I was or how "tough" I grew up or how "tough" guys are by nature. Besides, I saw nothing "soft" about it; I felt within me something as hard as diamond, and it was Love, and, as old legend says, diamonds were created by the flames of Love. 'See:' I said to myself later that day, 'dreams, fairytales, quixotic love, all doze stupid picturesque movies 'n' books—well, now it looks like all dose sentimental exaggerations *can* (to a certain realistic extent) akshly come true—*in the orchard.*'

So it goes, the winter only slightly curtailed our visits to, and when we went, our time in, the orchard. We went about five times just to "play in the snow." The greatest sensation would surge and swirl deep within whenever I'd look around at the naked apple trees and the dense naked forest on the other side of the creek, all shadowed over with snow where, on the undersides, gleamed the definitive browns of wet bark. That starkness and duality helped keep me warm, along with wintry sentiments where the idea of returning home to drink hot chocolate, while wearing a comfortable hoodie and relaxing in a state of tender reflection, slithered into my blood in nostalgic wisps. The one time, right after the heaviest snowfall of the year, we ventured to the orchard to make a snowman. We artistically fashioned it with the three traditional sections of the body: head, thorax, plump base. We didn't bring a hat, so I styled on its head five liberty spikes: a tall emphatic Mohawk. We didn't have a corncob pipe, so she broke from a tree a short twig and stuck it inside its rounded-out mouth. We didn't have a button for its nose (or eyes), so I dug up three little rocks then stuck 'em in its face with authority. It was looking rather archetypical and dignified, save for the liberty spikes. Then out of the blue she said that it was missing something. Without explaining what was missing she sculpted a girthy ten-inch penis! I was so shocked! What snowy salaciousness! However, I couldn't let her outdo me at my own game, so I karate-chopped the massive snow-penis to the ground. 'Whaddya do that for?' she asked. In response, I pulled out my frigid penis and stuck it into the snowman where the snow-penis had been. 'There!' I exclaimed with pride. 'Now Frosty has a vagina 'n' will be known as Frostuna!'[7] I didn't put my penis away either because I needed to pee. So off to the side I peed Ivy's name into the snow. 'Look, Ivy!' I said childishly. She came over and observed with laughter. But before she could laugh too much, I picked her up over my shoulder like a sack of potatoes—my penis still dangling out for frigid comical effect—and pretended I was gonna launch her into her yellow name. She was screaming in merriment tinged with slight concern. But instead of throwing her down in the yellow snow, I carried her over to our creation, readjusted her into a cradled two-armed grip, then gave her a mighty heave-ho and release forward. Big-boned Frostuna and her manmade vagina came crashing down. I dove into the remains. Panting with laughter, Ivy and I began caking each other's faces with snow...til she smacked me too hard with a two-handed heap and made my nose bleed. We promptly left the orchard, leaving behind in the snow blood, sweat, pee, a karate-chopped penis, and a tumbled-down vagina. We were still laughing as we exited the thicket, her apologizing not too apologetically, while I bantered with my head tilted back and nose pinched shut...

     ...Ehh, the heroin tragedy. It was out in the open in January. Pessi finally confessed to me that he snorted it "once in a while," to which I replied, 'Dere is no "once in a while" with H,' to which he replied with a dismissive h-nod as if I couldn't be more wrong. I even told him about my Sid and Nancy paranoia, which he smirkly huffed at then added: 'I ain't a fuckin' boy band member 'n' Teresa ain't a groupie.' When I returned to the real issue and asked what's the point, all he could come up with was the ol' "experimenting, boredom, bullshit, and fishsticks" reasoning of us drug users. My closing question was: 'So yir quitin' *when?*' And he replied, 'Whenever I think it's about da take over.' Kinda made sense seeing as he'd taken the same course with PCP in high school. So I concluded that Pessi was the type who needed to indulge in the hardest drugs from time-to-time in order to get that awakened sensation of living and moving forward in life: a paradoxical concept perhaps rooted in the desire to escape "his ennui, his contempt for life, his disillusionment." Although Ivy and I secretly shared our repulsion, we agreed not to intrude with drastic measures for the time being; I thought it best to be tolerant of Pessi's choices while subliminally trying to get him to wake up. As for Teresa, who fell in love with the cropped blonde hairstyle by keeping it—well, she had it hard being around me because I started treating her a million times worse than shit. However, buried far down in that shit remained that subservient disposition from when I spent the weekend at her house: something, for reasons unknown, I still felt guilty as shit about. There were no more buddy-buddy E-li fa-king Per-ez conversations or I'll-scratch-your-back-if-you-scratch-mine. I told her that not only did I feel it was completely her fault for the H-situation starting, but also now completely in her control to stop it, and if anything should happen to Pessi, then she would be dead—not verbally assaulted, or

---

[7] [scn] A big-boned female version of Frosty

materially vandalized, or physically beaten, but dead. 'Relax, you fa-king asshole!' she squawked. 'Dead,' I replied, grinding my teeth.

As for *my* drug use? Well, one night in March, the four of us had gone to Teresa's girlfriend's party. I got wasted on coke and booze. Then I became fixated on this big jock dude who was all drunk and kept introducing himself to chicks with: 'I'm Sal—the Italian fuckin' Sallion.' Since everyone absolutely adored the harebrained horse, I angled in and blindsided him so hard with a right jab that he fell straight back into the wall, which caused several of his friends to instantly jump me, while Pessi begin beating them off with a metal chair. I didn't see it but Pessi smacked one so hard across the face that he shattered his nose to pieces: the blood squirted all over my back. Those beating me down quickly backed off and away from me. But the cacophonic noise of everyone shouting was deafening. Consumed by a heavy metallic dizziness, I stood up with my nose was pissing all over me: my second bloody nose of the year. Teresa's "friend" came running over, pushing at us, telling Teresa to get her white-trash friends the fuck outta her house. Teresa said fuck off, cunt. Out of nowhere, the Italian fuckin' Sallion—now being restrained by his pussy ponies—had the audacity to spit on me. So I lunged forward swinging away, while Pessi attempted to swing the chair again, but a division of people swarmed between us, trying to separate the numerically disparate sides. Teresa was laughing haughtily, Pessi was laughing provokingly, I (in a blind rage) was threatening to kill everyone in my way, and Ivy was back behind us, shaking in silence, scared shitless, probably having never witnessed such a spectacle. The next day, she sat me down and told me to quit the drugs, chill on the booze, and "absolutely no more fighting!" I promised to comply; so right then, I quit all drugs besides the green, and still drank on Friday or Saturday, but not hard, not with the intent to hurt myself or anyone else: I gradually began feeling better too. Convincent Ivy had drank twice over the past year, the one time drinking herself into her first truly drunken state where, in my room, I had to hold her ophidian mocha, while she blew chocolate-colored chunks into my garbage can. Meanwhile, Luke was aiding us with water, washcloths, and silent prayers. 'Never again!' she sobbed. 'Never again!' I told her, yeah, I'm always saying that too...

...As soon as I returned for the spring semester Dr. Rosenbaum had a job lined up for me: a writing tutor at the writing center, making minimum wage, working three to four nights a week, and never passed 10 p.m. Perfect timing, too, because between Christmas, the hospital bill, getting car insurance (finally), inspection stickers, new tires, along with everything else too superfluous to list—it had all wiped me out. Further help came as I received another refund from my school loans. But since it wasn't as much as before, the job was essential. Not that bad of a job either. First, I had steady "spending money" coming in. Second, not many students came to the writing center for help, and when they did, it was either for a run-through edit or help writing their theses and conclusions. Third, since work was usually idle, I did my studying there, freeing up the nights for Ivy. And we spent nearly every night together. Whenever we didn't stay in together and pass the time away in her room, we went to the movies, museums, out to eat, and few times out of state: a scenic drive through the Blue Ridge

Mountains along the Shenandoah River, a couple kick-ass weekends in Da Burgh with my friends, and a four-day weekend in New York City.

...Ahh, spring came and spring went. A quiet, relatively uneventful time. Everyone had settled into their ways: Ivy and I were attached at the hip. Luke and I were so far apart five-feet away. Teresa and Pessi were attached to their pimp. Pessi and I were still best friends, bantering the same as always, just with more disappointed h-nods. Dr. Rosenbaum and I were bonding in his office. Ma and I were keeping in touch over the phone, her resorting to anecdotes about Aunt Stella and Uncle Alfonse's insanity. While she crooned in Sicilian, trying to sound happy, I would drift off into thoughts about how she was too young to be living there like that. But they were financially taking care of her, as former bills continued accumulating. The box in the middle of the block remained dead since no one had come up with an idea of what to do yet. Ma kept claiming that she wanted to get a job, but the outside world was also something she hadn't experienced in nearly twenty years. And the sad truth is: she was unskilled, illiterate, introverted, and so emotionally unstable that, even if she resorted to fast food, she was bound to breakdown at the drop of a fry...

...Ahh, summer came and summer went. Ivy and I decided to take summer classes for both sessions; this way we could be together, and I really had nowhere else to go anyway. But in order to take summer classes, I had to take out *private* loans because they had to be paid *before* the summer ended in order to get credit for the classes. From the start, Ivy and I had been in competition to get the best grades: I beat her fall semester 3.7 to 3.6; she beat me spring semester 4.0 to 3.6; and she won both summer sessions 4.0 to 3.8 then 4.0 to 3.4. But to digress a lot: I told Ivy about Rick's death the Monday after he died. She began crying til I began telling her about him. Anyway, back to summertime at Aristod with Ivy Pineda: wow what a summer! Visible on the surface, as if wearing her heart on her face, Ivy struggled through a very emotional summer: the numbing anesthetics of love flowing through me were like sharp pinpricks for her, like getting injected with the needle but no feel-good shooting into the bloodstream. She found many truths about my adolescence to be shocking and revolting: and I hadn't even told her the half of it! When I told her stories about Rick, all of which amounted to reasons why I didn't go to the funeral, she cried, only *admonishing* me for not telling her about his death right away. And when I told her Ma's version of Razzle's death, adding in my own conjecture, she was, by appearance, so equally horror-struck and enraged, and thereafter so crestfallen, that she couldn't even cry about it. But when I finally took her home to meet Ma (which was of course at Aunt Stella's) she went into my temporary bedroom and cried some more. That time I asked her why she was crying, to which she answered, 'I dunno; Life's just so unfair!' God, observing her prostrated on my temporary bed in her bleary-eyed solicitude, with her face down in the pillow, allowing the wild waves of mocha to drop down and hide her wild-thyme face...and knowing that her pear-shaped tears were now under the shroud like the shade of Pomona's fruit trees, in which the pruning-knife was carving out from Ivy's red heart to her emerald eyes a ravine to let flow fruitful tears for the entire loveless and lovelorn, world to drink and thus become healed through her sweet fruited love—yes, I realized then that, once opening up her cultivated orchard for everyone in need, Ivy was the most compassionate person in the world, and I (her chosen Vertumnus exalted above all) was just so thankful that this grenadine sugar was now the world to ME!...[8]

...And so it flows, in late July, Ivy and I were eating at Dawn Valley, an upscale restaurant located on the campus-side of LaSalle. We just finished dinner and were moving onto cheesecake when I spotted Dr. Rosenbaum on the other side of the restaurant. He appeared to be walking around aimlessly as if he'd forgotten the location of his table or was looking for a blind-date in which he only had a vague description to go on. He was dressed how he would for class: a pale-blue dress shirt with a red tie, navy blue slacks just long enough to cover his legs and just loose enough to conceal his lankiness, and generic white tennis shoes to keep it casual. The shoes—a stark disparity to the rest of his attire—were heavily scuffed and worn: a soft pedal to his prestige, and indicative of his humility. Then, by chance, he took a distant survey to my side where Ivy and I were placed against a wall of lighted glass. As if he'd finally found what he'd been looking for, he headed towards our table in a swift gait. Not that I was expecting a change, but his face still transmitted outward with incredible reach a natural clemency: his glacier-blue eyes made even more cheerful by his beautiful browstachios breathing just above the bone; his long silvery cheeks, which were home to two kavorkic dimples of seduction, along with the other small crevices that formed whenever he shined his straight sanguine smile; and of course his definitive silvery mustachio suggestive of a philosopher of pacifism and philanthropy.
　　Before addressing me, he clasped his hands together and gyrated 'em around in a paroxysm of idiosyncrasy. 'Hey, look who it is! My main man, Mr. Vincent Vallano.' For my name, he sunk into a deeper tone. Then his thin lips parted into a tremendous smile, manipulating his wiry mustachio into an upward curvature.
　　'Well, well. Surprised da see you round here with us rich folk. How ya doin', Dr. Rosenbaum?'
　　'Oh, fine, I suppose. Just meetin' with some—' he stopped with a puckered lip as if he was about to swear '—some colleagues from the department. We're tryin' to work out the direction of our curriculum. I'm tellin' you, these younger pricks—' Again he stopped, this time sighing as if no words could explain who or what he was dealing with.
　　'You order the bucket of fun huh?'

---

[8] In Roman mythology, Pomona was the goddess of fruit trees. She presided over a large orchard and relentlessly prevented outsiders from joining her, particularly men trying to woo her; it was because of her beauty that everyone desired to gain her love. Finally, Vertummnus (disguised as an old lady) tricks Pomona into marrying him, thereby opening up her abundant orchard, along with the vast surrounding gardens, to someone else. Pomona's attribution was the pruning-knife.

'I swear, it's like if I wanna serve Edgar Allen's poetatoes, they wanna serve Anne's Allen's rice.[9] If I wanna coronate Lord Byron, they wanna hail King Stephen.'

The three of us chuckled at the wordplay, at which time he nodded a greeting to Ivy.

'Well I suppose 'at's juss the fine tastes of our modern world.'

'Perhaps you know someone with a time machine?'

'Mmm, I'll hafta make some caws 'n' get back da ya on that one.'

'Well hook me up like I hooked you up.' Slouching a bit, he crossed his arms over as if to tame his unruly hands; at rest or in motion, Dr. Rosenbaum's energy was always a galvanizing centrifugal force. 'So how's those weeds and seeds treatin' ya?' he asked distantly, as he glanced at Ivy who was being respectfully attentive—and patient.

'Priddy good. Still pickin' some weeds. Buh dis here—' (I held out my hand to present Ivy with no further delay) '—is my most cherished seed, Ivy Pineda. Ivy, dis is Dr. Rosenbaum, da teacher I'm always talkin' about. Ya know, the pearl of the Aristod's English Department, 'n' my sagacious mentor, 'n' of course da guy responsible for gih'n my ass a job.'

In the middle of my half-serious introduction full of glorification, they shook hands and exchanged hellos. He said, 'Vallano, you're a very lucky man.' Then he told Ivy that if things ever fell through with me, he was single, to which Ivy replied—(I think jokingly because she shot a smile at me)—that she *did* prefer taller guys. She went on to ask him if he knew of her family; he said that he heard of the name but she was surely the first Pineda he ever met. Then he began beseeching me to schedule, if I could, his class in the fall. He said that he missed me and was also having trouble filling seats. He also encouraged Ivy to register the class since it didn't require prerequisites and would count towards her Gen Eds. So after considering our current schedules, given that we already scheduled months prior but could still add classes, we both promised him, and each other, that we would register the class. Inside, I was already burning with a thrilling sensation because I wanted to show off—show Ivy how smart her man was amongst worthy challengers, and, given that I had the right teacher to work with, it couldn't work against me! The class was three days a week but unfortunately at 8 a.m. Alwaysthemore, in the mornings, as of late, I was often found sleeping on Ivy's bed, her nestled on the inside against the wall, I on the outside. She was always up first, waking me with an embracive kiss with her soft protuberant lips...then gleaming down on me a tonic smile that willed me straight up...*ahhh*...

...First Wednesday back at school for the second fall semester. After leaving our class with Dr. Rosenbaum where we'd abstained from any class discussion simply because there wasn't one, Ivy went off to work for a few hours before her afternoon classes, and I (also not having classes again til the afternoon but no work) went back to Philemon to get high out my window. By now, I'd perfected the motions of caution and execution. Even if I *never* smoked in front of Luke, my renewed roommate, he had to know

---

[9] Anne Rice was born Howard Allen O'Brien.

because opening the door to walk into a wall of air freshener was a sure giveaway. But he would never say anything anyway.

Anyway, I entered Philemon to find the Hi-I'm-Thai chick still stationed behind the desk inside the fluorescent cubicle. She was twirling her boney brown finger inside a lock of her straight black hair, apparently bored. When she saw me, she smiled: her teeth large and white as milk. She gave me the ol' affable hello. Then, as if forcing a way into conversation, she asked if I'd completed and turned in my new paperwork for the semester. I asked what paperwork. She said it should be in my mailbox. I explained that I hadn't checked my mail in a while. Still twirling her hair around, she said, in a strange provocative way, that I should go fill it out then bring it back to her. I told her that I would. So I retrieved the heap of mail from my box. Filing through, looking for the new paperwork, I came upon a letter from Ma. It was postmarked three days prior. Ma never sent mail, so that too was strange.

Heading down the hall, anxious to read it, Agent Ralphie came out of his room, the timely bastard. As always, the tall and deceptively-bulky behemoth, who I found out was twenty and from Jersey, was wearing his tinted glasses: they looked more for style than prescription but might've possessed those gadget powers promised to the naïve in comic books ads. I tried my best to hide my mail because who knew what his intentions were. But another strange thing happened: he spoke to me for the first time.

He dipped his head down stylishly, but his glasses stayed up on his face as if bolted in. Then: 'Hey, you go to the floor meeting last night?' A deep, indifferent voice, but by effect, hypnotic; I was resisting against its powers to prevent being vanquished in his linguistic power-game.

'Yeah, I went,' I replied coolly. 'Same shit as always, ya know. I don't think Jeff rilly cares about much anyway.'

'For sure,' he rejoined diabolically. 'Well—I'll check ya later.' He walked away robotically.

In front of my door, I pretended to be fumbling around for my keys because I wanted to see if he would turn around and give me a "look"; I was seriously beginning to believe something was up with him. But without giving a "look," he cut the corner left with geometrical retardation as if his joints desperately needed oiled, even though he was the slickest person I'd ever encountered! Smirking, I entered my room, sat down at my desk, and immediately opened the letter from Ma. Translated, it roughly read:

Sorry, my sweet little wine cork. You know that I'm not the best at writing in English, so I write to you in Sicilian, and I must spell it as I say it. Please don't show this letter to anybody from Palermo! They will laugh at our precious Catanisi dialect! Anyway, I want to tell that I love you so much. Sometimes life makes it hard for us to say the things we really feel inside, right? At first, I was angry with you for the things you said over phone when your father died. Then for not coming home for the funeral. Truth is, I didn't want to go either. But I had to make my last peace and pray his soul into Heaven. I know it has been a very hard time on you. But the Lord giveth and the Lord taketh away. Lately I've been talking on the phone with Filomena. I really miss her. She says that the family misses me. I thought they hated me! But she said it's not true. She has been asking me to come visit. I told her that I have no money and I have to deal with the problems with our house. She said that I should just move back to Catania, and everybody will help me. I told her no, not with you here. I could never leave you behind. But she said that her husband would send me a plane ticket just to visit for a while. Maybe that would be all right? You'll think this is funny. When I told Aunt Stella, she said, 'Good riddance!' I didn't know what that meant. In Italian, I asked Joe, the owner of Castelli's. He said, 'To be happy someone has left.' But I'm sure you know that. You're probably wondering why I decided to write and not call. A much easier thing to go through with and explain for me. On the phone I would lose my nerve. Plus, it feels good to see Sicilian words again! This (present situation) gave me a reason (to write). But it would be nice if you called me with your response. Should I go visit for a while? If you don't mind, I will. But I promise with all of my heart that I will come back. It seems that my whole life has involved leaving people behind. Oh, and that sweet Ivy Pineda! She is so beautiful and polite! A little angel from God! Treat her right! Girls like her are rare and precious. And please tell Zach that I love him and miss him as well. Tell him that he can call me any time, and I won't tease him in Sicilian. Poor little Peppered Head! Ah Ah Ah! And Vinny, I'm just so proud of you! I now understand that you think different than most people. But the greatest people think like that! Look at Luigi Pirandello, Salvatore Quasimodo, and Giovanni Verga! So just keep thinking like that! And do good in school! And stay out of trouble! Please try to call soon with the answer regarding me visiting Catania. Okay? I love you, Vinny! Remember: you will always be my little baby boy no matter how big and old you get! God bless!

{On the envelope: *Teodora Scandurra Vallano*}

I left the letter lay on the desk. Then I went to the window, drew the blinds to the side, and stared deep into a large orange sun, looking for the answers...to Life. Out beyond, the large orange sun was set softly within a gray-blue sky flecked with yellow...almost protrusive in its grandeur...a voluptuous mass of rays billowing up and down...waving out interminably from the sides...two nearby blackbirds with red epaulettes on their inner wings swooping down...then ascending back up under one's lead—the more docile one of a shorter wingspan—both, bill and coo, flying away amorously—fawningly into the gray clouds slowly passing by...the soft eyes of the clouds turned away from me and towards that large orange sun dancing us *(down here)* around on the large dance floor grounded in gravity...dancing us *(down here)* around in dreamy swirls of emotions and thoughts too grand to be subjected to the word *rational*...dancing us *(down here)* around and around and around on the large dance floor presently becoming, through the absorption of the sun's bliss, ungrounded from the gravity *(down there)*—like a weightless ascension felt just for a second—only to fall back down to the ground *(down here)*...wistful...so wistful the wisp was!...but, yes, now back down here where *(from above)* transcendent tunes trickle down—stopping somewhere in between—and thus reaching *(down here)* in deafening silence.

I called Ma and told her that a visit to Catania would do her good.

The ticket to the sky would be on its way...

AND NOW WE DANCE

"He's got eyes like raindrops: (That's my man, that's my man),
And the way he turns to glance: (He's my man, he's my man),
Oh how my heart stops: (It just stops, it just stops),
Now it's time for us to dance: (And so we danced),
We danced all night, (Ah-ah-ah),
Through the streets and through the rain, (Woah-oh),
We danced all night, (Oh yeah)
No more tears, no more pain..." [1]

Already substantiated to a repetitive end: I began experiencing various types of violence at a young age. And yet my experiences with poetry, and on the larger scale, Art, would seem to be located on the other end of the spectrum, which according to that logic suggests either prevarication of my adolescence or my knowledge of Art. But I find fallacy in a theory that infers disparity in, and detachment between, *violence* and *poetry;* in other words, that poetry (regardless of a dark or merry nature) is tantamount with *feminine sensitivity.* NO! BALANCE IS KEY AS IT IS WITH NATURE! With that said, at a young age I knew what a poet was because in 6th grade we had one week of English class devoted to poetry. The only poet I can recall from the experience is William Blake: mostly likely approved for the school's curriculum because he was a humble, clean-mouthed, God-inclined mystic, although the school must not have overstood his dissidence in turning away from the superfetation of aristocratic logic plaguing his time, which, despite the reign of the Romantics, the plague would prove to be lying dormant, restrengthening, til (again) spreading its infirmity in imperceptible degrees with the commencement of the Hemorrhagingway Movement when the blood of Art was transfused with the oil of Roboticism. Well-oiled machines? NO! SPOILED-BAD ROBOTS! Anyway, as Ms. McKie read Blake's poem aloud, I sat back in my seat and shut my eyes, for she said, 'Try *reflecting* on the poem.' In retrospect, the "class reflection" had been an opprobrium because the subject had been handled blasphemously not just by the students but also by Ms. McKie, who later that year ripped up a poem of mine because I wasn't doing my class exercises on syntax. Regarding the students' behavior during the "class reflection": one student would project I-didn't-do-it sounds as the rest fell to laughter—except for me, unfortunately. It was very strange that I wasn't participating since I was usually troublemaker #1. But I couldn't this time, for I'd been impregnated. I began pushing them and their sounds far away. Although I didn't overstand the context of the poem, I remember feeling for the first time a sensation similar to intuition, and being "conscious" of it. From an epiphanal sensation whirling inside, I suddenly overstood the basic concepts of Art and Man, feelings and thoughts, aspirations and capitulations, joys and sorrows, peace and violence, love and hatred. Of course it wasn't the first time those

---

[1] Lyrics from "Dance Medicine" by Bree Brunette and the Blonde Hive, from the album *On a Moonlit Bridge*

thoughts and sensations had befallen me, for things like a love for my mother and a hatred for my father had long been established. But it *was* the first time that I began to overstand within those thoughts and sensations the ~~art~~istic instinct of birth, projection, and form. But perhaps more importantly—(going in reverse-order)—void, barrier, and confinement.

...eyes closed, a chill shook through me...distant words of a sick rose...a slimy animal from the ground is coming...now flying in the sky through a dark storm...while down below on the bed a crimson joy throbs in imagery...but it brings misery, for the shackled passions of Love and Dreams, the lack of actions and fulfillment, is destroying Life...it's a dark secret that's destroying Life...and the dark secret is, everything has become so ugly, so sick, so enslaved and deprived...but who knows everything is being destroyed: internally, externally, one soul, all souls, grain of sand, gobs of clouds[2]...*shhhh, it will be all right, for Life—if better days rise again—will soon give another birth*...And now I'm pregnant, inseminated by the chill of epiphany, the first manifestation: baptismal submergence, drop of chrism.

...eyes closed, in a natal gasp of hush, I could feel something within me beginning to kick like the nascent legs of a baby in the womb: and how Life comes about by the violence of man's seed! *and yet made beautiful and tranquil through the nurturing of a woman's womb.* William Blake (to be sure, a man) had planted within me a violent seed: his godly words. But I was not a woman, and thus didn't have a womb—(the void)—so the seed could only fester violently in my gut with no way to grow, to be born, to show itself in form—(the barrier)—my beauty and tranquility was damned, it seemed—(the confinement).

...And so there I was many years later, an ontogenetic man developing only in accordance with the flesh-and-bone of my age, walking down the florescent hallway, back towards the pretty lil Thai chick. In my tight, angry-like grip, I held papers just full of answers: on request, such easiness. I met her at the side-door, not the desk-window. She said, 'All done?' while fashioning a subtle inviting smile. And bearing a superficial smile on mine, while experiencing a sense of restriction in my gut, unable to gratify capricious desires, I handed her the papers...then walked away without a word, unable to decide if I wanted to make love to her, fuck her, or choke her to death...

...My skateboard had five year's worth of grinding scratching up the belly of the board where an emblem of two boxing gloves once touched fist-to-fist, but it still knocked $40 into my corner; because of my ankle, I figured it would be some time, if ever, before I could kick the board back up in the air. The twenty CDs I chose to sacrifice—the ones I listened to the least—rang out $58 notes. With the deadline not yet expired, I was able to sell my summer textbooks back to the bookstore, allowing $190 to fall into my pile. And the budgeting of my tutoring paycheck had worked itself up to

---

[2] Allusion to and dramatization of Blake's poem *The Sick Rose*

$413. Total: $701. I had $701 to be creative with. It was my only recourse since the newest refund from the school loans had gone straight to my textbooks for the fall semester, with the rest paying off the remainder of the hospital bill. I had to get the bill off my ankle because (from my own conjecturing) it was part of my mild OCD (or my strong perfectionist qualities) to loathe outstanding debts. To boot, after applying for my second-year loans, my financial situation changed significantly. In short, I switched over to being independent since Rick could no longer be used as a cosigner, which, before I even left for college, I'd stolen his tax forms and forged his information on the loan applications, thinking I would receive more money with parental auspices. Be that as it may, it turned out that having a dead father, a mother with no credit, and being responsible by having a minimum-wage job, afforded me *less* loan money: of course who would ever argue with that logic?! So I was now living paycheck-to-paycheck, which is why I had to sell some things for *the thing*.

Anyway, I had, for the present moment, not a penny more than what I had: I had $701 to be creative with. And I suppose I did just that. It was a hell of a lot of money to spend, but heaven isn't cheap. One muggy night in July, when we were in that other world called Orchard, Ivy told me that she'd missed out on the prom, and to her parent's dismay, even though they seemed to have been the reason why. But it was from that that I came up with idea of surprising her with a rendition of the prom for our one-year anniversary, which, despite some ambiguity over when we'd became "official," we set our anniversary date as October 10th because it had a nice ring to it; my unreliable memory, however, knew for a fact that the first night in the orchard was October 3rd—to be sure, a Friday night of perfect weather and undying echoes.

In late September, I tallied up my earnings and began spending the $701 as follows:

After a personal call with Bob Fontana—co-owner of Fontana Fashions in Pittsburgh and friend of the family—he charged me a generous $50-even to rent the tux and the dress, which would have to be fitted on prom day in order to keep everything in cadence. $300 went to Jean-Pierre—owner of Lefèvre—to rent out a banquet hall inside his famous French restaurant dahntahn. Also to Jean-Pierre: $60 for two French cuisines; *hors d'oeuvres* and desserts were *gratuites* with the hall rental. $100 went to the DJ to serenade the prom, and no one more fitting to do it than Eddie Hughes. $70 went to Rosa's Floral: $50 for an extravagant bouquet of red roses; $20 for the vase: a long crystal piece burnt in soft blue tones, with an ascending angel (also of a sacred blue tone) jutting out a good half-inch. $20 went to a local gas station for gas so I could carry out the necessary errands. $100 was set aside for future trips and tips. And finally, $1 to be given to Ivy Pineda when the time came.

When the time came, Ivy Pineda was confused. She'd been under the impression that I had no money because I'd given her the impression that I had no money. And since old-fashion values said that she couldn't contribute a dime to the day, we, according to her assumption based on my hoodiewinking, would be spending our one-year anniversary at a modest restaurant in LaSalle, followed by a flick. It was a banal choice from which a few arguments arose, given that she wanted the stars, and I was offering some sand. But when I called her late afternoon and told her to start styling up her hair like never before, she was confused. And I planned to keep her confusion hanging out there like someone left on a dance floor who's too mortified to make a move to the sidelines. Confusion is like a box of money: you never know what you're gonna get (once you get it), but you're always leaning towards a certain something. In cargos and a hoodie, I capered up to her dorm with the flowers in the vase...She was waiting outside and accepted the roses with no great surprise but with a look that said, 'Well, at least you did *something* right.' Once she took the flowers up to her room and returned, I informed her that we were using her Beemer for the night. No problem there. A nice car was certainly needed to compliment the nice way *she* was dressed. Yes, *she* was all dressed up, but I wasn't! Making sure I was the first to barb, I mock complained about the way *she* was dressed, to which she replied, 'You told me to do my hair, and I'm not gonna do my hair without dressing nice. But look at *you*! You look like a bum! People are gonna think you kidnapped me!' But my sweet little rose didn't know I was about to look like seven hundred and one bucks...

...Niki Fontana—Bob's wife and co-owner of Fontana Fashions—was in her early forties. She had chromatic blonde hair that dropped linearly to her lower back. Violet eyes that sparkled like two Hope diamonds. Full, firm breasts. Cheeks naturally blushed the color of pomegranate. And although a statuesque woman, like a Greek goddess, she had the voice of a little girl. So phenomenal and titillating it was to look at Aphrodite and yet hear soft suppliant sounds coming from large moist lips. Just the mere thought of Niki would swallow me whole in the desire to quit caring about everything else, to abandon once and for all the tussle between good and evil, because such a sublimation of the imagination, of the capitulation to the mere thought, inevitably leads to the process of transcending all earthly values...allowing yourself to nestle inside this elevated "space" of perfect infinity known as her essence. In other words, when I first hit puberty, Niki Fontana was "the one." Memory tells it that she was the first person to divert elsewhere the enamoring of my mother: those parental transferences happen instantaneously at the point when you question the morality of the impulses within your monstrous sexuality which is now burgeoning exponentially as if someone is fucking around with your internal calculator, and, repulsed by the "tally" of the impulses brought to your new frame of consciousness, you quickly shun and push 'em away, and in lieu fill yourself with guilt and disgust. With that said, Niki Fontana took a one heaven of a precedence in my heart! I mostly knew her from church; the angel sat in the pew in front of me; I would stare at her wings, listen to her sing, thinking about God knows what. I even had a song for us: an 80s love ballad. The heartrending song struck up at the strangest times in my head, but I didn't know who sung it or what it was called; I suppose I'd heard it on the radio and there was an instant connection for reasons beyond language, especially in the reasoning of this confused young boy. As the years passed, and the memory of the song started carrying more nostalgic worth, I would, whenever it came to mind, ask anyone around what it was called, but to no avail; it felt as if I was trying to sing something in a foreign language, leading me to wonder if it was perhaps a song I dreamt up. But Niki herself, in her powerful air of divinity, was anything but a dream—well, besides her *seeming* unreachable to the young desperate me, despite hugging her many times. 'Peace be with you.' – "N' also witchu.' A handshake? No, hug me! Ahh, yes, church, church, chirp, to once again feel the inflaming tactility of those real touches! to wit, the wings on your back! I wanchu baaaack!

To move from the worldly to the ethereal: In my old Grecian daydreams, I was gratified by the *cooler* end of the spectrum of sensations. Thick buoyant clouds abound, the ground a million miles away, I would lay cradled in her cool lap. Both naked, I would purposely squirm underneath her breasts just to feel the tepidity of the friction, slowly sliding my legs down her legs: the comfort in gentle reflexes when slightly cold. She had perfect feet as well as perfect teeth, but for the sake of my melancholy her teeth were rarely seen in my imagination. Without a word (by my design) she would touch and nurture all my physical scars, then listen to all the embarrassing things about me, which wasn't necessarily expounded in these reveries but *presumed* to have taken place. Yet all that in itself was only a gentle build up to the climax. Although in the earliest fancies there was nothing sexually explicit going on between us, I—for lack of better words to describe the pinnacle of the sensation that was void of the act itself—pined for her to "get me off" in the miracle of one split-second but to have it last forever. And as that imaginary sensation would tickle me in chilly methodical vibes, she would pet my head, pushing back my shiny black hair with motherly strokes, while crying down on me river-cold tears of joy because she was so obliged to make me feel so good. Yes, Niki Fontana, the avatar of Aphrodite! the goddess of my youth! the moralized replacement for my mother! "the one"!—the one who, like William Blake, took my deepest feelings out of nativity (out of the shell of innocence) and cast 'em into dark woods for futile pursuit, left in the present with schmaltzy recollections! Alwaysthemore, Niki had been getting pounded by Bob long before I was even born. Bob too was in his early forties, a tall, dark-blonde, attractive man—a man who always carried himself with professional equanimity. But fuck Bob. Fuck Bob with a high-powered Taser! *Bzzzzz-ZAP!*

Anyway, I'd explained the situation to Bob and Niki, letting 'em know not to say *anything* to Ivy no matter how much she questioned what was going on. Niki had told me how sweet I was, and I wanted to tell her that it *could've* been her. But fuckin' Bob...

...When Ivy and I entered Fontana's Fashions, located in South Side, Pittsburgh, I was quick to hug Niki, and I think the miracle of the split-second actually worked. *Wink, wink.* I took off my hoodie. Then everyone went straight to work. A bit later, with my tux not quite fitted yet, I was momentarily clad in jealously: I realized that everyone was touching—well, dressing the wrong people! After we reconvened in a backroom cluttered with clothes and all the things that make clothes, Ivy and I had transformed into something so celebrous—swathed in colors the world would never forget:

Ivy's gown was metallic ivory lace. The lace itself inconsistent: more thorough at the bottom end where it hid *all* skin, unlike the top where it increasingly became more see-through. On the bottom fringe of the gown were thin slants of violet silk. Like the ivory, the violet sparkled like tiny stars. A strapless piece, the gown revealed all the subtle freckles on her bronze shoulders. The upper portion of the gown was tight and tuckered in even further around the waist. (Ivy's chest had never seemed so defined; I would've believed Ds even though I very well knew she bore two Cs; either way I gave her an *A!*) With her curves, including hips, hugged, the gown tailored off and out a bit at the ankles. Save for the slight bell at the bottom, the dress was firm and classy. Since Ivy had, without fault, worn brown Chickee Docs, Niki lent her a pair of white dress shoes. But Ivy's hair, by request, was already there and prepared: up in a chignon with long waves of mocha flowing down the sides, waiting to be homed inside my mouth.

While making smalltalk with Bob, I kept my focus on Niki and Ivy, about ten yards away. Niki was hunched down a bit, focused on her own hands, as she clipped an ivory choker with a small locket in the middle around Ivy's neck. Then she grabbed a little bottle and flicked glitter on Ivy's arms. When Niki stepped back, she, in that soft suppliant voice, said, 'You're an absolute doll, Ivy! You ever thought about modeling?'

Ivy lowered her head with a modest smile and replied in the negative. She looked so overwhelmed—so in shock—so thankful, like she grew up poor on the streets and this was the first time she was ever dolled up.

Bob turned away from hemming my black overcoat to stare at Ivy and his wife's mastery of trade, giving an approving nod and a Bond-like smile that would make any woman unravel like a ball of yarn thrown out in the air. Bob stuck a needle between his lips, while he continued molesting me around the waist as if, deep-down, it was a vicarious way to rub in my crotch what he was rubbing his face in every night. Fuck Bob! Fuck Bob with a dirty stick of dynamite! And fuck Bob for purposely making my tux loose in the rear just to make me look stupid! Nice black bowtie and cummerbund, Bobby! But look at my fuckin' sag-ass!

After being fitted and over-stuffed with compliments, Ivy and I over-stuffed them with gratitude; for Bobby, I only did so because I *had to.* Too bad during the goodbye hug with Niki, I went again, then pretended to be whispering the sticky details in her ear. Then Ivy and I headed out the door and down the steps, expecting to be showered in rice, or whatever the contemporary confetti had become. Stupid exploding pigeons! Ahh, but the sun—so radiant! spilling its golden exuberance into the Mon! And the air— an autumnal blessing, blowing love all through South Side! I looked around, far out, and *all* of Pittsburgh was in high blowing spirits! The bovine picking it up an extra step! All noises amalgamated into a cheery whistle! All neon signs the signs of positive progress like they all read JUST MARRIED!...

...After bridging over the Mon, now inching through the streets of dahntahn, Ivy was still pleading with me to polish clean the details.

'Come on! Please tell me! I can't take it anymore! *Pleeeeease!'*

'I tolja, hun, you'll find out soon. Akshly in about five minutes.'

'Okay, but *hey.'* (I looked over.) 'I seriously love you *soooo* much.'

While playing *Frogger* through the lanes—with Chris Isaak serenading us on the radio—I couldn't stop from taking glances at the prom queen. She was squirming restlessly in her leather seat, peering out the window, hands on the upholstery below, like she was expecting, in the midst of the high-and-mighties, to come upon a surprising—but not so surprising—skyscraping statue of herself: a dedication from me to her, and the least I could do for her given what she'd done for me. But soon enough, what was in plan came into sight as I pulled into the arched valet roadway for Lefèvre.

'Vinny!' she cried out. 'Is this like a fancy French restaurant?!'

'Yeah, you could say that.'

'Wow!—Wait, do you know if they serve veggie? 'Cause ya know that's rare in French cuisine.'

'So I found out. But dey gadda couple vegetarian meals.'

'Oh my God, you're so sweet! I think you're makin' me love you *too* much!'

Pulling in front of the glassy, multi-level restaurant, I stopped underneath a red marquee. I left the yellow Beemer idling for the valet. A handsome young man, red-vested with taut black pants, was quick to open the door for Ivy, but I too was quick to open mine without any aide: *aide-toi, le ciel t'aidera!* [3] Ivy ran around the back of the Beemer, and quixotically threw her arms around my neck and lip-kissed me.

'Well, Ms. Pineda:' I said after the embrace, 'would you care da join me inside?'

'I sure would, Mr. Vallano.'

Around the back of the car we headed towards the doors of Lefèvre, holding hands; fitting that only days prior she'd went and had a French manicure done. As she proceeded, I had to stop to thank and tip the valet, as I thought was the custom whether coming or going. When I caught up to Ivy, another red-vested man opened the door with a grand smile. I convinced myself that I didn't have to tip him for that, not even a pittance no matter how fawningly he kept shinning his face for me, from which I found out that even a smartly dressed man can, for not dropping a dime, make you feel the way you do when you decline charity to a raggedy ol' bum. Oh well! Fuck him too! Fuck *all* these quarter-quenched queers! Fuck the world: I'm hanging out with Ivy tonight!

Lefèvre's foyer was aromatic (not from food but from polished elegance) with red walls that had black felt curtains running along the low border; French paintings hung up on the red; exotic flowers festooned across the trim; lavish garden sceneries in the corners—golden ivy strewn everywhere. Peeking to the left and straight ahead, I saw that the dining rooms were even fancier and sculpted in the Rococo style. A tall man with a sullen monkey face and blonde monkey hair (dressed in the same red monkey-suit the entire waitstaff was wearing) stepped forward and asked for my surname. 'Vallano,' I answered with an unprecedented pride.

'Ahh! *Vallano*. The banquet hall is right this way, *monsieur*.'

'*Banquet hall?*' said Ivy, standing behind me, perplexed.

Shrugging my shoulders, I flashed a naïve monkey face. So we followed Blonde Monkey Man down the red aisle...turned right and went up five red steps...down a quiet hall...then left into a large banquet hall, empty

---

[3] [fre] help yourself, and heaven will help you!

of souls besides Eddie. He was setting up his equipment on a gray hard-carpeted stage at the fore. With both hands gripped underneath a PA speaker, he looked over, smooth-cheeked, flat-topped, and composed, winking without breaking stride or saying anything. It was as if he didn't know us or was keeping quiet because he didn't want to spoil the secret that was no longer a secret. Although my closest guy friend next to Pessi, I never overstood Eddie, although, unlike Pessi, he was a pleasant enigma who hardly brought any concern or glum to my senses. Eddie and I shared back-to-back birthdays in mid-July, which meant we (with our friends) always had an annual joint-celebration. Alwaysthemore, despite growing up on the same block, I'd never been able to bring Eddie over whenever Rick was around out of fear that something racial might get said. The word *embarrassment* would be a gross understatement. Eddie had two younger sisters in elementary school. His mother was a frumpish cow with hair so disheveled you'd think she hadn't combed it in years; it stuck straight up in the front, and in the back, hung down in a grotesque manner, almost like a mullet. Whenever I'd hangout at his place, she was usually found on their ugly brown couch wearing a yellow muumuu mobbed with horrid flowers. She was always humming old jazz songs in between scoffs of food. She worked a few blocks away at a convenient store. Eddie's father was bald, short, and carried his weight around like a worm; as if to compliment his wife's humming, he looked like a failed jazz musician. He appeared to be about seventy but was only in his early fifties. Falling far from the tree, Eddie was a glowing natural athlete. Always smiling. Always saying agreeable things. Frequently spaced-out in his own world. And rarely mad. When ominous situations arose, and Eddie was dragged in, he'd get psyched just enough to do what he had to do then shake it off like a petty gadfly. He'd go back to wondering around, cheerfully shadowboxing or whistling—he whistled a lot. Such an enigma! Sometimes when I thought about him, I'd say to myself: *who is 'at kid?...have I rilly known HIM all these years?...I wonder whadee does when no one's around?* Then I'd resort to analyzing past conversations to see if I'd somehow been mistaken about Eddie being my so-called second-closest friend. I believe that in itself—contrary to the brotherhood qualities of Da Hoolies—proved that I wasn't close with anyone besides Pessi: the substance of *that* relationship covered, for me, all the philosophical measures of *friendship.* But of course that was all before Ivy Pineda, the girl whose color was perfectly balanced between black and white, although, to be frank, if Rick had ever met her, he would've considered her a "spic" or a "wetback," which, to be frank, if he would've ever said anything like that to me or her, I would've been liable to put a hole in him. 'Eh, a wetback. Go gitchirself a good Italian girl.' Turns away from me in disgust, and—*BANG!*—now he's gotta wet back. In mafioso culture, they say that's how you kill a man you don't respect: right in the fuckin' back.

'What's goin' on? Why's there a DJ up there'—Ivy pointed to Eddie—'and no one else here? Don't tell me you're throwin' me some kinda party.'

'No, not rilly. But 'member that night in the orchard when ya tol' me about not goin' da the prom, 'n' how much you'd wanted to?'

'Yeah?'

'Well—TA-DA! It's prom night, baby! See, I figured sincha missed out on da prom 'n' ya like French culture, I'd combine a nice French dinner with some prom stuff, like the music 'n' 'at.' (We observed the white and burgundy balloons and streamers hanging all around the commodious room, and above the buffet table hung a white banner that said Happy Anniversary!) ''N 'at's wunna my good friends—Eddie Hughes; he's our DJ for the night. 'Member me talkin' about 'im?'

'Yeah. I, uhh—' Standing with her sparkling naked shoulders and arms dropped like they wanted to collapse to the ground, she surveyed the decorated room, so transfixed by the sight. Couldn't even finish her sentence! Yes! Swoon, Ivy, swoon!

'Yep. Dis *entiiiiire* room is all ours tonight,' I superfluously added. With a mature turn of the hips, and my hands shoved down in my slacks, I focused my attention to the fore. 'Yo, Eddie Spagheddi! Why ya late?!'

'Ya know how idd is: *I missed da bus. (Ohhh.) I missed da bus...*' After breaking into song—a song we used to make fun of—Eddie began mimicking old-school Hip-Hop hand-gestures. '... *'n' 'at's sum'n I'll neva eva eva do again!*'

Amused, I walked towards Eddie up on the little stage, leaving Ivy alone in her state of transfixion at our table-for-two with a short candelabra set in the middle; the table was at the forefront of many larger banquet tables. After having lighted our three-pronged candelabra, Blonde Monkey Man made sure to step in my path *en route* to Eddie. Blonde Monkey Man said something inconsequential, so I sent him on his way with the tip of a rich thank-you. *Have merci on me, and also on you!*

Eddie was quick to bring up Pessi's newest drug situation; he seemed just as confused, concerned, and disheartened as everyone else. Thoughts therefrom were bound to bring me down, so I shot into Tonight's Rules. 'Look here, Wangsta: no Hardcore Punk, no Hardcore Rap. Dis is like *her* night, ya know. She likes R&B 'n' shit like 'at. But play some Oldies too...' I'd already informed Eddie of all this. '...Only thing you gadda abide by if ya want paid is no Celine Dion. I fuckin' hate her voice so much thit it's uncompromisable, her night or not.'

He laxly dropped his features. 'Come on, V; you akshly think I got Celine Dion?'

'Who knows. You've always seemed a liddle strange da me, like a closet homo or sum'n.'

'Oh yeah? Keep it up 'n' I'll run dahn the block 'n' buy every Celine record dere is 'n' 'en play 'em all night long.'

'I'd rilly appreciate that, cumface.' I turned around to call Ivy over, but she was busy walking around, checking the place out. I turned back to Eddie. 'Hey, wha' da fuck's Dante been up to? Ya know, I've prahblee talked do 'im maybe three times since I been at school. He never caws, 'n' whenever I caw him, he's never home 'n' he don't return my messages. Couldn't even come up 'at one weekend.' (One weekend, while Ivy was with her family on vacation, Jeremiah and Eddie drove down to LaSalle to hangout with me and Pessi. All of us spent the night at Teresa's. From observing her body language, I had a strong feeling that she was racist: squirming her reed around all night, never getting too close to Eddie, although I'd yet to hear her say anything outright.)

'Well one night he'z all about joinin'ah army. But den he started seein' 'iss Anna chick from Monport. Now he always dahn 'ere with her.'

'Oh yeah? I bet Anthony's jealous as fuck. 'N' if you see that liddle amoebic whore, make sure da tell 'im when *I* see 'im, I'm gonna knock his fuckin' teeth out for sayin' 'at shit about me bein' a referee 'n' thinkin' I'm bedder den everyone 'cause I'm at Aristod. No, ya know wha': *don't* tell 'im; I'd rather juss blindside 'im.'

Shaking his head agreeably, Eddie laughed; he was plugging in wires on the turntable. 'So why donchu, uhh, caw shordy over here?'

''Cause she hates blacks, 'specially ones 'at yuzza word *shordy*.'

Flashing a wide smile, Eddie came at me with a salvo of wild slaps, while verbally dogging my attire. After dodging most, I called Shorty the Shrinking Violet over to give improper introductions. Us three talked at the fore til our waiter, *Roland le Maître D,*[4] came in to greet us and tell us our food was on the way. Roland was a coastal-looking man in his sixties with reddened skin, a shiny bald head, brows white, thin, and high, and the stilted gait of someone who has something large and hard rammed up an orifice. Eek! don't fuck him with anything; his ass has already been had!

Ivy and I sat down at our fancy ecru-clothed table, and under my educational leadership, we talked about doublespeak, til Roland rolled in with the salads. I leaned back so I could *thoroughly* observe *him* serve *me* in the *proper* fashion. But an emergence of thought robbed me of my snobbery: there was one thing I hadn't taken into my calculations: what to do with Eddie while we ate! Eek! He'd soon be done setting everything up, and to leave him up on the stage to watch us eat would be awkward; but to invite him to sit with us and watch us eat at a closer range would be even more awkward. So like a Buddhist, I found the answer in the middle; but unlike a Buddhist, I shouted across the room, 'Eh, Wangsta! When yir done ya can grab summa that food over dere! Whore-derves 'n' deeee-zerts!'—and I shouted that as Roland was finishing up his proprieties. 'Bahchu gadda ee'dit up 'ere, or adda table far away from us 'cause yir black! Yir black, boy! Yir black!' Rigid Roland was holding himself up as if unaffected, but I was certain he'd return to the kitchen and talk shit on me, not knowing that I (who would've been more of a laugher had I been in my normal attire) was probably more culturally refined in my nineteen years than he would ever be. I wanted to stand up, rip my dress shirt off, and say: 'Wanna judge me by my earrings? tattoos? idiolect? Well, do ya *Monsieur Bourgeois?* Den come on! If you rilly think *yir* da "master of the house" den let's dance for da throne! Two-step, two-step, pirouette—kick ta da face! Fuck yeah! Now lemme sing, for Cervantes said he who sings frightens away his ills! 'N' lemme dance, for Nietzsche said a day ya don't dance at least once is a day lost! So sing 'n' dance with me, Mr. Rollie Fingers In The Butt, 'n' 'en we'll see who's so ill thit da other gets lost in his tracks! Come on; don't make me provoooooke youuuuuu! Oh, fine 'en! *Roland, Roland, Roland, let's get dishit rollin'—raw hiiiide! (WHAP!)* Now grab yir partners 'n' let us dance! *Dance like a thrown knife! It don't madder where yir from! Juss how ya come! Let's dance the Dance of Life! (WHAP!)* Now all you men, pull dahn

---

[4] [fre] the headwaiter; maître d'hôtel literally means "master of the house"

yir pants! 'N' all you chicks, tear off 'oze shirts! Step 'n' twist! while we honk yir tits, 'n' you grab our dicks! Let's dance the Dance of Life! (WHAAAAAP!)
 Since Roland backed down to the dance-off, he served our food then left. Then *la mademoiselle et je* began eating, while Eddie snacked on whore-derves behind his secret fort that was a table, turntable, speakers, and boxes of records. For Ivy and I, I'd pre-ordered French vegetarian meals, *a la nouvelle cuisine.*[5] *Yuck à foie gras!* For the *salade: chicorées frisées es/scarole Belges.* And for the *entrée: pâtes avec pistou.* In other words: a Belgian salad of dandelionesque leaves, with pine nuts, saturated with a strong French cheese veined with an exquisite mold. And for the main course: a bow-tie pasta seasoned with basil and garlic, garnished with goat cheese. Also included by my request: *baguette* with vegetarian *pâté*, and a side of wild rice pilaf to be served with the *entrée.* What a mindful meal!
 After eating the salad, Roland rolled in, cleared the plates, left stiffly, then rolled back in with the *entrée.* It was fancy: not overly garnished; just something I'd never had before. But it was a first-time experience without fear because the smell drew me straight into it. Hands-down-the-throat the most scrumptious food I'd had all year! I was tearing into it like a hog, stabbing at the pasta and cramming it down into my maw, chewing so obstreperously! But why o' why my pigsty? Perhaps Eddie's presence was making me feel the need to act improper and personify Verna? Or perhaps I was just really immature? Probably the latter. Ivy, though, she was eating so slow and urbanely, like an experienced aristocrat with her ecru linen folded and draped across her lap, her wineglass of cranberry juice set up and to the right of her plate, each piece of silverware serving a certain purpose: salad fork and place fork to the left, French blade knife and teaspoon to the right. In between her gentle bites, she kept giving me that ol' coy look in furtive glances like it was our first date and she was somehow really diggin' ol' streety me, and of course the unmeaty food...

 ...In the middle of the meal, Jean-Pierre paid us a brief visit to congratulate us on our one-year anniversary, and to make sure we were receiving A-one service and that the food was grade-A: all done in a queer, awkward way, for he was a native Parisian with an unaffected accent. Raising up his thin oily 'stache, he wandered off, satisfied, hands clasped behind his back, walking like Roland had given him whatever had been given to Roland. Eek! Somebody buttered and toasted their buns! Eeeeeeeeek!
 'So tell me:' began Ivy, wiping the corner her mouth, the meal finished, 'how did you honestly afford all this? You said you were broke and livin' paycheck-to-paycheck. I'm just—I dunno—still in shock.' She put her right hand atop mine in her *fifth* attempt to have me detail the behind-the-scenes making of tonight; I'd circumvented the first four attempts with off-the-wall comments and childish facial expressions. This time, I tried the parodical sentimental technique:

---

[5] [fre] French style of cooking that emphasizes quicker cooking times, less sauces, and smaller proportions. *Foie gras:* traditional French style; literally means the fattened liver of a duck or goose that has been overfed; it's usually buttery and served with saucy dishes

'Don't worry boud it,' I crowed. 'Juss enjoy it. Besides, *nuh'n's* too much for the prom queen.' With a wink, I held up my wineglass of cranberry juice for a toast. 'Here's lookin' at you, kid.' We mockingly clanged our wineglasses together, and drank to the look. Then I grabbed her hand and kissed it, instantly lighting up the classic scene with thousands of colors. 'Ya know I love you more than my words could ever express, right? I swear, every day I try da think of howda say it right—howda put inside you what's inside me. Buh da frustration only ends up hurtin' my he~~art~~—literally.'

'Awww!'

'Aht-aht-ahhh. You know how much I hate that *"Awww"* shit.'

'Saw-wee...' Again, she placed her hand atop mine and began purring in sweet, sonorous vibrations: 'Purrrrrrrrrr. Purrrrrrrrrr...' Whenever I was stressed out, Ivy would intuitively cuddle into my chest and purr into my he~~art~~, unbroken and divine, blindly sweeping her hands through my hair and all around my face, while I ravenously chewed on her hair, powering up at will.

'Now I got one lass thing for ya,' I said humbly, reaching deep into my pocket. 'It's nuh'n big.'

For a moment, her delighted visage was one of wishful-thinking, overstanding at this point in our relationship that I was inclined to use, with such swiftness, ironic wordplay; meaning, if I was gauging her face right, she was thinking that the "nuh'n big" was, in fact, something small but *represented* something big.

'Really? There's *more?'* She lowered her head with an evocative sigh.

'Why da long face, budder-c-cups? Yir should be all smiles 'n' tits tonight.'

Just then, a loud reverberation of metal static boomed throughout the room: engaged in last preparations, Eddie committed a *faux pas*. He whoopsed an apology.

'I dunno; I just feel really stupid. I mean, you did all this for me—well, for *us*—but still, I only got you that stupid tattoo.'

'It's not stupid! You asked me whad I wanted 'n' *that's* whad I asked for. Besides, I fuckin' love it.' Underneath the table, I reflexively reached towards my left calf where the two-day-old tattoo was still healing. The Misfit's *Crimson Ghost:* a hands-crossed-over-the-chest grim reaper with a ghoulish smile. My gift came early due to appointment availability. I'd implored Ivy to get inked, even if something small, but she, perhaps because of Leviticus, or simply, femininity, refused to have anything to do with a needle poking her with permanency. 'Don't worry,' I assured with another satirical wink, 'you already gave me da greatest gift ever—*besides* a skull on the leg.'

'Yeah? What's that?' Her cheeks were burning with skepticism; I let it burn for a few moments for my own pleasure. 'Well? What's this "greatest gift" I gave you?'

'A skull on the road.'

'Oh come on; tell me for real...' With a subtle head tilt, she was batting her long Latinas at me like the execution of one's greatest power. '...*Pleeeease. Puurrrrrrr. Purrrrrr...'*

I exhaled. 'Well, if ya rilly need sincerity da survive, it was when we were standin' at da bus stop 'n' you walked over witchir number. 'At's wha' rilly allowed us da stay in touch without relyin' on unreliable liaisons. If you hadn't done that—ya know, uhh...' (her hand was suddenly underneath the table, rubbing my leg) '...we might not be where we are now. 'N' my life woulda never been so great...' (with a further reach, the friction was now rising! rising! rising! galvanizing! animal magnetism! meow! meow! MEOW!) '...Uhh, so yeah, dat liddle piece a paper, was like, uhh, a magical magnet for us. That's the "greatest gift": you bein' drawn towards me.'

'Awww—' Immediately she slung her hands up to her mouth as if to block or retract the accidental slip of the worst swearword, in the process, banging her hands off the edge of the table, causing the wineglasses to jump and chime. She laughed, 'I mean: good point: that *was* a great gift.'

'*Non, ma chérie!*' I reproached in jest. '*Touché. Dire touché!*'

'Okay, who are you now? Juan-Pierre?'

'More like Napoleon.'

'Yeah, you're about as tall as Napoleon.'

'Maybe, but earlier Eddie cawed *youuu* shordy, not me. So there.'

'Fine, let's just be even and you can give me this other "not so big" thing.'

On request, I pulled out from my pocket the dollar bill, the last dollar that would remain after paying Eddie, Roland, and the valet (again!). I tried to get one last good feel of the bill: no special tactility besides what a bill feels like: dry and rough but malleable. I wanted to smell it, to get a better sense of things, but I didn't want to be weird, so I held it out over the table. As she took it, her genteel eyebrows folded inward.

'*Uhhh. A dollar? Hmm...*I don't get it.'

I took a moment to observe the perplexity spread so lavishly across her face...down into the shallow winkles caused by her bemused smile...edging around her pink bubbled lips...invisible on her rounded chin...mingled in the dark-honey hue of her cheeks, which chubbed just enough to be cherubic...then the perplexity stretched like a budget up to her green eyes and black mascara...and there it began its final draw into the chinks between each crescent-moon eyelash: *blinkity-blink-blink*...snaking centripetally and musically into the greenness, like the slippery notes of a flute playing on high bonny banks. And that richness of perplexity came about for just a moment after she said, '*Uhhh. A dollar? Hmm...*I don't get it,' to which I replied, 'No, you got it. Look in your hand: you got it.'

'So wait, is this like the I-love-you box?—*a cute and clever trick?*' she asked babyishly, shaking the dollar out before her like a pleasurable find or a comical piece of evidence.

'All I'm permitted da say is yir the one.'

'*Okaaay. If you saaaay sooo.*' She put the dollar away with no further delay or response besides a thanking smile and a reinstated upright posture. Just then, Roland rolled in to clear our dinner plates and ask if we needed anything else; we didn't. Securely holding the polished-white tray at his shoulder, like a deep-seated notion that never gets too heavy to endure, he walked off in measured, evolutionary steps, both cheeks puckered tautly in concert with the preposterousness of his ape-suit.

So with all my surprises jumped up from behind the couch—the red roses in the blue angel vase handed over, the ivory gown with violet tinges hand-sewn and hewn to the curves of her body, the one dollar bill shoved down into her ivory hand-purse, and the scrumptious food hands-down-the-throated into our bellies—I led Ivy over to the buffet table, not to eat but to impress her and take a closer look at the Happy Anniversary! sign. Below, on the ecru skirted table, sat crackers, cheeses, fruits, *crêpes, mille-feuilles, pâte à choux,* and other *entre-mets et délicatesses.*[6] Ceremoniously, we decided to try a sweet strawberry *crêpe.* Seeing that it wouldn't be an interruption to do so, Eddie came over to talk about Teresa and Pessi's situation again, as if he wanted to see if he could piece together more of the puzzle with Ivy added into the equation. But again, I didn't want my night ruined, so I made sure that the conversation went straight into the good ol' days in Verna; this way, I thought, Ivy could piece together more of *my* puzzle through another's perspective, which, in turn, might validate stories she might have found hard to believe.

Before Eddie retreated to his post to get the prom on the floor, I told him that at the end of the night we'd split the remaining food for "tamarra's supper"—well, supper for him; just snacks for Ivy and I. Yeah, the good ol' days, Eddie.

In position, his chocolate jaw dropped: long and leno, going slack. The PA speakers popped a noise of congested air. Suddenly, his hands made the first record go *er-er-er-er-err!* And so, like tin wind-up toys just wound and set down on the ground, we, *mademoiselle et monsieur, danseuse et danseur,*[7] moved to the dance floor. Eddie decided to start off with a clubby song, and to be randy about it, I hated *this* kind of dancing but rather enjoyed watching girls shake their asses. Alwaysthemore, I was feeling very uncomfortable dancing in front of Eddie. Now had I been drunk, then more power to me: I'd cut and puke on the rug with no problem. But thankfully Eddie was so in love with his musical play that, for his reasons and my own, as the music played on, he slipped away for good, like something thrown into a black hole...

...God, her long ophidian hair: when did snakes begin smellin like pomade! or playin the game of nature so fair!...go ahead: chew on it: mmm, so yummy...my neck tickles too much da think of poetry: so let us dance n slip away from everything, juss you n me...hard gray floor: soft sentimental tunes: harmonic voice carryin us in steps n mocking pirouettes: easy embraces hard da let go: breezy whispers euphoric like a sneeze: liddle fluffy cloud sixty-nine: nibble nibble: always hungry for a taste: if i could choose my death idd be da choke da death on her hair: mmm her knee: such a sensuous tap: sensuous chill: wow her back feels so silky: i wanna melt n die in iss moment: no school work politics opinions choosin sides: hate: nobody'd hate me now if dey knew me rectified in my compassion: i

---

[6] [fre] a sweetened, stuffed, rolled-up pancake, a flakey puff pastry, pastries like éclairs and profiteroles...and other desserts and delicacies

[7] [fre] Mr. and Ms., male dancer and female dancer

love all yinz: come inside me: im puttin yinz inside me: pas de deux[8] in the name of—marital peace!: no such thing as divorce in a lilt: wish i could block iss song out: fuckin hate it: but still feels sentimental: who am i now: whadve i become in one critical year: wonder if sumn in mes fake: too contrasted too contradictory...ahhh i love iss song: cant believe shes sicilian: this song still kills me: so good...LYing in my HAMmock, i SEE a bug and THINK of you, CAUght up in the ZAPPer, it's NOTHing new...mmm i wonder if you know that if i should ever turn up missing, just look in the shed and i will be found – and if you should have to leave for a while, i will be waiting, always, always, always.........oh man: music: dunno wha idd do without it: my hearts explodin: cant even think it hurts so much: my hearts all over da grahn: haha drop my heart n hope ta die: funny: electric slide right over guts: stupid dance stupid song: fuckin eddie tryina be funny haha........think ill double english lit with french: love language: ill be a polyglot paradox me not—okay stop thinkin: juss enjoy the moment: maybe dis night n feelin could last FOREVER (inshallah): arabic: shhhhhah-la-la-la-la.........body so warm like bonfire glow: pleasant taste of pomade n perfume: mists like the night ocean: could throw you acrossa room my delicate liddle rose..........oh yir tits: i cant keep my fuckin hands da myself: touch me secretly: please touch me: ere ya go: i looooove yooooou.........oh bella: its been pure bliss with you in my arms promenadin at da prom: you remind me of da color mauve with at dahny spirit of yirs...smaaaart guuuys say only buffooons ruuush iiiin but i – mmmmm: you feel so good, baby...tastes so good...like a brook flows (*der durrr*) your kitty kat is so perfect (*der durrr*) make it purr for me, baby (*der durr*) some thiiiings are meant to beeeeee-eeee...

    ...As the last wistful note rang out, we crowned it with a small kiss. Then we trudged our way through the pile of guts on the dance floor. I was about to drop; losing your guts like that can really be exhausting. Although my overcoat was off, and my dress shirt unbuttoned, I was drenched in sweat. The only thing flashing through my mind now was *SHOWER UP!* Looking up at Eddie, he flashed a wily smile and that three-fingers-rubbing-together pay-me-nigga sign. I apathetically flipped him off. From his "tamarra's supper" plate he snatched up some kind of cupcake and threw it at me—but missed. I walked over, picked it up, and fired back—but it smacked off the wall behind him. Just then, Jean-Pierre entered the hall. Though the rest of the restaurant had closed, he extended our invitation til the employees were finished cleaning and he was ready to lock up. Looking back and forth from me to Ivy, he spoke a quick summary of French; I only caught the ending: *'Bon Anniversaire...et reviens me voir bientôt...Bonne nuit.'*[9] Perhaps he thought it a *lagniappe*—no, no, *un petit cadeau*[10]—for us to hear French before we left, and fuck, at least it was *gratuitement!* And

---

[8] [fre] A dance for two in which each have different steps while following a cadence; it can also mean a close relationship between two people.
[9] Happy Anniversary...and come back to see me soon...Good night.
[10] Both mean "a free gift" but *lagniappe* (literally, "a little something extra") is a Louisiana French word derived from Spanish. It likely wouldn't be used by a Parisian, thus the self-correction. *Gratuitement:* free of charge

whoever said the French were rude and snobby?! They just walk and sound funny—like fuckin' frogs!

After handing over dough to everyone with their pay-me-nigga hands held out, I sat down at our table to rest a bit. Ivy followed.

'Wow, Vinny. Tonight's been—I don't even know what to say. But I had so much fun! The food. The music. You actually *dancing*.' She scooted her chair around the table, next to mine, slouching her shoulders inwards, tilting her head down in coy love. I started chewing on her hair, with my overcoat draped across my lap. Her head gradually slid down to that spot like a musical finale in a slow, sucking pianissimo. 'I love you so much—more than you could ever imagine. Do you love me?'

'I love *boo-bees*.' I honked her left boo-bee.

In her repose, she lazily swung her hand upward and slapped me on the shoulder. 'No, baby, say it for real.'

I turned to Eddie. 'Hey, Eddie! Ivy's makin' racist remarks again!'

That shot Ivy straight up from her repose.

'I did not, Eddie! He's lyin'!'

'Don't worry, Ivy; I believe ya! V's the biggest bullshitter around!'

'Technically, I'm a cordon bleu-shitter; I only deal with white lies! Figure that one out, bitch!' I turned back to Ivy, who was now upright in her padded chair. 'Well let's take 'ose pictures so we can skedaddle—*Minchia!*'

'What?'

'Nuh'n. I left my fuckin' phone out inna car. I'll be back in a minute.'

But when I stood up she jerked me back down. 'Wait!'

'Come on; I'm way too tired for S&M.'

'No, just listen. I wanna be serious here for a minute. And I'm gonna try to say this like you do whenever you end up gettin' what *you* want.'

I smirked, taking that as a compliment. Then, on the whim, I began singing out '*Ut-oh! Spagheddi-ohs!*' like an incorrigible child in a highchair who thinks it's funny every time red sauce splatters on the floor, looking so disastrous and fatal, just like my phantasmal guts already splattered all over on the dance floor. '*Ut-oh! Spagheddi-ohs!*'

'Stop!...Quit singin'!...' She was trying to smack my hands down— but to no avail as I continued singing the jingle. '...Stop! This is serious! Stop! *Pleeeease!*'

'Fine. Say yir peace, fair child.' But in my head I kept singing *Ut-oh! Spagheddi-ohs!* but now in gothic tones like a love-song playing in the background of a horror movie just as a teenager is about to get his guts sliced into from the blindside.

'Now I know this might sound kinda crazy, but—' she paused to snatch *her* nerves back up from the ground, '—I wanna marry you, but, but, not like an engagement or anything. No rings or announcements. Just like a pre-engagement. I know I'm always gonna love you. And I would hope, after a year, you feel the same about me. I'm seriously not tryin' to rush anything; I just need to know we're both lookin' to head in the same direction. Okay?...Vinny?...Hello?...*Okay?*'

Nothing from me; only *Ut-oh! Speghe*—suddenly sliced into from the blindside.

The silence was deafening, but bodies were squirming: her lips quivering against each other, her hand trembling atop mine. Then she began to fret: 'Oh no, this isn't good. I knew I shoulda just kept my big mouth shut. Just forget I said anything—*Okay?*'

After withdrawing my hand from beneath hers, and wiping some warm guts from my face—trying to look respectable—I coolly said, 'Ar'ight. I'm dahn. If love is love, den what's age or time madder besides the mistake in lettin' it pass us by, right?'

She wiped freshly busted guts off herself; I'd playfully flicked some at her.

'Exactly!' (An effusive shriek!) 'I love you so much!' She lunged into my arms, crying, spilling out her bethetics while squeezing out the rest of my pathetic guts. Oh, the floor is becoming rated-R! Cover your eyes, underagers! Cover your fuckin' eyes!

At the fore, Eddie must've been eavesdropping—frozen in musical anticipation—because promptly after the rejoice of 'Exactly! I love you so much!' he shouted, 'Congratulations on whadever the fuck all that meant, yinz racist crackers! Dis final song, ladies 'n' gentleman,' he pretended to be talking into a microphone to an anticipating crowd, 'is for dat pre-engaged couple over dere. Umm—' After scratching his head, he broke into song, clearly spelling out what I might have just lost. '*...Sock it to me! Sock it me! Sock it me!...*' Oh yeah, Eddie, sock it to me. I seriously need it. SOCK – ME.

And he did, in mocking musical fashion, dancing while packing up the last of his equipment—and his equipment had been hauled by way of Jeremiah's truck; he didn't actually "miss da bus" and catch another: just the dry sarcastic humor of Verna, the place I grew up before becoming an engaged-to-be-engaged nineteen-year-old student down in Maryland at Aristod. In the moment—as Ivy snuggled her somnolent head back into my lap—I was actually (in every sense of the word) *diverted:* I just couldn't believe she'd been so forthright about it! The week-long thoughts about how *I* had to handle the whole event financially and creatively were at once quashed since she'd broken one of the strongest tenets of the traditional woman. I just didn't know what to think anymore! Likewise, I didn't know *who* we were anymore! God, can God make bullets out of Life!...

...After a late-night drive back to Aristod—(the prom queen was committed to tomorrow's classes)—we went straight to bed in her room. She fell fast asleep, but I wasn't quite ready. Some swirly-twirly time passed before I cautiously crawled out of bed to fetch my cell phone. Returning to my supine state, I held it out before me. The cell phone: such a funny piece of technology. 'Hello?...Hello?' – 'I'm not here right now, but next time I'm anywhere, I'll get back to you.' After pressing some buttons, and navigating my way through computerlike files, I came upon the pictures; Ivy had said she'd transfer 'em to her computer at her parents' so they'd be secure. With the screen lit, I found one particular picture-in-pixel and just stared deep into it: we were in front of the buffet table, beneath the Happy Anniversary! sign. Ivy was standing camera-right...swathed in that classy ivory gown with violet tinges running in thin slants at the belled-bottom...her ophidian mocha up in that messy-looking bun with ribbony strands snaking down the sides...her green doe-eyes (despite the diminution of the picture) glowing vibrantly like the verdure of the orchard underneath the moonlight...a wide, protrusive, opaline smile: again similar to that great mystical moon...and her skin (although a shade darker than lighter) the color of neutrality from which any sensible onlooker would immediately overstand both colorblindness and rainbows. Standing camera-left with his arms around her wild rocking hips was me, whoever I'd become...stashed inside a black tux, the one Bob Fontana had purposely loosened the rear in just to make me look stupider...my black spiky hair just long enough to have a punkish flare...both of my slightly large ears pierced here and there...my fine, pointy eyebrows my only aristocratic feature...on my left temple a tiny chunk of skin missing from when I was eight and two Dobermans attacked me...on my right cheek a purplish circular scar from when an intoxicated me burnt myself with a cigarette...my copper-brown eyes squinted like someone burning with the intensity to execute a humanitarian's kindest intentions—that, or a psycho's plans of vengeance...my complimentary nose pointing out towards my targets....and, shining above all, my half-cocked smile. My smile seemed to say a lot; from it, you could tell that I had "intentions," but of the universal sort, one after another like crocodile teeth, in which my gun was cocked and ready to blow away all the plaque and tarter of the world, as well as ready to bring to the cavities of the past the sweet filling of rectification. What a feeling that would be!

Tinkering around with the options, I found a way to zoom in on the picture. I couldn't help from squaring-in on Ivy's breasts; I loved to spontaneously cup 'em, and whenever in bed, put my tongue and teeth to her nipples. Imbibing two memories and wordplays at once, I laughed, thinking, 'It's *all in the frame.*'

Time past and memory: those are some pretty funny concepts. Proust once wrote, 'And so it is with our past. It is a labor in vain to attempt to recapture it: all the efforts of our intellect must prove futile. The past is hidden somewhere outside the realm, beyond the reach of intellect, in some material object (in the sensation which that material object will give us) of which we have no inkling. And it depends on chance whether or not we come upon this object before we ourselves must die.'[11] The picture and phone itself, to be sure, material objects; and the picture *did* give me a sensation—an extraordinary sensation, for I was instantly connected to a time when I was leaving behind in a small dusty room a part of my essence—a bittersweet memory then and thereafter—along with a connection to a more recent time, only hours past, when I was in a large clean room, moving forward the rest of my essence: a memory still in incubation. But all of that—the notions of *essence* and *time*—was why I knew that I hadn't yet "come upon this object" of a recaptured past holding phenomena and epiphanies, for I was too close to my past, too aware of the inkling. Besides, a picture had never been worth a thousand words to me. More like one worthless thief of a thousand parts of my essence, leaving me no chance to "come upon" *anything* ever again. I believe I was born with an intuitive odium for pictures of myself: the reason why only a few were floating around. Even if one would open up my four high school yearbooks they'd only find me once. What had happened (after the freshman year picture) is

---

[11] Passage from Marcel Proust's *In Search of Lost Time* (also known as *Remembrance of Things Past)*

this: sophomore year, when my homeroom was huddling together for the snapshot, I went to the top row to stand next to a friend, who happened to be eight inches taller than me. Annoyed, the photographer told me that I was too short and would ruin the picture and so I had to get down from the last row where people stood and move down to the first row where people sat. I said, 'Fuck you,' walked away, and was consequently suspended for a week. Then junior year, with the same photographer, it happened again. 'You're too short to be in the back row!' he said sneeringly, waiting for me to move down. 'Yeah, 'n' yir sercly too cute da be straight, you fuckin' queer,' I calmly said, strutting away. This time, I was suspended for *two* weeks because the school took "queer" to be a slur against the photographer's sexuality, when, in fact, it was just my way of calling him a "crybaby asshole wanting his way because someone else wants their way and *should* have their way over his way." Why did he care where I fucking stood?! Sorry I took a stand because I wanted to stand next to my friend! The only thing that ended up ruining the picture was not having me and my awesome smile in it! (Cheese: I'm just kidding, ddikts.) Anyway, by the time senior pictures came I said fuck it and took a seat at home, while everyone else took their long-awaited solos. They even got to put a quote underneath. Pessi's was: "I can't wait to clean your closet out." The meaning behind it: absurdity: the lack of meaning. Once I got to Aristod and started overstanding philosophy, objects, forms, and reality on a different level, I developed a philosophy for why I didn't like my picture taken. Nothing grand or founded on any principle—or perhaps one already propounded brilliantly by others. But having your picture taken is thievery of the essence, especially when your picture is given to another. What they're getting and taking away is *you,* a small piece of you, and not being there connected to yourself, they have a form of control over you; hence, why it's "thievery"—thievery of your will. And the more pictures you take and leave behind, the more scattered you become from yourself. All over the place: snippets of *you* and *your* memories—frozen and disconnected from the original movement of the scene, as well as from the present movement of yourself, as you move further away from the past, never able to "come upon" that "material object" again. For me, a "direct sensuous apprehension of thought."[12] Thus, my intuitive odium for pictures of myself was a small part of a larger endeavor to keep all of me *with me,* not wanting to experience the horrible feeling of dissociation.

Becoming sleepy, I took one last look at the picture: so bright and colorful—yet so still and confined. A strong trance fell over me: it flushed out, and at the same time, let in, a deep, dreamy, downy stare into what was becoming an expanding blur of rainbow, or a constricting vacuum of colorblindness, from which slow-spoken (nearly musically-hummed) thoughts emerged and carried me down into slumber: *where's the sounds of Eddie's PA and Jean-Pierre's accent?...the tastes of our hands-down-the-throat dinner and the sweetness of that strawberry crêpe?...the sights of*

---

[12] A phrase used by T.S. Elliot in the essay *The Metaphysical Poets* to describe the fusion of thought and emotion, a "mechanism of sensibility" that had been lost by the modern poets

Roland's stuckup ass and that cupcake flying through the air?...the scent of purple pomade in Ivy's hair and the ocean-mist perfume waving across her neck?...and all those supreme touches, as I honked her tits, and she grabbed my dick, while we danced the Dance of Li...

AROUND AND AROUND

"Let's dance through the ghetto like Pinocchio and Geppetto,
Envision our slum as a plush green meadow,
See, politicians don't care about your plight,
Politicians don't care if you're black or white,
You gotta take hold of your own reality,
Gotta have the attitude of positive mentality,
Or else you're gonna be livin' in their brutality,
So don't smoke their meth, don't sniff their coke,
While we be clear sailin', others be like, 'Yo, I miss the boat?'..." [1]

Yo, I miss da boat? 'Cause it feels like I'm inna middle of da ocean, juss tryin'ah stay afloat. I mean, did Ivy P rilly mean she wansta get engaged? Now I'm wonderin' wha' da fuck's waitin' for me on the next page—AHH! she juss confessed da carryin' my kid! *Shiiiit!* Juss kiddin', ddikss. I know exactly wha' she meant, 'n' exactly I whad I did. Buh diija (diija) eva (eva) wonder so much abouchirself ditcha thought it wasn't *you*, (juss couldn't be *true*), gadda be *her* or *him?*—Damn, watch out, Kim, 'cuzza way Vallano be rappin', he might juss be da next Eminem! Please stand aside, please stand aside. But for rill, yo—da chances a me ever bein' a rapper? Da same as me grabbin' Ivy up by her throat 'n' slappin' her. Neva! See, we be in heaven foreva! 'N' dohnchu snakes in the garden *eva* forget where I fuckin' stand: I piss off my back porch 'cause I cayn, mayn!

The lion's share of Hip-Hop's life has been contaminated with misconceptions; namely, that its essence is misogynistic, homophobic, unintelligent, derivative, and a catalyst for drugs, violence, and crimes that support the Machiavellian cause. But perhaps before one speaks on it, one must first overstand big puns and da LA soul, da NY soul, and every soul of mischief, living legend, and public enemy that tries to come in between the two. And perhaps one shouldn't assume that what's promoted through the Industry is reflective of what's found in the Underground, where, in the roots, music originates, establishes its cause, and stays true to it, as long as it doesn't come up to touch the grass. Ya digg?

I started listening to Hip-Hop when I was fourteen. I was already a punk rocker, rocking out to bands down in DC like Bad Brains and Minor Threat: ironic that Minor Threat influenced me so much since Ian MacKaye, the singer, inadvertently started the straightedge movement which advocates no drugs, alcohol, meat, violence, and promiscuous sex (exact definition of abstinence varies); alwaysthemore, something I wasn't a part of *per se*. Up in Olympia, I heard Bikini Kill, the godmothers of Riot Grrrl, calling for revolution chick-style. Terrorizing the City of Los Angeles, Fear wasn't too concerned with feminism, but Fear was the first band I saw in concert, the most riotous band I ever saw, and interesting enough, John Belushi's favorite band! Across the Atlantic, in England, I was boot-stomping with 4 Skins, Sham 69, The Business—The Cockney Rejects: Oi! Oi!

---

[1] Lyrics from "Envision Your Reality" by B-Love, from the album *P.M.A.*

Oi! And of course I was real tight with my brothas up in NYC: Cro-Mags, Gorilla Biscuits, Murphy's Law, Youth of Today, Warzone, and the four horsebands that always picked me up by the bootstraps whenever I was so sick of life: Biohazard, H2O, Sick of It All, and Agnostic Front; and since I consider AF's singer Roger Miret, a Cuban-descendent, *thee* voice of Hardcore, doesn't that ostracized island *dahn 'ere* deserves some kind of *positive* sanction? HIS AND LOU'S LYRICS HAVE BUILT SANCTUARIES FOR SO MANY PEOPLE AROUND THE WORLD! I was also gracing land in Memphis with Elvis. And vagabonding across no man's land when I was broke with Cash—til we got detained in Folsom: so blue we were! Then I felt good again gettin' funky and down with the Brown: so dark-complected and proud I was! I also remember rolling with the Stones. And going underground the Velvet. (Hey, who's Who down here?) And how I could I ever forget kicking out the jams with Tyner! Iggy! Cave! Bowie! Patti! and all the other proto-punks! And what about the role of The Situationists, and the situation concerning the filth and the fury behind the great Rock 'n' Roll swindle suffered by so many of the original Punk bands?! And what about all the motifs and philosophies within the subcultures?! Ahh! I couldn't even begin to scratch the surface here! See, the truth is, Punk isn't as limited as it's been portrayed: it's actually connected with many other genres, arts, and cultures. Now, I state all this not to get people to like my music since I like all kinds of music anyway, but because it seems no one else ever has the time to set the little things straight that have big (but hard-to-see) consequences—but see, I *do* have the time, 24/7!

Anyway, when I was fourteen, Eddie introduced me to KRS-One, and I instantly related to what he—this God-fearing black man from the Bronx—was saying too. In his academic and spiritual raps, he was telling me to open my eyes to the things around me, become educated about it, and never stop that process of education: just overcome all oppressive things through the power of body, mind, and soul: let Knowledge Reign Supreme Over Nearly Everyone—overstand? Alwaysthemore, just like Punk Rock, Hip-Hop has long had its misconceptions, and different musicians, even those within the same genre, are going to offer up different solutions to Life's problems, many that mainstream society will disagree with, or, because of their ignorance or agenda, will misinterpret, distort, or manipulate the contextual meanings and functional intentions of the lyrics. Pick and chose! pick and choose! as long as you keep in the underground what wouldn't be good for the news! Ya digg-in yet?

...A semi-automatic GLOCK 22c: a small powerful pistol. The polymer barrel: black as death. The caliber: .44 mm. The magazine capacity: 10. The bullets: shiny-silver life-savers laced in adrenaline. *Ten shiny-silver life-savers: plenny enough*. I unlocked the safety...tightly squeezed the grip...then aimed it at nothing but the spaciousness beyond the windshield...able to feel the power within its firm black chambers transferring into the red chambers pumping out of rhythm within my chest. I wrapped my finger around the trigger for a brief second—the touch itself so intimidating and lethal—before putting the safety back on. Using the butt end of the barrel, I scratched my thigh. Just then, he made a break like a little kid running for his life. So with ironic casualness, I placed it beneath my seat, relieved of the external responsibility, although not a bit of the internal guilt. Pessi had warned me that I might *have to* "juss in case." He'd admitted that going in on the blind was "a liddle risky," and for that, he really appreciated my "help"—all sincerely spoken too...

...Dr. Rosenbaum was speaking to Ivy and I with elation. 'Cahoots!' he said with elation, standing outside Bloy Hall after class. The Bloy Preacher was at the bottom of the snow-salted steps, preaching to the cold air, the choir over in the Middle Ages, still busy with the inquisitions. 'I think you two are in academic cahoots to con me into givin' you both *A*s! But,' he dropped into a devious tone, 'as of now, I think Ivy here has the better chance in pullin' off the feat.' He put his hand on my shoulder, smiling down on me his sagacious, silvery countenance. I didn't know whether to laugh at the thought or begin expostulating how Ivy's work was slightly below the quality of mine. I'd read all her papers, even *helped* her, so how could *she* be in a better position to receive an *A?!* Delighted by the news, Ivy started pushing me around, and Dr. Rosenbaum not only egged her on but also gave me a few pushes. In a visible breath, I told 'em, 'We'll see'...went boot-stompin' down the snow-salted stairs...accidentally bumped into the Bloy Preacher at the bottom...apologized...then headed off in a speedwalk towards my dorm, leaving *them two* in cahoots, as they taunted me with "waah-waahs!"...til I could no longer hear 'em...

...And who else could be in cahoots besides Agent Ralphie? Yes, that slickster was still stationed on the first floor of Philemon, just waiting to crack open the case that wasn't a case. Coming out of his room in his timely ways, as I was heading into mine, he said, 'What's up, Vin?' like we were friends. I said, 'Not much,' like we weren't friends and didn't care to reply because we weren't friends and I didn't care to reply. On the other side of 122, Luke was down-and-out, in cahoots with influenza. It made me sick. I hated being around sick people—not terminally-ill sick, but I'll-cough-and-sneeze-my-flu-onto-you sick. I was burning like a high-fever to tell him to go home for the weekend and have his mommy take care of him, and if he couldn't drive, then I would take the money I didn't have and send him home on a bus! He just sneezed! Eek!

I sat down at my desk and locked in as far as I could, preparing to write a paper for my Latin class, my hardest class to date. It wasn't a language class *per se* (like Aristod's tongue mandate that had me set to take of twelve credits of French) but more of a thorough examination of Latin's origins: Greek and Roman history evaluated through architecture, music, literature, philosophy, theology, mathematics, linguistics, polity, sociology, archaeology, papyrology, epigraphy, numismatics: the terminology alone was daunting! But the thing I loved about the class was learning about poets, philosophers, and dignitaries whom I hadn't known much about, like Catullus, Thales, and Nero. Since it was a four-credit honors course, and I hadn't enter Aristod as an honors student but was likely to become one in the backstretch, I could only take the class after passing a placement test. Ivy, who was edging me in our "friendly" GPA-contest, only because, in my opinion, I took harder classes with more arbitrary grading techniques—well, she'd been *matriculated* as an honors student. But I wasn't crying about it, or jealous, or driven into a deeper competition which she was unaware of. No! the thought of *her* being an *honors* student and receiving an *A* in *my* major with the teacher who was *my* friend and *my* mentor never even crossed my mind! and so surety not bringing any ruin to it—my mind![2]

With a wan, scaly face (his cheeks drooping like the skin of a gutted fish) Luke squirmed out of bed. Wrapped up in a feminine burgundy robe, he was making repulsive drippy sounds with his nose. He lumbered over to his desk...then emitted a sound similar to *ugghh!* Ahh! it was making me so sick—so sick that I couldn't even vocally wish him to get better, although I desperately wanted him to get better, or just get out. Like a clued-in fish out of water, he got out by heading down to the big water closet, which is *probably* where he got sick; I'd been sick twice so far and that's *exactly* where I put the blame: the white germ-tile nation!

After Luke returned and went back to sleep, Ma called: the second time since she took flight to Catania two weeks prior. During the first call, she'd been bent on assuring me that she was coming back soon so she could be there for me by being hundreds of miles away from me. But I could tell she was happy right where she was. She *had to* be happier over in Catania, especially in comparison to being beaten by Rick, belittled by Aunt Stella, or beguiled into Uncle Alfonse's crazyland of dogbones, seddes, and clickerthings. This time I asked if she'd heard anything from or about Milvio and Gennaro. '*Nu, Tappiceddu. Nun nni ntisi nenti.*'[3] Alwaysthemore, I told her to just stay and relax for a while, and to take pictures of my "family": yes, pictures! how much they *do* depict! Before hanging up, I told her not to worry: the box in the middle of the block wasn't going anywhere besides straight to Hell in a broken handbasket. So we gave each other imaginary hugs and kisses. '*Ti vogghiu beni!*' Then *click.* Hook-line-and-sinker! An Ionian catch, previously full fathoms five, finally being pulled up from the sea of oblivion by the saving net of her holey adolescence...

...Three hours later, I put the Latin paper aside. Ivy was on her way over to visit before she left for the weekend. She, Teresa, and several of Teresa's friends were going to the mountains to ski. Two days prior, there'd been a light snowfall: just enough to give the resort the incentive to get the powder machines pumping on the piste. Ivy seemed a bit excited that I didn't ski because, every since we all paired up accordingly, she and Teresa rarely hungout alone, and even less so since the advent of H, which was now just over a year in the brew. Pessi and Teresa were still clinging to the claim that they only snorted it occasionally and in small amounts—what's called a "chicken shit habit"—to which I was habitually clucking back that they're so full of shit. Yet, to their credit, they didn't *look* any different: no gauntness in the cheeks, scabs on the arms, or shakes in the legs: things I'd been keeping an eye on. Even behavior-wise, they were holding steady to their typical unsteadiness. Unfortunately, though, with Ivy, school, and work, I couldn't supervise as much as I wanted to for the sake of Pessi. I could only wonder: 'Where's the *parents* at for these adults?' Teresa's

---

[2] Play on "To bring surety brings ruins" by Thales of Miletus, one of the Seven Sages of Ancient Greek Philosophy
[3] [scn] No, Vinny. I haven't heard anything.

father: still hadn't met him. He'd been home a few times in the past year, and was now enjoying life in a new swanky condo overseas. Despite seeing pictures of him at Teresa's, I couldn't help but craft him in my imagination as a pile of shit with a greasy brown moustache.

I met Ivy outside on the plaza because I needed a smoke. It was twenty degrees out and flurries were falling, causing the passing bundled-up bodies—short and tall alike—to look like toddling sfingi and cannoli. A hoodie sufficed for me. Ivy had on a white fuzzy coat, with a purple scarf and matching ear muffs. She looked so funny, that is, in a cute-funny way, from which, I became, at the thought, so sad that she was leaving. She had yet to leave my sight for very long; thus, what if some guy, seeing she's not around another guy, should happen to advance on her cutefunniness?

'So I was thinkin' about sum'n—' I took in a drag, '—how's Teresa's gonna make it through da weekend without *it?*'

'Oh I'm sure she'll survive. Besides, the fresh air and exercise will do her good. Help keep her mind off it.'

I took in another hit—and when I exhaled, it expanded because of the cold. Several Philemonian chicks passed through the cloud, laughing. After they went inside, I said in a privatelike tone: 'Juss seems strange she'd wanna leave Pessi *and it* behin'.'

'Okay. *And?*' Apparently, Ivy took my aforesaid comment to be suspicion of *her* intentions, as if the ski plan was all a hoax and I thought that she had "other things" in mind. However, I didn't poke the bear in hibernation. Instead, I used the Vallanic method of questioning: inquiring only about Teresa's intentions, as if I was just overly curious, in an attempt (unbeknownst to Ivy) to bring out the truth (about Ivy's intentions). It was a failure. The only hard truths she had to offer was the location she would be at, and that she was *making* Teresa ride up with her, leaving one of the other chicks—Cindy, Jen, or Meg—to drive Teresa's gear-hauling SUV.

I put my cigarette out, shaking my head as if still unsatisfied with her "truths." But since, deep-down, I knew I *could* trust her, and that I was starting to sound a bit crazealous, I decided to turn it into deadpan teasing.

'What, do you think we're up to somethin'? Do you think—'

'I don't think; I *know.*'

'Know what?'

'Ditchir goin' out dere with Eli Perez da engage in a Mexican Milkdud orgy.'

'How *diiid* you find out?'

'A guy I know. Works under the alias "Agent Ralphie."'

'Well would you like me to tell Eli you said hello?'

'No, a simple "goodbye" will suffice for the summation of my sentiments.' Then in a quick robotic tone, I added: 'He shall be dead.'

Minutes later, we were hugging and kissing goodbye: her tongue like a shot of passivity to my mock suspicions that she might be heading somewhere to have a Mexican Milkdud orgy with Eli Perez, or just doing anything other than hitting the slopes with a bunch of stupid druggies who might influence my little Christian bunny from bunny-hopping over her morals.

'Juss be careful drivin'; the roads are sposta get slippy out tonight. Ar'ight?'

'Okay. I'll call you when I get there. I love you.'

'I love you too.'

As I watched her hop on down the snow-covered bunny trail, a wicked sensation of loss began stinging through my veins. Hippity-hoppity loneliness is on its waaaaay.

I went back inside, and to prevent Boredom from being on its way to join Loneliness, I called Pessi: no answer. For the next hour: no answer. Into the evening: no answer. Ring, ring, ring halfway into the night: no answer.

Finally, the heavy roof of apprehension that had been building over me caved in. I drove over to Teresa's at breakneck speed, paying no heed to the brakes even though the roads were real slippy.

After ten minutes of pounding on the front door, I went around to the back. Burning with fatal trepidation, I used my elbow to smash out rectangular pane of glass (one of six) on the back door. Something wasn't right! Not with me, but with the rest of the world spinning around me! No brakes! Shaking, I stuck my hand in—trying not to cut myself on the serrated shards of glass jutting around the casing—and reached down, unlocking the door. I shot inside and went straight into the heart of the house, foregoing the mess. Clean it up later! Don't have time to be cleaning up messes!...After tearing the house apart in a state of hysteria—finding nothing! no one!—I cleaned up the glass then left out the back door. I lit a cigarette and jumped back into my car, not knowing what to do next. I just sat there in the dark, shaking like a nervous wreck, with my cell phone out in my hand, ready to call someone who would know what to do: no point in calling Ivy, for she wouldn't know what to do...Sometime later, having slipped into another world, someone who would know what to do knocked on my window: Pessi, smirking. I rolled down my window. He said that he'd been at a local arcade that's open 24/7, playing games with friends. 'Wha' fuckin' friends?' I shot back defensively, again being overwhelmed by that wicked sensation of loss. He thought my parental tone of concern was funny. He said that he was pretty tired but I could come in. He began walking up to the house insouciantly, hands shoved in pocket. My window still down, I told him to fuck off and just send me the bill. He turned around—probably about to say, '*What bill?*'—but I pealed out of the driveway, a laugh a million miles away...

...For the rest of the night—deep into it—I watched black-and-white movies on the only station left that played 'em regularly, musing over pixels, color, form, space, reality, copy, the essence of time, the movement of essence, the Unmoved Mover...

...In the morning I remembered (or woke up to), as if by phenomenon, my last image of the night: with the light of the television casting an eerie luminosity on Luke and me, and sharply reflected upward as if breaking the Laws of Nature, I was drawn into a profound stare: he looked gaunt and wounded: but not shaking or irritable: just frozen in the darkness...

...Everyone was pissed off Saturday afternoon. I was still lying in bed, pissed off. My dorm phone was ringing and ringing. Two seconds later my cell phone was ringing and ringing. A cycle of rings barking at each other from which I regretted "being cute" when, picking on Ivy, I made "Latin Loops" my cell phone ring: the most annoying preinstalled tune. Deep-down I had a desire to reach for the phone but on the surface I felt like a clump of rubber. The barking contest continued. *Ring! Ring! Ring! Doot-doot-doot-doot-doot-da-doot! Ring! Ring! Ring! Doot-doot-doot-doot-doot-da-doot!* I was tossing and turning—ready to start punching Darby on the wall!—but pretending to be asleep just so down-and-out Luke wouldn't disturb me. He was groaning incongruently, probably ready to get up and silence Satan's calling himself! Finally—I was seriously ready to fuckin' fistfight someone!—I jumped up from my bed in a blind rage and vehemently answered my cell! On the other end, Pessi shot back just as enraged! I had ten minutes to get over to Teresa's and do some explaining! or he's gonna smash out all the windows in my car! Although I knew he never would, I wanted to assuage him because I actually felt bad about it, embarrassed that I cared enough about my best friend to smash out a window and break into a house because I thought that he might be dead (just not enough to throw his ass into detox). I told him to shudup! I'll be over in a bit! For the sake of the few hours of sleep I *did* get, I was just happy that he evidently didn't go into the kitchen last night—and of course, happy that he was still alive...

...Hours later, when I legally entered through the front door, Pessi was reclined back in the ponderous green chair, dozing. He jerked up and turned his head backwards: a flash of stupefaction. His skin had a hazel shimmer to it—perhaps from the chair, perhaps from the fresh prismatic winter shining into the room. From a distance, I looked into his eyes: that bleary profundity: the spirit of James Dean present: gentle melancholy filling his eye: a continuous flow throughout the entire capsule. And all around—his brow, the puff underneath his lids, into his cheeks—enigmatic shadows that make you want to get close and examine, wondering if you'll be treated welcomingly or haunted for the rest of your life for ever looking so close at something so unorthodox. He caught me, then turned back around, face forward. Yes, just when you think you're looking straight on the mark, you're actually looking east of Eden.

Moving into the room, I felt strange about the usual sensation he gave me in times of his reticent disposition. I sensed a conflictive energy hovering around him, like a force field beyond his control in which domination over it was the vying between his vindictive father and deceased mother. More measured steps: ten steps, ten seconds, ten thousand sensations, a giant chain around my heart. About to sit down on the couch, I was smitten with strongest feeling yet—almost extraneous in its character—of something hanging above me, violently jerking me by the shoulders over towards him—then away: over and over, back and forth between Mediation and Abstention. I sat down, already exhausted.

Quiet and lax in his movements, Pessi got up from the chair and walked into the kitchen, not knowing how exhausted I was, yet knowing that I'd inevitably follow. He'd taped a black garbage bag over the missing panel. Figured he'd know to do *that*. Now he wanted to know why I did *it*. I just wanted to know why he was doing *IT*. After talking about how *I* would pay for the window and why *I* did *it*—I segued into the *real* issue:

'I juss don't overstand, Pess. Is it Teresa? Like, is she *makin'* you do it with her? or is she the reason ya started in the firss place? *'Cuzza* her or juss *with* her? Whad is it? Why woncha ever tell me anything anymore? I don't see why it's gadda be like a big fuckin' secret.'

'You know me: I'm an experimentalist. But I'm about done with it anyways. Thinkin' about movin' onda bedder things.'

'HA! Whachir gonna be movin' onda is fuckin' death if ya don't stop immediately. I mean, you *akshly* think quittin's gonna be easy now?'

'Yep.' He was oscillating between sarcasm and nonchalance about everything, even in his body language.

'Well I think whacha should do is juss suck in yir pride 'n' godda fuckin' detox. You nee'dda get it through that thick head a yirs atchur not playin' with aspirin 'iss time.'

'Nope. No detox.'

'Fine 'en. But at least start decreasin' yir intake da gitchirself on the wane, ya know.'

'Maybe. Maybe not.'

'Yir fuckin' attitude is sercly startin'ah make me sick!'

'Well yir sercly startin'ah make' *me* fuckin' sick with yir *holier-than-thou* attitude.' He walked passed me, towards the living room, with an apparent disgust over my existence. In a murmur, he said, 'Fuckin' yuppie asshole.'

'Whaju juss say da me?'

'I said, "FUCK – YOU – YUPPIE." Why donchu godda class or sum'n 'n' gih da fuck oudda my house.'

'Wha' da fuck's yir problem, dude?'

'You think yir so much bedder then me: that's my fuckin' problem.'

'Right. Dis comin' from someone thit punched Anthony in the face for sayin'ah same fuckin' thing about me. 'At makes *alaaawda* fuckin' sense.'

'Wha' does?' he rejoined indifferently, sitting back down in the ponderous green chair. He began flipping through channels, yawning. As static moments passed, I began flipping through the TV guide in my head, wondering how people can fall into the snare of mindless programming. I wanted to leave but I felt stuck to the couch, fossilized by awkwardness, like an emotional adhesive. My mouth kept opening, ready to apologize, comfort, or just go back to the friends we've always been—perhaps restore our brotherly concord by suggesting we mellow out on the green. But there was just too much oppressiveness in the air, too much tension in the distance between us, too much embarrassment in the botched compassion. So I lit a cigarette...began thinking of Ivy...her shooting down a dangerous slope...looking ridiculous...shifting left to right, up and down, with athletic retardation...comically crashing into a bushy pine...thankfully coming out unscathed, as the other girls laughed *at* her, not *with* her...Teresa pointing her finger out the furthest, squawking the loudest, saying something condescending like, 'Dolly-Doll, how *have* we managed to stay friends for so long?' Yeah, I couldn't agree more: how *have* they managed to stay friends for so long? Why? Because the kindest hearts are also the most naïve—the hungriest hearts the ones quickest to eat poison—the truest hearts (the ones on the sleeve) the easiest target for rocks: and how many times til it shatters irrevocably? Just change your pebbles to boulders, black hearts, and get it done and over with!

 I finally broke the silence with more persistence but now with a cautious, empathetic temperament, as if reverse-psychology—a method that I usually used tongue-in-cheek—was my newfound facility for serious matters. Perhaps the television could even abet the situation by serving as a hypnotic. After wetting my tongue with premeditation, I casually asked how often. – Once or twice a day—well, sometimes like three or four on a miss. (He meant three or four times a day if a heroin-sober day slipped into the cycle.) That led to me asking when was the last time he *didn't* do it in the course of a day. – Juss yesterday. – Rilly? you didn't do it yesterday? – Nope. – Dat's cool. – Yep. Sometimes we'll juss do yey if our dude's out or da shit's dirt. – Oh. Dija plan on doin' it taday? – I dunno; I guess. – Alone? – I guess. – How mahcha got? – Haven't looked yet. Priddy much been asleep since I got back lass night. But Teresa said she left me some; she bought a load[4] da take up ta da mountains, so there's enough da go around. – *(Oh there's a lovely surprise for Ivy da find out about! I fuckin' knew it!)* So those other girls do it too? – I dunno; prahblee. – *(Poor Ivy, PRAHBLEE bein' ostracized!)* Hey, ya wanna smoke a blunt? I got one out inna car. – Nah, I think I'm quittin'. – What?! – Well, maybe juss for a liddle. Teresa's uncle's a contractor 'n' might be gih'n me a job 'n' he's legit: no under-the-table shit 'n' gives random drug-tests. – 'N' you think *H* isn't gonna show up? – I dunno, man; maybe. I been waitin' weeks for 'im da caw, so it's prahblee not gonna happen anyway. – You—

 He shot up the steps before I could pry any further. I wiped my hand down over my face, restrategizing. Suddenly 'Fuck!' echoed from above. He came back down, swinging into the kitchen, and started dialing numbers on the phone. *HA! She didn't leave ya any, did she?! Well, GOOD! Dat's how dose greedy backstabbin' junkies are! Poor Ivy, I bet she's wishin' she never went: prahblee feelin' like a penguin oudda ice water!...Ahh! I hate when sober people are ostracized: juss as much as I hate when drug-users are: it's like only DRUNKS are accepted: 'n' alcohol's the most lethal drug!: I guess legal things dit can cause bad are ar'ight as long as its badness can be justified in its illegality: 'n' yet wherezza application of consistency for THAT logic?!...*

 'Yir gonna do me a favor,' Pessi said authoritatively, walking back into the living room.

 'No. 'N' don't even bother fuckin' askin' 'cause it's not happenin'.'

 'Why?'

 ''Cause I'm not bein' the accomplice da yir death.'

 'Here he goes again!' he griped, throwing his arms up in the air emphatically. 'Mr. Holier-Than-Thou!'

 I stood up so he wasn't literally talking down to me and thus asserting linguistic power over me. 'Honestly, Pess, ya might as well juss shudup right now. If you nee'dda get some, you can find yir own ride or even have da dude come here—'

 'He won't. I've only met 'im twice 'n' he's rill shady. Teresa always deals with 'im.' He turned his head to the side and gritted. '*Fuckin' cunt.*'

---

[4] Twenty-five bags of heroin

Back to me, impassioned: 'Now she's sayin' she *didn't* get a fuckin' load. But ya know, I coulda sworn I saw her with it 'fore she left. She said she thought I still had a bag left...*Fffuck*,' he said in a vicious whisper. He paced a few steps into kitchen...then returned with a devious smile. 'Oh in the background Ivy was sayin' hi—while gettin' fucked by some guy. Ya know, *hi-hi-hi-hi-hi-hi-hi*.'

'Wouldn't doubt it hangin' around *yir* girl.'

'Well look,' he exhaled, looking down and rubbing his head, 'Teresa gave meedda dude's number 'n' said he'd *prahblee* meet us somewhere. He don't push shit from his house, so I'm guessin' we'd be meetin'—'

'No: *we* won't be meetin' shit,' I interjected. 'I mean, don't Teresa's dad got another car inna garage you can take?'

'Yeah, but it's a three-hundred-thousand dollar Bentley 'n' he takes da keys wid 'im 'cause he's an asshole like 'at.'

'Sounds like a s~~mart~~ asshole if ya ask me, 'specially with yinz two sneaky fucks livin' here.' For the first time of the day, a true comical wave passed over me as the image of Teresa's father became restored to a true father figure. Alwaysthemore, Pessi duped me into arguing for another five minutes about me not wanting to take him. Bracing his hands on the back of the chair, he glared at me contemptuously. 'You sercly want meedda get fuckin' sick or sum'n?'

'Yeah. I think 'at's *exactly* whacha nee'dda wake da fuck up: get *riiiiiill* sick, come face-da-face with Death.'

'Look—I'm not the junkie you think I am. But if you can't help me 'iss one time—ya know, after breakin' her fuckin' window out, which *I'm* the one thit's gonna hafta deal with her shit, not *you*—well, V—den I guess I been wrong all deez years. Maybe yir not rilly my best friend after all, 'specially if ya wanna see me "get *riiiiill* sick." Ya know, you've honestly changed so much since you been in cawidge 'n' with Ivy. Maybe you can't see it, but *I* can. Fuck, I think *any* junkie-piece-a-shit like me could. Dat's whad I am, right? A *junkie?* But hey, look atchu! Yir juss so fuckin' great now! Takin' it easy on the booze. No more yey. No more nuh'n. Juss a liddle harmless weed, right? By da way, you find a Catholic church around here yet? You a choir boy again?' (Now *I* gave the contemptuous glare as I clinched my fists.) 'I dunno; maybe you'll be up for da Nobel Peace Prize soon. Maybe—'

'Juss shuh da fuck up 'n' lemme think for a minute!'

'What's 'ere da think about? Either yir my fuckin' friend or yir not.'

If my h~~eart~~ was made of glass, then it felt like it had just been shattered by an avalanche with a titanic snowboot further pulverizing the shards into the tundra. He'd never once talked to me like *that*, never once put our friendship in an *ultimatum*, turning what was permanent into something *conditional*. And I didn't even know what I needed a minute to think about anyway: I'd already told him with conviction my answer before he even asked. And yet there I was capitulating like a fiend to the call, as I (in a desperate attempt to fall to deafness) called for a moment of silence. My plan was to perform a logical diagnosis on the situation by looking inward—then outward. The results: Introspection: m r y. Eyesight: b i d.

'So what's it gonna be, V? Ya gonna help me out juss 'iss one time or not?'

Well, you would've thought Pessi had majored in Cognitive Psychology at Carnegie Mellon because he'd just used some kind of psychological technique beyond my comprehension that had me sitting my ass back down on the couch while he made the call. I guess in my b i d e s— after full capitulation—I was looking at it like this: I'd rather have my best friend flirting with Death than have no best friend at all. Which is why, while sitting on the plush couch, it felt like I was stuck between a cock and hard place. Seemed the fine horsehair hanging above me had finally snapped, leaving the Sword of Damocles to slice right through me. Indeed how quick the powerful becomes powerless! the strategist inefficacious! the narcissist full of shame!

Pessi set the phone down on the counter, coming in with greedy green eyes.

'Wanna go in on a half pound?'

'*What?*' I spat incredulously.

'Dude says he'll throw me a half pound for $600. It's only shwag, but still. Cut it up in eighths 'n' we can make aboudda grand with 'eez idiots around here.'

'Wha' idiots? Who you know around here da be sellin'?'

'I know a few people.'

'*Mmm,* I know a few too thit've asked me before.' (A few seconds to pretend to be thinking hard.) 'Well I *could* yuzza money. I'm guessin' we gadda pay up front?'

'Yeah, but I got my half. You?'

'Sure. Bahchu gadda scale?'

'No, but when Teresa gets a cut it always seems right on.'

'No, I mean for when we break it up.'

'Come on, V; we can juss stop at da store 'n' get one.'

Right: wha' da fuck was I thinkin': we can juss stop at da store so we can sell drugs! Come on, V! Come on! 'Whadever. I guess I'm in.'

We ended up having to wait a couple hours for dude to have the time to meet us—well, to meet Pessi because I didn't want to approach and see the face that was defacing my best friend's soul. I needed to feel as if there was *some* detachment so that I didn't accrue more weight to the heaviness of my "involvement." I was looking at my "involvement" as if I was a dispassionate chauffer driving the feeble to the devil just for the buck—but only getting my buck by having to take off my black bowler hat and fine white gloves, ditching the ride, then putting on the same dark cape of the devil, prowling through the devil's playground looking for souls to deface: yep, that's right: what's the weight of one's conscience mean when, case in point, it's nothing but cash fiends and dope fiends chasing each other around and around, everyone in the world wearing one face or the other: how then, when it all circles back around, could I ever feel *less* "involved" by pointing the finger here and there without having to turn it around on myself at some point? *However,* my defense against my conscience was that what *I* was pushing was no different than fast food, major label CDs, or books and DVDs by Marvin Morrison, and, if truth be told, my product of Nature of a less harmful nature. I mean, heroin, street meat, MTV, Marvin Morrison: it's all opiates of the "dissident" masses!

When the time came to leave, Pessi, in a high-stepping gait, went upstairs—then came plopping back down the steps with stolen money in his hand and a black bookbag drawn over both shoulders. It was the one he'd used in high school; now being used a drug concealer. In stark contrast to the Dean's shadow around his eyes, the ambiance had turned friendly, bright, sober: a reconciliation that brought to my senses a summertime nostalgia when Pessi and I (circa age twelve) would walk around Verna, smoking cigarettes, strolling down alleyways, pulling out from dumpsters things like chairs and glass objects just to smash up, on our way to get nachos and slushies at Rizzo's, then consuming the food and drink outside on the concrete slab running below the windowsill with our shirts off and wrapped around our heads like turbans, even if the heat wasn't as bothersome as it became with each passing year. That whole summertime sensation—I dunno—it was like I could taste three month's experience, many years past, in my breath. But as we headed out Teresa's front door it was undoubtedly wintertime, mid-December, and I was undoubtedly five months past year nineteen. As I sucked in the cool awakening air, Pessi suddenly slapped the back of my neck. Confused, I turned around, and Pessi quietly shut the door...

...First, using up two dollars worth of gas, I drove back up to the other side of campus to go to my bank so that I could withdraw money from the ATM without being charged a two-dollar fee. There, the coolest coincidence occurred: as I was walking back to my car with the wad in my hand, I ran into Andrea, a chick many would consider the likes of a two-dollar whore. We talked for about two minutes. She asked how my girlfriend was; I said good. In a facetious tone, I asked if *she'd* found anyone worth keeping. Pushing me in the chest, she said, 'Come on, Vinny-pie! You know me: I ain't inda the whole serious thing! 'At shit's for suckas!' I told her good point, look at me. She laughed, said she missed me, gave me a hug, and that was it—not even one bite. Back in the car, Pessi got a kick out of finding out the identity of Vampira. Next, we stopped at an office supplies store to get a scale. I paid for it: around two dollars—no, just measuring the weight of credibility; it was around six. So having taken care of the prerequisites, I began steering out towards the purple mountain outlining the bright-white horizon of LaSalle, being guided by Pessi's directions which he had to yell because the music that could never be turned down for such trivialities was blaring...

...We were heading down the same straight country road that led to the orchard. Passing Chow Down, I tried peering in through the windows to see if Ruby was working—she was! And I think I caught a glimpse of her still holding her hand up to her face like a telephone, shaking it a bit as a reminder for me to call some time. The flat fields on both sides of the road were covered with a film of dry snow. In some patches here and there you could see the brownish ground where the snow had melted or drifted. The mid-afternoon sky lacked a forefront sun but was cloud-bright and made appealing by the last flock of migrating birds: so black, fine, and linear, with a few in the back struggling to keep form. Approaching the orchard, which couldn't be seen *into* and which Pessi knew nothing *about*, there remained trees in the thicket with brittle brown leaves. Making the bend to the right, heading in the direction I'd never gone, the wind gusted fiercely: I saw leaves break from the branches: it had the feel of slow motion seeing as I couldn't hear the outside world with the windows up and the radio blaring. Yet with keen observation I watched the dead leaves rock back and forth like little canoes in a wild but invisible current, alwaysthemore, driving on at a steady speed, never to witness 'em settle on the ground...

...Still in Maniwaki, nearing the village of Wakanda Fields, we were cruising down a rickety road, passing by an enormous trailer park to the left, when, taken aback, I shouted, 'Wha' inna fuck is 'at?!' Reflexively, I hit the brakes: not to the floor but enough to jar the backend of the car forward. The momentum slung beltless Pessi against the dashboard: a minor shoulder collision from which he merrily bounced back.

'My liddle buddy,' he replied with soft coughing laughter. When I looked over, he was smirking as if he'd just experienced the best rush ever. This is when I realized how dangerous it had been to hit the brakes in such a situation, for Pessi had pulled out from his bookbag a black pistol.

Letting the car drift down the barren road, my eyes locked onto his face while I clinched my teeth in anger: *his* eyes, for a brief moment, were closed as if lost in sweet reverie; it only made me madder. I turned the radio down: the real bloodboiler.

'Wha' da fuck you bring a gun for? Am I takin' you do a fuckin' shootout now?'

Before answering, he, vanquishing the smirk, examined the gun with religious admiration as if beholding the most mysterious of sacraments from which symbolism lay in the grip, and the divine grace—the formal cause for justification, as the law of sacrament states—lay in the chamber. The gun (through the orifice of its barrel) seemed to be the one smirking now.

'Hey, *I* don't rilly know this dude. So here's whad I's thinkin'—'

'Fuck 'iss! I'm turnin' around. First heroin! Now a fuckin' gun!—'

'Cahm dahn, V.' He turned the radio all the way down. 'Look, I'm not plannin' a jack-move or anything; I juss wanchadda have my back juss in case 'iss dude tries anything, ya know. Think about it: a half pound; smack; alawda money involved; in the middle of a vacant playground. I'll be honest: yeah, it's a liddle risky. 'N' dis dude's shady. A big motherfucker too. I'd take da gun myself but I'm thinkin' since he don't rilly know me, 'nna two times we met he'z all cold 'n' shit da me, he might pat me dahn for weapons or wires. Big ballers[5] don't fuck around, ya know.'

'Shuh da fuck up. Da point *is:* yir sayin' if sum'n *should* happen, den it's *my* responsibility da start firin' off shots? I mean, wha' da fuck?! Have you gone insane or sum'n? Canchu even see wha' kinda situations yir startin'ah fall inda? Where ju even get dat at?'

'It's Teresa's dad's. A GLOCK 22c.' He held it out in front of the dashboard gangsta-style.[6] Looks like Mr. Cazzata shoulda worried about lockin' sum'n else up.'

'Well Mr. Pessini shoulda worried about gettin' *himself* locked up 'cause he juss bauddimself a ticket da rehab. I'm seris, Pess, soon as ya snort dishit up, I'm throwin' yir ass in. 'N' if ya try da resist, I'll fuckin' shoochu.'

---

[5] Someone who sells a variety of drugs and has street-credential
[6] Sideways

He laughed. 'Dere ya go: now ya sound like yir riddy da peel some fuckin' caps back. Juss kiddin'. Nuh'n's gonna happen. Badda-bing, badda-bang, 'n' we'll be out.'

'*Mmhmm*.' I gassed the car up again. 'So is 'at thing rilly loaded?'

'Ten in the clip, bitch. (Make 'iss next left.)'

'Ya know, Pess, it's funny how yir in such a good mood all of sudden now ditchir gonna sell yir soul out for dat shit.'

'Shaachir mouth, fool, 'fore I putchir fuckin' brains in yir lap.'

As hard as I tried, I couldn't help from letting out a little laughter: quality banter had been scarce lately—well, *everything* between us had been scarce lately. I made the turn onto the final road, heading into a woodsy area where the park/playground was. Before arriving, Pessi, in the most sincere tone I'd heard from him in a while, breaking the rules of sarcasm that had bonded us for so many years, came out and bravely said, 'Sorry about dat shit earlier. I didn't mean da come across like 'at. I know yir my best friend 'n' 'at. 'N' I wouldn'ah rilly hated ya if you *didn't* take me. Bahchu sercly don't know how much I appreciatcha lookin' out for me, 'n' at da same time, helpin' me. Who knows: maybe I *will* godda rehab.'

At the secluded park/playground, which, from where I parked, was directly in front of us, down in a large flat field surrounded in the back by woods and preceded by the same creek of the orchard, the obscured figure had his back towards us, kicking a red seesaw up and down underneath the authority of his wheat-colored boot. The snow was lying on the playground equipment like prostrated tenderness but had been shaken off the seesaw, leaving it, in its bright redness, to look stark-naked, glaring up towards me like a symbolic hell. I looked around on both sides for his vehicle—but nowhere to be seen; he must've lived close by and walked: probably in a villa back in the woods, for it's been known to be the Devil's earthly abode. I handed Pessi my money; in exchange, he handed me the gun on the low. Silently, he picked up the bookbag and went outside.

It was difficult making out any distinctions of the figure besides being black, about six foot something, having a trunk like Atlas, and a scruffy beard. Otherwise, from my view, he was all clothes: homogeneously sandy-colored, a bit baggy, with a beanie-visor cap pulled down over his bullhead. The soft vibe of the colors came off as an ironic air of purity. At first, for reasons unknown, I thought of a young black man going to church and holding *The Bible* in veiled mockery. Then I told myself that I could recognize him hereafter even without having examined his eyes and the lines of his face: probably because of his godly size and posture. I didn't want to see him up close anyway.

Anyway, Pessi's street-smarts turned out to be infallible: the figure patted him down, looked through the bookbag, and then, I believe, asked Pessi who was sitting in the car. Seemingly satisfied by his response, the figure continued with the deal by walking Pessi over behind a yellow jungle-gym placed inside a square of snowy mulch where he'd evidently stashed the drugs just in case there would be a case. They were now out of my view...A semi-automatic GLOCK 22c: a small powerful pistol. The polymer barrel: black as death. The caliber: .44 mm. The magazine capacity: 10. The bullets: shiny-silver life-savers laced in adrenaline. *Ten shiny-silver life-savers: plenny enough*. I unlocked the safety...tightly squeezed the grip...then aimed it at nothing but the spaciousness beyond the windshield...able to feel the power within its firm black chambers transferring into the red chambers pumping out of rhythm within my chest. I wrapped my finger around the trigger for a brief second—the touch itself so intimidating and lethal—before putting the safety back on. Using the butt end of the barrel, I scratched my thigh, as Pessi, with the bookbag pulled over both shoulders, made a break across the snowy field...running without caution like an ecstatic kindergartener to his mommy after an unbearable half-day away from his eternal solace. So with ironic casualness, I placed the gun beneath my seat as if by habit. Back upright, I surveyed the playground...gone.

As I backed out—swinging the car around—Pessi began informing me that dude had brought a hand-scale and weighed out the eight ounces in front of him. Then he said that dude warned him never to bring someone dude didn't know without bringing the unknown face-to-face with him, which wasn't a problem with me because I wasn't doing it again. Before pulling back onto the road, I reached beneath the seat to return the gun to Pessi. He asked why I put it *there*, thinking I hadn't had it cocked and ready during the deal; I told him to shut his mouth or I'd put his fuckin' brains on his lap...

...On the way back, it started snowing. I was already driving slowly anyway. Driving with drugs and a loaded weapon is a million times more nerve-racking than the actual process of being in a risky drug deal. If we were to get pulled over—(the thought was lurking in my head the entire time)—my life would literally be over because I'd probably hang myself in jail like my old friend Paul Motka did after robbing a bank with a gun, then escaping to New York City, getting spotted on a live MTV show, after which he was quickly apprehended. Such an idiot for going on television, no less MTV! Even stranger: he wasn't from a poor family. Father owned a Cadillac dealership, mother the vice-president of the school board. So no one overstood why he robbed the bank in the first place since it didn't seem to be for money. They hadn't even prosecuted him yet when he hung himself with his bed sheets, leaving nothing behind but the sway of his body. Every now and then I'd see Motka swaying in the abyss behind my eyes. But on the way back I wasn't even thinking about Motka or what I'd do if I'd happen to get caught til Pessi mentioned deceased friends. I was thinking more singularly about getting caught like: '*Is 'at a cop?! Is 'at a cop?!*'

'Hey, you still think about Paul 'n' Matty? 'N' Brian, Chris—April?'

'All the time. Why?'

'I dunno; lass night I had dis weird dream about April. She'z drivin' 'iss white car dit was comin' right at me—well, like my view was like I's layin' onna hood. 'N' she kept screamin', but nuh'n'z rilly happenin' do her. But lookin' at her face you'd think she'z bein'—well, stabbed, ya know. Den all of a sudden dere'z 'iss clown in the driver seat 'n' his eyes were shaped like big diamonds. Dat's when I woke up 'n' couldn't breathe. Completely drenched in sweat. Bugged me the fuck out, man.'

'Yeah, I have dreams like 'at too.'

A rundown on the people Pessi mentioned: Brian Pietra blew his brains out when we were fifteen; Matty McCoo was recently in a car accident in which the driver Jake Wexler, another friend of ours, was drunk and nodding off, while Matty was hanging out the window, screaming just for drunken fun, before the car veered off the road, and a telephone pole ripped off half his head; Paul Motka already explained; Chris Ulman got drunk and pilled up then romantically slit his wrists in the bathtub; and April Barone had been drinking underage at a dive bar, then came out in the alleyway to get stabbed nine times by a crazed ex-boyfriend, who was chased, apprehended, and beaten by Dante (who'd heard the screams from inside the bar) til the police arrived; to boot, April left behind a three-year-old daughter whose father wasn't the murderer but a friend of ours—all of which seems like extreme exaggeration for *any* story, but any skeptic is free to check the records. We all grew up in this little southeast slice of Pittsburgh, on Da Steel City's crust—though the northsiders, eastsiders, and dahntahners can tell the same kind of stories. It's funny: that one tragic story you see on the news everyday seems like nothing, so inconsequential, til you look back and realize your entire community, from dahntahn out to the rural lands, is flipping through the same elegiac scrapbook that just keeps webbing out in our hands as we turn the pages.

'Man, I miss 'em all, but I rilly miss Matty,' Pessi said wistfully. He turned the music down a couple notches. "Member when he fuckin' pissed in Nichole's car?'

I vaddled. 'Yeah, 'n' he'z always wearin' 'ose cop glasses whenever he'z drunk. He'd come up from behin' me 'n' grab my ass 'n' say I's under arrest. Man—I still don't think his death has even hit me yet. It's like I keep thinkin' he's alive but I juss haven't talked do 'im in a while 'cause I been away at school, ya know.'

I glanced over at Pessi. He was now looking outside the window with a simper on his face as if up in the sky he could see all our past friends singing and dancing, like a phantasmal assurance that, no matter what, everything would be all right. At that moment, we were passing back by the orchard. The snow coming down looked more tempestuous than it really was due to the wind. However, the long thicket protecting the orchard seemed placid—removed from the present weather as if its existence was only a figment in the minds of Ivy and I: an unsettling thought about existence that, at the prod into the feeblest part of my brain, and the distorted cognizance that followed, caused me to feel as if Ivy and I were not real but modernized, perhaps reincarnated, or entrapped, versions of the mythical beings who burned in that village in times of yore: but in whose head if not mine? in what time? and for what purpose(s)? Thankfully, the trepidation over my existence quickly dissipated without much physical effect. Still, all the memories I had thus far accrued of the orchard *did* seem mythical and detached from reality, reinforced by never telling anyone about the orchard because (to me) it would be like bearing Ivy's nudity to another; I was very protective of her and the orchard even though neither "belonged" to me. Yes, a very strange sensation driving by the orchard and "knowing" while Pessi didn't. I had no way of gauging *his* thoughts on what I was looking at over on his side (if he was even paying attention, which he was almost surely lost in thought over past friends), but it could've only came into his eyes as more naked trees and underbrush being covered in snow, and thus (without an electric stimulus) registering in his head as an automatic discard of memory.

'Lemme ask you sum'n, V. 'N' I wancha da tell me whacha rilly believe. But you think we akshly go heaven or hell?' That was Pessi's naïve response to my *noti nivicusi nuvulusi nigghiusi* [7] on Matty McCoo, only seconds later, and the reason my thoughts on my existence didn't have the chance to eat me alive. I replied:

'I dunno—there, or Wendy's or Burger King but definitely not McDonalds.' Yes, The Great American Brushoff. Cranking the music back up to maxvol, I caught (out of the corner of my eye) Pessi looking down into his palms. Frozen: face down, palms up. Not even moving his lips to Social Distortion, his favorite band. (He was a habitual lip-syncer; I a habitual singer.) I lit a cigarette, inched the window down, and enjoyed the music as much as the phantasmal cops would allow...

...Safely back at Teresa's, Pessi dumped out the half pound on the kitchen table, each ounce in individual baggies but wrapped within a larger baggie. Next, he took the gun out and set it down; it clanked ominously against the wood: one last coppish vestige. Finally, he pulled *it* out. *It* was also inside two bags, the first a small plastic baggie and the product itself inside a hard white packet, the bindle: a cut that probably cost ten to twenty bucks. I told him that I was taking my half back in his bookbag. Even though I needed the money, I had a strong feeling that I'd end up smoking my profit; while my investment would be made back by selling to the Philemonians I knew smoked, for they were always asking me if I knew where they could get some; and now I did: me. As I put my half in the bookbag, I told Pessi that we should've bought two scales; he said, yeah, but he'll get one for himself tomorrow. He sat down, looking wan and lethargic, his special little bag staring up at him mockingly like a fly that won't go away no matter how many times you swat at it.

'Hey—wanna do me one lass favor?' he asked with a fleck of forced bravery.

'What's 'at?'

'I dunno...' Secretly, he moved his hand down and across his gut, his face suggestive of a battle against simultaneous fears. It took some wincing and sighing before he could muster the strength and courage to speak, in a cowardly whisper: 'Well, I rilly don't wanna do it alone. Never have before. Teresa's always with me. The thought kinda scares me, ya know. Not thit I ever do dangerous amounts, but ya know.'

'Well, Pess, 'at's why I've always stayed away from the shit. I mean, wha' happened ta da days when we yoosta make fun a people who did H or smoked crack? I mean, 'member ol' Crackhead Willie at da potato factory? You wanna end up like *him?*'

He didn't answer. Instead, he took my jab as a definite "no," falling further into a yellowish look of sickness and regret: it almost seemed as if he was faking it. Alwaysthemore, I didn't want to see him do it. Even thinking about witnessing it made me just as sick and regretful. And yet if I *were* to leave him alone, and something *were* to happen, it would be a burden of regret that I wouldn't be able to endure. In a sudden impulse to see what the weather was up to, I looked out the kitchen window—but the darkness had settled in, and the back porch light was off. I looked at the blue digital

[7] [scn] snowy, cloudy, foggy notes

clock on the microwave: 7:25 p.m. I looked around the moderate-sized posh kitchen. There seemed to be nothing else to look at with the prospect of delaying time. So I was left to ask him when he planned on doing it because I was really tired from last night's sleeplessness and had work in the morning: he was ready *now;* I wasn't.

I went outside into the snowy darkness to get my blunt. I decided that I couldn't watch him get high sober. On the way down the steps of the sidewalk I slipped and nearly fell. My ankle still acted up on occasion, especially in cold weather, but I could no longer tame it with painkillers— well, I *could* find 'em "on the street," but using 'em with the other things I did, along with my usual state of mind, made me *too* out-of-touch. Down at my car, I saw my cell phone lying on my seat; it had slipped out of my pocket, as it frequently did. I looked at it: four missed calls: all from Ivy's cell. She was probably calling to keep our streak going: we'd talked at least once a day ever since the day she'd came over to my room after breaking my ankle. I planned to return her calls once I dealt with Pessi. So I tossed the phone over on the passenger seat, grabbed the blunt out of the glove-department, shut the door, then headed back up to the house...

...Pessi was standing by the kitchen table. Instinctively, I was about to ask if he was going to smoke with me til I saw the rail on the table. It was tan, almost brown, which meant it had been cut with diluting substances, such as cocoa, several times during the process of distribution. Before turning around to sit in the living room, I noticed that lying next to the gun on the table was his fake ID—so fitting too: who was he for real? He looked at me: everything was officially ready to go—besides me.

I sparked the blunt and let it rest in my lips (the smoke wafting up in front my eyes) while I turned the television on to hear an audience applauding in harmony with the snort. As much as I didn't want to look over, I did. Blinking, he was fingering his nose, heading towards me but without looking at me. He sat down in the ponderous green chair. He leaned back, with his arms on the arms like two bodies converging into one. He was staring at an indeterminate spot somewhere around the television. After smoking half the blunt, I lit a cigarette, smoking it slowly. Five minutes later, through the last whorl of smoke, I watched his eyes close in the rush. The audience kept applauding and laughing, but the sound was becoming more distant. He scratched his neck—emitted a ghostly sigh—his right knee jerked once—his right arm slid off the arm—his back lax into a tender slant— then peace: the process was almost beautiful.

I extinguished the cigarette. 'Pess? You cool?' My voice didn't sound right; it was coming out of someone else's mouth. 'Pess?' Still didn't sound right.

'Yeah. I'm cool, bro.'

Before he finished answering, I'd stood up. I suddenly realized that I wasn't me. Never was. All this time, I hadn't been living life. I began pacing around the living room, hand over my heart. It quit beating! No, it was beating too fast! I was having a heart attack! I was trying to tell Pessi to get up and call the ambulance because I was having a heart attack but I was already in the kitchen. I opened the refrigerator and moved things around...til a wave of scorching numbness swept over me. My hands were shaking violently as I tried to hold a glass underneath the spigot. I left the sink, running, and ran outside on the back porch. It wasn't outside outside. All the lights of the neighbor's houses weren't right. The cold air was too thin. It wouldn't let me breathe it. I was rubbing my hands over my head because the heart attack was about to take effect any second. I ran back inside so Pessi would know. Something was shaking my body so violently as I stood at the kitchen sink, throwing water into my face. 'Pess!—Pessi!' I started screaming, clutching my heart harder. I started running my hand through my hair; my head was missing, empty. Pessi came in. I couldn't make out what he was whispering from miles away. *BANG!* The gun: it shot me. A metal barking. Breathing convulsing. Pain suffusing. I stumbled passed him. I needed to escape this and go back to a long time ago. I circled around the living room a few times. I wanted to throw myself down to the ground, as if that decisive move would exorcise the evilness right out of me—leaving it to hang above—then grovel out to my car—(crawling through the cool snow would keep me conscious: putting some in my mouth would slake the dryness wilting my insides)—then up into the car like a snake, lying down in the backseat to shut my eyes til I could wake up during a better time in life, or perhaps just die there.

Heading swiftly out the front door, I was being applauded, laughed at: a staccato frenzy. Behind me, Pessi was telling me to cahm dahn, cahm dahn in a calm voice. But the entire world was exploding! and exploding! in a war! as my heart headed into its final thumps! I told him I have to go. Outside was still not outside. I booked through it as quickly as I could. In the car, I kept rubbing my face with one hand while holding my cell phone with the other. I had to call 911 while I was still able to. I had the number punched in the phone but then a mantra began sneaking up on me: '*Cahm dahn...Cahm dahn...Cahm dahn.*' I erased the number and began playing one of the preinstalled games. But I couldn't concentrate. All of a sudden it started all over again: heart pounding! limbs shaking! vision blurry! mouth dry! the numbness fatal! I started the car...now careening towards the hospital. On the way, I called Ivy to tell her to come home to see me before I died. When she picked up, she was already mourning, already on her way home, only an hour away. 'Where have you been?!' she cried. On the other end of that little thing so difficult to hold up to my ear, she was bawling, and so much that it scared me and sent me irretrievably deeper into the last stage of life. Since my life was over, I hung up for the experience. She called right back. 'I've been calling you for the last hour!' – 'I'm on my way da the hospital!' – 'Why?! What happened?! Did somethin' happen to Pessi?!' As I was about to tell her, no, it was because *I* was dying, I braked the car off the road, hitting the bank prematurely. I let the car idle and set the phone on my lap—still able to hear her voice—taking in deep breaths. When I put the phone back up to my ear, she was sobbing my name. My heart was beating itself back into normality; outside was now returning to outside. Retracting, I informed her that I wasn't going to the hospital, that I'd just had a severe panic attack, but what's wrong with her. Although it was hard to make out what she was saying, it was something about Teresa and how she *hates* her and that she's coming home *right now* to see me and that she's *never* leaving my side again and that she loves me *sooo* much. I told her that I love her so much too. But she continued with her sobs because she didn't like Teresa anymore. I told her to just cahm dahn, cahm dahn, and because of the snow, just concentrate on driving. In her last hour of driving she might get caught in the imminent snowstorm. To make sure she fully overstood, I told her to be careful again and to drive slowly, but hurry up so everything will be all right...

...Turns out nothing really bad happened with Ivy up in the mountains. On Friday night, after everyone but Ivy put forth a lethargic attempt to ski, the girls went back to their cabin for the *après-ski*.[8] Doing the things girls do whenever they hangout together, Teresa pulled out her little bag and chalked up a few lines for her and her friends: they went skiing on the sink counter. Then on Saturday, after returning from another "standing outside in ski gear but not doing much skiing," Teresa went to pull out her little bag to chalk up some lines—but found it missing. And when confronted about it, Ivy told her that she—being what they would call a "tow-woman"—had taken the drugs when no one was paying attention and flushed everything down the toilet: over two hundred dollars worth. Well, that's when Teresa attacked her, pulling her hair and doing the things girls do whenever they fight...til Ivy broke away...packed up her things...told 'em that they'd just have to find a way to put everything in Teresa's SUV...then, alone and in tears, started hitting the slopes back to Aristod. Nothing really bad happened with Ivy up in the mountains. She just got a little scared...

---

[8] [fre] Social activities that take place after skiing

CARRY ME NAKED

"I've come to the conclusion that I'm aware of my delusion,
And I'm completely confused about my complete confusion,
And my convictions, oh, they're all crumbling away,
I've made my poor decisions then decided against them anyway,
Now I'm taking my time on the whim,
So that I can reminisce about the day I can remember this:
I was someone somebody called a friend..." [1]

...Pessi hopped in my car, leaving Teresa behind to sulk since there was just no way *she* was partaking. Who the fuck was I! Ivy! Pessi! or anyone else! to tell *her* what to do?! she'd squawked just minutes earlier, when, inside, I gave it one last try with *her.* Who the fuck was *I*, a worthless *user* myself, to tell her that she was a worthless *junkie*, she'd fired out, adding (in a whisper) that she'd tell Ivy, to which I replied, tell Ivy what—leaning in even closer with her pointy nose almost touching my ear, that I'd spent the night at her place several times, had seen her naked *sooo* many times, and once tried to have a threesome with her and Pessi, which the latter never happened, but to which I asked her how much she valued her life to be making such threats. Well, in any event, Teresa wasn't partaking in rehab at a local outpatient clinic. But after I threatened her life again—this time lunging for her throat to choke her to death because she kept saying no! she ain't paying for shit!—Teresa *was* going to partake in the costs with Ivy and I, seeing as Pessi had neither a cent nor health insurance. Since I'd been the one who called the clinic to get the basic information, I knew that the three months of dedication would total over $7,000. Ivy already had her share of the costs saved because she'd been working since she was sixteen, had frugality self-instilled in her bones, and, although she used to tell me that she accepted nothing from her parents, she accepted everything from her parents, having covered for her every last peso of college expenses; *aparentemente cuando Edwardo Pineda sentado en el cagadero, mucho dinero fluía de su nalgas pomposa como—Montezuma's revenge!* [2] Teresa would likely call her fa-king father and make up some lie to get a tip added to her filial stipend, and the piece of shit would surely oblige because that's how you shut your kid's mouth from thousands of miles away. And contrary to my natural disposition, I assumed a realpolitik stance, making politics my technique, taking Machiavelli's hand in order to do whatever it took to get my best friend clean; even my thoughts were now grounded in pure manipulation with regard to getting him out of *that* house and away from *her* shit, and of course, *it.* Ivy and I agreed that, at best, things were bound to crash between 'em once Pessi got clean, or, at worst, Pessi would end up relapsing. The entire world, it seemed, was pulling for the former.

---

[1] Lyrics from "Someone Called a Friend" by One Step Ahead, from the album *The Art of Coming to Terms*
[2] [spa] on the shitter, tons of money apparently flowed out of Mr. Pineda's pompous ass like a bad case of diarrhea contracted in Mexico!

I drove Pessi to the hospital where the clinic existed within a plastic blue wing. We went inside, waited an hour, then a lady came to escort him to where aliens worked on out-of-whack workings. Flush in the plush, I thought back to the catalyst for this cathartic moment in the nonce: two nights passed, when Pessi gave us a "little scare" during a lame New Year's celebration at Teresa's. To my knowledge, he hadn't even been on H; instead, the culprit seemed to be Synergy, for he brought in the New Year with a bang by going Baby Blue then shoveling enough snow to have him shaking in the worst fit, talking violent nonsense. While trying to calm him down, I was making him drink as water much as I could, which, from his swinging anger, ran counter to the breathing techniques I was trying to have him do. It was on the verge of a hospital visit but I ultimately deemed it unnecessary, for he replied in the negative to my questions regarding chest pains and high temperature; he just wanted to kill people: that's all: mostly psychological crap. When he finally seemed all right, I left him to sit on the steps—halfway up—looking like a pouty little boy. Then I returned to entertaining Ivy and two of her girlfriends from school, who had no better place to spend the holiday, and therefore had to find out what it's like to witness a nightmare with their eyes open. Well, twenty minutes later, Pessi *still* wasn't all right: *all* psychological crap at this point. It culminated in him coming down the steps, brandishing the gun, apparently ready to kill people. When Ivy saw him, her jaw dropped: might've been the first time she'd ever seen a gun, to wit, a handgun, outside television. Snowed under with embarrassment for Ivy (because her friends had to witness it), I asked Pessi what he was doing without sounding too reprimanding. Imitating a hillbilly in both vernacular and body language, he said that he was going outside to shoot the moon. He kept singing out in twang: '*Hey, V—Yeeee-haaaaw! Happy fuckin' New Year's, BOY!*' Fortunately, I was able to trick him into letting me hold the gun. After taking possession, I went outside and locked it inside my trunk. Then I asked Teresa if there were any more guns in the house, for it had become evident they didn't need to be around weapons. Since she was too wasted to answer, I searched the house the best I could—but found nothing. To Pessi's dismay, I told him that he could have the gun back when they became stable: seemingly years away. Something told me they were bound to shoot or stab each other—ya know, Sid and Nancy were. Yet I couldn't move myself to take all the knives out of the kitchen; if I did, then *I'd* be the one who looked like a nut. As I was conducting the investigation, Ivy's friends had decided to call it an early night: *Happy fuckin' New Year's whoever yinz two were!* And in her embarrassment, whom did Ivy blame? Me, the bad guy. She wouldn't shut up about it. So an hour later, after Pessi had eased into a sober but irritable mood, I, looking to make amends, crafted his New Year's resolution: 'I, Zachary David Pessini, gadda seris drug problem 'n've become mentally instable. So tamarra, January 2, 2001, I'll enter rehab. If I don't, I'll luzza two people I love the most, V 'n' Ivy.' Although it took me a while to get him to *agree* to it—(he refused to say it verbatim)—he did. This was all happening in front of Teresa, but too bad she was lying on the couch, oblivious to it all. Alwaysthemore, I woke up on this present day, called him, and clarified that the New Year's Intervention was serious: no choice but to get in my car when I came to take him in, because, yes, our friendship was now *conditional!* I was just so fucking sick of the whole situation! I was no longer going to be passive in my threats! Sure, he technically had the freedom to continue "experimenting" but only at the cost of me turning my back on him for good! Of course I would've never done that, but people in his state can hardly analyze another's linguistics because all that power is transferred over to how to construct their own linguistics into forms of manipulation to convince others to do things for 'em such as take 'em to get it or lend 'em money "juss 'iss one time 'n' I promise I'll pay ya back next week when my grandma sends me my birthday money." Fuck her and fuck you! Get the fuck in the car *right now!* I'm finally putting the balances of power back in check! Yeah, Pess, you're yee-hawing your ass right to rehab!

Finished with the analysis, Pessi came out and told me that he was going to be undergoing treatment everyday because they had to give him a daily dose of methadone, which also carried a risk of addiction. (He tried getting "take-home meth," but they refused to sell it to him because they had no medical history on him.) They were also putting him on a strict diet with an overdose of vitamins. But the crux of the treatment was the behavioral-therapy five days a week for the first two weeks—the most critical and difficult stage—then three days a week for the last two and a half months. They said even after the treatment was finished there was a good chance that he'd crave it for years, and therefore, psychological-therapy, even if only twice a month, was strongly suggested. But like when I'd broken my ankle, and they'd suggested further therapy, Pessi, for the same reasons, knew that it wasn't going to happen whenever the time came. Notstandingvandivylessness, he agreed to everything else put before him. He was just so sick of the sickness and slavery, and perhaps had came to the realization that he was on the brink of *irretrievable addiction.*

Pessi was doing the last of the paperwork when he called me over to the desk. Across from him sat a flaxen scarecrowette with gossamer hair and moldy gray eyes, perhaps a recovering addict herself, for they're known to hold such prophylactic positions.

'She wansta know about da payments 'n' 'at?'

I addressed her: 'You need money now or sum'n?'

'Well what we'd like to do is get a down-payment in order—say, around $2,000—then we can set up the rest in monthly payments. Since Zach doesn't have healthcare, it's the only way we can establish a line of credit with him.'

'I see,' said the blind man. 'Well, umm, I dunno.' I turned and looked down at Pessi; I could see (in his rolled eyes) how much he hated the subordinate position he was in. 'I guess I can I juss put the dahn payment on my credit card. Den I'll get Ivy da make a few a da monthlies til me 'n' Teresa get some more money together—'

"N' me. I'm gonna help pay for it. Den pay yinz all back.'

'You juss nee'dda worry about gih'n yirself clean. Da money means nuh'n.' I looked up at the scarecrowette—who returned a sympathetic I've-been-there-before look. I said, '*Take Discover?*'

She said, 'Yep. Have a seat while I get a form for you.'

Ahh, it certainly does pay to discover what you'll do for a friend! But I had a feeling Poor Pessi was already deep in internal debt, making the toughest payment: the silent transaction to the Givers in the currency of

Indebtedness, which accrues Inferiority. Of course he needn't feel that way with *me*. But his internal inevitability matched my external awkwardness as I pulled out my newest credit card right in front of his flushed face.

After the clinic "spotted" us, they, just like any other drug dealer or healer, let us walk away with what we wanted, and enough incentive to return for more. In silence (save for the music), I drove Pessi back to Teresa's to deal with the worst addiction, the one that you'll spend everything you got to discover, then spend a lifetime just trying to overstand what it is you've found: Dislover.

As much as it was a relief to my conscience to see Pessi getting help, it was also a shock, but not in which to make complaint. I was just so proud of him, my best friend, for breaking through the walls of pessimism surrounding him, and seeing, even if only the faintest ray, the light of optimism in a world of darkness. I even shocked *myself* when, returning to my room, I made an expensive long-distance call to Ma to inform her of what's been going on. Kinda funny because she didn't know much about heroin. Once I parentally explained everything to her, she whimpered then said a quick prayer to God. Although she'd yet to hear anything from or about Milvio and Gennaro, she was, save for the moment in which the news on Pessi was revealed, in high spirits. Catania was like geographical-therapy for her: I could sense the purification and renaissance of her soul through my own like when standing on the cool sands of a beach at night, with the tide crashing into your shins, looking far out above the ocean at certain star in memory of a beloved face, and experiencing, without formal penitence, that elevated sensation of being absolved, knowing through intuition that everything's going to be all right. That said, right after the fall semester had ended—(Ivy and I both received *As* in Dr. Rosenbaum's class!)—Ma called, wanting to know what she should do *now*. What else is there to do *now?* 'Juss stay 'n' spend Christmas witchir family.' – 'Stay *here?*' she asked with a restrained tone; her tsunamic waves of anticipation for my sanction, however, were crossing the Atlantic and causing the phone to bang against my head. 'Yeah. Ivy's parents are forcin' meedda go over der place anyway.' So Ma stayed in Catania for Christmas but almost backed out at the last moment when Aunt Stella called her to criticize her for what could be summarized as Ma's "abandonment." That's when Ma, beaten back into reservation and guilt, called one last time. I asked if she knew the saying "Bah! Humbug!"; meaning, tell that to Aunt Scrooge. Ma laughed, almost unreservedly, and said that she missed me and loved me and would be home soon, whereupon, in my mind, I saw, from the token of the word *home*, the jaundiced box in the middle of the block halfway sunken into the ground, and further down, Rick's flesh degenerating. Unfortunately, I could also see Razzle's gray pelt fading way, his to that fragile hillside loam. Boy, I missed him so much! Here, boy, here!

Anyway, regressing to Christmas time with the Pinedas: wow! what a time! Just kidding, ddikts—kinda ;) Once again, Edward and Sandy splurged on me: this time the highlight was a laptop computer! I did my best to decline it, but Sandy assured me of the great deal their friend in-the-business gave 'em for buying three, one for each of their children, me being the missing link to the trinity. I bought Edward this, and Sandy that. And in comparison to the previous Christmas, Ivy took half as much with a half-grain of salt. But that didn't stop her from filling my closet with clothes I tried not to wear, as if by allergy I simply couldn't. Besides, being overtaken and smashed together by the better breed of fabric, the orphans were beginning to feel subordinate, cheap, and unloved: something any good father must jump in and reconcile by wearing his heart on his sleeves and legs. Here, cordurboys, here.

The most interesting, and by effect, the strangest, present came in the mail a week after receiving the already-opened present that was Pessi-in-the-detox-box. Ma sent me the pile of pictures I'd asked for. She labeled who was who and what was what. I laid down on my bed to focus in. Zia Filomena (who I'd already seen in pictures) was a bombshell: slightly taller than Ma with larger breasts and hips, and straight brown hair to the elbows. Even though she wasn't younger than Ma, she *looked* it. (The one time I was on the phone with Ma, Zia Filomena wanted to say hello and hear my voice. In Sicilian, I said, 'Hello, Aunt Filomena. It's nice to finally talk to you.' She said, '*Ciau, Vinny*—Hello!' then pulled the phone away to titter like a little girl who just got a magic trick pulled on her. Then we talked about me being in college til she implored me to come visit. That was the very first time we talked.) Ogling the pictures of Zia Filomena—fixated on her dark, athletic exoticness—I felt satyric. Might sound sick, but given the chance I would've fucked the Sicilian right out of her: that's how much of a knockout she was! Kissing-cousins, fondling-siblings, fucking-aunts-and-nephews-from-two-different-walks-of-life-who-don't-even-know-each-other: what's the fucking difference! Just kidding, ddikts ;) Then there were my other aunts, Caterina, Gianna, Nicola, and my uncles, Salvatore and Pasquale. Although semimatte photos, they clearly exuded the humility of my zii. Physically, they, both sexes, were on the shorter side and thicker than Ma, which meant my assumption that my natural girth, especially in the chest and arms, came solely from Rick's side was wrong: Ma was just an anomaly. Other Scandurresi traits: thick black/dark brown hair, besides Gianna the dark blonde; sleepy-eyed almonds; small pointy noses; melancholy smiles; and deep swarthy skin suggestive of Greek blood. My cucini, at least the younger ones, looked like beggars, complimented by the raggedy scenes of their hillside huts. Unlike the majority of the Americanizing Sicilians, they were dressed in antiquated clothes that reminded me of kids who had one "good" outfit that they wore everyday as they went out into the streets, *trying* to look respectable, while hustling for bread money. But there was something else about my cousins—perhaps the lack of propinquity, and with it, the absence of tactility in the present, and more so, the touch never had—or perhaps the sensation of pre-eminence I felt, and with good reason, for their education would most likely never exceed high school—but whatever it was locked into the stillness of the pictures, it made me gauge 'em as anything but my cousins, *me cucini*. I even felt rich and fat looking at 'em in their frozen destitution, but also very saddened by it. For some reason, there weren't any pictures of Nanna Maria Grazia, and only one of Nannu Ignazio. His picture was smaller than the others: apparently very old, for it was monochromatic, wrinkled, and foxed. Perhaps my nannu had qualms with pictures too: his disposition was more twisted than the photo itself! In frayed overalls, he was sitting outside on a wicker chair, all wrinkly and slouched, with a sagging gut; dark hair combed over; eyes squinted down into an angry state; and a furrowed mouth (no lips) as if sucker-punched before the snap, with a cigarillo poked directly into the missing hole as if by force. Yes, a real bitterness about my nannu from which he instantly gained my respect. Someone stole his essence.

The next set of pictures were recent because they had a present-age Ma, with her present-age siblings, in various places around Catania—a low-lying city, atop vast level land, situated between the Ionian Sea and Mt. Etna. In plain sight anywhere in the city, the active volcano dominates the horizon. The mountain is called Mungibeddu by the locals (Mongibello by the Italian mainlanders) and is accompanied by Trifoglietto and other smaller peaks. The pictures of the range illuminate the power that lies behind the city: these big, dark-based, upside-down Vs—some white-peaked; but from the eyes of the Ionian, sharp shadow-casters on the outskirts. There were several pictures of the Ionian Sea and the wharfs, with hundreds of small boats docked and at sail; in one prurient photo, Zia Filomena was standing in a shark-finned felucca, wearing a white bikini top—oww! Anyway, some majestic waves emerged in a perfect blend of blue and green as if The Creator had mixed the colors that later came to make the irises of Dr. Rosenbaum and Ivy, and from that tropical concoction, filled the Ionian hole with life. The water had such a strong appeal that I wanted to drink it, believing it would taste like an exotic juice.

At a distance, Catania is chaotic with whites, bronzes, grays, and peaches. Zooming in, you can see the abundance of Baroque churches and palaces, glossy sculptures, and multicolored *palazzi:* very clean in comparison to where my family lives in the *borghetto* [3] which is, in fact, a poor ghetto. Even though certain parts of Catania are pristine and angelic, it's also known as "the dark city" or "the city of black and white" due to Mt. Etna's numerous destructions of the city. Former resolute and ironic Catanisi even used the black and gray volcanic stone (from the lava flows) to fashion ashy facades all across the city. This gloomy look, however, together with the various causes of Catania's urban sprawl, has left many European critics to consider Catania a city in degradation. But from *my* perspective, even in the nighttime pictures, with yellow and pearl lights burning amid wide boulevards and inside imperial palaces, Catania symbolized anything but darkness, ominousness, or degradation. Rather, it gave off an image of extravagance and palatialness, much like Naples, where you'd think not a poor person existed. In other places, which I couldn't quite mentally map out the relation to the rest of the city, there was the Cathedral of St. Agatha: a dedication to Catania's patroness; Elephant Fountain: a monument of a dark gray elephant (Catania's guardian against Mt. Etna, also made of its volcanic stone) with an extended trunk and an Egyptian obelisk rising high off its back; House of Bellini; Chierici Palace; Ursino Castle; Roman Theatre; Odeon; University of Catania; the famous fish market in a frenzy; the Piazza Stesicoro where the remains of the Roman-Age Catania lie; and above, *palazzi* abound, which the building of these *palazzi* led to the unending socio-economic rivalry between Catania and Palermo.

---

[3] [ita] *a small borough*

Photographically speaking, between the humble but perseverant disposition of the citizens, and the intense glow of the architecture not without the kind of grim that produces a working-class pride like that of Pittsburgh, and the viridian sea that I wanted to sit by and sip, Catania looked like the perfect home for the ~~art~~ist who was twisted up in violence but looking to unwind in peace. Seemed like a sleeper-city, and one I *did* want to sleep in. *Sè, rintra nni mia,*[4] I was beginning to develop a strong feeling (like a rising tide of prospect) as to where I wanted to move after college; just had to keep Ma over there in the meantime.

The last set of pictures was of Caltagirone: a city still in the province of Catania but about forty miles southwest of the port. Like Catania, Caltagirone is very Old World and ~~art~~istic-looking: a mecca centered around fine ceramics and renowned for its terra-cotta. Flipping through the pictures, I saw why it's the essential place for a craftsman's pilgrimage: a rich colorful spirit spread all across the city on the hill, magnetically drawing one into its ~~ear~~thenware sanctuary; the pilgrims probably even made their way up and across the hill with their cockle hats and staffs and sandal shoons![5] The city itself is filled with gardens, plazas, palaces, churches, monuments, all adorned with Old World pottery, hanging lanterns, and smiling flowers so vivid and alive. But the most fantastical attraction in Caltagirone is the Santa Maria del Monte staircase. 142 steps connecting the low end of the city to the high end. Each step is decorated differently with multi-colored ceramics in tiles of *maiolica.*[6] In one picture, Ma was waving to me with one foot on step-71 and the other on step-72. In another, she was standing in front of a large circular fountain, its inner bowl decorated like the glazed steps of Santa Maria del Monte. Posed in her finest style of innocence, she was smiling so effortlessly, so youthfully, like the face of a baby rolling around in the nude. And the naked sun in the background was shinning enough to produce a large glare across the top of the photo. In the middle, standing brilliantly behind her, was an enormous sculpture of—(if I had to guess, or pretend for the cause, since it wasn't labeled on the back of the photo)—of Eros: naked, short-bodied, cherubic cheeks, spread wings, one leg lifted and bent inward to where it was flush with the other, spitting water out in the direction of Ma's head. It looked like a constant stream of purified love coming down on her, or like the sacrament of baptism in hyperbole. At any rate of flow, from the burst of energy breaking through the photo, she looked so revivified, *me bedda matri.*

Having produced a new tatse of oddity, the pictures stirred up some serious confliction in my soul. As soon as I set 'em down, they seemed to be calling me back as if I'd overlooked something. So I picked 'em up and began flipping through again but with more attention to detail...almost to the point of futility...seeking meaning behind the surface: *there's XXXXXXXXXXXXXXXXXXXXXXXX*[7]...Surely no answers were coming to me in my room. But I could still he~~ar t~~he call of the pictures, as if they, the answers,

---

[4] [scn] Yes, inside myself
[5] Allusion to lines 25-26 (IV, v) in *Hamlet* in which the dress described is typical of those on a pilgrimage
[6] [ita] highly decorated ~~ear~~thenware glazed with tin oxide
[7] ???

needed to be sought out, not thought out, and *touched*. After getting up and setting the pictures down on my desk—alone on a cold January night—I closed my eyes in wistful reflection. *(A youthful sigh.)* For as one intelligent, sensitive, benign animal loves helping another, I could see myself riding on a dolphin, finning out across the sea to see if I could find myself...

     ...As Pessi lunged into month-two of rehab with promising growth, Ivy decided to stem the tide of something else that was, up until now, also growing quite richly by breaking up with me for two weeks for two reasons: 1) a stupid issue with name-calling; 2) failing to heed to her parents' call. On the first matter: She started being persistent about wanting a cute petname. She made it seem that, without one, I really didn't love her. She hated her mother's "Iv" and Teresa's "Dolly-Doll," and was fed up with my "stupid names," the ones I randomly said in jest or out of childishness: but more or less a linguistic indication of when I was in a good mood. She even stated that "bella-loo" was probably something I had called every girl I liked. So she wanted something *genuine* and *everlasting*, something I could call her in our 80s, while swinging on a front porch and reminiscing about Love as a baby. She would say, 'Oh, can you believe Alana'—a grandchild of ours—'got in on a full-scholarship?' And I would reply, 'Yep. Liddle Alana is gonna blow 'em all oudda the wudder at Aristod.' *(An elderly sigh.)* 'Good ol' Aristod. 'Member when you yoosta sneak me inda yir dorm room so I could spend the night? We got away with it every time too! After makin' love, you'd cuddle inda my chest, 'n' I'd put a sweet lock of yir mocha hair in my mouth 'n' rotate it around, while you purred 'n' ran yir fingers all along me like a playful cat. Remember dat, Sciancatedda?' That's an endearing Sicilian diminutive that roughly translates as "goofy-walking girl." I assumed that was something similar to what she wanted, only something in English; I just hadn't come up with anything yet! And when the facades of Obstinacy wouldn't let me tell her that I *was* thinking about it, Ivy would come down on me, saying that I wasn't like how I *used to be*, which caused me to shoot back in the name of the things *I* was still waiting for, the things she'd never given *me*. (Ya know how that goes.) But I guess when it comes down to it: 'Let men tremble to win the hand of a woman, unless they win along with it the utmost passion of her heart! Else it may be their miserable fortune when some mightier touch than their own may have awakened all her sensibilities, to be reproached even for the calm content, the marble image of happiness, which they have imposed upon her as the warm reality.'[8]
     Anyway, the DNA-strand that broke the politician's back was the thing about her parents. First, Ivy expected me to eat dinner with them every time *she* did. I wasn't used to eating with a family except on holidays, and even then, if I could, I would sneak off with my plate. Despite the *bel espirt*[9] façade I'd put on for Edward and Sandy, I felt uncomfortable about it, and Ivy didn't overstand why. Nor did she overstand that families that eat together do so because there's an easiness about it due to a cultivated bond—one in which its fibers have become tightly stitched together from the accumulation of many small measures such as regularly asking *how was*

---

[8] Passage from Nathaniel Hawthorne's novel *The Scarlet Letter*
[9] [fre] A cultivated, highly intelligent person

your day? and *would you like to talk about it?*, and having participated together in things like Little League games and school activities. And just because my girlfriend's family had the "cultivated bond" didn't mean *I* was part of it or could be because of their cordial invitations and lavish Christmas gifts. They just didn't overstand that I'd been irretrievably *damaged* by the family.

But to put the Pinedas on the backburner: I could only hope and believe that the "diseases" that had afflicted my family weren't genetic and thus wouldn't be borne into my future family, the one of my direct seed. Despite my dark past, which thanks to education, reflection, compassion, and connection, ran deep into the recesses of History and Dem ol' Graphics, I planned to see my future as a bright one. I concluded that I *will* be a good father and I *will* have a healthy family; I'd just never be a son to anyone other than my mother, no matter how tightly whatever family had stitched their fibers together before my coming...

...By mid-March it was becoming clear that Ma didn't want to return to America. Ever since finding out about Pessi, she'd been calling every week just to see how he was doing. Then she'd embark on her guilt-trip til she heard what she tacitly called to hear: 'Ma, juss stay 'n' relax! Dere's nuh'n for you here anyway.' As for what's *over there* for her? Well, still no word from or about Milvio and Gennaro. But the good news was that Zia Filomena was teaching her how to do shit with ceramics; that's what Zia Filomena did for extra money. Perhaps they could open up a shop together? That would surely keep Ma over there! Meanwhile, Jealous the Elder was *still* down Ma's throat every given chance, telling Ma that it wasn't right to leave me behind after losing my father; yeah, seems like Aunt Stella could've come up with something better than that, but she couldn't. However, she *did* trick Ma into believing that she missed me and wanted to keep in touch, from which Ma made the mistake of giving her my dorm phone number. Consequently, Aunt Stella started calling me all the time, telling me all this stupid shit about her friends til she could find a way to complain about Ma, hoping that I'd backbite too; I never did. Sometimes, whenever I'd tell her that I was doing work or heading to class even if I wasn't doing either, she'd resort to putting Uncle Alfonse on, thinking it would keep me on and her "plan" intact. He'd scream Nonsense for a few seconds til swatting or throwing the phone to the ground. If I allowed it, she'd get back on and translate whatever Uncle Alfonse had said as more disparagements to Ma's "abandonment." After putting up with that for two weeks, I called the phone company and had her number blocked. Then I called Ma and told her that, as far as she was concerned, I didn't have a cell phone, and now, with my new laptop hooked up to Aristod's free internet server, an email address either. Aunt Stella was suspended indefinitely from communicating with me by *any* means. Nothing feels more liberating than being incommunicado with the insane!...

...In April, Teresa, Pessi, and I celebrated Pessi's successful completion of rehabilitation with cocaine confetti. 'Let's do some fa-king yey tonight!' Squawk suggested. As far as I knew, for the past three months Pessi had only been taking the prescribed meth, perhaps popping the ol'

Baby Blues. But I was worried about him doing coke. Seemed like the quickest route to relapse. I told him that he should really think about it. But he said, 'Fuck, yey ain't *shit* comparedda H or meth. But I need *sum'n* with a liddle kick so I won't get sick or anything. Besides, you never had a problem with yey before—ya know, before I started doin' H.' *Touché,* Pushi. Truth is: I hadn't done yey in a while either and was burning to get that "kick." I liked that "kick" once in a while. Perhaps it could be like an ice-cream habit this time around, considering I didn't have the money to be doing it all the time anyway. Sure, Ivy would go banana-split if she knew both Pessi and I had done coke, taking it all out on me by doing another temporary split to teach me a lesson that I'd pretend to fully lick up. But she wouldn't know about *this* late-night dessert because she had to work til eight, and afterward, had a group meeting—one, as she informed me, might go into the wee hours of the morning because the work was due soon and her group was behind. That's college life when it comes to group work: a bunch of procrastinating drunks with one studious person who wants to get everything done promptly and with quality but is dragged down by a group that cares more about dipsomaniacal traditions. So while Ivy was dealing with *that,* Squawky Skank, Squeaky Clean, and Stupid Genius—The Three Sneeketeers—were on their way to party with the dipsomaniacs who didn't have to deal with any Ivys on this lushious school night.

Located on the most popular and populated street off campus, the destination was Kelly, Danielle, and Cindy's apartment: three of Teresa's mysterious friends, probably bound to be short-lived ones, because the girls she associated with, save for Ivy, were only in her life for some kind of materialistic purpose whether it be drugs or keeping a good tipper...til something involving drugs ruined it: a permanent hairy cycle continually being filled with new chemicals in the turn: friendships feigned and dyed with promises of permanence, but like a perm, it soon fades.

Well, we kicked off the night by getting that "kick." While the rest partied loudly throughout the apartment, The Three Sneeketeers, along with two skeezers[10] riding on Squawky Skank's coketails, snuck into the bathroom. I shut the door behind me. The music was still blaring. A Thursday night—but, hey, fuck the neighboring students who have class in the morning! they're obviously not cool! they'll just *have to* deal with it because we came to college to get fucked up! and our parents paid a shit load of money so we could! so crank up the music and let's party, motherfuckers! That's the attitude floating through every crack in the place, especially in the mouths of the two little skeezers crowding around me, waiting to indulge in what *we* brought. Squawky Skank was chalking up lines on the marble counter. Meanwhile, the one little bitch was bragging to the other little bitch how she's been *sooo* drunk all week and how she blew off *this* class and *that* meeting and how she can't *wait* for the *big* party at Sig Pi tomorrow. I looked at Squeaky Clean with a sarcastic look that said: 'Dis girl's *sooo* fuckin' cool.' But he just outright spat, *'Shudup, you dirdy*

---

[10] A word with various meanings, but meant here as a woman with lax morals, only concerned with doing whatever it takes (usually sex) to gain money, fame, or material objects such as drugs or clothes

whooores!' That ol' Pittsburgh corrosiveness instilled in blue-collar yinzers, slathered all over our Steel Walls like   .[11]

The still-cropped-blonde Squawky Skank snorted her line up with the authority of a true addict. Next was a quick hit by the no-longer-coke-clean Squeaky Clean. After Squeaky Clean maneuvered out of the way, Stupid Genius was about to step up to plate and get a hit—til that little bitch pushed him aside. He could only shake his head and mumble something; he didn't even try to go next; he let the other little bitch go to bat. Finally, Stupid Genius snorted up his thick line in anger—really thick anger like he just broke a nail doin' the rail. When he turned around, sniffling, he accidentally nudged that little bitch who'd cut in front. Glaring back, she hissed; glaring back, he was wondering if she lived in the apartment because he suddenly had to take a wicked piss. Pinching it for now, he, Teresa, Pessi, and the two skeezers who got their hits via base-on-balls, headed back into the party, sniffling...

...And hey! Just more and more anger! I didn't like these people! I didn't like this music! I didn't like how these people were dancing to this stupid music! I didn't like the way Teresa immediately ignored Pessi as she gallivanted all around the party in her black miniskirt! squawking real close to rouge faces! holding a yellow plastic cup of beer by the tips of her boney fingers like a witch practicing Wicca! her powers inherited from the darkest side of Nature! nine layers deep in the Netherworld! treacherous hex! treacherous hex! treacherous hex! I could hear her incantations over the music! And I couldn't decide which one was worse to listen to! It was like choosing between getting your ears stabbed or getting your ears speared! Neverthehex, I *did* like the way I went into the kitchen...grabbed a bottle of beer from the fridge...then a bag of pretzels from the cupboard, probably doing it out of a subconscious hope that it would start a fight so I could throw a fist at whoever had something to say about it. Sniff, sniff.

Leaned back against a pomelo wall with Pessi, we looked out at college life, hardly separated from it, in the physical. We were actually having a good time fuckin' with people without them knowing. Everyone knows you can't fight pompousness with propriety! Well, after I finished off the pretzels, we snuck outside and smoked. Well, when we came back in, I was higher. Well, after I drank some more, I was drunker. Well, that's when I started grabbing Pessi by the back of the neck, head-butting him, telling him that if he ever touched H again I'd kill him. Well, that's when Pessi threw me a hard kidney shot. 'Fuckin' right,' I said to myself. 'Ain't nuh'n like da good ol' days!'

'Same fuckin' shit, huh,' I slurred. 'Jussa different fuckin' place.'

'You got it, bro.' (Seemed like Pessi was laughing without emitting the sound.)

'So, skipper—where you wanna go next, huh? Why 'on't we go over da—da Catania with Ma, 'n' you can marry her, 'n'—'n' I'll get me wanna dose nice liddle *beddi siciliani* who say, "*Ooo-la-la-la-LA! Rip off my shirt 'n' BRA! Vinny! Vinny! VINNY! Stick it in me! in me! IN MEEEEE!"*'

Arms crossed, Pessi let out a casual laugh. 'Whaddabout Ivy?'

---

[11] ???

'*Sheeee* don't fuckin' overstand me!' I dumped out from my gut a sound similar to a dumptruck unloading rocks. 'No one 'stands me 'roun' here. Looky here, skipper: me 'n' you go over dere 'n' I'll—I dunno—I'll buy 'at whole fuckin' place for us!'

'With what money?'

Grunting, I spilled beer on his leg. What money?! What MONEY?! Yaw'n crack, kid?! I'm gonna fuckin' write books addle blow 'er mind 'cause no one 'roun' here likes me. Everyone says, "*EH!—Arenchu motherfuckin' Vincent Ig-ignazio Scandurra Vallano?*" (We both let out a burst of laughter over my absurd voice and my struggle to make it through my name.) "'*Cause I'll tell ya what, BOY: we don't like yir kind 'roun' here. We like dem der movies where dey blow things up, 'n' dey got dose sparkly things comin' atcha, 'n' dem der simple books 'bout luuuuv—'n' mysterieeees—'n'—'n' 'em thrilleeeeers. Yes, sir-ee bob! See, BOB: you don't know da first thing about writin' stuff for US!*" (I pointed hard into Pessi's chest, nearly falling over, not sure what was coming out of my mouth next but it was a-comin'.) "'*'N' if you don't like it here—den you can GIIIIIIT OOOOUT!!!*"

Well, about five minutes later I got out the rest of whatever was going on inside my head by puking my brains out all over the bathroom. I don't know who took my shirt off, but it was off and missing. Some flashes of consciousness: violently pushing bodies out of the way...a canary toilet...pretzels twisted in a grotesque form...Teresa laughing from the doorway...Pessi kicking my leg as I was head-down, saying, 'Wow, I ain't seen ya this bad in a while.' Somewhere in the mix, I splashed water on my face and brushed my teeth with someone's toothpaste using my finger; for some reason, the toothpaste was in my pocket as if I was attempting to steal it. Then I grabbed another bottle of beer, walked downstairs by myself, and, through the back doors of the apartment complex, went outside. (After throwing up, I'd sobered up a good bit, and planned to take it easy this time around in the early night. I knew it wasn't the booze *per se* that had sent me quickly into heavy intoxication; it was the mixture of three drugs: and how hard and unexpected it can hit you!)

Outside. Nighttime. I faced the bricked apartment. Right above the door: a plastic yellow lantern. Like an imp on the spy, something inside its disciform shield was clicking spiritedly. All along the bottom windows: a row of bushes. Off to my right, in the yard: a collapsed lawn chair, its weavings pulled and tattered: evidence of the imp's past mischievousness, or symbolic of my present state. Two floors up, behind the patio door: the music still blaring but with a muted effect. Turning around, off in the distance, somewhere down the alley: the sound of more music playing, along with the faint smell of bonfire. I stepped further into the small dark yard as if to get away from all the things I couldn't get away from. After sparking a cigarette, I looked deep into the sky to see the other side of the world—no other side of the world to be seen—or a moon—just a lot of blackness with a few pristine stars taking advantage of the moon's absence with a jazzy twinkle. Lip-puffing on the cigarette, I patted at my pockets, stumbling upon the tube of toothpaste and, from the absence of the small bulge, the realization that I forgot my cell back in my room, on purpose— *Eeeeerk! Click!* As the back door opened and shut, I turned around.

'Hey, you all right? I saw you from the patio and thought you might be passin' out in the yard.'

My rheumy eyes couldn't gauge the countenance moving towards me. Seems all the energies of my body were fixated on an internal vision, trying to ameliorate myself: although my buzz had waned, the back of my head, eyes, and throat were throbbing, my stomach feeling ominously sour, breathing on its own accord.

'Yeah, I'm ar'ight,' I laughed quietly, flicking a long ash from the cigarette. As if for my own enlightenment, I added, 'I think it was from 'eez fuckin' nasty pretzels some chick gamme earlier.'

'Oh, you mean the nasty pretzels you took out of my cupboard? And the nasty pretzels you threw on the ground after finishing the whole bag off and started stompin' on it with your friend?'

'Depends. You a detective or sum'n?'

'No, but I'm the girl you owe $1.29 to.'

I yawned down a swig of beer. 'Well sen' me the bill, hun, 'cause I ain't gahdinee cash on me.'

'That's all right; I have collateral til then.' She held out my shirt, the little bitch did, waving it around with one hand, a bottle of beer held still in the other.

'Umm—can I have my shirt back?'

'Maybe.'

My retort: yawned down another swig.

'How much do you want it back?'

Impassively: 'I don't. Juss keep it. Iddle be worth a lot one day.' Naked from the waist up, I flicked the cigarette up into the black sky: it valiantly shot upwards like a little orange firework...doing hundreds of cartwheels over the polestar—pausing for a split-second at the zenith—before orbiting back down to ground-zero...sparking out a few flickers on impact...a gray smolder left rising up from the blades. When I looked over at her, she, biting her lip and squinting her eyes quizzically, seemed to have watched with adoration the butt's phenomenal line of trajectory, however quick it may have been. Suddenly, above me, the music and voices got louder: a postnatal screaming as if a hundred people just popped out of the gravitational clutch of a wet vortex.

'Hey, VinnYYYYY! I fa-king SEEEEE youuuuu! I'm te-lling IIIvyy!'

'Hey, V, some bitch—oh it's 'at chick! Yeah, I's juss gonna tell ya some chick founjer shirt 'n'—'

'Hey, VinnYYYYY! I fa-king SEEEEE youuuuu! I'm te-lling IIIvyy!'

Trying to think up a slick rejoinder that wasn't coming—interrupted by an urge to launch my beer bottle up at her that didn't finish itself—I puked. Hunched over, it came again. Laughing, Teresa spit-sprayed beer down from the balcony—but not a drop hit me. Pessi threw something—yelled something too. After flinging off gooey strings from my lips, I snagged my shirt out of her hand. I told her to hold my beer for a second. I put on my shirt. Then I took the toothpaste from my pocket...squeezed some into my mouth...took the beer bottle back...put the rest in my mouth...swigged it around...spit, spit...handed her the toothpaste and empty bottle...then headed back inside, feeling much better now, ready to get drunk.

Well, back inside, after getting drunk again, things really started getting out of control. Everything around me was spinning around like those metal contraptions you get inside to simulate what it's like being in outer space. Everything was blending together with sporadic flashes of slow motion. My movements were tilting from side to side in great sways like a ship in a storm. The music and voices were going *waah! waah! wwyyyuuuaaaaaww!* And in our small click, our laughter, in a strange visual sense, was like looking like soundwaves stuck on repeat. My consciousness had completely melted away. Felt like I'd grown another heart in its place. In a way, it felt like I was tripping: not a favorite feeling of mine. Alwaysthemore, I was laughing uncontrollably over these explicit stories about Pessi and Teresa in bed, Teresa doing most of the narrating. The little bitch, christened Cindy Something, was hanging on my shoulder, laughing, sharing her cigarettes with me. Every now and then, Teresa would flash us a cunning look in our close embrace, then say in her drunken, childish voice that she was telling Ivy; but not only was she saying it in a way that undercut her seriousness, but it was also like she was indirectly making fun of Ivy, the naïve simpleton. And manifest in my guffawing, I thought it was really funny. I had no idea who Teresa was even talking about, really. Yeah, Squawk was an all right chick. Kinda like me: a sarcastic comedian with an anarchic soul and twisted imagination, always throwing it into the best form possible—a chick that, just like me, drinks and does drugs because she's been through some shit, not to be cool or get that first taste of experience like all the fresh bloods around us. Besides me deeming her H-habit pure stupidity, we overstood each other. In another fork in Time, I, not Pessi, could've even been with her. But maybe Mormonism, or to be less religious and more political, libertarianism, or to be less political and more literary, bacchanalia, or to be less literary and more philosophical, hedonism, was just right around the corner for us three, or four, or whoever else wanted to join The Fuckin' Freaketeers.

And fuck, did shit get freaky! OWW! Not sure what time it was but Satan showed up with a keg of sin and ten trays of hell-red jello-shots! The fuckin' place was burnin' down! Burnin' dahn, I tell ya! Out in front of me, assholes were bumpin' 'n' grindin' inside the Lake of Fire and Brimstone! Sweatin' to the old thing—Aerobic Lust! Gropin', grabbin', slappin', keepin' things happenin', while the music kept rappin'. Put 'em on the glass! Put 'em on the glass! That's what Pessi and I were yellin'. Put 'em on the glass! At who? Whoever had 'em to put on the glass! Sir, my thoughts were mixed A LOT! I was just yellin' and touchin' and takin' down into the steel walls inside me more material for King Transgression's servants to expand my Kingdom of Sin, all of which—in each moment of material ingestion—was absent of pleasure, pain, and conscience. It was all just fuckin' n(d)umbness!

Catching my stumble, Pessi lifted me back upright with the right kind of idea. He said Teresa should start dancin' with Cindy. Noooo! Teresa declined, but how 'bout this? She lunged forward like a hawk, clawing her talons onto Cindy's shoulders and throwing her tongue right into Cindy's mouth. A couple walls in the apartment caved in because the heat had just reached the degree of disintegration. Teresa's left talons flung her cup to the side—the little amount of beer left splashing out merrily. Ahh! how sensuous talons can be! She slowly moved her hand up to little Cindy's cheek. Judging from what I could see, I'd never seen two people so in love! When they stopped, by Pessi's intervening hand, I tried pushin' Teresa back at Cindy, laughin'. What's next? someone inside my throat spoke up. What do you *want* to be next? asked little Cindy. Yir fuckin' tits! answered Pessi. Well, before the its in tits was out of his mouth, Teresa's shirt was up in the heavens, leaving two circles of flesh for viewing. Sweet little Cindy, she was courteous and copped a feel. And right then, I fell in love with the idea of taking pictures! What couldn't be captured in those things! Losin' the essence? Fuck no! Holdin' onto the mammary! Go ahead, Teresa lured her prey in a bit further. So sweet little Cindy began flickin' and twistin' 'em like doin' a little dance with her fingers. And Teresa began laughin' so much from the titillation. We were all laughin'! Then some big meathead came struttin' by, sayin' something like, Damn! look at this! Pessi told him to scram. He did, kinda, but he couldn't stop lookin'. But who wasn't by now?! Everyone was green eyein' the red eyes! Hell yeah! When I looked around the room as best as I could I realized that we were the areola of attention! The boob I was, I hadn't noticed all along! Wow! I'm a star! A burnin' star! In front of so many people with two girls who'll do anything anywhere! And they're all mine! Someone touch me! Someone ask for my autograph so I can spit on you! That's right, Cindy Something, you go right ahead and show us *your* tits! Fuck those things are huge for a little girl! Now suck 'em Teresa, I dare you! Make her do it, Pess! Yeaahhhhhhhhhhhh! Par-dee! Par-dee! Par-dee! Now go put 'em on the glass, you stupid bitch! Hahaha! I'm a fuckin' star, bitches! A fuckin' burnin' star!...

...The ground looked brindled and split...on his way back to wherever, Satan had thrown paint thinner all over the world; it was floating around in the air...we were slogging through it all the same. Click! Clack! Click! Clack! Click! Clack! Squuuueak!—BLACKNESS—then a revival of light. From their shouldered grip, they tossed me on the couch. I was laughing wildly while trying to rip my shirt off. He just slapped her boney ass! Haha! So funny! That's why I said, Hey, Pess, I'll fuckin' kill you! He said, Why? (I threw my shirt right at his face.) I'm gonna tell Teresa! Tell Teresa what? She's right here. No! Fuck all yinz motherfuckers! (In a new fit, I began struggling to rip my pants off.) Hey, Pess! What? Come back dahn here! I'm gonna—look, I'm gonna tell you, sum'n—

It might've been three minutes later, it might've been three hours later—most likely three hours later because I could actually make out the standard form of the world when I opened my eyes to her sucking on my neck, grabbing me. Instantly, I pushed her away, hard. She tripped backwards to the ground. For a while, I watched her carry herself up the steps despondently, holding a glass of water, naked...

...In the early afternoon—before driving back to my room to sleep for the rest of the day—Pessi recounted all the hysterical details of the recently-deceased night. I didn't have much to add that he didn't already know, kinda...

LAST BELIEVER

"I saw a woman, I saw a black man,
I saw a guy with a turban and a blind man,
I saw a Democrat, I saw Republican,
I saw a German, a Russian, and a Mexican,
I saw poor man, I saw a rich man,
I saw a Christian, a Jew, and a Muslim,
I traveled around the world and saw it all,
But I let demographics stack bricks on a wall
Around my mind where I took a fall
Into this place I like to call—
Our Cultural Devolution!..." [1]

...The burgundy curtains were pulled back and the windows were pushed up. Lukewarm rays were shining in on Luke and I. A cool breeze was whistling through the micro-mesh screen—sweeping in and wrapping around my neck like the unconditional hug of a child. It felt so good because the child just wouldn't let go! On his stomach, pawing at a pine-green book, Luke chuckled: the child hugging my neck must've had a sibling tickling the back of his fat naked calves, or perhaps it was something funny in the material he was reading for his last final. Upon completion, Luke would be going home for the summer, unlike me who had a full summer of classes lined up; I had no choice for my summer-life, although I would've chose it all the same.

Already finished with my finals for the second spring semester, I lay on my bed, flossing my teeth with not much else to do besides picking up a new personal read; but I was getting sick of getting smart when it seemed to only be making me most stupider. I had every book I owned knocked down besides *War and Peace*, and that's something that just never ends, including its eyemark on two words that I was so sick of seeing; I'd rather just be stuck in the *and*. Furthermore, I quit taking my bi-monthly trips to the bookstore; I was *really* getting sick of going to the graveyard. I mean, how many times can you mourn a friend that's been dead for over a century? I read that Wardo's literary nemesis, Zuckerman, had just put out a new book, but even my sex drive was six inches under.

Grunting in mental exhaustion, Luke rolled over to face me. 'You know what *mollify* means?'

Locked into unneeded thought, I froze, leaving the string of white floss between my two front teeth to hang down like emaciated walrus tusks. 'Whatsah sentence? It's gadda few meanings with subtle differences.'

'"The letters were innumerable that came to my hands, without knowing who brought them, farsed too full of amorous conceits and offers, and containing more promises and protestations than characters. All of

---

[1] Lyrics from "Our Cultural Devolution" by Peeled Off Labels, from the album *Psychological Term Oil*

which not only could not mollify my mind, but rather hardened it so much as if he were my mortal enemy."'

'Ahh, sounds like ol' *Don Quixote.*'

'Wow, you're right on!'

'Should be; it's one of my favorite works. Anyway, *mollify*, uhh, it can mean da physically soften sum'n, or da emotionally soothe sum'n. Cervantes uses both meanings. It literally means da *soothe* her mind, but he follows up by sayin' it, so to speak, *hardened* her mind as if it became a steel shield against her "mortal enemy."'

'Kewl way to put it, man! Thanks.'

I went back to flossing my teeth. I loved that acute burn against my gums, up in the root's abyss, from the saw of self-incision. Afterward, though, it always made me thirsty, creating a discomforting itch that could only be mollified by more flossing. Mmm, a mollified mind: that's something I hadn't had since that night, now a month in the brew. Daily, my mind had been turning over in brutal revolutions the scorning and condemnations. It was like an abysmally loud engine in which no matter how hard I tried I couldn't throw a wrench in the gears. There was hardly a moment's rest from what some might call a trivial problem: something some would easily fix with the tool of dismissal. But I couldn't resort to such uncleanly mechanics; it would've been like turning my mind into a lemon, and I'm the one left driving it.

Musically speaking, my cerebral drum was pounding excruciatingly to the beat of perfidy! There was just no doubt that I was a deceitful traitor like Judas Iscariot! A slimy amoebic whore like Anthony Durkin! A full-fledged sellout to everything I believed in and cared about beyond my own welfare! However, in spite of it all, there seemed to be *one* superhero fighting for me in my head: Captain Pragma. It was through his pragmatic power-punches to the Army of Principles that my reasoning for external silence gained enough vitality to sustain itself hitherto, but not without busting open from their bellies more armies, such as the Babies of Doubt and the Toddlers of Regret. But the reasoning behind not telling Pessi (and Ivy: to be discussed subsequently) about that fateful night came primarily from two notions which intertwined into the rope that noosed me, but also kept me from falling off the cliff and down into the hell of fellow turncoats. I guess at this point I was still hanging around in mental purgatory til I made an ultimate decision one way or another, from which the ultimate judgment upon my character would be delivered.

The first and foremost reason that I didn't tell Pessi was *relapse.* I had visions of candidly telling him about the incident, and, as a result, him blindly jamming a needle full of death into his vein out of the anger and pain induced not just by Teresa, but also by me, his best friend. Involuntarily—(and hidden from his consciousness)—he'd equate me (the person who pushed him into rehab) with the devastating upshot of his relationship with Teresa; this, however, would not appear in such a manner to his consciousness; it would be distorted. Unbeknownst to him, the rehab would now seem a failure because, in a sense, I *was* the rehab. Therefore, by telling him, as well as being "involved" to whatever degree he'd deem appropriate, I'd also become part of the new poison flowing through him: that sick feeling you get when you know you've been betrayed by one you hold close to your he̶a̶r̶t. He'd go back to H not out of anger and depression, but because rehab and getting clean only brought his girlfriend to be underhanded and to have recreant desires towards his best friend who, despite putting him in rehab, was only doing so to become the target of his girlfriend's intentions. That's most likely how his mind (for the body's needs) would find validation for relapse: showing how something once thought as positive only led to a negative, and therefore he *must* return to the last state before any "deception" occurred—as paradoxical as that may seem. But consciously, it would be projected to him backwards: he'd almost instantly develop an *appetite for destruction;* namely, mind via body. In other words, he'd want to put a stop to the thoughts of what had happened by *hurting* his body, and there wouldn't be much else in his decision-making. This is the façade of the junkie that projects to us how parochially destructive they are when, in fact, they're thinking even more than us! especially with regard to health and survival! Beneath his consciousness, his foreconscious would be in liaison with his body by pushing distortions up to his consciousness in order to get the body what it wants: the drugs it's still craving: simil̶a̶r̶ ̶t̶o the undying wish retained in the unconscious that's found a new way to bring its desires to the attention of the consciousness but in a disguised manner. In this process, there would be little concern over me and Teresa; namely, no ethical considerations. His unconscious wouldn't be "thinking suicidal" like conscious Pessi, but rather trying to get back that sweet taste of life found in the powder. His unconscious would be trying to *heal,* not hurt.

As I said, this developed idea not to tell Pessi "intertwined" with the second primary reason; that is, the two formed a correlate. The second reason: *the view he would develop of me,* not with regard to the rectitude of my character, but *my connection to Teresa's choice of behavior—* including, even if she was *removed* from the picture, the leftover feeling that would linger throughout the years like a stench hanging over us when together. One might be too quick to assume that Friend-A telling an honest account of something unpleasant to Friend-B concerning Friend-B (and in this case, both) registers into Friend-B's mind as nothing but a true friend standing before them. But as it so often said, the truth is "the truth hurts": and where else to transfer that hurt but to the bringer of the truth? Me! Friend-A! Under the assumption that I told him, and he and Teresa "worked it out," there could no longer be anymore hanging out between all of us. It would turn into two people vying for custody of him. And although I considered Pessi as loyal as one could be, he was in love with *her,* and he was living with *her,* and she *did* have that power of physical intimacy (and the unique attachment that comes with it) that I would never have with him. So there were several things Teresa had on her side to at least hold her own weight, if not tip the scales her way for the time being. Now even if I told him, and he "left that bitch," there would still be this attitude on the surface where he might say, 'Ehh, fuck 'at bitch.' But how incomplete that statement would be! To bring his *unspoken consciousness* to the podium, the statement can be completed as: 'Ehh, fuck 'at bitch because now every time I think of why we broke up, I automatically think of *you,* even'o you were a "good" friend for tellin' me. But every time I see you, I see Teresa naked, suckin' on yir neck 'n' grabbin' yir dick, even'o you were an "honest" friend for tellin' me.' To be sure: a horrible stench we'd smell but never talk about just like when a girl farts. Simply put: that false-hearted bitch had made such a critical move beyond my control but from which I (no matter my choice) was involved in and fucked no matter how I looked at it: Pessi relapsing; or us four as a tight clique; or his view on me ; or the internal me, the one presently being fucked.

I also resorted to the fruitless "what ifs" and "maybe ifs": What if Pessi would've never touched H in the first place? Well, I would've told him the very minute it happened! I would've drug that bitch right up the steps by her hair and told him, with her nakedness, my neck, and my anger as the evidence (under the assumption that, in the heat of the moment, the basic nature our relationship thereafter wouldn't have hit me yet). And maybe if Pessi would've never touched H, it would've never happened anyway, at least not in such a problematic circumstance. And maybe if I was unacquainted with the idea that being an honest person to my best friend would ultimately change our friendship for the worse in the sense that it would leave an awkward, bitter, suspicious redolence thereafter, *then* I would've told him. And maybe if Teresa would kill-over, *then* I could tell him without any malicious rebuttals to worry about. Yet the nature of our relationship thereafter would still be an issue: essentially the same as if they broke up!

Much of the same pattern of thought applied to Ivy. That irretrievable way she'd look at me, seeing Teresa, naked, sucking on my neck and grabbing me. Always lurking in her mind the suspicions of whether there were *other* things being concealed. To be sure, her friendship with Teresa would cease, even though that in itself wouldn't necessarily be a bad thing, just more hurt to deal with, just more awkwardness, bitterness, and division between everyone. Lastly, she'd lose a great deal of trust in me: something, as they say, so hard to gain back once lost. 'Why were you there to begin with?' she would ask. 'Why did you lie to me? and sneak around on me? and relapse yourself? You said you would quit coke for good—for me! And only God knows what *else* has been goin' on!' That last suspicion-laden statement was the one ringing the loudest in my head.

Finally: Teresa Cazzata. To think she'd easily submit if I called her out would be sheer stupidity. She'd lie to Ivy and Pessi just to save herself, or if it came down to it, which it was seemed inevitable it would, she'd do whatever it took to bring me down with her. Over the years, I'd dealt with people like her. Even outside empirical evidence, it's common knowledge that unethical fuckheads exist: unfortunately too many. And it doesn't take a genius to take a stab at what tactics she'd employ in her defense. Some might call me a narcissist and not be far from hitting the stigma of a narcissus, but technically there's nothing in the definition of *narcissist* that states his love can't also be given *elsewhere*. Whereas Teresa was just plain selfish and outwardly heartless, with a loud, boorish, senseless mouth that got her off like having, from just yapping her jaws, the ability to self-engender and disseminate throughout herself a free drug or self-erotic stimulation: she was a squawkissus to dirty up the word a little more. Yet she was also a genius in her own right because she'd set up a nice impenetrable wall to her ways, just like any genius tries to do with their ideas. So what else could I do but try getting through patiently by removing it brick by brick? And believing you have the wrecking ball you don't can *really* be destructive.

Even the most righteous and nurtured conscience will never overstand how badly I wanted to convince myself that doing the "right" thing would also bring about the "right" situation. (But it's not always so.) And to speak the whole truth and nothing but the truth, more than anything in the world. (But I didn't.) In action, I took a vow of silence, shunning intimacy by tossing my he~~art~~ over in the corner, and consequently paid for it internally—so to speak, morally. *(Shhhhh...)*

Much more going on inside my mind. If the Teresa-issue was the drum playing to the beat of perfidy, then it was only a *concerto* within an orchestra of chaos: her drum would take a solo but fall into accompaniment as another took solo. And the baritone voice of Razzle (sometimes yelping in falsetto) was the *cantata* both cuing in the first movement (the instruments) and initiating the finale for the main and oldest burden of the grand composition, the *ritornello:* Richard Vallano: the evil maestro of my he~~art~~! Why was he still just dead? Why had he lived his life as he had, and yet been allowed to escape so easily and freely through death without paying what he owed? Sure, some of us put faith in Ultimate Justice. But what about the little justice going on here? the one, and most likely the only one, involving human rationalization and sensibility? Why had he been allowed to evade all of us?—"all of us" under the assumption that justice, to be the least bit consistent and meaningful, encompasses *everyone* despite the scale of an issue. Why?! Ever since his death, I hadn't been feeling the relief I thought I would. There was only relief insofar as I didn't have to deal with his shit anymore in the present. But what about the unrectified past? Although in effect only *I* felt it (and perhaps Ma) there seemed to be a great injustice weighing the world down because of that pathetic whisper in the wind. Seemed my nemesis had somehow une~~art~~hed the location of The Erinnyes,[2] and found a way to evade their stings. But ya know—perhaps there is *no* justice; perhaps there's just us ☹

And now the sickening music segues into the *intermezzo:* the nightmares.

They st~~art~~ed creeping up on me again, but detached from the marred painting or the nocturnal fairy, at least in the manifest content. George Carlin once said there's nothing more boring than listening to someone else try to describe their dream. When I first heard that, I laughed because it's true! However, I've always been fascinated by dreams, and through Freud, realized that, yes, every dream detail has *meaning*, along with *the fulfillment of a wish*, whether or not you're conscious of it. A week after the incident at Teresa's, I had a dream that Carlin might actually find interesting. On one lobe, the fabric of dream blew my mind: perhaps the longest, most vivid, extensive dream I ever recalled: a true *hypermnesic phenomenon.* On the other lobe, it ruined my entire day: displaced from reality, I had the desire to sink to the bottom of Lethe just so I could forget *everything.* (I swear, despite the temporary displacements from reality that I suffered, something inexplicable happened in my life, at an indiscriminate

---

[2] Three avenging goddesses who seek out those who have transgressed natural laws but never paid for it; they symbolize the guilty conscience

point in time, in which Reality slapped me in the face—like I'd just been born and had to learn the simple nature of myself then the complexity that evolves as humanity gradually enters into the mix; it felt like I'd suddenly imbibed the lives of both Victor Frankenstein and his monster.)

Anyway, as Freud explained, as a general rule for the disturbed, dreams aren't just about our present life but also our childhood; specifically, past events that have unreconciled issues. What happens is something in the present will trigger our dreams, and in 'em, we'll see present ideas and settings that are essentially symbolic of the past. Even if we believe (and feel) our feelings about the past have waned, they hardly have. They can hold just as much or even more weight than the most traumatic events in the present; this happens whenever the unconscious is presented with an opportunity to bring to the foreconscious (the middleman) instances of the past, which makes them, the instances, feel as if they just occurred.

So my fascinating dream—which, like all others, I wrote down as much as I could as soon as I woke up—was preceded by two weeks of a recurring dream set in an exotic but darkened scene with daunting waterfalls everywhere. Covered in amniotic fluid, I was always running away (but with difficulty) from multi-colored snakes, some which bit me. Suffice it to say, as much as I'd always been fascinated by waterfalls, those ankle-snapping snakes chasing me across paved hillsides and through amniotic streams made me want to put off the vacation to Niagara Falls that Ivy and I had planned for the upcoming summer. Anyway, my key dream begins in an upper story of an apartment building in an unknown city. Everything is chalky and sooty: reminiscent of the 30s. I'm with this girl I knew from high school, Sophie Driscoll, who'd had sex with her boyfriend on video in 10th grade, and we (his friends at the time) got to watch it. I'm sleeping in the corner when Sophie wakes me up. It becomes tacitly overstood that she works for a nude cleaning service, although she's not nude. Suddenly, on a large floor with no divisions, there's three families lying in gigantic beds. Sophie wants me to work with her, and says something about being paid extra for the one guy who's a fat slob. It's also implied that he masturbated on the sheets. Then the scene changes. Now I'm downstairs on the first floor, lying on a bed in front of a television; it's on. I sit up on the edge of the bed. An enormous black guy is sitting next to me. He has huge lips, a huge box head, and the tender eyes of a horse: a six-foot-six, three-hundred-pound slave in overalls. Tacitly overstood, I'm on community service with him. He talks in whispers about "cleaning," but it seems he doesn't mean the room. Then it flashes to me running down a snow-covered hill in Pittsburgh. I have a large bag of cocaine on me. I start throwing it in the snow like how one feeds a bird. Suddenly I turn around and scoop it all up, the bag becoming bigger than before. I head down this alley. Soon I go blind, or the scene does. Again, I'm back in the room with the black guy. We're talking about life in general, agreeing on everything, such as the unsolved problems with society. However, we keep having these minor confusions; on the last confusion, I say something like, 'Yeah, if *I* went out 'n' shot someone—' making a gun out of my hand, I point down the street we can see out the window above the television '—I'd only get twenty years. But if *you* did it, you'd get life.' But he's offended by this as if I was making fun of him in a racist way. I put my hand on his massive shoulder. Forlornly, he says that it's time to go. We walk up several flights of steps where his car is parked in a parking garage; seems to be in the same location of the initial room with Sophie. I'm shocked because his tiny blue car was literally my first car (only in the dream). I get in on the passenger side. I try shutting the door but it won't shut, which was, in the dream, an assurance that it *was* my old car. When I tell him that it's my old car, we're suddenly driving down another hill in Pittsburgh. He says, 'Now you tell yir mamma I said hello.' I start arguing with him that he doesn't even know my mother, pleading with him to state where she's from. His guess is "Da Angle in Abruzzi." Then, in abstruse ways, he starts implying that he used to have sex with Ma "before she moved." Then comes a conversational gap in which I can't remember what was being said but it opens back up to us talking about drugs. The bag of cocaine from before is now tucked in around my waist. I take it out and put it down beside the seat, premeditating that we are about to get caught, yet I can't get in trouble for a certain reason left unknown. At that moment, going around a bend, several cop cars are now chasing us. I'm now in the backseat, struggling to put my seatbelt on. He says something like, 'Figers, e'er time I gots bad drugs wif me, dey a-cumin' affa me.' I start begging him to take the blame; he says he will. So he veers off the road. All of a sudden, a cop, whose head I can't see, starts punching him so hard in the face. A swarm of cops is coming up the driver's side. One cop, with blonde hair, starts shooting him repeatedly. A shot deflects off him and hits me in the shoulder. I grab the big black guy for a shield because they are about to shoot me. Pushing him aside—(he's presumably dead)—I jump out the passenger's side of the tiny blue car. I grab the closest cop as a new shield. They fire into him, while I shoot back. Then they call themselves together to look for me, even though I'm still right there. So I take off running, clamber up over a fence, then dive into a river with the gun. Just beneath the surface, I'm swimming against what's supposed to be a strong current, but, for me, it's so easy to move through, face up, stroking backward. I'm also able to breathe underneath the water. The shot that I suffered in the car is bleeding into the water: my blood is whitish, jelly-like, looking, by effect, like the ink ejections of an octopus, but it hardly hurts. (That sequence went on for a while.) Another *flash*, and now I'm running down an alley in an unknown part of the city. The cops have found me. They're firing shots into me left and right, as I try to do something with the bag of cocaine. I jump another fence. Now I'm in front of an alga-green house. I contemplate entering since it would be a crime, but I'm bleeding to death in copious streams of translucent blood. So I burst in though the front door, pick up the phone to the left, and try telling the female operator the address. '6th! 6th! 6th!' I scream. But she says that's not the right one. Then I scream, 'Oblation!' which I only say once and protractedly; it resounds in my head for a while. (To my knowledge, I'd never said or heard that word before. Once I looked it up, and pondered, I realized it was comparable to, or literally in the rhetoric, when Father Carr would say, 'And communicants give...the offering to the Eucharist...and communicants receive...from the Mystery of Life...the ciborium and the chalice...Body and Blood...Blessed Sacrament of the Altar.') As my vision starts becoming blurrier, I scream upstairs. Seems someone is in the shower. I scream up to whoever it is that I'm not a criminal but I have a gun and I've been shot. 'I rilly need yir address!!!' I scream in the last desperate moment for help. That's when, all alone, I begin stumbling...circling around and around this strange dark living room which has tinges of hay-yellow light here and there, spotting, in my moribundity, a self-portrait of Van Gogh and an old fashion rag doll sitting in a miniature rocking chair...before collapsing to the ground, dead.

Fascinating! But to pay respect to Carlin, because dreams *can* get annoying, I won't bother with some of the interpretations I came up with after weeks of analysis. Suffice it to say, it involved, via the dream itself, other dreams, and daily circumstances, a lot of interwoven notions on the behaviors of my parents, not being able to masturbate at will in my dorm room, heartfelt issues I've had with linguistics, taking Pessi to get the H, the night Satan threw a party, violent tendencies, feelings of estrangement, future "success" as an artist, and lastly a battle between God and *Übermensch:* one fighting for my heart; the other, my mind.

Clap! Luke shut the book. He rolled over like a cub, yawning. He stood up...moved in a sulk to his desk...then began stuffing things into his backpack. Before heading to take his final final, I wished him good luck as if through those two words I'd just broken two years of reticence—or even better, ameliorated the situation with two therapeutic syllables. He thanked me in his southern way, and left brightly. In harmony with the door shutting, another gust of wind came into the room. I licked my lips; they'd become dry; I was still flossing. I pointed out the remote and turned the television on, hoping there would be an afternoon ballgame on; the season was just underway. No game was on, so I popped in my *Annie Hall* DVD. Lying back down, a narrative Woody Allen brought Dr. Rosenbaum to mind. As I learned through our private meetings, Dr. Rosenbaum didn't practice Judaism but was brought up in a strict Jewish family. He had a critical approach towards both Jews and Gentiles: similar to Zuckerman: but I always imagined Zuckerman to be a pompous asshole in real life; whereas Dr. Rosenbaum was a man I couldn't imagine a soul in the world disliking. Too friendly, too slick. Unfortunately, I didn't have him for class this semester, but sometimes I'd see him around, and whenever I had the time, I'd swing by his office just to fire at the wind. We'd turn the universe inside-out. His take on Rick was to forgive but never forget. I disagreed. I explained how *that* attitude is just like the passive neo-Jew philosophy that essentially allows neo-Nazis to retain a sense of pride for their Nazi forefathers. He retorted by explaining the importance of forgiveness, and how it can heal the soul of perpetrators and victims alike. I gave the last retort by explaining, in sum, that our forgiveness now will, in fact, become our forgetfulness in the future: no firm stand now and all will fall to ruins when our forgiveness, and for that matter, our collective memory, fades or starts anew with today's circumstances and problems; more or less using the logic of "History repeats itself" as my foundation, while advocating a new approach: "History *teaches* itself," as in let what's been done be our reasoning for being proactive with a "never forgiveness for *that* kinda shit" attitude; seemingly at odds with the teachings of Christ, but even God limits his mercy, and thus the reason for, and logic behind, Hell. But besides that passive vs. proactive debate, Dr. Rosenbaum was downright cynical about many things, and I deeply admired his ability to hide it! Had yet to see a spark of anger from him! He converted everything, such as cynicism, into subtle complex-irony. If I was shaking the passion right up out of my skin as I criticized some teacher who'd said this and that, he'd agree with a neutral smile while twirling his fingers around with a positive spin. Then he'd say that the "this and that" is like this other "this and that"—sometimes speaking very stoically. But sometimes he'd fly into this overwhelming energy about a sudden emergence of thought, memory, or circumstance that seemed wholly detached from the this-and-thats. Whatever we'd been talking about would drift far away, and yet, after I'd leave, all of his words would sneak back up on me, like a puzzle putting itself together right before my eyes. It was such a creepy, stunning sensation, culminating in such a body-shaking phenomenon that I wanted to reach into my chest, tear out my ~~heart~~, run back to his office, open the door, and hold it up, smiling just to let him know I got it—I got it right where it counts!

But that certainly wasn't the case of the me lying on the bed, waiting for Ivy, violently tossing and turning every which way, not getting *anything*. Felt like I was sinking down into the bed further than its actual confines: and it was *down there* where my mind was the ululating engine, my ~~heart~~ just an organ sustaining me physically. I could even *feel* my ~~heart~~ turning sable. Which is why, in May 2001, I decided the time had come for me to pull my ~~heart~~ off my sleeve (so nobody could see its nascent blackness), throw it over into the cloistered corner, and just leave everything else on the inside to burn, while lying on my back, sinking further down warmeal, looking upward at the rest of the blackness painted across the canvas so congruently to the point that there wasn't one trace of stroke, one disparity in shade, and it, the darkness, all sunk down heavily on my chest, as the red coals burnt my backside; all alone, locked inside a world of hate, to wit, stuck in between it, I lay, flossing my teeth...

...After a perfunctory knock, Ivy swung inside. Instantly, I put on my façade: the dark comedian who's not *too* dark because he's just so damn funny and cute that everyone wants to be his friend! Ivy was wearing tight white shorts, a tight fuchsia shirt with tight half-ass sleeves, and platform sandals. She came over, dipped down, and kissed me because she loved me. With the floss hanging down from my teeth, I did my new walrus impersonation for her. It received a bubbly giggle. She sat down flush with my midsection, asking me to touch her freshly-shaved legs. I combed my hand over both thighs at the same time...down to her knees. It panged me with melancholy and confusion. Then she dropped backwards on my midsection and began rolling around on me like a little girl would do on her daddy's stomach in those times of jocular bonding done on the living room floor. She was being really affectionate and touchy.

'So what's the plans for tonight?' she asked upside-down: her neck arched backward.

I stuck a lock of mocha in my mouth. '*POWER UP!!!*' Instantly revitalized throughout! I hummed an *I-dunno* in the squirrel voice. 'Wanna go feed the squirrels.'

'No. They don't like me.'

'How you ever gonna be a veterinarian if animals don't like you?'

'First off, I won't be working with those evil little things. I mean, you ever see how beady their eyes are? and the way they run around with their little acorns? I swe~ar~ _they're_ the Devil's animal, not snakes.'

'Well that ain't gonna stop me from bein' a squirrel when I grow up. 'N' I'm bein' seris about whad I said: I wanna squirrel suit for my birthday.' That's seriously what I asked her to find: a full-body squirrel suit simil~ar to~ the one used as the mall Easter Bunny. And I knew squirrel ones existed because I'd seen 'em in English comedy skits. Once I got a hold of one, I was living out the rest of my days inside it.

'Baby, I don't think that's happenin'. Knowin' you, you _would_ try wearin' it in public, and there's _no way_ I'm marrying a guy who walks around in a squirrel costume!'

Oh yes—_marriage_. She sporadically hinted at it; namely, the next step: pre-engagement to engagement. But that was like an interlude of _commedia_ in the haunting symphony playing upstairs. Several times, I told her that marriage wasn't even an option til after graduation, and she said that's fine but engagement is. I think Edward and Sandy were involved insofar as young but certain marriage was better than a continuance in the depravity going on outside of wedlock.

After making out 'n' 'at, I convinced Ivy that we should go to the orchard til we figured out what to do for the night. We hadn't been there since the season turned. The last time had been a brief winter trip after eating at Chow Down. Ivy seemed to like the orchard in the winter more, as if enduring the cold was a test of her fidelity. I simply liked going to the orchard _whenever:_ always had that musical sensation of secluded Nature to distract the sickening symphony upstairs: always had that blended tune of nostalgia and heaven, spinning its two weightless children around and around all year round, like a calendrical carousel...

...The sky was vast. Cotton-white. So many clouds that little distinction could be made in the form. The few things that tend be found in the sky were unified, coated over with a thick marshmallow gumminess that hid the sun well enough that you could look directly into it, for it was just a nebulous spot out there. The sun's weak effusion made all the colors around us soft and subservient. Perhaps that's why I felt a great sense of power and eminence walking through; usually the orchard (just from its size and grandeur) put into check any arrogance I carried in with me: and I appreciated that: it let me know that I could prove nothing here: and yet there was never a need, for what would it mean on the way back out? After inspection, Ivy and I each grabbed a premature green apple and decided to sit under the forefront weeping willow, which was like our way of taking a vacation from her tree. Down through the field we walked like neighborhood children in love, while the wind sung this silly song about a chipmunk that tried to ride on the back of a squirrel but kept falling off. Tongue and mushed apple in cheek, I p~art~ed back the sinewy branches like a man politely opening the door for a lady...then pinched her ass as she passed through. She squealed like that little neighborhood girl. Such sweet music!

'Can you believe it,' she began, chewing on her apple, 'we're goin' into our junior year of college? God, it's goin' by way too fast.'

'Bedder watch 'ose words 'cauzsha know yir gih'n old when ya start talkin' about how time's goin' by too fast. Stay young, stay gold, liddle girl.' Standing, I yanked a branch like I would a strand of her hair. 'So ya think yir gonna finish in four or wha'?'

'Highly doubt it.'

'Why not? I gadda chance da finish in four 'n' I'm pickin' up a second major. I think Classics—ya know, Greek 'n' Roman studies?'

'I know what Classics is,' she said in a haughty tone. Then more naturally, while chewing: 'But it's still probably gonna take me five because, one, you've taken more classes than me, and you have those extra classes from the first summer. Plus, since my classes are about to get a lot harder, I might cut back to four a semester.'

'Like mine aren't gih'n harder? I mean, all I know is, if I can graduate in four or even four 'n' a half with two degrees, den you can with one. All ya gadda do is push yirself a liddle more. I mean, whaddum I gonna do if I graduate a year before you? I won't be able da live in the dorms, 'n' I'm not tryin'ah move back da Pixburgh.'

'Well maybe we can get an apartment together.'

She was sitting with her back against the truck; I was walking around, playing with the branches, occasionally taking bites of my green apple. I wanted to swing on the branches like Tarzan, but the one time I tried, I accidentally ripped half the branch off. Ivy made it out to be like a human limb, adding that I needed to start working out because I was getting chubby, even though I—drum roll!—was now a vegetarian, yet one who ate loads of pasta and fries. So not wanting to start working out as much as she did, or change my diet any further, I just quit trying to swing from the branches like Tarzan.

'Pessi told he might be getting' a job at the mall, at Yo! Records.'

'When ju talk do him?'

'When I dropped Teresa off yesterday. He was outside washin' her car.'

'HA! Dat's about the only work that lazy fuck'll be doin'.'

'God, Vinny,' she began with a tone that suggested a quick change of subject, 'have you noticed Teresa lately? I'm actually startin' to get scared now. She's startin' to look like she *does* do it, don't you think? I just wish we could just figure out a way to get *her* into rehab.'

'Not me. I could care less what happens ta that fuckin' cunt.'

'Stop it! You know how much I hate that word.'

'Fine. That piece a fuckin' shit.'

'That's enough! You know she's goin' through a really hard time just like *Pessi* did. And her bein' your best friend's girlfriend and all , you'd think you'd at least care *a little*.'

'Nope; I don't—at all. I hope she ODs 'n' dies.'

'Don't you *ever* say anything like that again! I'm bein' serious! Get away from me! You make me so sick!'

'What?! Calm the fuck dahn, Ivy.'

'No! That's my best friend you're talkin' about!'

"At's wha' you think.'

'And what's that supposed to mean?'

Pause. Pause. 'It mean she's a worthless fuckin' junkie thit turned my best friend inda one too. Ya know, it's funny how me 'n' Pessi come from the city where there's drugs everywhere, 'n' we'd been doin' 'em for *sooo* long, 'n' yet we come da this liddle fuckin' snuburban tahn 'n' he's suddenly doin' fuckin' heroin!'

'Ya know, it's funny,' she mocked my voice, 'you'd think comin' from the city he'd have the know-how to make the better choice. So seriously shut up and quit tryin' to blame everything on Teresa.'

'I honestly can't believe you'd fuckin' stick up for her—'

'I'm not! You're the one makin' me take sides, and all I'm tryin' to say is that it's *equally* their fault, and Pessi has the free-will to make his *own* decisions.'

'Free-will! HA! No such thing when yir within a system, hun. Da revolutions of yir "wheel" turn in relation da the weight of the barrow on toppa ya 'n' the invisible hands pushin' it forward. But hey—as long as you *think* there's free-will, then that in itself must be da proof, right? I mean, *hey, look at me: I have the free-will da say I do. I have the free-will da walk around in a circle. Hey, I'm so fuckin' free! Just call me fuckin' WILL!'*

'What are you even talkin' about?—Why are you actin' like this?'

Pause. Pause. 'I dunno; prahblee the nascence of insanity...I honestly think one day I'm juss gonna fuckin' lose it. Everything's gonna flash black 'n' when I open my eyes I'm not gonna be me anymore. Someone else'll be controllin' me 'n'—I dunno.'

She stood up and came towards me. 'Seriously, hun, what's wrong? Talk about to me. You don't open up like you used to.' (Again, Used To shows up: but now in the Holy Orchard!) 'You know, like about *personal* things. I mean, is it you dad? Has that started botherin' you now or somethin'? I could see why it would.'

No, she just couldn't keep her blasphemous mouth shut! My "dad": now in the Holy Orchard! Get out! Get out! Get – the fuck – OUUUUUUUT!

'Come on, Ivy; you know that didn't bother me like it would someone else. Him dyin' was like hittin'ah loddery for a million bucks.'

'Then what is it? Your mom bein' away?'

'Again, a *good* thing: she's *happy* now. Idd be fuckin' *selfish* of me da make her stay here juss 'cause I'm here. I'm a big boy now. Certainly no fuckin' *mammone*. So that's not it either.'

'Well I dunno, Vinny! It just feels like you've been keepin' somethin' locked up. I mean, I shouldn't have to tell you that you can open up to me about anything no matter how hard you feel you have to act around everyone else.'

'How hard I *act?* I don't fuckin' *act* hard; I *am* hard. 'N' it's not sum'n I'm proud of either. Trust me: I've opened up da you way more den anyone else. It's juss a slow process for me, so chill the fuck out, ar'ight?'

'Yeah. Well I still think we don't talk like we used to,' she whispered. As Used To squalled in my ear, Ivy walked back to the trunk, doing one of her fastidious bark inspections. The subject needed changed before things got to me and I really exploded.

'Hey, ya know whadda bearcat is?'

'Yeah, it's a mongoose.'

'Wow, I'm impressed: 'at's a tough one. I saw one on *Leno* lass night. It's funny 'cause 'er neither bear *nor* cat,' I said this like a little kid. 'I sercly can't wait da turn indua squirrel, den everything'll be ar'ight. Whad animal suit you want for *yir* b-day? Whoozza squirrel gonna be matin' with?'

'Please. I told you, if you ever wore a squirrel suit, I'd disown you.'

'No. Juss pick one. I juss wanna know whachu'd be.' I ran up behind her and poked her in this ticklish spot on the small of her back. 'Tell me!'

'Stop! Hahaha! Stop! Fine! Fine! I'd be a—a—I dunno—a bearcat!'

'No, yir juss sayin' 'at 'cause it's fresh in yir mind. Pick again.' I wouldn't stop poking her til she gave a real answer.

'Haha! Stop, Vinny! Haha! Stop!'

'Den pick!'

'Fine! A kangaroo!'

"*Ere ya go, mate!*' I said in Aussie. Then, in a formal announcement: 'Whenever I, Screwy Squirrel, get tired, I can climb insijir pouch 'n' you can carry me around.' Transitioning into another voice—the one of the squirrel—I wooingly yelled, '*Roo-Roo!*' just to light up her pouch.

We kissed 'n' 'at for a while. Then we walked down to the creek to see how cold the water was. We'd yet to take a swim in it, but I had plans of throwing her in one day just to see how she'd react. Dipping my hand down in, the water was still cold from the winter. But it seemed clearer from the year before because in some places I could see rocks on the bottom that I couldn't before. Plus, I could actually *see* the fish. Even all the new ones, the little-bitty ones, getting acquainted with their new home. The mild current was sending 'em without recourse in the direction that led down to the cove...then around the bend into the wooded area beyond. Since Ivy and I had messed around for close to an hour, and the day was marching on, we were about to head back to her car. However, when I thought of her car parked on Jack's road, Jack came to mind, and the conversation continued down at the creek.

'Hey, you think Jack'll ever catch us?'

'Catch us? I'm allowed here.'

'No, I mean whad if he came hobblin' in while we were whistlin' or sum'n? That would be pretty awkward, at least for you.'

'Guess we shouldn't do that here anymore then.'

'I agree. No madder *where* we are. But sercly, I juss think tha'd be fucked up if he caught us? I can't even imagine whachu'd even say do 'im.'

Uninterested in my hypothetical, she started throwing rocks into the water.

'If he came in, wouju try da have a threesome with 'im?'

'Oh come on! You're seriously sick! He's like eighty years old!'

'Ohhh, so yir sayin' is if he'z *younger*, you would?'

'No. Not in a million years.'

'Why? It might be fun.'

'You'd actually want another guy touchin' me?'

'See, girls always gadda word it like 'at. I'm juss sayin' every now 'n' 'en 'ere's nuh'n wrong with doin' a lidde a this 'n' 'at with the person ya love. As long as it's not behin' anyone's back, it's not wrong or cheatin'. Plus, it keeps things fresh—'

'Oh, so you're sayin' you wanna have sex with other people now because things between us aren't *fresh* anymore?'

'See, I knew you were gonna say *that* too. So I'm juss gonna drop the subject 'cause it's not even an issue; a mere suggestion; juss *free-will* of thought, right?'

'You're crazy.'

'Yir lazy.'

'I'm hardly lazy.'

'Den yir flayze.'

'That's not even a word!'

'Prove it!'

'I will. When we go back, I'll have *Webster* prove it.'

'Oh please: My mom told me thit Noah Webster started readin' when he was four, 'n' he'd learned a new word every day, but when was twelve he began readin' articles in—in *Colonial Cockmaster* 'n' wound up masturbatin' til he went blind. He became *noawebbledareed,* if ya wanna pardon my French. So there; whaddaya think about yir liddle puddin'-in-the-eye now, biatch?!'

She pretended not to find that funny, even though I'd said it in such a crazy, tone-shifting, off-the-wall way in which I felt she was both amused by it and, in general, happy that I was all hers. If anything, it was conveyed through her green eyes: in the movements they made when I said those strange words: coy blinking...perplexed wondering...that returned look of I-really-don't-get-you-sometimes-but-I-really-do-love-you. I stepped down over the bank and kicked the surface of the water for no good reason. Huck Finn flashed before my eyes. I dunno why. Then a cool gust of wind swept in, and I suddenly felt romantic. I dunno why. But what I do know is that I wasn't horny in this feeling of romance. *Asexual* romance? Yes, almost that fairytale sensation where I wanted to drop all my hardness, pick Ivy up by the waist, and swing her around, while telling her all the reasons why I love her, in a poetic song—*a little ditty for the pretty kitty!* Me-OWW!

'So I's thinkin' about sum'n,' I began in a serious tone, "n' I wanchada be honest with me—do you still love me like ya *use to?* I mean, priddy soon we'll be headin' inda year three 'n' things we'll be gih'n *rilly* deep—ya know, with the time invested. I juss don't wanna get left behin' one day when all of a sudden ya decide I'm not the person you wanna be with. 'Cause I've noticed lately yir always sayin' *used to be.* You *used to be* like this 'n' you *used to be* like that—'

'Honestly, Vinny, that's exactly what I think about: how one day *I'll* be the one left behind. *You're* the one with the free-spirited personality. *You're* the one who's more inclined to want new things; not me.'

'Only insofar as I'd want new things da keep happenin' with us.'

'I dunno; that thought scares me sometimes, especially with you bein' so much smarter than me. You're gonna want someone like that soon enough.' (I gave her a curious but amused look.) 'You will! I mean, what if you suddenly come across this girl who's a genius and real sexual and likes Punk Rock? You'd leave me in a heartbeat!'

'First: don't ever compare us by wits. Yir smart as fuck, 'n' you know it. Besides, I been thinkin' about how arbitrary intelligence is anyway.'

Turning her back to me, she huffed as if I just said that comparative intelligence *was* an issue; but it really wasn't; I couldn't have asked for a brighter half!

"N' ya know wunna the reasons I'm with a girl like you 'n' not a so-called punk rocker? It's 'cause I know 'em *aaaaall* too well. Most are so fuckin' fake: all about the look; so elitist towards those who aren't. Der love for you mounts according da how many tats you get. But see, I want someone dit *lives* Punk Rock, not *looks* it. I want substance and sweetness, not juss matchin' records 'n' wild sex. Got it?'

'*Riiight,*' she replied, swinging around. 'You want someone with that look just as much as they do. It's what you're most attracted to: you even said it yourself.'

'Hun, no madder what *any* girl of *any* look or *any* belief had da offer me, idd never happen; idd juss never be enough 'cause no girl in the world has whachu do.' Briskly, I grabbed a lock of her silky mocha hair, stuck it in my mouth, and in that special funny voice let her know what only *she* possessed: '*CHEWY POWER UP HAIR!!!*'

Then I made her power up, which she'd always do with petty reluctance.

'Anyway, whaddabout *me?* So whad if I'm short, dark, 'n' handsome? 'At's no guarantee thit one day you won't leave *me*. I mean, whaddaya rilly love about *me?* Name summa da things thit hookcha from the start 'n' is still caught in yir jaw?'

'Vinny, you don't even understand. When I first met you, I was head-over hills. I'd lay on my bed and just think about you nonstop—'

'Yiiiiiiir bein' evAAAsiiive.'

'Nooo I'm nAAAOt. I still love everything aboooooout yoUUU—'

'Such as?'

'Let's see: you're smart and funny. You're a Christian but open-minded. When you spike your hair you're the most gorgeous guy in the world. And whenever you *do* decide to be romantic, you're pretty creative about it. Umm, you chilled out on the booze and stuff when I asked you to , which shows you actually care about my feelings. What more could I ask for?'

'Free—whaa-ah-ah-I won't even say it. But do ya like the power up?'

'I guess. But that's just weird.'

'No it's not. You don't even overstand it yet, do ya?'

'No, not really. But please enlighten me.'

'Sorry, can't do that. Overstanding it must come through epiphany. But lemme ask you *this:* since I'm a priddy passionate person, 'n' tenda bitch about a few things—'

'Everything!'

'Ha! No, not *everything*. But whenever I do bitch 'n' 'at, does it annoy you? I mean, is *'at* sum'n you hate about me?'

'Does it *annoy* me sometimes? Of course. Is it somethin' I *hate* about you? Not at all. If you were completely passionless, I wouldn't even be with you. I love that you care about things (even if I don't always agree with your solutions). But the fact that you love animals makes me melt knowin' I'm with a guy like that. I mean, if I met someone like you, like with your background and the way you dress, and had to guess if they loved animals enough to become a vegetarian without really *knowing* 'em, I'd automatically think, "*No way.*"'

'Well do ya like da fact thit I'm not afraid da throw a fist?'

'I—'

'Wait, before ya answer: Now thit I'm a liddle older, 'n' have more responsibilities, I wouldn't juss fight da fight like I yoostu. So whad I rilly mean is: you know if anyone ever fucked with you, I'd drop 'em in a second—I'd do whadever I gadda do da keep you safe.'

'I know that, Vinny. And it does give me a sense of security, but I just don't believe violence never solves anything.'

'Oh, it can solve things all right. Say some guy comes up da ya 'n' grabs yir tits—*BAM!*—knocked the fuck out. Then they'll think twice 'fore they do sum'n like 'at again—da *anyone.*'

'*Or* people could just raise their kids better and stuff like that wouldn't happen in the first place. Kids would grow up with more respect for people.'

'Hey, I todally agree with 'at too. But til families become healthy, we nee'dda knock people like 'at da fuck out. It's one thing da do whacha will around people ya know, but it's another da bring yir ways da someone ya *don't* know 'n' expect dill like it without rilly knowin'. 'N see, when *those* kinda people think the world's in *their* hands—well, that's when ya juss gadda raise yir own 'n' show 'em it's not.'

Ivy simply shrugged then tossed her last rock into the creek. 'Well what about me?' she delicately returned to the original issue: 'Do you still love everything about me?'

'Whaddaya think?'

'No, no. Just like you said, I want you to "name some things."'

Just then, the wind blew whimsical music into me. 'Shit, girl; I love every-mavurfuckin'-thang abouchu. *Inside-out, upside- dahn, front 'n' back; eww, girl, shake dat ass, shake dat ass...*' (She was smiling because I was "acting black" in hyperbole. From the way I'd move my body, touch up on hers, and pretend to be spittin' slick game, she'd jokingly say, 'What, are you black now?!' And the one time I said, 'I'm gih'n 'ere.') '*...da way ya move dose hips, 'n' pop dose lips. PLOP! Oh baby, you's so fine I GOTSTA make you mine!*—No doubt, shordy, I be lovin' absolutely every-mavurfuckin'-thang abouchu. Biatch.'

'Right. You mean everything *so far?*' Her tone was so ironical.

My response so musical: '*HEEEEELL NAW!*' I moved in real close, putting my hands underneath her silky elbows. 'When I say *every-mavurfuckin'-thang*, I mean *every-mavurfuckin'-thang FOREVA!...*'

Removing my right hand from her silky elbow, I made sure she witnessed how pleasurestakingly I was inserting a lickable lock into the depths of my mouth. 'Now lookie here, honkey-tits: I'm gonna prove it to ya right – *now—*' (A sudden squirrelly change of voice, but so explosive this time) '*—POWER UP!!! HMHMHMHMHM!!!...*'

BLEEDING IN MISERY

"Hammered down since the day you were born,
Misunderstood, criticized, and scorned,
The things you loved were taken and replaced,
The pain mounted and your soul was disgraced,
You tried so hard to rise to the occasion,
You turned away from the parade of evil persuasion,
To become a man that triumphed over 'never',
To overcome the pain that tries to burn on forever,
Will the pain burn on forever?!..." [1]

...I called Ma in Catania to tell her that I was going blind. The doctor gave it to me straight: 'If you keep sleeping with your contacts in, there's a serious possibility that you *will* go blind. There's also an increasing chance every time you *do* decide to take 'em out—after prolonged periods of wear—you'll tear your cornea.' In the meantime, though, the doctor gave me a stronger prescription—because the gigantic E was blurrier than the year before—and said she'd see me next year, although by then I might not be able to see her back. So knowing I was only making my eye complications worse, why would I continue sleeping with my contacts in? I dunno! Probably because I was crazy, lazy, flayze—ya know, just didn't care if I was noawebbledareed anymore! Ma reminded me how she'd warned me a thousand times not to wear my contacts to bed. But she's the one who really needed admonished. See, she told me that she'd saved up some money from her job as the neighborhood babysitter/maid, then sent the money to Aunt Stella to make payments on outstanding telephone, gas, and electric bills from the box, which was now three-quarters sunken into the ground. That's when I finally decided to come out with my intentions, and Ma was happy about it when I did; it grounded her further into her roots. I told her fuck all those bills and let 'em pile sky-high because as soon as I graduate Ivy and I are moving to Catania. I'm going to be a writer, one who needs no specific place to work, and Ivy's going to be a veterinarian, and she might have to travel around at times, but together we'll take care of everything *over there*. Whatever's left behind *here* can remain unrequited and unresolved because that's how everything else works. So *my* ticket to the sky was also on its way, in a couple years...

...Aristod's classical campus was a nice place to be in the summer: most classes done, less students around! While enjoying that cozy sensation of loss for the tenth time—ten days into the 2001 summer classes—I was strolling along the white coiling pathway, just having left Dr. Rosenbaum's class. He said to stop by his office after his next class so we could catch up. In the nicetime, I planned to spend some time with my future brethren: the

---

[1] Lyrics from "The Parade of Evil Persuasion" by Bare Knuckle Discussion, from the album *Tales from the Victim Vault*

squirrels! I guess everything was finally starting to fall into place: Ivy and I were going to get married, which would have to be done in LaSalle so as not to leave on a bad note with the royal family. Then I'll put on my squirrel suit, board the plane, and fly to Catania, where I'll become a writer, financially living off the European market, and dietarily off the local acorns and hazelnuts: *yum, ghiandi ie nuciddi siciliani!* As for Pessi? Well, I was just waiting for Teresa to die so I could include him in the plans with more certainty.

Back behind Philemon, under the shade of a mighty green oak, I sat down on a white bench. I was prepared for times like this because I started keeping a bag of mixed nuts in my backpack, in the pouch where you're supposed to put your pens, pencils, and calculator. With the bag resting in my lap, I looked around for potential human interlopers—NONE! So I shook the bag out in the air to let the nuts rattle. They'd be coming soon! (Any choler that any squirrel might've once had with me was now gone; each one really did know and love me; I could do whatever I wished without 'em displaying any temper or timidity!)

The new June air, filled with expanding bugs, had a light breath of moist earth around its expanded buds. Up above, 'the sun was warm; the sky was clear,' as Shelley would say.[2] Just real nice out, ya know. As soon as I lit up a cigarette, my thigh started vibrating: that intrusive cell phone! I answered; it was Ivy seeing if I wanted to have lunch. I wasn't hungry, and didn't plan on going, but I conned her into meeting me at the bench so we could further discuss it; I just wanted her to watch me with the squirrels. While awaiting her arrival, I finished the smoke, threw in a piece of gum, and continued feeding those fuzzy little heathens.

'Hop like a kangaroo, Roo-Roo!'

'I'm not hoppin'!'

Nope, once Ivy was in sight, and I told her that, she didn't hop the rest of the way; she walked in the manner she usually did: slightly, just ever so slightly, like a duck; after the one time I braved to make *that* comparison (in jest), I learned never to do it again (seriously!); thus, to prevent getting slapped upside the head again, she walked exactly like a runway model thereafter. Gracefully, she sat down on the bench and slightly, just ever so slightly, puckered out her protrusive lips for a kiss. But I said, 'Nope. No kiss unless ya feed the squirrels.' Emphatically, she dug down into the bag of nuts. Pulled out a handful. Then blindly tossed 'em out to the side. 'There! Now kiss me.' Since she'd grabbed so many nuts, I was so turned on that I frenched her!

'See, Woo-Woo: dat's Screwy, Stewy, 'n' Spewy.' I pointed out to the first squirrels to arrive. *'Wook! Wook! It's Chewy Chipmunk! He don't wike Screwy 'cause Screwy don't even know whadda million times a billion is!...'* (Whenever I was around the squirrels [and chipmunks], nearly everything I said was in that quirky, cartoonish voice: so energized and huffy and full of nonsensical statements. And like a little kid, it consequently altered pronunciations. For instance, a word that starts with TH- usually came out

---

[2] "The breath of the moist earth is light around its unexpanded buds...the sun was warm; the sky was clear," from Percy Bysshe Shelley's poem *Stanzas Written in Dejection near Naples*

as F, and Ls and Rs frequently became Ws or Ys; such as, wook, I'm ownwee fwee years ode. Also, the middle of words were emptied out and filled in with "whine," glides, and sometimes an exaggerated ch-sound.) *Screwy said he ate free seahawks, 'n' a wahrus, 'an''an''an''an' 'N' 'EN HE ATE AHWEE AHDER!!! HMHMHMHMHM!!!—'*

'Are we going to lunch or not?'
'Screwy says I'm not awowed.'
'Stop. Are we goin' or not? I'm hungry and I have class again in like an hour.'

A very tattletale tone: *'Screwy says he's gonna bang you.'*
'Well tell Screwy if he tries, I'll kick him in the nuts.'
I laughed and pulled out of the voice. 'Well played, squirrel hater.'
'Well are we goin' or not?'
'I dunno; I'm not rilly hungry, 'n' I gadda meet Dr. Rosenbaum soon.'
In a huff, she turned away, her hands clawing her naked knees.
'Wha' inna F is wrong with you, Roo-Roo?'
'Nothin'. I just wanted to go to lunch with you: that's all.'
'Well my man onna inside said der gonna be servin' lunch again tamarra, all over da place.'
'But I had somethin' I wanted to tell you—like *now*—and I wanted to do it in a private setting.'
'*A private setting?* Wha' inna F do you caw this?' I used my hands to present the glimmering greenness. As I continued opening up the vista through the V of my arms, the scattered yellowness of dandelions shot into my eyes with authority. Seemed to be the first time I made the connection how cosmopolitan they were, as if never noticing 'em before in Pittsburgh, the place that (by design, ethos, and narrative) was nothing like LaSalle. *It's all da same? All juss THIS? Juss WEEDS?* Trying to shake off the sensation of the absurd, I did a quick fling with the V as if conducting the choir of birds to commence. 'Come on: juss spit it out.' I moved back into the voice, secretive now: *'(Screwy won't tell anyone.)'*

She let out a deep, ever so slightly annoyed, breath. 'Fine, Vinny. My parents aren't likin' the idea of us goin' up to Niagara Falls—'

Mad, almost-twenty-years-old voice: 'You fuckin' seris?! Dey didn't have a problem with us goin' anywhere else 'n' stayin' alone.'

'Oh yes they did; I just defied them. Now they're tellin' me that if I'm gonna be goin' all over the place with you, and spendin' the night in hotels all the time, then I better be gettin' engaged—I better start takin' on *all* the responsibilities of bein' an adult.'

I laughed. 'You akshly think I'm gonna fall for that? Yir juss tryin'ah trick me inda gih'n ya a ring so you can go around showin' everyone.'

'No I'm not! And who am I gonna show? Teresa? But if you don't believe me, ask 'em yourself. My dad's not happy *at all.*'

'Ya know; I juss don't fuckin' get that guy. I mean, yir almost twenty years old; he don't control you anymore. 'N' I've done nuh'n—absolutely *nuh'n*—where dey shouldn't trust me. It sercly makes me so fuckin' mad. It's time dey cutchir fuckin' cord 'n' gimme some fuckin' respect.'

'Hey, then you go tell 'em that. I mean, I might not agree with 'em either, but that's just the way our family is. And I'm not gonna keep defyin' 'em and end up losin' my family over somethin' that can be so easily settled...Really, Vinny, I don't think it's *too* much to ask to be engaged. I feel pathetic that I practically have to *beg* you. But you say I'm twenty years old now, so maybe you should be ready to treat me like one.'

Dismissively, I went back to tossing out nuts to my heathen brethren. There were five now. And they were bumbling, fumbling, and stumbling over the nuts. Chasing each other around and around, swatting tails. Zipping up and down trees. Into bushes at will. Gradually, I could feel the simper come to my face as I slipped into a reverie about being a little kid...*far away: lost in innocence, down on dry grass...chewing on things, dirt, flinging pebbles...digging holes, own nation...covering holes, trapped invisible beings...silly noises, laughter...ear to the ground, calmness...no worries, nothing...innocence, alone, dirt, nothing at all—*

'Hello!'

'What?!'

'Nothin'! I have to go now so I can go eat by myself! Maybe I'll meet someone who cares enough about me to understand the situations *I* have to deal with.' She shot up, and began booking down the white coiling path.

'Good luck with 'at! 'N' if you *do* meet that special guy, make sure ya send me a wedding invitation! If ya meet 'im taday, I betcha can getchirself in 'at gahn 'n' dahn the aisle by Christmas!' Before I got it all out, she was already far down the path, slightly, ever so slightly, furious...

...I walked into Dr. Rosenbaum's office. It was a rather small room for a professor of tenure. The walls were celadon (a pale sea-green), adorned with three educational promo-posters, which promoted Dr. Rosenbaum's self-imposed irony: for who else would ever be influenced by 'em besides those with degrees or already in the process? The rest of the furniture-polish-scented office was disorganized with books, papers, and folders piled on the shelves behind him and on his desk where a computer was pushed off to his right, the window side. With his red tie slackened, he had his face pushed down into a paper even though he was wearing his small invisible glasses. He blindly motioned for me to sit down in my usual seat, putting three-feet of cluttered but low-lying woods between us.

'Interesting,' he said seconds later. He took his glasses off and handed me the paper. It was a memorandum from Harvard stating *Nigger of the Narcissus* was now banned from their curriculum, and they're encouraging the other seven Ivy League schools, along with other top private schools, to do the same. That's how the pecking-order of education works. Typically, Ivy League with Stanford and MIT (the exceptions but for all practical purposes part of the League) sends "the word" to other private schools, whereby Academic Diffusion begins by letting it be known what knowledge *is*, as well as what knowledge is *proper* for the times. It goes back to when I first met Ivy and discussed the concept of the "trendy intellectual" where those trying to revive Nietzschean thought were doing so against the grain of those dictating the trends, as if education is an article of clothing to be worn accordingly! (A fitting analogy: Ivy League : other private schools : public universities = Paris : New York City : Stamford.) Before leaving for college, I read about the "trendy intellectual" in a journal at the library, authored by a distinguished Ivy League professor. And this dictation of educational dos-and-donts usually comes from the professors with seniority, on the boards, and published outside the university press. Collectively, they wear white horsehair wigs and black silkworm robes—if I may speaketh in that manner, and if I may maketh no sense at all just to starteth a new trend. Order! Order! Order!

'"It is obvious how one could easily find the title of the work disparaging to African-Americans,"' I began reading aloud sections of what I'd just skimmed silently. '"In no way are we implying Conrad was a racist. But since we are in a time when our country is still suffering from racial injustices, while claiming to be an egalitarian state, we, as the leaders of education, must fulfill our civic duties by paying more attention to where modern racist attitudes may be deriving from...Recently, several African-Americans students complained that the work is causing unneeded stress and awkwardness in the classroom. Furthermore, they allege that they have caught several Caucasian students tittering at the mention of the word "nigger." Although no professor has yet to witness such inappropriate behavior, the veracity of these allegations should not be undermined or dismissed...Perhaps it is harder from a Caucasian's perspective to understand"—Ar'ight, enougha dishit.' Looking at Dr. Rosenbaum, I rubbed my hand over my face as if I was part of the Aristod faculty about to go to into a heated debate with the opposition. 'I mean, personally I think Conrad's overrated as a writer, but that's not the issue: seems we're either dealin' with immature white yuppies, or my hunch, black liars thit juss have a problem with it 'cause Conrad was white. If Baldwin's name was on the spine, idd be a whole different story. I mean, not da sound racist, Dr. Rosenbaum, but I think 'ezz blacks nee'dda quit thinkin' 'ey own slices of language. All they're rilly doin' is exhumin' the hate within the word. Relinquishin' 'er power over it. Obliterating History 'n' the collective memory for their own selfish reasons. Thinkin' you got hereditary entitlements in language is juss another form of superiority. Sercly, why is it some blacks think their own sensitivity doesn't exist in anyone else, 'specially not in whites who've—I dunno. You think Aristod's akshly gonna comply?'

'Who knows. Thing is, no one here has taught Conrad in years. The nucleus of the problem seems to be Kennedy's new book *Nigger: The Strange Career of a Troublesome Word.* He's a professor of Law at Harvard. He wrote the book with the hope that we'd take a look *behind* the word and into world of *etymology* and *context.* But since most understand neither, the protests are growing and leaking elsewhere. Ironic that he wanted to lessen the fear in tackling the word, and now it looks like it will all come to be for future reference: fear works with offensive titles and works that use epithets "inappropriately," as the memorandum states. So—'

'So context 'n' message don't count anymore? Vernacular don't count anymore? I sercly don't get it. Don't both blacks 'n' whites thit claim *not* da be racist see that this *is* racist. It's a form of segregation: it *differentiates* in manner where we gadda be a liddle more careful around blacks. I think if we're *truly* equal now, den we can only look back collectively at doze cawed "niggers" as *everyone's* brothers 'n' sisters, *everyone's* painful memory. 'N' yet why do I feel like shit for be—' (*cough* cough* cough* *cough* cough* cough*) '—for believin' in whad I say?' (*HACK!*)

'Need some water there?' Dr. Rosenbaum joked.

I managed to emit a sputter of laughter. My face had to be beet red.

'Maybe you should debate it in lieu of me because I'm certainly not up for it.'

I coughed, but this time in preparation. 'Nah. Ya know, maybe they *should* ban it from the classroom: give us another chance dahn the line da learn from our mistakes. 'N' maybe everyone *should* caw black Americans "African-Americans" since 'er so special, so sensitive, 'n' so in touch with an African culture dit's nuh'n like their life here. I think sometimes we forget how Black History Month tends da highlight da achievements of doze in the celeber sphere, 'n' not dose who *rilly* battled shit out. It's like every February all I see is Holly Cherry 'n' Gil Smitt glorifyin' 'er peddy accomplishments but makin' sure 'ey link it da MLK, Malcolm Little, 'n' Big Rosa P. I mean, nuh'n against 'em or anything bahcha *rarely* hear about people like Akhenaton, St. Benedict the Moor, Edward Wilmot Blyden, Jane Bolin, August Wilson—or even the ol' white-African Albert Camus!'

'*Akhenaton?*' he inquired with a look of concern.

'Yeah, Akhenaton was 'iss revolutionary king of Egypt. Sometimes considered the founder of monotheism. He basically uprooted ancient religion 'n' gave it the structure it has taday. But how many people are taught *that* when talkin' about systematic Christianity? Or thit there were tons of non-black slaves for longer periods of times 'n' under worse conditions than black slaves in America. Or juss the simple honesty thit the exclusion 'n' segregation subtly promoted through things like Black History Month 'n' 'iss limelight we put on pseudos like Gil Smitt 'n' Marley Hartley is *not* wha' we as a nation have fought for. It's like I gadda fuckin' square white boy from the suburbs 'n' a dumb racist jock tryin'ah tell me howda treat *them* right 'n' live *my* life when 'ey dunno the first thing about shhhit. I swear it's so fuckin' pathetic thit we'll go inda race wars over a fuckin' word but won't even give a ~~quarter~~ of that energy for things like improvin' health care or endin' poverty.'

'*Hmmm. Akhenaton,*' he repeated in self-whisper as if he was busy running the reels of his memory to see if amnesia was now in effect.

'Oh well, fuck it. But ya know what? I think *I* should file complaints too. See, I wanna be cawed an *Avezzano-Abruzzese-Taliano-Catanisi-Sicilianu-Vernanite-Pixburgher-Pennsylvanian-United-Statesian-American-~~Earthling!~~*'N' hey, I have juss as much da right da complain 'cause I grew up in the same conditions as poor urban blacks, 'n' I have Sicilian ancestors thit suffered oppression from many, many countries for *three thousand years*, 'n' still continue to! I mean, you'd think when Italy annexed Sicily in 1860, they woulda been the most sympathetic towards Sicilians; but no! Can't let 'em have 'er own identity! Banned 'er own language from 'er schools! 'N' wha' can you do about it when ya don't have the resources, education, 'n' power? I mean, Palermo tried revoltin' against it in (I think) 1866, 'n' the fuckin' Italian Navy bombed 'em! Ma told me thit alawda Sicilians tried revoltin', but Italy issued marshal law 'n' took prisoners 'n' destroyed villages. 'N' 'en from 'at rose the Mafia, 'n' now ya got fuckin' "Italian-Americans"—deez, uhh, blind-priders wavin'ah green, white, 'n' red around without overstandin' the history, culture, 'n' the poor motherfuckers who, whether in Sicily or New York, gadda live under the fear of tyrants. Dey think it's a fuckin' joke—sum'n'ah be proud of—sum'n'ah *associate* with.' I paused. 'Ehh, sorry if it sounds like I'm goin' off on *you*, Dr. Rosenbaum. I'm juss gih'n rilly fed up with everything.'

'Ehh, Dr. Vallano,' he sighed dismissively. 'This is why I invite you into my relief-box: you give the vocal cords of my brain a breather.'

Things died down like a *carillons à musique* making its last crank, with the last chime one to reflect upon. The moment had been a spark-'n'-spat of passion-'n'-parody, forgoing the complex-irony Dr. Rosenbaum would've used. We glanced out the window to make sure no outsider had been eavesdropping and heard those vicious words lest we be hung by our tongues. To be sure, it was the most heated I'd ever been in front of Dr. Rosenbaum and I didn't even know why. It's not something I'd premeditated, for I was blindsided with the issues; and looking back, there would be alterations not only to my views but also the presentation of those views. However, how's that possible when it's unscripted words only left in the minds of the two who heard 'em?

Thankfully, *Nigger of the Narcissus* was just the thing to have mentioned because, after all the colors melted away, it was a clear segue to talk about me, someone who had become blacker than ink, on the inside.

'Question: so I been feelin' the urge da start my first extensive work, but I'm alriddy stuck on a few things 'n' need some direction.'

'Sure. First, don't start a sentence by stating you're gonna ask a question without askin' a question.'

'Well in light of race talks, I finely see why the Jews run the comedy industry. You must be workin' behinda *second* set of curtains 'cause I never even heard of *you*.'

He throat-laughed, as he reclined back in his flexible swivel chair. Scratching at his stubbled jaw, he dryly said, 'So my main man is finally ready to tour his forces.'

'I guess. But it's funny the word *narcissus* was brought up 'cause 'at's wunna the concepts I'm contemplatin' 'fore I even drop a word.'

'You mean *narcissism?*'

'Yeah. Here, lemme stream summa my thoughts: Is the narcissist only capable of self-love? Izza problem with the narcissist their *confidence* 'n' *honesty*, or rather their *cocksureness* 'n' *delusion?* 'If in fact dey only comprise the former set, den aren't dose *virtues* 'n' not *problems?* 'n' 'erefore it's everyone else's *denial* thit's the *rill* problem? Here's my hypothetical: First lemme say thit I've always thought one requirement of the genius is da be udderly honest, never modest. So say ya gadda guy who invents da infallible flyin' car. Everyone would caw 'im a *genius*. No one would doubt it since his invention has such stand-alone significance; it exists outside opinion insofar as his work *is* an incredible tangible invention; it's uses are another madder. But now say ya gadda creative writer who can tackle *many* issues, all of which have 'at philosophic nature people are so quick da equate with *opinion*. Dere's nuh'n tangible about their work besides the book itself, so it's like *after* they're done, 'ey still gadda get dose sells. If they're lucky, they might be dubbed a genius by those who "get it," or agree on a moral level, even if wha' they've done required more exertion den the scientist 'cause not only did they hafta gauge 'er heart 'n' mind on the inside but they also hadda look outward in their calculations: it's truly an all-inclusive, complex process. 'N' face it: makin' things purely out of material substance—it's *all* rationalizations, even if the person *does* have a *passion* for it; it's parochial 'n' very well could prove da be a provisional benefit for society since technology always changes, or rather piles up. But human emotions don't work like 'at; they don't evolve historically; they're innate; 'n' even if 'er mutable in the individual, in the external network, dey've functioned the same since the beginning. Now comin' back da my point here: literary writers are usually shit on. I always hear people say' 'ey mean nuh'n' da the functioning-society, 'n' change nuh'n in a practical sense. 'N' 'er kinda right. Any significance ~~Art~~ has is either unseen, unmentioned, or undermined. So what good's ~~Art~~ if there's no praxis? 'n' if there is, it's always so far dahn the road when the old problems once addressed by the ~~artists~~ are finely acknowledged by the masses but are now under the pile of all the new shit thit's accumulated since 'en? I mean, is ~~Art~~ juss a reflection twice-removed like Plato said? or how Aristotle said ~~Art~~ is imitation of our actions? But if ya think about it, that in itself doesn't require any further action in the reaction da ~~Art~~. It's priddy much useless except for sensual reasons. I mean, right now I'm kinda agreein' with Tolstoy's ~~Art~~ is *not* for our pleasure or amusement—ya know, what Gautier would say is *"l'~~art~~ pour l'~~art~~"*[3]—but rather ~~Art~~ is a very serious madder.'

'Actually,' Dr. Rosenbaum calmly interrupted, 'it was Victor Cousin who said *"l'~~art~~ pour l'~~art~~"*—not Gautier. And Tolstoy wouldn't have been too amused or pleasured to know that one day historians would claim that he perhaps borrowed his serious point from his contemporary, Paul Gauguin, who said, "~~Art~~ is either plagiarism or revolution." Personally, I'm not sure who was the plagiarist and who was the revolutionary.'

'Well, either way, I juss don't get it: if we can clearly see in hindsight dis pattern of apathy 'n' passivity all throughout History, 'n' how it's hurtin' us, which ~~Art~~ "reflects" or "imitates" so brilliantly, den why not take a more aggressive stand *now?* Why's it narcissistic for the great ~~artist~~ da be blunt about bein' the *true* comprehensive genius? the one with a manifold of disciplines at der disposal? the one who *truly* cares about the welfare of humanity? who's not juss tryin'ah make a livin' or give people materialistic luxury? Da way I see it: dis modest 'n' passive nature ~~artists~~ tend da have has only gotten us where? whozza ones *rilly* bein' heard? Sure, ~~artists~~ might never be silenced as long as 'ey can produce their ~~art~~. But our *soul*, past 'n' present, *is*. I mean, is 'iss sercly the way Life's saposta be: dis never-endin' resistance?—dis fight thit's not bein' won but dey continue da say never give up 'cause one day it *will* be won? 'N' why da fuck does shit like Tom Clancy sell over 'n' over, but never Thomas Mann? Why's Mann's work uncool for the younger generations 'n' considered irrelevant for today's issues? Why do those chompin' bias idiots on TV get da tell us about politics, but never Chomsky? Whyzza soldier *always* the hero, but *never* the pacifist? See, Dr. Rosenbaum, 'ezzer summadda things I juss don't get. Wha' do we gadda lose at dis point? 'N' why are deez very words comin' oudda my mouth those of the narcissist? the misanthropist? the fuckin' "traitor"? Yes! the subversive one *must be* the enemy here! 'N' ya know, it kinda does make ya feel like you *are* evil, thit you *are* wrong, or at da very least, as many like da say, "Juss – not – ril – lis – tic."' Ahh – so – breath – less!

---

[3] [fre] ~~Art~~ for ~~Art~~'s sake

'Hmm...' He scratched around on his silvery face, rocked his head around, and breathed in some idiosyncratic breathes before responding. 'Certainly all legitimate concerns, Vallano. Nothin' I've never thought of myself. But are these your *real* concerns with *writing?* What does Chomsky not bein' heard have to do with you creating a̶r̶t?'

'I dunno; guess I'm afraid iddle happendda me: like everything I do will be done in vain.'

'Then don't take your fear intravenously; juss swallow it whole.'

'You know whadda mean: I juss don't wanna be misoverstood, or worse, *ignored.* Even if I wrote a book thit akshly got published, I'd prahblee get lambasted by the critics, den the masses would fall in line, 'n' 'ere my history would be written: Vincent Vallano, the crazy "outsider." People juss *love* da find truth in numbers. It's like the rapist is in the right if nine says he is 'n' only one thit says he's not; the bulk majority the sane, the few who stray the insane.'

'So what is it you're lookin' for—*easy fame?'* he asked with a calm smile.

'No, fame alone would suffice. I'll gladly give away all da money 'n' privilege 'at comes along with it. I juss wanna remain me 'n' know I'll have *some* significance outside of people *like* me. I'm not tryin'ah preach ta da choir. I wanna reach people *not* like me, which,' I laughed, 'would be nearly everyone. But it's like Hawthorne said in the intro da *The Scarlet Letter:* "It's a good lesson—though it may often be a hard one—for a man who's dreamed of literary fame, 'n' of makin' for himself a rank among the world's dignitaries by such means, da step aside oudda the narrow circle in which he claims are recognized, 'n' find how udderly devoid of significance, beyond that circle, is all that he achieves, 'n' all that he aims at."'

'Ha! Yes, that's certainly the sad but true realization for the a̶r̶tist. And, hell, Vallano, that might be your best use of a quote yet! Sure beats that Rousseau you tried on me—the first one ever. Remember?' (We laughed.) 'But question: how in the hell do you remember all these passages and be able to bring 'em up in the most timely fashion? It's really remarkable. Hey! there ya go! That's somethin' you can be narcissistic about,' he joked energetically. But quickly shifting back into the dry tone: 'I've seen it in books and movies with super pedagogues, but never met anyone in person who could do it as much and as well as you.'

'Well much thanks. But I dunno; I cheat a liddle. My memory isn't *that* good. See, whenever I come across a sentence or a passage thit strikes me, I'll read it like five da ten times, reflect on it for a while, think about its relevance outside its literary context, den read it like five more times til I feel like iddle stay in my memory. 'N' the remarkableness of it is seein' if its value was as true as I thought. Most fade, but a few stick. Like I can still quote verbatim about ten opening 'n' closing lines da summa my favorite works. I'm in love with great quotes. I'd prahblee engage one if I wasn't so sure thit our marriage would end up bein' terse. Ya gahdeeny favorite quotes?'

Suddenly, Dr. Rosenbaum spun around in his chair like a little kid: one of his capricious gestures that he'd do just to, so to speak, keep you on the edge of your seat. 'You know what: a few minutes ago you mentioned how a majority has nothing to do with the truth, which brings to mind what I guess I'd consider one of my favorite quotes. It's by ol' Samuel Adams.'

'The revolutionary or brewmaster?' I joked—but not sure if there's a difference.

'I'm not even sure if there's a difference. Is there?'

'Beats me. But, hey, if they're one 'n' the same, then what's bedder then a drunken revolutionary?'

'Well, whatever or whichever, he said, "It doesn't require a majority to prevail, but rather an irate, tireless minority keen to set brush fires in people's minds." Kinda reminds me of you.'

'You callin' me an arsonist?'

'You callin' me a firefighter?'

I vaddled, feeling as far away from the heat as possible. 'Don't worry, Dr. Rosenbaum; I'll getcha one a deez days, 'n' when I do it's gonna be a fuckin' blaze.'

'That's fine; I'll just seek refuge inside the *cool* bulk majority.'

I dunno where it came from, but he flung a gumband at me. I picked it up and played with it, getting back on target.

'So whaddaya think about me tryin'ah reach an audience who'd prahblee hate me, 'n' yet, from my end, not do it in a purely antagonistic, "political" way?'

'Let me begin by sayin' that I've never written anything outside poetry and short stories, all of it very amateurish. I write just to see some smoggy reflections and leave it at that. But if I know you, you're gonna be tryin' to make your ~~art~~ like a freshly-polished mirror. And I would think you, as a writer who's gonna be slugging through these long periods of torture, would not be so concerned with the effects your work will have on the world nor what audience you may gain. Shouldn't your main concern with *the process of creating* ~~art~~ be with figuring out how to get it *out of* you and not *into* others? Just finding that black grain and then polishing it til it looks as bright and as big as the sun can be the most rewarding thing of all. I know you're really diggin' Romanticism, right?'

'Yeah, I kinda considered that: writin' a Romantic novel but with my own stylistic touches, 'specially since I'm ~~startin~~'ah see how intellectualism outsida one's self is shit.'

'Ahh! Well, Vallano, I think I really got you on this one. Now isn't this renowned genius you just referred to—you know, the one who everyone admires, who gets to draw upon all audiences, who gets to live lavishly his accomplishments in the here-and-now—so to speak, the non-Chomskies—aren't those geniuses defined solely according to their *brain?*'

'No,' I replied confidently, while mentally backtracking through what I'd said.

'Sure they are! You just said the outward intellect is shit, but you also wanna be *called* a genius, and yet the genius is entirely based on the brain insofar as it all comes from outer perspective, which is contrary to your discovery that "intellectualism outside of one's self is shit."' Just then, to prove his point, he pulled out a large dictionary and read five definitions of *genius*, all of which related to the brain in one way or another, without, contrary to Romanticism, mention of the ~~heart~~ and its qualities. 'So maybe you should abandon this idea of the genius if you think intellectualism is arbitrary, manipulated, and over- or undervalued by those who look upon it. Now, Vallano, I never been one to give strict definitions, but to be a

Romantic is, in essence, to quit worrying about the outside world, insofar as thinkin' the aftermath of your art is what holds all value. Don't worry about how smart people may think you are, for their power of judgment is just as skewed as yours is to theirs; it's all, so to speak, pulled from the dictionary.' He held it up for effect. 'So let 'em all go or else they'll only bleed you dry and fill you back up with misery. See, the world has a way of working itself out for future fates—and perhaps its *final* fate—that no one genius, good or evil, will ever be able to control. *That Dame Fortune is a bitch like that.'*

(I laughed at his shift in tone, while knowing the reference and getting the pun.)

'Maybe when you begin your work,' he continued, 'you should let the reader see your protagonist as someone they'll love to hate, or as someone they, the reader, feels must feed off their "listening-in." Give the reader that sense of power over your character. And then, as the story goes on—give it all up! Yes! give up all fears of not bein' heard, all notions of someone "listening-in." Quit tryin' so hard to change a world you're no longer a part of. Don't even take the time to swat the flies. Just fall away from it all. Turn to the *inner-life of emotion,* and seek your value *there.* And don't stress over tryin' to produce exact imitation because perhaps it's all an illusion anyway. Try finding the *unseen* things: what we tend to believe is the *real* illusion, but what Kant referred to as the *metaphysical,* or the real Reality—*Nature;* that's where I think the essence of Art lies; not in the superficial, or on the surface, but underneath in the *intangible.*

'That's my advice, Vallano: *don't kill yourself tryin' to become a fly-flap.* Just relax, fall away, and seek your genius for your own sake, not for the sake of any insight it might provide others. Everyone on the outside will soon disappear anyway. Everything they think, say, and do will no longer matter—not to you as the artist or you as one embodied in your characters. Their laws, religions, convictions, and lifestyles you'll no longer seek to change whenever you're involved in producing art in *this* manner because you'll be so far inside yourself that you won't even see how it affects someone like you, the person so embedded in their pure emotions.'

After a long reflective pause, I chose not to rejoinder...

...From minutes later to the two weeks later of the present, there could be but one result of that conversation: Dr. Rosenbaum's words weighed heavily on my mind, not my heart, for I had yet to fall into the state of the artist in the toil; thus, I could only *think* about the grand feeling of liberation, not *feel* the grand feeling of liberation. Alwaysthemore, I now had the "directions" to trek in the right direction. 'Question: so I been feelin' da urge da start my first extensive work, but I'm alriddy stuck on a few things 'n' need some direction.' – 'Turn to the *inner-life of emotion,* and find your value *there.'* That's how amazing Dr. Rosenbaum was when looking back at what he just did to you; it was another instance where I wanted to run back to his office to let him know the phantasmal puzzle started doing it again right before my eyes! But sometimes, I must admit, Dr. Rosenbaum's modes of thinking were far too complex for me. In the midst of it all, I was always worried that I wasn't getting the *real* point. I also began wondering if perhaps he *had* written masterpieces but neither spoken of nor published 'em because, to be Vallanic about it, it would mutilate the essences of the works whenever another hand takes a malicious strike at it; even the most benign set of eyes are fated to alter essences and corrupt purity.

To me, a work of a̶r̶t̶ (in which the a̶r̶t̶ist has cathected the human quintessence in blood) takes on a humanlike existence in its own right, from which an outsider can change, and *always* takes pa̶r̶t̶s away from, its essence. The a̶r̶t̶ist and their a̶r̶t̶, as one, are both hurt or healed accordingly by the outside world, for a work of a̶r̶t̶ can *only* be separated from the a̶r̶t̶ist in the physical; and in this respect, it's much the same as a photograph of the a̶r̶t̶ist (or anyone else) where, when given or taken away, it creates that abysmal fragmentation and incompleteness. This notion of what effects us and in what manners is illustrated brilliantly in the song "Marked" by Bad Religion. In the song, Greg Gaffin sings about how everything, big or small, ultimately effects us, not just on the surface where it might be manifest in our demeanor, but also deep within where you never really know about the significance of a "mark" until you take an introspective look at it. Therefore—(under the assumption that a work of a̶r̶t̶ can't be hidden, and we ourselves can neither seek protection nor abscond from the outside world)—if A̶r̶t̶ *is* Us, and a "mark" effects Us, then a "mark" must also effect A̶r̶t̶ in the same manner with the same consequences. Now even though I don't always see eye-to-eye with Bad Religion's philosophies—seeing as Greg Gaffin's a Biological-Humanist, and I'm of the Mythical-Godist sort—I'm still going to share the song in its entirety because it has a phenomenal non-linear narrative that I think, with healthy reflection, can open up how one views the world underneath the straight-forward hustle that we're all pa̶r̶t̶ of, and you could even say guilty of staying chained to. And if anyone is in a rush and has a problem with this disruption from the linear, speak up because I'm not listening.

"If I'm a **MONSTER**, I'm a **WILLING ONE**,
This roller **coaster** ride **is** an **enticing** one,
On the tip of a continuum flowing wavelike through disorder,
carry me like a vessel to water~~~~~~~~~~
EVERYTHING YOU SEE LEAVES A MARK ON YOUR SOUL
EVERYTHING YOU FEEL LEAVES A MARK ON YOUR SOUL
EVERYTHING YOU TOUCH LEAVES A MARK ON YOUR SOUL
EVERYTHING YOU MAKE LEAVES A MARK ON YOUR SOUL

If I can touch it, I can destroy it,
If it's imaginable to some degree, I can become it.
Like a hungry turning vortex that just flickers to existence, consuming bits
and pieces until I'm finally extinguished——————
EVERYONE YOU SEE LEAVES A MARK ON YOUR SOUL
EVERYONE YOU BARE LEAVES A MARK ON YOUR SOUL

EVERYONE YOU TOUCH LEAVES A MARK ON YOUR SOUL
EVERYONE YOU LOVE LEAVES A MARK ON YOUR SOUL
EVERYTHING YOU TAKE LEAVES A MARK ON YOUR SOUL
EVERYTHING YOU GIVE LEAVES A MARK ON YOUR SOUL

AND ALL THE FEAR AND LONELINESS THAT'S IMPOSSIBLE TO CONTROL
(AND EVERY TEAR YOU CRY) LEAVES A MARK ON YOUR SOUL"

Reeeeeeeeeeeeeeeeeeeeefffffffffffffffflllllllllllllleeeeeeeeeeeeeeeeeect

The following weekend Ivy and I drove up to Niagara Falls. No snakes attacked me—well, not literally. But it had been another defiant stand against her venomous parents, which, to me, had hardly been a stand of defiance, and it wouldn't have been to them either if Ivy had been wearing a diamond on her finger that emitted a blinding sparkle like the waterfalls we could see from our hotel room. The room itself was breathtaking: twenty-two floors up in a building that was real skinny in the middle because there were no floors between the first and twentieth. When I walked into the room, the entire wall before us was sheer glass, right above the misty Horseshoe Falls. To the left I could see American Falls, Bridal Veil Falls, and the plains far out beyond. I almost passed out at first-sight: that's how hard it hit me.

Well, we had a pretty good time during the days (doing all the tourist crap)...til the nights came. See, I wanted to gamble all Ivy's money away; and it worked the first night. Then she cut me off the second night. So I decided to stick my new credit card into the ATM, taking out $500 in cash-advance. Why did that bother her so much? I dunno. But she went back to the hotel for the night, while I, sitting around the rest of the degenerates, smoking, drinking, and bullshitting, turned that $500 into over $1,500. Why did it still bother her so much when she found out in the morning? I dunno. But I was coming back across the border with enough money to finally contribute to Pessi's rehab bill and have a little something for myself, along with gaining a priceless feel for the phenomenality of a waterfall—and that's all it had been: a feeling, trapped. No matter if down in the water on a boat, or standing level with the top of the waterfalls, or far above in the hotel, it was like watching and listening to an infinite amount of poetry pouring down over the crest in a deafening gush, like the constant crash of thunder where you think you'd finally "wake up." But, there and afterward, I was just stuck and struck speechless—so damn thunderstruck—as if I'd taken in too much of it and had consequently became waterlogged—permanently! ~~~~~)Just kidding, ddikts(~~~~~

Two days after returning—(~~~~~I missed my Monday and Tuesday classes to catch up on sleeeeeeeeeeeep ~~~~~)—Pessi called. He was fighting with Teresa, but she just left for work, and so he wanted me to stop over with Mary Jane to make everything just merry again. He sounded very dry, very ryd, very dyr: ~~~{{{{{{{{{{{{{{(hey what's in here?)}}}}}}}}}}}}}}} ~~~

...Inside the haunted house, I sat down on the coffee table so I could be close to Pessi sitting in the ponderous green chair as we passed a blunt back and forth. He looked exhausted in the face—Dean's ghost written all over it—but healthy everywhere else. Hitherto, it had been a mystery to me as to what had been going on between him and Teresa since he, so to speak, got "clean-arms." I'd been staying away as much as possible, and certainly couldn't find the nerve to inquire without feeling guiltier. It pained me so much to be there so close to my best friend and yet so far away—so withdrawn from our normal relations that I was hoping a slip-of-the-tongue would do what my will could not. And with all the things going on with the Pinedas, Ma, Dr. Rosenbaum, Aristod, and my internal troupe of demons, I hadn't realized that it was the time of the year when his mother died in that drunken car crash (on her birthday) many years ago, but it was quickly brought to the surface when he said:

'Hey, ya wanna do me a favor 'n' drive me back home for a liddle bit on Saturday? I didn't gih da godda Mum's grave lass year 'cuzza everything.'

'So weird 'cause Jeremiah cawed me lass night, 'n' guess who's comin'ah Co's on Friday?' (Dis Co's is a venue in Punksburgh for Indie bands.)

With smoke slowly waft from his mouth, Pessi passed the blunt. *cough* *cough* 'Who?'

'Yir sercly not gonna believe 'iss—' (I started hitting the blunt) '—Dropkick, Floggin' Molly, Da Unseen, 'n' Middle Class Trash. Only fifteen bucks too. I's thinkin' we can leave right after my classes on Friday, godda the show, maybe stay at Dante's or wherever. Den on Saturday, we'll go see yir mum. Den we can either come back then or juss stay another night 'n' come back Sunday.'

'Sounds good da me.'

Coughing, I passed the blunt back. A thick cloud was taking over the room.

'Jeremiah said da show is da help raise awareness 'n' support all the workers bein' laid off in the area. He said Pixburgh was ranked high in the most layoffs lass year: mostly blue-collar jobs thit were *saposta* be protected by da union—ya know, like Rick's. It's fucked up, man: even union workers are no longer protected. No warnin', no protest, no recourse, no nuh'n: yir juss done.'

'Yeah: another reason for me not da godda trade school. I'll juss end up gih'n laid off 'n' forced da work at Wal-mart, 'n' I'd rather be dead.'

'Yeah, Wal-mart epitomizes how stupid poor people rilly are. Only contributing to their own demise. But hey! look! it's the smiley face sayin' it's the cheapest prices around! so it *must* be a good deal! hurry! grab yir buggy 'n' buy! buy! buy! a hundred things for the price of one! Excess'll definitely come in handy when we're either oudduvva job or workin' in the only place we shop! 'n' soon, the only place we'll be *able to* shop! hurry! hurry! hurry! buy! buy! buy!'

Pessi vaddled at this, overstanding what I meant. Despite being in different circumstances, we were both still poor in the pockets and rich enough in the mind to know the basics of economics; back in Greater Pittsburgh, all you had to do was drive around and look out your windshield and past all the deceptive smiley faces to overstand (both inside and outside of the economy, if there's such a thing) the things they call "consequence" and "entrapment."

After we finished smoking, I moved over to the couch. Pessi popped in *South Park* on DVD. He waited til the Hillbilly theme-song ended to speak.

Ner ner neeeer.

'Ya know, V, we should use our IDs at Co's da drink at the bar.'

Huh? 'Huh?'

'I dunno; lately I been thinkin' about Mum a lot. 'N' everyone obviously knows I don't drink 'cuzza her death. But I realized it's not like I do it oudda respect for her or anything, or 'cause both of 'em drank 'n' were always at it. I mean, *you* drink even'o Rick was like he was—'

'Yeah, 'cause I'm a fuckin' idiot.'

'Well either way, I realized *I* don't drink simply oudda fear, 'n' I nee'dda conquer it. I mean, I've done so much other shit juss da do whad I wanna do. But it's funny how I've never drank but *that's* the thing keepin' me feelin' like I'm—I dunno—like I'm trapped. 'N' it's all based on fear.'

'Pess, whachir cawin' *fear* could also be considered *strength*. I mean, after all this time, why start now? Truss me, you've seen me, 'n' our friends, 'n' yir parents, 'n' Rick—it can get juss as ugly as H, or even worse. Even statistics show wha' da *rill* problem is no madder wha' law or social etiquette says.'

'Yeah; but look at me. It's not like it's gonna make a difference if I *do* start. I ain't got nuh'n'ah lose.' He turned his attention to his left, fingering with the extinguished roach in the golden ashtray-stand between the chair and wall; today seemed to be the first time I recognized it. 'Ya know, lately I been wonderin' wha' Mum would think of me if she could see me now. No cawidge, no job, already been in rehab, livin' off someone else—basically a waste a life. So who cares if I start drinkin'?'

'*I* fuckin' care, you asshole. Plus, if you consider yirself a waste a life, den 'at's even more of a reason *not* da drink 'n' get yir shit together. I swear, you drink at the show, juss stay da fuck away from me 'cause I'm not gonna be in any mood da talk da ya, look at you, or even be around you.'

'My first time gih'n drunk 'n' you wouldn't wanna live it up with me? I know everyone else is gonna be pumped.'

'Dat's 'cuzzer only gonna be thinkin' in the moment 'n' nawda the aftermath.'

'*Da aftermath?* Wha', the hangover?'

'No, you stupid fuck. Da aftermath as in yir fall from manhood.'

He threw his neck back and let out a boomerang laugh into the ceiling. 'So if I drink, I'm not a man? I'll be a kid?'

'No, you'll be neither.'

'Oh man, I'm so glad I didn't godda cawidge; dey been teachin' ya alawda fuckin' nonsense, ya know that, V. Or maybe 'at's juss the "thought-process of the sophisticated adult,"' he mocked. 'But you said you'd never grow up, Peter Pan.'

'I haven't 'n' never will. It's funny you'd even say that 'cause Ivy's always tellin' me for how smart I am I still act like a liddle kid. Trust me, I'd rather be that naïve kid den the sophisticated adult.'

'I'd rather juss be stuck in the middle 'n' be a reckless teenager thit fights, fucks, 'n' gets fucked up til the end.'

'Well yir fuckin' 'n' still gih'n fucked up, so ya juss nee'dda start gih'n in fights again—get a few more bawdles across yir head. Den everything'll be ar'ight.'

'Nah. I might still get high, but me 'n' her never fuck anymore. All we do's fight. She'll come home from work 'n' I'll be fuckin' horny; 'n' what's she do? Straight upstairs da snort some shit. 'N' whenever I do the right thing by stayin' dahn here so I don't hafta see it, she gets all pissed 'n' starts throwin' shit dahn the stairs. Sercly, V, people are right whenever 'ey say relationships only work when two people are da same. Two crackheads can live happily ever after. But a vegetarian 'n' a hunter are bound da crash.'

I paused to watch Cartman hit an underpants gnome with a stick.

"'I'm not a pussy; you're a pussy,'" Pessi mimicked Cartman.

'Hey, you, uhh,' I began stammering, ill at ease, 'you didn't plan on bringin' Squawk back with us, right?'

'Fuck no. She's hardly around on the weekends anyway. Always out with dose stupid bitches, comin' in all wasted. Den she'll wake up da next day 'n' start a fight over sum'n stupid. Cryin' 'n' tellin' me how much she hates me. I know it's juss da H talkin', but it gets me so fuckin' mad sometimes. Da one time, she threw da fuckin' cordless phone at me, smacked me in the back of the head, 'n' I juss lost it, man. I took 'at snowboard she bought me for Christmas, propped it against the bed, 'n' jumped on it til it snapped in half. Den she grabbed her shit 'n' drove ofta who knows where 'n' didn't come back til da middle of the next night. The shit never ends. Every liddle thing dit happens, she leaves like she's in *my* house. I'm juss waitin' for the day she kicks *me* out. Sometimes I kinda hope she does. I mean, can you imagine dealin' with wakin' up 'n' checkin' yir girlfriend's pulse da see if she's alive? den have her turn around 'n' not appreciate it?—have her say "I fuckin' hate you" 'n' 'en walk out on ya?'

'Well, Pess, my advice is give 'er da boot or take da boot, 'n' do it sooner than later. It's only bound da get worse, know whadda mean.'

'Who knows...I swear, oudda all da people I've known, she's by far the biggest headcase of 'em all—'n' she's my fuckin' girlfriend!' He lowered his head. 'But as much as I hate da admit it, I still love her. I juss don't want her da be like 'iss anymore. I want us da go back da how it yoosta be. Believe it or not, V,' he looked over, 'she's akshly not dat bad whenever she's sober 'n' yir alone with her. She acts different then 'cause she don't gadda impress anyone. But *nooo*, now I gadda take fuckin' pulses.' He raised his hands and laughed in a slightly, ever so slightly, bitter timbre. 'Like, where'd my life sercly go so wrong? How'd I get stuck here in 'iss fuckin' misery? It juss all seems so unreal whenever I think about it—ya know, like 'iss is juss some bad dream, 'n' I'm rilly back in Verna, juss havin' fun with the crew, like always.'

'It's cawed growin' up, Pess. 'At's why I'm doin' all I can da resist it.'

'Why ja godda cawidge 'en? That ain't resistin' shit.'

'Well, I've always wanted da meet someone like Dr. Rosenbaum 'n' get some direction in life.' (Pessi knew who Dr. Rosenbaum was from various conversations.) "N', ya know, I like da learn about different things; hear wha' different people hafta say. But as for me gih'n a degree 'n' meetin' "people who madder" so I can get a "good" job? Not why I came dahn here. 'At's sercly all deez kids talk about: how they know *this* person 'n' *'at* person; how they gadda internship *here* 'n' *there;* how they'll be makin' *this* much 'n' *'at* much. I swear, their god's Money. Let's juss pray God's a commie...' I found that amusing but, getting up from the ponderous green chair, Pessi grunted perfunctorily as if I'd been talking to and amusing myself. As he went off to the bathroom, I reclined back into the couch, lit a cigarette, and focused on *South Park* but absentmindedly. I was high but comfortably high. Thankfully, the sense of paranoia that started sneaking up on me when Teresa was the topic had tapered off. And now that I had the opportunity to give full attention to that funny sensation I smoked into my body, I simply felt relaxed. It's a simulated feeling that tends to become mundane after years of frequent use, and to the point where you don't even take notice in the enjoyment: you essentially function the same as if sober. But that's also when you find yourself focusing in on it, causing a resurgence in the appreciation you have for the moment of peace it affords you...*ahhhhhhh...*

When Pessi came back in, he did a clean hurdle over the arm of the chair. 'Hey, where's 'at gun at?' he asked casually, turning the television up a couple notches.

'In the drawer of my desk. Why?'

'Need it back soon.'

'Decide da shoot Squawk? I know a good place we can dump the body.'

'Nah, her dad's comin' home in a few weeks. He's stayin' for like a month, so he might notice it's gone.'

'I dunno, Pess. I mean, I'm not worried abouchu goin' crazy with it anymore, but ya never know with her.' In an ashtray sitting on the coffee table, I extinguished my cigarette with an angry twist. 'I sercly can't wait for Friday. I wanna see Floggin' Molly.'

'You rilly like 'at Celtic shit, huh? Like the fuckin' Pogues.'

'Fuck yeah. Sum'n so nostalgic about it. Combinin' Punk with Irish—I dunno—like, it makes me feel I'm in Ireland durin' the 1800s in some remote gheddo out inna greenland havin'ah best time ever dancin' life away with peasants. Da pub's undergrahn 'n' the lighting's dim! Everyone's close together, decked in rags, dancin' with every bone in 'er body! Eclectic, rebellious sounds flyin' all around us! Over there's da Wild Geese dancin' before they leave for international bloodshed! Over here's da Fenian Brothers stayin' home da keep the British Pigs out! 'N' scattered throughout are the proud Bog Trotters ready da dance through *any* marsh, at *any* time, 'n' *never* let their spirits be suppressed! Aldagether, the freckled antecedents of the Punks! Workin' class roots! with potato buds stemmed of politics! Our only concern tonight is drinkin' cheap booze 'n' dancin' with hot raggedy-dressed women! As long as 'iss wild music plays, we don't give a fuck about anything else in the world! Not even leprechauns 'n' Lucky Charms!'

I finally got a long, healthy laugh out of Pessi, followed by that you're-seriously-crazy head nod. But what could I do? As of late, I'd been getting a bit fiery over descendant-talk, and even if I had not a trace of Irish blood, there was an energy whirling through my heart that said otherwise. So kiss me: I'm Irish.

'Yeah, I like Floggin' Molly too. But I like Dropkick more. But I'm wanna see The Unseen 'cause I've never seen 'em before, 'n' 'ey fuckin' rock.'

'True. Ya know, I juss don't get how bands like The Unseen aren't bigger. It's like all deez new punks have no concern for where Punk came from 'n' whad it's all about. I mean, I like alwada the bands 'at blossomed in the 90s with 'at catchier melodic sound, but that's *all* these punks like anymore. Even'ah kids...' By now my heart was pounding so fast; I couldn't stop singing! '...Well, ya know wha': I'm akshly wrong about deez newer bands 'cause I'm startin'ah sense a disconnection between them 'n' us; shows are gih'n too big. It's openin' up the floodgates for ruin: 'n' 'atsah *last* thing we need. God—*everything's* goin' da hell, huh?'

'Yep. The Black Flag's at half-mast.' Absolutely one of the most amazing and cleverest things Pessi ever said! I was wishing I'd been the one who said it! So succinct too! 'But I don't care as much about new punks not knowin' about da roots as I do deez liddle fuckin' faggot bands on MTV exploitin' our sound, wearin' 'er liddle patches 'n' dyin' 'er hair juss da be cool 'n' stand out.'

"At's what I meant by "openin' up the floodgates."'

'Yep. Face it: our scene was *meant* da be small. Now that it's not, look who's comin' in da ruin it. I'd sercly like da knock 'em all the fuck out.' He clinched his fists together and then punched inward. 'Sercly, fuck 'at wanna-be emo shit 'n' fuck 'at Bad Charlene shit. I hope all dem fuckin' faggots choke 'n' die on the shit thit comes oudda their mouff.'

'Well we *do* have a gun with ten bullets in it. Iddle be juss enough for dem, 'n' 'en we can go after Mama Spliff or Floppy Nuggitz.'

Pessi grunted in agreement. Then he picked up a bottle of iced-tea sitting along the blindside of the chair. He took a big swig and set it back down, wiping his mouth. Looking into the television, he seemed to be seeing not *South Park* but a taped memory, which might've been true because he said, 'Ya know, it's like Gustapo[4] told us, "Da scene ain't nuh'n but a joke anymore; even Harry Roddins thinks he's a superstar, drivin' around in his Porsche, gettin' all politically bias, actin' like his opinions mean more den everyone else's." 'N', fuck, dazz back before all deez wanna-bes even got big on MTV. Now ya gadda million parents with kids listenin'ah Bad Charlene 'n' Floppy Nuggitz 'n' thinkin' *that's* wha' Punk 'n' Hardcore is. I'd honestly rather have people hate us for who we rilly are den love us for who we're not. I can juss hear 'em sayin', "*Oh, it's just a liddle rebellious trend my liddle Johnny's goin' through.*"'

'Well who cares wha' they think? We know what's up: 'n' 'at's all thit madders.' I went into the kitchen to get a drink of water. When I came back in, I sat down, facing him intently. 'Hey, 'member when Blood for Blood firss came out 'n' we heard "Wasted Youth Crew" at Dante's? We all started goin' nuts 'n' piled on 'im. 'N' Eddie—' I burst out in laughter before I could say it, and kept laughing as I talked: "N' fuckin' Eddie took his bawdle 'n' juss threw it across'ah room 'n' it smashed off the wall. 'N' 'en I flipped over the fuckin' coffee table—'

Pessi was laughing so hard. 'Yeah. Wha' da fuck happened? Oudda nowhere we juss snapped 'n' started trashin' his place. The music was up so loud too. I 'member his neighbors were poundin' onna walls, 'n' we kept screamin' back all 'iss stupid shit. Haha, Dante was so fuckin' mad. Even Jeremiah was all in'do'it, pilin' on, droppin' 'bows, throwin' whadever was in reach—'

'Yeah, 'n' 'en I went inda the kitchen 'n' started firin' food inda the livin' room!'

'Yeah, 'n' ya fuckin' smacked Dante inna face with a hotdog!' (He was still laughing.) 'Fuck, even Matty was 'ere! Him 'n' Eddie grabbed the

---

[4] Lead singer of the Hardcore band Murphy's Law

couch 'n' turned it over while Dante was tryin'ah stop ya from throwin' hotdogs! That was sercly wunna da funnest nights ever! Izz like, yeah, get Da Wasted Youth Crew involved with us hooligans 'n' we'll fuckin' destroy this entire fuckin' society—startin' with Dante's livin' room.'

'Yeah,' I sighed with an ironic smile. 'We're trapped like 'at. In fuckin' livin' rooms...'

Two night days later—Thursday night—I was lying in bed. As usual, I was a bit paranoid about falling asleep because I dreaded the thought of having a nightmare and waking up in convulsions with no understanding of reality and existence. But I *had to* call it an early night and execute it since I had work in the morning, then classes, then drive back to Pittsburgh with Pessi. Although I had no desire to go to work, and there, waste my time, in the summer it wasn't *too* bad since there wasn't much tutoring to do: they found other ways to waste my time. So all I had to do was make sure I got up on time then grind through the monotony: that's all.

Breaking tradition, I clicked off the television. They say even if you *do* sleep regular hours in a regular fashion, it's more effective whenever you sleep in silence and darkness; you can make eight hours feel like twelve, they say. So it was dark now but not all in silence, kinda. Like last summer, Luke had gone back home where I imagined he lived a simple, quiet life: one that mirrored his ascetic life at Aristod, kinda. But over on his empty bed, made so tight before he left, I could kinda hear his gentle snore and that piggish grunt he'd make whenever he tussled with the sheets: kinda funny to witness, especially when his gut was hanging out. But in the physical, Luke was gone. However, Jesus Christ was still with me, still on the wall, still in his confined world of soft, sad greens and golds, still standing emaciated and despondent in front of that dark wooden door—so still, not making a sound, unlike phantasmal Luke, but looking as if he ever did, it would be the knock heard around the world...

...with a steady focus out and slightly above me the darkness soon began consuming me...in steady, powerful tows, pulling me into that mystifying state where you can't really tell if your eyes are open or closed...it swirls and pulsates like a vortex in outer-space...pops and dances like visible atoms....every now and then, whenever that sensation of colorful darkness (with its little atomic sparkles) befell me too intensely, I'd blink willfully or touch my face quirkily to know whether I was in inner- or outerspace...later on, since "execution" was failing, I got up and opened the window, hoping there would be a *zefiru câ ninna nanna* [5]: particularly at night, I loved that ghostly whistle, and the soft chill that came in with it...to breathe it in was like inhaling lotus dust, perhaps while lying alone on a hillside somewhere far away...who then could ever know of my indolence?...to sink down in clover and narcissus amid soft wavy lovegrass, gathering my black wool: *duci far nenti: oh duci vita* [6]...ahh, so there I shall go where my lonely but breezy senescence will be reflected in a plane-mirror propped on the

---

[5] [scn] lullaby breeze
[6] [scn] care-free idleness or a self-indulgent life; literally, "sweet doing nothing...oh sweet life"

hillside, right below my feet, tilted upwards, so I can see better this test of languorous strength...

...ribbons of Time passed by in the breeze, each wisp (and there were many) taking a second away...never seems to be much thievery in a second—at least not til the whole windy gang gets away from you, their bags filled with months and years, leaving you with one will-o'-the-wisp to mull over in vain for the rest of your days...la la la la LA!...HEY! look at you! this lazy decrepitude is PATHETIC! using the last of your energy to shuffle off the rest of your mortal coil in order to prepare for the soil that awaits you...ahh! but methinks, old and listless one lying on the hillside far away, that the very last second will flash before you in the mirror so mockingly! for sooooo looooooooong!...

...*whispers...whispers...an echo...the mock...*now *sliiiiiide* down the long slope of the hillside, old shell, and hope there's a lake to drown your shock!...

...ahhh! there is! and it's frozen!...Cocytus!...I – I – I—yes! / the old shell on the hillside!...how did I forget?!...it's all coming back to me, and so excruciatingly, how I always knew *this* would my fate for my sins!...into Caïna: I'm sorry Scandurras, Pessinis, Pinedas, Vallanos...into Antenora: I'm sorry, America, for I caused a war and—why isn't this working?!...into Ptolomea: I'm sorry, Luke...into Judecca: I'm most sorry to You, God! so very sorr—instantly shot under the flapping wings fanning the Lake of Eternal Rebuke!...(it's so cold here...I wonder which monstrous mouth will eat this dead traitor alive?)...fall from the teeth, Judas, Brutus, Cassius, for I deserve it all!...and who knows all my guilt and iniquity but Him thrice!...Ahh! He calls!...

...*(sustained sibilance of the mind for a while)*...

...some time later—drained both physically and mentally, ready to succumb to the spell of Night—I began musing, slipping, in time, into a lighter state of mind as if gradually being absolved for no good reason...in the dark vortex spread out interminably before me, I was seeing his face and the satellite scenes, with all the images coming into me, down on me, like falling swarf...in accompaniment, there seemed to be the sound of light chiming...at first, I believe, he came to mind because I realized I hadn't talked to him since I left that day but would have to call him tomorrow after classes...I kinda sighed thinking how it was such a somber thing he had to go through on Saturday: standing above his mother who was no longer much of anything down in the dirt...a really depressing ceremony to partake in: rest in peace but not in piece...oh dear mother, I really hope God stole your essence away because there's not much left of you here...rest in peace...rest in p e e—

—ahh the wind suddenly swirled in and shot up my body so violently!...the curtains snapped back like black flags at half-mast!...in the inhale—the breath being drawn back into the wild beast's mouth!—they huddled back together silently like frightened children lest they (and I) be whipped again...lest they (and) be w i p'd again...w i p'd again...and again...a...a...n...wisped again...tick-tock tick-tock...don't mean nothin' to me...leave me alone!...leave us alone!...sum' a noel or leavee!...

...soon enough I was consumed whole...body gone, just eyes...every colorful twinkle before them seemed to be evolving, thankfully, into visible confirmations of how glad I was that Pessi and I had talked the way we had on Tuesday...the ol' revolutionary discourse...and it wasn't necessarily about revolution, rarely was in the political sense of the word, but it just had that pushing-forward energy...and yet in this most recent example swirling in the vortex right before me, with the falling swarf and the light chiming of the night, I could only reminisce about the good ol' days, the ones furthest away from the present, and draw comparisons, like making new constellations in the sky out of the old ones...things had certainly changed in the ol' revolutionary discourse...the linguistics was more advanced...the topics mostly the same but deeper in severity and desperation outside the personal level, that is, in the general narrative...and the ideas and solutions proposed were more...rationalized? passionate? serious? flippant?...well, if anything, not *too* serious considering one proposal was to shoot the exploitative bands we hated, which was like divine comedy for us...in any case, this time Pessi was talking like he'd been doing some meditating on his own and was ready to become his own speaker, like he could now start up a discourse without me present...it was just sad the other things he was meditating, the things he'd never discuss without me present...if I would've had to guess after the first five minutes of the conversation that we would end up having fun I would've guessed in the negative...there was his nine-years-dead mother who he once favored over his father...then there was the hopefully dying-soon girlfriend who was, for however long she'd been at it, selling him out: that straight-forward but condensed concept that means to betray your soul, your principles, or anything you once held dear, for more trivial, usually fleeting, reasons, such as once being loyal to your love...only to turn your back on 'em when they prove to be a bit different in lifestyle whereby you flee to the crowd with the powder...and selling out at night, as he said she'd been doing, seems to make it that much worse for no logical reason besides the feeling attached to the dark which is just a sensory "product of the culture" shared by the majority of the world, but certainly nothing innate unless the physical presence in darkness, or knowing an event is taking place in the dark, creates in *all of us, at all times, everywhere*, ominous feelings, which isn't and never has been the case...alwaysthemore, when Pessi said that thing about how Teresa wasn't that bad whenever she was sober and not around people she had to impress...might've been my first true hunger for self-inflicted pain, or death...nothing more painful than looking at a friend talking a certain way, believing in a certain something, whenever you know they're oblivious to a certain horrible truth that *you're* involved in too...but Pessi wasn't *entirely* oblivious to Teresa's ways...he was well aware of the things he could *see*...but in the same way the rest of us suffer, he was being duped by those blindsides...sometimes, I often thought, maybe having *all* my sides be a blindside would be for the best...just complete visual darkness in exchange for the invisible darkness on the inside that comes from seeing things on the outside...the latter is worse because it's a continuous wave of pain to the brain and heart, and whenever that happens, it ultimately brings everything to the soul...then *it* becomes black, this stinging blackness you can feel even though you have no idea where it's at...but it's there...if you can feel it time and time again no matter where you are, it's there...*hmmm*...I feel, therefore *I* exist...I feel *it*, therefore it exists...thank God for intuition...into this, onto God...

...lying there in the darkness, still thinking about Pessi, another thought entered the vortex...encouraged by the two Latin classes I'd taken thus far, I decided to do linguistic research on the computer, coming across something that, to my knowledge, has no true connection, but it came to my senses as something very strange...the English use of the word *love* has its roots in the Latin word *lubere* which means "to please"...one of my favorite English words based on sound alone is *lugubrious* which comes from the Latin word *lugubris* which before conjugation comes from *lugere* meaning "to mourn"...so here we have *lubere* (love) being very similar to *lugere* (to mourn)...*lubere, lugere*...only one letter differentiates the two...and that letter must mean everything...   perhaps it's Divine or phenomenal symbolism of how just *one* difference between two people, whether a small difference in opinion that we wish we could change, all the way up to something more momentous like being separated in the physical, in which it's brought to light why love is to mourn...*lubere est lugere*...love is to mourn...there is no love if there is no pain...even in Sicilian, "to love" is *amari*, and "bitter" is *amaru:* again, only one letter of difference...so perhaps when *in* love we can only know it for sure when we are *out of* love, and accordingly mourn, and thereafter become bitter...ahh! now if we could only get away with seeing *ourselves* in the mirror *at all times,* then it might never get so bad...we'd never even know what is to mourn...*but just when you think yourself safe, Intuition destroys your perfect self, and from that, you seek out the missing pieces, in another, so that one day (bless the day) you can mourn, and thereafter become bitter...descending like rain...*

...the wind begin dying down...for a while it had seemed in labor wherein the contractions were getting closer together...and perhaps that was true in a sense because water broke from the sky...falling heavily at first...then after a few minutes, conforming to a drizzle: another lullaby I loved: *la ninna nanna ri l'acqua* [7]...much peace in the sadness of rain...much loneliness in the company of infinity[8]...the drops tapping down on the sills in syncopated rhythm like a trillion wistful mothers rolling their fingernails on a table...getting very sleepy now, yet keeping my open?closed? eyes—the only thing left of me—focused into the vortex where Pessi finished off my last remembrance of the night...very strange comparing us...why did it seem like I had all these lofty goals, and Pessi had none?...couldn't be because I was in college, and even before then, had put forth effort in high school; formal education has nothing to do with sowing dreams and aspirations...it's just a tool (one among many) to attain 'em, sometimes broaden 'em, but it's certainly not the architect of dreams...despite his hebetudinous mien and phlegmatic attitude, Pessi *had* to have dreams too...but why didn't I know what they were?...even the most pessimistic person has at least *one* dream, and most likely it would be to change whatever they think is causing those nihilistic feelings, and as a result, to live in the opposite...maybe the dream is even larger like a utopia...yeah, Pessi seemed like a utopist, like me...he just wasn't one to bother mentioning it...but if I ever had a million dollars to bet I'd put it all on the

---

[7] [scn] the lullaby of rain

[8] ∞

fact that it was there inside him, designed perfectly like New Jerusalem...when we got to talking and bitching about this and that, and that somber mood of the beginning progressed into this amazing ambiance wherein we began discoursing fervently but almost in that Rosenbaumist sense where our visions of the world spinning around us were not about the outer *per se*, and rather, they, our zealous sentiments, were more like small snacks for our minds because our real hunger, the place where we really were feasting, the place we had utopia, was in our hearts, for it all came down to our selfish concerns of how whatever it was affected *us*, and more so, how two souls related to each other, and in that, we found comfort and a sense of peace...nothing "real" on the outside mattered as much as it seemed in our rhetoric because there was someone right there whose familiar tactility—whether it be a kiss, a hug, a handshake, a stroke of hair, wild sex, soft love, or just the warmth of their breath coming at you in slight caresses—could soothe all outer pains, could make a dictionary of outer convictions and crucifixions seem nonexistent, could, through that intimacy, take both souls far away and deep into the inner-life of emotion which may lie separately in both bodies but are only separated in the physical, only in the physical...ahhh! what a sensation!...yes, after all that talking without having any serious concerns about the outside world, and I got up to leave later on, and we did that special handshake of ours, saying how the plans for the weekend were set, and I looked at his face where the shadows were drifting away like clouds from the sun, leaving rays of light to beam into me, and there he was so close to me, unlike the sun, yet almost appearing sublime and ready as he smirked that same ol' smirk that seemed to be developing into the first memory I had of him—what a powerful, resplendent smirk!—yes, I realized then that whatever it was making me feel the way I did, it was, in that fleeting moment, just a small instance or pixel of my dream, my utopia, *our* utopia, the one thing I wanted to live out til the day I died...this feeling—for that's all it was—a lustful, gem-gilded feeling, a desire for this internal consummation stitched together with and by the few whom I called family...but it was all so fleeting, for the feeling, the actual burning sensation of it, would abate with each step I took further away from him, almost like leaving behind in that house a piece of my essence as if the house within that specific scene was one big picture of a moment in time I'd never be able to get back...and the remnant you get from something like *that* is the wistfulness you must take along with you...for, as Life dances you on in the most awkward, muscle-stretching steps—til the music stops—you'll inevitably experience it again and again in times of solitary...

     ...Friday morning came too quick...I didn't have to wait til my alarm clock sounded to wake up, for Ivy called me about half-past eight to tell me that Pessi was dead...Teresa found him dead an hour ago...after whatever had happened in between that slot of time, Teresa called Ivy, then Ivy called me, hysterical. '*Viiinnnyyy! Vi-vi-viinnnyyy!...*' went on for a while til I lashed out in anger to tell me what it was, while, outside the anger, being completely immersed in *déjà vu:* obviously from Rick's death and how Ma had cried over the phone in a similar manner...however, when Ma had called and procrastinated, I had a feeling what it was...but this time, I don't know what was going on...hearing Ivy's voice in a foreign manner seemed to kill my ability to conjecture...til she, halting the hysteria and dropping into a low-key tremble, said, 'She founda, she founda him deaa-auda in – in the be-be-drooom. He's deea-udda, Vinny. Pessi's de–' at which point I hung up, instantly embodying the sickest, most ineffable feeling from which I pulled out from my desk drawer the gun, released the clip, mentally counted in counterclockwise revolutions of redness, then stuck the clip back up in with authority, ready...ready for war...

...Several hours later, the police showed up at my room. Ivy had stopped over since then, but I refused to let her in, telling her to just go the fuck away; and she did; to make sure there wouldn't be any more disturbances, I shut off my phones. The police knocked again, authoritatively stating who was on the other side. Before opening the door, I put the gun back inside the drawer. Smoking the butt-end of a cigarette, I opened the door apathetically. Two badged men: both tall, broad, and clean-cut, one black, one white, the black one differentiated by his grotesquely tapered waist. While the black cop eyed my room, the white cop asked if it was okay for them to come in and talk, or did I prefer to go somewhere else. I didn't know what he meant by the latter given that cops tend to be sarcastic and crafty, so I told 'em to come in and feel free to sit on Luke's bed; they moved in but remained standing. Putting the cigarette out, I sat down on my bed, as hard and dry as a desert rock, conscious of every breath and word I let out, already premeditating the future.
Gravely, they introduced themselves as Frank and Mike, of the local, not the state. Then Frank, the white cop, asked if I'd been contacted by anyone. I said, yes, by my girlfriend, and all I knew was my best friend was dead because I couldn't listen to her say anymore over the phone, but if it was a heroin overdose, I didn't want to know. In a routine manner they apologized, commiserated, then Frank told me that, yes, unfortunately, it was a heroin overdose—*kind of.* They were investigating because there were several mysterious things about the situation. *'Murdered?'* I suddenly thought with a curious burn, almost saying it aloud. But that wasn't it—well, it was *kinda* what they were implying: suicide: murder of the self. Frank began running through the basic questions—but stopped, and before going any further, asked how much of the details I wanted to hear at this point since it could technically be done later when my mind became clearer—that is, if I just couldn't go through with it now—but best to get at things as early as possible. I said I am—I was his best friend, and I'm holding together as best as I can, so just give me all the details. He said good because they—he made sure to stress *they*—want to work with me to see if we can situate this and discover the truth.
Yes, deez noble men are on a mission for the truth so their justice can be served. We'll see. Inconspicuously, I gritted my teeth, telling myself that I might have an "in" here if I just lose a grip on their names.
The black cop seemed enthralled with my edgy posters, as the white cop talked:
'...and Ms. Cazzata said that she spent the night at her boyfriend's and came home this morning and found Zach upstairs in the bedroom collapsed on the floor. She called 911 but unfortunately he was already gone. The paramedics could've possibly administered nalorphine, an

antidote, if he'd been found sooner. Thing is, the needle was still in his left arm, which means several things could've happened. First, a needle still in the arm *usually* signifies suffocation and—do you know anything about heroin?' Frank stopped to ask this question with a skeptical tone and visage.

'Somewhat. He was in rehab this past January thru March for it.'

'Did you know he was doin' it again?'

'He wasn't doin' it again,' I replied impassively.

'What do you mean?'

Pause. Pause. Diversion. 'I'm the one thit got him into rehab. I tried to get Teresa to go too, not only because it was more incentive for him, but so she could get clean too. Did she happen to mention she's still doin' it?'

His face took a curious investigation of mine before asking why.

'Well it's not that I'm tryin'ah get her in trouble or blame her, but where do ya think he got the heroin from after bein' clean for so long?'

No matter how you speak to cops, they don't like when you ask 'em challenging questions. 'Let's start at a different point. Did Zach drink?'

'No. Never. I've known him my entire life 'n' he's never drank once. When he was ten, his mother died in car wreck—his father was drivin', *drunk*.' (Of course they knew this already. There was just one word flashing before my eyes since he said it: *BOYFRIEND*.) 'Why do you ask that?'

'We found a six-pack in the bedroom,' he replied dispassionately. 'Five had been busted off the wall in the same area—like he'd thrown them one after another. The floor was still damp in that area. But they're going to run tests to see how much he actually drank and shot, and for anything else he might've done. But right now it's not looking like a heroin overdose in the sense that he took too much for his body. See, usually when someone is found with the needle still in the arm, it means they suffocated. What happens is they have an allergic reaction to the dose since heroin is continually cut different and no one really knows what the next dose may have in it. If that's the case, the allergic reaction would've filled his lungs with fluid; however, it's such a quick process that he wouldn't have suffered any pain—it's almost instant coma or death. Mr. Vallano? Mr. Vallano? Are you sure you're up to this? We can—'

'No, I'm fine. This isn't the first time I've gone through this—ya know, a friend dyin'.' Yes, look at me: know that I'm just an angel who'd been born around devils.

He turned to his partner. 'Go get a few bottles of water from the soda machine.'

As the black cop exited, Frank sat down on Luke's bed; it made a crunchy sound from his 'form. He continued: 'What we really need to know—and for Zach's sake, just be honest here—but did he ever have suicidal tendencies? every try hurting himself? mention it? give things away? fall into prolonged periods of depression?—anything that might've suggested he wasn't happy with his life?'

'No. None of that stuff. 'N' I'm positive he didn't kill himself. He always told me he believed those who commit suicide godda Hell. We're both Catholic, 'n' although he might not have gone to church as much as I would've liked, he was still very religious. He was the most optimistic, brightest, levelheaded person I knew. That's why the whole heroin thing was a shock to everyone who knew him.'

'Had he done other drugs prior?'

'Not really. I mean, in high school he went through a phase where he smoked marijuana, 'n' he took LSD once, but that's it. Unfortunately, some people come to a point in their life where they feel they need to "experiment"—'

'Well—'

'Oh—sorry; I was just gonna say that when he first started seein' Teresa, she was alriddy doin' heroin, 'n' he said he didn't wanna try it, but she got him da try this drug he cawed Baby Blues, which I *think* is oxycontin. Either way, it was from that thit he ended up movin' onda heroin. But what's strange is he told me he never shot it. Always through the nose. Which means there's a chance he didn't know what he was doin' 'n' juss injected it wrong.'

'That's also what they're lookin' into: a collapsed artery. The needle was pushed in deeper than normal which might've happened on the fall or—' he paused, gauging my blank face, 'or from self-harm. D—'

'I just don't get it. The first time around, he worked so hard to quit. He juss told me on Tuesday (the last time I saw him) how he'd stay downstairs whenever she was doin' it, 'n' how she'd throw things down the stairs or take off for days 'cause she was mad he wasn't doin' it anymore. He was actin' like he at least had *himself* under control. But I guess when yir ex-girlfriend is doin' it all the time, and yir livin' with her, it's not that easy da escape.'

'Yeah. Unfortunately, if one's still doin' it, they'll end up draggin' the other into the cycle again and again. Let me ask you another question here: You said this was the first time you knew of him doin' it since the rehab, right?'

'To my knowledge, yes. Like I said, I was juss with him on Tuesday. No signs. I developed a habit of observin' the signs the rehab clinic had explained.'

He effortlessly scribbled something on his pad as if whatever he was writing had nothing to do with what I said or the situation. 'And tell me about the rehab?'

'Well, it was for three months at the hospital's drug-clinic. He told me the only way he'd agree da accept help is if he could convince 'em that he was at a stage where he could get methadone in lieu of heroin. I couldn't tell ya if he really needed it or not; the behavioral-therapy he had five days a week *might've* sufficed, but I juss wanted him da see him get clean period.'

'What was he like when he was done?'

'Honestly, back to normal. He had remarkable resiliency. I mean, I was watchin' over him as much as I could with school 'n' work. Prahblee stupid for takin' his word on *everything*. But I truly think he was over it at that point. Maybe he'd gone back to those pills da help him get through the transition; I'm not sure. I'm not very up on how things work when yir deep in it. I never experimented with drugs—I've only drank like twice since bein' in cawidge—so it was the worst feeling in the world for me da witness my best friend bein' like that but not rilly knowin' what he was goin' through.'

He scanned my face; perhaps I'd over done it; I rubbed my forehead forlornly.

'How had he been dealin' with the break up?'

'Rilly good,' I responded quickly but evenly. I proceeded in the same even manner: 'He told me it was the best decision they ever made together. It's juss that he had nowhere else da live in the meantime since he didn't get along with his father back home in Pixburgh. But can I ask you sum'n'?'

'Sure.'

Just then, the black cop came back in. He handed me a bottle of water. I didn't thank him. He backed up and remained standing over by Luke's desk. I asked if they minded if I smoked, but I said it directly to the white cop; he said he didn't mind; I lit it up; I was so much thinner than the gray smoke; I was nothing; I was Rational Man.

'You able da tell me anything about Teresa's account? I mean, I'm guessin' it'll all be public anyway, right?'

'It depends. What do you wanna know?' Spoken very conspiratorially by the white cop. And right then, I had the strangest sensation come over me, something like being in my thirties and working undercover with cops, as if they knew me already or knew I was someone who'd previously dealt with cops. However, it didn't feel like that at all, but it kinda did, but Rational Man doesn't *feel* much besides the basic bodily functions; Rational Man is a man of pursuing Truth and Justice via Logic.

I blew a hit of smoke upward, and fixated on it—like how rich white people do whenever they're stressed out. 'Well, Pessi—that was his nickname—he never told me much about her new boyfriend, juss thit he was, uhh—*mmm*, what was it: a janitor?—no, maybe a clerk at a gas station...' I fell into false meditation, looking for assistance.

'He owns a detail shop,' replied the black cop.

'Yes, that's it. Anyway, Pessi *didn't* have a job, 'n' hasn't in years. He said that was wunna the reasons Teresa didn't wanna be with him: because she's materialistic 'n' he could never give her all the things she wanted. Then, last week, he said that Teresa's boyfriend was askin' her da throw him out, but she told him she was still friends with him 'n' wouldn't do it—that Pessi would find a place soon enough. But Pessi told me that he had a fear her boyfriend was gonna—I dunno—start threatenin' him, perhaps physically harm him. Did Teresa happen da say anything about her boyfriend havin' those kind of intentions towards Pessi?'

'Honestly, didn't talk about it much,' replied the white cop, with signs of deceit. 'But she did say her and Zach were still good friends and she didn't want that to end—'

'Did she say she still does heroin?'

'Why, is there somethin' you want to say about that?' he asked, sounding a bit irked by me bringing it up again.

'Not rilly. I guess when it comes dahn do it, it's fuckin'—sorry—it's juss thit Pessi was so much smarter than that. He should've known da stay away whether or not she was doin' it. I juss doesn't get why all a sudden—' I stopped, pretending to be flabbergasted, even though I was about *other* things.

'Yeah, we certainly share your confusion over all this,' said the white cop, now looking truly sorry for me. 'And we're gonna do whatever we can to give him, his friends, and his family a sense of peace. The main question here is what his motivation was if he'd completed rehab successfully, had given no signs of suicidal tendencies, and had everything smoothed over with the relationship. Doesn't seem to make any sense.' He scratched his blonde head, exhaling.

'Did you happen to talk to my girlfriend—Ivy Pineda?'

'Briefly. She was with Teresa.'

'How is she?'

'Just tryin'ah hang in there,' the black cop edged in. 'Ya know, when I was sixteen I had a friend who OD'ed. Just gadda stay strong and have faith in God in times like this. He can help you get through. Here—' He handed me a tan business card. 'We offer free counseling for family and friends. We want you to at least come to a few sessions. We have a councilor who'll talk to Zach's family and friends in group-sessions, even privately. It's a good way to keep one another strong and sort things out.'

Taking a drink of water, I nodded my head. Then I extinguished the unfinished cigarette, and I did it with such feminine compassion as if I didn't want to apply too much pressure to the butt while pushing its head down into the thick glass.

'So you're positive Zach didn't have suicidal tendencies?'

'Positive. He was never one da let life get him dahn no matter what. It's juss thit heroin's such a powerful drug thit I guess he couldn't conquer the crave...' I wasn't listening to myself talk now; I was trying to think of a way to weave back into the boyfriend-issue, but I was aware it could start to look suspicious, so til I had a better segue, I kept my head hung and my tone melancholy and dry.

'You all right?' asked the white cop, gauging my demeanor. 'You need us to get you anything? Take you anywhere?'

'Thanks but I'm ar'ight. This may sound strange, but I'm not much of a mourner over death. My father juss died about a year 'n' a half ago. It's juss the facts of life we all gadda go sometime, 'n' God picks as He sees fit. There's always a Higher Reason behind it all. I mean, not da sound pessimistic, but in my opinion, life's gonna be short whether you live twenty years or a hundred; it's nothin' compared to Eternity. So I'm not upset in the way everyone else will be. No doubt I'm gonna miss Pessi every single day of my life, but he's in a much better place now—forever.'

'You're exactly right,' said the black cop. 'That's a good way to look at things.' With a raised brow, he turned to the white cop: 'We'll, Frank?'

'Is that all?' I asked weakly; too much for a white person to bear in one day.

'For now,' said the white cop. 'We're gonna wait to hear from the coroner, and then go from there. Do you mind if we call you if we need to ask any more questions? We can set up an appointment if needed.'

I stood up. 'Sure, no problem. Do you need my number?'

They already had my information, but they still took down all they could get from me; I didn't mind: there's a Higher Reason for everything. Again, they expressed their heartfelt condolences, adding in all this other bullshit that I nodded agreeably to.

'Hey, I have a question,' I said as they were heading out the door. 'N' I certainly don't mean this in a racist way, but I'm juss not rilly sure on the matter since it wasn't wunna Pessi's favorite subjects da talk about. But Teresa's boyfriend is that big black guy, right? I believe he lives out by Wakanda Fields. I'm not sure if it's the same guy I'm thinkin' of, but I think I saw him once, right before Teresa 'n' him started dating. Teresa 'n' I haven't rilly talked much since she broke up with Pessi, so if Pessi didn't tell me sum'n it was kinda hard for me da know what was what. So I only ask oudda curiosity because—I dunno—well, I juss feel like I've been left in the dark about so many things. I'm juss tryin'ah figure out what might've been goin' on inside Pessi's head. But he's that big black guy, right?'

From the doorway, they both gave me a quizzical look. 'His *name* is Jackson,' said the black cop, almost defensively...

...So just when I thought I was an excellent judge of character it turns out that Teresa wasn't racist after all, or at least not enough to refuse sleeping with a black man. However, it wasn't that simple, for the reason *behind* it would spell out her true character: was it really for love? or just drugs?—in the name of hedonism? or simply whoredom?—a fetish for the forbidden taste? or a desire to get away from commitment? Although I could see the plate of the problem, I couldn't see the provisions. It reminded me of a Sicilian proverb Ma taught me: *Tinemu d'occhiu û scurpiuni ie û sirpenti, ma nun nni guardamu dû millipedi.* "We keep an eye on the scorpions and serpents but don't look for the millipede." In other words, the Devil dwells in details, so pay attention to everything. Perhaps then it was for the best that I *couldn't* see the provisions on the plate, because, at the moment, I didn't have the strength to go down and take on the Devil and the minutiae of Hell, for above up, God and that strength seemed to have abandoned me: I looked up to see if any intuitive answers were blowing in the wind—only to see a mass of gray clouds—while knowing many irretrievable concrete answers were about to be buried beneath the ground. But at least one thing (general in nature but perhaps giving me direction for the future) became unearthed and crystal clear: all white people, like Teresa, and all black people, like Mike, have their weak spots, just like everyone has their blindspots...

...For the next two days, hardened Rational Man kept away from everyone, including himself, as he stepped into an insensible shell, trying to put things together before making a move. That was me: hardened Rational Man whose heart, if there was anything left of it, had become blacker than coal. The lack of feeling I had was actually remarkable. Although it didn't allow me to think clearer, it did allow me to think without concern for anything; perhaps a sense of freedom in its own right....

...As if I would've expected anything less from Teresa, I knew she pulled the wool over the cops' eyes, just as I did, although I likely did it more proficiently and methodically owing to my linguistic virtuosity. Yet it didn't mean a damn thing when it came down to what existed within *our* world outside the police, coroner, and whoever else was bound to get involved; seemed Teresa and I saw them as intruders in some tacit war?game?story? going on underneath it all—something that, when all was said and done, would most likely evade everyone but us. Rational Man just knew *prima facie* [9] that something wasn't right here—well, nothing wasn't right here. First postulation: *Teresa was doing so much now that she couldn't keep up*

---

[9] [lat] before closer inspection

with the costs and so she started fucking Jackson to get her fix for free.
Another: Jackson had a monopoly over the local H distribution and used it
to his advantage by fucking Teresa knowing she couldn't deny him. Either
way, Pessi hadn't known she was with Jackson, no less (if it was true) to the
point of constituting a *bona fide* relationship. Pessi was a nut just like me:
you touch or disrespect our chick, and you're getting fucked up by any
means necessary. Like Túpac Amaru when it comes to protecting our loved
ones: willing to take it straight to the end til the enemies shed our blood in
the face of God. And if Pessi *had* known beforehand, it would've been the
first thing he said to me. He would've been calling for war, with me as his
auxiliary force. I was positive of that. I was also positive (as were the police)
that something more than a crave triggered him to do it, and by the needle,
in such a violent fashion, so abruptly. And the alcohol? Just more evidence
that a big piece of the puzzle was missing; although perhaps *that*, as he
said, was all about conquering a fear; and what better thing to do than
conquering it before taking on the biggest fear of 'em all? Anyway, one
thing required no further probing: now that Jackson had been placed
conspicuously in the picture, it was likely that Teresa had been going to *him*
all this time when Pessi thought she was out with those girls she called her
friends. So what was it? Teresa finally told Pessi about it? Pessi had
somehow caught her? Jackson had actually said something to Pessi? None
of those seemed like a reason for suicide, but, to be sure, relapse. Even if
he'd found out and had taken it hard, along with dealing with those
thoughts he'd been having of his mother and being a waste of life, it still
wasn't a solid reason for suicide, but, to be sure, relapse. But relapse wasn't
cutting it for me. He undoubtedly killed himself; that is, he did the drugs
with the intentions to die—even if it *was* done in an ambiguous way where
the "evidence" could easily say otherwise. But all the outsiders could ever
know was the *physical* evidence, not the *mental* and *emotional* wherein the
truth resides. But why, Pess? What happened?...

...During those two days, I, as Rational Man, sat at my desk, fighting
against a pine for yesterdays, while listening to nostalgic music, so fucked
up on whatever I put into my body, trying so hard to find the answers in the
wind, the music, the drugs, the deductions, the yesterdays—just *anywhere—*
but unable to stop from hearing over top of everything the echo of *but why,*
Pess? what happened? like a vinyl record stuck on a haunting note...*maybe*
she'd given him a bad dose on purpose...maybe—oh God! whaddum I
doin?! whaddum I sayin?! my best friend's dead!...no, this isn't rill...no, juss
crazy again...another mental breakdown, another bad dream...please be
alive when I wake up, Pess!—PESSI! WAKE – THE – FUCK – UP!!!...Pess?...

...I don't remember saying it, but according to Ivy I told her: 'Juss
stay the fuck away from me; don't try talkin'ah me; don't ask meedda go
with the funeral with you; juss leave me the fuck alone til I'm riddy, 'cause if
I do anything besides whad I'm doin' right now in my head, I'm gonna go
fuckin' crazy 'n' people are gonna die.' I also don't remember calling Ma, but
she flew in from Catania to attend the funeral. How everyone else found
out really didn't matter: there's always that way in which they do which is
why everyone was at the funeral home...

....Alone, I drove back to Verna: that's where they took him so the father who had lukewarm affection for him could attend then bury him in a local cemetery. When I pulled in, I waited til I finished my smoke...When I stood up out of the car, it felt like I was going to faint. But I went on; *had to* go on...A suited old man opened the door; he said something polite...In the red-carpeted, bright vestibule, I caught a glimpse of Jeremiah, Dante, Eddie, Anson, a bunch of other friends from back in the day who always showed up at our yearly funerals for the young, then, next to the water fountain, that backboneless amoeba who didn't dare look at me when I shot him a cold glance. Should've walked up and decked him right there just to get him back for what he said about me, and more so, to make Pessi laugh. But didn't. No one approached me. They were all blurs anyway, as perhaps as I was to them. In the background, there was this strange dirgelike music playing but it wasn't anything Pessi would like. Why would they do that to him? I stopped and thought about going back out to my car to get his favorite Social Distortion CD. But didn't. I walked across the threshold into the viewing room. Think it was the perfumed scent in the air almost causing me to vomit. Think my head was shaking back and forth. Think I was trembling uncontrollably. Think everyone parted to the sides as I made my way up to him. Suddenly Ma came flying at me. Mechanically, I stuck my left hand out to keep her away. She started bawling more. I heard hateful gasping. I mumbled something, clinching my fists at my waist. Kept walking forward. But he was too far away. Seemed I'd never make it. Couldn't see him either. All I could see, since my head was fixated downward, was the bright red carpet...But I finally made it, somehow. Somehow the course of my life had brought me to this point: right back where I came from, a little less of me left upon arrival—no, a lot less, in this reunion of departure...

....In a strange glare, I saw on the bier that his casket was white, bejeweled with gold stuff. To my left, at the fore, stood his father. He was a scraggly rough-faced man who was somehow scrawny even though he was an Italian working-class drunk. His short blob of a mother was standing next to him, locked into his arm. I could see the movement of handshakes, cycles of 'em. He was saying thank-you, thank-you. What was he thankful for? I clinched my fists tighter. A vision of decking him passed before my eyes. Somewhere behind me and to the left, Teresa screamed out. Suddenly I disappeared. I was no longer with all the surrounding people either walking around balling or sitting in somber silence. I was in the car with Pessi, driving passed the orchard...before my eyes, the scene kept repeating on the same spot of the road...a light snow falling all around us...him looking out and up into his own kind of orchard where the gray matter of the sky unraveled for him whatever mysteries had brought to his face that enigmatic smirk, allowing him to look down into the palms of his hands with new wonderment...

....At the front of the casket but not right up on him, already knowing I wouldn't be returning for any more viewings, I said the following words to Pessi through the inner life, the very last words I'd ever share with him in the physical. I didn't—just couldn't look up at him, and so I kept my head hung down, near his head, my hands folded down in front of me, just like his were by force and custom. I gagged back a breath, using all the strength I had to focus in on the slant of view that shone my plain black t-shirt, knee-ripped blue jeans, and black skater shoes. I refused to change into anything else because Pessi and I had always hated that kind of formal shit. I was sure neither of us would like what he was wearing either. So for both of our sakes, I didn't—just couldn't for the life me look at him—nor could he look at me...

> hey pess: im not gonna look up but dont be mad at me: n im not gonna yell atcha either not even for not cawin me n lettin me help ya juss one more time: so ill stop there n proceed with wha rilly madders now: so many things da address but my heads spinnin so juss try n stick with me: first ill never forget at day when i drove ya da get the dope: thats where i see us right now: were on our way back n im lookin at dis orchard me n ivy go: its a priddy cool place: deres all deez apple trees n weepin willows n iss arbor with grapes n flowers n a crick n its all circled in by woods except dahn by da willows where a cliff goes up n out towards at wooded mountain: it seacly minds me of a place huck n tom woulda gone n had all deez imaginary adventures n maybe float dahn the crick: ju ever read huck n tom: i told ivy we yoosta be like da urban version of em: they smoked tobacco n sold things but we smoked chronic n stole things: haha...i dunno pess: whenever i looked over atcha that day i didnt see you as lookin like a waste a life: i guess through dose liddle reflections in snowflakes is seein you up in heaven with our friends as if from a combination of visual n mental phenomena: prahblee makes no sense huh: well anyway you were thinkin hard about yir life huh: firscha had that dream about april den you were talkin about our other friends: i mean as far as i can member youd never bothered askin me a question about da afterlife: izz always the ol revolutionary discourse: you loved at shit huh...man we rilly had it out lass tuesday: youll never know how good that shit made me feel: eres no one in the world i can talk to like at: its like you were the only one thit truly overstood me: (hold on pess)...anyway: at day when i took ya ta da playgrahn it came da me in retrospect datchir eyes had been so focused inda yir palms like you were suddenly amazed by da nature of the human body: n en ya asked me where we go when we die: n i blew it off: but i do have an intuitive feelin: deres juss no words or any rational way da explain it: n its stuff like at thit causes so much pain whenever you cant express it: when eres feelings n thoughts trapped in us n ey cant get out: well anyway whachir unanswered question has done is left me feelin like i letcha dahn: maybe ya knew you were on yir way out n only wanted a comforting answer or anything at all from me da make the new journey ahead an anticipated one not a scary one: but I shrugged it off n turned the music back up in lieu of an answer: n i guess i priddy much lefcha hangin in purgatory like i internally promised id never do da any of my friends: did i sell you out...guess ats sumn ill never rilly know: but i know ya wouldnt want meedda bother myself about it too much...ya know i once read dis proverb thit said sumn about i think thirtysix people carry da weight of the world: n its not a literal thing: but it signifies how a few people feel things most never will: the pain of everything: its kinda like the poets: da best people with words with the most powerful things da say are also doom da the terse paradox: n it gets so intensified when ya add years of stupid education: always tryina do sumn with it cause ya cant cant break away from it...well maybe its bedder not da be tortured by such things: maybe its

bedder da stay at the bottom of the steps n never climb cause it only feels like a walk dahn inda hell...man i wish i could see yir smirk right now: izz natural ~~art~~*: bahda course i coulda never said: hey pess i juss absolutely love yir smirk: cause you woulda put it indua different context: but im tellin ya now i fuckin loved at smirk: buh i know theres alawda hidden pain in it: juss like my halfcocked smile: but we juss kept showin it n let the sarcasm n banter flow oudduve it like we didnt care much about nuhn: but if anything we cared about one thing: each other: right: but i guess we couldnt come together juss a liddle bit more da stop da clawin hands from finely pullin ya under: n da be honest i only feel half guilty: i tried many times ya know...now whad all dis leads to is wha went wrong: wanna know wha da cops tol me: teresa was at her boyfriends n came back da fineja dead: ya didnt know bout dat huh: but i mean face it: thats where shed go whenever shed leave: n i dont hafta tell ya all the reasons why some deceitful junkie cunt would do that: but i juss dont overstand why youd do whacha did: da paper said it was a possible massive pulmonary edema: but were still waitin on the coroners report: either way i know it was more then at physical bullshit: izz suicide: either cuzza sumn festerin inside for a long time or sumn rilly big put on ya that day: like maybe she tolja about bein with im...but deres gadda be sumn else dit juss pushja over da edge...(hey pess i know dis might sound rilly dumb but if ya can somehow whisper the reason ill keep it da myself)...hmm haha: didnt think add work ya fuckin lockedup asshole: dont madder: ill find out wha happened: n when i do ill do ya good: promise...ehh the worst* ~~part~~*: i have a very bad confession da make: n the image of you in iss fuckin casket is the main reason i never tolja: but please believe me: i rilly did plan on tellin ya once ya gadda liddle bedder: like a liddle more removed from the h or her...man ya dont even know how hard dis is for meedda say even like iss: but after i tell ya n explain why i juss hope youll overstand the decision i made eveno its still not one im comfortable with havin made: so i guess ill juss come out n say it: teresa tried gihn on me one night: after that one pardy when yinz carried me back: i woke up some time durin the night ta her kissin my neck n grabbin my dick: n shez completely naked: but i immediately pushed her away: den she went back upstairs: n you dont know da hell i been goin through since en: i kept tryina make myself believe if i tolja then things would turn out for da bedder: but its juss not like at: i thoucha might go back ta da h: or see me differently even if i juss bein honest n didnt do anything wrong: n youd always feel awkward around me: n if ya stayed with her den youd look like an idiot: but thats juss how strong love can be: plus us four couldve never hungout again: n i also thought teresa might attack my credibility n try da tear us* ~~apart~~*: n say ya woulda left her dohncha think she woulda made up lies da ivy da get her away from me too: i mean sercly pess it mighta seemed so simple da juss be honest but it wasnt...(is iss makin any sense)...well if truth be told n i could do it all over again i woulda drug at bitch right up da steps: tolja: taken ya back da my room: n kept an eye on ya til ya healed...(pess deez people around us are makin me so sick with er stupid selfish tears n the way theyre talkin: ivy n teresa are huggin which makes me wonder wha da fuck ivy knows or has known: i swear she bedder notve known anything about teresas fuckin shit: but shezza one pissed cause im not consolin her: but shell never get people like us pess: never: how is it we can be such hard* *people n yet so emotional n sensitive in our own way: but juss da letcha know sumn about ivy: she rilly does loves you: eveno me n her are from different worlds shes still an awesome chick: i think she saved my life in a way: but den eres you: never gihn one fuckin break like at: but pess i gadda leave soon: im startina get rilly sick)...so back da whad is sayin: im sercly sorry for not tellin ya bro: n im gonna do all i can da find out wha happened: but is thinkin maybe deres one other thing i can do da make up for my disloyalty: its at question ya asked in the car: i know i dont have a definite answer but it rilly bothers me how i blew it off: i think it was a crucial point in yir life where you were lookin for direction or juss some comfort: but i dunno: if i could go back da that day da give ya dat sense of peace i think ya wanted i coulda tolja whad an irish man once sang in a sad song: but in at sadness i heard the answer da yir question n its rilly not that sad at all: i came across the song on the computer when is readin up on irish history juss for the hell of it: whatever izz cawed i dont even member now: but izz iss rill slow melancholic song with a fiddle n some instrument dit sounded like izz cryin: but at da end of the song i had an epiphany n thankfully one that has at least one word da go on: n its so simple so dont over complicate it: i juss wanchada accept da peace within: so when we die...we...(ahhh fuck pess why why why: i juss dont fuckin overstand why youd: no i promised i wouldnt do this) i juss (hold on pess: i needda breathe for a second).........aright pess listen: when we die we all godda same way home: yep: thats it: dont madder whad anything else is or was or will be cause we all godda same way home...dont madder where yir from or where youve been or where ya thouchad be goin: its now the same exact way da the same exact home...home: yir home now pess: with yir mum n god...now look: im gonna leave iss fuckin place: i cant take eez fuckin people anymore...ahh ya know dickhead i gadda drive all da way fuckin back dahn da school cuzza you: but dont worry: im gonna get so fuckin high n lissina some dropkick n social d juss for you...hey pess check iss one out: you do realize once ey putcha under n time passes by iddle rilly look like ya got...struck by da yuck: hahahahaha...ahh if i could only see yir smirk one more time...well in a way i still can: juss in a different way: kinda like how well still be talkin all the time ya know...(prayer)...well bro uhh guess ill see ya soon: whenever i get home...i love you.*

FOR PESSIMISM'S DELIGHT

What does it mean to be a dreamer? : a meticulous planner of small facets and big circumstances? : one that clutches to, and rides on, a destiny they want to control? : they *believe* they can control? : perhaps one who's ready to face disappointment? : perhaps not? : but you've become so sick of the perhaps and perhaps-nots that you feel like collapsing your body down and stretching your arm upward to embrace the dream : yes, just snatch that silk-spun dream right out of its phantasmal carapace! : for, at a distance, the dream is just like a rainbow : a vision of utopia : a glimmering palatial haven just beyond the horizon : and although you can't reach it from here you're sure you know the roads to get there : so you're thinking : if these dreams, hopes, and visions spawn in the mind then shouldn't they become alive through the industrial creations also spawned by the mind? : the tactile worldly things we can touch and feel and manipulate for our own welfare? : exactly so! : therefore, knowing you can't reach it from here, and the journey is too far by foot, your acumen encourages you to use those tactile industrializations so capturing your dream is all the more obtainable : sooooo—BAM!—the incredible inventions spawned from our incredible minds come into tangible existence : ready to accommodate the arduousness of—hurry! hurry! hurry! start the engine! can't hesitate : for the dreamy rainbow is trickery in perception and you don't have much time : and the car might only last a two hundred thousand miles : the rainbow is surely at least three hundred thousand! : surely so! : go! go! go! : *quo vadis? redivivus!*[1] : no! no! no!: gooooooooooo!...and now the years of aimless traveling has taken a toll on your composure : you're weathered and beaten like a battered piñata : and look at the car : it's damaged and rusted like something in a junkyard : but who looks worse? : its life will respawn in the earth, once again able to be what it was before : but not yours : at least not in whole : but wait! fear not! hope is still in sight! : for the rainbow shines on! : I can see it! can you! (could he?) : certainly so! : because after all these long senescent years spent on this expedition searching for the visionary land, you're convinced you must be closer : true, the dream might seem too utopian and curious at times : but it *must* be genuine : yes! because the expectation of validity is why we foster dreams in the first place, right? : right! : so we must strive on! : in haste! : so let's gooooooooooo!...and now you're *in articulo mortis*[2] : HA! yes, the end is near! : AH! *tempus fugit!*[3] : BUT! the car, the good ol' industry, decides not to endure another inch : perhaps (or perhaps not) due to your reckless driving from your sudden disregard not to preserve the standard condition : have you've finally realized what you had to do all along? : doesn't matter: all industrialization desists alongside the road that you're about to stray from : a road that seems to be right back where you started : and after all (that is, after all your

---

[1] [lat] where are you going? come back to life!
[2] [lat] at the moment of death
[3] [lat] time flies!

dedication), the industrialization has left you nothing besides the remnants of loathing and dissatisfaction to choke on : but you've already been so overconsumed by such trifles that immunity is now your newfound friend : notwithstanding, what you're consumed by now which offers no immunity is the trepidation burning inside you, aware you must go on all alone : that it doesn't stop here : it can't stop here : it *won't* stop here : so you bolt from the vehicle which you now curse as fallacious, twisted, wasted, and damned, and you, you brave soul, you step off the road and lunge your body out and up towards the sky, trying in your final attempt to be answered : one final attempt to read your heart, your mind, your entire self, by untying all the ties tied up in Gordian knots : to cut 'em all loose and let everything that's been concealed underneath beating up through with incessant knocks of desperation explode : you must now bring to this final endeavor nothing but successful fruition before it's too late because there's so much more for you : there's so much more than this : there just has to be so much more! : so in supplication, you brave, brave soul, you step, you lunge, you collapse, you exhaust, and, *sub dio, inter spem et metum, superne nitens,*[4] you stretch your beaten, battered, bruised, cut, gashed, slashed, manipulated, exploited, labored arm, and with your desperate up-to-heaven clawing hand, embrace..

---

[4] [lat] under the open sky, between hope and fear, striving upwards

PART III

A ONE-WAY FLIGHT TO HELL

"Close your eyes, child...there's nothing to see...close your eyes, child...and got to sleep...dream of clouds, child...soft and white...dreams of clouds, child...then hold on tight...feel the breeze, child...the window's open...feel the breeze, child...and keep on hopin'...for something sweet...close your eyes, child...something's coming...but not for you, child...not for you...it's reality and it's mean, child...now close your eyes and go to sleep..." [1]

...After reversing its itinerary, the commercial airplane zipped back over an inlet of the Atlantic...then slipped inside the upper windows of the silver skyscraper, like a charmed snake taking refuge in a large metal basket then striking up a symphony of burning sorrow. Instantly, with such indignation and vengeance, an explosion of flames shot sideways into the air. Engulfing the spacious skies, the variegated orangeness expanded...rolled...then curled like a demonic tongue. When the ball of flame reached the apex of combustion, ember waves of pain began falling from its belly...all the way down to the fruited plain and pilgrims' feet. A rain of black flakes. An abortion of a flight that just became the plight of the alabaster city, New York City, which could only look up at this monstrosity with dimmed tears. The tears, the shock, the Manhattan Concourse had started seventeen minutes earlier when the *first* snake slipped inside the cranium of the twin's sibling; *that* snake was slithering...constricting...and strangulating...while smoldering out- and upward a plume of black magic. If you transfixed on the lines of the smoke you could see an antithetical SOS. It read *FUCK – YOUR – GOD*

Yes, when I opened my eyes at a quarter-past nine—(an unexpected time for me to wake up, given that my alarm clock wasn't set to go off for another hour)—it was to witness the upshot of America being the world's p(l)eace-maker. Perhaps it proved my intuition was stronger than my unconsciousness? Either way, my body was awakened by an ominous chill, while the flames on the television screen corresponded with the burning sensation in my gut, assuring me the entire world was (or was about to be) tuned-in to watch the grotesque results. Coughing from a week-old cold, I turned on my side and started flipping through the channels...hoping *it* would stop...hoping a cartoon would appear...but nothing on the whole suggestive of innocence. That's when I yelled out in a hoarse voice: 'Wha' inna *fuck* is goin' on?!' Luke woke up. Humped on his side, he rubbed his sticking eyelids and groggily asked, 'What's wrong?' Once he saw the television: 'What's goin' on?' I said that I wasn't really sure, but whatever it was, it wasn't good. Luke sat up on his bed like a chubby Buddhist, and once overstanding the gist of the situation, he bowed his head down in prayer. Seemed like a good idea, so I too decided to pray in the way I do. Then, together, we watched people die...

---

[1] Lyrics from "Close Your Eyes, Child" by Hawa Halo, from the album *Our Cloud of Witnesses*

...Out on the warring streets of New York City, the reporters and their crews were in disarray, pushing and shoving, vying for the best position—trying to establish for the audience the best aesthetic background. Shapeless bodies were speeding by, heading for harbor, heading for waters—subways to the suburbs! But underneath the black flakes, the reporters erected themselves fearlessly and began disclosing the details behind "this breaking story" which varied between each reporter, and with each reporter, changed every other minute. Some knew this, some knew that, some never saw it coming, some saw it coming, so to speak, from a mile away; meaning, in measures of time, years prior. Yet none could stop it—*could've* stopped it...

...Meanwhile, the police and firefighters (even undeterred locals) were working in harmony to evacuate those trapped inside the burning buildings and surrounding areas. But the task was already proving to be convoluted, oppressive, and dangerous. The two thick almost-rock-solid clouds of amalgamated smoke, fire, and metal were doggedly and downwardly fighting against them. These dark waves of muscle that had ripped up through the cemented ground, straight from Hell...rose as high as the clouds...then flexed their arms outward like Agrios and Oreios on the verge of bringing their prey into inexorable bearlike grips, ready to crush the entire city into pebbles. Even the way the two manbeasts were huffing smoke in measured draws was simil~~ar to~~ the premeditations of large predators about to give a deathblow to millions in one fell swoop: *Born to slay like their mal-mother; manbeasts to carnivorous birds; swooping down for bloody remnants; feasting lawlessly on innocence; they can fly away—but never land.*[2] So grotesque and unreal, like something pealed from classic pages but animated by the greatest brand of modern technology. But how real it would become every time the cameras panned from the smoking monsters up in the sky...down to the flesh and blood of those made from the same mold as me, except they were becoming grimy and charred and I was clean in my bed. You would've thought the firefighters would've turned the fire hose around and stuck it in their mouth just to quench an apparent thirst from the stinging metallic particles beating against their blistered faces, and whenever they breathed, the chunks of xerotes shooting down

---

[2] Agrios and Oreios were half-human/half-bear Gigantes in Greek mythology that feasted lawlessly on humans. "Born to slay like their mal-mother..." and the lines that follow allude to their mother Polyphonte whose name is translated "Slayer of Many." However, even she feared her sons because, lacking respect for the ancient pecking-order, Agrios and Oreios feared neither god nor man. For this reason, Zeus sent them to Hades to let Hermes (the interventionist of the gods) punish them. But before Hermes could cut off their limbs, Ares intervened and helped him turn the Gigantes, along with Polyphonte, into ominous, carnivorous birds: Agrios the vulture, Oreios the eagle-owl, and Polyphonte the owl who portends war and sedition. "They can flay away—but never land" alludes to the fact that Agrios and Oreios, detested by both good and evil gods, weren't allowed in any realm. The tale is recounted in *Metamorphoses* (21) by Antoninus Liberalis.

their inflamed throats. But not one soul did: forward and together, they labored on in blood, sweat, and tears—and filth—such filth!—pushing back, whenever they had to, those getting in the way, the ones trying to make morbid photo albums.

Although appearing ominous through the camera lenses, the situation *did* (as I look back into the lenses of my mind) seem containable via Work and Time. That ol' split catchphrase "in time, in time" seemed to be the historical crutch to start leaning on. But what could we do in the meantime? Could we lessen the devastation? Were we now dealing with the inevitable? Had the wheels of the world been placed in another's hands? Seemed so. Seemed as if we'd woken up inside an opera house with a twisted tragedy underway on stage, with a few actors playing to a soldout crowd in the millions, because in the 8th hour of September 11, 2001, we as a nation instantly split: there was those who could only watch, and those who were *had to* perform—perform the daring hard work...til "in time, in time" allowed everyone to reconvene backstage: almost like meeting back inside the frames of the day before, just with a few less people. Only the two-crutched hopefuls would believe *no one* had died yet. So in this state of mind, I lay back on my bed thinking that this combination of hard work by the New Yorkers, coupled with the slow passing of time the rest of us were experiencing passively, was our best hope—that blood will *have to* bleed til we find a big enough Band-Aid to fix this gash in the heart of our nation.

However, that all began falling apart. My rationalizations, hopes, and solutions came crashing back down into darkest recesses of my inner world. My emotions were piquing my rationalizations—gradual but harrowing like measured drops of water falling on my forehead, each one that much closer to insanity—for if truth be told, I was well aware that I wasn't sure *what* was about to happen in New York City: how demonstrative the scene was, how expansive it could become. Thoughts of little cuts (a few casualties) quickly began turning into images of an urban slaughterhouse...into a flattened nation...into worldwide holocaust.

I picked up the phone and called Ma, just in case there would be a case. As the phone kept ringing—so torturously it kept ringing!—I was trying to subdue any physical signs of apprehension in front of Luke whose face was like a large frozen tear. Thankfully, finally, surprisingly, Ma answered the phone. In the background, Aunt Stella was already bellowing out convictions and instructions. Come home, Vincent! the world's ending! her friends were right! she was right for believing her friends! how could they let these foreign monsters into our country! these sandniggers are gonna kill us all! (By now, reporters had the scoop on the hijackers' identity: their nationality and dogmas, based on physical descriptions and language. Initially, the information had been relayed from those on the planes before crashing. They'd been on cell phones, and the information had been sent to the primary sources, then to the media, then ultimately to us with slight delay and spin.) Before Ma could even speak anything more than hello, Aunt Stella bellowed out in love, fear, and delirium: 'Vincent, you come home right away!' By "home" she meant her house where Ma had once again found herself stuck after Pessi died because for whatever reason—(her weak inclination to obey? the strength of her loyalty? the rampant fears?

the utter confusion? the guilt from her so-called "abandonment"?)—she couldn't make it back to Catania. For her to return, it seemed, would be to sanction another young death; yet to stay in America might now be her own. Desperately trying to establish authority over Background Stella, Ma went into a tearful jumpy tone, telling me to please come home. However, I was neither externally nor internally as shaken, for her heightened sense of fear didn't come from the television *per se*, but from Aunt Stella's rhetoric: her selfish brainwashing to have (no matter the external circumstances) someone to hold onto who wasn't "crazy" or an invalid like Uncle Alfonse.

'Ma—MA! Juss cahm dahn. Everything's gonna be ar'ight. Juss stay inside, 'n'—'n' I'll caw back in a liddle when I know what's goin' on. Ar'ight?'

'Okay. Dat's-ah fine. Call back soon. *Ti vogghiu beni, Vinny.'*

'Ti vogghiu beni macari.' Click.

Holding the phone at my knee, I wondered if that was the last time I'd say *I love you* in *any* language: was the world really heading into its final fate? was the Second Coming coming? Just in case there would be a case—just in case this *was* our last chance to speak our peace and say our goodbyes—I called Ivy; I never dialed a number so fast before. *Punchpunchpunchpunchpunchpunchpunchpunchpunchpunch.* With the phone pressed tightly against my ear all I could hear was that fucking torturous ringing again!...But no answer! I hung up and tried again...three times!...four times! Fucking answer! I looked over at Luke: seemed he was trying to read my face, flashing me a tinge of sympathy in the process, just in case there—it suddenly came to mind that perhaps he *could* see how much I was agonizing inside. I couldn't show any weakness because I was as strong and hard as humanly possible. I couldn't let it be seen that inside me was fear simply because Ivy wasn't answering, which could mean Aristod too might be under attack and she could be suffering from some horrible act of crime and therefore I needed to hurry up, go outside, and find her—no, SAVE her!

I took the phone away from my ear and set it on my lap. Indifferently, I told Luke that I was going out to have a smoke. But inside I was so anxious to make sure nothing abysmal was happening beyond our secure walls: a decisive moment upon which I made my first major break from Rational Man since Pessi had died (nearly three months prior). I grabbed my smokes off my desk, already clutching my cell phone, then stepped out into the hall. Walking down through the fluorescence several doors were swung open because Scholars were popping in and out of each other's room, probably scared to be alone, finding strength in numbers. As I passed by, peaking into each room, I saw on their televisions the same catastrophe I'd seen on mine, the same catastrophe I was hoping not to find outside the dormitory, as irrational as that may seem...

...In terms of the foreground proximity, all was safe outside. Yet the faces passing by were blank, perplexed, nervous, crestfallen: maybe all in one. I sat down on a bench and scuffed my shoes on the concrete as I lit a cigarette. The smoke only further agitated my cough, but I persevered. Looking around with a sharp eye, I saw less bodies walking to and fro class than usual. In all probability, Aristod was just a microcosm of *every* community in the nation: everyone watching (or on their way to watch) people die on television, while lacing up their strings real tight, preparing to run to the edge of the world and (if necessary) jump; the pluckier ones loading up the clip, preparing to fight back; and the profiteers—the "heroic entrepreneurs" (as Max Weber would say)—only had to glance at the television once before—

Halfway through the smoke Ivy *finally* returned my calls to tell me that she was home with her family (a relief); and that all classes at Aristod had just been cancelled because of the general proximity of the full-blown sadism (didn't plan on going to classes anyway); and the updated news that purportedly other hijacked planes were flying around the northeast (???).

'Who the fuck opened up Pandora's box?' Taking the question as rhetorical, Ivy didn't bother replying. But I said it with Pessi, Rick, and Razzle in mind. The recent past still seemed as surreal and brutal as the mythical nature of the events occurring in present in which I knew people were dying as we talked on the phone. What could I do though? What could I have done? Could I have stopped 'em from falling? Stopped Pessi from shooting? Stopped my dog's innards from mushing? Stopped my father's heart from exploding? Solemnly, I started to accept my guilt, and—

'...Fine!' she screamed. 'It's not like I expected you to anyway! God, you're so stubborn I can't stand it!'

While she waited for a response, I coughed violently, almost without end. Amid the blur and hacking (with an acute pounding in my head!) I realized everything, everywhere, was taking the form of irritability and intolerance in the name of love. She was imploring me to come over to her parents' *right now:* another behind-the-scenes demand by her parents who, as of late, kept asking her where I've been: this, knowing I was still severely depressed over Pessi. But who was I to want time alone to pretend to be healing? to slow down the craziness of my life that had escalated to psychotic degrees since leaving for college? the place I went to find peace, relaxation, and normality. But like being mocked by an echo that took a while to carom back, the concept of college as a retirement home for the youth *had* come true, for there *was* peace and relaxation in the deaths occurring during my time at college; namely, within the souls retired from their bodies; and ultimately, they say death *is* normal.

After telling Ivy that I wasn't coming over because I wasn't in any mood for family shit, and from the way her parents had a tendency to talk about me behind my back, I'd *never* be in the mood—well, Ivy, in one of her most ferocious tones ever, told me that she was so sick of my "ways" and not to call back. *Click!* But I let it go: stress was just getting the better of us on this tragic day of combustion. And to speak of myself, in addition to the stress, I was afflicted with a farrago of anger, anxiety, confusion, chaos, curiosity, cough, and phlegm. Feeling like this, I stood up and smashed the cigarette into a ceramic tray. Before going back inside I surveyed the side yard. Behind it all—that is, the bodies and buildings—the weather was pleasant: in a mild temper, the amber sun was relaxing low in a chalk-white sky; from an even strain of wind, loose leaves were curling upward like flexing smiles; uncut blades of grass were rolling out collectively towards the east as if fanning the sun into its mild temper...

...With his arms crossed over like a bad-ass bouncer, Agent Ralphie was standing in the middle of my dim room, conversing with Luke. From behind, he looked like he'd lost weight; his unwieldiness seemed more compacted and now capable of professional stealth. Moving in, I coughed and sniffed a few times. He slowly turned around: a prismatic grayness flashed on his arms: the sun clashing with his gray t-shirt. In a heavy drop, he nodded his large head at me—then turned back towards the television. I sat down on my bed, knees towards Agent Ralphie's hip. He whispered something I didn't catch, but to which Luke, sitting on his bed, solemnly agreed to. I felt awkward and left out, so I leaned back and turned the television up a few notches. The chaos became louder. Agent Ralphie began talking about the '93 terrorist attack, which I'd forgotten all about. He mentioned that his uncle lives in Manhattan, and had been five blocks away during the '93 underground bombing of the same building that now had a snake stuck inside its cranium. Agent Ralphie quieted as we listened to a reporter discussing the other purported hijacked planes—but nothing could be confirmed at this time. While we waited for more concrete information, we watched the smoke swelling around the twins, becoming blacker and thicker...converging together in a magnificent stream lurking out to the left in the skyline...slowly leaving the contained space...some of it, out to the sea, the rest seeping into nearby buildings...

...Then at 9:41 a.m. the concrete information we'd been waiting for came when another plane came crashing down into the wall of the Five-Star. The explosion of flames went twice as high as the short cream wall. Within minutes the scene was nothing more than a parade of gray and black smoke...most of it rolling out to the right...and slightly upward in uniform slants...being guided by the natural wind. After a sudden swell of hell, the building disappeared. But shining through where the plane had hit was this phenomenal ovular flame. The colors so enticing. There seemed to be a grand answer within...but too hot to approach...too hot.

As if the area was prepared for it—and why wouldn't the Capitol be on the highest alert?—the firefighters were immediately on the scene, ready to fight the newest monster. And this one seemed to have its puissance, its nefarious soul, deep within that ovular flame glowing so mockingly behind the smoke. They stood back, braced themselves, then fired away into the ganglionic too-hot. But some firefighters ran outward, and with motioning arms, began coordinating the evacuation of all government buildings, although many were already running for their life, the more youthful ones pushing seniors and women out of the way: Survival-of-the-Fittest clearly visible in the place founded on and sustained by that very principle. And then—

The clock struck 9:59 a.m. Flash to New York City. Evidently those within the buildings had been informed or had a good idea the buildings weren't going to withstand the damage. Too much too late: the building that had been hit second looked like its neck had just been snapped. It titled to the left—paused—almost staring us right in the face with self-disappointment like the hero who fails to win in the end—then collapsed straight to the ground in a matter of seconds. There was a horrible grumble like rolling thunder...*everything falling to blackness...(silence)...the feeling all heartbeats have stopped*...before the remnants came storming back up from the ground, lashing outward in a mobile mass of Grayness symbolic our past sensibilities. Now this thing so real and animated (yet made of the earth's most stolid elements) was coming straight towards us with obstreperous vengeance. As this thing—this fuckin' steel monster on the hunt moved forward with aggression and abomination, I could feel myself running away with those terrified souls in New York City. The sound was horrifying. I closed my eyes in desperation: to take everyone away to a better world. But even there I could still see 'em running towards me...still hear their cries and screams coupled with the amelodic crashing of instructions and metal...still smell the stench of smoke on their bodies...still taste the salt of their tears...still feel my heart (in a fast rhythmic beat) yearning and striving for utopia. And then—

The clock struck 10:06 a.m. Flash to Shanksville, PA. The aftermath reported: another plane had just came down through the sky, wobbly at first...but steadying out, upside-down...torching the top of a forest with the meticulousness of a barber...before crossing a barren country road...then plunging deep into pastoral ground. Focus on the crater: no remnants of a plane to be seen; just a gigantic sooty hole. I thought, '*Fuck, 'at's near Pixburgh!*' Then I fell into a frozen state of mind: astonishment keeping my mouth held open: a microcosm of the crater—as everything else in the world rushed on in vengeful vicissitudes. Although I didn't want to face Luke or Agent Ralphie, I couldn't control my urge to gauge their reaction: but I couldn't even discern their basic states or shapes in the haziness of my own. And then—

The clock struck 10:10 a.m. Luke gagged back a breath. Twenty-nine minutes after being hit, the walls of the Five-Star crashed to the ground; the walls were too weak, too light, too unsecured, so naturally they fell quicker. You could see the firefighters still fighting, but they could only get so close, could only do so much. The camera panned across the scene slowly: the ovular flame had become a shoddy-looking V with its sides being stretched outward...further and further like arms being bent behind its back...til they, the arms, snapped...then vitriolic ash quickly extinguished the V...

...As silence reigned over the room, save for the television, a song began playing inside my head: "Curse of a Fallen Soul" by Dropkick. Dunno why. Dunno why the song fluently slipped into another Dropkick song "Wheel of Misfortune." Then into "Amazing Grace." Then fluently back into the first. Dunno how long those songs played til I witnessed him falling. (At this point, my memory becomes severely distorted: mostly likely from the amalgamation and swelling of emotions. It's hard to say if I'd seen it that day, live or delayed, or days after when that brilliantly morbid collage began stitching together, snugly draped across the fabric of the media like a homespun quilt, *in memoriam* to the body-count still in progress. How *do* you keep the dead warm?) Again, I'm just not sure when I saw it, but I know my eyes had to be open really wide because I could see half of the building to his left and the entire sky behind him as I watched him fall through the air...rotating around and around like a cent to split a head...his tiny elastic arms and legs flailing clockwise-to-counterclockwise like a tribal dance taken to new heights...a freer space to move around and around...heaven now his dance floor til—*BAM!*

The television audience didn't *see* him hit the ground, but *the impact* split the ground of the entire nation: so secure and positive it once was. Then more, one after another, men and women (some hand-in-hand) following him to the promise land, jumping to save their lives through death...on the way down, dancing in silence...looking like dexterous spiders coming down an unseen string...hitting like clashing temperatures, or when worlds collide. They, those desperate souls, just evaporated. As a distant witness, I was being knocked more senseless each time the last remaining building quivered or another person jumped. But my eyes were being held opened, not allowed to quiver, forced to witness. But I wanted to shut 'em, fall back asleep, st<u>art</u> the day anew, st<u>art</u> my life anew—the world anew. But I was stuck in—*the screaming the running the pushing the shoving the shouting the loving the hating the money, our truth is debris wafting in black seas, across the land twirl tornadoes of misery—whose God blessed this divine tragedy?!—now black birds once white, once flying, are now falling, now dying, and voices once right are now lying, now selling, so compelling, but the signs on the stage are always trailing—the observer, the audience—can't you sense you've been blind all this time?!: rewind, play it again, and catch what you failed to find...*

Ahhh! I flipped to different coverage. I had no other choice. This channel was driving me insane...The new one the same!...Flip, flip, flip...All the same! But I had to stop cold and stick to one because I couldn't stop watching what I didn't want to watch...

...Then I could sense it. Even the reporters were *affirming* the improbability. My eyes might've been wide-open and technically focused on *it*, and my ears might've been unplugged and aligned with the speakers, but I was busy backpedaling through my mind, seeing *other* images, the superimposition of symbols over symbols, trying to figure out how to stop that last building from falling: walk backwards two thousand years: stop the cross from going upright...walk back another fifteen hundred: stop the water from p<u>art</u>ing aside...another million billion trillion years: stop the apple from being plucked...ceaselessly backwards...til there was nowhere else to go besides inward, perhaps into the nativity of the first sun: an impetus sucking me and the entire universe inside its nucleus, closing up— an indescribable implosion!—then evaporating, just like the desperate souls who jumped. But I couldn't do anything to stop the last building from falling. At 10:28 a.m. it too looked like its neck had just been snapped—a *coup de grâce*[3] from an invisible force lurking within the fire and smoke— then it came dropping down, layer-by-layer, in succession, in a matter of four seconds...*(a sustained sensation of heaviness)*...then rising back up in the shape of a giant gray weeping willow. And emerging from the metallic shade came the neck-snapper: another fuckin' monster moving forward on the prowl! Seemed nobody could stop these brutal p<u>art</u>uritions! Seemed millions more were to come: one in every American building! I was calling

---

[3] [fre] a deathblow delivered to end the misery of a wounded victim

for Beowulf or *San Giorgiu la spata vita*[4] (ol' horseback Heros) to come and slay these dragons of the Old World!

Demoted, Deputy Ralphie couldn't bear anymore of this sick surreality: powerless, and without a farewell, he decamped to his room. Luke Adagio finally rose from his bed. He gloomily slipped on a pair of wrinkled khakis. Clad and sad, he picked up his cell from his desk. His Adam's apple convulsed as he dialed home. I was surprised his mother hadn't already called. (Of course, Luke's hadn't because he had to be respectful to Agent Ralphie.) Listening in, I found out his mother's reasoning was that she'd been asleep, sick with the flu. He told her to turn on the television. Then came the questions. Luke's responses came in short affirmations. When he moved back to his bed, I could hear his mother a little better. She didn't sound like Aunt Stella had, but there was still a tone of concern, but within a modest, prayerlike voice. They talked for ten minutes before exchanging goodbyes and I-love-yous. Luke set his cell beside him on the bed. He clutched his knees: couldn't have free hands. When we made eye contact, his nervousness asked if I wanted to go to the commons to eat. I said that I wasn't hungry; hadn't been in days. So like always, he got ready despondently...and left the room despondently—that sad, lonely, slow-moving deportment that often made me question my reserved attitude towards him. But there was a deeper tragedy at play other than my collegial caginess. Besides, it might've been a bittersweet blessing for him to be going out alone this time; probably wanted to find a place to hide away and cry.

After he left, I shot up with unseen strength, kicked a white undershirt towards my closet, and marched as far as I could without exiting, which left me standing militarily in front of my desk. It was unusually messy, but I didn't have time to be militarily fastidious, only the time to keep on high-alert. I could feel it—so intense and intensifying—that something was about to blindside me. Preparing myself, I began shuffling through papers, folders—an array of things on the desk...til I found the bottle. I shot two doses of bitter orange medicine down my throat. It would do me good. Then I did an about-face and began shuffling through the orphans. I pulled out a black hoodie and threw it on. It would do me good. I spun back around and stared at my small silver stereo jammed into the corner of my desk. I knew music would also do me good: the music that had been my salvation all other times when I needed some rugged angels to lift me up by the bootstraps. So I picked up a black vinyl case, set it on the desk, and began flipping through...til stopping on the Ds. I pressed my forefinger down on an army-green Dropkick Murphys CD, the one with all the songs that had been playing in my head earlier; seemed to be a touch of fate or a small necessity. But I couldn't take it out. The television—it was yelling at me. Telling me to sit back down and watch. Watch and listen to *this!* Now!!! (But I didn't want to.) I sat down at my desk, cowering behind the shelf, positioning myself as far against the wall as I could. No you don't! Take a peak! (I did: they were coming after me.) I hunkered back down. But I could still hear 'em—abysmal sounds calling out for help—calling out to *me*, the

---

[4] [scn] the living sword, St. George

failed-hero in the audience...perhaps an embryonic chickenshit seeing as a pusillanimous feeling was now twitching in my cheeks. But I could still hear the shriek of every victim—and my name within: *vaaaahh!...laaaahh!...nooooo!* This dirgelike shrill ripping through my ears but stripped of the formalities of melody: *vaaaahh!...laaahh!...nooooo!* Meanwhile, every journalist's account seemed to be blaming me for *it* while commanding me to stop *it;* they'd done and were still doing *their* job, but I wasn't doing *mine* and hadn't been. Their fingers were gripped so boldly around their black wands, but I could see their pointer-fingers secretly pointing out at *me* on behalf of the ones dropping dead around 'em. It's my passivity, they seemed to be saying—my hands were red because of my passivity. As they continued yelling at me, I looked over my hands...the reporters were right: my hands *were* reddening; and now they, the reporters, were mocking me even louder, more viciously. It felt like blood was going to emerge from my fuckin' ears: a cerebral explosion, the blood squirting out everywhere, filling up the holes and tubes in my head, methodically thumping down on the drums to the beat of "The Tyranny of Tympanic." Panic! Panic! Panic! I needed to deafen my ears! I would've cut 'em off or stabbed into the drums if I didn't need 'em to listen to the music that I presently couldn't listen to. And the remote control—well, it was *waaaay* over there on the bed, three-feet away; I couldn't leave my bunker: I could be sucked into it—the war on the streets—where they would surely maul me.

On a yellow piece of paper I began jotting down poetic observations and blunt condemnations, trying to exorcise from my head the age-old demons, along with the newest haunting images and sounds...but it was proving in vain. I'd *have to* suffer. Besides, who was I to try escaping when no one else could? So I put down the paper and pen, then pulled out a bag, a blunt, and a razor blade; from this, I created something more effective. Afterward, I held the little creation of ephemeral salvation in my hand. As I eyed it up to the tip, I found myself shifting over, peeking out, focusing back into the screen, trying to find answers...but nothing could be discerned amid all the fallen debris; and the leftover metal banging clangorously against leftover metal; and the warlike sirens ripping through thick, darkened, fiery air; and the outraged reporters clashing with the piteous reporters; and the physical victims flying by, trying to escape the streets of Armageddon—the suave suits now all haphazard and ragged—who, on their way out, if they could even get out, looked like they were either shrinking into children or aging into cripples: that too couldn't be discerned. Out of the blue, Ivy Pineda (the Spanish angel whose wings could take us high away from this mess [God bless the thought]) flashed before my eyes. I wanted to be lying down with her, nestled underneath her soft wings, resting my head on her peaceful breasts, chewing on her ophidian mocha...in the orchard...up on cloud nine...far away from here...far away.

I realized that I *had to* leave this place. If Luke should happen to return before I had the chance, I'd feel obligated to stick around and exchange words. But no time for words. Not even a syllable. I *had to* go! I quickly grabbed up a few things...*got 'em!*...but on the way out unfortunately remembered that I was supposed to tutor Gabby Williams at 3 p.m.; it was now almost 11:30 a.m. I wasn't sure if canceled classes meant everything else affiliated with college was automatically canceled; Gabby and I had set up our meeting in a private, which meant I was helping her off-the-clock, and therefore it was probably up to *us* to cancel or continue. I went back to my desk...ransacking through the mess...my backpack...the pockets of my jeans, searching for her number...but couldn't find it anywhere! Frustrated and ready to punch something, I caught a glimpse of Jesus: a reminder that Luke could be back any minute. I *had to* go. If Gabby Williams was still expecting me to show up, although people were dying, she'd just have to fuckin' overstand I *had to* go really far away from *here*. I really, really had to go. In an involuntary jerk, I looked back up at Jesus still knocking on the door not being opened...then down to the television I left on. I looked at both, one above the other, for another second or two. It was time to go. Confused, I turned around and quietly shut the door...

....The road was winding through the mountains like a snake. It was an old gray road: rough and narrow, like a snake. Chips of gravel were kicking up against the chassis, probably putting nicks in the quarter-panels. But I didn't care: my rust-laden light-brown car had now become *nu cavaddu ri battaglia*: a warhorse. Besides, I liked the sound of pinging gravel. In some parts (where I was driving too fast on the 40 mph country road) it sounded like a heavenly hailstorm turned upside-down...

....The mountain that I was gradually ascending (and now driving straighter and deeper into the heart) was dense with bluish evergreens and fading-green oaks whose arms extended over top of the road to hold boughs on the other side. The woods, in some parts, looked like it had been sent through a paper-shredder because the trees were skinnier with thin, wavy, white strips of light separating 'em. Overall, though, the forest was heavily shaded and solitary: the amber sun could only spy on me around certain bends; passing humans were few and far between; even the animals were out of sight, besides two opossums who made no attempt to flee from the road, which I had to cater to their lethargy, four deer who squirmed through the thicket, which I slowed down to observe, and one dead skunk lying in the middle of the road, which I—an accidental *PLUMP!* Yep, I was virtually all alone, cruising through unknown territories, listening to my blazing, blessed music, three CDs in, on my way to reach the unseen horizon...

....I lit a cigarette. Rolled the window down all the way. Ejected Cockney Rejects. Slid in Hank III. Turned it up. And kept driving through the wooded mountain. A very pleasant monotony. Gobs of greens. Slivers of silver. Blotches of brown. White, yellow. White, orange. AMBER! The whole shrouded land engulfing my eyeballs, with a creeping cocksure feeling that many unseen animals were all around me but not bothered by my presence. The wind—the unseen wind....*shwoooooooooo!*...beating against my naked left arm with such intimacy! As true country music blared through my speakers, I was being filled up and overwhelmed by a nostalgia that wasn't my own, which wasn't right...til it finally broke wide-open.

Before me now was the same sole rickety road but completely straightened out...the road slightly dipping down...then shooting ahead three visible miles...before ascending back up into a blind horizon. The road itself a fantastic sight. Not too much to the sides besides stretching green fields that rolled up and down til reaching (far out on the left) a yellowish hill with short shrubbery, evidently planted, for they were in symmetrical rows. Preceding that: colorful green fields wild with yellow buttercups, grainy white clovers, and elongated clusters of Viper's Bugloss: fluorescent-purple. Lonely maples sat here and there: some mountain maples with short drab trunks and bushy foliage; others brilliantly orange massive sugar maples with lustrous gray trunks and leaves in an upright ovular shape. I wanted to go lie under one! on the backside! where no one would ever see me way out there! But I couldn't stop the ol' warhorse; I was buckled into the saddle.

Up high, in the blue, invasive clouds just moved away from the amber sun. The sky suddenly brightened like the flick of a switch. The sun was at my northwest, half aligned with the open window, half with the windshield, and although bright, appearing smaller than the trees. I focused back ahead—straight ahead where the long road was set before me like a challenge—and with a wild urge surging through me I put the pedal to the metal to see how fast the ol' warhorse could go. *Vrooooooooom!...VROOOOOOOM!...*just striding ahead!...til topping out at a shaky-89. The ol' warhorse jerked left, so I gradually pulled the reins back to prevent from fishtailing. *Ahhh! but who cares if I wreck anyway? Prahblee juss roll out inda the field. Da ol' warhorse might explode. I'll purposely leave my cell inside its belly juss in case. As long as I can manage da escape den—well, the closest tree won't take long da get to...unless I lose use of my limbs. MY LIMBS!* Put in check by catastrophic thoughts, I used my left foot and right hand to shift into cruise for the other two wide-open miles...

...Back into the woods, I began coming upon steep slopes that the ol' warhorse was struggling to climb. *Rump-thump-glump-pump...ump-ump-and-away!* After the gray road leveled out a bit, and I passed a series of private driveways, it began looking like sheer night from the density of trees and hills within the mountain. It was only 1:06 p.m. But since I had no intentions on turning around, time meant nothing. I popped another cigarette in my mouth, fishing around for my lighter. Meanwhile, the last song on the Lucinda Williams CD had just begun, so I was also contemplating what to put on next. But my attention to the lighter and music was diverted when, going around an elevated bend shaped like a wide upside-down U, I met with a mint station wagon padded with wooden panels. The driver appeared to be a portly lady with graying brown hair, while the rest of the paddy wagon was filled to the brim with unruly matmice. She was driving too fast, while I was driving too far on the other side: caused by fishing for the lighter. As I swerved back to the right, she braked to a near stop, honking twice. I looked back through the rearview mirror. The matmice were laughing, the ones in far back (where there wasn't a seat) falling all over each other like kids playing in a pool of plastic balls. But there was this one matmouse—this one kid who stood out. He was plumb against the back window. It looked as if he was trying to plant his lips against the window but couldn't because as she gassed it around the elbow of the U, the posse wagon began bouncing up and down while jerking forward, and his shaven head swiveled to the side and his cheek smacked off the glass; he flashed a cheesy smile, then vanished. It was only a glimpse, but I swear that kid looked just like Pessi when he was little.

A little trace of an old face can really get the thoughts a-pumpin'! So alive!—yes, Pessi! And why not? If I still couldn't get the death of years-deceased Matty to shake me in the present, then how could I even fathom Pessi to be months-dead? He wasn't—simply *couldn't* be dead. Either too unreal or too real. Either way, how could I believe it when it still made no sense? And since I and Ivy disconnected ourselves from Teresa, there was no way of knowing what really happened. It was pointless to question Teresa anyway because she was so full of lies, and with me being so full of rage, someone else would've—I dunno. Anyway, I settled for patiently waiting for the answers to come in with the wind. *Shwoooooooooo!* But so far all it bought were ear infections—and explosive nightmares of him lying on the ground, quivering, foaming, then blowing up, while she sat on the bed, smoking a cigarette, not laughing, but certainly amused behind her blasé expression. Yes, my mind's symbolism perfectly played out their final irony: her *content* in her quietude, and him *causing a scene* in his lunge into quietus, after it had, for the most part, for years, been the other way around. That's how Pessi became the fusion bomb in the light of things, and Teresa the fission bomb. Unlike Teresa's unremitting diffusion, her constant blitzkrieging, Pessi had a proclivity to let things build up, slowly but surely, with a few instances where he just blew everything up in one fell swoop. After the results came back, the coroner said he'd used X amount of alcohol to help X amount of oxycodone slide down his throat. Then he intravenously shot X amount of heroin into his arm: not even a dime's worth,[5] but within that small worth a large amount of quinine, the cutting agent. And after nineteen and a half years of all that had accrued inside, it only took a split-second to trigger the big bang—and he blew up. The amount of drugs was relatively small *per se*, they said. An allergic reaction to the quinine, they said. *Massive pulmonary edema*, they officially stated. Suffocation in the act, they explained to the lay. Suicide heading into the act, I said...to myself. But the coroner overruled suicide, going on the same logic that the police had half-outlined, and bolstered by the information Pessi's best friend had provided. As far as I know, that was it: the "investigation" went no further than that day. On my end: no more phone calls or visits. The newspaper had a follow-up article with general drug statistics. It also stated that "Officer Jenkins reported that Zach's long-time best friend Vincent Vallano, a junior at Aristod, said he never saw it coming since Zach had successfully completed rehab at..." None of the information came *directly* from me; I refused to talk to the papers whenever they called. Nor did I (or any of our friends) attend the group meetings to "keep one another strong and sort things out." I hardly discussed it with the crew. I just couldn't. So I let them, along with other friends, former classmates, neighbors—just anyone who ever knew Pessi—all the punks, skins, jocks,

---

[5] The relative amount of heroin to cause death

'necks, metalheads, fiends, queens, kings, hippies, yuppies, nerds, dropouts, wiggers, gangstas—the unlabeled nothings!—yes! even though Pessi had stayed away from so many people, so many people knew and liked Pessi!—you could feel it in the air!—you could see it in their body language and hear it in their words the respect he commanded and the concern he could provoke from Anyone's rumor, or simply from his silent smirk—yes! everyone loved his silence! the silence that killed him and yet brought alive the spirit of everyone's curiosity! But by keeping my suspicions inside, I let everyone believe in the oh-so-unfortunate relapse/allergic reaction/overdose raft of rubbish for the riffraff. Funny thing is: after knowing it wasn't from the *amount of* drugs, the coroner still considered it, generally speaking, an *overdose;* thus, just another story for the stats and a cause for a commercial. However, I did some research and found out that in circumstances like this—for *massive pulmonary endema*—it's an incorrect diagnosis to deem it an overdose, that the majority of deaths from heroin are *not* overdoses, and rather the result of abstruse chemical complexities. But given that no one (especially those within the rank of highly-educated doctors) likes to admit they're purblind, the matter is carelessly, frustratedly, categorically, thrown into OVERDOSE in order to provide us with certainty and closure, and yet that closure, in the larger scheme of things, is certainly the beginning (or rather at this point, the expanding) of an array of other societal sicknesses. Then again, perhaps it's like a *faux pas.* No big deal, really. Live and learn, live and let live. But since *he's* dead, just let go...let – it – go.

After going around the other side of the big U, a small town appeared. A stout green sign with white lettering read WELCOME TO THE TOWN OF LEY. Immediately to the right sat a ratty trailer park: the ratty trailers (mostly white, brown, and yellow) were in measured slants, edged against three rows of ratty roads (mostly busted up blacktop). I took a guess that the lady I passed lived there, and inside her pathetic trailer was the same as inside her paddy wagon: chaos packed with matmice—and mice. Cruising along, I passed, on the left, in solitary, that same church you see in the brochure for every small town in America: white, rectangular, one-story, with a brown cross nailed up on the gable. (Steeple churches must come free if you're starting up a small town.) Just past Ley's staple, I was stopped by a red light, the only one in sight. Two cars to my left and three to my right began taking turns. To my left, the church-side, but beyond the intersection, sat a large vacant parking lot...then a post office...then a large orange-bricked hall with a belfry at the top for a large golden bell: this was both the police and fire station. On the right side, close together, sat a clothing store called Dee's...a supermarket called Rick's...an electronics shop called Shaler's...a hobby shop called Adam and Eve's...then an old-fashion service station called Ley Garage and Food (est. 1937). I looked around this tiny business district...good and hard...and...and...and no Wal-mart! Wow! I vaddled. Straight and further ahead of this Wal-martless business district was a quaint residential area with a tree-lined street with three-story houses with round porches and pointy dormers. Evidently a few other businesses existed in the mix because I could see thick signs in some yards, as you see, in many places, dentists and lawyers do: locate their offices right among the families. Alwaysthemore, the wind-worn houses still had breathing-room. I could also see, far out on both sides of the yellowish land, a few ranches with fenced-in yards, as well as up on the bluish hills beyond, where they sat an acre apart. To get out that way you had to turn either way at the red light then travel down backroads, which the roads *furthest* away looked like long dying worms. When the light turned green, I went forward a quarter-mile and turned into the service station; I needed gas and a drink.

Unsure of how this old-fashion business worked, I reduced the ol' warhorse from a trot to a walk. The off-white service station had three parts: from left to right, a small dinner (a beat-up pickup truck parked in front) connected to a soda shop (with foggy windows) connected to a garage (with its door shut)—all welcomed by a bulky rusted sign and a gas area with only two pumps. Seemed like a potential murder scene for a b-film. Despite being from an area full of hunters, and the street ahead of me was full of friendly-looking houses, I felt a bit vulnerable. *Maybe Ley's a cult town—a real life Nilbog! Looks similar da Nilbog: small normal tahn in the middle of nowhere, but den oudda nowhere—GOBLINS!* I double-checked my gas gauge to see if I could make it to the next town: the thin needle was petting big E's head. I warily pulled in. The closest pump (on my right) had a full-serve sign posted on the side. So I figured the one ahead must be self-serve. I pulled up to that one, checked down the ol' warhorse, picked my nose real quick, exhaled, then stepped outside. The scent of hay and fertilizer smacked me right in the nose—jammed right up into my freshly tunneled nostrils. I tried spitting the taste out, but it didn't work. (Smell: city or rural, you're still breathing in shit!) Ready to gas and go, I tromped around the back and up to the pump. The top of the pump was made of thick bubbled plastic, adorned with a Coke bottle emblem. It didn't have digital numbers; just those ol' turnovers that make a quick-spinning sound for every tenth of a gallon and a clicking sound for every cent. Luckily I had cash on me because it obviously didn't accept credit cards, and who knew what the deal was inside the foggy windows of the soda shop. Visa, Discover, and Mastercard accepted everywhere my ass! Not here! Not *here!*

As soon as I stuck the stick in the ol' warhorse's ass, I heard a grotesque phlegm-sucking sound behind me. I quickly turned around to see if an ax was heading straight for my head—Nope! But *something* potentially lethal was! This hideous thing in grimy black workbooks, grimy Prussian-blue workpants, with a matching short-sleeve workshirt that had an oval nametag that read "Bill." Yes, how common! But who's *inside* Bill's uniform? I'll tell you who! This monstrous thing with a head that's all forehead and chin, upon which winkles washed away the middle—no mouth! which means he must eat through a slimy lipped orifice in his chest. And look, there *is* an indentation! And conversely, a huge bulge on his back! So short and turned aside! Looks and walks like Quasimodo—Quasimodo with no hair!—

'How ya doin', stranger?' drawled Billy Modo. (More like *shtraain'jur.*) 'Purrdy sure I ain't seen yir face around here before.' Although slimy, grimy, wrinkly, bald, and bent up, Billy Modo was likely in his fifties. I actually felt safe once he was standing next to me—about three inches shorter!—reaching out with his tiny greased hands to take over the pumping. Apparently *neither* pump was self-serve. (Stupid modern me.)

'Yir right: you haven't seen me around here before 'cause I never been here before. 'N' go ahead 'n' fill it up, please.'

'Where ya from?'

'Well I's born 'n' raised in Pixburgh but I godda college at Aristod up by LaSalle. I ended up dahn here 'cause I couldn't sit dere 'n' keep watchin' 'at shit on TV, ya know. Figured bein' deep in the mountains would do me some good.'

'Usually does. But e'erybody here's up in a tizzy too. Hell, I ain't even *seen* it yet. Juss bin listenin' on the radio—*Dang it.*' He let go of the pump handle. Jiggled it. Then rejammed it back in like a trick-to-the-tic. 'Yeah, I called a few folks up 'n' tol' 'em spread the word thit I'm shuttin' down soon. 'Cause 'ey shut down the borders, 'n' I'm shuttin' mine down too, ya hear.' Where there was once no mouth appeared a wide smile: he held it open, too, as if trying to show and warn me of the horrifying results of tobacco use; his teeth were chew-grained, chew-stained, and as crooked as the humor.

'Dey shut the boarders dahn?'

'Yes-sir-ree. 'Bout an hour ago president put us on 'at Defcon Delta. That's, uhh, two notches below an all-out nuclear war, ya hear. Seems ain't much happenin' now besides puttin' out the fires 'n' tryin'ah save as many people as 'ey can, but ya never know what's bouna happen. The way I see it: if 'ey can hit liddle ol' Shanksville, they may very well hit here too. So, hell, I'm lockin' 'n loadin'.'

'Yeah, I dunno. It's juss so unrill. Like oudda nowhere. I'm juss—'

He looked me over. For some reason I thought how I probably looked like a cocky urban toughguy to him. But no black ink, black hoodie, big chest, or clinched fist could save me now. He seemed to know this, too, because, with a tone of serious inquiry, he said, 'You carry a gun?'

'Yeah, I got one, but I usually don't carry it in my car. I don't gadda permit for it.'

'*Permit?* In times like 'iss ya gadda *permit* yirself da protect yirself.'

Just then, the pump gulped to stop, and just as I was thinking how urban his maxim was, and how city, suburb, and rural were becoming one, developing the same mindset. But those true New Yorkers of the streety type were no longer standing around with their arms crossed over like punk-rocked monoliths, hiding their teeth, epitomizing the hardness of the streets, using their cold eyes to tell passersby: 'Yo, ya gadda do wha' ya gadda do, ya know?' No, *in times like this* they were running for their lives.

'That'll be $29.25, sir.'

'Can I still gidda pop?'

'Yeppers. Juss follow me inside.'

Billy Modo began gimping the way with his lumpy legs. As we were sluggishly crossing the lot, out from the diner came a tall skinny guy wearing a red trucker hat with long ginger ribbons stringing down the sides. In stride, he yelled, 'Ar'ight, Bill!'

'Take it easy, Randy,' replied Billy Modo with no enthusiasm. He turned to me: 'Biggest drunk in Ley. One night, drove 'at damn pickup right through the firestation door; damn-near crashed inda the firetruck. Five thousand dollars of damage 'n' he spends one night in jail—*only* night he's ever spent in jail. See, his uncle's the sheriff here, 'n' his mother's the mayor. She's the one thit ended up payin' for it. Told 'im, "That's it, Randy, no more drinkin' 'n' drivin' or I'm havin' the pickup impounded." 'N' yet *eeeev*ery night he's drivin' around drunk as a skunk.'

'What's he nee'dda be drivin' for anyway?' We walked through the clouded door; two bells clanked and quickly dulled; he headed around the back of the counter. 'Seems like ya could walk da wherever ya need around here.'

'Well, his girlfriend lives over in Beckville, about thirty minutes west of here. So he'll go over there. Start drinkin' with her. They'll get in a fight. She'll kick 'im out. 'N' here he comes stormin' back home, shit-faced.' He turned around and turned down a transistor radio sitting on the shelf behind the counter as if to respect my wishes: silencing what I was trying to get away from. 'Damn kid. He'll lay on the horn all the way down the road. People'll tell 'im, "Come on, Randy; grow up. *Some* of us gadda sleep. *Some* of us got work in the mornin'." Well, he'll apologize for it. Say he's done drinkin'. 'N' won't be two hours before he's drinkin' over at Zola's. 'N' 'at's the only bar we got around here, 'n' 'ey take any business 'ey can get, ya hear.'

I had now made my way to the back of the cramped dusty shop, surveying the drinking selection in the cooler. To compensate for the twenty feet and the for-aging dust, we were speaking a bit louder. 'Yeah, I know people like 'at. In my old neighborhood we yoosta have 'iss dude who'd get all drunk, go stand out inna front yard, 'n' juss yell at da top of his lungs—not even sayin' anything, juss yellin'—til the cops came 'n' locked 'im up for the night.'

'Well, see, ya can't rilly call the cops on Randy; he's damn-near grown immune ta all the stings on his wrists.'

I grabbed a Dr. Pepper out of the cooler then peppered back down the aisle, observing an array of funny snacks and candy; each silver pole only had one or two items, and they were pulled damn-near to the front to make things look full. A seedy package of sunflower seeds caught my eye, so I pulled it off, leaving the horizontal pole naked.

I set the pop and seeds down on the counter. 'What, don't his uncle wanna punish 'im 'cause his mum's the mayor or sum'n?'

'Well, his uncle's always sayin' he'll *talk* to 'im 'n' he'll *straighten* 'im out, but, hell, that kid's about as straight as Liberace in a maze.' (I liked that one and let Billy Modo know with a vaddle.) 'N', yeah, his mum's *riiiiill* protective of 'im, so nobody ever wantsta get *too* involved, know whadda mean.' He stopped to give me an involved look, squeezing his sandy eyebrows inward. 'Whachir name, son?'

'Vinny.'

'Nice ta meetcha, Vinny. Name's Bill.' We shook hands across the counter. 'See, Vinny, nobody ever does time round here. Years back 'ere yoosta be 'iss one fella—Johnny Fritz. But alwada folks called 'im Johnny Fists 'cause he yoosta beat his wife all the time. Now whenever *he'd* do that, they'd lock 'im up for a week or so. Try talkin' sense into 'im, ya hear. Then they'd let 'im out. A week later: *right back in*. 'N', hell, he's rilly the only one thit gadda good taste of the tank here.' He looked up in a closed-eye reflection. 'Let' see. Johnny was in 'n' out for about—six years, I think.' He looked back at me with a crooked eye. ''Til his wife shot 'n' killed the damn sonuvabitch. Damn-near blew his head off! She got sent straight da county.'

'Wow. Guess country life has its war-stories too.'

'*Ehh*, not rilly,' he sighed. ''At's about the only big thing thit's e'er happened around here. I mean, you'll see yir fights: guys findin' out his buddy's been sleepin' with his wife, so he'll bust his face up a bit.' He huffed as if a specific instance busted into his head. ''N' e'ery now 'n' 'en a kid'll get caught with pot or booze. But times are changin'. See, Vinny, I's born 'n' raised here, 'n' I raised my own family here. My granddaddy, my daddy, 'n' his brother in-law are the ones thit built this service station back in '37. My granddaddy yoosta run the gas, my daddy ran the garage, 'n' my uncle ran the diner. Now my wife runs the diner, I take care of the gas 'n' garage, 'n' I got my son Nathaniel helpin' with summa the garage work. Now eventually—if he can keep his head on straight—he'll own the place. I'd rilly like ta see it stay in the family.' He looked beyond me towards the coolers against the backwall. 'Iss is about the only place left thit's still the same as when I was a kid—this 'n' Rick's Supermarket. Yoosta be about ten houses on Main, a couple on Zola and Brandy, 'n' the rest of 'em are all out in the fields. Shit, I bet the population's at least tripled since I was yir age. Don't get me wrong: it's still an e'erybody-knows-e'erybody town, but yoosta be on the weekends the entire town would meet at the firehall 'n' we'd have hootenannies; e'erybody'd bring a dish 'n' some booze. 'N', see, we kept the food inside the firehall, opened up the door, set up tables 'n' chairs, 'n', hell, we just danced all around—in the firestation, the parkin' lot, out in the yard—in the street! 'N' we're talkin' *live* music, ya hear. The Horvats had a Bluegrass band called The Fat Horvats. Seven of 'em. Rill fat 'n' rill good.'

'Ha, 'at's awesome. So yinz still do that?'

'Every now 'n' then; only difference izza booze. 'Ere'z a time when ya could juss show up, 'n' if ya didn't have money for booze ya could juss take a couple shots of someone's moonshine 'n', hell, 'at's all you'd need for the night.'

'Yeah, I drank pure grain before: 190 proof Everclear, which is illegal in PA. Da one night I drank it...'

Amid the exchange of memories, we'd been being slow to finalize the transaction, but I just received an unannounced amount of money back, which I shoved into my pocket without looking.

'When I's a teenager, Vinny, we had what they called a ridge-runner,' he began with his elbow pivoted on the counter. ''N' he'd drive down'ah Franklin County, Virginia where shiners docked along the Roanoke. I 'member he had this orange supped-up Nova juss in case the cops ever try da pull 'im over. 'N' he'd bring back a whole trunkload of shine. Made a killin' doin' it. His daddy was best friends with my granddaddy, 'n' they'd both been ridge-runners durin' Prohibition when *nuh'n* was allowed. But then in '72, the ATF finely took the distillery down. 'N' that was the end of us drinkin' shine. Might seem kinda strange, but that kinda changed life 'round here.'

'Yeah...' I didn't know what else to say, but Billy's story was painting dusty images of the outlaw life in my head; I liked the thoughts—and that nostalgic feeling.

'But I guess the topper was about five years ago when they built a mall 'n' a bunch a shoppin' centers for the folks over in Beckville. (Beckville's about five times the size of Ley. You'll pass right through it if ya keep goin' straight on Main 'cause it merges right onda 119.) Anyways, it brought in a good bit of business; created alwada jobs. Let's see, they gadda Wal-mart, a Home Depot, a Lowes, Dick's, Best Buy,' he was counting out the stores with his grimy fingers, "'n', uhh—what's 'at one store called?—oh! A Target. But anyways, the suburbs 'er are gettin' purrdy big. Now all the kids here wanna go over *there* on the weekends 'n' hangout at the mall 'n' stuff. But whaddaya think ends up happenin'?'

'"*But the kids in Beckville are allowed da do this 'n' that.*"'

'Ha, purrdy much. But they also been bringin' them hard drugs back. We *never* had any of that here. *Never.* Yoosta be juss whiskey 'n' pot. Now I ain't too sure how many colored people live over that way, but now our kids listen'ah music in their car with enough bass da shakes calves right oudda the springers up in the fields!' (I was vaddling as he continued.) "N' maybe *you* can tell me since ya come from the city: *how inna HELL* can you walk with yir pants damn-near 'round the ankles?'

'Guess it's an acquired walk.' As he chuckled, my laughter was still catching up from calves dropping from springers because of Rap music!

'Hell, Vinny, I'm serious: I can't tell if my son's from the country or the streets of, oh, I dunno—Pittsburgh or Baltimore or wherever. (Ain't rilly a big city close ta here.) But that's the thing now: e'erybody wants ta be someone they ain't. I call 'eez younger ones "The Backfused Generation." That's backwards fused with confused, ya hear.'

I nodded my head in agreement, feeling a bit prideful that Billy Modo apparently assumed *I* wasn't part of The Backfused Generation, even if I was a younger one and from a city named, thus making me a potential corruptor of country youth. Perhaps he'd already developed a sense of trust in me?—or he trusted that I had sense *in* me? Who knows?!

Right after coining a generation, Billy Modo knocked something onto the floor, which chimed against the green tile: perhaps a cent? Who knows?! But he hunched over and began searching around for whatever it was. It gave me a moment to observe the three wooden shelves hooked on the wall behind him: a panoply of Coke memorabilia, including original soda bottles still unopened; metal model cars, a bit dusty but all classics between the 30s and 60s; a framed dollar bill from times of yore; and photographs of Ley, showing the progression of development over the years, which seemed to be proof that Billy Modo told no lie in his folk. Like he said, still an everybody-knows-everybody town, but now with overburdened ankles, springers springing prematurely in the fields, and lurking around the fences, a big yellow happy-face steered by a singular goal but strategically having herd a million ways to sell it backwards in order to confuse a generation.

The hump rose again. Upright as best as he could, he tossed a penny into the give-a-penny-take-a-penny tray next to the cash register. He smiled ironically, respectfully, as if deep-down he was working his way through serious back pain but had to uphold a hospitable face.

'Well, Bill, I should get back da the unknown roads. Bahdiz rilly good talkin'ah ya; got my mind off things for a bit. I think I'm gonna go check 'iss Beckville out. Comin' back, I can catch 22 from 119 by cuttin' straight across, right?'

'Well, whacha wanna do is...' (He discoursed an itinerary) '...'Get off 'ere 'n' 'en make a left at the first red light. You'll pass the mall on yir left: the Wal-mart's over on 'at side. 'N' Dick's 'n' Lowes 'n' a buncha restaurants'll be on yir right. But juss keep goin' straight. I dunno exactly how far back north you gadda go, but you'll eventually start seein' signs for 22 East.'

'Ar'ight. Thanks a lot, Bill.' With my left hand, I picked up the pop and seeds. Then we joined right hands across the counter: a nice firm grip: a symbolic exchange of grease stains and a solidification of our blue-collared unity, even if I was in college and he, so to speak, owned the instruments of production. 'Take care.'

'You too, Vinny. 'N' 'member whad I said: screw dim damn gun permits. Ya only got one life, so don't let anybody rob ya of it.'

As I walked out the door, I heard him saying, "N' don't be skurr'dda come back now, ya hear?' But I didn't need to reply, for he knew I heard him. I heard that nostalgic working-class country voice let out into the autumnal wind: *shwoooooooooooo!!!* In the city it sounds like *oiiiiiiiiiiiiiii!!!*

I ventured safely through what Billy Modo had called "no man's land," and made my way onto 119. With the window down, and the cigarettes leaving a trail of smoke, I was careening through the recesses of my mind, while wondering on an even deeper level where the unknown Romantic roads that led to the heart of my heart were. But it was all broken—blown out the window, falling wistfully by the wayside—when Ivy called. I turned the radio down and put the cell up to my ear, coughing a little, which I believe was more from the smoke than the cold, for the couple of shots of orange medicine *had* done me good.

'Yeah?'

'What are you up to?'

'Drivin'.'

'*Driving?* Where ya goin'?'

'What's it madder? Yir mad at me.'

Pause. 'I just want you to come over, okay? To my dorm. I'll leave here and meet you out front in fifteen minutes... *Okay?*'

'Can't be done.'

'Why not?'

'Too far away.'

'Where are you?'

'Who knows?'

'Vinny, tell me right now where you're goin'!'

'Straight da Hell.'

'I'm bein' serious!'

'I'm bein' comical.'

'Do you seriously think this is funny? The country is under attack, people are dyin', and you're out drivin' around like it's a nice Sunday afternoon!'

'Hey.'

'What?'

Click.

I shut the phone off and kept driving...kept driving down 119...and through the small suburbs of Beckville...passing the stores Billy Modo said I would...down through the quaint center of Beckville...steadily sinking in elevation...dropping down a massive hill...but when I found myself heading back up towards 22, I kept driving elsewhere...who knows why I didn't want to catch 22 or turn around and go back down 119...but I didn't...so into the next mysterious mountain, and through the next set of mysterious woods, I drove...Viatic Vallano drove as if he was never going back...

...Around 5 p.m.—(and God only knows where I was)—I came upon a peculiar scene to the right: another serendipity of Van Gogh's spoors, for it looked like one of his famous olive grove paintings. Of course it wasn't—geographically *couldn't be*—an olive grove. But the trees had those gnarled trucks slanting to the side. Spooky-looking trees. Spooky-looking grass too: tall, tufted, nimble, sickly greens and yellows. A real haunting atmosphere. Secluded enough for someone to dispose of me with ease. Alwaysthemore, I decided to guide the ol' warhorse off the dusty trail because I had to race to piss. Before dismounting, I pulled off my hoodie because the sun was now close, full, and warm. From the ashtray, I grabbed the green bedded in the brown (only a quarter left but it would do me good); I slid it into my cigarette pack. Then I left the ol' warhorse to graze along the roadside.

I walked forward and a bit to the right where thick yellow brush flourished, as well as orange-berried mountain ash, and wild flowers of white, yellow, pink, purple; and all throughout: wild blackberries, jagger bushes, and miniature trees that seemed to lack branches, for they were of the vertical biceps-pressed-against-the-head kind, but copious with dulled carmine leaves. I moved to the fringe of the brush and squared up. But having that stupid kind of luck, as soon as I pull out here comes a car driving passed real slow as if observing a car wreck. Oh well! Too late! *Psssssssssssssssssssssssssssssssssss...pssssssssssssssssss...psssssssss...ssss...sss...ss...s*

I walked out to the closest spooky tree. It was only about eight-foot high, with the prospect of an additional three if it had good posture. I circled around it, observing with curious eyes, then up into it: slanting, wrinkly, knotted, skeletal, tired, faded of any vibrancy...like an old man. But I wasn't sure if the tree was actually old or just naturally cursed with the look of senescence. As I scraped my hands along the jagged bark, a memory from elementary school popped into mind: the day I learned that to know a tree's age you count the rings inside its trunk. My teacher—*Mrs. Andrews?*—passed around large colored pictures showing the inner trunk of different trees. There was one with over a hundred rings. For some reason I thought she'd *drawn* the circles over top of the pictures just to play a trick on us. Then Melissa Curry, the little bright blonde sitting next to me, added confusion to the mix when she privately swore to me that we too have rings inside us: one for each year. She said that her mother *told her* and her mother *knows everything* and her mother has *thirty perfect rings.* And who was I to challenge Melissa Curry?! that spboiled egghead! No one cracks a joke on her! NO ONE! So when I came home I immediately asked Ma how many rings *she* had. Holding her left hand up (wiggling her ring-finger back and forth) she said, 'Just-ah one.' Ahh! I remember standing in the kitchen with my backpack still on, pointing and yelling, 'No! Inside you! Not *that* ring! NOOOO!' At my fury, she froze with a wild-eyed quizzical look: this irritated me beyond belief! Melissa Curry's mother didn't play games with her like this! Melissa Curry's mother didn't joke with her little yolk like this! NO! Melissa Curry's mother told her *exactly* how many rings she had! Thirty! And they were all perfect! Trying to clarify myself to get the diamond out of the rough,[6] I said, 'No! *Inside* you! The age rings *inside* you!' Ma just laughed, and mocking my tone, replied, '*Age rings?* I don't have no-ah *age rings!*' Before marching off to my room, I said, 'Den yir not even born yet— BABY!' Ahh! so strange I was! Anyway, the tree's little olive-esque leaves were shimmering in the breeze. A light but constant whip-and-crackle as they trembled against each other, pushing eastward: the direction most trees were slanting. Everything seemed to be pushing eastward against the sun; and yet who knew if *unnatural* things were still pushing into the west? I didn't know, nor did I care to. I was finally where I wanted to be, doing what I wanted to be doing: standing in the middle of nowhere, musing...slipping into contemplation over what it would be like to be a tree branch: to bear fruit...to be the sanctuary for a nest of birds...to be part of something so secure and true, rooted straight into the ground, its premise unquestionable, its purpose simple, its effects complex. *If I was a branch would my worth lessen? become greater? remain the same? hmmmm...mmmm...mmm....*All thoughts began fading away, as I swirled into a state of nonexistence: a feeling close to supreme limberness...a soul floating in limbo...

    ...I might've only stayed in the middle of nowhere for a few minutes, I might've stayed there forever, but as I mused and petted, toked and smoked, coughed and fretted, smiled and frowned, walked around and sat down, it was so hard to believe that it was a September 11th like no other—that things were still going on, perhaps getting worse—that the borders of my country had been closed to the world as I closed my own to all. It's true that my physical body returned to the ol' warhorse...and headed back down through the mountain and woods...cruised musically underneath a peaking sun that had turned into something that looked like it had been drawn with pastels...and eventually found my way back to LaSalle, at which time, I called Ma back and tried to answer her

---

[6] The idiom "diamond in the rough" is someone with a good character but lacking social graces; *clarify* is punned here ("to illuminate," as in to make something clear, and "to refine," as in to remove impurities); the idiom itself plays on the notion of a ring, to wit, a diamond ring. It can also be read as irony, for the diamond is symbolic of lasting marriage, and detesting the idea of the tacit power that he, deceased Rick, still has over his mother, V is, in the recollection of the memory, trying to get the diamond (his mother) out of the rough [times]; that is, her eternal commitment to Rick.

unanswerable questions...then called Ivy back and apologized by going over to her dorm just in time for the president's worldwide address...and that our gloomy but resolute president said that something very bad happened today but we're now on the hunt to punish those who did this to us...then later in the night, New York City proved it truly is the city that never sleeps—no, not tonight, and, no, never again—because it was burning with too much anger and sadness and confusion, while trying to stay focused on saving the remnants of the better day just here the day before...and finally, with a head growing more cloudy by the minute and detail, I'd fallen asleep next to Ivy with one arm wrapped around her so tightly, and one eye open. I know all of that, in its simple encapsulation, had happened on September 11, 2001...but it still seems as if there was another me left driving down the roads snaking through that mountain and out into the unknown, where I embarked on my escape from the world and myself...

...There was no relief when I woke up on September 12, 2001. It took a million blinks to get my eyes to remain open. Yet the crevices in my dried contacts caused Ivy to look fragmented and dreamlike, although it *was* clear it hadn't all been a nightmare, at least not one of the sleeping world. Ivy was already up, getting dressed for class. She flashed me a blank expression—then went about her business. I gulped down a painful bowling ball—winced—then looked straight ahead at her flatscreen: it was smoking black and white, as debris wafted throughout the city. Such a cataclysmic wave of obscurity. I began doing false mathematics in my head to figure out if the mass-energy-momentum of the wave could carry it to nearby cities like Philly or Baltimore...or maybe even *here.* Meanwhile, a reporter was explaining a simpler science: the color-code. I hadn't known much about it til now, nor did I care to. I already knew what I needed to know. Billy Modo had said it: screw the nuances of the terror alert, screw the subtle differences in color, screw gun permits, for "in times like 'iss ya gadda *permit* yirself da protect yirself." Which is why no explanation of alertness could adjust my position of defense anymore than it already was: it was locked and tight.
'You goin' to class?' Ivy asked, slipping a mauve shirt over her head.
'I dunno. Don't rilly feel like it. I didn't get much sleep lass night.'
'Me neither.'
'You sure we even got classes?'
'Yeah. I asked my RA.'
'Oh.' I rolled out of bed. 'So did they say anything new about why?'
'Not really. But one guy was sayin' it's just part of the Islamic
religion.'
'Whad is? *kamikaze?*'
'Yeah, they do it all the time over there. You'd know that if you ever watched the news.'
'Uhh, well if you ever read about Islam you'd know bein' a kamikaze *isn't* part of the mainstream religion. This shit *here,*' I pointed to the television, 'if it rilly *is* a religious or political issue, would be called *fundamentalism,* 'n' it's exists in *every* religion, *every* government, *every* epoch; it juss changes its clothes over time. People doin' whatever it takes

da implement *their* way of life on everyone else 'cause nobody can be content with personal salvation.'

Questioning me with a stern face, she said, 'So what are you tryin' to say?'

'Juss thit whoever did this should be burned at the stake juss like anyone else thit can't keep da themselves.'

'Well, Vinny, how are they gonna be burned at the stake when they're already dead? Besides, *these* kinda people don't even care about death, or who they kill. So—so how are you gonna stop 'em or punish 'em? That's the problem.'

I could only shrug my shoulders.

'I mean, it's like a gateway to anarchy!' she said with authority and exasperation.

'No, unfortunately we're not headin' in that direction,' I yawned. 'But I'm gonna get goin'.' (We kissed on the lips.) 'I guess caw me in a liddle.'

'Okay. Just make sure you keep your cell on and *by* you.' Just then, she pulled me into an I'm-scared hug and kissed me again. 'I love you.'

'I love you too...' I grabbed a handful of her backside curls and began falling away...melting...disappearing...taking a taste of peace on the side. *'...POWER UP!!!...'*

...I had no power. During the walk down to Philemon, the wind fully knocked me aware of that. When I entered my room, I kicked my shoes off and fell straight down on my bed. Unfortunately, I couldn't avoid conversing with Luke, as he too got ready for class. But *I* wasn't moving at all: not today, maybe not tomorrow, maybe never again. I was sick. My face felt like mush. My eyes were trying to turn themselves inside out and into utter blindness. My nose was stuffed up and sore. My throat was on fire. My stomach was turning over in cycles of acidic abuse. The cold had apparently turned into a flu: just like the world's change of condition: the pile of shit now had a stronger odor to it.

'Well I'll see ya in a bit,' said Luke, picking up his cell from the desk and placing it in the pocket of his khakis. 'Sure you don't want me to pick ya up anything?'

'No, I'm good; I have some medicine 'n' 'at. Thanks'o.'

'Okay. Well I hope ya feel better.'

The door shut. We were alone again: the television and I. It wasted no time execrating me for not having watched one of the twins' ancillary buildings fall at 5:20 p.m. the day before. Probably around the time when I was turning into a branch. But now I got to see all forty-seven stories drop to the ground over and over. Then the other two buildings: the snakes sneaking inside...the excretion of an orange ball of flame...the air-dancers...the dropping stories...the ashy silhouettes trying to make it through the clouds being kicked up by the Pale Horse...but the ashy silhouettes being engulfed by the cloud, many crashing to the ground, some falling dead, trampled in their wake, over and over. And to compliment these horrific scenes: commentary from pundits either giving rhetorical wakes for the dead or exhibiting their finest stiff finger for those who *will* pay. Still seemed as if they were pointing their finger at me; not only did I fail to save anyone but it was also all my fault. Funny thing is: as I lay on my back during the morning of Day Two, musing, I realized that my hand *was* resting atop my he~~art~~, the pointer-finger doing its job: pointing right at me. I'd been treacherous before. I'd hidden the truth before. So point and fire away.

I must've been absorbed by the television and its death/blame games, along with my shame and despair and self-loathing and longing for a time long ago and yet longing for better days to come—for me, for everyone—and the sick static swirling through me well into the afternoon before I was finally allowed to sleep...

...The next week was filled with elegies and encomiums, as the nation continued to burn with tears of sadness and pride. While mourning with us, most of the world was commending us for pulling together and putting forth the effort we had—well, that *some of us* had. Most had only been spectators and commiserators. But some had been much more in the moment; that is to say, the rescue personnel had been much more. And there was no doubt that those fighting to save lives *had* given their all. Even if they hadn't saved everyone—(no one could've nor was anyone expecting 'em to)—they were still heroes in our he~~arts~~. But 346 heroes didn't make it, 76 of which were firefighters. It was from them—the *fallen* heroes—that I realized *heroism* is about the ability to step in lands others won't: whether you fall down and go nowhere, or make it all the way across, doesn't matter—you're still a hero.

The notion of *needing a hero* inevitably signifies *tragedy already exists:* the empirical proof in NYC, the enormous city now shrunken down to one block where the ruins lay. Day after day, people dug through the heat-deprived remnants—these big black piles that collectively looked like a tarred junkyard—while bulldozers cautiously plowed charnel paths with a sole purpose: to find souls, ones still in-body, although they were finding more of the opposite. At this point, the body-count was indefinite because there were over 10,000 unidentified fragments of bone and tissue that couldn't be matched with the dead already identified. The present number was 1,600 dead, with an estimated 1,000-1,500 to be identified. Not much else could be identified besides a piece of the south tower wall, still standing like a dusty relic from ancient Rome; the Islamic fundamentalist organization, al-Qaeda; and accordingly, nineteen terrorists commanded by the world's most hated man, Osama bin Laden, who at first claimed to be unassociated with the attacks, only to take full responsibility when the pride of it seemed priceless.

Although Dr. Rosenbaum had no sympathy for *whoever* the perpetrators were—insofar as he believed they deserved severe punishment—he explained that a terrorist to one is a hero to another. Without thinking it through, I almost got mad, almost said, 'I don't give a fuck. Terrorize me or anyone else, physically *or* mentally, then expect something fierce. I mean, you rilly think *they* could be considered *heroes?* HA! Heroism is *reactionary!—the reaction to the tragic!*' I was so glad that I didn't say that because I didn't have to walk away from Dr. Rosenbaum and wait for everything to connect right before my eyes for me to overstand my ignorance. But even *if* he might've been right as far as perspective goes, I was still burning to say, 'So how's yir forgive-but-never-forget philosophy lookin' now?' But I didn't say that either. I don't even think *he* (a Jew who'd made peace with the Nazis) was anywhere close to being ready for the process of forgiving. I knew I never would be. *Forgive* these sick twisted fucks? Never! As for Ivy, her family, and Aunt Stella: they wanted death for *anyone* mentioned negatively on television. The difference between them and I was that I wanted more information before casting my stones. I was aware nothing is as simple as: 'They don't like the way we Americans live. It conflicts with their religion. So they finally took the initiative to kill us.' No, the problem was historical—an accumulation—multifarious—multinational—multieverything—filled with mistakes and mis-takes—within the balance of perspectives, the problem so reactionary—yet so provoking.

Goodbye, Middle Ground; Hello, Ground Zero. That's what everyone was looking at, facing an ultimatum: *either you're with us or you're against us in the fight against terrorism:* the expedient message from the burning bush, sent out to every country and individual coherent enough to overstand what the underbrush meant: *either you support America's political decisions, or you support the evil actions of Terrorism.* I certainly didn't support the evil actions of terrorism, ya know. Even if my intuition said, 'Beware of simplistic convictions, of logical fallacies, for whoever supports the murder of who *they* consider the innocent? and when do only the truly guilty die? and what is *guilty* anyway? and wouldn't the hero/terrorist role-switch also apply to the innocent/guilty?'—well, even though questions like that arose in me, I didn't have time to think things through; I had to make my pick before I was picked out as something that I wasn't: one of the guilty terrorists! *I* didn't fuckin' kill anyone! But someone (or something) seemed to have killed my dog, my father, my best friend, my other friends, and millions of innocent Americans!...The terrorists?!

Welcome to the United States of Hysteria!!! But truth is: sometimes terror *can* produce the best defensive strategies. And *our* strategy? *Hunt down the terrorists.* Not just a job for the government and military, but also US. And why not us? Most were already aware this wasn't going to be a normal war; these terrorists could be *anywhere*, could move *anywhere*, could have support *anywhere*—they could even be right here in our backyards! And the evidence was showing they were or had been. (I must admit that I looked up how many terrorists attended Aristod: 32. That's a lot. Glad I still had Teresa's dad's gun.) As we continued watching television to become more educated on the matters, we learned that the terrorists, or at the very least, the *supporters* of terrorism, weren't very hard to find: all you had to do was see who didn't have an American flag sticker on their car or an American flag in their front yard. Thank God the patriot's kit-and-apparel companies were officially back in business. And business in general? *So essential:* the country *had to* keep the wheels of their SUVS turning or—well, it's simple logic: if you don't sell your product, then your business goes out of business. For example, if you don't drive your SUV, then the oil companies go out of business—then the terrorists win! I know *I* didn't want the terrorists to win, which is why I began buying groceries and smokes every single week. The terrorists were *not* going to win on *my* wallet!

As the nation marched on to the beat of the patriot's drum, Time began tripping over its own two feet, not knowing how to dance. And although I was doing my best to keep up, I couldn't get a grip on anything. I was all over the place. The linear of my life no longer seemed existent. So much information, so much misinformation. So many innocent confirmed dead, so many heroes rising in their place. So many I-told-you-not-to's from this person, so many I-told-you-so's from that person. Meanwhile, amid the fervor and turmoil, the hard-skinned patriots seemed to have a synoptic effect on the mind of the nation, but certainly not its eyes: they were wide-open: glaring...peering...profiling. But enough! For it's time to – get – things – done. It's time for the pros to get in file and git 'er done!

And done it was about to git! The breadbasket of America was a big buff chest and the coasts were huge flexing biceps! Not to underestimate the west coast, but the east was so tense that if you touched it, it would fly back and knock you outta the universe! In a strange way, it was great. Something long overdue. I guess from growing up listening to Oi! music I had a longing for unity: not in the Nazi sense, but for brother- and sisterhood: a strong apolitical family ready to fight for what's right! Although not without compunction, I saw the horrible happening on 9/11 as a great opportunity for a revolution of thinking and living (in the name everyone); not as a reinforcement of the arrogance and ignorance (in the name of the few). (God forgive me for that, for what do I really know?) I dunno—for a moment, amid the darkness, I saw a flicker of hope. I swear to God, it really did seem like an opportunity for *real* change! But unfortunately, things kept taking a turn for the worse, *everywhere.* I could no longer look out anymore, *anywhere.* I didn't want to know *anything* about *anything.* Thus, the narcissist in me *finally* took over, as I fell down, turned inward, and began writing—trying so hard each and every single day hereafter to get away from all the senseless fighting. I said to myself: 'Why not take the biggest risk of all and go to war with *myself?* And go all-out as if there's no other feat? Plus, there's plenty of snake oil around me if I should happen to hurt myself and need to retreat.' So I snaked my ass over to my dark desk, fell down on the chair, slid far in, and began looking for the switch to the inner light. The time had finally come to fight with myself, as the fate of the world was (in a sense too dark for ordinary sight) being orchestrated in stealth...

Love,

Vincent Ignazio Scandurra Vallano

(P.S. - Violent Ivestigations Soothe Victims?)

As Time fell apart so did my memory : sailed to the pit of snakes it did ; there were only wisps left in my head, but wisps that hissed hysterically in the westerly wind : the crackpot of tele-geniuses telling us the world will never be the same ; either you're with us or against us—hey, what's *your* name? ; blasphemers of the nation = traitors of the nation ; the nation splitting like a mad-scientist's pacified ass-lying patient : the one half splitting halfheartedly—ignorantly ; the other half arrogantly—ignorantly ; I know who the terrorists are : anyone and everyone who's *not* me ; security versus privacy ; security versus freedom ; security versus heretics ; we'll have to wait another year to take care of New York's *other* derelicts ; necessity knows no law ; law before all ; all before nothing ; nothing for all ; all for nothing ; one for all ; come on now! : consume, consume, consume or the terrorists win ; now do it again and again and again : march, march, march til justice is served ; every one of these sandniggers will finally learn when they die for this tragedy (a tragedy among millions of forgotten tragedies, but please remember to forget the tragedies never acknowledged, for knowledge is not needed to lead my country 'tis of thee) ; these sandniggers' resources, the ones they don't own, the ones of the mother-country close enough for a connection to direct the sword forward through their bones, will serve as retribution for what they've done to our dead brethren : call it compensation for our frantic ones who survived like Temptation lying dead at the feet of the good reverend ; fathers will be rectified in the belated completion ; brothers will be resurrected in the patriotic memory of their deletion ; and the mothers and sisters of the East will be deniggerfied and revivified when their garbs fall into pools of blood ; in sum, in the end, with Time's helping hand, Democracy will spoon-feed these uncivilized barbarians ; and all fathers and mothers sinking in the sand will soon rise up with richness in their whitewashed brown hands ; and their unbound children will never be hungry or uneducated again ; just like ours here in America where there's white feathers on all our beds, right? ; right : there's white feathers on my bed.

Dear everyone:

You can clearly see that my hands are full but not red; they've bled but they're not red...

MEASURE THE TIME

"Oh! do not attack me with your watch. A watch is always too fast or too slow. I cannot be dictated by a watch."[1]

"Oh! do not attack me with your contemporary writers. Contemporary writers are always too formulaic or too simple. I cannot be dictated by contemporary writers."[2]

This chapter is a hole, and I'm going to continue returning to it, steadfast to the belief that one day I can fill it up and bring to the surface an overstanding of what occurs subsequently in the linear of what was/is my life moving on in the physical. Ahh! how do I even begin to explain what's going on here?! Well, first, this chapter might annoy you. In several parts, it might push to the threshold a bitchy, contentious attitude I can have at times. I'm warning you that you seriously might get acute headaches from reading this chapter. Plus it's really long! So stop for a moment and consider if this is something you don't feel like pursuing; if not, flip to the next chapter: you won't be missing much here, kinda. Now to the others who might really be diggin' me: I think you'll absolutely love being in this chapter—I mean, this hole. And to the wiser ones, with wide eyes and adventurous hearts—well, I think the way in which you'll read this chapter, the manner in which you'll reflect on its structure and significance, both in the minutiae and on the aggregate, will be like going on a magic carpet ride. However, at this moment, writing *this* line, it seems inevitable that *everyone who can endure* will be picked up and taken far down the road. Please don't try to read too much into that last line, or anything else in this hole. In the words of a person I just made up—umm, Jack Stemless Pumpkinhead: 'Don't get squashed by the cumber. On cue, carry on, my little seeds, carry on—and keep your eyes on the pie in the sky!'

See how I'm talking in the present and *to you* as I've done here and there prior to this? Kinda confusing isn't it? Makes it seem like I'm a physical orator of this story. But truth is: I'm not, kind of, kinda. First, this is all typography: no physical audience here with me. As for *my* physical presence: well, I wrote *this* line while living out the events of chapter 24. Overstand: this here is Vincent Vallano the writer. Yeah, it should now become clear that everything you've read so far is something I've only recently lived out in "reality" and then started writing about after the events of the last chapter. I know: I'm sorry, I'm gonna try to explain this as best as I can for those of you who are confused. (Fuck, I'm 21 when I wrote this line and I'm still confused!) (22 here, and I'm still caught up without being caught up!) (16 here! <—just kidding, ddikts.)

First, those inclined to outline the "correct" ways to write a novel would say that I'm doing everything so wrong right now, that I just ruined it

---

[1] Passage from *Mansfield Park* by Jane Austen
[2] Passage from the work presently titled *Vanishing Inside Silent Violence* by Vincent Ignazio Scandurra Vallano

all, that I'm simultaneously breaking two of the ten commandments of writing that says never deviate from the linear in such a manner and never deviate from the tense you start out with because it's confusing, unrealistic, and—I dunno, perhaps narcissistic for a first-person narrator to do such a thing. But who cares about them: they're stupid and bitter over someone like me who can get away with it. Let them go "do their own thing" and revel in the froth of their mimicry. However, don't think for one minute that this is some effort to "be different." It's so not! You just gotta trust me on that. In that respect, I think my life in the physical will suffice. (Yeah I know to think about that last line in relation to me as the one writing is a paradox. But maybe it's like one of those paradoxes that appears to be false at first but turns out to be true [my favorite definition of *paradox*]. Or maybe this splitting is my point, you pair of clocks!) Anyway, *somehow*, in the end, all the multiple contradictions and subtle divisions add up to a lot of sense. So to recap before moving on: If you decide to read this chapter, I'm either gonna blow your mind—(which will hit its peak during retrospection, not right here in the present, given that I've now come to the point where I'm kinda two people since I'm living out my life in the physical and yet I'm also the writer who's going back over and "trying to catch up to myself")—or else all this rubbish will just annoy you, give you a headache, or perhaps create a loophole to discredit me mainly because you don't like me. But I'm guessing anyone who's made it this far has to like me just a little bit, or at least be interested in "how it all ends," which right now I don't even know: *isn't that strange and contradicting?* And I'm certainly not trying to make enemies by doing this; more like hoping to make friends, if I can, because the me who's outside this hole seems to be losing 'em left and right. But that doesn't mean I'm gonna kiss your ass. I'm still gonna keep doin' my own thing. <— these last few sentences were part of the original ones once I started this work (the day of 9/11); but technically this "separate" chapter precedes even the beginning of the story because I was around sixteen when I began writing a collection of notes with the intent to one day embark on an extensive work (aka this). But I reordered this section...up until the months after graduation, which it would (or will) end up taking me five years to graduate; remember, in the linear I've just started my junior (3rd) year of college when the buildings fell.

All right. Let's begin the dirty work. First, one of the points of this hole is to show you what the underground artist—and more so in my case, the *unknown* artist—is *truly* like: not always a pretty portrait: the illusion, delusion, disillusion 'n' 'at will be shown progressively and aggregately <— and this line was added later on. Another point is to talk about language. So we're gonna begin with Writing Incorrectly 101. Woah! Wait! I forgot to put these lines in. (It was in my head but Agent Ralphie just came in the room to talk to Luke. I think they're friends now, which is fuckin' weird. Agent Ralphie is a senior and on his way out. I think he's trying to get the last scoop on me since he previously made no attempt to be friends with Luke besides smalltalk. I mean, come on! What do they have in common? Agent Ralphie doesn't seem very religious to me. He stinks of that air of someone who, in the first ten minutes of a conversation, has to state how they're a science-based atheist, or part of Hollywood's mock-religion, Scientology. Fuckin' celebrities. Hey, ya know how people love to say: 'Don't push your religion on me!' Well, how about this one: 'Don't push your science on me!' Haha.) Whoops! Those lines: 'Unless I denote otherwise, the passages below are *not* crafted. I wrote each one in a single sitting, or a sitting only split by having to go to class. I don't have the time to craft this shit; I have a book to write and a life to live. Hey, would it help if I gave you a better idea where I am; that is, state the frame of time for each passage? Hey! What did Jane Austen tell you for me?! That's right! Do not dictate me by your watch! Close me! Oh I fuckin' dare you! Close me like a pocket watch and see if I don't I don't take this whole blankity-blank thing right back to 1901!

Huh? Oh! "1901": a Vallanian slip-of-the-finger. (Later on, when you feel me deeper inside you—*Fehlleistung!*[3]—as I talk about how music played a major role in my writing, I'll sing the song I made up about me being insane called: "Called Insane Being Me.")+%wewq433434.

Out of respect to those who don't like me, I just now decided months from now to designate the passages where I get a little out of control; this way if you read 'em, *after* I've warned you, it's not my fault and you can't hold it against me, at least beyond this hole. It's like: 'What happens in Las Holez, stays in Las Holez.' And how true that is! HOs and LEZes! From Las Vegas to Las Holez! (These trees are rocking me to sleep. *Bona notti, Ma.*)

(Hold up! Don't you even think about editing this. I see you! Put the blue pencil down and nobody will get hurt! If it's here, it's here for a reason, and if there's no reason, there's a reason. Hey, everyone, watch this: huj380hdoedhorhuenuebufb4uhdn!!! You know how mad that just made some people? It's kinda funny and strange and sad—mostly sad. Like what the—(*gotta go to class; brb* <—computer lingo)—well, it's getting old now so let's move on with what MUST be said before I do my thing here.)

The following passage might bore those who don't care about writing (or speaking) so yinz can just flip ahead a few pages and pick out a random spot like a Burroughs novel. Anyway, ya ever read one of those how-to-write books? Well, like many others, I had to read Strunk in high school. And man, it stunk! Made me think twice about the message of *Fahrenheit 451*. I mean, we *do* need firewood from time-to-time >:] Nevertheless (<—haha), there's this teacher I have in the linear who told me to read *The Proper Way to Speak and Write* by Vliden. I was a bit hesitant because I've been writing since 6th grade (well, technically since I was like 4) but I'm well-read and -written, so there's really no need. Still, I read the piece of shit, and I would like to share three key passages from Hitler—I mean, Vliden, and from there I'll proceed with how I feel. Wait! Let's get this out in the open *right now:* I'm not just a literary character. Do you overstand that yet? I'm only a literary character insofar as I've made myself one. Yes! I'm real! I'm a *real* motherfuckin' G, and one hell of a character >:] See, I have opinions and feelings and I don't wanna follow literary techniques where I always have to be so freakin' mysterious about things. Does that ever bother you: whenever you read a book in which the author concentrates so much on the physical movement while the protagonist is always so indecisive and everything's so obscure and poetic? I mean, poetry is my first-

---

[3] [deu] A slip of phrase, otherwise known as a "slip-of-the-tongue"; coined by Freud but punned here as a "slip-of-the-finger" since it's being typed

love, but it's not *all* of me. I'm just like you: things make me mad, sad, happy, and I wanna come out with it. I'm just like any other person you can meet and greet on the street and like or not like. I'm not Holden or Humbert. You can really touch me! If you don't believe me, come to Aristod right now. Come hold and hump me! Oh am I just rambling now? Well who doesn't? Maybe that just *proves* I'm real. *Now* do you overstand? Anyway, I read this piece of shit book on how to write properly. The overall tone—and so fear-provoking it would sound in person!—is like: *You are forever forbidden to use demonstratives or else Hell awaits you, young writer!* Bullshit and fuck you. Seriously, who the fuck do these people think they are? They're demons! and me can demonstrate it!

So here's the 2 + 1 passages from Vliden; and if he wants to sue me—although as far as I'm concerned he can't since it's in the name of literary criticism—then I'll hunt him down and treat him like I'm a boy named Sue. I love Johnny Cash so much. But he just died.[4] [Everyone's dying ☹]

Anyway, Vliden says: 'The three fundamental components of the English language are: *Purity, Clarity* and *Exactitude*.'

Law 1: 'Purity is realized in the use of good English. It excludes all antiquated words, foreign idioms, ambiguous phrases, slang, vulgarity, and all ungrammatical language whatsoever. It also denounces neologisms until adopted by the leading writers and speakers.' So I guess what he means is that the leading writers and speakers would be of the Puritan kind; hence, his comical explicitness in using *purity* and then CAPITALIZING it. Yeah, Vliden capitalizes his shit to show us who's the boss, and it ain't no slangy New Yorka like Tony Danza!

Law 2: 'Clarity is————————————————————————————————strictly forbidden. ————————————————without pomp, ostentation and mannerism or any strenuous result.' So I guess what he means is that Joyce wrote incorrectly, and for that matter, anyone who crafts wordplays or incorporates poetry. Plus, "without pomp, ostentation and mannerism or any strenuous result" implies that to create a character with an ounce of personality and dimension, or to portray yourself or any other real person as is (like I'm doing in my work) is to write incorrectly. And just look at *his* language: *strictly forbidden.* Sound a little nazi-esque or puritanical to you? Sound a little POMP-OUS?

Law 3: 'Exactitude requires————————————————, while abstaining from redundancy and tautology. The style must be terse and unambiguous and————————————. It forbids all long and involved sentences, and————————.' Hmm, I wonder if he knows that *redundancy* and *tautology* is the same thing, or rather not different. Either way, I've had it with this Blackshirted Pantaloon. Brought to you by the III Van Covenant, emit to give you *Speek-king 'n' Right-ting Prop-'er-, Lee.*

Here's my only rule: Learn all the rules then break 'em whenever you want no matter what kinda writing you're engaged in. Whenever a teacher or an editor tells you to change B to A, and you don't wanna, then

[4] The influential role of Johnny Cash (both his life and death) isn't discussed at length but it's not to be undermined or overlooked.

return with C. For example: you like *bitter,* they tell you *angry,* return with *choleric.* Whenever they tell you a sentence is a run-on, take the sentence and sprint another hundred miles with it. Whenever you create a word and they tell you that you're not famous or powerful enough to do such a thing, create another one in lieu of their name or profession like *peesacrapologist.* Whenever they tell you to delete a swearword common in everyday life, say it aloud and direct it at 'em even if it wouldn't make sense to. *Fuuuuuuck!* Seriously *fuck* this Demon! The purpose, or rather, the effect, of *any* rule is constriction, and that's exactly what will happen to your mind if you fall into linguistic subservience; by applying "etiquette rules" to language we *do* become constricted: it can easily be proven by the logic of linguistics, psychological deductions, empiricism, the reaction and reflection of Art, and an array of other measures. And given that language on the whole is already so futile, why make it worse? why let this serpent both poison and throttle us with what he, the evilinguistic *snaca,* hisses as right. Vliden honestly reminds me of some pompous Cockasian who not only dreams necrophilically about sucking Hemmingway's journalistic (terse?) wang, but also, in the awake life, condemns Ebonics because it didn't pass through the etymo-embryo incubation of European Whiteness; that is, he hates Ebonics because it didn't fall into the arms of Journalism to be rocked and nurtured...only to grow up to be one of Spartan's bastard children which are all named Laconic! Yuck-ewwe! And how interesting is it that the first five letters of his surname can spell—well, you can see it. The leftover *n* probably stands for *niger:* the color of his *lingua.* And he thinks it's so silver! Haha! Well, that's the end of this lesson. You can pay me for my services by writing whatever you want however you want, and if they refuse to publish you, and you actually *are* a fine writer—(and please be honest with yourself because, in my opinion, it takes years at the craft to become publishable)— then go back to the linear and find—sorry, this isn't Vincent Vallano; this is the publishing company and we could not permit the end of his last sentence due to—sorry, this *is* Vincent Vallano, and nobody's gonna tell me what to do! And if you wanna know what I meant, figure it out yourself because I'm starting to feel a little dictatorial myself. Goodnight!

"The English language is not crowded with words beginning with the letter "v" that suggest anything but trouble. After violence and vengeance, there is also vulgar, vicious, victim, vermin, vain, vacant, vile, vampire...the list is long, with not a lot of smiles."[5]

When I first started writing my book I was listening to a lot of Punk Rock because there's so many songs within the genre that convey different emotions. That's what I wanted: specific songs that corresponded with whatever I was writing about; seemed to help the memory resurface with more vividness. However, given that I did a lot of my writing at night, (after the present semester in the linear I started scheduling late afternoon classes so I could stay up all night and sleep half the day), I couldn't always play music above the sinless level with the bear in half-hibernation...*til I bought earphones for my laptop and cranked it the fuck back up!* I took Diversity to

[5] Awesome lines from *A Death in the Family* by Hunter S. Thompson ☺

a whole new decibel, bringing in Jazz, Blues, Reggae, Hip-Hop, Doo-Wop, Hillbilly, American Folk, Traditional Irish, Italian Balladry, Sicilian Peasantry, even Classical like Tchaikovsky, Schubert, and Schumann. Ahhh! what a way to get an array of emotions and perspectives pumping! See, I believe there's a music for everything as well as *in* everything. I even see music within situations and in everyone—well, of course, it's a "seeing" that plays a phantasmal melody. Just walking by people I can hear their music. But it's not a specific song I hear; meaning, it's not one you'd hear on the radio, or for that matter, one ever recorded, but a melody of emotion both dancing around and within them. Maybe that sounds a little crazy. Which is funny. As the semesters passed I was singing all these made up songs to myself because I was ¾-outta my mind. I know I said I would share those lyrics but I need to go to the dentist now. I'm getting a cap put on my front tooth. (It's cool like Coolgate because I had to apply for another credit card to pay for it since I don't have health insurance, and even if I did, the plans for people like me don't cover such dental costs; gotta be rich to get the good discounts.) Anyway, I got into a fistfight in a grocery store parking lot. I didn't tell anyone what really happened, but it started with some asshole's buggy getting away from him; the parking lot is sloped and I was on the lower end. Well, I was backing out and next thing I know—WHACK! So I alight from the ol' warhorse and see the guy had watched it hit and was about to retreat, but I call him down; you could tell he was pissed at himself for getting caught. After showing him how he bruised the flank and discolored the coat, I calmly say, 'Can I gitchur info?' But he tries actin' like it's no big deal and refuses! So we start arguing. And this guy was about 35—stocky too—about as short as me and you know I'm pretty short. Maybe we both have a Napoleon complex, a theory that's mostly bullshit (hey! wanna fight about it: just kidding, ddikts). Anyway, since I'm not one to bother getting professionals to solve my problems, especially not for small problems like this, I lose it and deck him. The thought then crosses my mind to see if anyone witnessed it and what's their reaction since they could call the police—no shoppers looking!—but my concern only hurt me. It was only a second but enough time for him to come back and catch me with a hard uppercut. My lower teeth jarred into my upper, chipping my left front tooth. Then he quickly pops me in the nose. Busts it wide-open! Now I'm bleeding and can't see where I'm at! He slams me against the ol' warhorse, knees me, then takes off like he's the one who just got roughed up! Yeah, me and the ol' warhorse got our asses whipped! First time in a long while; and I've been exercising everyday to counter the smoking, so I could've fought for a while because, like Danzig, I don't mind the pain, but I had to leave anyway 'cause I had ice cream in the trunk and I was starving—shit! gotta go!

[WARNING: A PASSAGE THAT MAY CAUSE YOU TO HATE ME FOR GOOD] They don't want my in their world. I'll never be in their world. They're gonna do everything they can to keep me out. Find any way to discredit me. And that's not self-pity; it's the fuckin' truth. So why would I have to reword it? why do my purest feelings mean nothing? why do I need an agreeable façade? Why?! Why don't *you* shut up and quit telling me how to be. Besides, where have *you* gotten us? You're so agreeable, but so is not this fuckin' shit piling up on my streets. Haha. Fuck you. Seriously: FUCK – YOU.

Ma foi! I never realized how callous, bitter, and mean I can be! I'm sorry—well, actually I'm not. I really am trying to become more delicate, being a poet and all. But it's just how I feel right now, and they say—meaning, *I* say—the two fuels of sustaining power for any artist is their candor and courageousness. (Gadda 500 cc here.) So please try to overstand; I would do the same for you no matter what you believe in as long as you're not a full-blown hypocrite or blinkered.

Anyway, who turned on the blinkers and steered us so far off course? This has *nothing* to do with what's going on; meanwhile, it has *everything* to do with what's going on! Hey watch this. It kinda has a strange feel to it...

...Luke walked in. In the course of a heavy yawn, his matted eyelashes fanned the sap on his cheeks. After a quick change of clothes, he crawled into bed. I hadn't been aware it was the midnight hour til the creak of the door snapped me from a deep drone. The radiant computer screen was burning my itchy retinae—(Peek-a-boo! Isn't this already feeling so superficial?)—I think the radiance of the screen was gradually dissolving my contacts; I never took 'em out, not even for sleep. Luke yawned again, this time causing a chain-reaction. I rubbed my forehead like a middle-aged man ready to retire from the daily grind. I just finished the first draft of "Alter of Repose," proud of myself for the titled wordplay since it's a slick Catholic allusion to an "altar of repose." That chapter (just like the preceding ones) started out as hundreds of passages and snippets I'd written down on paper. To type the story from scratch on the computer seemed superficial, insincere, and too easy. I was old-school in that sense. I wanted my hands to cramp into paralysis. Wanted 'em to *bleed*. Wanted to grip the pencil and push it down on the paper, feeling more directly the emotional transference. And if the tip of the pencil snapped, I wanted my hand to fall down to the paper with a hard thump, with the tip jabbing deep into my skin...Transferring the written word up to the computer screen wasn't as arousing. It was relatively easy except for the strain on my eyes after sitting there many hours straight. But that's what I wanted: *everything* to be hard, *every* nuance of the process to sting me like I'd just been hit by the entire hive. Whenever I was done writing for the time being, I wanted it to come because I was on the brink of a nervous breakdown. Wanted to stand up knowing I might not be able to walk. Wanted to labor. Wanted to feel *pain*. And many times it ended up just like that, although more mental than physical, nevertheless, psychosomatic...Something I was finding really hard to write about was Pessi. To go back and show him alive, to craft all those funny and happy moments together, was painful knowing the tragic dénouement that awaited him in the chapters to come. I decided not to write about the rest of the summer after his death because my pen could never do justice to the haunting anguish (though tearless) that followed; besides, it seems I had a hand in the tragedy; and it was stuck there in the tragedy, too occupied to write. I just wanted to catch up to myself as quickly as possible and go from there in a breezier manner. And yet, as I said, I thrived on the pain of the past. Perhaps from seeing myself in the past on a different level, with a different perspective, I was burning to punish myself in order to rectify the things I'd gotten away with. But I don't think the past was as sympathetic of the present me, for I could sense the past wanted to do something more painful to me than what I was already doing to myself, like keep things hidden from me...I was also finding it hard as a writer to separate what I knew in the present from what I knew back then. I wanted to show my thoughts and philosophies of the past as immature. By the same token, since I consider emotions to be beyond the realm of immaturity and maturity, I at least wanted to present my past emotions as having a genuine quality. However, a fictionalization of my life, by my own hand, seemed inevitable. That's not to say that I was intentionally lying but rather could only draw from the my present consciousness with the hope that past moments hadn't fallen into my unconscious with no free path upward, and thereby whatever I assumed now, in retrospect, was not wholly true, falling to fragmentation, suppression, repression, and all that other shit. I can't even imagine what older writers have to go through whenever they have to recall things from 20-some years ago! All the same, no matter the distance in between, whether a second or a millennium, it's only human fact that in this process, whether writing or reflecting, there'll always be distorted truths here and there. E.g.: recalling the panic attack I had when walking to the fair: I remember the gist of the sensations, and Pessi hitting the back of my head, and being taunted with the tongue-in-cheek shouts of "Sellout!" but everything else, in hindsight, is perhaps what I *want* to believe or what I *assume* happened while knowing what I know in the present; hence, "filling in the gaps" with more recent, sometimes related, memories...Speaking of distance, my character *back 'ere* doesn't seem like me. Probably rewrote 0 and 1 over 100 times; and instead of my older character "youthanizing" and becoming more "real," it seems to be "aging" and becoming more "detached." I mean, my narration sounds as if I'm a septuagenarian! But this is my first such endeavor so I know there's still spit on my neck...These reflections on my writing caused me to have distorted images of myself, while outside the process of writing, I was desperately trying to put my life back together. It was too much for me to comprehend. (It's even hard for me to explain it; it's all seeming futile but I'll continue anyway.) On one hand, I felt harmony and had further overstanding. On the other, I felt chaos and had more confusion added to the two mes who were but one. I began wondering if, in fact, there *was* a difference between me as the literary character and me as the one portraying myself to be a real person just within a different form-at. (Where'm I at!) I was (am?) becoming so displaced from—I guess—from reality, even if I can't overstand why reality has to be a concept of the present, why the past I've fallen into is *nonreality.* I keep telling myself, 'Only in the physical.'...It's true I wouldn't consider my work to be autobiographical, for, as I see it, that implies one is writing about themselves usually in a straightforward, bland, all-knowing, self-glorified manner. I was (am) on a mission to relive my life to discover what I missed due to the speed and chaos of The Dance, and to acknowledge my ignorance so that I can rectify the results here in the present...To return fully to the present, I'm learning that to live a life at the artist's desk (*escritoire* is a nice synonym), while tunneling deep into something so intricate, is to toil through phantasmal trenches. But no matter how deep I drop in I can't find refuge because I am after I. As I try to put tangible things down on the paper, I'm also sending all these thoughts, emotions, and images at myself, which cause me to duck and miss the target with my blood-tool:

chickenscratch is the visible aftermath! Cluck! Cluck! Fuuuuuck! I'm all scratched up! It's a vicious full-scale war: I against I, good guy versus bad guy, each embodying a thousand voices, all of which come up through my gut like missiles, and drop down from my head like bombs, simultaneously shooting out of my mouth via the blood-tool, with the intentions *to be one person in whole*, but, in fact, in pieces, only this young shattered existence with emotional shrapnel, fragmented thoughts, and broken memories as the only remnants to go on: that of my phantomlike essence yet to fall to personal abandonment, or into Time's bag of thievery.

"The trouble is,' sighed the Doctor, grasping her meaning intuitively, 'that youth is given up to illusions. It seems to be a provision of Nature; a decoy to secure mothers for the race. And Nature takes no account of moral consequences, of arbitrary conditions which we create, and which we feel obliged to maintain at any cost.' 'Yes,' she said. 'The years that are gone seem like dreams— if one might go on sleeping and dreaming— but to wake up and find—oh! well! perhaps it is better to wake up after all, even to suffer, rather than to remain a dupe to illusions all one's life.'"[6]

<u>interpolate</u> (v.); <u>interpolation</u> (n.); <u>interpolative</u> (adj.); <u>interpolator</u> (n.)

1a: to alter or corrupt (as a text) by inserting new or foreign matter; b: to insert (words) into a text or into a conversation
2: to insert between other things or parts: intercalate
3: to estimate values of (a function) between two known values
4: *intransitive senses:* to make insertions (as of estimated values)[7]

1) Aren't all written works *interpolations?* Do they not suffer the alterations and corruptions of craft, namely, by *the hand* committing the half-sin of craft? And what about the full-sin of others *editing* a work that isn't their own? Therefore, any author who claims to adhere only to the linear, pointing to the solidity and imperviousness of their forward-moving plot, is either a bold-faced liar or a cerebral tenderfoot in denial.

2) Aren't all lives in the physical *interpolations?* Do they, our lives, not suffer alterations and corruptions with every mark put upon 'em, as well as from every flash of memory and reflection, no matter one's age or perspicacity? Therefore, any person who claims to adhere only to the linear, pointing to the solidity and imperviousness of their forward-moving life, is merely under the façade of *being in* Reality.

3) Thus, one function of Art, which can't be avoided, is to reflect our constant slips from Reality. How much we're *in* Reality at any given point is indeterminable, but to be sure, it's never in whole, for interpolations are ubiquitous and unavoidable, running deeply all the way into Nature, the harshest interpolator, as well as the least acknowledged.

[6] Passage from *The Awakening* by Kate Chopin
[7] http://www.m-w.com (Merriam-Webster Online, 2002)

Why do only movies get big-time promotion? They get so many commercials, plugs, and attention from the media and other branches of the industry, which is why no one reads anymore! I mean, why can't literature have commercials too? That's what publishing companies need to do. It might not pay off right away, but it will in time. It's all psychology. Minds are easily manipulated. You put it out there as something "cool" and "necessary" and the masses will hardly disagree. This whole tragic reality really irks me. Of course I love movies, but where's the promotion of imagination? creativity? depth? endurance? all coming from the mind of ONE person. It's so amazing if you think about. I just don't overstand why some shitty movie (the product of mediocre-mind teamwork) that will soon be forgotten can garner national attention, yet an amazing inclusive book that's bound to transcend the times can't. I guess it's just another example of History spanking us in the rear. That, or there's nobody writing amazing inclusive books anymore, haha.

I've been thinking about *fame* since I was sixteen and made the decision to go to college and come out as an equipped writer, one who's able to make a living at it. Now any career ~~art~~ist (no matter how "underground" they are) who tells you they don't wanna be famous is a liar. I would think whenever you create ~~art~~ you're doing so in order to share it with as many people as possible. Of course I overstand why ~~art~~ists wouldn't sell themselves out by using *certain* outlets. But I've been thinking about what it would be like to have other famous people know me; that is, read my work. Who would hate me and who would love me? I certainly have a good idea. But contrary to what I said to Dr. R in the linear about wanting to be read by people *opposite of* me, I wanna make friends who are *like* me. I admit it: Pessi's gone, I'm lonely, and I really wanna network with people who can relate. And celebrities are the ones with the resources to "get around" and be heard; the rest of us are left to the chance of the street. I wonder what Nas would say about my work? What about De Niro? I think he would hate me; besides being Italian, I doubt we have much in common; HA! just found out he's only $1/4$ Italian: his paternal grandfather was "of Italian ancestry," and yet yinz "Italian-Americans" epitomize *him* as *Italian*. Ya know, I'm just so sick of these "Italian-Americans" who exploit the actions of such a small percent. And I'm so sick of these mushmouth goombahs bastardizing the language and dialects, like squashing the characteristic vowels! And I'm so sick of these surname-touters who might very well be only $1/8$ Italian while someone with a non-Italian name might be $7/8$ Italian, yet these in-name minuscules attach themselves to a culture they know nothing about, or rather to the Americanized image of it, glorifying it, like 'I'm Italian; therefore, I'm connected.' *Se, aviti i nessi a cosa nostra—ie i romanzi ri dan brown annu i virità ri storia cristiana.*[8] Believe it or not, most Italians are peaceful, loving, hard-working people. Sooo...fuck *Sopranos:* there, I said it! ☺ Anyway, Drew Barrymore might like me til she reads this—> I hate that fake bitch! Now she thinks she's a political scientist/activist? Haha! Please, bitch. Eat Teat and go home! My capricious intuition just told me that

---

[8] [scn] Yeah, yinz have connections to Our Thing (The Mafia)—and Dan Brown's novels contain the truths of Catholic History.

Woody Allen would love me. (Bonerific!) I think a lot of screenwriters and directors would love me because they usually overstand the significance of a work: not talking about the empty works of violence exploiters like Tarantino. Another "Italian"! Haha! Yeah, okay, mafioso, keep shootin' 'em down. But again, do celebrities ever read *literature?* and not just for work? I know Bill Maher does. I think he's one of the few celebs who would overstand me attitude-wise. Although I don't agree with all of his political views, he's a lot like myself: a seriocomic Renaissance man—ya know, a jack of all trades/master of some—has a degree in English from a top-tier school, but also educated beyond school; loves animals; isn't afraid to tell you fuck-you to your face because if you come back and say something like, 'Oh you can only use vulgar language!' he can discuss, with thoroughness and perspicacity, whatever you wanna get into. And I love his method: use comedy first, and if people remain uptight and insular, then break open the books and show 'em they don't know as much as they think they do. At least *he's* having his say, even if he's still preaching to the choir or blowing into the wind: both futile if ya ask me. He's like looking in the mirror except he's flaxen and I'm much darker, all around. He kinda has that Jew nose too. Mine is smaller and pointy. Did I ever describe my nose in the linear? I can't smell very well from smoking, which kinda sucks, but kinda doesn't since there's a lot of stench floating around. Wow! Once again I'm so far off-course. Actually, I have no course here. I might shovel this passage outta the hole since it doesn't seem to serve a purpose. (Well, I'm writing *this* line sometime down the line and not everything is answered concretely, just like not everything has concrete significance. I guess that's just Life. Oh! I've been doing some thinking and researching, connecting and philosophizing, and want to say some amazing things about Christ.... *Well?*...Nothing...Just leave me alone...Fuck fame.)

Ya know, if you only ever listen to what *I* have to say, you fall ignorant to the other 6,520,737,247 people around you, not counting the countless who've already come and gone, although most have forever fallen into the oppressive hands of Silence, crushed like they never existed.

How am I supposed to remember everything that's been said? How every little detail turned itself in the moment? I'm a liar! My life in the neck-turn is a lie! Niceties! Subtleties! Nuances! So what?! It's still a lie! Just cut this knavish noose strung around my neck and let me fall into the Lake of Lies and drooooooooooown!

[*I whisper this:* Not to sound conspiratorial but I honestly believe the bestseller lists are rigged. It's not about what books are actually good; they just ram down your throat whatever they need to by listing it "in place," whether or not it's selling well yet. This way when we pick up the paper or log onto the Internet, we assume *these* books *are* the ones selling; and so *we* buy 'em; and so *it* works. Same thing with movies and television ratings. And the thing is: you'll never know: it can easily be controlled behind the scenes. But if you *did* know, would you still sit for this? Either way, if a publishing company *needs* to sell a book, they will. If a network *needs* to sell a show, they will. They'll make it a blockbuster. Well, more precisely, they'll make you make it a blockbuster. Think about it. (*Care* about it.)]

[WARNING PASSAGE] I don't fucking care! I'll come right out and say that any author who mulls over a plot beforehand rather than fall into one is—I dunno—I honestly dunno what to call 'em but they make me SICK! And I don't care if it *is* fiction: to outline a story, to center everything around a plot, is how formulas begin. You'll never discover anything that way. 'Don't write what you already know; write what you're willing to discover,' which is a quote from some lady I can't recall (sorry!). Even I who seems to have this autobiographical work in progress is, in a sense, writing about what I'm willing to discover because not only am I reevaluating my past, and experimenting in style, language, and philosophies, but I'm also writing blindly as I'm living out this plotless life of mine. But everything out there, everything they tell you, is plot! plot! plot! Well you tell me the fuckin' plot of *your* life. Like I said, I don't have one. Out *there*, I'm heading from birth to death like a fuckin' comet. And suspense? HA! I get it from the sound of the fuckin' phone ringing cause it might be another person dead. Satire? irony? wordplay? complexity? Love it all but I might be growing too bitter to do it "right." Why can't I just be angry and nothing else for one fuckin' minute without someone waging their finger at me, telling me to calm down, rebuking me, or judging my character as if my anger, if shown, must be all that constitutes me? People are always saying, 'Let it go! Let it go!' No! fuck you! I'll never let it go! <—Why can't I be angry like that, without your permission? Why can't I let myself do what I want? That's the problem: it's beaten into your head that everything has to be downplayed, dumb-down, and euphemized or else it gives everyone an easy opportunity to say you're a nutcase or immature. 'Just be polite and act like an adult and people will listen to you.' No! no! NO!: wake the fuck up, because we all know how you really get heard in this world: there's two ways, and if that's what it takes, I'll just keep talking to myself. Damn it, I just calmed down. Hold on. (Getting super angry again.) Why can't I write like this without feeling guilty! without fearing how everyone will bash me for it! without people saying it only drags me and my ~~art~~ down into the mud! without picking up my latest read and thinking how bad I suck! how I don't do my details like *them!* how I don't move my scenes like *them!* and all this after I write something that makes me feel so good, something that means something to me, something that has brought me an overstanding of some point in my life that I didn't get in the moment. Is my answer a fucking journal? A fucking diary! Is that what I'm destined to be: a bagger at a grocery store who in his spare time keeps a journal, while telling everyone he's an aspiring writer just to have everyone laugh at his back! some to his face! Doesn't anyone overstand? *(Written in: bathroom break, laughing at myself, making fun of myself by slamming my head off the bathroom wall, Agent Ralphie spotted me, I want to growl at him, grrrr...back)* Here I am, this lad who knows a little about literature, language, and life, whose "real" life has already entailed enough details to write a solid version of the Book of Life, and yet what will I become? I know: a joke, a sad, sad joke. Someone who's always gonna be told by "those who matter" that *this* won't cut it. Well, I *am* diverse, at least give me that, but— Fuck me. Seriously, I hate myself! I hate this fuckin' book. I hate everyone else's too. I liked Tom Wolfe til I read him after I started writing this. You just open his book and there everyone is praising him for every shit he's ever taken! But what about me? Someone, *anyone*—I don't even care if you don't give a fuck about literature—just tell me *I'm* gonna make it too. Just one person tell me I touched 'em. That my anger brought 'em peace. I seriously don't give a fuck anymore if I sell well. I'll take what Hawthorne said about writers only having fame in their little circles and be happy about. I just can't be all alone...Oh God my fears are eating me alive. Look at me! I just looked at myself. I'm a monster! I need to get help for my head everyone knows it now. Because this bitterness that used to be my blood I want you to taste so bad—I want to pour it right down your fuckin' throat—and yet I love you, I really do. No I don't who am I kidding. It's all over for me I've fucked myself so bad. I'm not turning back and reportraying myself cause that would be such an extensive lie (perhaps I could be other characters in my future works? of course I can be but it wont matter they'll always see me this way) Fuck $\sqrt{}$! What the fuck's wrong with me? Why do I know I'm gonna die a nothing? I know it. I *am* History. I really am. Let it go. Let it go. Just like History, let me go. I'm so scared of everyone winning at least once in their life except for me. Please someone come comfort me. I promise I'll give everything up. I'll shut up forever if you just hold and coddle me forever while whispering into my ear warm dualhearted lullabies. Help me let it go. Please. I just wanna stop this war exploding inside me and just be a little kid again only this time with a childhood. Please hurry. Someone come save this hero. Hello? Hello? Hell

So I stayed in tonight to drink and play Texas Hold 'em on the computer. Nowadays the set-up is very fast and intricate. You can play all kinds of live games (for money) with people all over the world. Within the format of the website I was on, there's a box to the side where you can chat with the other players. This lady had read my profile which states that I'm a writer. She asked what I write. I told her poetry. She asked who my favorite poet is. Not wanting to go into depth about how I don't have a favorite, I typed, 'Vinson Vulkano.' She never heard of him. Although I made no inquiry, the lady behind the screen told me that she's a drug councilor. I quote: 'I teach drug addicts not to use drugs because they (the drugs) are evil.' I said nothing. Someone else remarked, 'Hard work. U gotta b strong.' She replied, 'Love it. That's why I don't retire.' Uncontrollably, I typed, 'Moralists never do,' as in they never retire. She didn't reply to that but (I believe in response to the other person) typed, 'It's very hard but it's my job to teach them what they can't see for themselves. Sad how helpless they are.' Then the other person typed, 'I retired but went back. I teach the problem child how 2 obey.' The drug councilor typed, 'That's hard too.' Before switching to a different poker room, I typed, 'I teach people not to listen to everyone else trying to run their life. Hardest job in the world.' Then, biting my lip, I folded an ace-high flush just to feel the pain of something so trivial.

To turn a phrase then hump half-round the body of passages before returning to a phrase; to pun a word then bring into play a barbaristic word; to throw down a barb just to exhume an antiquated word...then rise back up holding a neologistic word in my fledhant; to pitch out fastballs of pop-culture references then follow up with curves of ancient allusions; all of it just to take us far away to somewhere close by. I felt it: not just the process of creating ~~art~~ but also the ~~art~~ of story-telling, knowing others will be along for the ride: but when are we going? where to? and on what course?

> "Clocks slay time...time is dead as long as it is being clicked off by little wheels; only when the clock stops does time come to life." [9]

I spent the evening watching television: Reality TV has become the new thing: it got really creative when every network st~~art~~ed doing it: now there's so much Reality that Plato, Kant, and co. have all been proven completely wrong by the networks: *all* is right before us: people in their *realest* moments: and, politically speaking, privacy is for the communists anyway—wait, isn't it the other way around? Well, who cares: I'm enthralled: pacified: a little pacifier in my mouth: Waah? Waah? Waah? Nah! Nah! NAH! cause I'm just so fucking passive here on my ass by these shows that are just so creative and emotional and wise and eye-opening: I SEE they *have* outdone us all: and for that, I've been thinking about abandoning my efforts: just kidding, ddikts: but seriously, almost every one of 'em blows, but so does the wind...*so this is where we're gooooiiiiiin*...

[WARNING PASSAGE] I find this quota shit racist, b(l)acklashing, and degrading. Blacks should just bust the walls down and bring in their whole blackballed crew. As long as it's not a rapper's crew aka an entourage. Seriously, Rap music today is fuckin' shit. It's just a bunch of stupid fucks who brag about their "creativity" and "greatness," but (pardon any racist undertones) they all look and act the same! Nothing but "my bitch, my gat, my ice, my dubs, da club." And blacks think *that's* cultural progression? Nigga, please. Wake the fuck up. This shit today is fuckin' garbage: repetitive fuckin' garbage! Stands for nothing. Won't accomplish a thing. I'm sure you don't wanna hear it from a "white" person, so maybe Chuck D or KRS can take you back to the way it's supposed to be.

Ya know another rule they say I should never break? Well, I'm not even sure if it's a rule yet cause I can't recall anyone doing it inside a work of fiction; that is, if we're to call *this* fiction since, due to my take on the memory, *everything* becomes fictionalized in various ways at various degrees. Anyway: literary criticism. They would say I shouldn't evaluate my work or another's in the middle of *this* kind of work. I can already hear 'em: 'That's ridiculous! It ruins everything! Leave it to the critics and readers!' But so what if I do it? I have my reasons. And what they don't overstand is that just because *I'm* the one who's lived the life and who's writing about it, doesn't mean that *I'm* the one with the ultimate interpretation. I could interpret my life out-there and my life here on-the-page in a million different ways. There's many facets to this work: some I'd rather leave alone and some I

---

[9] My favorite lines from *The Sound and the Fury* by William Faulkner. (Side note: obviously not all the quotes in this work are mine, but the footnotes are. Love, V)

want to talk about it while I'm doing it. So tell me: why the fuck can't I speak my mind on what *I'm* doing? Well, I don't give a fuck about those who say it's "wrong"; I'm trying to overstand things here! And if *you* don't like it, put the fuckin' book down and walk away. Quit telling me how to write *my* book. *(Inserted: Gotta headache yet? Haha, sorry but I told ya!)* I'm not as stupid or as crazy as you might think. Sure, I might do a lot of stupid crazy things, and act immature at times, but I really am trying to do a few didactic things, at least til I can surrender *that* horrid state of ~~art~~ for "aesthetic bliss" (whenever it comes to me; that is, *if* I'm ever so blessed to have it come to me). So again, just shut the fuck up and leave me the fuck alone.

D
D
I
K
S
T

Why is everyone fighting with me?! I hate Dante! Fuckin' hate him! How could he do this?! ☹

Hahaha. What a nightmare! They just won't leave me the fuck alone. 'You can't promote your book inside your book! It's ridiculous! Narcissistic! UNPUBLISHABLE!...' Well, what can I say? This hole is getting deeper like the pain stinging through my he~~art~~. From now on let this whole fuckin' thing be the bludgeon for the slayers of my soul. I'm so fuckin' tired of this shit. I'm out to destroy *everything* you hold dear. And let me—Vincent Ignazio Scandurra Vallano—spit some fuckin' truth to yinz idiots who think these postmodern writers are soooo "creative," soooo "cult," soooo "underground." Guess what? They're not. They're no fuckin' different than the commercialized authors who've been at the top for years. It's all a marketing ploy. They're aaaall money-hungry elitists! And as far as I'm concerned if you're an elitist then you're not p~~art~~ of the Underground or any respectable Overground. Seriously, try contacting these so-called "cult writers" and "true ~~art~~ists" of our time. THEY'RE ALL FUCKIN' FAKE!!! And I'm so fuckin' sick of the term "postmodern." It's done, over, *finito.* I mean, do yinz realize that once Joyce penned *Finnegan's Wake* everything "stylistically out there" had been done? Even *Tristram Shandy* (1767) has most of the postmodern qualities. But postmodernism has turned into this devil's vortex where no matter what you do, your neck will be turned and your face shoved into a foreign example, and worse, no matter what you say, despite the context, it will be considered a postmodern device. That's the danger of postmodernism: it poses itself as something that can't be trumped, something you can't escape. It continually mocks your efforts for the sake of its name. I know even *this* will be seen as another postmodern bullet, and no matter what I say, critics and readers will be locked into how to lock me in. All prerequisites are present. 'Metafiction,' claims my imaginary critic. Or: 'It's like a satire of an ~~art~~ist's novel.' – 'No, it's like a satire of a satire.' – 'No it's like a satire of postmodernism.' STOP!!! It's just me doing what I wanna do. Okay? I don't force styles and have no respect for those who do. If you see postmodernism, it's because your head has already been fucked with, and not by me. See, many out there are jumping on the bucking bandwagon, but I fell off modern trails...through the dust, I saw that Art will always be about the liberation/entrapment from Beauty and the elucidation/blindness therein. Everything else belongs somewhere else. And just so yinz know—before you break out the critiques and comparisons—I've hardly been influenced by postmodern writers. Off the top of my head, the only ones I've read and admired are Pynchon, Borges, Kundera, Nabokov, Heller, Vonnegut, Burroughs, Salinger, Kerouac, and Thompson. I'm not even sure if Thompson is postmodern since Gonzo is more concerned with hands-on journalism (as opposed to plotted imagination). You could even make an argument that none of those writers are postmodern. Either way, they didn't affect my writing. Yes, I'm well aware that I've done the "anyway, anyway" thing; it's a homage to Salinger; and yes, I know my opening lines and the first few paragraphs play on *Lolita;* it's a homage to Nabokov; get over it. Point is: no author or work has control of mine; period. → Two months after that last line I figured (since I have a strong feeling this postmodern suction might be an issue) I'll insert every fuckin' work I've read right here; this way, if you're so bent on connections, you'll know where to look.[10][11] So don't you DARE say I'm like

---

[10] *1984; Absalom, Absalom!; Alcestis; Adventures of Huckleberry Finn, The; Adventures of Oliver Twist, The; Adventures of Tom Sawyer, The; Aeneid; Age of Innocence, The; Age of Reason, The; Alice in Wonderland; All the Pretty Horses; Al-Qur'an; American Indian Stories; American Pastoral; Amusing Ourselves to Death; Anarchism and Other Essays; Anarchy, State, and Utopia; Animal Farm; Anna Karenina; Antichrist, The; Antigone; Apology; Arabian Nights; Art of War, The; As I Lay Dying; Atlas Shrugged; Awakening, The; Bacchae, The; Being and Time; Bell Jar, The; Beloved; Beowulf; Beyond Good and Evil; Bhagavad Gita; Birth of Tragedy, The; Blood Meridian, or the Evening Redness in the West; Bodega Dreams; Bonfire of the Vanities; Book of Laughter and Forgetting, The; Brave New World, A; Bread Givers; Breakfast of Champions; Brothers Karamozov, The; Buddenbrooks; Bury My Heart at Wounded Knee; Candide, or Optimism; Cannery Row; Canterbury Tales; Catcher in the Rye, The; Catch-22; Cathedral; Ceremony; Cherry Orchard, The; China Men; Chomsky Reader, The; Chronicles of Narnia, The; Clockwork Orange, A; Color Purple, The; Communist Manifesto, The; Confederacy of Dunces, A; Confessions; Count of Monte Cristo, The; Crime and Punishment; Critique of Pure Reason; Crying Lot of 49, The; Culture Industry, The; David Copperfield; Dead Souls; Death in Venice; Death of Ivan Ilyich, The; Death of a Salesman; Decameron; Divine Comedy, The; Democracy in America; Demonology; Doctor Faustus; Doll's House, A; Don Quixote; Dr. Jekyll and Mr. Hyde; Dracula; Dubliners; East of Eden; Ecce Homo; Ego and the Id, The; Egyptian Book of the Dead, The; Electra; Electric Kool-Aid Acid Test; Elements of Law, Natural and Political, The; Epic of Gilgamesh; Essay Concerning Human Understanding, An; Ethics; Even Cowgirls Get the Blues; Fables; Fahrenheit 451; Fall, The; Farewell to Arms, A; Faust; Fear and Loathing in Las Vegas: A Savage Journey to the Heart of the American Dream; Fear and Trembling; Finnegan's Wake; For Whom the Bell Tolls; Forever; Fountainhead, The;*

Frankenstein; Gay Science; Gift, The; Giovanni's Room; Go Tell It on a Mountain; Golems of Gotham, The; Good Woman of Setzuan, The; Goodbye, Columbus; Going to Meet the Man; Grapes of Wrath, The; Gravity's Rainbow; Great Expectations; Great Gatsby, The; Groundwork of the Metaphysics of Morals; Gulliver's Travels; Hamlet; Heart of Darkness; Heat and Other Stories; Hedda Gabler; Herzog; History of the World in 10½ Chapters, A; Holy Bible, The; House of Mirth, The; House of Sand and Fog; Human, All Too Human; Human Stain, The; Hunchback of Notre Dame; Idiot, The; Iliad, The; In Our Time; In Search of Lost Time; In the Lake of the Woods; Infinite Jest; Interpretation of Dreams, The; Interpreter of Maladies; Jane Eyre; Jitterbug Perfume; Journal of the Plague Year, A; Jude the Obscure; Julius Caesar; Jungle, The; Junkie; King Lear; Kingdom of God is within You, The; Koran, The; Labyrinths; Last Temptation of Christ, The; Lectures on Aesthetics; Les Misérables; Leviathan; Lies My Teacher Told Me; Life of a Slave Girl; Light in August; Little Novels of Sicily; Little Women; Lolita; Lord of the Flies; Lord Jim; Macbeth; Madame Bovary; Magic Barrel, The; Magic Mountain, The; Malcolm X: The Autobiography; Man without Qualities, The; Mansfield Park; Martian Chronicles, The; Master and Margarita, The; Medea; Mein Kampf; Metamorphosis, The; Metaphysics; Mezzanine, The; Middle Passage; Moby Dick; Moll Flanders; Mrs. Dalloway; Naked Lunch; Narrative of the Life of Frederick Douglass, an American Slave; Natural History; Nausea; Nicomachean Ethics; Nostromo; Notes from Underground; Odyssey; Of Grammatology; Of Mice and Men; Old Goriot; On Narcissism; On Photography; On the Genealogy of Morality; On the Road; On the Soul; One-Dimensional Man; One Hundred Years of Solitude; Origin of Species, The; Outsiders, The; Pagan Rabbi, The; Pale Fire; Paradise Lost; Passage to India, A; People's History of the United States, A; Periodic Table, The; Persians, The; Phaedra; Phenomenology of Spirit, The; Physics; Picture of Dorian Gray, The; Pilgrim's Progress; Plague, The; Poetics; Point Counter Point; Politics; Portnoy's Complaint; Portrait of the Artist as a Young Man, A; Pride and Prejudice; Prince, The; Princess of Clèves, The; Problems of Philosophy, The; Profit over People; Prophet, The; Psychology of the Unconscious, The; Queen of Spades, The; Ragged Dick; Rape of the Lock, The; Republic, The; Reservation Blues; Robinson Crusoe; Rotten: No Irish, No Blacks, No Dogs; Rum Diaries; Scarlet Letter, The; Second Sex, The; Secret Garden, The; Seize the Day; Self Reliance; Sense and Sensibility; Seven against Thebes; Simulacra and Simulation; Sister Carrie; Six Characters in Search of an Author; Slaughterhouse-Five; Social Contract, The; Song of Solomon; Sons and Lovers; Sorrows of Young Werther, The; Sound and the Fury, The; Stranger, The; Summa Theologica; Sun Also Rises, The; Suppliants, The; Syntactic Structures; Tale of Two Cities, A; Tao of Jeet Kune Do; Tar Baby; Tartuffe; Them; Theogony; Tender Is the Night; Theologico-Political Treatise; Theory of the Leisure Class, The; Things Fall Apart; Things They Carried, The; This Side of Paradise; Through the Looking-Glass; Thus Spake Zarathustra; Tibetan Book of the Dead, The; Tin Drum, The; To Kill a Mockingbird; Tragical History of Doctor Faustus, The; Trail, The; Treatise of Human Nature, A; Tristram Shandy; Tropic of Cancer; True History; Twilight of the Idols; Two Treatises of Government; Typical American; Ulysses; Uncle Tom's Cabin; Underworld; Utopia; V.; Valley of the Dolls; Waiting for Godot;

someone I haven't read or that I copied some fuckin' style-crazed story-void postmodern slave! This is MY style! MY revolution! You're dealing with a ONE-MAN ARMY! Those who have influenced me I've made pretty clear. So when it comes to today's authors you better keep me separated from EVERYONE or else I'll go around burning down every fuckin' bookstore in this country then murder your masters. I'm so fuckin' serious. I'm real and I really will do it. Go ahead and try me, masterfuckers.

[WARNING PASSAGE] As things are coming together, I've come to overstand that no one is shittier than me. Someone please just admit it: I'm the shittiest artist of my time: sure, in comparison, only a baby bristlemouth blown out of the sea by those starving sharks Shake, Kov, and ReJoice, but still, those ravenous word mavens would, if they could, wolf me and all I have to offer down by vomiting it back out that I'm the most dimensional, innovative artist of my time, especially since I (besides my demiurgic work on the human condition, and my willingness to forgo, obscure, or paradox many of my perspectives, while upholding my valor to write forthrightly in the scenes I've lived out) I, yes, me—I've added brands of humor never seen before in literature, which, Zuckerman (bless his milted attempts) has failed at this because apparently it took him (over forty years my senior) too many years to read enough to have referential wit—(I would think he could do better than throwing in a Conrad quote; but maybe *he's* the true mighty narcissist who believes his own intellect can sustain the rain)—and there's just been too many years at the craft for him not to have wordplay or some kind of creativity in his style—and since *Porter's Objection*, for his "humor" still relying so heavily on that explosive sexual explicitness he's yet to pinch: (time and time again, a freshly busted load eventually dries up, you fuck!): so someone please speak the truth: challenge me: don't spare the row: get

---

Walden; The Wapshot Chronicle; War and Peace; Watchmen; Way to Rainy Mountain, The; Wealth of Nations, The; Western Canon, The: The Books and School of the Ages; What Is Art?; White Noise; Will to Power, The; Winesburg, Ohio; World as Will and Representation, The; Wuthering Heights; Zorba the Greek [11]

[11] Includes works assigned in college (namely, modern novels that I wouldn't have read otherwise). Decided to leave out many academic, philosophical, and psychological works, children's books, Classics (works originally written in Greek or Latin), autobiographies, essays, short stories, novellas, poems, plays (wasn't going to list everything by Shakespeare), and all the garbage fiction that failed to assert any influence (keep in mind: I gave most best-selling authors—at least those who have been on top since I was young—one or two shots. I will only criticize those I've read. I also haven't got around to reading notable writers such as Douglas Adams, Margaret Atwood, Andrei Bely, T.C. Boyle, Pearl Buck, Italo Calvino, Truman Capote, Willa Cather, Paulo Coelho, John Dos Passos, Umberto Eco, Bret Easton Ellis, Ralph Ellison, Frank Herbert, Henry James, Yasunari Kawabata, Ken Kesey, Gaston Leroux, Sinclair Lewis, Jack London, Xun Lu, Norman Mailer, Somerset Maugham, Iris Murdoch, Marquis de Sade, Amy Tan, J.R.R. Tolkien, Ivan Turgenev, John Updike, Nathanael West, Elie Wiesel, Thomas Wolfe, and obviously a bunch more that I didn't get to list here or there).

the buzz out there that I want your top kite so I can just open my mouth and blow it outta the fuckin' sky. HA! I shaped that last wordplay to have six meanings! SIX! And it only took me and Screwy ten seconds to come up with it, then seven more seconds (totaling a hot minute) to overstand the other 1(0)(0)1 meanings! HAHAHAHAHA! HMHMHMHMHM! And I'm only TWENTY-ONE: that's gotta just-gust you! And Diana! Ohh! For all the money you're making—such a dedicated writer: over sixty books!—you sure do describe your scenes well, right? Well, wrong. Your steel is like paper: easily bent and crumbled. Both paraphrasing and quoting things you've said: you don't bother writing about "real people" or "reality"—(random note: the conventional definition of "the human condition" usually centers around the joys and terrors of physical and mental ontogeny, but that's such a pathetic, parochial view on something far more comprehensive)—and you didn't study literature because fashion design was more important—(sounds like good ol' corporeal materialism garmented in vogue, helping to keep women defined according to their bodies and what they put on their bodies; nevertheless, strip it all down and let us see the abuse language has suffered in your design to fill up the Silicon Valley with silver stacks)—but then again, with regard to studying literature, "who's to say I missed out on something important—then again, who's to say I didn't!" Very smart indeed! I mean, the only thing you missed out on was developing a basic underknitting on how to be an artist, and we all need *some* trend to follow. Moving along now, I'd like you to answer a few questions so my readers can hear it straight from your oral plate; that is, if you don't me metaling in your affairs. First, who's one of your favorite writers? 'French literature is my favorite, but recently I've been reading a lot of Grisham.' Yes! bring the steel house down! Bring it down! *Quel bouleversement! Oui! oui! l'art de Grisham est la plus bonne! Crème de la crème! MWAAH!*[12] Next, Miss Steel-the-show, how *do* you find time to put your nose to grindstone—ya know, put the pedal to the metal? or rather, how does it all materialize? Tell us! 'Well, over weeks and months—it's a long process!—scribbling on notepads and sketching out scenes, I gradually slip into my new world, and my new world gradually flowers, and my characters become *real*, then I'm left on the sidelines, watching an unfolding drama!' Wow! don't you just love her galvanizing spirit?! I do! I'm instantly drawn to her like a magnet! I wonder why?! (Fuck yeah! it's such a wonderful thing to be unfolding the material of truth!) One last question, if I may? 'Sure!' All right, calm down there, you mettled lightening bolt. Now, with sixty-five books published to date—"it's a long process!"—tell us, how long *does* it take you to write a book? 'To get from A to Z, two and a half years.' *Hmmm*...I was never good at math but let me think here: 65 books multiplied by 2½ years equals...162½ years. Wow! You're simply striking for your age! And you didn't finish your first novel til you were nineteen! You seriously must be made of stainless steel! Well, you just keep hashing out those scenes with that mettle because you're obviously one precious element. Yes, any petty scientist knows that steel is commercial iron. (Hey, let me cut in here with

---

[12] [fre] What an incitement for revolution! Yes, Grisham's art is the best! It's superlative! [Also a play on words, for its alternate meaning refers to people of the highest social level.]

my cleaverness and tell you that I just found out that sometimes she works on *three* books at a time: now that's what I call an ~~art~~istic trinity!) Now, little ol' me, Mr. VV, the varcissistic vobody, the pile of dirt in the hole—well, not to steal your thunder but I'm gonna return to my case not in print and state that, besides your fabrications, we can all walk outside and see "scenes" for ourselves. So fuck the steely constraints of details and constant upkeep on the action of the physical scene. And I seriously don't care about all that humanitarian shit you and your marketing minions put on the façade to make it seem like you're "involved" and making "real changes." I won't let the steel wool be pulled over *my* eyes! Let's bust out the snips and cut the shit because you're not gonna fool me: when you break it down it's all stinkin' greed! I can only ask all yinz this: where's your philosophy: poetry: spirituality: consciousness: conscience: he~~art~~: wit: questions: opinions: intentions: functions: imitation: character: ingenuity: your power over language and the power of language over you: your absorption of and reflections on "the scene" instead of writing for "weeks and months" the hackneyed photographic depictions that we, as readers, continue to get shoved down our throats by the bestsellers lists; that we, as readers, continue to settle for, seeing as there's nothing else available besides formulaic potboilers without having to dig past the rock bottom remainders clear into the core of the ~~ear~~th to une~~art~~h it; that we, as resigned humans who've been massacred and thrown into the large pile of what was once our souls, continue to believe that this excrement we call our culture is what we want because everything else is suppressed and therefore we don't know any better and can only defend what we know; notably, above all, all you noble, thought-provoking, he~~art~~-stirring, soul-lifting cyn?-o-sure!-s living it up on top of the world bejeweled and crowned in all your exaltation, where's your ~~ART~~: "tell me" *that*, and don't bother to "show me" because (sales receipts aside) you obviously think it rests in trite descriptions of the pure physical, such as "let me show you what the apple looked like and how she handed it over to him" with same lame joke thrown in—seriously, you dirty mutts, break out of your dogmas!!! And *THAT*, my readers, is the facet of the human condition when concerned with the exploitation, plight, and necrosis of ~~ART~~, in all its forms, including us humans as the tissues that stitch together the Body of ~~ART~~, which is decaying cancerously, so very close to death. Ahh! but fear not! I'm still young, with (thanks to self-criticism) some of my own literary shit to work out before I'm completely unstoppable. But soon we'll be going so deep into Life, and yet from that liberating expedition down into our souls, so much *higher!* Now, in sum, in cum, my income is still zero—wait, let me st~~art~~ over the end and say: as I'm looking at what I've been writing, while writing "over top of it" in the present, to my knowledge, there is, in today's world, no other ~~art~~ist as comprehensive and ingenious as me, but of course there *are* a few others I would tip my hat to but never show 'em my mind if full effect, if you know what I mean: so take one last look at me telling you who's doing this before I slip out of the present state of the abject ~~art~~ist: yes, hello! it's me: Vincent Ignazio Scandurra Vallano: how the fuck yinz doin'?: haha, doesn't really matter if ya don't even know what the fuck's goin' on, does it? Well, in cum, I think I just unpinched it and busted one all over your face, Mr. Phial Zuckerman. I hope you find that funny, you stuck-up asshole. Haha, yes, I know who the *real* asshole is, but at least mine isn't getting fucked. (Phallus Scrautum: you just gotta love my balls.)

I would remain in the confines of my desk for hours on end, writing, researching, revising, crafting, mastering, drawing on memories past, reflecting on the present, painting both hopeful and dismal pictures of the future, my head spinning around like a top! with the midnight oil burning in cadence! the fuckin' chaos of cadence!!! I would exaggerate my experiences—then retract my exaggerations. Release poetic flow—then release the flow of consciousness. Randomly shoot my mouth off—then conscientiously censor myself for the sake of my mystique. And then—after laughing a little like a madman-squirrelman, hahahahmhmhm—I would retract all shots and censorship for the sake of my mission. All the while, the rhythm was so Punk Rock: hard and straightforward...before moving over a mellisonant bridge, for, after grinding the blood-tool down on the ancient paper, I would move up to the shining new screen, my fingers now moving sensuously like inching caterpillars: silky, measured—indefatigable!

I was becoming so caught up in the idea that if *I* could write over sixty books by my fifties, then, at that point, my life would be nothing but incomplete, inconsistent, and insincere. Keep filling in the spaces for the buck and see how many holes perforate your soul for being such a materialistic fuck. And yet it continues throughout the ages: Stone Age, Bronze Age, Iron Age—Steel Age! Hey, to pop back into the present: I'm just playin' with you, Diana. If I get on the bestsellers with the rest of yinz geni-hands, which market my word, I don't stand a chance til posthumousness exhumes me from the grave, then us genii—me in the form of a zombie—can go out for a drink and spend money that wouldn't be better spent on the poor, the sick, and the uneducated (oh! and maybe the dead, but fuck the restitution of those wronged throughout History: they're all dead anyway!). In toast to the literary dystopia instilled in your books—(that lovely anti-artism soldering your lines together)—I'll even spit ya a slick endearing line and buy ya a drink—if you'll kiss my rotting black ass! Anyway, any way the agent or publishing company can bowdlerize the last few paragraphs so people won't hate me in my living years?

Nah. Do what you will. I just don't give a fuck anymore. I think I'm falling so far into myself now that it won't matter! Just let go, V! Let 'em go! And fall *awaaayyyyyyyyyyyyyyyyyyyyyyyyyyyyyyyyyyyyyyyyyyyyyyyyyyyyyyyy*...

Hi! Who's still here? ☺ Just remember: there's one simple end to this: shut the book. There's so many better things out there. And I might be a sarcastic asshole at times, but I'm being dead-serious about that. Put this book down. Go outside. Take a walk in the country. If you live in the city: drive out to the country. It's a dying thing. Enjoy it while you can. Hey, ya like it better when I write in short sentences? I kinda like to mix it up. There's a point when I write longer sentences. Sometimes it's to make your head spin. Sometimes it's a release of emotion or thoughts. Sometimes, to be honest, I just don't like putting in a period for a while cause I don't ever want this to end do you Hey! I thought I told ya to go to the fuckin' country! Go! *Right now!...Aaaaand* we're back. ☺ One thing I should say about Steel is that I only attack her as a writer because from what I've read she's an amazing mother, and being a parent comes before everything else. One thing though: if she's writing so many books, and has so many children, when *does* she find time to be with 'em? I mean, can you imagine how much money she already has? If I were at that point, I would put the pen down, jump into the playpen, and play around with my real loves. Still, I can't judge Diana on a personal level because I don't know her. And despite being skeptical about what I read concerning her family life—cause face it: those quotes and that information were on her website so she's not gonna say otherwise—I actually have a feeling she *is* a good mother; I believe so not because of her charity work, but because her soft smile and peaceful eyes give her that kind parental face. (Sure, I still judge books by their covers from bind to bind; and truth is she *does* deal with a lot children-in-jeopardy issues, inside and outside of her billion-gastillion books.) Anyway, that's what I really want to be: a parent. I want a family. I guess that's another "conservative" side of me because I believe in the strong traditional family, although I know little about it. But common sense tells me that a healthy family has to be better than the sick family I knew, or rather, kinda know. See, I wanna be with this amazing girl who I love more than anything in the world: we talk about everything so freely, and everything for us is a passionate adventure. I repeatedly and vividly play out the birth of our first baby girl whose name is something natural, mellifluous, surreal, poetic, religious, or allusive, like Autumn, Layla, Cinderella, Visola, Donata, or Quorra, respectively.[13] She has tan skin, protrusive lips, a tiny pixie nose, and soon grows long black curly hair. Yes! I can see my little girl so clearly! She's five now and the brightest kid in kindergarten. Mommy's just picked her up from school. For whatever reason, I'm down on the living room floor, reading. She comes in and jumps on top of my chest, wraps her arms around my neck, and says, 'I love you, Daddy. Power up! Power up!' And so I throw the worthless book to wherever, grab a lock of her hair, put it in my mouth, and then power up in my squirrel voice: '*POWER UP!!!*' She lifts herself up—gives me that Daddy-you're-so-crazy look—and starts giggling as she falls back down on my chest, squeezing me with all the love she has to give. Then Mommy comes in and joins us down on the floor. We're wiggling, giggling, poking, kissing, and waiting for more to join the party; in the nicetime, just loving and laughing life away. God that would be the greatest feeling in the world! Wow! I want a family right now! I really do! Family! Frame me in a family! Hey mothers: go tell your kids right now how much you love 'em and how you'll always support 'em no matter what. Fathers: why don't you call that brother of yours you haven't talk to in years and tell him the feud is over. Let's just drop all this stupid shit. Let's all be a family again. I love you, brother. You should finally meet my wife. I love her so much. Well—go tell her! Put this fuckin' book down right now, go grab her up by the waist, spin her around, kiss her for sooo long, then say, 'God bless us!' or 'I'm so happy to have you in my life!' Hey high schoolers: I know you might be rebelling against your parents but listen: sometimes parents *do* know best. Unfortunately (because mine didn't) I know parents can also

---

[13] Autumn (natural) is Latin and means what is says; Layla (mellifluous) is Arabic for "dark beauty"; Cinderella (surreal) is Latin for "girl by the cinders"; Visola (poetic) is African for "longings are waterfalls"; Donata (religious) is Italian for "gift from God" [note: Teodora comes from Greek and also means "gift from God"]; Quorra (allusive) is Old Italian for "heart."

suck: some have good intentions but take 'em in the wrong direction (Ma), and some just don't give a fuck about you (Rick). Try to have good judgment on what you have. Try to overstand your parents before you think you know it all. More often than not, you'll be just as justified as your parents because most parents out there are ill. (But maybe we can heal together?) Also high schoolers: you might be in school as you're reading this; you might not. But next time you're in school and one of those self-righteous teachers tries to lay down the law, say, 'Listen here, you fuck! I'm so sick of your fuckin' shit! Ya know, education might be interesting if you'd get off your power-trip. Don't worry about my opinions. Don't worry about who my friends are. Don't worry about what I do after school. Either teach me and keep your police-morals to yourself, or I'm outta here! There's better places to learn than school anyway!' (And there is.) Now if they come down on you even harder, gather up all your classmates and strike. Seriously. Walk right the fuck out. Go home. Protest in the lawn. Whatever. Just don't put up with it any longer. Age means shit. Don't let that magical number 18 ever define you. You have feelings and rights too. And remember: no matter what the school threatens you with, you have something to counter that's much stronger: your *soul*, and the other souls around you. In the words of one of my favorite Oi! bands, Sham 69: 'If the kids are united, they will never be divided!' And just think about this hypothetical: what's the schools gonna do? throw *everyone* into bootcamp? Not a chance. With everyone united, they'll shut up and do the job they're paid to do. And if they refuse, call me. I'll never be too cool to talk to anyone. I'll give you the best advice I can. I know how pathetic high school is; don't let my efforts to be educated fool you, for I consider myself mostly self-educated: I've learned more through experience and novels than teachers and text books. Now back to *everyone:* We can really make this work, right? They've just created complex ways to separate us, to keep us divided and ununited. But no longer! Mothers, fathers, teenagers, whoever you are: why don't we all get together and have a vegetarian cookout, drink some beer, smoke weed if ya want, and—well, let's just relax for once, and for a while. Go tell your bosses to fuck off, which is exactly what I'm gonna do right now: tell myself to fuck off—(I'm my own boss now because I recently quit my job, haha)—and rest for a while. But my phone number is—sorry, the publishing company took it out. See, what they're doin' to us? Goodnight all. I love you. And of course hate so, so many of you.

(I still don't overstand all my contradictions, but at least I acknowledge 'em. It's just that there's so many things dancing me around and around, violently jerking me to go this way, then that way. However, either below or above everything—well, perhaps it's only *within*—there's a much stronger Dance with a music that comes into my ears in wisps...whispers. I just really hope this Big Tease, one day, sooner than later, blares out the never-ending melody that leads me to where I wanna be—where I need to be...to be.)

Apparently I have an incurable infection called rejection ☹

So sad but true what Musil said in *The Man without Qualities:* "A particularly fine head on a man usually means that he is stupid; particularly deep philosophers are usually shallow thinkers; in literature, talents not much above the average are usually regarded by their contemporaries as geniuses." God, don't let me die honest, bitter, and defeated like Musil ☹

[WARNING PASSAGE] Still don't overstand why publishing companies allow this suppression. Why couldn't I sell well too? Keep the money; I just wanna be read on a large scale ONE time, given ONE chance. Yes, like The Temptations or TLC, I ain't too proud to beg—for ONE chance. King's been given over a hundred and has yet to say anything! I mean, is there one good reason why my story *wouldn't* be "marketable"? I guess some might say that I get too hostile or maudlin at times. But what do you want me to do? This is my life, this is how I feel, this is the shit I've really been through. I guess if you don't like how I poeticize certain things, then you have a reason to hate me, or how I can be philosophical, if that's not your thing, or when I'm biting and straightforward, or ironical, or immature, or loquacious, or pretentious, or pedantic. Well, I guess I've given everyone a reason not to like me, or rather, read me. But by the same token, that's also the reason why I would be relevant to everyone: that diversity. Everyone's invited to my smorgasbord: I made it by taking a taste of whatever I can. Sure, I end up spitting most of it out but I still shovel shit in like Marvin Morrison at a fastfood restaurant. Did I ever say I don't care for him? First, let me state that I'm not political in the sense that—(to use the American paradigm here)—I'm not a liberal or a conservative. I won't go into the long explanation why or what's my take on every little matter under the political sun, but I will go into why Marvin Morrison repulses me. Let's call this "Ten Reasons to Bitchslap Marvin Morrison" 1) ...clearly making *him* the single biggest profiteer 2) XXXXX 3) XXXXX 4) XXXXX 5) XXXXX 6) XXXXX[14] (I know "fascism" is often misused but...and I'm willing to share it in depth with anyone who will call me on my cell; the number is—see! they did it to me again!); 7) XXXXX 8) in these warring events going on outside this hole, he's claiming to speak on behalf of people he doesn't; the fact of the matter is, most war vets do *not* like him; one may agree or disagree with the principles of the vets themselves or the larger issue—(not my point here)—but to go around saying so-and-so is on *my* side, when, in fact, they're not, is just sickening; I have more respect for people who do things I morally disagree with, who aren't afraid to show their true colors, who will stand alone if necessary, than people who, to feel justified, are always grabbing people to stand behind 'em whether or not those people want to be grabbed; 9) XXXXX 10) I just figured out something by pondering over this morron. Earlier I was talking about why I perhaps wouldn't sell well, and how it's sad but true that an artist must also partake in the world of marketing if they're to "make it." So maybe I'll sell myself out by devoting Ten to promoting my work; thus, in order to get known or sell—that is, if History is right and a writer like me is damned to Hawthorne's "small circle" if I remain passive—I promise to pay the fines of anyone who bitchslaps Marvin Morrison as hard as they can if they can provide me with a receipt that shows they purchased my book; this way, I'll prove I would rather be read than make money because all my profits will go back to you via the State for doing a noble

---

[14] Removed pending lawsuit. –Ed.

thing by fighting back against someone who's pretending to fight against what's "wrong" but is only trying to get *his* god in power to rule over everyone; hence, fascism. It doesn't matter if you agree with him: his *principles* aren't important here, but rather his slimy *method.* So seriously, if you see him don't be afraid to slap the fuck outta him. What's the worst that'll happen? He'll choke to death on a triple-decker cheeseburger?! And if he would somehow die, then I think the world of *true* dissenters will be thankful, for his "efforts" will stop and soon fade from our memories, thereby giving the world of *true* dissenters, in time, another chance not to be laughed at—also allowing, in lessmorobesitee, for the word *dissenter* to become unbastardized. Hey, Marvin Morrison: Go ahead and sue me if ya want because I assign little to value material possessions. You and the others could even rally together and go class-action style and teach me a lesson about Freedom of Speech; file libel charges, then claim "reckless disregard," not "actual malice," since what I say is true, and "reckless disregard" takes no regard on that point, while "actual malice" does. Neverthemorr, let me say in my defense: *mono-a-mono*—ya know, without pulling anyone to your side, (not that you can reach far enough to place someone waaaaay over there)—but it would be best to keep your mouth shut when it comes to me and just save your fat face, because any way you wanna have it out, on any matter you wanna choose, I *will* prevail. I'm not one of your insular politicians isolated on the Fruitless Island! So if you can ever overstand anything let it be that you don't have the arsenal to take on someone like me, you condescending, "truth"-spinning, oblique, fascist piece of shit. Hey, name-calling! The aggregation and underpinning of your work, eh? (Peace Solution: If *you,* Marvin "Must Eat" Morrison, buy my book, I'll buy you a super-sized fry and personally ram it down your fuckin' throat. Do we have a meal—I mean, a deal?)

*Days later...*I realized the last passage could be used against me in the sense that some might say I had to exploit another's fame to gain my own. I thought about it for a while because I *have* dropped a lot of names in this hole. So should I take 'em out? Well, obviously I decided not to, for this hole isn't even in the linear. This is all "outside" my life and the art itself, although it's also very much *inside* it. The way I see it is: anything within this hole can be evaluated in its own right, as in outside the literary context. Conversely, all this (although it would be a hard task for the reader) could even be dismissed. I would like to believe I could cut out any reference to scum like him and still have a masterpiece. If anything (and I think some critics would agree) it actually *hurts* my work. But as I explained, these passages (so deceptively "present" in their tenses, while together serving as a historical and personal backdrop) are just raw sentiments of mine occurring in the process of writing as I try to "catch up to myself." Hmmm...perhaps this is all coming outta me because I no longer have Pessi to share the ol' revolutionary discourse with? Well, if you're not liking this, it just proves how great it was to have Pessi in my physical life. If you *are* liking this, just face it: it's only because you agree with me, so that, in itself, is no great accomplishment; does nothing for me. You're not Pessi. I can't even see you! I mean, who am I even talking to?! I hope these words get covered over with dirt. I have a budding urge not to share *any* of this, *ever.* Didn't someone tell me I have other things to worry about?

[I'm not sure if I still agree with the following passage. DFW—I'm just torn. I respect his courageous endeavor but hang my head at the results.]

{Never mind. I deleted the passage. After reading his essays, I realized that I was letting my criticism of his fiction get in the way of our personal bond. I still disagree that irony is adverse to fiction and communication but agree that "after the pioneers...the crank-turners capitalize for a while on sheer fashion, and they get their plaudits and grants and buy their IRAs and retire to the Hamptons well out of range of the eventual blast radius." Yep, but let our illumination in dark times (not a focus on the darkness itself) see us through. Maintain your PMA, DFW. Much love.}

My, my, B.R. So whaddaya think of *my* pretentiousness? Like McCarthy's or DeLillo's? Seriously, who the fuck are you?! Go ahead and mac on Moody; when I was two, I used to do my coloring books with more style. But the Mac and Don would go outside the line and do circles around you! And me? Just get in line with the rest who want a shot at the new world-beater >:]

Christian Moorenko is so not funny in real life. The fakest and most vicious of them all! A bloodsucking arrogant crybaby douchebag—another Pete Townshend delivering a blow to Abbie Hoffman then proclaiming it *his* fucking stage! Ahh, I'm shaking uncontrollably right now. I seriously can't believe this. Is there some secret group out to destroy me before I get known?! At least I documented everything just in case there's a case. I can only wonder: if people knew about this, would they continue to buy into all the sea-blueshit? Probably. But one moore ounce of that putrid lamb and I'll XXXXX[15]

I can't wait to write sick poetry. I just can't break all the way inside yet. I have too much bitterness to conquer first. Seems if I'm openly "scathing" and "pretentious," or if my work has to "insist upon itself" at times, it just might do the trick. I know poets usually aren't such assholes, but you have to take into consideration that I've been molded by a lot more than erudition and antiquity. Besides, fuck-you attitudes fit in well with today's society. It only seems "rude" whenever it's directed at you or something you hold dear. Yet people love it when it's bashing what they want bashed; they just can't take a bashing themselves. People also can't stand for someone to admit that they're better than them at something. In that respect, we're expected to be modest (and lie) unless we have a fat bank account to back it up—and mine is anorexic ☹ but my work isn't ☺

---

[15] Removed pending lawsuit. For a detailed account of expurgated and banned material, see Mark Danielewski's essay "V Follows You: So Why X'ed?" in *The Yale Review* (Vol. 95, No. 1, 2007). Professor Kathleen Leshner expanded on the essay with "The Z Factor" in *Book History: Volume 11* (State College: The Pennsylvania State University Press, 2008). –Ed.

After watching Priscilla of Quincy's celebutante show, I wrote this joke: "How do you make one of those hard-to-please celebrities wet?————— You spit on 'em." Thank you! Thank you! I know: *That's hot!* Hahaha. I hate you, you meretricious bitch. It's just a façade, you dirty whore. A mask, you stupid skank. Now get back under the fuckin' covers where you belong, you ugly slut.

1% of America owns 38.5% of the wealth. Poverty-rate is at 12.5%, totaling 35.9 million people, of which 12.9 million are children. Now imagine 12.9 million children of poverty lined up before you. What would you do? Doesn't matter! In "reality," we can't see things in such a manner. But looking at the statistics, and thus statistically speaking, I can conclude that to achieve the venerated American Dream (be part of the 1%, or in other words, be the lucky 1 out of 100) you only have to beat 99 people into the ground—again, statistically speaking. Hey, that's not really *too* bad if you look at it as "outdoing" 99 others instead of "overlooking" 12,900,000 children of poverty.

"Money rests on the axiom that every man is the owner of his mind and his effort but money is only a tool, it will give you the means for the satisfaction of your desires but it will not provide you with desires. Money will not purchase happiness for the man that has no concept of what he wants; money will not give him a code of values." '...an' ran far away from 'at shit as I could. I didn't even stop da shrug! At lass, I know: objective is, umm, dumb!'

Way shorter, way better: "The New Idol" in *Thus Spake Zarathustra* (XI)

Some of you will hate me because of what I hate, some of you will love me because of what I love, some of you will hate me because of what I love, and some of you will love me because of what I hate, but it will make a fool of each and every one of you.

If you only embrace one thing I say in this hole, let it be this: Despite my conflicted feelings for each, neither G—, nor O—, nor B— are humanitarians. It doesn't matter how much one "gives," or how tactfully (or craftily) one promotes their "charitableness," if one has a penny more than what they and their family needs, while others suffer around the world, they are NOT a humanitarian. And with *these* superfluous ones, we're talking about *billions* being sat on. (Just remember: Gandhi sat on nothing but the ground and wouldn't even take a piece of bread for the sake of peace; now *that's* humanitarian.) Anyway, it's time for us who get by from paycheck-to-paycheck to stand up and put these Hollywood and CEO fucks in check. We might not have the cameras and mics, but let it be known down here, where *we* dwell, that we will no longer let these dogs in the manger debase us; that we will no longer give our spare change to agreeable fatcats just to have 'em swat it back in exchange for their teeth-bearing titles; that we are prepared to revoke their titles and bestow 'em upon each one of us down here, as we walk up the steps together, never proceeding til we're all on the same step. This isn't a clarion call for socialism or communism. This is a clarion call for dignity and compassion!

"There are those who give little of the much which they have – and they give it for recognition, and their hidden desire makes their gifts unwholesome...And there are those who have little and give it all."[16]

I want Harold Bloom to live long enough to read my work then replace Beckett with me as the latest writer to be "the most authentic" since I actually am. That's all I really want regarding praise. [Insert laughter.]

Forgot to say, especially to the blind defenders of postmodern conceit: FOOTNOTES DO NOT MAKE YOU CREATIVE! NEITHER DOES THIS! AND JUST BECAUSE A WRITER TRICKED YOU BY DESIGN DOES NOT MAKE THE WRITER A GENIUS! AGAIN, NEITHER DOES THIS! BUT IT DOES MAKE ME SOMETHING MOST WRITERS AREN'T: HONEST![17]

So there's this up-and-coming writer Nigel Spargle who's writing one bestseller after another, and they're all turning into movies. Of course it's because he writes in formulas and caters to women (and the industry) by writing exactly what they want to hear. Well, it's no great surprise to say that he makes me fuckin' sick; and just like everything else, there's not much I can do about it besides express myself in words. But how I'd love to fuckin' XXXXX.[18] But ya know what's strange about him? I was looking on his website and he supports classic literature. I was shocked because 1) as part of the Commercialized Writers Guild, he primarily supports dumbing-down this country, and 2) it's blasphemous for him even to dare connecting himself with artists like—(hold on, let me look again)—like Dante, Chaucer, Shakespeare, Dostoevsky, Tolstoy, Wilde, Nietzsche, Kafka, Fitzgerald, Salinger, Heller, Nabokov, and Bellow. He's so full of shit! Does he actually believe they would support his work? not be enraged at what he's part of? I mean, each one (in one way or another) has criticized the kind of work he produces. I'm just taking the notion to be more forthright about it. Anyway, look at this quote from Spargle: 'Although many of these authors date back centuries ago, I usually find the development of their characters more alluring, unique, and dimensional than what's being written today.' Hahaha! Honestly hold on. I have to stop because he just sparked all my funnies into conflagration...*(stop, drop, and rollin' around on the ground!!!)*...All right, upright again. I agree with Mr. Spargle. I really do. I guess the difference between us is that I'm *doing* something about what's being written today. But ya know what? I think I'm growing too bitter, and I'm sure you think so too. I'm setting myself up for a hard fall. Straight into inferno. I know it! But ya know what? I'm nowhere high up to fall down much further anyway. It's like I'm Anne Welles down in the valley of the

---

[16] Passage from *The Prophet* by Khalil Gibran, a true Christian and humanitarian
[17] See? Fuckin' retarded. Got it? Re-tar-ded. (P.S. – I can see the footnote above this. OoOoOoOo, how crazy, right? So weird, right? Re-tar-ded.)
[18] Removed pending lawsuit. –Ed.

dolls, except I never even got to touch Mount Everest. Speaking of Welles and co.: I've been eating a lot of painkillers lately. They only work in the physical. But I'm gonna go eat a bunch anyway then spark it up. ☹ ☹ ☹

Yes, Ms. Austen, I overstand you: it *is* my pen dwelling on guilt and misery. But could it be any other way?

It's so hard to pick out what exactly to write about my life. Not even sure what approach I'll take once I "catch up to myself." But I've had to and still am jumping over hurdles of time just to get there, or else this will end up being millions of pages long. Sometimes, when I go back and read what I've chosen and the sequence of it, it seems like everything happened bang-bang-bang, but I've left out so many "normal" days and periods of time that, upstairs, seem to lack physicalness...*and yet now there's something so nostalgic, dimensional, and dynamic about all those missing days.*

[WARPING PASSAGE] Can't get away from the TV yelling at me. Superficial TV faces telling me *they're* everything and *I'm* nothing. Now they're trying to own language. "You're fired!" How's that entertaining?...*(written in: classes, squirrels, hittin' the weights, joggin', showerin', eatin', piiiiiills)*...How?! Behind that phrase and show there's a telling psychology, along with unsettling effects almost concreted in our culture. Is "You're fired!" seriously funny to you? Is that what humor has come to? Well, come to my old neighborhood and see how "You're fired!" only sets afire the angry passions of the struggling working class. Come here and tell me "You're fired!" and see if I don't bash your fuckin' head in. And besides— outside the pathetic defense of "hey, calm down; it's only entertainment"— the idea of *legally owning* those words is violence to every single person in the world. Owning words in *any* manner is like dropping a guillotine down on our collective soul, or playing global hangman with letters we can't use: we're all gonna end up hung. But what can *I* do? I can't stop it; therefore, I'm subjected to this violence. Yet if *I* would impose a form of violence on the first perpetrator—say, smash his fuckin' toupee in like he deserves for as many reasons as he has dollar bills—they (no matter wherever I may be in the world) would lock me up—*pour la vie—bien sûr!* [19]—because *that* violence is as tangible as the Eiffel Tower: like the Leaning Tower of Pisa it has that aesthetic form that can turn a stomach. But no one seems to see how the former violence has *already* ripped our stomachs right out, as some alligator boot stomps the remnants into the ground like a boy stomping ants. Yes, we're fuckin' myrmidons: we'll continue to listen, watch, and march on command! Besides, *I* have a job, and nevertheless it's *just* entertainment. *Touché!* It's *just* words, and no one at all, *in reality,* is being trumped. Unawareass, please...*(Long cigarette break; darkness falls over me like a blanket of anger)*...This notion of not accepting the matters *within* a realization brings to mind a passage from Freud on this lonely sleepless night. Let me go find it...Ahh! Found it! "A way in which such mental streams are kept from consciousness is the following: Our conscious reflection teaches us that when exercising attention we pursue a definite

[19] [fre] for life—without a doubt!

course. But if that course leads us to an idea which does not hold its own with the critic, we discontinue and cease to apply our attention. Now, apparently, the stream of thought thus started and abandoned may spin on without regaining attention unless it reaches a spot of especially marked intensity which forces the return of attention. An initial rejection, perhaps consciously brought about by the judgment on the ground of incorrectness or unfitness for the actual purpose of the mental act, may therefore account for the fact that a mental process continues until the onset of sleep unnoticed by consciousness." Yes! it falls to the sleepyheads! However, perhaps because *I'm* the one up in the middle of the night, being a crybaby about it, it's only I who suffers, for, as the unwise one says, "What you don't know, won't kill you." And since what the unwise one means by "know" is something at the attention of one's consciousness, it's *I* who's killing myself. Oh Night, I beg you to cast just enough light tonight to lead me to Lethe, and there I'll show you a real murder by extinguishing this fire inside of me. I'll dip my head down under and never think to withdraw it. (I want to sleep. I want to forget. But I can never have both.)

I've been in an all right mood lately. But I swear I'll quit complaining if someone will just buy or make me a full-body squirrel suit! It has to be fuzzy and have a big bushy tail and little brown feet and the whole twenty-seven feet! I would be the happiest person in the world! I would wear it everywhere! throwing over my fuzzy shoulder a satchel of acorns! You don't even overstand how happy I would be and perhaps how happy I could make the world if I was only a widdle squirrel like Screwy. I'll never speak English again; just Squirrelese >:] And I wanna procreate so much! Have hundreds of kids and dress 'em up as squirrels too! But I wanna be a species-mixer and have some chipmunks, raccoons, skunks, otters, foxes, and—just whoever else wants to fuck me like an animal! Please someone hurry up and send me one. If I receive it before this is done, I'll quit—and I mean quit school too—and just be a widdle squirrel forever. *POWER UP, SCREWY!!! HMHMHMHMHM!!!*

Woah! Ms. Rice, I *do* apologize! You got some bad-ass flare! I like that! However, here's a grain of truth: money owns and motivates you. Come on: admit it. *(Screwy won't tell anywon. Screwy wikes wrice.)* Seriously, how easy it is for ric-h/e people to say they'd still be doing whatever?! Truth is, they wouldn't—just *couldn't*. They'd be forced into the working class—hushed—their dreams crushed. But not me. You'll see. I *will* fail, I *will* be in the gutter, but my hand will still be chasing after the light of stars. So please, people, quit acting like pseudo-philosophical vampires belong with the greats in literature. You may hate me for saying it, you may sink your teeth into *my* work (go ahead, I need it, I'm only 21), but all this shit today *will* be forgotten as Time moves on. In the year 3000, all these flat fakes will be as good as dead, and no vampire's eternity will be able to save them. But robust literary heroes like Achilles, Bloom, Bovary, Caulfield, Dedalus, Frankenstein, Hamlet, Humbert, Odysseus, Quixote, Raskolnikov, and Yossarian will still be alive, and so will Vallano. Now will you beg to digger?

(((((Diana, why do I keep thinking about you? Am I really this jealous? I mean, I thought I hated you, and here I am admitting a strange love for you. Now I'm not sure if it's right for me to bring it up, but your son. Ya know, he was around the same age as Pessi. Your son, my "brother": same kind of tragedy, a lot of unanswered questions. I feel so stupid now because I didn't even realize all the shit you've been through, and look how mean I've been. Even worse, I didn't even know your son was Nate Pietra of Chain 40. I love that band. "I feel like I'm the only one left who's true, and no matter what I do, I'll lose. Everybody is always trying to dictate my life. Waking up to their hands putting on my suit and tie. But I push their hands away and run. Some say I'm copping out but what else can I do?" [20] *Yeah, now what else can IIIII do but feel like the worst person in the world? But to push my selfishness aside for once, what should we as a people do: keep repeating aloft the roots of all evil? or is it time to dig down for the root of all good? I know you probably won't believe this, but if we ever meet, I'll hug you before I yell at you because I know there's deeper things that bind us besides a passion for writing. I'm just pissed about so many things in my life and the lives all around me—from Oakland...down to New Orleans...up to Detroit...down to Atlanta...up to Baltimore...out to Camden—I'm just so sick of seeing people forced to live this way and everyone else acting like there's no practical solutions. Ya know, sometimes I like to believe I'm the one holding all the solutions...but then I look down and see nothing but two hands that can write and punch: and I can only write to the ghosts floating in the ether and punch the half-innocent faces I encounter in the physical. Besides, whenever I was younger and got into trouble for fighting, Ma would say, "Nun si pò pigghiari u celu a pugna!" You can't punch your way into Heaven! Yep, maybe I'm just writing myself into Hell. Oh well. I just feel so sick and discouraged anymore, to the point where I pray every night that I don't wake up in the morning...Anyway, Ms. Steel, I just wanted you to know I'm not gonna take out all the things I said about you. I can't. I'm sure deep-down you overstand why. But I do apologize. I wish I could offer more than that. I know money's never a real solution, but I vow to donate to your charities in due time. For now I'll just do what we do where I'm from: turn on "Bro Hymn" by Pennywise and have a drink in memory of the ones we've lost...So this drink in my hand is for Nate, Pessi, all our departed friends and family, and of course for all those in the present going to bed tonight, feeling like they got left behind.)))))*

Including what's between the lines, this book is now over a million pages long.

[NOT SURE IF THIS IS A WARNING PASSAGE OR JUST A WAR PASSAGE] Today in my Political Science class, my professor said it's common sense not go to war. He arrived at his "common sense" not through any meditation, or even a gut feeling, which seems to be the point of common sense, but simply because he hates the president. How do I know that's his sole reasoning? Because all semester long he's done nothing but bitch about

---

[20] Lyrics from "Hands of the Clan" by Chain 40, from the album *How to Be a Kid Again*

those running the present government, and he's spoken every word in the most bias manner. I mean, I've agreed with things he's said, but it's just his slimy method and arrogance, coupled with his lack of ethical and pragmatic considerations, that make me loathe him. And I don't even know how I feel about "common sense." To me, that implies it's something shared by 99.9% of the people, with room for extraordinary exceptions that stem from reasons too superfluous to expound here. But outside this hole, it's about 50/50 on what to do in the broadest sense of things, then it gets broken down even further when it gets into the particulars. So evidently, there's nothing "common" about it; seems we all have different gut-feelings. Maybe I'm contradicting myself according to other things I've discussed. Maybe Analysis would say I'm not. I certainly believe in intuition—ya know, gut-feelings to guide ethics—but there's also the pragmatic side where it can only exist *within*, for whenever you *push it onto others*, it becomes, in fact, the attempt to implement *law*. Now is war itself that *push onto others?* Well, I believe that's where the heart of the issue lies, which to be sure exists outside politics; that is, its "rightness" can be determined before circumstance. I think that makes sense, but I'm too tired right now to continue with the thought. Anyway, after class, I went to Dr. Rosenbaum to bitch about it. He had one of those clever succinct comments, but of course stuffed with complex-irony both within the statement and outside the context; namely, concerning our relationship and past conversations. After I was finished turning my face red, he calmly replied, 'Vallano, if I'm Benjamin Franklin, you're Thomas Paine.' I won't explain everything, but Franklin was thirty-years older: the calmer mentor-type. Whereas Paine was more obstinate, anarchic, and—well, a passionate temperamental man like...umm...*Rousseau*. And guess what? Paine wrote *Common Sense*.

IT'S

LIKE

COMM

ON!

BRING

THE

PAIN!

For as twisted as my sense of humor can be, I think I've done a decent job in not exploiting sex, drugs, and violence; of course, there's a good bit found throughout the work but it's true to my reality. On this subject, I believe the reader needs to be ever prudent, always pondering: *is this done merely for shock value and thus likely for profit? or is this done in good taste with the intent either to illustrate an important aesthetic or to provide social commentary?* Now what's *not* done in good taste and has *horrible* aesthetics and *no* social commentary—just something stupid I had planned to include no matter what—is the surprise waiting for you on the next page:

V

This dialogue is driving me fuckin' insane! You'd think writing the way you really speak would be easy, right? Well, I'll let you in on two secrets. 1) When I first started this work I wasn't writing in the dialects; the only thing I was doing was droppin' Gs 'n' 'at. What you read came later on. 2) Nearly everything me and Ma say to each other say is in Sicilian; it's our conversation language. So for the work, I've had to pick and choose and do a little more than translating; I basically had to create an entirely new dialogue for what we supposedly said in English. Nevertheless, I wanted to introduce a considerable amount of Sicilian to English prose, help preserve a dying language, and give you a feel for it while keeping the dialogue somewhat coherent. See, I wanted *everything* to be "authentic." But *nothing* seems real anymore so why should I put so much effort into the way I and others talk? And why does everything have to be so polished and consistent anyway? Life's not polished and consistent! Why does everything have to be a certain and strict way to be "publishable" or "real"? Why can't there be immature lines here and there? What's wrong with showing rawness and void? then complexity and superfluity? You know how Steel said after months at the craft it starts to become "real"? Well, not (for) me. Every time I craft, I feel that much more disconnected, even if the "literary me" is becoming more like the "real me." Does that make any sense? Well, I don't care; it does to me. Don't you see THIS is real? THIS IS RAW ART FROM HEART. God, I gadda gihdoudda here 'n' fuckin' do sum'n.

What's up with chicks nowadays? It's like they either starve themselves down to a size 0 because they see these disgusting celebrities and models doing it and think *that's* what men really want, or they never put down the fork and balloon into what men also don't want. But it's true for both sexes. Government statistics show that 64.5%, or about 120 million American adults ages 20 and up, are overweight, with 59 million considered obese, which is 30 or more pounds overweight. (To return to drug comparisons: go look up how many people die a year from illegal drugs, then compare it to heart disease and eating-related diseases; you'll be shocked at the disparity.) Anyway, tell me: what happened to the Lorens, Pages, and Monroes? Although the exactitude has been disputed, Monroe was around size 12. And she would put any current celebrity to shame! It's like now you have a choice between a toothpick in which you have nothing to eat, or a family-sized meat log in which you alone are forced to eat for four, whereby after you're done you explode in the bad way. Although Buddha might've been a bit chubby, it's like we've totally lost sense of the middle-ground whenever it would make sense to go that way. But, hey, fuck it: let's just keep driving-thru or heading down the fast lane.

What's up with cartoons nowadays? It's like we treat five-year-olds like twenty-year-olds, and twenty-year-olds like five-year-olds. Children cartoons have become so graphic, violent, and adultlike. I'm a fan of the ones all the way up thru the 80s; I was a kid in the last phase before the full-blown commercialism of children transpired. The violence in the older cartoons is a lot different than the violence in today's cartoons, because 1) the violence in the older ones was off-the-wall and comical; whereas now it's portrayed as straight-forward and necessary, (nothing funny about it); and 2) in the older cartoons the context was more mythical and surreal, as were the characters (animals or animal-like in many cases), and thus less imitable for children; you'd be surprised how good children are at differentiating. But whenever you have cartoons with characters who look and act exactly like their slutty big sister or their fake-gangsta big brother, then perhaps children assume *this cartoon is no different than the "real" world and the behavior of those I look up to, and so this must be how I should act.* Anyway, wanna hear something funny? *The Smurfs* recently came back on here: one of my favorites! I decided to look up some stuff on the Internet to get reacquainted with the cartoon. One website has an analysis that says *The Smurfs* is actually a Marxist utopia with Papa Smurf being Marx and Brainy being Trotsky. It explains how there's no money in the Smurf Village; hence, communism. No Priest Smurf; hence, atheism. And Gargomel represents all that is evil with capitalism. Then it moves into a discussion on sexism/feminism because Smurfette is the only female and is solely defined by sex, not occupation; *however*, she was "made" by Gargomel the capitalist. This leads into the last analysis: that the Smurf Village is also a homotopia because the male smurfs never have relations with Smurfette. So now whenever I watch it, I can see it so clearly. And it's ruined it for me! I wanna watch *The Smurfs* to get my mind *off* things, especially socio-political issues. Still, it's kinda funny there's the narcissistic smurf Vanity. Is that me? Haha...Seriously, is it? Noooooo! I wanna be Brainy! Just kidding, ddikts ;) Oh well, I'm just gonna try to block it all out and go back to what's always occupied my mind while watching it: how I want to smurf the shit outta Smurfette. Is that sexist or just abnormal?

Dear whomever is ready to do business:
         Even if this work turns out to suck, and I'm smurfing it up by doing this and that, at least let it make a name for me. Go ahead and criticize me; I can take it; I can be your whore if that's what it takes. I just need to get out there, have people anticipating my second work in which I promise to open my mouth and blow people away with a whole new squall if nobody's feeling this. I just need it make it. I'm so hungry. I'm so ready to smash my 99 into the ground so I can get higher in the sky. I'll personally put a million more into poverty if I have to. Shit, I'll even steal a little from Steel and gradually start writing like her because I'm *that* damn hungry! Sooo—*PILFER UP!!!* [Hahaha, just kidding, ddikts ;) But I had ya goin' huh? Well, that's just my breezy way. Wait til I start putting lightning bolts through you; it'll be shocking! You'll see. That's right, Zeus: this is Poseidon of the Sea; don't think I won't come up there and pull a Prometheus on you in the name of my people. Let my people blooooooooow!!!]

Wow, I'm so happy right now! I haven't felt this good in a long time! I'm not sure if it was putting into this hole some of my anger, along with what didn't fit well with my story on the outside, but whatever it was I feel like I've put so much bitterness to rest! I feel like I no longer have anything to complain about with sheer anger! that I've made peace with people who've upset me! that I can perhaps "normalize" now! yes! normalize! and not feel so estranged from myself and this wonderful world spinning around me

AND 99% of these people I love no matter what because they're all my brothers and sisters! Yes, I still BELIEVE most people have good HEARTS! And I still BELIEVE people are capable of WAKING UP! And even if I'm still a bit CYNICAL about people in their PRESENT STATE, there's still ME, and that's all the hope I NEED! GOD! I feel so lighthearted! My heart is racing from natural euphoria! Somehow I've been dipped into pure waters, revived, and made weightless! 'Saved!' as the religious one says. 'You've been SAVED!' Which seems true because I feel the world is no longer on my back; I'm on top of the world in my own right, willing to give anyone and everyone a helping-hand up! Once again I feel comical! and young! and just—I don't know—just ME! Thank you! Thank you so much you piece of hole! you dirty nothing! you shallow clod! God! I never thought I'd feel this way again! God! I never felt I'd ever think this way! God! it's just ME!

"There would have been a time for such a word. To-morrow, and to-morrow, and to-morrow, creeps in this petty pace from day to day, to the last syllable of recorded time; And all our yesterdays have lighted fools the way to dusty death. Out, out, brief candle! Life's but a walking shadow; a poor player, that struts and frets his hour upon the stage, and then is heard no more: it is a tale told by an idiot, full of sound and fury, signifying nothing."[21]

* * *

P.S. - By burning the midnight oil, he might've fell out of the outer, but that doesn't mean he fell into the inner-life of emotion—the fall into the rise of utopia—the fall into his self where a world of light awaits the one who can strike up a wild fire inside just by rubbing two wits together—for his abscond from the outer was only in the physical, only this bitter man locked into a cloistered desk, with busy fingers and a searing mind, rambling to himself with no concern for the clock...til one day he suddenly realized so much time had passed while sinking down in the hole, heading completely backward from the direction his mentor had given him; to be sure, it wasn't an inward turn like a finger pointing back into his chest, but rather like a decent straight down, masqueraded and sustained by his high-flying cocksureness; alas, he was just an ass who in reality had "fallen down into the hole" only according to figurative terms that appeased his eccentric mind and conformed to his twist of linguistics, for (to be very literal) he still existed within the horizontal linear—that spectrum one can never escape *in the physical* with vertical movement, since there is no "top of the world" and likewise no "bottom of the hole," again *in the physical*—from which, upon seeing the break of day, he lowered his head like a nocturnal creature abashed by the light, soliciting the darkness to return just to hide his shame and regret, for he now knew that in this very straight line that drives our bodies from beginning to end, birth to death, he unwittingly pulled himself away from one thing only ♡ (22)

---

[21] Passage from Shakespeare's *Macbeth* (Vv)

IT TAKES ONE TO DANCE

"Well I didn't care much for high school,
It was the beating-grounds for the estranged and the poor,
The snobs and slicks made fun of the clothes I wore,
Which cost my mother spare change and my chances of being cool,
La la la la la, I only wanted to fall in love,
La la la la la, I just wanted to succeed in life,
La la la la la—but my past ate me alive,
My past ate me alive..." [1]

(...Ha-ha. Baa-baa. This stupid black sheep has been laughing and saying bye-bye to his future as a writer because he realized he's not cut out for it. See, Today's ~~art~~ requires a contract hand, 'n' I got workin'-man hands. But I have no choice now but to move on with the details and scenes as best as I can. That's right, I admit it: I tend to live in dreams, but sometimes there's no better feeling than livin' 'em out to the max. Alwaysthemore, I'll never again bitch [well, it's bound to happen in the actual moments of my life, such as in the dialogue, but not me as the disruptive writer]; never again break tense [well, maybe once or twice]; never again break rules [well, not any important ones]; never again stray from the linear [well, except for the occasional memory]; or do anything besides move this along as quick as my physical life will allow. So while writing and crafting what you've already read—strange concept huh?—I'll be *trying* to do everything henceforth, whenever the time comes, in a manner that has nice breezy feel to it like one of those horses that can lollop over fence after fence without breaking stride. So are you happy now? Good. So me am not...)

...Ever since the giants crashed to the ground, and I slipped into the confines of my desk, two more deaths occurred in my little world: one of flesh, one of bricks...

...The whole month of July '02 had been wet and muggy. I never knew there could be disparate climates between relatively short distances: Pittsburgh seemed more humid in the summer, with snowier winters, while my time in LaSalle had thus far been slightly snowy, with lots of rain but without the humidity surrounding Pittsburgh rains. It's not that I was longing for the cloud-heavy humidity of my past, and hating the common cool rains of the present, because I wasn't. First, no sane person likes humidity. Second, I was born in love with *everything* about rain and its process: the cinematic calm set upon the dry world...the oily scent of petrichor about to waft through the air...the chromatic colors disoriented in the sky between dawn and dusk (vivid yellows, pinks, greens—sometimes

---

[1] Lyrics from "Monsters of the Past" by The Static Take, from the album *Nostalgic Rev*

that scattered fleck [or broad undertone] of cerise]...the viscid pools of metallic blues and flushed violets at night...any-time flashes of electric-white...the surreal drift of gray clouds...the vocal hunger stirring in their bellies...the whirl of the wind...the whistling of the leaves...the crackling and rubbing of boughs...and then the rhythmic impact of the rain...whereupon there becomes only the sound of that, the wind, the leaves, and the faint rivulets in the ground, as sleep and silence consumes everything else—if truth be told, times when I feel closest to myself, almost feeling omniscient, for rain is like the medium connecting the divine beyond the sky to the mud beneath my feet. Withal, rain is also *fragmented*—so bittersweet, tears themselves—bringing a sense of darkness and ruin over your slice of the world...perhaps bringing a wisp of wistfulness, or in someone like me, a deluge of dejection, to the soul whenever reflecting on the nature of essence: *Is man truly God in ruins?* [2] *if so, is this rain falling from there to here symbolic of the fragmented connection between us?...but how could this puzzle of drops, this deity shattered in a thousand bits sinking down into infinitely deep chasms and vast vacuities, ever be put back together to form His image?* [3] *and yet look at how man's innate fascination to construct The Eternal wets my hands so acquisitively!...*

...Alone I treaded into the orchard: mid-afternoon, mid-July. The ground was still sodden from last night's storm. The sun, however, was brilliant, pouring its golden exuberance into the wild greenness everywhere. Walking towards the hub of the orchard, I carried a pen and notebook to take notes, for it had come time to write about my first time in the orchard. Although the first time had been at night, I still thought if I could be *in* the place that I was presently writing about, then best to do so: moment before memory if possible. Coming upon the closest tree, I set my utensils down on a dry spot near the trunk. Using one hand to hold the back of an apple to keep it still, I firmly ran my free forefinger down its green skin: it squeaked from the drop of water trapped beneath the tip of my finger. Like a rabbit's habit, I smelled the apple...then the leaves...then the tiny white flowers. Couldn't think of anything to describe it. So I tore the apple off the bough. Tasted it with the chaw of a horse. Couldn't think of anything to say about it besides tasting a little sweet, a little sour as a green apple does. Not frustrated, but driven further into the depths of curiosity, I picked up my utensils and headed over to the arbor. Diligently, I drew a picture of it, although it would've been a comical sight for another set of eyes. Closing mine, I thought back to that first night...when I was at the front of my car before we entered through the thicket...then when we stood underneath the arbor and looked up at the moon through the lattice...I opened my eyes: the present moment having done my memory good. I jotted down some notes: *opaline moon...as conspicuous as a moon can be...incandescent and prismatic like a large celestial opal flawlessly cut in half...couldn't talk if I tried...shoots and slats of hazel...eclipsed light...creating perfect penumbrae all around us...*Afterward, I picked up a clump of loose grass, and with it, motioned my fingers back and forth like

[2] Ralph Waldo Emerson: "A man is God in ruins" from *Humanity*
[3] Allusion to Rosalìa de Castro's poem *A Glowworm Scatters Flashes*

how ones does when asking for money. I wanted to taste it, but it was freshly cut grass—as was the whole orchard—and because of that, I didn't want to taste the dead. So I released the clump of grass. Set the utensils atop the arbor. Dropped down on my hands and knees. And then, like a cow, began masticating the blades of grass still within the ground. Damp, minty, leathery—but all in all, not that bad. I realized this—the present moment—wasn't anything I was likely to write about, and was one of those moments where I found myself to be my own comedian; alwaysthemore, perhaps it would fill me with esoteric knowledge that would materialize in other ways, down the road.

Down the row, between the roll of vegetation to the left and the outer set of green apple trees to the right, I looked up from all-fours to see ol' Jack McArdle hobbling towards me, a caramel cane in one hand, pruning shears in the other. It was the first time I encountered the legend, and fate couldn't have picked a better time. Quickly, but with composure, I picked myself up from the ground, brushing blades off my jeans. Funny thing is: he'd undoubtedly spotted me but stopped and leaned the cane against his leg to chop off a skinny limb jutting into the walkway. Then he hobbled up, hunching about five-feet away. He was wearing ragged overalls without an undershirt, bearing the farmer's tan, and a straw hat casting a shadow over the wrinkles, tracks, and the smash-and-dip of his thin dusty brow. His natural countenance would make a freight train take a dirt road, with his angry-looking lantern jaw—jutted and stern—causing his lower teeth to snap upward at his wide crooked nose as he spoke:

'The bad farmer: the one who forgets to prune year round eh.' At this, he lifted up the sheers for display, snipping the tips together briskly. I thought maybe *I* was about to get snipped, but his opening comment—spoken in a mild New England accent—suggested he didn't seem to care who I was or what I was doing on his property, even though I had a burning desire to let him know.

'Sorry I'm here withouchir permission, but I'm, uhh, Ivy Pineda's—'

'I know who you are. Two years I been seein' ya here.'

He's been seein' me here for two years? yet I've never seen HIM?—

'Ain't my land either,' he mumbled to himself, inspecting the tree closest to us. 'It's God's land. I just work it for 'im.'

As he turned his attention back to the trees, I spoke to his wrinkly side: 'See, I'm writin' a book, 'n' summa the scenes—'

'A what?'

'Well, I'm a writer 'n'—'

'A writer?' he huffed, without looking at me. 'Whaddaya write?' *(snap!)*

'Like—'

'I saw Kinsey speak before,' he interjected with a brilliant tone of senility and cantankerousness; perhaps an Uncle Alfonse with Irish blood and working legs?

'Oh, Kinsey...' I took a minute to think of who Kinsey was—but didn't know. So I asked: 'Does he still write?'

'He's dead.'

'Oh. Whaddee write about?'

'Many a thing from the ground up.'

(It wasn't until I returned and researched Kinsey did I learn he was a biologist, sexologist, zoologist, entomologist, among other things; basically the intellectual trigger-puller for the Sexual Revolution. But with God in his lips, and canny in his myth, Jack McArdle likely held Alfred Kinsey in high esteem for purely Green reasons.)

As Jack began expounding on gall wasps, and the subtle difference in every creature, I carried on with my note-taking, trying to feign a professional disposition, while sweating violently from the awkwardness, even if Jack carried on all the same. His energy struck me as very bitter. After he would make some botanic comment, I would respond as much as I could til he cut me off with a mocking half-grunt. Evidently, ever since Eleanor died he'd become a lonely man, but as I came to find out, he hid his loneliness, like an imploded form of bitterness, or perhaps he simply didn't mind the loneliness out of the philosophy borne in certain older men. Who knew with this enigma!

Weaving through the orchard, Jack began telling me all about his roots. In 1867, his grandfather was born in Aye, Scotland but planted his seeds in Dun Laoghaire, Ireland. In 1916—when Easter Rising was occurring in nearby Dublin—Jack's father, mother, and two bothers immigrated to Boston; Jack was born a year later. (It went into the typical struggling-immigrant family story.) In 1925, the McArdles moved to a small town north of New Haven because his father's friend in Boston was going there to do vegetable farming, and said he (Jack's father) could come learn the trade. Well, soon enough Jack was learning the trade! 'Didn't spend a nickel of my earnings,' he boasted. In '41, Jack met Eleanor: didn't say how but they married four months later. The same year, they moved to Maniwaki, MD, where Eleanor's sister lived. This sister's husband got Jack a farming job offering benefits, which Jack and Eleanor needed because they just had their first child...in the years to come, three more...from them, seven grandchildren. Now the McArdles had seeds planted in Quebec, Connecticut, and again back in Massachusetts. Jack's daughter, Abigail, and her immediate family, were the only McArdles left in the area. After Eleanor died from cancer in '87, Abigail began calling her father daily, and frequently stopped over, but he would shoo her and her husband away because he neither needed nor wanted to be taken care of. At this point, he made me touch his naked bicep: beneath the flab was a small bulge of muscle, but more like a big bulge of delusion. Even so, relatively healthy for a man of eighty-six years; they just all tend to have that touch of delusion.

After the family story, Jack took me down to the weeping willows. Owing to his gimpy leg, it took us about ten minutes to traverse fifty yards, during which time the sun became hotter, or rather, the lack of shade displayed for us a better picture of reality. While finessing and examining the trees like Ivy would—(evidently she'd become horticultured by observing Jack)—he began explaining the history of the weeping willows: when he planted them; how they grew over the years (the one in the back-right had been nipped by lightning in '84); and what likely would've been a poignant story about him and Eleanor sleeping underneath them on hot summer nights if I'd heard the half of it: concerning Eleanor, he mumbled a good bit. I did, however, catch the gist of everything else, for he talked much about Nature and sex, much in the manner of Kinsey (openly but dispassionately), and seemed to be trying to reach a philosophical conclusion before he went to the grave. At one point, while circling around the willow in the back-left, I was moved to tell him that I loved the myth about the orchard. *'Myth?'* he huffed, stroking one of the interminable branches. I replied, 'Yeah, the story about da village 'n'—' He interrupted by shaking his head disappointedly. 'Daddle be from the Book of James and Proverbs. Lil Ivy rightly knows that.' Right, lil Ivy: evidently one heaven of an improviser, because, with this revelation, I was reconnected to the "Tongue of Fire" and "Warning to Rich Oppressors" passages. It had been years since I read 'em, but *some* pieces of *her* myth made sense now, as in where her plot and details came from. It brought me a sense of amazement how I couldn't recall something I should've known when she first told me. But perhaps I *had* known. Perhaps it had been a fleeting moment of knowing something seemed familiar about it. Yet I couldn't really remember. As if to assure Jack that there had been no paganism in her account—(although not letting him know what inevitably happens with the oral tradition)—I lamely said, 'Yeah, Ivy loves the *Bible.*' Out of nowhere he cursed Edward. Why? Stories left untold. Stories taken to the grave. Which is exactly where he went three weeks later after a peaceful passing in the night.

The day after his passing, the local newspaper reported that Jack McArdle had owned the most land in Maniwaki—> population of 548, with $^1/_4$ living in the trailer park up the road, so Jack's predominance on the page was a little misleading. Anyway, Jack bequeathed the little house and fifty acres to Abigail. But for reasons unknown—perhaps for the love of money or eradicating roots?—she soon stuck a FOR SALE sign in front of the driveway. *Nevertheless, the sign gradually began drawing dandelion dust, for no one was looking to pay so much money for such a little house with so much worthless land; it was now marked another no-man's land waiting to become a blip on the Wal-Mart radar.*

...Before Jack died—more precisely, hours after leaving the orchard on that muggy day—I confronted Ivy about her exaggeration of the myth. Teasing her, I called it blasphemous, but in all seriousness, I was shocked. She asked why. I said that to expand on a story like that is a sure sign she should be a writer too. Excited by the thought, I began telling her stories about Percy and Mary—only to find out she truly didn't care to be a writer. Apparently, we'd been fighting for close to a year now about *me* writing "all the time" and "ignoring" her: the things on *her* mind. But I didn't overstand what she was talking about. I was only worried about my frivolous jealously, for the myth she'd crafted orally, which I would recraft on the page, seemed so effortless on her part, and there I was fighting with every word about a life that was my own. I didn't—perhaps *couldn't*—tell her about that. She wouldn't stop talking like we were fighting...

...Before Jack died—more precisely, in the hours of the night that followed that muggy day in the orchard—words among his last began echoing within me, and occasionally thereafter. Seemingly wise words, but words only causing more confliction: two more hands upon my shoulders, violently jerking me this way, then that way. In response to me explaining how Ivy wanted to get married after college, Jack—clipping branches and kicking them off to the side—said, *'Aye, Carpe Diem,* lad.' *(snap!)* 'Seize the day.' *(snap!)* 'For a man's tomorrow may never come.' *(snap!)* 'A man's today may never join hands with the night.' *(snap!)* 'And when a man turns to look at yestaday—he can barely see his own memories sourin'.' *(snap!)*

Although I didn't want to, Ivy forced me to go to the funeral. Jack just looked so bitter lying there with his hands folded over his chest, his skin like an apple tree in the winter: leathery, wrinkled, and silent, but screaming for a new season to come...

...In October, '02, the fiscal year of Pittsburgh, and that of its the brother and sister districts, began anew: drained from the previous year, needing a little something for the next swing around; namely, for the new plans under construction dahntahn and other places that needed to update to keep property value up. The preparation began in August, a very small part of it being the state putting the Vallano house up for auction. My attention was immediately drawn to the parallelism between the two houses going up for sell around the same time. But for the Vallano house it was "mandatory" or "a contractual matter." No payments had been made since Rick's death; but on the other land, no feasible payment options had been available. Be that as it may, the sign in the yard informed any hungry onlookers that our ol' palatial mansion was soon to be "on the block"; in between the lines, the sign read PAY UP IN *FULL*, OR LIVE OUTSIDE, *FOOL!* It brought to memory the same thing happening to the Hughes over three years prior, but, because they both worked, they'd found a way to save their house by going further into debt.

In late August—after finding out the auction-date was set, and Ma was upset because she was now claiming that she wanted to keep the house—I decided to go home for the weekend before fall classes started. True, I wanted to comfort her, but selfishness is what saddled the horse, for I needed to take notes on the house before it was too late for *that:* again, moment before memory if possible...til I found myself standing alone in front of the faded yellow box, looking at the AUCTION sign, realizing *everything* I was indulging in *was* a memory. In the moment I walked around the small front yard: instantly a memory. Around the circle of dirt in the back where Razzle had lived his life: that itself a memory; my reflection of it: instantly a memory atop the original. Then I put my key in the back door, wondering if it would still work. It did—yes, the locks hadn't been changed yet because it was still the Vallano house that the Vallanos had never owned. I went inside: so musty, so disconnected, while my thoughts pushed for the realization of a connection. I bit down on my lip and just stared into the dead room. On the verge of something I hadn't done since diaper-days, I stopped myself. Became overheated. Vomited in the kitchen sink. Couldn't make it to the bathroom. Turned back around. And began driving towards Aunt Stella's. Moments, memories, moments, memories, all fused together, muddied with and buried in Bitterness. I couldn't believe on the drive over that I actually admitted to myself that, as much as much as I hated that little shack of violence and death, I didn't want to see it sink all the way under ☹

'See, Vinny,' Ma began sententiously, sitting in Aunt Stella's poop-brown recliner suffocated in plastic, 'here in America, dey don't-ah care about poor widows. No, no,' she shook her head in self-correction, 'dey don't-ah care about women at all unless she works a *beeeg job!'*

Huh? Wuzzer a feminist movement in Catania or sum'n? Now she's talkin' about rights 'n' equality?! 'Well, I dunno if it's all about gender. It's more about havin'ah big job: money 'n' connections make the world go round, but thing is: you can't get one without the other. Where the hell's Heller when ya need 'im?'

'*Eller?'*

'Juss an ol' friend of mine.' Every now and then, I got a kick out of messing with Ma in the aforesaid manner. *EL-ler?* Haha. So cute! Wish you could hear it!

'Well, I-ah want to keep dee house for *you.* But nobody will give me loans!'

'Did ju see if, uhh, maybe you could get loans in Aunt Stella's name?'

'Yes. I ask. She tries for me. But nope!'

'*Riiight,'* I whispered, knowing very well Aunt Stella hadn't tried shit.

'Vincent, when you graduatin'?' ol' Owl Ears butted in. She entered the living room carrying a plate of chocolate chip cannoli: another one of her grandmother's *true* Italian recipes. Straight across the room from me, Ma took one. I took two. Then Aunt Stella placed the plate atop Uncle Alfonse's lap since the coffee table had a better chance of moving. Uncle Alfonse was placed to my right, in front of the television just like anywhere else he was taken; he was watching CNN, engrossed in the escalating debate on who needs to die.

'Uhh, I don't think I'll be done til the middle of next year since I picked up another major. But five years is priddy good for two degrees, ya know.'

'Maybe if ya didn't drink like a fish you'd alriddy be done.'

'Yeah you should prahblee getchir ass back in the kitchen 'n' grab me a cold one, toots.'

Ignoring that remark, she said, 'Prahblee out every night with 'oze dirdy *putannas!*'[4]

'Nah, I like my dirdy whores fresh in the morn.'

'Stella!' Ma interjected. 'Vinny has a wonderful girlfriend. Right, Vinny?'

'*Mmhmm.'* (After Ma finished her cannolu, she stood up to get a drink of water in the kitchen.) 'Hey, Aunt Fella. You gadda meet dis *new* girlfriend of mine.'

'Oh yeah?'

'Yeah oh. That's what I said, Fred.'

'Is she Italian?' <— Aunt Stella being a True Italian-American.

'No. She's akshly born in, uhh, Iraq. Right outside Baghdad.' <— Me being a True Dickbag.

'What?!' <— Aunt Stella in disbelief, glaring at me.

'Shudup!' <— Uncle Alfonse, pushing the piled-up plate off his lap.

---

[4] [ita] whores

Swearing to high heaven, Aunt Stella bent down and began restacking the plate of cannoli just for our epicurean pleasure because carpet-hair won't kill anyone.

'Yeah, wait til ya see her, Aunt Fella—well, ya can't rilly see her 'cause she hasta wear a burqa, but—'

Just then, Ma returned from the kitchen, unaware that I'd decided to mess with Aunt Stella. 'Who wears a burqa, Vinny?'

'My girlfriend from Iraq.'

'She is not from Iraq!' <—Ma, still out of the loop but being oddly playful.

'She bedder not be.' <—Guess who? 'For God's sake, that's the last thing we need in our family: a sandnigger! Bad enough Marissa had a nigger baby.'

'Ya know what? Why you gadda be so fuckin' racist all the time?'

After setting the plate on the coffee table, she walked over, leaned down, and pointed her long boney finger right in my face. 'Jaw'riddy forget wha' dey did do us?!'

I slapped her hand away, laughing. 'Honestly, you have no clue whachir talkin' about. 'N' you see 'at woman over dere?' I pointed at Ma. 'Look at *her* skin? She's a hellava lot closer to an Arab or an African den a German, you *dumb* Nazi. Sercly, start watchin' yir fuckin' mouth around me 'cause I'm gih'n rill fed up with yir shit. Juss 'cause you believe whatever yir told, 'n' yir driven by fear, don't give you the right da do it da her. Yir nuh'n bahda *allarmista scimunita*.[5] Right, Ma?' (I looked over at Ma; shaking her head, she gave one of those in-the-know smiles.) 'I mean, look at my poor dark-skinned mother, wastin' away her bright youth 'n' beauty with ol' fear foggies. She should be back in Catania.'

'She doesn't wanna go back, you liddle foulmouthed prick!'

'How the fuck do you know wha' she wants? If she can't keep the house, wha' makes ya think she'd wanna live here with *you?*'

Simultaneously, we both looked at Ma. She had her head dipped to the side with her hand covering her eyes like a visor. A classic moment of confrontation and conclusion. In the fourteen months since Pessi died, and she "moved back," it was the first time we were in a situation where I was openly showing Ma she didn't need to stay here any longer, not for me or anyone else other than herself, and I couldn't think of one reason why she would want to stay for herself, especially since deep-down we all knew she wasn't "keeping the house." To boot, if she was shooing away the old shell, talking about women, choice, and freedom, after knowing nothing about it for the majority of her life—well, then now was also the time to put it into praxis by deciding once and for all where she really wanted to be.

'Well, Ma? Tell us where ya rilly wanna be. AND!' (She was about to reply but with a look that suggested she was either going to be indecisive or neutral.) 'Don't include me in yir considerations. I tolja I wanna move da Catania whenever I graduate anyway; Ivy too. 'N' Aunt Fella here doesn't nee'ja around. She's juss fine. It's juss a ploy of hers—'

WHAP! Aunt Fella slapped the side of my head. 'A ploy! For wha'?! How do you know *she* doesn't need *ME?!*'

---

[5] [scn] stupid scaremonger

'Shudup, hammerdogs!' <—Uncle Alfonse.
"Cause she has her *rill* family over dere. Yir juss—'
'*Sbuddiriccilla!*'[6] <—Ma.

'Den answer the question: Where ya wanna live? 'N' face it: da house is gonna be gone soon; dere's no way da save it now. 'N' soon 'er gonna be comin' after *you* for all the other money ya owe—ya know, wha' Rick left for us in his will. You could sercly godda jail.' <—great fear tactics, but at least mine were kinda true.

'*Ahh, c'ù sapi?*'[7] said Ma, flabbergasted. 'Filomena *does* want me to come ba—'

'Ma!—dohncha fuckin' get it yet? It's about wha*chu* want. *Youuuu.*'
'Dohnchu talk da yir mudder that way, you liddle prick!'
'Sercly, fuck off, you *fuckin'* hag. I'm so fu—'

Aunt Stella took a hard slapping-swing at my face, half-connecting. But in the process of protecting my face, my second cannolu jumped out of my hand and went flying up towards a muttering Uncle Alfonse. Enraged, I jolted up, pushing the fuckin' hag out of the way, storming over to Ma to give her a quick kiss goodbye.

'Sorry, Ma, but I'm not puttin' up with her shit anymore. I'm goin' out with my friends. I'll stop by tamarra 'n' stay a bit before I go back.' I decisively turned away.

And while Ma came chasing after me, pleading in Sicilian for me to stay, Aunt Stella came chasing after Ma, pleading in English for her to stay, meaning in her house—'Let that miserable foulmouthed brat go!'—and of course, in America—'He's not gonna tell you wha' da do!' But *she* certainly could...

...Oh! the tragic sacrifices of love! After having my roots permanently uprooted, I sold every stand of hair on my body to an opulent wig factory just so I could buy you that soccer field down the street you always wanted; after selling your athletic legs to medical science, you bought me a lifetime supply of my favorite hair gel.[8] Oh! the comical compromises of love!... *Well?*...

...After my evening French class, I sped back to my room...got cleaned up...got dressed...then sped over to Ivy's to see what she got herself into. I didn't call when I arrived; her dorm was more apt to enforce the escort-rule than Philemon. So I shot inside...took the stairwell without concern...but snuck down the hall and gently knocked. She opened the door, smiling, dangling it out in the air like a snack for a dog; and how I would soon be chewing on it like a tasty dogbone! Without using my hands, I crouched underneath it and had her insert it into my gaping mouth. *Woof!*

'*Sooo?*' She moved into the middle of the room, twirling around. 'You like it?'

---

[6] [scn] Both of you knock it off!
[7] [scn] Who knows?
[8] Travesty of some short story I can't remember

'Yeah, looks rilly good, Wimp-Wimp.' After powering up on the tress—the first power up on detached hair!—I took it out of my mouth to examine it. So long and thick that in three places she had to loop and tie it with violet lace! And how it waved! like someone saying goodbye to one they wouldn't be seeing for a long time. I wasn't expecting such a gift! I'd told her that three inches would do!

'Well? Is that all you have to say about it?'

I looked Ivy over. Her hair was chopped to the shoulder and straightened out. She had a large red flower tucked into the side to compliment her tight white shirt with a red flowery trim. I'd told her that getting a haircut in the fall didn't make sense, especially since she would have to bear through the winter with half a head; still, I liked the change: a sense of loss I could handle. Moreover, the tress in my hand, for inexplicable reasons, knocked me absolutely senseless: with *this* in my possession, there could never be a sense of loss, *for me*. I kinda stole someone's essence!

'It's a liddle strange da see ya like 'iss, but yir definitely one sexy flower.'

'Which way do you like better?'

'Whichever way makesha happiest. I mean, you can make either way work. But you could be fuckin' bald 'n' I'd still like ya.'

'Oh, just *like?* Not *love?*'

'Exactly. You know how shallow I am.'

'Oh I know all right.'

I shot up on her and snuck a kiss on her neck. Holding her in my arms, I said, 'I *love* you,' implying the *unconditional* nature of that love. Sounding like she was pulling the words from the bottom of her heart, she returned the ILY. (Seemed it had been a while since we shared such an expressive moment, but I wasn't really sure.) We cycled tongues for a minute (although I was more concerned with finding out what it was like to cycle her short straight hair around my finger). Afterward, I laid back on her fluffy bed of lilac and turned the television on. But something else was keeping my attention: the long luxurious lock! I put it back in my mouth, clenching it in the middle, leaving the sides to hang down like a long moustache. Sure, it tasted like she'd doused it in perfume, but I didn't mind because the indescribable sensation was shampooly blowing my mind!

As I chomped away, Ivy was talking about how tough her new classes were; she was doing this while getting ready for our dinner-date with her parents. Going out with her parents the compromise? Haha, yeah right. The compromise: she could get a drastic haircut without being harassed if I got a lock of hair and she a tolerable petname. Soon after, "Wimp-Wimp" had slipped out, spoken in the squirrel voice. She'd asked what it meant. Having no idea, I improvised: 'It's whachu've done da my hardened heart: made it a wimp. 'N' sayin' it twice is juss for the sake of euphony. See, in Sicilian you can say sum'n twice da make it an absolute superlative. Like, *"Eh, Peppi, ddà Wimp-Wimp iè bedda bedda, sè? Piddaveru, so biddizza mi fa me cori affumari, bruciari—ie poi esplodiri!"* Hey, Joe. Dat Wimp-Wimp over dere is *extremely* beautiful, right? No joke, her beauty makes my heart smoke, roast—den explode!' Ivy had no response at the time, but apparently putting "Wimp-Wimp" into satirical Sicilian sufficed because it stuck. Besides, Ivy probably thought it cuter and cleaner than my other off-the-wall names. To pull the wool up, I think she was just happy I was talking to her in one way or another, making an effort to show I still cared, because I guess I'd been away for a while and she wasn't too happy about it. Anyway, *I* liked "Wimp-Wimp" because it sounded so awesome in the squirrel voice and was easy to inflect into different sounds with varying speeds of delivery; i.e., it was easy to alter and convey the emotion I wanted to express, if that makes any sense. (Hard to write, so only the ear knows what I'm really saying. Hey, since I'm rambling here, can I pop back into the "present," or the real me writing this? Haha, this is so weird. Hi, everyone! Hi, Diana! *[Ça roule?]* [9] Look, what I'm trying to say is that sometimes Ivy would say, 'No, Vinny, I don't wanna,' and I would say, *'SEE, WIMP-WIMP?! Ya don't even wike me'* in a brokenhearted tone, which is supposed to have the effect of "being cute" so she would think *Oh, he's so cute sometimes,* and thereby I would get what I wanted. I guess imagine a silly cartoon squirrel getting all huffy and guttural, and how it actually comes across as harmless and comical. Oh! then there's the squirrel laugh. Whenever I say something in the squirrel voice that's supposed to be funny (or funny according to the squirrels), I do this two-noted trilled but muted laugh. I do it with my mouth closed in which neither my tongue nor teeth move: all done in the upper throat. Done correctly, it sounds like a benevolent machine gun. And while human laughter is written as "Haha!" squirrel laughter[10] is *"Hmhm!"* That screwy shift: perhaps an exhibition of my most sensitive side. Or an attempt to revive my childhood innocence since it was stolen away some time before memory. Well, I gadda leave now, sooooo— *POWER DOWN!!! HMHMHMHMHM!!!)*

'Hey! Hell-ooooh!'

'What?!'

'I just asked you twice if your mother decided what she's gonna do.'

'Oh.' I shook my head; for about five minutes I'd been musing over Pessi. 'Thought I tolja she's goin' back da Catania next week.'

'Nooooo.'

'Well she is. I sat dahn 'n' explained to her thit even though the house is gone she still owes a good bit of money to the state. I told her they're gonna hunt her dahn 'n' rip her oudda wherever 'n' toss her in jail. Prahblee scared the shit oudda her.'

'Vinny, that's not very nice.'

'I agree. That's why sum'n' needs da be done about it.'

'Huh?'

I pulled out my wallet. Delicately folded up the tress. And carefully placed it inside. Then, in a more secretive manner, I made another adjustment. 'Hey.'

'What?'

'Turn around.'

Sitting at her desk, painting her face in the reflection of a pearl-rimmed mirror, she turned around to look at me doing something lewd.

'*Come 'ere, Wimp-Wimp,'* I said devilishly as the squirrel. *'Screwy's gadda widdle sah-pwiiiize for you, hmhmhmhmhm!'*

---

[9] [fre] How's life rolling along?

[10] Grammatically and phonetically expressed the same as squirrel whimper

'Well tell Screwy to put his widdle surprise away. We're leaving soon.'

'Oh come on; not for like another half an hour,' I asserted in my normal voice. 'Hey! I said come 'ere for a minute. I wanna tell ya a secret.'

'Nice try.'

'*SEE, WIMP-WIMP?! Ya don't even wike me—ya don't even wike me, hmhmhm.'* <—the brokenhearted tone.

'Oh you know I love you more than anything in the world.' She leaned inward, getting more personal with the mirror to apply eyeliner. '*You're* the one who doesn't like me. First time we've been out with my parents in how long?'

Ironic deadpan voice—> 'Prahblee since the lass time we had sex.'

'Hardly.'

'More like *not hard.*'

'Gawd, you're so perverted sometimes.'

A sick thought split me down the middle; the mood instantly wilted. '*Gawd?* Please don't tell me you been hangin' out with her.' Hot steam began flushing over me, as I flashed a disgusted, boiling, hateful look her way; she looked back at me through the mirror: an ominous paused reflection. 'Have you?'

'*Nooooo.'*

'Who cuhchir hair?'

'Not her.'

'Ivy, I'm not fuckin' around: if I find out yir even at the same *place* as 'at stupid bitch, we're gonna have a seris problem.'

'Well I never see her around anymore. But I'll be friends with whomever I want. I've known her a lot longer than I've known you.'

'Wha' da fuck's 'at saposta mean?'

'Let's not start.'

'Oh of course not!' I moaned. 'Let's not start on how yir subtly stickin' up for a fuckin' murderer!'

'You're crazy. *He's* the one—'

'Shudup! Don't even fuckin' *think* about sayin' a word about Pessi. It's not his fault he got ensnared by some junkie whore fuck thit turned out da be a MURDERER. 'N' 'at's not even my "opinion"; 'juss da fuckin' facts. You wait 'n' see.'

'Wait and see what?'

'Da truth when it comes out. Den we'll see how quick you are da stick up for a murderer. I'm gonna be laughin' so hard at all yinz when 'at fuckin' bitch is on death row.'

'Hey, look! I loved Pessi *sooo* much, and I would never side against him and blame *everything* on him, but that certainly doesn't make Teresa's a murderer. No one will ever know exactly what was goin' on with him, or with her, or if they'd really broken up, because you're right: she does lie. But still, you just can't go around callin' her a murderer. You'll—'

I shot up from the bed. 'Okay. Goodnight, Ivy. I can't put up with dishit anymore. Tell yir parents I said fuck off!'

She'd shot up when I had, grabbing me by the wrists. 'I don't think so! You're comin' out tonight!'

'Den say she's a murderer.'

'Have you seriously lost your mind?'

'Say it or else I'm out.'

'I'm not sayin'—'

'Peace.' I shook my wrists free with a brisk downward jerk, gnarled up my face at her, then headed for the door.

'Fine!' she cried complaisantly.

I turned around at the threshold, my bitter bones freezing, even though they felt like they were on fire. After spotting the vindictiveness within my eyes, she dropped her head down...*sighing...sighing*...her eyebrows wavering: obviously contemplating. Her makeup was only half-done, but her face looked so pretty, and also pretty sad. The silvery sparkle throughout her cropped hair with that red flower tucked in on the side brought to mind a black canvas highlighting a razorblade and a pool of blood.

'*Well?* You gonna say it or not?'

No response, so with a turn of waist I feigned another I'm-leaving move.

'I—she—jeez—she's a murderer.' After forcing it out, she looked up for a second, maybe two, her cheeks reddening as if embarrassed or smitten by an invisible hand. 'Happy now?' Sullenly, she turned around, sat down, and returned to her makeup. Like a ghost with body weight, I hoped back on her fluffy bed—quietly sank in—and stared violently into the television...til she was finished, then we went out to eat with her parents. Just another compromise, but this time neither of us were happy...

...Standing next to Ivy, watching the plane take off, I internally sighed out of mental relief and sexual frustration: one because of Ma, the other, Ivy. The former was on board, heading back to Catania, expecting my—well, *our* arrival in a year and a half. Girl, was she crying so much when, on the way to the airport, we drove by the officially-auctioned-off-for-pennies box in the middle of the block. The only reason I drove by was for closure. But the way she was spending her tears, you would've thought she once loved the place. You would've thought she once called the place *home*...

...The following week, I stopped in Dr. Rosenbaum's office to spend the latest details of my life I'd been saving up. Jokingly, I said, 'So should I let *this* go?' meaning not just the house but also the politics behind it. And he said, 'Sure. Unless you have, or come to have, the money to buy it back. But I would think—from what you've told me—that you'd rather spend the money on other things. More important things, right?' Yeah, nothing too ironic, witty, or sagacious on the surface, except that he purposely overlooked the target of my anger ("the politics behind it"), which tacitly coincided with his trademark advice: always forgive but never forget. Furthermore, with fame and one-day-I'm-gonna-come-back-and-set-things-straight burning in my mind owing to my promising work, it *had* crossed my mind to buy the house back one day, as he was suggesting was my hidden desire. Unbeknownst to him, however, I wanted to buy it back just to blow it up. Soon, my life would be moving to Sicily, so literally burning the bridges behind me would be something heartening, heroic, romantic, triumphant, utopian, and just—just something that would surely spark my he̲a̲r̲t!—that is, whenever I got a hold of some kerosene; already had the matches; slowly but surely developing the fortitude to strike one or two...

For weeks wielding wood pressed into the pain swelling in the bell of me.
Come out little monster and play!
Tell why the Devil would sustain
The pain in the bell of me; is he who knows Hell god of poetry?

Toll! Toll! Toll! I pay the price to toil a field but not eat its fruit?
Adam, this is NOT a dam game!
Go tell Eve I-am so hungry,
From feeding Swell in the bell of me; A, did E pluck copiously? [11]

Screw you all; go to Hell; and tell the Devil I'm so sick of wordplay;
My widdle baby needs muuuuuch more!
"Weeds and seeds": oh, Vallano, please!
Yo, I don't disagree; so, Red, let me sign the same line as Shelley! [12]

(Senseless! Senseless! How much time's passed since this!)

'Hey, Luke: what's taday's date?'

My laptop was gone for the night, getting a tune-up, and I didn't feel like getting up to find my cell. Sitting at his desk, parallel with me at mine, Luke looked over and giggled. 'Friday, January 31st. Sta̲r̲t̲in' to lose track of time huh?'

'Yeah, juss goes da show ya how reliant on computers we're becomin'.'

'And how gettin' swamped with work kills the calendar.' Since I didn't reply, he turned back to his work. But the revelation of Friday meant I hadn't been to classes in three days. Cogitating the notion of time more broadly, I realized I hadn't talked to Ivy in two days, Dr. Rosenbaum fourteen, Ma twenty-some, Eddie months, Jeremiah months, Dante who? clock what? Pessi still hasn't woken from his opioid dream? my father's still degenerating? he squashed Razzle? ol' Jack passed peacefully? orchard now abandoned? new family in my old house? New York City swept up in ashes? commencement of war imminent?

'Were you good friends with Ralphie? like dija think he wuzza like, uhh, a sincere kinda person?' <—where did this question come from?

---

[11] Asking Adam if Eve sinned a lot. Also, a double-entendre, for "pluck" is a double-sound pun for "fuck." The hyphen in I-am is intentional and plays on the name of Adam; the same with dropping the "n" from "damn" so it says "a dam."

[12] One of the few Romantics who didn't believe in God. Vallano is jokingly saying that he is so frustrated with his poetry that he would reconsider his religious beliefs just to be a great poet like Shelley, who, according to Christian belief, secured his place in Hell by being an atheist.

Luke turned back across his shoulder, smiling. 'Yeah. He was all right. A bit mysterious. Seemed like there was somethin' he was hidin' deep-down.'

'Yeah, 'at's the vibe I got too...' I began jotting down the conversation, as well as my immediate thoughts on it, Luke unaware of this. 'This might sound a bit paranoid, but it felt like he was always watchin' me. 'N' a couple times, I think I caught him eyein' yir painting: he would kinda develop this scowl on his face. But I wasn't sure if it was all in my head.'

'Well, he *is* an atheist. I found that out during a friendly discussion on religion. His basic argument was: "If I can't see it, then it doesn't exist." But he said he's still respectful of everyone's beliefs.'

'Rilly? An *atheist?*' I feigned a tone of surprise; I *knew* Agent Ralphie had been up to something with his nothingness.

'Yep. Isn't that what you are?'

I vaddled 'Nah, I think 'at whole "If I can't see it, den it don't exist" shit is for blind fools.' I took a moment to let the writing catch up. 'It's funny: 'at line-of-thought reminds me of the logic behind "I think; derefore, I am."'

'Really? How so?' Luke sat back in his chair like an indication that we'd actually slipped into *conversation* and he was aware of it, trying with a steady approach not to let this blow over. 'I mean, what exactly are you? I never fully caught the grip.'

'Well ya know I's raised Catholic. 'N' I still share many of those beliefs, but dere's things that the Church can't capture in my spiritual identity. I'm not even sure if there's words thit could describe it, ya know. But I'm not an atheist. I think atheism is dangerous insofar as it deflates the imagination 'n' thus creativity, not da exclude the fact thit it's just another blind organized religion. I think the absence of traditional myth in our culture is also dangerous 'cause wherever myth *does* exist, it's mocked 'cause it's "not rill" when, in fact, myths, in a deeper sense, are more indicative of reality than our own singular perspective, which is why I think classical myth needs revived 'n' taught with an intellectual seriousness.'

'Well I haven't read much of the mythology you have,'—(he was referring to my second major in Classics)—'but I definitely agree that, because of its dimensionality, fiction allows us to build strong interpretive skills: somethin' I think most people lack without knowin' they lack it.'

'Exactly...' I just developed a newfound respect for Luke; what I thought would be an insular major had apparently turned Luke into a critical thinker while remaining dogmatic in conduct. You could say that the coddled cub had grown into a barefaced bear in my eyes. After a breath of preparation, I *tried* to readdress the issue I really didn't know how to describe: 'Ya know, Luke, I rilly don't know howda describe my spirituality. It's not an *agnostic* sentiment since 'at would imply the afterlife 'n' God can never be proven; hence, don't bother with it. I guess—I dunno—I guess it's like I'll bother-with-it-while-both-enjoyin'-'n'-bein'-humble-of-my-ignorance. Kinda like never *shun* the Impossible, yet never *grossly* copulate with the Air. If 'at makes any sense.'

'Yeah—it does. Just never heard it put like that before,' he chuckled. 'Now I can see why you're a writer: you have a unique way with words.'

'Thanks.'

'So generally speaking then, you still believe in the *monotheistic* notion of God as what exists above all things?'

'Sure.' I stood up then, needing to go the bathroom: I drank way too much iced-tea whenever I wrote! During the walk down the hall, one thing was occupying my mind: while replaying the conversation in my head, I was trying to decide if Luke had asked that last question just because it was the proper conclusive question or because I'd mentioned the importance of traditional myths and thus he might've thought I actually *worshiped* the ancient gods (ya know, polytheism); I concluded the former— for God's sake, hopefully the former...

...Entering the white germ-tile nation, I was instantly lambasted across the face with that sickening scent of bleach mixed with aftershave! Yuck! After pisstol-whipping the porcelain, I embraced John and relieved a shitload of thoughts into his ear—well, as much as he could handle...*shit, I sercly nee'dda take a break from writin'...it's fuckin' killin' me...I should caw Ivy 'n' take her out tonight...wait, is this the weekend she has da godda her aunt's?...no, she woulda cawed before leavin'...I know she's not happy with my dedication ta the book...juss wish I could explain how it's gonna support us...a liddle sacrifice now will pay off big when we're oudda school 'n' need some extra money...I should take her out da eat at Donalucci's, have a nice dinner, 'n' finely tell her where we'll be goin' after graduation...tell her how we're gonna raise our family Sicilian-style...wonder if she knows how much I wanna st<u>art</u> a family...God, I wish I could juss tell her these things with ease!...why's it so hard for meedda juss be open up about da big things?......don't you see how after the honeymoon phase ended you slowly went back under the façade you used for your friends...just let it go and open up to her...let that go and let this out—wha' da fuck is 'iss jag-off lookin' at?!*—

'What's up, Vin?' <—one of the new kids in the hall: Mike, three doors down.

'Not much. You?'

'Gettin' ready to go to a pledge p<u>art</u>y.'

'Cool.' *(shake, shake, shake...shake...shake...shaaaa-KAH...)* 'See ya, John.'

Mike's face = bewilderment. 'Yeah. See ya, Vin.'

...Back in the room, I dialed up Ivy's dorm number. No answer. Cell phone. No answer. After calling ten more times I went out into the stairwell and began leaving voice-mails of sycophancy. Then ones of desperate beseeching, revealing the plans I made for us: *so caw me back—ar'ight, Wimp-Wimp?* An hour later, her cell phone quit ringing, going straight to voice-mail, which meant it had been shut off. At midnight, I broke down and trudged through the freshly-fallen snow up to her dorm...I stood in front of the building, a little off to the side, by a bench...lit a cigarette in the twenty-degree air...no one else directly around but a few people out on the hilled street, probably returning early from p<u>art</u>ies...I was contemplating how to go about this...but the coldness seemed to be slowing my brainwaves...cold brain, cold skin: didn't make sense, for I was burning up inside...a few minutes later I flicked the cigarette and walked down to her parking lot...far enough to where I could clearly see her yellow Beemer right in the first slot, third row...so I walked back up to the dorm, thinking how a present car didn't necessarily mean she was in her room: could be around campus, downtown, or *anywhere* thanks to the billions of other cars in the world!...I was starting to shake a little...I was kinda peaking around and through the front door because I didn't want to be spotted by the fat girl behind the cubicle...Ivy's dorm was all-girls: always needed an escort to walk down the halls, and despite her frequently sneaking me in through the ID-locked back door, no male visitors whatsoever allowed after midnight...it was past midnight...I wanted to go to her room to see if she was inside, and with anyone else...lighting another cigarette sparked a novel idea: go around back to where her window is...I crept around the back of the dorm...through the unpathed snow...but five floors up I couldn't tell if her light was on because she had a thick blanket-like thing draped over the window...I bought her that because it had a big butterfly on it and she likes butterflies, and now it damns me!...I crafted a snowball and threw it up towards her window...but missed...made another one, only bigger and more compact...this time, before launching it, I slogged halfway up the steep hillside to level myself with the window...then—ready—aim—FIRE!—(!!!X!!!)—TARGET HIT!—(???)—nothing: no crack of light, no parting wings, no peering eyes, so I hurried back around to the front because I couldn't miss her coming in...

...Out there in the late-night chill, I stood off to the right side of the entry, perched behind the bench, underneath the highlight of a mocking lamp, smoking cigarettes one after another to keep warm, to tame hot nerves...I kept calling her dorm number...kept getting this mocking reply: 'Hi, this is Ivy. I'm not here right now. Try the cell, or leave a message and I just might get back to you.'...but the cell's shut off!...I kept peaking around and into the building as if at some point I could make a break inside and dash to my destiny...I was eyeing every drunken passerby without trying to look like a stalker, trying to look like I was waiting for someone, even though I was...for a few minutes I fell into a deep stare directed at the corner of the bricked wall...when I snapped out of it I wanted to smash it in, see what the fuck was going on inside!...then I started shaking: it was getting colder—too cold: it was now getting to me...didn't have a coat on either because I didn't own one: hoodies usually sufficed, but the hoodie wasn't cutting it!...the thought even crosses my mind to take the tress out of my wallet and power up for magical warmth, but that wasn't going to cut it either...so dejected I returned to my room...and lay on my bed, thinking up scenarios of the most abysmal, upsetting, painful nature...my teeth squeezed tightly together...but nothing compared to my hands...I just wanted to go hangout with Pessi to get my mind off things....wanted to relax my teeth and laugh, relax my hands and run one through his hair so it would make that rough sandpaper sound...around 3 a.m. I became so sick of the way I was breathing, so I stood up and pulled out from my desk drawer a bottle of comfort...underneath the highlight of a mocking lamp I began trading off paragraphs for shots...every so often getting up from the desk, going over to the window on my side, cracking it open, and smoking a cigarette, the cold air blowing into my face...must've been around 6 a.m. when I finally made it back over to the bed, burning in anger...

...As soon as I woke up the next evening, I assailed the rubber buttons again. She answered promptly but wouldn't answer my questions sufficiently. 'Where were you lass night?' – '*Weeeell,* since you never wanna go out anymore, I decided to go out with my friends.' – "Wha' friends? What's his name?' (She laughed.) 'Hun, believe it or not, I *have* friends; I've just put 'em aside for you. And I'm not even gonna lower myself by responding to "his name."' – 'Whadever. I'm comin' over; we nee'dda talk about some shit.' – 'No. I—' *Click!...practically running through the snow...right through the front door of the dorm...straight up the steps...down the hall... *knock*knock*knock*knock* knock*—*

'Are you insane?'

I moved into the bedroom with grit and stompin' boots, ready to look underneath the bed, between the sheets, through the closet—perhaps below the windowsill outside.

'Wha' da fuck? I cawed you all fuckin' night long. Den ya shut yir cell off? How many messages I leave, huh? You heard 'em: I had plans made for us. But *nooo!* as soon as I try da do sum'n nice, you gadda fuck it up. Where were you, huh? 'N' who were ya with? Was—'

'Just sit down and breathe. You're gettin' all worked up over nothin'.'

'*Nuh'n?* All of a sudden yir actin' shady; I haven't heard from ya in like a fuckin' week; you won't fuckin' answer yir phone; you haven't been cawin' me; 'n' *I'm* gih'n worked up over *nuh'n?*'

'Hey, I call you all the time, but ever since you started your little book, you never have time for me. Sorry but I'm gettin' sick of sittin' here or at home by myself, especially on the weekends—'

'Wha', you a big pardy animal now or sum'n?'

'No, but I do like to go out on occasion.'

'So where ja go? a party? I betcha went to a pardy. I can sense it.'

Indifferently, she turned away from me and lay back on her bed. She was in tight black shorts and an oversized purple t-shirt. She gave me this coy look, which disgusted me, followed by a giggle, probably for me standing out in front of her, huffing like a fat man but staring at her as if I was a sculpted statue about to flex.

'Sum'n fuckin' funny?'

'Yeah. You're insanity.'

'I'm not insane; I juss wanna know if ya went do a party lass night?'

'Yes, I did.'

The next breath I took stung real bad. 'With who? I mean, I thoucha didn't know anybody. Thought poor lonesome Ivy didn't have any friends.'

'I have one or two.'

'Den which one ju go with?'

'Luke,' she laughed.

'I'm not fuckin' jokin', Ivy. Tell me right now before I start breakin' shit.'

'You touch anything and I'll have you thrown out of here.'

'You fuckin' seris?! You do drugs lass night or sum'n?! I mean, juss listen'ah whachir sayin': tellin' me you'll have me thrown out!'

'Just listen to what *you're* sayin': tellin' me you'll break my stuff!'

'Den tell me who ya went out with. Ivy, I'm bein' so fuckin' seris, please don't tell me—' I stopped. Scanned her face. Seeing the truth hurts. But once you know, you need it told to you, and not just once but again and again so you can feel more and more pain til you feel it's equaled the seriousness of the matter. 'Don't tell me you went out with her. Please don't. Diju?'

'Well when the person you love turns away from you, and you have no one else in your life, you tend to turn to old friends.'

'Fuck 'at shit. Right now: me or her. I refuse da be with someone thit's friends with the fuckin' cunt who murdered my best friend—no! don't even try da argue with me! Juss pick: me or her. Who's it gonna be?'

'This is stupid, Vinny. You don't have to see her or be friends with her, but I've known her for so long and she's still *my* friend. I mean, how pathetic is it that you're just now findin' this out?'

'*What?*'

'Umm, we never really stopped bein' friends. I mean, we don't hangout like we *used to*, but we still go out once in a while. But you're so lost in your little world that you didn't even know til now. Says it all.'

I threw my hands up in the air. 'Un-fuckin'-believable! Dis can't be happenin'ah me! Da girl I love is backstabbin' me!—no! she's stabbin' me right in the front! She's choosin'ah be friends with a junkie—a fuckin' murderer!'

'Oh God, Vinny, you're so dramatic. You just have this narrow view of what happened. And you're so bitter over it—'

'Yir fuckin' right I am,' I shot back. 'You lose five friends by da time yir twenty, den yir *best* friend, 'n' see how *you* feel.'

'Now if you would've let me finish. You're so bitter over it and I completely understand because I am too. But you turn your bitterness to blame then direct it to whoever you think is the closest to bein' responsible for it.'

I laughed in a supercilious huff. 'You a fuckin' psychologist now?'

'You a homicide detective?'

'Is my best friend's death a fuckin' joke da you or sum'n?'

'Of course not, Vinny! But you're just actin' like a, like a—I dunno, but you just need to settle down.' She patted down on the empty space beside her. 'Come here, hunny-bun. Come lay down with me for a while til I have to get ready.'

'Where you goin' now?!'

'Come lay down with Wimp-Wimp. You can *power up!*' She held out a piece of her hair in temptation. But I surveyed the room; I needed to break something, and quickly. Breathing heavily, but with self-suppression, I began walking around the reddening room, throwing the unbreakable shit aside, looking for the breakable shit.

She stood up. 'What are you doin'?'

I turned around. We were face-to-face. 'Me or her: pick right now.'

'I'm not pickin' between you two.'

'Wha'? You shouldn't even hafta *think* about it.'

'Vinny, look: we're almost done with school, and I'm sure we'll be movin' away together. And I'll probably never see her again. So why can't I spend some time with her now?'

'Because – of – what – she – did.'

'She – did – nothin' – Pessi – didn't – do – himself.'

'Wow. If you only knew how fuckin' naïve you are. You rilly do like da believe in whachu can't fully see, huh?'

'What's that mean? I know her better than you do.'

I wisely retracted. 'Come on, Ivy; let's juss quit playin' 'iss stupid one-up game 'n' be rational here: juss tell me ya won't talk da her anymore 'cause you know she's no good for you as a friend or for our relationship. Get dressed, 'n' we'll go wherever you wanna go.'

'Sorry, Vinny, I already have plans.'

'With her?—With her?!'

'Shouldn't have ignored me for so long.'

'I never ignored ju. Sorry I'm a fuckin' writer 'n' I'm workin' hard da provija with a nice life.'

She laughed right in my face. 'Oh, I think we'll be fine either way. Veterinarians make over a hundred thousand a year, and writers are lucky if they make thirty.'

'Not me. I guarantee I'll be a fuckin' millionaire!'

'I hope so. I really do.'

'Well?'

'Well what?'

'Caw her right now 'n' tell her it's over. Let's go out.' I grabbed her by the elbow; she shook me away then shook her head, implying that *all* attempts would be futile. Still, I asked again. The same cold response. Seeing nothing but red, I started swearing at her, so much and so furiously that, in hindsight, I couldn't logically piece it together if I tried. The conversation just kept getting deeper and deeper, more truth, more pain. And she wasn't even crying! And it hurt me *not* to see her crying. She actually seemed rather happy at my misery. Like it was funny! It drove me straight to the fuckin' breaking point! I snatched up one of her stuffed animals—the one I bought for her last birthday—and ripped its little yellow head clean off. As I continued trying to rend it apart, she began pounding on my back. 'Leave! Leave right now!' she cried. 'Fine,' I replied, 'I got somewhere I gadda go anyway—*you fuckin' traitor!*'

I slammed the door behind me...flew down the hallway nearly knocking over some blur in the general shape of a human...crashed right though the hallway door...descended the stairs without caution...crashed right through the main door...then began storming through the snow...back at Philemon, I swung myself up on the ol' warhorse, gave a tug to a blur in the general shape of reins, revved up the ol' warhorse's heart by applying pressure to its girth one time but relentlessly, walked the ol' warhorse out without caution, then began charging in a gallop down the white stormy road...

...don't care if her dad's home, don't care if Jackson's 'ere, don't care if she's fuckin' junked out—I'm tellin' her how it's gonna be: she's not gonna take away the last thing I have left in this miserable piece a shit world!...I sercly hope 'at fuck's 'ere: tries sayin' sum'n—BAM!—knocked da fuck out...don't care how big or black he is: no one's gonna stop me, no one's gonna take her away from me—NO ONE!.........don't worry, Pess; I know yir still with me too...gimme some extra strength...

...I violently swung the ol' warhorse into Teresa's driveway, almost hitting her white SUV in the process; no other cars to be seen. I was so mad—so immersed in this blind rage—that I pulled the e-reins before stopping, while simultaneously letting off the stirrup too soon: the ol' warhorse jerk forward and stalled. I was so irate—so immersed in this redness before my eyes—that I forgot to close the stall gate, or tie the ol' warhorse to a hitching post, or whatever. I stormed right up the snowy steps...and as soon as I got close enough, I kicked straight into the door...and again...and again.

'Open'ah door, you fuckin' cunt!'

She opened the door, giggling. 'Hello, Val-lano. Iv just called all upset and said you might be stop-ping over to visit. Nice to see you. Been a while.'

'Fuck you. Sercly, stay the fuck away from her. Your days with her are over. O-VER! Overstand me, you fuckin' murderer?'

'*Murderer?*' she laughed with high eyes. On the whole, she looked like a crack-whore in stylish clothes, with her hair now styled like Ivy's and dyed as black as Ivy's; the only difference: Teresa's thinness and greasiness. 'That's libel.'

'Nah, it's the truth 'n' you know it. But I honestly don't give a fuck whachu or anyone else wantsta caw it. Yir a murderer, 'n' yir gonna stay away from Ivy or else I'm gonna murder *you*.'

'Ut-oh, I wouldn't be ma-king threats like tha—'

I charged right in, knocking her backwards to the ground, leaving her body half on the living room rug, half on the wood of the foyer. I spoke downward with a strong finger: 'Listen here, you stupid whore: dohnchu *ever* try threatenin' me. You rilly wanna caw da pleece? Go right ahead. Have 'em come right now, 'n' we'll go pull out da H for 'em...Well? Go ahead! Get up 'n' caw 'em 'n' I guarantee I'll ruin yir life like you've ruined mine! Or how 'bouchu go caw yir big badass boyfriend; have 'im come over da protectcha 'n' see if I don't put that motherfucker six-feet deep too. You sercly don't know who yir fuckin' with, bitch.'

She stood up awkwardly. 'Just get the fuck out.'

'Den tell me yir cuttin' all ties with Ivy. I mean, juss fuckin' look atchu: she's goin' somewhere in life; yir not. Me 'n' her are gonna live a rich, happy life far away from here. But you—yir gonna be dead soon 'cause yir a dumb junkie.'

'That's what *you* think. I'll be more successful than you ever will.' She crossed her skinny arms over with bold conceit. '*You're* the one who's gonna be a complete failure; I bet you can't even write worth shit.'

I just laughed that off. She was a brave girl for standing in front of me like that, talking back like that; actually seemed to calm me down. 'Well while I'm here, why dohncha fill me in on the whole boyfriend thing. Ya know when the cops told me that, I juss played along as if I alriddy knew. But I knew right then, for you da say that juss meanchu were obviously hidin' sum'n—'

'HA! You ever think Zach was hi-ding some-thing from *you?*' She tried pointing for effect, but I slapped her hand away.

'Nah, I don't think so, bitch. He told me *everything:* how ya started sneakin' out all the time; how you were always tryin'ah get 'im da start again but he stayed away—'

'He stayed away my ass! He quit for like a month. Then he was right back at it. *I* was the one who actually got mad at him for star-ting again.'

Again, I could only laugh. 'Yir such a pathetic lyin' piece a shit.'

'*Vaffanculo,* you god-damn asshole! You're so fa-king stubborn that you can't even face the fa-king truth that your best friend was a weak—'

The moment of calmness ended: I swiftly grabbed her up by the arm and slung her down on the couch. I pinned her down, got up on her thighs, and stared right in her face. A slow, calm, biting voice: 'Listen, Teresa: I'm not fuckin' around. No madder wha' happenedda Pessi, it all comes back da *you. Yir* the reason he's dead, not the drugs. Sum'n triggered 'im da do it that night. Sum'n triggered 'im da drink the bir. Sum'n triggered 'im da violently jab the needle in his arm. 'N' I *will* find out the truth one day, 'n' when I do, you bedder start runnin' 'cause you'll find no protection from the pleece or yir boyfriend. 'N' anytime you even *think* about gih'nah pleece involved, juss remember: I'm a million times smarter than you. You can lie all ya want, but I'll always outsmart you. 'N' don't forgichir boyfriend's a drug dealer; whether or not ya rilly like 'im doesn't madder, but I can get *him* put away like nuh'n, 'n' then yir out yir black connection da yir precious white master. 'N' I'll make sure *you* go dahn too. So, yeah, donchu ever think you have the advantage here...' (I took a moment to stare, almost sympathetically, at the sweat running down her temple, and to listen to the tremble in her breaths. Then I pushed back a strand of dyed-black hair hanging down in her eyes, seeing the Italian in her face, bringing to mind an image of something I'd seen on her bedroom wall.) 'Ya know, Teresa, sercly don't ever say "*vaffanculo*" da me again, 'n' go take 'at fuckin' Sopranos poster dahn in yir room. It's such a disgrace da yir blood. I'm juss so glad my mother wasn't born here.' I huffed at the thought. 'I betchir a spittin' image of yir whore of a mother, huh? You should rilly try learnin' from the mistakes you see around you. But anyway—for now things are gonna go back da how dey've been since Pessi died except yir not gonna talk da Ivy anymore. Or else—*t'ammazzu.*[13] *U capisci?* I'm sure you overstand *that,* right? Ya know: *kah-peeshhh.'*

'Fuck – you.'

Just then she tried breaking free, so with one hand I pushed down into her chest, restraining her with my forearm; with my other hand I grabbed her hair and wrenched her neck back. She was screaming and squirming and trying to kick but I put all my weight atop her legs and left arm. Meanwhile, I continued asking if she overstood that her days with Ivy are over, but she kept responding defiantly. So I pulled her head back further and asked again, this time very slow and sternly. She managed to free her left arm from underneath my knee and scratched me across the face hard enough to draw blood; I managed to clutch her head long and steady enough to spit cleanly in her face. Then, by the hair, a mighty handful of it, I slung her from the couch down to the floor.

---

[13] [scn] I'll kill you.

'Get the fuck out!—GET OUT OF MY FA-KING HOOOOOUSE!!!' She was bawling, clutching her arm.

'Fine. Bahcha caw da pleece, 'n' yir done. Talk da Ivy: the same.'

Confused, I turned around and quietly shut the door. But she was sprawled on the floor, crying hysterically, clutching her dope-arm...

...Back in my room—after mending my face—I was torn between two conflicting emotions: fear that she *was* going to call the police, and relief that I got a little piece of her, perhaps fully got *to* her. Moreover, I was somewhat glad it was the weekend and Luke was gone for the moment: probably gallivanting all over campus, practicing peace, love, and charity. Still, the present solitariness could bring *me* no peace. Neither could a kind attentive ear. I sat down at my desk, brooding in the mind, steaming in the heart, my soul in chains, contemplating my next move. Besides the fear of flashing lights and cuffs on my wrists, there was still the other immediate problem of Ivy going out with her; that is, for the night. If Teresa would happen to tell Ivy what had just happened, then the problems with Ivy would only escalade; I would undoubtedly seem the bad guy. I couldn't stop myself from calling to find out if I'd acted amiss.

'So Teresa caw ya?'

'Yes, she's on the other line,' she replied casually; casually = good.

'What's she sayin'?'

'Why?'

'Is it a secret or sum'n?'

'No. She just said you went over there and told her to stay away from me, then you left and tore up some of her yard. But look, I told you: me and her already made plans for the night, so she called to find out when I'm pickin' her up.'

'*Fuckin' bullshit,*' I muttered; picking her up = bad; bad = fuckin' bullshit.

'But, hey, now you know how I feel about you ignorin' me, maybe you can fix the problem; I just have plans I refuse to break. And even if I *didn't* have plans, I couldn't be around you after your episode earlier.'

'*My episode?*'

'Yes: your episode. You're always taking things out on *me.*'

'You juss said earlier we never talk anymore, so yir contradictin' yirself.'

'We *don't* talk like we used to, but whenever we do, you're always in a bad mood, actin' like everything's *my* fault.' (She paused as if waiting for me to respond, but I decided to let her listen to the heaviness of anger in my breath.) 'Hun, listen: I know you're used to chaos and tough situations, and I *do* try to sympathize with you, but I didn't grow up like you, and—and I just can't handle this.' (She fell silent again; I kept breathing angrily; a good fifteen seconds passed.) 'Look, I know you're still upset—'

'Juss save it. You don't know fuckin' shit about me.' *Click!*

...Whatever happened hereafter in the course of my physical, I'll never know: probably never drank so much in my life. I woke up early the next morning, in the backseat of my car, vomit spewed all over the floor. Woebegone, I dragged myself through the windy coldness, back through the doors of Philemon, ready to give up on everything. And just as I probably never drank so much, I probably never wished so hard that I hadn't gone to college. I would've done anything—*anything*—just to be back in Verna, rich as dearth, with no prospects, but with my friends, being the wasted youth we were, with Pessi alive, discoursing the ol' revolution, high on weed, with my father alive, marching around the dead room, drunk on bourbon, with my mother half-alive, hiding herself in the walls, drunk on tears, with my dog alive, chained to the tree with flees and skin disease, dehydrated and starving—just have back that whole life of hell I was born into, instead of the one I chose...

...After waking up for the second time on Sunday—although I didn't sleep very long or well—I spent some quality time with John. Out of nowhere, I started getting real emotional, letting it all out, all that he could handle. (I was whisking him with the key to what made me tick.) When I was done, I gave him a sloppy kiss goodbye on the lips, flushing like a little schoolgirl afterward. Then I went to the commons and forced myself to eat. Physically, I felt better. Mentally—well, why even bother with what's not level?

I returned to my room with the intention to restrain my desire to call Ivy. I figured she *really* has the ball in her court now, and by me calling her, whether to harass or kiss ass, it would only make it worse, for me. So why not lie back down and catch twenty-two winks? or get chapter 12 into flight? or just plain do some school work? Well, intentions are intentions, and executions are executions, for everything flew away or went down the drain all the same. In other words, I didn't have to worry about restraining myself from checking in on Ivy because I picked up my cell phone to see that she'd left two voices-mails the night before when I was drinking in my car. So without hesitation I pressed the key keys, then listened to what was left of my life come crashing down. It's simply inevitable: a wing comes off a plane in flight, or an engine drops, and the rest follows: it's only a matter of time before it catches up to you: and when you're flying, "a matter of time" comes in no time at all.

Message 1: '*Why? Seriously, why?*...' (There was no anger in the question, nor was it spoken loud; just the tone of bereavement and misery in the midst of crying.) '...I can't—I can't be –beli–' *Click.*

Message 2: 'Please just, please just leave me ah– alone – forever.' (Her breathing was huffier now.) 'She told me – she, she told me. You—you're the one who – I just—' (an explosive bawl) 'I can never talk to either of you ever again!' Another burst of tears, followed by *click.*

I dialed her number faster than a speeding bullet. Thankfully, she answered; unfortunately, she was still in tears. I asked what's going on, why was she saying that she never wanted to talk to me again; I assumed Teresa went ahead and told Ivy the unpleasant details of yesterday, and so this was Sensit-Ive's response: crestfallen because of my broken promise—my return to violence—greatly worsened because it involved a girl, to speak euphemistically of Teresa, that nefarious bitch from Hell.

'Well I'm gonna stop over now. Ar'ight?'

'No, don't. I'm packing.'

'*Packin'?* For wha'? Wha' da fuck's goin' on?'

Click. She hung up then shut off her phones.

So I was back storming through the snow...passing by hundreds of blurs in the general shape of humans...many of the blurs out in the snow-covered yards, playing, sculpting, echoing cries of laughter and joy which, hitting me, seemed to add to the resistance of the slog...but soon (shooting forth like an indomitable snowman) I made it through the slog...crashing through the main door...ascending the stairs with persistence...crashing through the hallway door...storming down the hallway...finally crashing through her door without knocking.

An ivory valise sat atop her fluffy bed of lilac: she had the side of her head dropped down on it, facing the window. She was filling it up with tears—sobbing so hard that the possibility of feinting was in each next-breath. I knew she didn't want me there, but she didn't do anything besides cry and tremble, not even a glance behind her, towards me at the door. I shut it and stepped forward. Seemed inevitable I would start firing out questions, but her unchecked tears checked me. My gut was burning with fear, but somewhere deep within my heart, and carried out through my quiet breaths, I felt a pleasant warmth suggestive of some eventless summer night long ago; it sparked a memory with no details, bodies, or movement, only the sensation of a warm, calm, summer night from which I couldn't even overstand or explain its significance to myself, couldn't draw the location of the scene within the eyes of my mind—almost as if it wasn't a memory at all, and rather deceitful *déjà vu.* In any event, while experiencing one of the greatest sensational wisps of my life, I just stared at her, wanting selfishly to place my hand on her shoulder just to keep myself from collapsing. My eyes closed shut...opened quickly on the rebound...but again, fell downward heavily, sticking, as if a great redemptive sleep was soon approaching...*(Is it twisted to feel soothed to the point of falling into a wispy, blissful apathy as you watch the one you love weep?)*...

...I opened my eyes. Looked around the room. The lighting was dim and shadowy: an unusual day-setting for her, but the butterfly had its wings spread. It held power like a by-the-grace-of-God monarch with the power to hide the sun from his kingdom. I cracked my neck and no longer felt soothed; I felt—well, like what a butterfly must feel like after having its wings ripped off. Mystified with equivocal feelings, I couldn't comprehend a thing, couldn't speak a word, couldn't write one sensical word if I had a pen. I dunno: the crying, the darkness, the bag of clothes: you would've thought someone far away yet so close to the heart had died.

Finally, her crying shook me sober. 'Ivy, turn around 'n' let's talk.'

'Please just-ah leave. I can never – look at you again. Never.' All trembly.

'Whaddaya talkin' about?' I moved over to her and tried touching her pulsating shoulder—but she shook me off and burst into fresh tears.

'Leave! Pleeeeeease juh, just leave-ah!' Her breathing fluctuated with the sobbing, as she lay on her side, facing the butterfly.

'I'm not leavin' til I know what's wrong. I mean, I've never seen ya act like 'iss 'n' you juss expect meedda not be concerned? I mean, come on.'

'Oh God!' she cried abruptly, clutching her stomach like a woman going into contractions. 'Your voice is-ah making me-ah so nauseous.'

'Yeah, my voice tends da have 'at effect on people; 'at's why I'm a writer.' But no laughter. I walked around to the other side of the bed to face her...but she only shifted herself, burying her face down into her comforter. I sat down on the edge, my waist twisted a bit, my arm down and outward as a sign of affection. 'Come on; ya can't get all upset without even tellin' me wha' she said. I mean, wha' vicious lies—'

'How could-ah you, you do this to me?' she sobbed into the pillow. "What did I ever do-ah so—so wrong? Wh-what?'

'Whaddaya talkin' about? Wha'd I doddaya? Juss tell me 'n' I'll explain as best as I can.' Again, I tried touching her—her short straight hair, then her curvaceous hip—but she just twisted and jerked and continued sobbing, even heavier at my touch. 'Well, fine then; I'll leave 'n' we can juss talk about dis—'

'Nooo!' she cried out. 'We can never talk again!'

'Oh yes we can, 'n' we will—I'm sure of it.'

'Nooo!' she cried out again, this time in a convinced tone that really started to worry me, like this was something *real* serious.

'Come on; yir rilly startin'ah worry me. I mean, are you sick or sum'n?' I went to touch her forehead but she slung my hand away. In a sudden urge to be affectionate, I cuddled in close to the side of her head, and, switching into what I thought would be a therapeutic tone for her, musically said: '*Wimp-Wimp. Screwy's heeeere.*' I put a lock of her hair into my mouth. But as I went to say, '*POWER UP!!!*' she yanked it out without looking up.

'*Now Screwy's mad! Hmhmhmhmhm!*'

'Can you-ah just promise me you'll leave me alone forever? Can you-ah – at least do tha-a-a-at for me?'

'*But Screwy didn't do anyfang wrong!*'

'She told me wh-what you did – because, because she wanted to ruin my life too. She was ju, just waitin' for it. And I never did anything to either of you. *Never.*'

'Wha'd she say I did?' I said in my normal voice; now I was starting to get really annoyed as the thought of Teresa and her schemes began burning the underside of my skin; thus, Real Worried retracted a bit, for it seemed it *was* over the episode at Teresa's since Ivy validated it with "she told me what you did." I mentally prepared myself, ready to justify it, while downplaying it—basically ready to lie. 'Juss come out with it. I mean, whatever idd is, I'm sure it's one hellava lie if yir *this* upset.'

'Unt-uhh. There's-ah proof. She showed me. I saw it with my own eyes. *Oh God, I can't take this! I don't deserve this!*' Fresh heavy tears.

Suddenly Real Worried returned with colossal manifestation and intensification. I grabbed her by the arm and turned her over with force. Slow austere voice: 'Quit – fuckin' – cryin' – 'n' *tell* me. I been patient long enough. Now wha' da fuck did she "show" you? Huh? Tell me right now 'fore I fuckin' lose it.'

'The papers.'

'*The papers?* Wha' fuckin' papers?'

'You, you were there; you know wh-what papers. You and her were there t-t-together. You t-t-took her there. You, you helped fix *your* mistake. You helped hide it from me and, and Pessi—'

'I swear da God, Ivy, I've never been anywhere with 'at stupid bitch when you or Pessi wasn't with us. I mean, dohncha overstand she's gonna lie about whadever she can juss da stay in yir life 'cause she's miserable her life's in shambles? Dohncha see she's a junkie out da ruin everyone else's life? She don't wanna see us happy 'cause she's not 'n' never will be...Well? What's 'eez 'papers' all about? Wha'd she lie about? Huh? Fuckin' tell me!'

'Just please leave me alone,' she whimpered.

I vaddled because she sounded so cute when she said that. I wanted to tease her like I would when she was in one of her moods. I wanted to use the squirrel voice to make a mockery of all this. I wanted to say, *'Screwy says weave ME awone!'* Instead, I fell back into a cool, rational tone. 'Ya know, Ivy, you shouldn't be so assumptive 'n' actin' all dramatic over wha' dat stupid junkie says, 'specially not 'fore ya talk da me. I mean, who da fuck you trust here: someone you *know's* a liar, someone all strung out on hard drugs, or da person you love, the one yir gonna marry 'n' spen' the rest a yir life with? I mean—'

'The papers, Vinny – from, from – the abortion. It was ya-yours. And you two hid it from us. And when she finally told him, he, he couldn't believe it. He just couldn't believe it was *you*, Vinny—Pessi killed himself because of *you*—'

Snapping and flying straight at her, I flipped her on her back, pinned her down by the arms, and looked straight into her tear-covered face. 'Dohnchu *ever* fuckin' say anything like 'at again. I swear I'm gonna go kill her. She sercly say 'at? Huh?! HUH?!'

She began pushing me back with the strength of her shoulders...til she wrestled her arms free, although I wasn't attempting to keep her restrained anyway. But now she was bawling uncontrollably as if I'd physically hurt her.

'You seriously need help! And so does she! You two deserve each other! I just don't see how I was so blind to it all this time! I really thought she was, she was my friend! I really thought you—I wish I would've never met you! You've ruined so many lives! You're the reason your best friend killed himself! *You-ugh-ugh! You-ugh-ugh!'*

'Fuck you, bitch! Sercly: *fuck – you.'*

'Get out!!!' As she rose up, angered, she began trying to push me off the bed. 'Oh my God, I'm callin' my dad to come pick me up! And he'll call the cops if you're here! Leave, you lying, disgusting pig! I hate you! Get – GET OOOUT!!!'

I stood up, smiling—smiling because she called me a lying, disgusting pig. 'Come on, Ivy—'iss is all juss so fuckin' stupid. I mean, honestly I'm not even mad now that I think about it 'cause iddle take me like one day da prove who's tellin' the truth here, 'n' when I do, yir gonna laugh 'cause you'll see how fuckin' true I am 'n' how thankful you'll be da have 'at fuckin' bitch oudda our lives for good. So I'm akshly glad she tolja some bullshit like 'iss. It's juss thit *I'm* the one thit's crushed now 'cause if the *premise* of 'at's true, den I finely know wha' rilly happened da Pessi. (Wow, idd all make so much sense.) Think about it: If she did that—with *his* kid—he prahblee juss went overboard. 'N' bein' a sneaky bitch, she prahblee waited a while da tell 'im 'n' 'en coincidentally told 'im around the time his mother died. Musta triggered all these horrible thoughts 'n' feelings. He musta juss lost all hope, became so filled with the notion of death: his dead mom, his deadbeat dad, our dead friends he'd been talkin' about right before he died—the dead relationship with her, then, da top it all off, a kid he coulda had, like spawnin' new hope, but it too ended up dead—or wait! I bet that fuckin' cunt *did* tell 'im izz mine—'

'It was!' she cried out with conviction.

'Ivy, please—honestly, please do not accuse me of ever touchin' 'at fuckin' whore. I'll sercly go nuts. I mean, ju see my name on 'eez 'papers'?'

She paused. 'No—but only because they, they don't put the guy's name on 'em.'

'Exactly. Now think about how easy it is for her da lie about it. I mean, you know how I feel about abortion; 'n' besides, I'd never *ever* do sum'n like 'at da my best friend *or* you. Dohncha overstand yet: I'm true through 'n' through. I mean, yeah, it mighta taken me some time—('n' it was only 'cause I was worried abou' da fuckin' aftermath)—but I told Pessi how *she* tried gih'n on *me* that one ni-(ght)—' The last syllable faded in a whisper, at which time she stopped crying. The room was dead silent and heavenly bright. I just incriminated myself. And I never even did anything wrong besides delay my loyalty; namely, my loyalty to Pessi. But it had now been confirmed once and for all, in her eyes. I—Out of the blur, something came flying at my head. Something thumped off the wall. Someone was pushing me out of the room. Someone was slamming the door in my face. Someone was twisting the lock. Someone was on the phone, crying, 'Daddy, Daddy, please come pick me up!...Just come! I'll—yes, I'm all right...No, I am. I just wanna come home...Because I'm too upset to drive...Okay. I love you.'

I realized several girls were out in the hall, seeing what the disturbance was. Parting through was the RA. She approached me, not looking overly concerned because I guess girls had similar issues all the time. Besides, she knew me; I'd always been nice to her; she'd seen Ivy and I together many times; so there was no reason for her to think I'd hit her or anything. She asked, 'Is everything all right with Ivy?' (Yeah, she's juss upset about sum'n.) 'Well, you know you need an escort if she's not comin' out.' (I—) 'I'll walk you downstairs.' (I—) I looked at the door. I went to lift my hand...but it couldn't be lifted. I went to step forward...but I couldn't step. So I opened my mouth—only enough to feel the air coming in—about to tell Ivy how it's all a lie and how once she finds out the truth I won't be mad at her because I love her so much and how soon we're moving to Catania and we're gonna get married and have this great big happy family...but nothing came out.

THE HUNGER IN THE BEAST

"I turn off the lights in my bedroom,
The horrors of my life hit the walls,
Seeing the shadows of defeat mock me,
The wick of rage fires up, fires up inside, oh yeah,
I'm a motherfuckin' lit stick of dynamite,
A stick of motherfuckin' lit dynamite,
I'm a motherfuckin' lit stick of dynamite,
A stick of motherfuckin' lit dynamite,
All I need is a target, a target for my grief,
All I need is a reason, a reason to self-destruct,
Every night I pray for relief,
Knowing I'll only get fucked over again, oh yeah,
I'm a motherfuckin' lit stick of dynamite,
A stick of motherfuckin' lit dynamite,
I'm a motherfuckin' lit stick of dynamite,
A stick of motherfuckin' lit dynamite, oh yeah,
I turn off the lights in my bedroom,
The horrors of my future hit the wall,
Seeing my fuse winding down,
And when the spark draws to an end,
A lot of people are going to die..."[1]

...Once Ivy broke the news to him that he'd broken her heart, and now they had to part, he set upon the course to "get her back," as Life marched him forward like a soldier on the front line. And how brutal and demanding the straightest paths can be! Thus far, his life—in ways he could never fully detail on paper—had been chaotic: nowhere close to straight: rather a rough winding road full of philosophical cul-de-sacs, which circled him right back to square-one, along with the everyday roadblocks—from the estrangement, to the financial hardships, to the battles with violence, to the death of loved-ones, to the death of those at Ground-Zero, to the death of those who leave everyday without a sound—all of which made him want to choke Raison D'être[2] to death. But *nothing*—not even Pessi's death, even though it was so closely related to the following—*nothing* filled him with such violent intentions and visions of red than Ivy wanting to walk away for good, especially since it was based on such a horrible lie. She couldn't have had any other reasons, right? Hypothetically speaking: If Teresa had never told Ivy that she'd slept with him, murdered "their baby" for whatever reason, which he and Teresa kept secret from Ivy and Pessi—well, if that lie would have never happened, then Ivy would have no other reason for leaving him, right? Everything else was all right, right?

---

[1] Lyrics from "Insanity Deluxe Package" by Death to Hope, from the album *From Hell's Heart*
[2] [fre] The reason for living

Wrong directions can still lead one to where they want to be: a notion as strange as how knowledge of histories, together with observing Nature, will show a certain order to the chaos in the Circle of Life. And many things he'd been through, such as the death of his father, are considered part of It: things we tend to call *natural* and *essential*. (Even if there seemed to be something very systematic behind his father's relatively early death.) Nevertheless, losing Ivy is *not*, in essence, *natural—not* what makes the world spin: at least that's what he was desperately trying to believe, very well knowing on a deeper level his folly in denying the truth of his intuition which said that the grease of suffering *is* vital to the wheels of the world, and not just the suffering of the loss of life, but also lack and loss in general, no matter how unfairly the lack and loss (and the sense of loss) is divided among the world. Still, in his new state of mind—this deep depression and anguish bringing fever to his face, nausea to his gut, and rubberness to his extremities—he thought, and not without good sense, that people in-love leaving each other (besides through death) might be *common* but that doesn't mean it *has to* happen—doesn't mean that the divorce of love we have so much of nowadays is *natural*. But wait—maybe it is too! Along with all the other contretemps! So maybe his sick subcutaneous burn is just part of God's Plan! Maybe it's Luck of the Draw from which only a select few have to suffer from that which enrages the heart! Either way, why blunt the shards when you can enrage them![3] Yes! for if you have ever been in love and then had it torn away from you, then you know what the feeling is like: pure hell! And if you ever had to suffer from an injustice of lies that greatly alters your life, or that life, then you what that's like too: pure hell! and just like love-lost it burns and burns, oh how it fucking burns! So why not enrage your heart into an intimidating muscle...til the anger becomes sheer and palpable, whereupon you begin pushing for sweet rectification...and if that sweet rectification won't come—well, that's when and why man turns into BEAST! However, even the beast can have its day, for there shall come the exception: a turning-point, a halt, a confirmation, a spark of hope, a taste of sweetness, a road up ahead leading back into an old one—something that will change his life forever...although that is true of everything else...

...The life of the solitary beast begins right after Ivy felt the need to go home for a few days. At that point, he thought emotional overkill, a severe mood, or a great misovanderstanding had gotten the best of her. There was just no way she was walking away based on "the papers" and malicious words of a false-hearted junkie. And that—this accusation that he'd slept with his best friend's girlfriend (or his girlfriend's best friend), impregnated her, then took her to have an abortion—well, how could a smart girl like Ivy actually believe such a thing? He needed to find out before he went insane.

The first time he called—an hour after the fight—Ivy's sister answered and said, 'Don't ever call here again, asshole! If you do, we *will* press harassment charges!' *Click!* Well, perhaps *the whole family* was presently (and hopefully, temporarily) suffering from emotional overkill, a

---

[3] Allusion to "Do not blunt the heart; enrage it" from Shakespeare's *Macbeth* (IV, iii)

severe mood, or a great misoverstanding. Still, he couldn't stop the ignominy from bringing to his he~~art~~ more anger, from callousing more cells,[4] from tweaking more nerves into shapes criminal to the natural anatomy. After the call, he laid down on his bed. Trying to breathe normal. Straighten out his vision. Find recourse. Think logically. But all his tryings were in vain. He could almost feel his body transforming into something strange. It was scaring him. Thoughts of slipping into insanity were inducing a panic attack. But he couldn't differentiate between *anxiety* and *insanity.* Things no longer seemed normal. Sounds: foreign. Sensations: out-of-body. The world before him: swirling into a violent inexplicableness...

...Elsewhere in the world, it was a normal peaceful Sunday. There remained, however, a sense of bereavement in the air for those who died on September 11th, and it seemed there always would be. Also seemed even normal peaceful Sundays, the Holy Sabbath, would have to do away with the resting ~~part~~, for, after going to church, the government must return to its work with charities, social programs, and philanthropists to make sure the families of terrorist victims were financially taken care of, while the military, (the militaries of *all* pro-freedom countries), must remain vigilant for anti-freedom monsters. The American Government promised that all anti-freedom monsters *will* be hunted down, found, and tried, and that the families of victims *will* be aided and rectified. But Jesus Christ! somebody help this poor kid! (He looked up at the painting as if beseeching the man at the door to leave and come to his; Vallano would surely let him in.) But Jesus Christ was leaving in a matter of months, with Luke Adams. Besides, *this* situation wasn't bound to be solved with governmental strategy, or a sudden miracle. No, this was bound to be a covert mission—one not fit for the conventional missionary.

He moved to the desk and sat down. With the skill of a country boy, he stuck a large wad of snuff inside his bottom lip; he bought a can on the whim during the hour he'd driven around after the fight. He liked this new burn in his mouth. He also liked the idea of quitting smoking and thus breathing better and staying away from the coldness outside. As his mouth kept filling up, he kept spitting into the garbage can to his left. The gooey revolting stains on the plastic bag lining the garbage can were like running reminders of who the main culprit of all this seemed to be: Teresa Cazzata. He stared hard into the slow-moving disgust like how one looks into clouds to discover the shape of something. He wanted to be picturing—he was *trying so hard* to picture something soft and pure like Ivy. But Teresa, like a mark of mold indicative of all that is wrong with man,[5] kept flashing with authority before his bloodshot eyes. He was debating whether or not to pay

---

[4] Brain cells

[5] As in all that could be wrong with a person with regard to relationship issues, in contrast with what a person can do that significantly affects others on a larger scale. Yet don't matters at the local and personal levels carry upward and outward throughout society? And don't societal issues, in turn, cyclically push down to the local and personal levels? Be that as it may, "of all that is wrong with man" is clearly an exaggeration here, for nothing else in the work suggests such a simplistic remark or conclusion.

her another visit...but cruel thoughts of cuffs and clubs curbed him. Instead, he decided to call her...only to find out she already had his dorm phone number blocked. Had all this been planned beforehand? Had Ivy and Teresa been *conspiring* to break his heart? Why was everything and everyone already blocking him out without fair trial? Too quick! Too quick! Yes, things *must've* been building up behind his back for there to be (what seemed) a defensive strategy working against him. But he wasn't giving up just yet. No—no one outsmarts *him!* He switched over to his cell phone to find out that *it* hadn't been blocked. Ahh, hope was still alive.

'Teresa, yir done.'

'Are you threat-en-ing me? 'cause my boyfriend is here and he'll kick your fa-king ass. Come over and try to touch me now. Come on!'

He replied calmly, monotonically: 'You murdered my best friend. You got 'im hooked on H, you cheated on 'im, you treated 'im like shit, 'n' worst of all, you lied do 'im about wunna the most seris things ya could. Dunno why ya did. Dunno whether ya told 'im it was mine or his or wunna yir other boyfriends. Don't even know if it woulda made a difference. Plus, who knows if you bein' pregnant is even true?' (On the other line, she grunted a tiss, but didn't seem *too* interested in what he was saying.) 'Well, I guess if you showed Ivy deez, uhh, "abortion papers" den ya musta had one. But who's da say the baby's father wasn't 'at fuck—'

'A fuck?! A FUCK?! You wanna come say that to his face?'

'I juss don't overstand why ya had da push Pessi over the edge. He never did anything wrong. I mean, ya hid so many other things from 'im, so why not *that?* Dija need a way out or sum'n? Was it the H? Wh—'

'Quit your gawd-damn cry-ing, you abusive asshole! Just come over *now* and see what happens!' (Laughter in the background; closer to the receiver is the sound of her lighting a cigarette, sucking at it with a nervousness almost tangible.)

''N' I *rilly* don't overstand why you'd lie da *Ivy.* Me 'n' her never did nuh'n'ah deserve 'iss. We tried helpin' *you* too. But *this* problem's still fixable. It's juss thit God—'

'HA! "God." That's funny.'

'It's juss thit God's gonna punish you eternally for wha' you've done da my best friend 'cause he can *never* be brought back. As for Ivy: you have til the end of taday da caw her 'n' tell her ya lied about everything. I mean, 'ere's no reason not to, Teresa: she told me she can never be friends with you again anyway.'

'That's what *you* think. But too bad we're goi-ing out ta-night,' she laughed. She took a moment to indulge in the smoke and a delusional-like chuckling.

'Well juss caw her 'n' let her know, 'n' everything'll be ar'ight. Ar'ight?'

'No! You don't fa-king deserve her! She's too good for a piece a shit like you! See, Vinny, I know your type: you're just – like – me. Me and Zach should've never been together, just like you and Ivy should've never been together. Things would've been a hell of a lot better off if it would've been them two together and us.'

The voice in the background said, '*Daaamn!*' Vallano paid no mind though because he was wondering if there could be truth to what she just said. He *had* thought many times before Pessi *did* deserve someone like Ivy. But *him and Teresa?* Had he thought that too...before?

'Just let it go and move on. Become a successful writer; then you can get *any* girl you want,' Teresa said in a nice, caring tone, but then followed up with: 'But there's no point in hur-ting Ivy anymore. I *won't* let it happen.'

(Vallano spit in the garbage can.) 'Deep-down ya know I'm not da one who's hurt her. You know her pain right now might be real but it's all based on lies. *Yir* the one who's damaged us all. *You,* not me.'

'No. *You've* damaged her by ig-nor-ing her since you started that stu-pid fa-king book.'

'Oh, so then yir basically admitting I haven't hurt her by sleepin' with you, gih'n ya pregnant, 'n' 'en murderin' some imaginary kid of ours?'

'*Nooo.* You *did* do that—'

'Yir a motherfuckin' liar,' he shot back in a restrained, teeth-clinched voice. 'Yir juss tryin'ah provoke me inda fightin' with ya so it gives yir lie more authority, but it's not gonna happen. See, Teresa, it's *riiiiil* simple: when ya die yir gonna pay for whacha did da Pessi, but yir gonna rectify whachu've done between me 'n' Ivy *now.* You got til the end of the day.'

'Or else *what?*'

The thought of being tape-recorded passed through his mind; by now he'd lost track of who's said what and who would look the guiltiest, not just in the eyes of Ivy, but also the authorities. (He spit.) 'Juss be a good person for once in yir life.'

'I told her the fa-king truth so I'm not gonna call her and fa-king lie about it.'

'You—'

'Look here, dawg,' interjected a deep voice, 'don't be callin' here no more. 'N' you *ever* touch Teresa again, Imma hurcha.' The voice paused, waiting for a provoking response...but nothing but another spit; the spitter—picturing the ghost of his best friend—was saying: '*Don't worry, Pess; I'm not lettin' it go. Juss playin' it cool for now. Can't lose Ivy too, ya know.*' 'Seriously, dawg, I run this fuckin' area. I got liddle kids daddle hurcha if ya wanna play games wiff me. But you say gonna run da the cops on me? *Me,* dawg? Go right ahead; dey won't do shit. I keep der fuckin' mouths shut wit dough and dough-*nuts*—Yeah,' said Teresa, taking back the phone, 'and I'm in the process of get-ting your cell number blocked too. So just leave me the fuck alone. And Ivy too. We all hate you!' (She blurted a laugh.) 'Face it, Vinny: you'll never have Ivy back. Never, you short fa-king loser!' *Click!*

He exhaled deeply...listening to the silence on the phone...til it dully beeped and the background light went out. Dejected, he set the little phone down and began staring deep into the desk. He was beginning to hate it: that stupid, carved up desk, the desk he'd apparently been trapped behind for the last year. Maybe *the desk* was the one in cahoots with Teresa. Maybe *the desk* was also out to ruin his life, simply because the desk's life was dead and going nowhere just like Teresa's: while she worked on the outside, the desk, from the inside, could help petrify him by making it seem that Ivy *was* leaving him for good. As a forest of jagged thoughts began sprouting up in his mind, he began rubbing his knuckles up and down the desk as if to warn it: 'Priddy soon I'm gonna smash you indua million liddle pieces then burn yir existence inda oblivion.' As if trying to capitalize on the threat, he smashed his fist down. *THUMP!* The stinging pain shot up into his forearm—it went numb for a minute—but he didn't mind. Self-inflicted pain or self-inflicted numbness: what's the difference without her to console either? He slouched back in his wooden chair and went to swallow a gulp of air but forgot he had snuff in. His mouth was nearly full with harsh juice. Instead of spitting it out, he swallowed every last drop. It lay heavy in his stomach. He was frozen in place...til the bitterness abated. Then he pinched the snuff from his lip and flung it into the garbage can. With a free mouth, he wanted his lips to move and his voice to say aloud: 'But I rilly do love her, 'n' she rilly does love me!' He wanted those words to ring throughout the world just to have it confirmed, just to assure himself and everyone else that the truth's the truth and that's that...but nothing came out...

...The next morning, Luke was shaking him by the shoulder. The alarm clock was howling, but Luke was afraid to shut it off because it wasn't his to shut off.

'Vin—Vinny. Wake up, man. There's, uhh—vomit on your bed.'

Vallano rolled over into the puddle of vomit cupped within the mane of the fuzzy lion. He couldn't see straight. He was breathing funny. His viscera felt as dry as coal. A bitter stench was hanging in the air. With force—and the heaviness hurt—he opened up his contact-fogged eyes, trying to look around. *'Where am I?'* he wondered. He'd never seen this room before. Or this short chubby kid standing in the middle of the room. For a moment, a feeling passed over him that he'd just been born, that the beeping of the alarm was signifying his entrance into the world. Then he remembered that, no, it was letting him know that he'd been alive for a while—old enough to be in school—and so he needed to get ready so he could meet Pessi and Eddie in the alley behind Pessi's where they get high before heading to the bus stop. Knowing he was running late, he rose out of bed and slammed his hand down on the alarm clock. He ripped his shirt off. The pants he wore last night were sitting in front of the mini-fridge. He hurried to put 'em on. Then he went to the desk and dumped a gallon of contact solution into his eyes. Dripping wet, he started searching around for the things to put in his pants...smokes, lighter, wallet—make sure his reduced lunch card is in his wallet—keys...Meanwhile, the short chubby kid—he kinda looked like a bear—he was telling Vallano that he'd come in late last night and tried blasting his music, but he, the bear, had talked him out of it. 'Next thing I know, you're layin' on the floor. So I helped ya get up on the bed. And when I woke up, you were mumblin' weird things with, uhh, vomit on ya...Man, bet ya don't feel like goin' to class today, huh?' the bear kinda laughed.

'*Class?*'

'Yeah, today's Monday. Did you go out last night thinking it was Saturday?'

He didn't answer. He now knew who the bear-looking kid was. He knew who he was too: Vincent Ignazio Scandurra Vallano, from Pittsburgh, Pennsylvania, presently a fourth-year senior at Aristod College in LaSalle, Maryland. His mother was back in her homeland, Catania, Sicily. His father was dead and so was his best friend; he could never see them again. His girlfriend was five-minutes away, but she didn't want to see him ever again. Yes, it was all filling back into his dry, aching body. The realizations were making him want to lie back down and go to sleep forever, see and know *nothing* ever again. Instead, he apologized to Luke for whatever he'd done last night and for the room smelling like vomit and sour beer. He said that he would clean it up and spray it all down. Still shirtless, he went down to the bathroom, instinctively knowing he was about to throw up...And he did. His eyes were watering so much. They were so sore. He wanted to rip 'em out. But then what to do with his head? It felt like it was compressed with heavy air and an aneurism was about to happen at any second.

After his body dispelled the poison, he left the stall—still a bit tipsy in his walk—and approached the sink. A kid whom he hadn't seen before walked in. Vallano slowly washed his wands then pretended to be adjusting his contacts...til the kid left. He turned the cold spigot on and began splashing water all over himself. It felt good, real good, although inside he was reproaching himself for not having brought his toothbrush and toothpaste. Drenched from head to waist, he looked in the mirror—just a stranger staring back. So he shut his eyes and let the sickness pass over him...and just when he thought he was all better, it swelled up in his belly again. Back to the stall! Back to the hunch! And just let *goooooo!!!*...It was turning into one of those times most people would make that internal promise to never drink again. But through the waste he was well aware there was no need to make a commitment he knew he wouldn't keep. He wasn't about to quit drinking! No way! *(Puuuuke!)* However, he did tell himself that he *was* quitting—*(Puuuuke!)*—*was* quitting...*college.* Yes! and moving back to Verna to drink his life away! *(Puuuuuke!)* He just couldn't deal with this shit any longer!

'I gadda deal with 'iss shit right now,' he said to himself later in the day. He was downtown, just having bought cigarettes, snuff, water, and seeds. The sun was out and bright. The snow was melting in the yards, already absent from the wet roads and sidewalks. For the beginning of February, it was relatively warm: forty-five degrees. He was wearing an old pair of black Docs, blue jeans with the knees torn, a black 4 Skins hoodie, and a black ballcap with a golden "P" on it, the bill titled a bit to the right. He came upon the corner of the block where an anti-war protest was taking place, although there was no official war yet. Being a Catholic-dominate (not Catholic-required) private school, with most students coming from affluent families, Aristod's Liberal faction was small. These twenty rainbow chanters was probably it. Most were dressed in rags as if their attire was symbolic of the aftermath of war. Their self-induced stench: the same—or perhaps suggestive of a poor upbringing, or the poor who would be sent into war. 'Yeah, like 'er fuckin' poor!' he thought. '*Like 'er gonna be goin' anywhere besides Ben 'n' Jerry's or back da their white upper-middle-class suburbs!*' The mention of skin color suddenly brought him the realization that it was perhaps beyond the pale to be wearing a blatant skinhead-band hoodie. But he didn't care! Not around here! Besides, it wasn't *his* fault that people don't know most skinheads are *not* racist and have *nothing* to do with Nazism! That the media lies and distorts and practices obscurantism! That *real* skinheads, the *majority of* skinheads, are and always have been about the working class! OI! And *he's* from the working class! OI! He knows *all* about what the lower working class means! OIIIII!!! With a cold violent strut, he marched right through the rainbow of students—those fake dirty hippies!—hoping they would take notice of his skinhead hoodie. *'Come on: say sum'n'ah me, you acid-fried fucks! Spitchur pseudo-philosophy 'n' stupid politics at me 'n' I'll give yinz a fuckin' free reality trip. Si vis pacem, para bellum! Haha yeah, might as well be my father. Maybe we weren't so different after all!)...'* He kept rambling to himself, smoking one cigarette after another—with the chew can jammed down into his jeans pocket, the seeds slipped inside the pouch of his hoodie, the water already quaffed and tossed in the garbage—stomping—oh how he was boot-stompin'!—his way back up the hill and into the heart of Aristod. My God! you would've thought something really got under his skin!

Heading down the Gothic-clad street of Ovid, he could feel the beast slowly coming up out of his thick skin, in which the truths of this nightmare were manifesting right in the broad daylight: prowling around like a rapacious animal...wiping his face downward as if caked in blood...spasms visibly running up and down his body...even inside his mouth, the upper and lower teeth becoming well acquainted but grinding at each other with grit suggestive of hatred or pride...the air exiting his nose with such slow exhaustion you would think the particles had expanded into something visible...just so tense, so prepared to attack...to his left, quickly to his right, surveying around for the enemy: that wraithlike existence that had done this to his life—that murderer in the blindspot who caused thousands of knives to wrest and twist, briskly up and in, deep and gutting, some strikes viciously straight across, slicing open a throng of punishments—inescapable waves of torment and flame gushing over him as if trapped in the middle of the Lake of Fire and Brimstone—in the rending, allowing the inner walls to crumble down, allowing the suppressed monster to start climbing up through the subcutaneous confines to lead him instinctively on this beastly march of vengeance against the monsters of the outer world.

Yes, new instincts had been bestowed upon him. He could now sense the call of the wild in the wind. Hear the minutiae of meaning within the laughter of the instigators as they passed. Taste the emotional bitterness in his mouth as he huffed on his smoke. Then, off to his left, up on a small hill—so mockingly it stood!—he could see Ivy's dormitory. Frozen, he stared up at it, suddenly overstanding the essence of Love. He wanted to go see her. Seemed like he hadn't in years. She could touch him the way she used to—with her soft vulnerary hands—and all beastly thick-skinned feelings would instantly vanish. Then he could power up on her ophidian mocha, and she would laugh because she loved the funny sound of the squirrel voice. Then they could go to orchard and rip the FOR SALE sign out of the yard because that's *their* place! They could actually buy it! They could surely find a way! Yes! they'll surely find their way through *everything!* They *will* be together in the end!...Yet looking up at that mocking bricked monolith, he wanted to be together *now*—more than ever, *now.* '*So close but so far away*' passed through his head, as he headed the other way. She was probably at class or back home anyway. Besides, it would probably be best to let things cool off. But how long? A day? A week? A month?—A YEAR! MY GOD! a year and she would forget all about him! She would find someone new! and that someone new would father the children that should've been his! HIS! Wait—maybe he *should* turn back, run up there, and check. Wait—maybe he should just calm down, keep walking, and think it out. Yeah, just *think*...

'Just think of it this way:' Dr. Rosenbaum began, 'You have the rest of this semester, two more, then you'll have two fine diplomas in your hand. So just stick it out.'

After his *Women and Religion* and *Intermediate Creative Writing* classes—(these classes were his Tuesdays, making this the day *after* he wore the 4 Skins hoodie, now wearing a Murphy's Law hoodie)—Vallano stopped in on Dr. Rosenbaum's 1:30 p.m. lunch break to tell him that he was fed up with college and thinking about taking a year off. It was getting to be too much. He didn't like any of his professors. He didn't like the way they taught. His writing class with the snooty Mrs. Katarski was stressing him out so much that he couldn't sleep at night. (Hadn't said a word about Ivy.)

'I mean, my professors focus in on the stupidest things. I wrote a short story lass week in which 'ere's a fight, so I put a few *BAM*s 'n' *WHAM*s in it. So what's she do? She dedicates a class da writin' incorrectly; ya know, stylistically incorrect. She didn't mention my name or anything, but she glanced at me when she said several students had came up do her, askin' her about dos-'n'-donts. Which I didn't do 'cause I could sercly care less about wha' she has da say about it. But listen'ah this shit. She goes—'n' I quote—"Onomatopoeia is the most sophomoric technique in literature. *POW*s, *BAM*s, and *KABAM*s should be left to comic books, which, to use the word loosely here, is what I consider the lowest form of literature. Very lowbrow."'

'Should've told her you consider *that* the lowest form of teaching.'

'Shoulda. But den after class she pulls me aside, tells me da substance of my writing's good—which I guess by *substance* she meant *entertaining*—but I nee'dda hone *how* I write. Basically sayin' I'm grammatically retarded. She asked if I ever read Strunk, 'n' I said yeah. So she suggested I read *Vliden's* liddle writing bible'

'Nah, don't waste your time,' advised Dr. Rosenbaum, taking a sip of coffee.

'Well I prahblee will juss 'cause I haven't read a good comedy in a while. But for rill, dohncha think shit like 'at's poisonous for *anyone*, no madder how experienced they are? dit constrictin' writers from the get-go with dogmatic rules only pushes 'em right inda the hands of Formula 'n' thwarts creativity?'

'Well you need to learn the rules before you can break 'em. But you already know the rules.' From a plastic baggie, Dr. Rosenbaum pulled out a tuna sandwich cut in half. He bit into the first half like a lion. For such a sophisticated man—for someone who'd been raised by fastidious Jews—he ate so sloppily! Tuna was already dripping down from the bread and onto a paper towel he laid on the desk as a place mat. 'So anything else goin' on? How's your mother?'

'Priddy good. I juss talked do her yesterday 'n' she said she's back da babysittin' da *picciriddi sarvaggi:* the bad kids in the neighborhood. Don't pay much, but I think she's juss happy bein' back around her family 'n' 'at. At least she don't got Aunt Fella 'n' Uncle A tryin'ah shove cannoli 'n' dogbones dahn 'er throat.' (Dr. Rosenbaum was about to smile or chuckle but a chunk of tuna dropped to the ground, so he dipped down, fishing around for it.) Speaking to a headless Rosenbaum, Vallano continued: 'Man, I'd like da go over there too—ya know, *once* I graduate,' he stressed as if hinting to Dr. Rosenbaum that he wasn't actually quitting; suddenly, the head of Rosenbaum popped back up; he flicked the slimy chunk of meat into the garbage can. 'But I'm not sure how much I'd akshly like it. Ma said it's gih'n a lot like America: Italians wanna imitate Americans, especially Italian-Americans. Like Rick—his idea of Italian culture was pasta 'n' mob movies. 'N' if sum'n was mentioned onna news thit another Italian did sum'n *noble*, then idd strike him dit, "Hey, *I'm* Italian too!" He'd be riddy da pour some fuckin' Chianti 'n' sing *"Inno di Mameli."'*[6]

'*Aye, paesano*, at least-ah you got da eat da finest Italian food in town, *si?'* Roseno said satirically.[7]

'I guess. Buh'diz more about eatin' whadever we could afford—whadever da coupons said we could eat for da week, ya know. Whenever Ma would get sick—'cause 'ere'z times when she wouldn't get oudda bed for days, but we never rilly knew wha' was wrong 'cause she refused da godda the doctor—but when she'z like 'at, I'd cook myself fuckin' tayder tots or French fries, 'n' well, *French* fries sounds kinda *French* da me. '

'Best French cuisine out there.' Still being satirical, Dr. Rosenbaum kissed his trinity-pinched fingers then flung 'em out in a spray.

'I ate rill French cuisine once ba—'

Just then, a knock at the door. Dr. Rosenbaum set his sandwich down and ordered in the knocker. Entering: the professor whose office was next door: a young buck with thick fawn eyelashes, a shiny pole neck, and a big butt like an ostrich. He wanted to know if the professors in Zinn—(where the History professors had offices)—would get mad if he went over and used their copy machine. Dr. Rosenbaum let out a two-noted chuckle and asked rhetorically if they, the History professors, owned the copy machine. The ostrich looked flummoxed. So Dr. Rosenbaum told the slow-to-the-wit fledgling that the copy machine in the English Department is always breaking, so yeah, he uses the one in Zinn. 'Go on over, Randy; the History

---

[6] [ita] Mameli's Hymn [the Italian National Anthem]

[7] Americans frequently misuse *paesano* and *paesan* for "friend." *Paesano* is used among immigrants to address other immigrants who came from the same community. The word implies a feeling of alienation, and translates along the lines of "fellow countryman." Whether or not Dr. Rosenbaum knew of this nuance remains unknown.

professors only bite on the way back out.' Awkwardly, the fledgling thanked him then left.

'These newbies and their respect for History,' quipped Dr. Rosenbaum.

'Yep, 'n' like 'at copy machine, History repeats itself,' retorted Vallano. 'In other words: I'm sure he'll be back with more questions.'

'So tell me somethin': What's with the Murphy's Law?' He was using his pinky finger to point at Vallano's hoodie while shoving the second wedge back in his mouth. The black hoodie displayed in fluorescent green MURPHY'S LAW, and below that, a fluorescent green 13.

'"Whadever can go wrong will go wrong."'

'Since when did you—' *chew* *chew*'—become so positive about everything?'

Vallano made a sarcastic "positive" face for him. 'Nah, it's akshly a band. Ya know, it's strange but I've never asked you what kinda music ya listen'da.'

'Okay,' Dr. Rosenbaum replied dryly, not about to answer since no question had been asked.

'Yir such an asshole sometimes, you know that?'

'Yes—I know.'

'O-kay. What kind of mu-zik do you lih-sin to?' asked V-13 the Sarcastic Robot.

'Usually slurp up some Jazz and Classical for breakfast; munch on a few Punk bands for lunch; then chill out with some Bowie, Cave, or Drake for small late-night dinners.'

'Shuh da fuck up.'

'Okay.' Dr. Rosenbaum shuh da fuck up after swallowing the last of the tuna.

'You've seen me come in a hundred times with Punk shirts on 'n' never once said a word about.'

'Am I supposed to compliment the way you dress?'

'Well it *would* make me feel priddy. But for rill, wha' Punk bands you like? 'cause I'm in shock right now.'

'Just a few that were big back in the day. The Stooges, The Clash, The Sex Pistols, The Damned, The Buzzcocks. You know, all the "the" bands. *Umm*, The New York Dolls are pretty cool—'

'Shuh da fuck UP! Dere's no way you like da New York Dolls. Dat's *sooo* not yir music. Der like all fuckin' glammy 'n' faggish.'

'"*Trash—pick it up—take 'em lights away. Trash—go pick it up—go put that knife away. Trash—go pick it up—don't give your life away. Trash—pick it up—don't throw your love away. Trash—pick it up—don't take my knife away*'...'

By now Vallano had broken into such a hard laughter that his nose squirted goo onto the desk! Dr. Rosenbaum didn't mind; he was busy thumping his hand down on the desk in a Swingy-Rock style while singing New York Dolls with a straight face! No less *Trash!* Ahhhhh! Pick it up! No—*blow* it up, Dr. Rockin' Bomb! Then wipe it up!

After the singing ceased and the messes were cleaned, Vallano said, 'I dunno, Dr. Rosenbaum; for some reason I think yir juss fuckin' with me. Anyone alive back den could name 'ose bands or sing 'at song.'

'I dunno, Dr. Vallano; for some reason, I think Mr. Johnny Lydon would say otherwise—considering we've talked before.'

'Riiiight.'

'Twice actually.'

'Why not make it three times?'

'You think I'm bullshittin' you?'

'No doubt.'

'In '78 I was datin' a girl named Beth Kushner. Eight years younger than me. A fine little ass on her too—but you didn't say that to her. A feminist like you wouldn't believe. Didn't shave or *nothin'!* Of course I really didn't mind; I was smoking a lot of pot back then, and tootin' up lines—ya know, call it some small late-night Bowie.' They giggled and muttered for a moment. 'Anyway, Beth was into the whole Punk movement. We had plans to go see the Pistols in New York but it got cancelled. So we ended up drivin' all the way down to Memphis to see 'em play at the Taliesyn Ballroom.'

'No way! This is so fuckin' crazy!'

'Yeah, well you should've been there. Police *everywhere.* They wouldn't let half the people in because they changed the seating capacity at the last minute. The people outside ended up smashin' the front window in. And inside people were up on their chairs, throwing whatever they could at the Pistols. (You know, first time in America: people didn't know how to approach this type of music, especially people down South.) So apparently Rotten was gettin' mad. And Vicious—he wasn't even playin'; he's walkin' around instigatin' shit! Next thing you know, Rotten gets hit in the head with a big cup of ice and whatever was in it—I think it was just water. But he quits singin', picks up a hand full of ice off the stage, and throws it straight in my direction. Now I didn't get hit, but Beth did. So I go, "Hey, asshole! *We* didn't throw shit at you!" He mumbled somethin' and went back to singin'. So don't tell me I never talked to Mr. John Lydon before. And that was just the first time.'

Like a cube in the freezer, Vallano was frozen in disbelief. He wanted to ask about the second time but was so absorbed in the image of Dr. Rosenbaum at a '78 Sex Pistols show, getting ice cubes throw at him by Johnny Rotten!

'Second time was, I think, in '94 or '95. But he came right here to Aristod.'

'Sercly?! Wha', da promote *Rotten* or sum'n?'

'Yep, he talked a little about the book but didn't read from it. He mostly talked about growin' up in London and havin' Irish immigrant parents, and discoursed a few socio-political issues. Didn't talk much about music though. Said a few disparaging things about Malcolm McLaren, and today's music industry, but that's about it.'

'So how ja talk do 'im?'

'Well afterward, him and his entourage went to a conference room in Baughman. I, of course, was allowed back there. *All* faculty was. But he didn't have to worry about our professors botherin' him because he had pink streaks all through his hair and a completely pissed-off look on his face. Everyone was very intimidated by him. So anyway, he's sittin' down at the conference table, talkin' to some lady who I think was his publicist. I'm across the room, just bein' observant. Then someone brings him a plate of food and a drink. So as the lady's talkin' to him—and it looked like he didn't give a shit *what* she was sayin'—he grabs the sandwich, flips the top piece, and starts pickin' things off. Takes a few bites. Chomps it up real good. Swallows. Then yells out somethin' to one of the people he's with. Then he picks up the drink. So from across the room, I shout, "Don't you even think about it!" Then I left.'

'You did not say that.' Vallano tried gauging the truth of Dr. Rosenbaum's lines, but his head was spinning. The fluffy part going down the middle of Dr. Rosenbaum's silvery head was turning into a green Mohawk. He just couldn't believe any of this!

'No, you're right: I didn't say a word to him when he was here. But I *was* in the same room with him. It would've been funny though if I actually said that though, huh.'

'Yeah. But wow,' he shook his head in disbelief, 'I can't believe ya saw da original Pistols. I saw 'em too back in '96 on 'er reunion tour, of course *sans* Vicious. But it's funny, 'cause me 'n' my friends had da do the *opposite* of you: we drove *up* da New York da see 'em 'cuzza the show in Pixburgh got cancelled. Izz worth it though. Only thing I didn't like was too many people. Not da same kinda experience, ya know. I betchir show was small, huh.'

'Oh yeah. Not even a thousand.'

'So have you seen any other Punk bands?'

'Nope. I decided to go dry after the Pistols show.'

Vallano vaddled. 'I still go do alawda punk shows; seen alawda the original bands too. See, I started listenin'ah Punk when 80s Hardcore was makin'ah transition inda 90s Punk when it went back da the ol' melodic sound but gadda lot faster, da shows more crowded, 'n' the kids most stupidest. Things juss never seem da change for da best, ya know...' Vallano mused for a moment. 'Ya know, I sercly hate havin' such a strong passion for sum'n so true, 'n' for so long, 'n' 'en watchin' it be destroyed by others.'

'*Others*, paesano? "*All* things deteriorate—*in time*." (That's Virgil.)'

'Yeah, 'n' since when you start quotin' people?'

'Since when you start believin' in Murphy's Law?'

'I already tolja: it's a band.'

'So you really don't believe in it?'

'Should I?'

'You tell me. I mean, I know you've been through some shit. But hasn't just as many things gone right for you? You grow up poor; you end up here. Your father dies; your mother's happy in Catania. Your best friend Zach Pessini dies—well, that's what Ivy Pineda's for. If you ever have a boy you should think about namin' him Zach. That way you'll be keepin' Pessi's memory alive because one day you'll explain to your son *why* you named him Zach. And over the years you'll tell your son all about your time with Pessi. Sometimes you'll tell him about the bad things and use it as a lesson. And sometimes you'll tell him about the good things and use it as a lesson.

Whatever can go wrong will cause a right. *Nuhgihdouddahere. I gadda class da teach.*'

But he didn't gihdouddathere just like that. Vallano and Rosenbaum walked out into the hall *together,* talking about Rotten...til they reach the populated sidewalk, whereby they forked off in different paths, Rosenbaum going left, to teach a class, Vallano to the right, to sit in a class and think about Pessini and Pineda...

...The next evening Vallano was at work, helping a Pakistani-descendant freshman with a short story. Vallano was impressed with the story itself; the problem was the grammatical errors slowin' the flow. Since Vallano had recently been criticized for *his* style, he didn't want to dwell on it; he was simply showing him how to reword things for the sake of euphony. Meanwhile, the garrulous freshman was spilling out his frustrations to Vallano; he too wanted to write for a living. It was an opening for Vallano to pass on advice in his own words, just as Dr. Rosenbaum had done many times for him.

'...Yeah, I know whachir sayin'. I been writin' since I's eleven. Twenty now 'n' still tryin'ah figure things out. But my advice: don't listen'ah the professors here. I been havin' problems with 'em ever since I started. They like da judge accordin' da the current trend in criticism. But what's 'at rilly mean? Many of the greats weren't accepted in 'er time. Always misoverstood. Always put against the grain, ya know. Ya juss gadda decide wha' *you* want: Do you wanna release what's within in the way thaddle bring ouchir individuality 'n' reflectchir soul, even if it's only for *yir* eyes? Or do ya wanna conform a bit, gitchir skills 'n' 'er formulas dahn pat, 'n' from 'at, have much bedder chance for *financial* success?'

'Well I don't have a unique style that goes "against the grain" or any great personal stories to tell, so I should probably just worry about developing strong syntax.'

'Truss me, Anjum, I can sense a unique style buddin' here. As for personal stories: if you think you lack 'em, look inda Pakistan's histree, or ask yir parents or grandparents. Find some great untold stories. Yir parents speak Urdu?'

'Actually, my dad does. I don't know much. But how did you know what our language is called? I've never heard a white—I'm sorry, I—'

Laughing, Vallano cut in: 'Nah, it's ar'ight. You never heard a white dude randomly mention yir language. But see,' he laughed again, 'I dunno how "white" I am. First off, my mother's from Sicily, 'n' she taught me Sicilian 'n' English together. We use Sicilian as our conversational language, but I get frustrated 'cause I can't speak it with anyone but her. But that aside, I know wha' Urdu is 'cause I care da know. See, Anjum, I got bad eyes, so I'm forced da keep my ears open, 'n' 'cuzza that, I've heard about alwada different things from alwada different places.'

Anjum stared without awkwardness into Vallano's face as if he was seeing a *farishtaa,*[8] and because of that, he wanted to touch the umber cheek.

---

[8] "Angel" in Urdu, a language with over 100 million speakers worldwide

'Anyway, don't worry too much about syntax; juss find a way inside jirself da find *yir* words, 'n' once let loose, dill show demselves in whadever manner dey want—til ya raze 'er nature. Craft kills, but so does Abandonment, know whadda mean. I've learn the freedom *of* writing is a lot different den the freedom *in* writing.'

'Wow. But I bet you write some great stuff.'

'Ehh, not rilly. But maybe one day.'

'Well whenever the day comes I wanna know so I can read your work. What's your last name?'

'Vallano. I'll be keepin' an eye out for yir work too—' he looked down at the paper to reacquaint with his last name '—Mr. Saeed.'

'Thanks. So what do you think about changing...'

After going over a few more things in the short story, Anjum Saeed left the writing center probably feeling good about himself and his ability as a writer. Vallano too had one of those feelings which warms the heart for causing joy in another. But it was only momentary. The comfortable warmth turned to excruciating heat as she began passing through his mind. He only had thirty minutes of work left, then he would go to her room. He'd waited long enough to let things, so to speak, cool off. It was time to straighten this mess out. Explain the lies of Teresa, and the truth of his love. Just grab hold of her and never let go...

...He went around to the back of her dorm. All by her lonesome stood a gorgeous redhead in monkey-patterned pajamas smoking a cigarette. He quickly pulled out a smoke and asked her for a light then began talking about his girlfriend upstairs—in a relaxed manner that extinguished the cautious look initially on her face. He did this to gain her trust so that it would be nothing for him to walk in with her through the back door. The redhead said bye as she headed down the first floor and he ascended the steps in stealth. The dormitory itself was quiet: usually you would hear girls talking in the halls or girls coming up and down the steps, but no one to be seen or heard on this quiet February night. It was close to midnight now, so he assumed the RA would be behind closed doors. When he reached her floor, he peaked through the narrow window of the door: a wet blonde in a pink bathrobe heading towards him! He backed away and waited a minute...When he looked back through the narrow window he viewed a clear hallway. He slowly opened the door and slipped into dangerous grounds. Down the hallway he went with light steps...til reaching her room on the right. He tried looking through the peephole, hoping he wouldn't see distorted sights that would've confirmed the vivid images that had been running through his mind. But couldn't see anything. So he put his ear against the door, hoping he wouldn't hear muted sounds that would've confirmed the vivid images that had been running through his mind. All he could hear was the television (with voices that sounded like an old movie or an old show). He gave the door one light knock.

'Who is it?' sounded out Ivy in a startled voice.

He didn't answer. He heard approaching footsteps. For some reason he was so nervous. As he was taking in a deep breath, the door opened—and there she was: Ivy Pineda! Wow! looking so amazing in her silky purple pajamas and her fluffy purple slippers and her short messy black hair and her—

'What are you doin' here?' she whispered in an angered tone.

'We nee'dda talk. You juss left me hangin' without a chance da explain myself.'

'There's nothin'—' She suddenly grabbed him by the drawstring of his black hoodie. 'Just get in here. But you can't stay long. I can't even look at you.'

'Why not?' he asked with a sense of rejection, but happy to be pulled into her room.

'Because. I just can't.'

The room was dark besides the light of the television. She quickly crawled into bed, and as he went to follow her, she told him to stay standing by the door and to keep his voice down. She pulled the comforter up over her, to the neck, gracing her chin. Only when the television lit up with bright colors could he see her face.

'Look, Ivy. I swear I never slept with Teresa. I never did *anything* with her. You akshly think I'm the kinda person who'd do sum'n like that? I mean, even though I've hated her from day-one—back before I even knew you—she was still *my best friend's girl.* 'N' let's juss say you were *never* in the picture, 'n' that I *did* like her, 'n' *was* attracted to her—I would still never touch her. Wanna know why?' (She didn't respond.) 'Because I'm true. I believe in loyalty. Friends means everything da me. Besides, I've always considered you a best friend like Pessi. Yinz two 'n' Ma are da only people I ever loved 'n' been close to. I can't even tell ya how much you mean da me. I love you so much, Ivy. I rilly do. I wanna move away together after school 'n' start a family with you—'

'Stop, Vinny. It's too late. Somethin' tells me what she said is true. You know how you're always talkin' about intuition?' (He didn't respond.) 'Well, *my* intuition is tellin' me that it *did* happen. I've always had this weird feeling you were up to things whenever we weren't together; I just didn't wanna say anything and sound crazy. Plus, I've always been kinda afraid of you. After seein' you get into fights and drink and do so much drugs that you're half-dead—well, it really scared me. I'm not used to that. I didn't grow up around that. And just the way you talk—you're *sooo* intimidating. You get so violently passionate about things, and sometimes that can lead to bad things.'

'I ever hit you? Threaten you? Did anything "bad" do you?'

'You might've never *hit* me. But the point is: we're just too different. I wanna laid-back life. I wanna be with someone who has a *normal* job and who likes *normal* things. I don't wanna spend my life always fightin' everyone and everything.'

'Neither do I.'

'Yes you do. It's in your nature to fight, and there's nothin' wrong with that.'

'My nature? No; it's da way I was brought up. Buh dat don't mean I wanna be fightin' shit for the rest of my life. I been tryin' so hard da get away from it all, buh dat's juss sum'n you'll never overstand.'

'That's another thing: you think because you had it hard growin' up that no one else can relate to you. Maybe most people can't, but they can at least listen if—key word—*if* you try...I swear, Vinny, in the beginning it seemed like you were gonna be so open with me. I thought you were gonna keep lettin' me in. But then you became locked up once you knew you had me. Every conversation became so childish. If I mentioned marriage or the future, you turned it into a joke. And I don't think I pressured you or was incessant about things, was I?'

'No, but—'

'I mean, you think I dunno you don't like talkin' about that stuff? I do—I *did*—that's why I always tried to be careful about it. I understood your dad had just died and that you came from a home where your family had problems. But, jeez, discussin' it—your *past*, your *family*, *our* future, *our* family—just once in a while would've made me so happy. The next girlfriend you have—'

'Don't say that. I'm not gonna have a next girlfriend.'

'Yes you will. And I'm sure she'll be this beautiful little Punk Rock chick with tattoos and fluorescent blue hair and wears those boots up to the knee you used to bug me about buyin'. I just hope she's smarter than you. That would be really good for you.' There was a trace of laughter within her somber tone. 'But when you find her, let your guard down. Don't fight against her. Open up to her, and don't forget you have to keep doin' it; not just in the beginning. And please—*please* never cheat on *her*.'

'I didn't fuckin' cheat on you, Ivy.'

'You even said it yourself that Teresa tried gettin' on you before.'

'Yes, key word: *tried*. Key word: *tried*. Key words: *she tried*. Not me—'

'No, I'm sure you let her, or eventually let her. Just the way it slipped out and the look on your face—I could tell.'

'No, I juss didn't wanna say anything about it for this very reason: 'cause you'd think *I* was involved, dit I *put* myself in a situation with her. But it's not true. Here's wha' *rilly* happened: Me, her, 'n' Pessi went out drinkin' one night. I came back with 'em 'n' spent the night 'cause I's fuckin' hammered 'n' couldn't make it any further—'

'Couldn't have taken the bus or a taxi back to your room?'

'Ivy, I's fuckin' wasted. I didn't know *what* I's doin'. I mean, da me, izz like I's goin' back da my best friend's da spend the night; I didn't see it as goin' back da some girl's house, ya know.'

'I don't believe that for a minute.'

'Well ya bedder 'cause it's the truth.'

'So when did she *try* gettin' on you?'

'Some time after I passed out. I woke up—'n' mind you, I's sobered up a bit by then—'n' she's tryin'ah kiss all up on my neck. So I quickly pushed her away, 'n' so hard she fell dahn. Den she went back upstairs. 'N'—well, 'at's all that happened. If I had da guess, she'z on the junk 'cause she's walkin' 'n' movin' all funny.'

'Outta all the girls around here, you couldn't have picked someone other than Teresa?'

'Ju hear whad I juss said: there – was – no – me –'n' – Teresa. *Ever*.'

'And the abortion. God, you know how strongly I feel about that. Since I met you I've done alotta things I said I would never do, and put up with things I said I never would, but abortion is just somethin' I can't tolerate. I can't. It's like in so many ways you've ripped me apart from God.'

'Ivy: I wasn't – involved – in any – abortion. She's tellin' ya izz me 'cause she can—'cause she's all fucked up in the head, overstand? 'N' with Pessi dead now, dere's no one da say otherwise...Ya know, we should caw wherever she got dis abortion done 'n' find out who she *rilly* went with. Found out wha' *rilly* happened.'

'You know they can't say anything about it.'

'Well you can bet I'm gonna try. But whaddaya mean in so many ways I've rippchu apart from God? We've never had one single religious argument, have we? No, we haven't. Why? Because we're da same fuckin' religion, with the same core beliefs.'

'Vinny, I slept with you the second time we were together,' she answered sternly. 'I always told myself I would wait til marriage. So same core beliefs? I think not.'

'Well I'll take my sin again...' Not given a response, he exhaled, restrategizing. 'I mean, sercly, Ivy, almost every girl, religious or not, says 'er gonna wait til dey get married. But things change once ya get oudda high school.'

'Well, not for me. (At least I wish they hadn't.)'

'Do you rilly wish 'at? thit we woulda never slept together?'

'Yes. We should've waited.'

'I think we shoulda done it sooner.'

'You would say that.'

'Yir fuckin' right I would, 'cause I don't need no fuckin' church or state da tell me when I can consummate my love. I mean, sorry I couldn't get it on paper 'n' stamped da second I fell in love with you which was *at – first – sight*.' He took three silent steps forward; she didn't see because the television went black for a moment; besides, half her face was buried down in the pillow, and the comforter was bunched up in front of her shoulder. 'Ya know, I still 'member it like izz yesterday. I's sittin' 'ere inna corner, drinkin' alone. 'N' Pessi came oudda the hallway with his arms around two girls. The one daiz left was a devil; on the right, an angel. Once 'ey came over, 'n' we were introduced, I kinda leaned forward 'n' shook the angel's hand all nonchalant. Den she kinda backed up, lookin' all shy. I's thinkin' how I's juss gonna be laid back 'n' cool about it but I suddenly found myself so nervous inside. I'd never seen a girl like her before. 'N' I 'member Pessi 'n' the devil were makin' such a big deal oudda the whole situation. Then when they finely left us alone, the angel sat dahn, two seats away—'

'Stop, Vinny.'

'I's takin' glances at her—ya know, tryin' not da get caught. She was wearin' black Mary-Janes that had a large bubbled tip and a thick elevated back-heel, tight faded blue jeans, 'n' a vintage-style velour shirt (long-sleeve with belled-shaped cuffs) with a black, gold, 'n' maroon floral pattern. 'N' her hair—God, I'd never seen anything like it! All dis poetry started streamin' through my head. I's tellin' myself da say sum'n—juss *anything*—but I couldn't. 'N' ya know wha' slipped oudda my mouth? "I rilly like yir hair." 'N' she goes, "*What?*" with a confused smile. So I said, "Yir hair: it's rilly unique." She still seemed confused or surprised. Den—' He stopped to laugh at what he was about to say. 'Den I go, "Yir hair's so incredibly brown 'n' sinuously." Apparently, she thought izz funny I said *sinuous*. But me—I's feelin' so fuckin' lame. My face was prahblee as red as a fire hydrant. 'N' I rilly *did* need cooled off. So I got up da get another bir 'n' asked her if she wanted one. She said, no, but she'd like some wudder. I'm like *wudder? who da fuck drinks wudder at a party?* Wudder! So I went 'n' got her a liddle glass of wudder. 'N' when I got back we started talkin' about our families. 'N' 'iss is funny: After tellin' me her dad's Mexican 'n' Spanish, she cawed her mum *plain white.* For some reason, I thought that wuzza funniest thing ever. Den oudda nowhere she asks meedda stand up. When I did *she* laughed 'cause she was a bit taller den me—'

'Stop, Vinny. I don't wanna hear this anymore. I really don't.' The angel was beginning to whimper. The blanket was covering her arms but you could see her hands clinching the sides of the pillow. Certain flashes of light from the television were displaying the pained looks on her face, but light in motion within a dark atmosphere (with those shadows that quickly dance off into the abyss) can play such tricks on the mind.

'Well we ended up goin' outside so I could smoke. (She smelled so good. I could never rilly describe it but izz kinda like a flower thit's not overpowerin' but has a strong enough scent da taste, like sweet alyssum or water lilies.) Anyway, we were outside onna porch, off in our own liddle world. She'z talkin' about da moon, 'n' I's lookin' up at all da stars, so da speak, thankin' my lucky one. Den we started teasin' each other about school 'cause I thought she alriddy knew where I went, but apparently she didn't. I think when she found out we were both so excited inside 'cause seein' each other again was boundda happen. In my head, I's havin' wunna dose "fate versus coincidence" debates 'cause everything was workin' out so perfectly...Another funny thing I 'member is at one point, back inside, she said sum'n'—can't 'member wha'—but she'z mimickin' her father with 'iss strong Spanish accent, 'n' 'en kinda dipped her head dahn 'n' her curly hair swayed in front of her breasts. Izz like slow motion. 'N' I realized den she kinda looked like Elsa Aguirre,[9] this beautiful chick I saw in an old Mexican flick. But I didn't say anything.

'Anyway, after the pardy, I walked dahn da the bus stop with her. She went off 'n' started talkin'ah her so-called friend. 'N' I's talkin'ah my best friend. That night he'd taken all these crazy pills 'n' was actin' rill strange. Kept talkin' about how he knew all about da angel, but he wasn't makin' any sense. I's laughin' 'n' playin' along but rilly wantin'ah talk more with *her.* Den right before the bus came, she walks over, hands me her phone number, 'n' we kiss. Might sound cliché but it sercly felt like I's meltin' even after the bus pulled away...Hey, Ivy, 'member Pessi poundin' onna windows 'n' the bus driver yellin' at 'im?' he laughed; she didn't. 'Ya know, I walked all da way home 'at night, right through the ghetto. But I didn't care. Felt like I's untouchable. Felt like if any harm came my way, da angel I juss fell in love with would come dahn, pick me up, 'n' carry me home. 'N' when I *did* get

---

[9] Memory dispute: might have been a film with or photo of María Félix

home, I couldn't sleep! I juss kept thinkin' about her. I's playin' out all deez scenarios in my head. I kept askin' myself, "Could she rilly like *me?* A girl like *'at?'* Well soon enough I found out she *did:* she took me to an orchard where we made love. 'N' I swear it felt like it was God's Will—thit the church 'n' the state 'n' *aaaaall* the shit we create da keep us in check no longer maddered. I's consummated in 'iss divine trinity: me 'n' her (man 'n' woman) with Nature. 'N' it wasn't the feelin' of the sex itself; izz sum'n else burnin' inside. That night changed my life forever. I've thought about it a million times. All the symbolism is so surreal. Like the tree hangin' over us was like God: dis Thing protectin' us from the world outside. 'N' 'en 'ere's the apples: the temptation. Thing is, Eve didn't wanna eat it; Adam did—'

'Exactly, *you* lured *me* in,' she lashed out viciously. 'You were like the Snake.'

'No, we were lured in *together* by sum'n beyond our control. 'N' dere was no snake; only invisible doves flyin' all around us up in the night.'

'You're seriously insane.'

'Maybe a liddle bit. But I'm sane enough da know I truly love you.'

'Just leave. I let you say what you wanted, now leave. I don't wanna be up all night cryin' again.'

'Den don't. Let's juss relax 'n' watch some TV.'

'No!'

'Don't scream.'

'Then leave. I swear, if you don't leave, I'll call the cops.'

'Sercly, what's happened do you, Wimp-Wimp? You've suddenly become so cold. I mean, 'ere's no way you can juss stop bein' in love with me. Not dis easily. Not over some bullshit Teresa fedja.'

'I told you: it's not just that. It's everything. I don't even know you—I really don't. And I don't *wanna* know you now. I've seen and heard enough. Three and a half years was enough for me, Vinny. I've changed. You've changed. Life's changed.'

'Yes, everything changes in time—except *love.*'

'I'm sorry, Vinny, but I don't love you anymore. I really don't.'

'Yes, you do.'

'No, I don't.'

'(I know deep-down you don't believe her),' he whispered.

'(I *do* believe her),' she whispered back. 'And I believe you've ignored me since you started your stupid book. And I believe all the fights I've seen you get in. And all the drugs and alcohol I've seen you do. And my dad when he said he has a funny feeling about you. And I believe my heart when it says you're just not the one. I'm sorry, Vinny, but we just aren't meant to be together. Just deal with it. *I* am. I really am.'

'Have you found someone else or sum'n?'

'No. And I don't plan on it for a long time. I just wanna be left alone by everyone. So please leave, and don't call me or come here again. Please.'

'I think 'iss is all juss some phase yir goin' through. Yir juss stressed out from school 'n' all da shit on TV 'n' yir parents 'n' the fact ditchir best friend is a heroin addict. 'Iss is juss reality slappin' you in the face. Yir finely startin'ah get a taste of da *rill* world after bein' sheltered from it all yir life. I know it ain't easy. I mean, how you think I feel with all the shit *I've* been through. But, look, *I'm* still goin' strong. *I'm* not givin' up. *I'm* not takin' it out on you.'

'You have five seconds to leave or else I'm callin' the cops.'

'One, two, three, four, five.'

She swung up and jerked her head towards the right, towards her desk, either to seek her cell phone or cordless. He rushed over and grabbed her. She went to the scream out but only one syllable slipped, for he quickly put his hand over her mouth.

'Listen, Ivy. I didn't do anything wrong. I love you. I wanna spend the rest of my life with you. But if you need time, I'll give ya time. Juss don't give up. Please, don't give up on us. Yir all I got left...Now I'm gonna take my hand off yir mouth, but don't scream. Ar'ight? Dere's nuh'n'ah be afraid of. I'd never hurt you. You juss gadda overstand thit *I'm* hurt. I love you more den anything in the world, 'n' I came here da prove it. Now I'm gonna leave, 'n' if anything comes up, you know you can caw me whenever.' (He briefly paused.) 'I love you more than life, Ivy, 'n' nuh'n will ever change that. Don't ever forget that.'

Sitting on top of her, he lowered his face down and kissed her forehead...slowly letting his hand slide off her mouth. She didn't scream out because she was crying so hard that it was almost soundless.

'Don't cry. Things'll get bedder.'

'Okay, okay. Just go,' she cried, pushing at him to get off. He stood up and looked down with devotion at the crying angel balling herself back up in the comforter. He didn't want to walk away with her in tears; it didn't feel like the right thing to do.

'Look, if ya want meedda leave, you gadda stop cryin'. Show me some hope. I wanna see ya smile 'fore I walk out da door. Ar'ight?'

'I ca-can't,' she quavered. 'Please – go.'

'Fine. At least say you love me.'

'Naa-no.'

He moved back to the bed and sat down. 'Juss rill quick 'n' I'll leave.'

She wasn't looking at him. Her half-face was staring right through the door. The comforter was wrapped around her so tightly and her body was trembling so violently, as the tears poured down. She looked so petrified. The room chilled over in silence, as shadows continued dancing around them...before she, in a jumpy but empty voice, finally said, 'L-lav y-a. N-n-na go-ah.'

Yes! YES! It felt good to hear those three precious—those two precious words! He leaned back down towards her, but she jerked away. Before she burst out—because she probably thought he was trying to kiss her—he quickly assured her that he just wanted to power up. She said ur-ry up-ah. So he moved in close to her head and stuck a piquant lock in his mouth. '*POWER UP!!! HMHMHMHMHM!!!*' After an intense feeling of joy and passion swirled through his body, he stood up...walked to the door...put his hand on the knob...took in a deep, deep breath...then exhaaaaaaled, turning his head over his shoulder.

'I'll be waitin, Wimp-Wimp,' he said in a solemn breath.

'Don't. I'm never comin' back,' she whispered through her tears.

'I love you too.'

Confused, he turned around and quietly shut the door...

He'd been down this road so many times, but he didn't even know the name of it. From this unknown road, he'd pulled into Chow Down...crept up Jack McArdle's dirt-and-gravel driveway...went around the right bend at the orchard...up the hill...passed the trailer park...and down roads that led to the haunting playground...before turning around and heading back down towards *this* road—and he still didn't know the name of it. Not a street sign anywhere, not on one end...or the other.

As he passed Jack's driveway, he could still see (despite a foot of snow) the FOR SALE sign in the yard. A juvenile instinct urged him to stop the car, get out, rip it out of the ground, snap it in half, then drive off: this way no one could buy the orchard that he and Ivy were going to buy: the orchard is going to be their home away from home in Catania, one day. But he kept driving...driving down the country road, passing the snow-covered fields...passing Chow Down where they hadn't eaten in a while...til he came upon her neighborhood. It was Friday, around 5 p.m., so the darkness was soon approaching. He made a left onto Lily Drive. Not her road but he planned to drive around the back of her house first—peeping from above—then, coming back around, checking it out from the front. He wasn't even sure if she would be home, but that was his reasoning: he wanted to know what she was doing with her life without him.

The basic layout of Ivy's neighborhood was like that of the average suburban development: houses centered on a lot with moderate front and back yards but hardly any yard on the sides; a tree or two; smooth slightly-inclined driveways; two cars on display, perhaps two in the garage. In the magnitude and substance, however, it wasn't like the average suburb found in the intimate radius of a big city. Here, the cars were more expensive; the three-four-five-story houses much larger; (although some were *faux chateaux*, most were Victorians, some kept authentic, some modernized, but all gleaming and vibrant); even the grass and paint gleamed brighter here in these suburbs, because for one thing, many city-suburbs frequently deal with vandalism, and for another, the average city-suburban family brings home smaller paychecks and therefore doesn't hire landscaping services, as they do here in her suburban neighborhood. As he went around the bend, atop the hill, he caught a glimpse of the back of the Pineda's Victorian and its currently withered flower garden...but no action or bodies to be seen. Descending the hill, he returned to his suburban thoughts, wondering if there was an exact word for suburbs *not* around a large city. Are they even "suburbs" since they're not connected to a metropolis? He was thinking there should be a more specific word for *this*, because *this* suburban life—for it certainly isn't rural life either, nor even wholly a college town—but *here* is a lot different than the suburbs of Pittsburgh where the suburbs aren't exactly urban life since it's less populated and dangerous, and to boot, lack walking-districts, but it's certainly not *this*. A fistfight or a smashed mailbox must be scandalous here! No wonder she thought they were so different! Having a drug dealer here would be like having a hometown celebrity! (And yet he did know of *one* in the general area: a black suburban male with a heroin connection and purportedly a cop connection; needed to find out more about that oddity.)

Heading down Rose Boulevard—Ivy's road—Vallano felt determined but nervous. Her house sat in the middle of the road, and the neighboring houses seemed to be parted back, and the road so well structured and wide-open that a passing car could be seen coming and going for a minute if driving at the 25-mph speed limit. Since he couldn't take the chance of being spotted, he went flying by at 50 mph...(probably drawing the attention of a neighbor or two in the process)...but only concerned with whether her car was there...it wasn't, which meant she was elsewhere, and not in her dorm room either because he'd already surveyed her parking lot. What to do now?

He decided the only thing to do now was to drive by Teresa's. So he went down to the four-way at Rose Boulevard, made a left...passed three streets...then turned left on Iris Drive. Teresa's house was the second on the right...and as he passed the haunted house where his best friend died, he saw Teresa's car—no trace of Ivy's—but noticed that the pearl sedan usually in the garage was parked in the driveway, which meant her father was likely home. Vallano made a common-sense note to himself not to call or bother Teresa for a while no matter how drunk he may get—no matter how much the burgeoning beast inside starts begging him to. That aside, Vallano just couldn't bite the bullet that his best friend had taken his last breath in the house fading away in the rearview mirror...

...As he frequently did, Vallano, as he drove up towards Aristod, begin wondering what Teresa's father knew of the situation—his daughter's roles and habits—and of course if he noticed the missing gun yet. But why would he? When would he ever need a gun in *these* suburbs? And so what if his stupid gun *had* been stolen from his bedroom: *many* things had been stolen inside that bedroom. But what to do now? What – to – do.

He drove back to Philemon, swinging the ol' warhorse into the same spot it had stalled in for over three and half years. He alighted and stormed into Philemon where he'd been housed for over three and half years. As he passed the desk, he capriciously thought of the yumber-skinned Thai chick. But she was long gone now. When he reached his door he (because of the missing Thai chick) thought of Agent Ralphie who used to be housed right across from him, but he was long gone too. He went into his room where Jesus Christ was still hanging—thank the Lord!—and Luke was still present too! He was watching television. However, Vallano wasn't in the mood to put up with Jesus Christ hanging up and not knocking, and with Luke hanging out and not bothering him, so he quickly went to the commons to eat...When he finished he went back to the room and secretly retrieved his pipe and bag from his desk drawer.

'Later, Luke.'

'See ya, Vin.'

Back to the ol' warhorse! *GIDDEE UP!!!* ☺? ☹?...☹!!!

First, he drove through Ivy's parking lot: still gone. Then back to her house: still gone. Decided to pass by the haunted house again: too much reality, as well as no Ivy. Then he jumped on the highway: got high during the five-minute trip it took to pass all the strip malls and reach the mall mall.

He went inside the mall mall and bought three CDs. Charging back down the highway, he begin one-after-another calls to her cell: receiving one-after-another no answers, but leaving one-after-another voice mails. Then he maneuvered up and down every street on campus. Then off campus where the stores and bars were. Then off campus where the students lived. Nope, no sign of her tonight. So filled with painful anger and sadness, he headed back to Philemon. After swinging the ol' warhorse into the same spot it had stalled in for over three and half years, he alighted and walked up to the backside of her dorm, waiting, in the dark, for her light to come on. But as minutes passed by like snails, the coldness eventually got the better of him. So he went back to his room, and made a nightcap, as he sat down with the hope of discovering through words what had gone wrong...

Now, besides attending school full-time and his full-time job as an unpaid writer and his part-time job as minimum-wage tutor, the aforesaid is all that Vallano did February and half of March: a repetitive sequence of events that placed a TPO in his hands on Friday, March 15, 2003, passing on the word that he needed to be everywhere besides wherever Ivy Pineda was. The following day, he went outside to find on the saddle of the ol' warhorse many things he'd given her, like the I-love-you box (inside it lay that old worthless dollar), the acoustic guitar, books, movies, etc. etc.; apparently, Ivy didn't care if the items entered hands other than Vallano's. Oh, what's a TPO? A Temporary Protection Order—against Stalking and Harassment. On Friday, March 15, 2003, Ivy's parents spotted Vallano driving by their house. So chances are, they asked their daughter if he'd been bothering her—well, let's not be euphemistic, asked if he'd been *stalking and harassing* her, and she probably spilled her guts by saying that, yes, he has been, and from that, they *forced* her to get the TPO because *she* was in love with him and would've never done it herself, for she hadn't taken the initiative in the month and a half prior. (Fuckin' parents.)

Anyway, on Friday, March 15, 2003, the local police let Vallano know that he'd been issued a TPO. Thank God for a phone-serve! for it saved the embarrassment of having them explain in front of Luke that Vallano was to have no contact *whatsoever* with Ivy for the next thirty days, at which point she could decide if she wanted to go to court to attain an FPO, which would last a year; and if Vallano should happen to transgress the TPO, then he could face "a maximum of 90 days in jail and/or a maximum fine of $700." Yes! how embarrassing it would've been if the police had explained that in person with Luke there! Yet he couldn't stop the ignominy from bringing to his heart more anger, from callousing more cells, from tweaking more nerves into shapes criminal to the natural anatomy. After the call, he laid down on his bed. Trying to breathe normal. Trying to straighten out his vision. Trying to find recourse. Trying to think logically. But all his tryings were in vain. He could almost feel his body transforming into something strange. It was scaring him. Thoughts of slipping into insanity were inducing a panic attack. But he couldn't differentiate between *anxiety* and *insanity*. Things no longer seemed normal. Sounds: foreign. Sensations: out-of-body. The world before him: swirling into a violent inexplicableness...

...Ronald Adams (the mayor of Duneville) was a husky man. He had wet brown hair combed over to the side but untidy with curly cowlicks. His eyes were little and black: they sparkled benignly like a skunk's: a merry face, too, even though he appeared to have a jaw problem because his mouth barely moved whenever he talked. He gave off the air of a middle-aged man who managed a Denny's during the week, went bowling Friday night, fished Saturday morning, and Sunday, at church, never the one to make sure the congregation took note of his family's presence. Yet *he* was the mayor! And to boot mayoral stereotypes even further, on this May day— the day before Luke's graduation—he was dressed *nothing* like a mayor: a generic red-and-blue collared shirt (which was too small for him), blue jeans (which were too small for him), and red Velcro shoes (which looked like they were from the 80s). Grace Adams (the knickknack maker in Duneville) was a husky woman. She had miniature blonde curls. Her eyes were big and blue, with a big pocked nose below. Her skin was milky, the clothes on top modest and outdated. Despite her homely appearance, she had the nicest-sounding voice: very motherly and southern. On several occasions, Vallano had seen pictures of Luke's family but they were formal family portraits: Luke's mother was exactly what he'd been expecting in-person, but not his father.

Luke's four younger brothers (ranging from five to eleven) were running around like squirrels...doing circles in the room...then flying back into the hall...off to who knows where. (There were all sorts of people and animals invading the campus, just like at the end of every semester.) Luke's parents weren't concerned: his mother had told 'em to "stick together." Luke's older sister wasn't present yet: she was flying in from South Carolina tomorrow to attend the graduation ceremony.

'So, Vinny,' spoke Grace, 'would ya like to come out to eat with us?'

'Mmm, yinz guys goin' now?'

'Soon as we load the rest of his stuff up,' answered Ron. He turned away from the closet to look at Grace. 'Right, hun?' (Ron's voice shhh'ed a lot and he barely pronounced his t's: *Soonash we load a'rest ovis'shuff up. Rye, hun?* The mayor!)

'I suppose. Luke, now think: is there anything else ya need to do while we're here?'

'Nope. This is it. Everything else is taken care of.'

Grace turned back to her left to speak to Vallano. 'Yep, I guess soon. And don't worry about payin'; we got it; we'd just really enjoy your company. Four years and we're just now meetin', and just as we're leavin' for good!' she laughed. (Yep, just now meeting after four years: he'd done one heaven of a job at strategically going MIA, for this wasn't the first time the Adams had been in town—[there had been several Sunday afternoons they drove up just to break bread with Luke]—it was just the first time Vallano got stuck being around, but since this was *it,* he was overwhelmed with a sense of obligation, and so he decided to stay around to see Luke off "for good" and just drive back to Verna tomorrow.)

'I wish I could but a couple friends from back home are on 'er way dahn, 'n' I nee'dda be around whenever they arrive.'

'Well they can come too. We can wait for 'em. Can't we, Ron?'

'A coursh. We're in no rush.'

'Ehh, don't worry about it. I don't wanna tie yinz up. I'd caw 'em da see where they're at but neither have cell phones.' (Yeah, he'd caw 'em da see where they're at *if* his two unnamed friends were on the way: just an excuse not to spend quality time with the Adams. *Ehh, 'er jush bleshed dey even goddah medim.*)

With a stack of naked clothes laid across his forearms, Ron carried 'em from Luke's closet over to his bed, setting 'em down inside a big suitcase. He tucked the corners in then zipped it up. He firmly grabbed the handle like a mayoral handshake. As Ron exited, two of the little boys came flying back in. Grace asked 'em where Josh and Tim were. The one boy, who was out of breath, said, 'They went – outside with Daddy. Mommy, – can me and – Jake – have a dollar?'

'For what?'

'We want a – a pop.'

'No, you're wound up enough. Anyways, we're goin' out to eat soon.'

They must've took that as "you only have a few more minutes to run around like a nut" because they zipped right back out of the room, the one screaming for Mark, Tim, and Daddy to wait up.

Vallano wanted to be running around with 'em, without a care in the world. But, no, he was stuck with Luke who had just asked his mother if so-and-so back home had done something. As Luke and his mother begin talking about it, Vallano went off into his own world, for he noticed Luke had just picked up his desk chair and set it down beside the television: he was about to take remove Jesus Christ from the wall. Standing next to Grace, Vallano watched the bear climb up the chair, about to take Christ into his arms. '*Wow, can't believe it'* kept repeating in his head like waves of shock. Yes, it was *finally* coming down. In his eyes, his life thus far had been so ironic and symbolic, and it seemed there was going to be—*had to* be some great biblical ending with the painting. Yet here it is, being taken down so orthodoxly just like any other ol' thing hung on a wall. Just like that—*snatched!* away from the wall, an unceremonious Deposition—so many mysteries thrown into Time's bag of thievery, taken away, never explained, never solved, just like that hazy, intoxicated, delusional night when he'd had visions or a nightmare of smashing it into a million pieces...only to return Sunday to see it still up on the wall as it had been from day-one. He looked out at the empty space on the wall and felt so sad. Just a painting and he felt so sad it was no longer there.

'So, hun, ya sure you don't wanna go out to eat with us?'

'Thanks for da offer, but unfortunately I can't. Like I said, if it wasn't for my friends, I definitely would. Will yinz be stoppin' back here?'

She turned to Luke who was sliding the painting inside a large corrugated box. '*We're* stayin' the night in a hotel, and I assume Luke is too. Right?'

'I suppose. Dad already took my pillows,' he laughed. 'So unless I'm snugglin' up with you,' (he looked at Vallano) 'then I guess I'll have to.'

'Well deez beds are priddy small, but I'm sure we could make it work,' Vallano replied lamely, just trying to be jokeful in response to Luke's odd remark, while trying not to choke on the sadness of the debarkation of Christ.

'Are your friends stayin' here tonight?' asked Grace, meaning in the room.

'No. We gadda friend thit's gotta apartment off campus, so der juss gonna stay there. Our friend's graduatin' tamarra 'n' we're all gonna go watch 'im. 'N' of course, I'll be dere for Luke too. He'll get cawed early 'cause it goes in alphabetical order, but my friend's lass name is Williams.' Yeah, good thing he could quickly come up with a name aaaaaaall the way at the end of the alphabet.

'Lucky we don't go to a big college or you'd be waitin' all day for his name to get called,' said Luke, poor oblivious Luke.

'I know. Hey, ya sure ya don't want meedda help with anything?' Vallano had already offered to help carry at least ten times, but Ron—who just walked back into the room—wouldn't have it, even though Vallano *did* sneak in one trip thus far. But not much left now. Not much.

'No thanks, Vin. We're almost done anyway. I'm like you: don't have much, don't need much.'

Leaving with another box, Ron amened to that. Suddenly, one of the kids came flying back in and parted the small space between Vallano and Grace; Vallano was slightly moved aside. He kinda smiled at their naïveté, wondering if he had ever known such frivolous joy as a boy.

Grace said, 'You don't have any siblings, right?'

'Nope. I'm an only child.' His heart wanted to say a *lonely* child: 'Nope. I'm a *lonely* child.' Moreover, he kinda had a half-brother somewhere overseas; but how could he ever explain that to her? He never even mentioned it to Luke! The last day and Luke was probably listening so attentively to his mother's questions and Vallano's answers because he didn't even know who Vallano was—but neither did he!

Vallano crossed his arms. He needed to ask anyone anything just to get the attention away from him and his life. He spoke to Luke's sweaty back: 'So yir still not sure if yir gonna go straight inda grad school or look around for a job firss?'

'*Weeeeell.*' Luke propped the boxed painting up against the desk before turning around. 'For now, I'm just gonna go home and find whatever job I can and take a break from school. But I'm sure I'll end up in grad school eventually. Might end up teachin'.'

'Oh yeah? Wouju ever come back here da teach?'

'Yeah, I'd teach here. I'd be kewl with whatever as long as I'm not *too* far away.' The World Religions grad turned back around and picked up the boxed painting. He was about to carry it out til Ron came in and said that he would take it because he had a place for it in the van where it would be out of harm's way. (Since Ron's good friend had painted it, he likely had a different concern for its welfare.) So Luke handed Christ over to his father, and for himself picked up one of the last boxes. Luke's brother Jake, who just entered, said that he wanted to carry it, but Luke said, 'Jake, this box is bigger than you!' Jake stomped his foot down as if he was going to take a stand. But when Josh—was it Josh?—tagged Jake in the back, Jake went back to playing tag with the rest of biblical bunch. Then Luke, his father, Christ, and the biblical bunch went out into the hall, in pursuit of their oversized family van.

For the first time, Vallano found himself alone with Grace. As from the start, there was burning awkwardness beneath his skin because he was wearing a t-shirt and, strangely, shorts, and therefore many of his tattoos could be seen; he recently added three more images to his arms, and the skin around the images was adorned with little generic stars, fish, sparrows, and other traditional filler. Moreover, he still had those two posters hung by his bed: the feral Darby Crash and the tough-looking fully-inked New Yorkers, Agnostic Front. For God's sake, the words *Agnostic Front* were in plain view of Grace! And he couldn't explain to her what the band was really about, for they didn't even sing about religious issues. Oh well, his courtesy would just have to suffice. Besides, *he* was the one who'd been her son's roommate for *four* years, so he had to be *good* or else Luke would've switched rooms. Yes, *he* is Luke's *good* friend and a student at a *good* college going for *two* degrees. So judge not! Judge not! Here before you, Grace, is no agnostic or front!

'So Luke told me you have a girlfriend who goes to school here too.'

Watch this front—> 'Yeah. Well we're kinda on a break now. We been together since our first year. But we both decided idd be best if we took some time off da focus on our lass year, den go from there.'

'Oh. Well school *is* the most important thing. Plus, you have the rest of your lives to figure things out.' Grace moved to Luke's desk to look through a box filled up with knickknacks. Then, in a soft curious tone: 'Do you believe she's the one?'

Watch this agnosticism—> 'Well, I mean, I love her 'n' all, but thing is, after graduation I plan on movin' da Sicily da be with my mother. See, I wanna be a writer, 'n' I can do that *anywhere*, but she's gonna be a veterinarian, 'n' we're not sure if she'll be able da gidda job over there, ya know. So location's one of our big concerns.'

'Well Love can lead you all over the place, and at the same time, keep you right where you are. I'm sure if it was meant to be, it'll work out.'

'Yep.' Yuck! How he learned to hate that saying! If it was meant to be! Fuck that! He's gonna *make* it be! Yes, as soon as Ivy comes around! And things were already looking up, for the woman of mercy didn't even pursue the FPO; when the TPO expired in mid-April, she called to let him know that it would be wise for him to remain at a distance or else he would be in more trouble; and that she was getting a new cell phone number which he couldn't have; and...'seriously, Vinny, it just wasn't meant to be. I'm so much happier now. And soon enough, you will be too...I seriously can't wait to read your book. I'm sure it will be amazing. I know I'll never meet another person as smart as you.' – 'But I wanna be with you forever.' – 'No, Vinny; it's over, and nothin' can ever change that. I have to go now. Take care, all right? And even though I really don't like those little things, whenever I see a squirrel, I'll *always* think of you and smile.' – 'But—' *Click.*

'Vin? Are you?'

'Huh?'

'You gonna miss me?'

Time for Luke to leave already? 'Yeah, for sure. I couldnt've asked for a bedder roommate: four very enjoyable years. 'N', hey, we got each other's cell numbers, home numbers, home addresses, school addresses, 'n' email addresses, so da only way we *won't* be able da stay in touch is if wunna of us gives up all faith in technology.'

Huddled together in the doorway, the Adams took that to be a very funny litany and punchline because they laughed freely and looked at one another as if to say, 'Don't we all agree that Vincent Vallano is such a funny, sweet kid? Yes. Yes. Yes. Yes. Yes. Yes. Yes. Just too bad his friends are coming up and he can't come break bread with us, especially since we don't know if we'll ever see this good kid again.'

'Yeah...Well, Vin—' Suddenly, the harmless bear came wobbling towards him, throwing his paws around Vallano. Such an embrace! Yes! squeeeeeeze that fish! You got him! BEAR WITNESS! YOU FINALLY GOT HIM! 'Take care, Vin,' Luke whispered (whimpered?). Was Luke shedding tears on his shoulder? 'Good luck next year, and good luck with the book, and—' Oh such a divine whisper—> '—and I hope everything works out with Ivy. I'm sure it will.' Luke let go. And, yes, there *were* tears rolling down his chubby cheeks; but none on Vallano's. He was so absorbed in the thought of how so many people had come and gone. But this wasn't the final farewell: they had each other's cell numbers, home numbers, and so on. And no one was giving up all faith in technology! So, yes, emotional overkill isn't necessary! Luke was just going home!

'Oh! the pictures!' chimed Graced. Ron handed her the camera. 'You guys stand next to each other in front of the television.' She turned to Ron, and with a disappointed tone, said, 'We should've taken pictures of 'em before we tore the room apart.' Ron humbly agreed. Nevertheless, *now* was the time. So standing on his side of the room, Luke put his right arm around Vallano. Those two roommates—those good ol' friends stood upright in front the television, underneath the blank wall, while Grace placed the camera in front of her big blue eyes. 'Okay. Say cheese!'

'Chee—' *SNAP!...SNAP!...SNAP!...SNAP!*...Picture after picture! solos! duets! kids! adults! the whole family! the whole family and him! him and the whole family!...til the flash died out, whereupon Vallano and the Adams walked outside...hugged...said more goodbyes...watched the family van drive away...went back inside...down to his room...and from the doorway, stared at the missing spaces on the right side of the room...and on the center of the wall...then, confused, went inside, turned around, and quietly shut the door...

...In the morning, he packed up a good portion of his clothes, for he was spending the summer at Jeremiah's uncle's. This far into his curriculum, there were no longer summer classes available that would count on his audit; besides, the loans he'd taken out just for summer classes had amassed into an amount he didn't care to tally. He only needed seven more classes anyway: a bit too much for one semester, which is why he would have to schedule a few "fillers" for his final semester in the spring in order to be a full-time student and thus be eligible to receive more loans. So knowing he couldn't and shouldn't attend summer classes, as well as not having the spirit to spend any more time at college—he was just so sick of it!—Vallano called Jeremiah to ask if he could stay there for summer and do plumbing. Jeremiah had told him that he would talk to his uncle...then called back with: 'Yeah, he said we could yuzza another hand. 'N' he said he don't minja stayin' here 'n' 'at juss as long as yir riddy da get up early 'n' work yir ass off. Think you can handle it, cawidge boy?'

Of course! But what he *couldn't* handle was the thought of being far away from Ivy for so long, even if they were no longer spending time together or even talking. He knew, however, that to stay at Aristod for the summer (taking classes or not) would only bring long, lonely, miserable nights. He knew something bad was bound to happen. He would eventually catch Teresa and go ballistic. Eventually catch Jackson and go ballistic. Eventually catch Ivy and never let go. So what else could he do? Ivy, her family, Teresa, Jackson, the authorities: they all told him to stay far away or else he would be punished for being in love. The verdict was out, the majority had spoken: justice had been served, from which he was again hung up in the great Gordian knot. So what else could he do but suck in enough breath to sustain himself for the time being? It was only a few months anyway. And when he returned, he could still continue his mission to revivify his life with Ivy, as well as rectify the death of Pessi, and do it all with a clearer mind! In the vicioustime, he just had to tame the beast within, which he did by sucking that last painful breath out of the clear LaSalle sky—*huuuh!*—then crank the music up well above the non-sin level—*ahhhh!*—then pop a bunch of suckable seeds into his mouth—*yuuum!*—now ready to steer the ol' warhorse up towards those precarious hills of Pittsburgh, Pennsylvania: *GIDDEE UP!!!...*

J.C., W-C: TO SAY THE LEAST

"A steel-tough worker died today,
He spent forty years covered in grease,
His calloused hands were soft to his children,
Soft to his wife, soft to his neighbors,
He was a quiet man, a gentle, humble man,
Uneducated and underpaid but understood love,
He sacrificed for love, without complaint,
He spent forty years covered in grease,
The news said that a celebrity had sex last night,
And that a politician was mad at another politician,
And that a rock band just went platinum,
But they never said he spent forty years covered in grease..." [1]

Vallano's first hands-on experience with the working class was when Dante got him and Pessi jobs as potato sackers. There are five primary positions at the potato factory. An actual *potato sacker* is one of the five to eight people who stand around a circular conveyor-belt, taking off small bags of potatoes and methodically putting 'em inside larger, stronger bags that they erect at their flanks: Vallano had only done this for the first week. Once the big bag is full with small bags, the *potato sacker* shifts it backwards to the *potato stacker* who tapes it up then methodically stacks it on a pallet til it reaches the vertical limit: Vallano had also done this for a week. The *pallet driver* then drives the full pallet to the back of the factory: Vallano never did this job; this job is for those with seniority, as was Dante's case before quitting. At this point in the process (in the back of the factory) the potatoes are stationed both at the starting and ending point for the *potato dumper* (only two per shift). Even though the *potato dumper* has the job of helping the *pallet drivers* load and unload pallets into and from the trucks at the dock, the primary duty of the *potato dumper* is to set into position the heavy bags of loose potatoes fresh off the dock; then slice a bag open while it's still on the pallet; lift it off the pallet; carry it over to the tank; then dump it in. But before the *potato dumper* sends the loose potatoes ahead, they have to sort through and pull out the rotten ones, and there tend to be many, for they are potatoes-for-the-poor that arrive from unknown places: Vallano had never been sure of the logistics. Nevertheless, as the potatoes move along the belt, they are mechanically packaged in plastic, but there's also two *potato weighers* to make sure the small bags are weighed correctly and don't jam up on the belt. For the majority of the time they worked there, Pessi and Vallano had been *potato dumpers:* the most toilsome of the five positions. So hard on the back! But they'd been consoled by their budding muscles. Moreover, whenever the supervisor wasn't around, they would have a little fun by launching small potatoes up at the *potato sackers;* and sometimes the *potato sackers* would fire back! And Vallano could never forget Willie the black crackhead, who, whenever

---

[1] Lyrics from "Covered in Grease" by C(A)S, from the album *Skinhead Alley*

they took breaks, would always say: 'Why yinz throw dem tayders eh may? Yinz guys weh: imma gitcha ray inna noggin'.' Then crackhead Willie would whisper (to Pessi) in a musical, toothless tone: 'Yuzz-ah gahdeeny wee ta'ay? Some smokey-smokey f'ol' Willie?' Yeah, that was Vallano's first hands-on experience with the working class. Now, years later, college boy is doing commercial plumbing! Like most people, he thought plumbing meant dealing with feces and installing sinks and toilets. But that shit doesn't come til the end, if ever! How quickly college boy learns...

Late May
'Ya gahdit in yet, punk?!' yelled Big Joe from twenty-feet away.
'No! Gadda 'bout two more inches!'
Frustrated down inside a four-foot trench, Big Joe ripped the long iron digging bar out of the ground then rammed it back in. He leaned forward on the rooted bar, taking in heavy breaths of preparation. He couldn't rest too long because Steve was lurking around up on level ground. So using every ounce of might in his 6'5"/300 LBS of pure muscle, Big Joe began prying the main water line forward...pushing and pushing the heavy pipe...*aaaahggggh!*...til it was flush inside the bottom valve of a fire hydrant.
'Ar'ight!' yelled out Vallano. 'It's in!' He turned around. Big Joe had thrown the digging bar aside, now wiping the sweat from his face; it was a humid 90° out. 'Ready da roll this one dahn?' Vallano was referring to the long water main pipe to his left, up on high ground. There was an interminable row of pipes up there: a long mint-green snake. Thankfully, Danny (aka Curls [because of his hair]) had steered 'em over on the skid loader hours ago, when the fork piece was hooked up to the front; Curls now had the bucket piece hooked on, dumping gravel atop the pipes that Big Joe and Vallano had already connected. This was all part of doing the "underground" of a job. A relatively easy task: the mathematics were simple, or rather "flexible" since not much else was underway yet; just a lot of monotony with little shelter offered.
'Eh, Joe!' yelled out a whiny soprano voice from level ground. 'Joe! Fuck, man! Ya gadda make sure deez pipes are fuckin' straight!...Take 'at fuckin' board out 'n' put it up unner 'iss one 'n' kick it over my way!...Eh, Joe! Yinz guys makin' sure da glue dose fuckin' tablets in?!...Fuck, man! Dis is a fuckin' mess! Yinz wanna end up puttin' a 90 on 'at?!—Den make sure it's in fuckin' straight! Yinz guys gadda make sure 'iss line's fuckin' straight or yunz'll run it straight inda the bank! Eh, Joe!...'
As the commands and complaints spewed out, Vallano quaffed water and kept his eyes on Big Joe. Steve was talking directly to Big Joe, but Big Joe was looking at Vallano with a flustered look that said, 'Fuck this, man. I can't wait til dis asshole leaves.' Besides being Jeremiah's uncle, co-owner of O'Malley Brothers (Commercial Plumbing Experts), and a wealthy workaholic, Steve O'Malley is also Big Joe's best friend; they grew up together, but after high school parted ways when Big Joe left for Nebraska to play college football; but his time on the defensive line only lasted a year before he dropped out and returned to Da Burgh; then Big Joe joined Pittsburgh's police force, working in blue for fifteen years, but was fired when the department found out he had moved out to the eastern suburbs and was keeping an address on file that was actually his mother's residence,

and in Pittsburgh a police officer must *physically reside* in the city proper; how did the department find all this out?: well, a couple had moved in next door to Big Joe, and it wasn't long before neighborly love turned into suburban disputes; this led to Big Joe's neighbors making strategic calls to the local police with false complaints while Big Joe was working *dahntahn;* and from that, both police departments made the connection; yes, one would think Big Joe's neighbors would've been in trouble for the false complaints, and that the Pittsburgh police department would've taken into consideration that Big Joe was out in rough city streets dealing with dangerous people, and that those dangerous people could've easily went down the block to his house "in the city proper" and put his wife and two kids in harm's way; yes, one would think there's a slight problem Big Joe was fired by authorities in the force, and thereby forced to heed to the whiny authority of his old friend Steve for $9/hr as a non-union plumber's assistant.

Vallano retracted his progress in the trench to help Curls with the gravel dumping...*(a bunch of hand-signals)*...Afterward, he used a shovel to even out the waves of stones since Curls hadn't overstood the novice's confusing hand-signals. Setting the shovel aside, Vallano took a glove off and used his relatively clean hand to put chew in; he was allowed to smoke but it was bothersome whenever hard at it down in the trench. Big Joe yelled out, 'Hey, punk! 'Iss ain't fuckin' lunchtime. Putchir chew in 'n' grease 'at pipe up! Come on! 'Iss ain't cawidge, punk!' (Everyone teased Vallano about being in college. And once Jeremiah informed everyone that Vallano was an aspiring writer, he never heard the end of that either.) 'Come on! Quit thinkin' about suckin' Hemingway's dick 'n' grease 'at pipe up! We gaddabout two hundred more feet da lay so we can come back on Monday 'n' lay another two hundred!'

'*Hemingway!*' Vallano huffed in thought. '*Figures: a laborer akshly mentions a writer 'n' it's gadda be fuckin' Hemmingway!*' Never a fan of Hemingway's ambages, appendages, and axed anthems,[2] Vallano squatted down on the lengthy mint-green pipe, straddling it like a feral Spanish bull that could buck from side-to-side in the dirt, all the while mumbling windy expletives to the ghost of Hemingway. He pulled the bucket of grease over. He dipped the brush in and swirled his hand back and forth sensuously like a painter. The gooey grease was dirty-cream. He thought it looked like a bucket of mucus. With the fresh chew in his lip, and the windy expletives dropping from his mouth in between spits, the plumbing artist was having a grand ol' time plumb on the pipe, painting its mouth with mucus. Meanwhile, Big Joe was yelling out for the millionth time for him to make sure that he thoroughly applied mucus to the *under part* of the pipe—so to speak, on its nether lip: this bettered the chance of Big Joe pushing the pipe into the valve without being on the brink of a heart attack. Vallano wasn't annoyed that Big Joe had already given him the same instructions a million times because Steve had told Big Joe a million and one times. After all that

---

[2] *Ambages:* inability to convey emotions in a direct way (alluding to Hemingway's literary technique of emotional transferences/blocks); *appendages:* his penis (alluding to Hemingway's overkill of masculinity); *axed anthems:* the widely praised conciseness of Hemingway's works

he'd heard thus far, Vallano could only sympathize with Big Joe. It was only his fifth day—and although most jobs are somewhat pleasant til monotony takes hold—he was already disheartened from the slough of stories he'd been told. Well, none of the plumbers just *told* stories; they *bitched.* Such angry, bitter bitching too. Sure, they might've joked just as much, especially by ragging on each other, or bragging about some macho quality they had which no other could surpass, but it wasn't fooling Vallano...nor could he fool *himself.* Yes, underneath the toil, pipes, and ribs, he could feel a breathy compassion for his father burgeoning: this nagging regret deep within. He just wasn't sure *what would come of it...*

...Finally the end of the day arrived, and being Friday, the end of the work week; but the never-ending pipes always seemed to threaten the prospect of *end.* Big Joe and Vallano were now cruising down the highway in the company van, on the way back to the shop in Monport. They had strapped everything down in the back of the van with bungee cords, but the tools in buckets, the copper fittings in boxes, and the metal shelves against the walls were banging around cacophonously like a Scrap Yard Symphony; at first, Vallano frequently turned around, thinking things were spilling out everywhere, but he soon learned to block it all out.

Breaking for a red light, Big Joe took the pause as an opportunity to break the seal of a new snuff can, putting a fresh wad atop the old one. His double-chew lip jutted out comically like a stub-out with a test cap. Vallano thought Big Joe looked so funny in the driver's seat, too, because his tree-trunk legs engulfed the gray vinyl—so crammed in that it looked like an elephant on a tricycle; his head was almost as big as the steering wheel! After struggling to spit in between his legs and onto the floor (Big Joe rarely spit his chew so no puddles came of it), he asked Vallano if he wanted to stop at the gas station up ahead to get a drink or piss; Vallano said, 'Nah, I'm cool.' So with forty-five minutes to go, they kept going. Big Joe was passing the time with stories about drunken nights, bloody fights, and Steve's inept management because he kept his fist tight. (Sandino, another plumber, had told Vallano about Steve's tightfistedness the very first day. Sandino said that Steve will make sure you bring back every little piece of pipe so he can scrap it, yet he won't shell out the money to hire *licensed* plumbers—[Glenn the racist was the only one with a license]—and spending extra money in *that* manner, Sandino explained, would be the *real* way to save money. Sandino had *other* money-making strategies for Steve. But so did everyone else! Yes, *everyone* overflowed Vallano's mind with Steve's shortcomings, yet *none* bothered to present their suggestions to Steve in a serious manner because the highly-strung man signed their paychecks, and being non-union they had no "protection.")

Big Joe and Vallano were nearing the end of the rustic highway when Big Joe's anecdote about Steve's ineptness reached its conclusion. Vallano had been enjoying his stories, further amused by the idea that he was now kinda friends with a cop—an ex-cop. Big Joe flung his chew out the window. A comfortable silence befell the van. Vallano was looking out the window, musing. The calm green Mon had just come into sight. As he began drifting off into a dreamy state, music began playing in his head. Not the phantasmal melody *in* everything, but a true lyrical song. It perfectly matched the ambiance, and thus probably on track by his own will. The song was "Highwayman," a nostalgic piece in which Johnny Cash, Willie Nelson, Waylon Jennings, and Kris Kristofferson each sing a verse. The four singers take a role of a working man who dies at work but still lives on in what they've accomplished. Between-the-lines (as Vallano interpreted it) the song was about the *universal* working man who is killed time after time throughout History, and yet perseveres, as *Life* continues moving down the long straight highway. In the song, the working man shifts from the ancient solder who kills then gets hung, to the sea-born sailor who fights the storm then dies in a shipwreck, to the tight-roping dam builder who builds the dam high then slips and falls to the concrete down below, to the make-believe rocket man who's trying to "reach the other side" to *"find a place to rest my spirit if I can...perhaps I may become a highwayman again...or simply be a single drop of rain...but I will remain...and I'll be back again...and again...and again...and again...and again..."* Ahhhh! He could hear the music so loud and clearly! He could *feel* it thumping against the chambers of his heart! This rhythmic intimacy between souls unknown! And despite his focal attention soon turning elsewhere, the music continued playing in the background, still connected deep within, *in memoriam...*[3]

...As they careened alongside the Mon, they came upon one of the steel mills still in operation. In front of the murky green river lay a double-set of railroad tracks...followed by six smokestacks rising high into the sky, shooting out clouds of semen that consumed the troposphere...and down at the right end of the line (ruining the perfect spaces between the other six stacks) one much shorter which was presently dormant...in front of the stacks sat the main building: baby-blue metal, long and vast, with a rusty peaked roof with three large silver letters painted across it...the rest of the ground was populated with smaller blue and silver buildings....most were short and rectangular with dirty facades, altogether stirring up a sensation that would make you question if you'd fallen back into the late 1800s...some buildings had large grayish pipes coming out of the roof, many at odd angles...then straightening out as they hung in midair...before shooting perfectly, at an angle, down into the roof of another building...and some buildings—the ones close to the river—had sets of railroad tracks running around the premise. Vallano was wondering if trains still went *inside;* that is, into the cloistered docks. He couldn't remember if he'd ever been down there. But like a true yinzer, he did know with pride the basic history of the steel mills: *This* one (fading away in the review mirror) had helped to turn Pittsburgh into a city, a long time ago; had literally taken The Steel City into the sky! And he knew about the infamous strike of 1892 that occurred at a nearby steel mill, from which, in a fight to establish a union, blood reached a boiling-point...and spilled into the green river when The Steel Strikers fought in gunfire against The Pinkerton Agents; shortly after, Alexander Berkman, an anarchist, attempted to murder anti-unionist Henry Clay Frick, and from that, via the media, public opinion changed and turned against the anarchists, as the mill continued operating without a union: inept immigrants soon replaced skilled millers. And Vallano knew (through his own memory) about the drastic layoffs in the 80s that put most of metro Pittsburgh in economic turmoil, which gave some opportunities to join the

---

[3] [lat] in memory of

burgeoning medical and technological industries. Still, he never really knew what went on *inside* the steel mills, particularly *this* one. He always pictured big lava furnaces but wasn't sure if that's what the *modern* steel mill is like. Looking into the rearview mirror, he could sense (almost *see* behind the walls of one of those buildings) the ghost who *did* know. The ghost who hated blacks but would soon be going home blackened. The ghost who liked to drink but would soon be going home to eat food he worked so hard to put on the table. The ghost who was misogynistic but would soon be going home to kiss the wife he must've missed during his lonesome shifts. The ghost who was working to pay off all his debts and officially buy his house then save up a little extra so he could put his son through college because deep-down he truly loved him. Yes, inside one of those buildings, there was a ghost still working to dig his own grave...

Early June
        With six grocery bags occupying both hands, Vallano guided three fingers out of the plastic jungle and finessed the golden handle granting entrance into the O'Malley's pristine three-story house. Jeremiah's aunt and uncle, Kelly and Steve, were residents of Mannick, a middle-class borough ten miles east of Verna, but their house was located in an upper-middle-class enclave. Their cul-de-sac street was lined with fluffy trees, red-bricked sidewalks, and quaint streetlights. Their house was on the left within the bulb. It shined like crystal inside and out, the vanguard being the chandelier hanging down from the high ceiling in the foyer. The first floor smelled strongly of fresh wood: the large living room floor being honey oak: shiny like shampooed hair without a trace of flake. Steve O'Malley might've been a working-class entrepreneur who spent more time down in a muddy ditch than behind a clean desk, but he was also a neat freak who liked trendy furnishings; his wife, the same. In her late thirties, Kelly O'Malley was an attractive strawberry-blonde. Her fine, straight hair was usually pulled back in a tight ponytail. She had small pointy breasts and pointy hips that flared whenever she walked. Although Jeremiah and Steve made fun of Vallano for being a vegetarian, Kelly was overstanding, always making sure there were plenty of things on the table for him. A sweet woman. No, a *delicious* woman. Yes, Vallano had already fantasized many times her walking into the bedroom they'd put him up in (late at night when everyone else was asleep) and letting him clean her pipes: a pro's bono for the sake of *quid pro quo.* But from day one, it was already on the table: Kelly was married to Steve, and Vallano had a girlfriend—(wait, were they still *pre-engaged?)*—nevertheless, Vallano was taken by a girl at school. Everyone knew that. They knew he simply had nothing else better to do this summer since that girl at school had gone to Bolivia for an internship with Peace Corps—(wait, had he said she'd gone to *Belize?)*—nevertheless, that girl at school was out of the country for the summer. *Sic vita est...sunt lacrimae rerum!*[4]
        'Zatchu, Vin?!' rang Kelly's voice from the kitchen; the kitchen was straight ahead but mostly hidden by a peach-colored wall to the right.

---

[4] [lat] Such is life...there are tears to things. [The latter part is a quote by Virgil. *Tears* is also punned, for there are tears (to the fabric of truth) in his story to the O'Malleys.]

'Yeah, it's me.'

''Ey got everything?!'

Keeping his face in half-turn, he walked into the kitchen and set the bags atop the breakfast table. 'Yep. Here'shzur change.' He set it down and quickly turned around.

'Howda cake turn out?'

'Good,' he projected backwards. 'I'm goin' out da get it.'

Vallano had made a run to the grocery store to pick up a pre-ordered ice cream cake and a few other things because Kelly was busy getting things ready for Jeremiah's birthday dinner. Jeremiah and Steve were still at work because whenever you were on a job with Steve there really was no *end*. Besides, it was only 7 p.m., so Jeremiah had all night to celebrate his 24th birthday.

Once outside, he slowed his pace, trying to buy time to conjure up an excuse for his puffy upper cheek and chipped tooth. If he would've just kept his focus on that little asshole and not been so concerned with potential spectators and that damn melting ice cream and his growling stomach—he could've taken him!...

...7:30 and its sister minutes crept up on the house and left silently like tumbleweed. Kelly had been consoled by the fib that Vallano had ran into the automatic door at the grocery store after turning to look at something and the automatic door failed to open. (She actually fell for that?) Now she lay with her back sunken down in a white leather sofa, frustrated by her husband and nephew's absence. She had the dining room table set but left the food atop the stove and counter. Vallano was upstairs, lying with his belly on the bed, writing on his laptop. Like always, he had his cell close by just in case. Even though Ivy was somewhere in Latin America (*wink*wink*), she would surely be calling to find out why he wasn't at school. She must've noticed his absence by now. If not, it was sure to eat her up whenever she *did,* especially since he'd been so cool about it by not letting her know! Yes! He'll teach *her* a lesson! It will put the power ball back in *his* court! and she will come running back to him! and their dynamic love will again be a slam dunk! and vibrant confetti will fall from the rafters!!!...But as hard as he tried to paint the picture of the future with sanguine colors, he couldn't lessen the pain. Couldn't stop from seeing the *other* side of the sanguineous tracks where his heart had been ran over and the sky was raining down red angerdrops. At times, however, he tried to view the temporary separation as a boon with regard to his work in-progress: perhaps it had created a couple lively scenes to add to offset a period in his life that had been rather mundane, given that the past year had been filled with a lot of "catching up to himself." Alwaysthesame, it was that much more pain to write about. But what good art isn't inundated with pain? There was just one swamping problem on the rise: *now* (whenever he was attempting to express his pain through words, whether in a serious manner or veiled by comedy) the tides of guilt were mounting because of everything else going on in the world. Soldiers were dying; people dividing; hungry children crying; the gap between natural disasters shrinking at a hurricane speed so blinding. In his head, he was beginning to hear the voice of humbleness asking: '*What is your small measure of pain—that tiny incision with a sting so sufferable—when the whole world is sunk deep in a* salted wound? *Who are you to lament your life and his life, this life and that life, so discriminately? so selfishly? Who are you, as selfish as you have become, to seek the cure to that which is incurable?* Such bothersome questions! He was doing all he could to push that Rosenbaumesque voice away. So he kept at his writing, headstrong and self-exalted, thriving on his cuts and craft as if he was bleeding all man's blood. He sought to connect together his words with such beastly courage!—*while driven by a softer inspiration*—with the hope that he was, in fact, stitching together millions of bandages! Yes, he *would* be the one to unite the world, magnanimously, himself hidden, only concerned with the positive upshot. Sitting in his temporary bedroom, he looked down and audaciously told himself for the millionth time: '*I know deez words can somehow heal the sorrow 'n' make everything ar'ight, 'n' not juss for me, or me 'n' her, but for EVERYBODY. I know they can! All that's needed is right here between the lines!*' But his gift seemed but half a gift, leaving half unknown, and all the same.[5]

From upstairs, Vallano heard the front door slam shut. His meditations came to a screeching halt. Steve and Jeremiah were yelling back and forth at each other. Soon, someone was stomping up the steps—slamming the bathroom door shut. Vallano saved his writing on his laptop, stuck his cell inside his jeans pocket, then went downstairs to see what the situation was...

'...on the eskavidder 'n' blows da whole fuckin' unnergrahn at CTS,' Jeremiah was explaining to Kelly. 'We shouldn'ah even been 'ere that late. It's not even 'bout my birfday, ya know, but everyone else left four ahrs ago. Bahcha know him: he's gadda keep goin' til everybody hates 'im for the day. 'N' 'en he's mudderfuckin' Big Joe for everything like izz *his* fault. I'm tellin' ya, Aunt Kelly, no one can stand 'im anymore. He's sercly gonna end up losin' *everyone*—you watch.'

'I'll have a chat with 'im. Baffanah, go up 'n' take a quick shire so we can eat. I mayja yir favorite supper. 'N' Vin went 'n' baucha a cake 'n' 'at.' Kelly looked Jeremiah on with the compassion of a mother. 'Okay, birfday boy?' She gave him a hug. After they separated, Kelly started moving around the kitchen like a fly. 'Oh! Jeremiah, yir mum 'n' dad cawed. Dey wanchada stop over tamarra affernoon.'

'Yeah, dey cawed me earlier.'

Jeremiah's parents would've come over for dinner but Jeremiah's father and Steve didn't get along. Jeremiah still had a healthy relationship with his parents; it was just more convenient for him to live with his uncle since he was Steve's right-hand man, and sometimes they would wake up extra early and go straight to a job, sometimes staying out of town for a few days. Luckily for Vallano, this was never expected of him; he just had to be at the shop by 7 a.m.—(even if everyone else showed up late)—and from there, he was told where he would be working for the day. He prayed every morning that it was wherever Steve wasn't.

---

[5] This paragraph is an allusion to Tennyson's poem *In Memoria A.H.H.*; namely, Part V where it reads: "I sometimes hold it a half sin; To put it in words the grief I feel; For words, like Nature, half reveal; And half conceal the Soul within."

Jeremiah turned to Vallano and smiled. 'Ha, ju piss Sandino off n'ee popcha one?'

'Nah. I fuckin' ran inda the automatic door at the grocery store. I wasn't lookin' 'n' it didn't open. Chipped my fuckin' tooth too.'

Jeremiah shook his head, smiling. Kelly intervened with a few comments, handing each a glass of iced-tea. Then she began putting the food on the table in the adjoining dining room, as they remained standing in the kitchen.

'So wha' happened now? Steve blew da unnergahn at CTS?'

'Yeah. Now he wansta be oudda here by six tamarra so we can be dere by seven. 'N' I told 'im it ain't happenin'. I don't min' workin' Sadurdies, ya know, but it's my birfday 'n' I'm gih'n fuckin' hammered tanight. Ain't no way I'm gonna be able da git up at six. I told 'im I'll go in 'round twelve or so, 'n' 'at juss pissed 'im off even more. 'N' Big Joe alriddy told 'em lass week he's goin' oudda town 'iss weekend.'

'You don't think he's gonna ask me da go in, do ya?'

'I dunno; bedder hide juss in case.'

'You seris?'

Jeremiah smiled at the sudden twist of concern in Vallano's face, although his right puffy cheek hardly moved. 'Yeah, I'm fuckin' seris. He's prahblee gonna ask ya, 'n' if ya say no, who knows what's gonna happen. Might be packin' yir bags 'n' headin' back da cawidge.'

'Fuck 'at. Is he inna shire now?'

Jeremiah stopped to put a good ear to the pipes. 'Sounds like it.'

'If I sercly hafta get up at six 'n' work with him, my whole fuckin' weekend's gonna be ruined.'

'Welcome da my world, buddy.'

'Jeremiah,' interjected Kelly, 'you gonna shire 'fore we eat or not.'

'Nah. I'll juss worsh up.' Jeremiah wasn't all that dirty; however, Vallano had returned hours ago covered in mud, smelling of flux and solder-smoke, because he spent the whole day crawling around on the naked ground underneath a bus terminal—three feet of vertical space!—helping Glenn the racist put in new gas lines.

'So who ja work with taday?'

'Glenn again. We're still workin' dahn Greyhound. I swear, if Rick was still alive, he'd seem like a fuckin' NAACP member comparedda him.'

Vaddling the words, Jeremiah said, 'Whad I tell ya: he's a fuckin' nut, ain't he?'

Glenn the racist was a racist. Just from his aura, he could be mistaken for a potential Klan member, but he actually hated the Klan because he hated Christianity. Just from physical appearance, Glenn the racist could be mistaken for a human mole. He was fat, grayish, bald besides a few hairs in the back, with small mean-looking eyes. Everyone at work had asked Vallano to guess Glenn's age because he was forty-five but looked sixty-five. Strange thing is, despite having nothing in common, Vallano liked Glenn. He swore a lot, made up outrageous idioms, and used a strange mix of scholarly and antiquated words: called everyone "babe," money was accounted for in "beans," and he pronounced "squirrel" as scroll. DA SCROLLS! Apart from eating too much, Glenn had one lethal vice: the lottery. He played heavily everyday and lost heavily every day. But his lotteric hindsight was impeccable! He could tell you every number that's hit, when it hit, who won it, and what they did with every penny! He claimed his day was coming soon because every morning a guy in the mafia stopped in a gas station near the shop to buy "five-cent cahfee...meanwhile, da fuckin' jaggoff's wearin' ten Gs in julree!" And not one to let a once-in-a-lifetime opportunity pass by, Glenn would stop in the gas station every morning to "overhear" the "fixed" lottery numbers for the day. Vallano thought it all sounded crazy and would argue with Glenn that the lottery wasn't fixed, and Glenn would tell him that he's got a lot to learn. Well, Vallano learned when Glenn finally gave him a number to play. Vallano put twenty beans on it and lost the whole lot. Funny thing is, Vallano's pulse almost stopped when he was watching the drawing because he was only off by one number, on the fourth and final digit; Glenn *did* have genuine memory problems: not only did he come in every morning claiming to have been off by just one number in yesterday's number, but he would also forget to write down what he'd "overheard" from the mafioso. Oh well! After hearing his stories, Vallano found himself fond of Glenn the racist. Yeah, once he warmed up to you—barring you weren't colored, foreign, female, gay, Christian, Islamic, Jewish—(and joking around, or maybe not, Glenn had told Vallano that Italians were "just lighter-colored niggers," to which Vallano had said his mother was an Sicilian immigrant, and a dark one at that, to which Glenn asked if she had "nice tiddarellis"—[ahhh, you cocksuckin' prick]—eh, babe, why dohncha push 'at prick of a pipe up in 'ere for me)—yeah, once he warmed up to you, Glenn the racist was a real nice babe who was just trying to get his beans to roll around in.

'Yeah. Firss time I work with 'im,' began Vallano, 'we stop at Lowes over in Dunning da pick up some shit. 'N' he goes, "Lock up 'at side 'n' back door." 'N' it's not even eight yet, ya know. So I'm like, "Should I lock my door too?" 'N' he looks at me like he's all pissed off 'n' says, "Not unless ya wanna nigger stealin' yir lunch." I juss laughed, ya know. Den he goes, "I'm seris, babe; dill steal whatever dey can. Couple years ago 'ey stole over $3,000 in tools right oudda the back of my van dahn in Avelwood while I's inna gas station. Two minutes: bing! bang! boom! 'em mudderfuckers were gone quicker den a teenager's virginity at a sylvan keg-pardy."'

'He ever tell ya dat story about 'im shootin' 'at black kid inna leg?'

'*Noooo*. Wha' da fuck? On the job?'

'Nah. At his house. But he wouldn't hesitate da do it onna job either. Look unner his seat. Carries two loaded pistols.'

'Maybe I shoulda brought da Glock I got dahn at school.'

'Yeah, well I keep a pistol in my van too juss in case. But ain't much da worry 'bout long as ya lock yir shit up. We all learned our lesson 'cause we all been robbed. Buh da thing is—' Jeremiah peaked around the corner to make sure his aunt wasn't listening in—then continued in a lowered voice: 'See, summa da guys—'n' I ain't sayin' who—buh dill tell Steve shit's been stolen 'n' 'en go sell it for straight profit. 'N' he gets it all back through da insurance cumpnee.'

'Sercly? 'At's not a bad idea.'

'Well don't even think aboudit. One: ya ain't got tools worth anything. Plus, his insurance is alriddy oudda the ruff, 'n' it's only hurtin' *us* inna long run. Only keeps our wages dahn 'n' allows him da say he ain't got da backin' da join the union—even'o he'd never join anyway; gets away with more shit 'at way, ya know.'

Kelly returned. With rose-pink mitts on, she picked up a pot of stewed potatoes and carried it off. Vallano took a moment to watch her hips and ass sway.

'Yeah. It's only been a month 'n' I can already tell he don't know howda run shit. I don't see how he hasn't ran the place inda the grahn yet.'

'Well juss wait 'cause tamarra he's gonna be runnin' *you* inda the grahn. CTS ain't nuh'n bahda big fuckin' mess. But, look, if he starts gih'n on yir shit, juss tell 'im da fuck off: 'at's what everyone else does. When it comes dahn do it, we're *his* boss. 'At's like our perk: we can do whadever want, 'n' he's afraid da stop us 'cause he knows no one else'll work for 'im; we juss don't get paid as much if we worked somewhere else.'

'*Ahh, this sucks.* I wanna go out 'n' get fucked up tonight. We've had everything planned all week, ya know. Everybody's gonna be out 'n' it's been so long.' Frustrated by the thought of a "ruined weekend," he turned away from Jeremiah. '*Minchia!*'

Jeremiah spoke in a low-key: 'Well if ya rilly wanna get oudda've it, den ya bedder take off 'cuzza wudder juss shut off 'n' he's gonna be dahn soon.'

'But I'm fuckin' starvin',' half-joked Vallano. 'We still hittin' up Fat Kats first?'

'Fuck yeah. Bikini night.'

'Ya rilly think I should juss take off so he can't ask me?'

'Hey, I don't care. I alriddy told 'im: if he wants meedda work, it ain't gonna be til after noon.'

'Ar'ight, look: I'm gonna go over da Eddie's now—' He stopped and waited for Kelly to disappear again. 'So juss stop 'ere 'n' 'en we'll round everyone up. But I neeja da grab my hat oudda my room before ya leave.'

'Wha'?'

'Well, I got my wallet 'n' shit on me. But look at my fuckin' hair. I can't go out like 'iss. So juss grab it before ya leave, ar'ight?'

'No. Go up 'n' gidit chirself.'

'Don't be a dick.'

'*Aww,* cawidge boy gadda look all purrdy for da broads at Fat Kats.' Meowing, Jeremiah began throwing friendly swings at Vallano; Vallano was swatting 'em away, worried that Jeremiah was actually trying to get the cat stuck in the bag.

'Look, motherfucker, juss tell 'em I ran dahn the store da get chew. Den I'll caw yir cell in five minutes 'n' say my Aunt Stella juss cawed 'n' needs meedda stop over.'

'Stop over for wha'?'

'*Da fix her fuckin' toilet,* you fuckin' buttplug. Juss tell 'em whadever. 'N' if Steve asks da talk da me—' Vallano froze.

'Eh, Kelly!' rang out the whiney voice from upstairs. 'Where's my fuckin' hair gel at?! I can't fuckin' find it!'

'It's all gone, Steeeve! I threw the bawdle away dis mornin'...'

'(Shit, I gadda gihdoudda here.)'

'Eh, where's he goin'?' rang out the voice of Kelly from the kitchen.

Vallano was tearing up pipe towards the front door with a plastic smile. The boss was coming!

Mid June

After weeks of unreturned voice mails, text messages, and occasionally, whenever he blocked his number, a pick up followed by a quick hang up, Ivy finally called. Unfortunately, he was passed out at the time. So she left a sweet voice mail: 'Remember what happened last time, Vinny? I don't wanna call the police again. I really don't. But you have to leave me alone. I'm livin' at home for the summer, so half the time my parents can hear my cell ringin' like crazy, and I don't wanna put it on vibrate because I'm expecting other calls. So, look, if you wanna leave me a text message or a voice mail once in a while and let me know how things are, that's fine. But just stop with the harassment. Bye.'

She wants him to let her know how things are? That's fine with her? YES! She's finally coming around! Sweet! He knew she would! As soon as the voice mail ended—(he took a second to thank God)—he called her because he was just so happy! Ring-a-ling-a-ding! My baby's comin' back da me so my he~~art~~ can sing!

'Hello, Vinny,' she answered indifferently. She answered! Sweet!

'Hey, how ya doin?'

'Good. Just been busy workin' two jobs.'

'Two? Doin' wha'?'

'Redstone's of course,' (the veterinarian's office) 'and I st~~art~~ed waitressing.'

'Rilly? Where at?'

'Hooters.'

'Ha, like you'd rilly work there. So sercly, where at? Don't tell me Chow Down.'

She kinda laughed. 'No. Up by the mall.'

'Can ya be a liddle more specific?'

'So how's *your* job goin', Mr. Plumber?'

'Ehh, it sucks. Not whad I thought idd be. First, I never know where I'm gonna be or what time I'm gonna be workin' to. 'N' I haven't been sleepin' much lately, but I still gadda get up so early, 'n' I'm usually all hungover—' (Wait, should he have said that? Hungover?) '—Well, I'm not hungover all the time, but me 'n' the guys'll go out for a drink a couple times a week, ya know. Buh da whole experience has me realize: da workin' class ain't too fun.'

'Yeah, I can imagine. But at least you won't have to deal with it much longer.'

'Hey, lemme ask you sum'n—you miss me, Wimp-Wimp? 'Cause I miss you like crazy. Every day 'n' night, I'm tryin'ah figure out wha' went wrong—ya know, the mistakes I made—'n' juss prayin' thit the truth'll somehow come da light. I mean, I know there's things I shoulda—'

'Hold on, Vinny,' she said aloofly; she began talking to her mother or sister. He couldn't believe it: she was actually staying on the phone this long and hearing him out! 'Okay. Hey, I have to go help my family with a few things.'

'Cancha talk juss a liddle longer? I miss hearin' yir voice.'

'I dunno. How's your mother? She's so sweet. Is she still in Catania?'

'Yeah. I talked da her a couple times a week. She seems priddy happy. She rilly wants meedda move 'ere when I graduate.'

'Aww. You should. I'm sure you'll meet a nice Sicilian girl.'

'I don't wanna meet any other girl.'

'Well, still. I think that would do you good: just get out of America. I don't think you were meant to be here.'

'Wouju ever wanna move da Catania or somewhere else overseas?'

'No. I'm pretty happy here. I mean, I'll probably move away from here—maybe like California or Florida where the weather's nicer.'

'The weather in Catania is so amazin'. 'N' it's so scenic. You got da Ionian Sea 'n'—'

'Vinny, you've never even been there.'

'Yeah, but I know whad it's like. I've read about it, seen pictures, 'n' of course know people who *do* live 'ere. But I'd honestly move anywhere as long as yir with me.'

'Okay. I'm gonna go now. Take care of yourself. And have fun plumbin'.' *Wait—Okay? She said okay?!* Did she really just consent to moving anywhere with him?! She did! Sweet!

'You rilly gadda go?'

'Yes. I'm bein' called.'

He sighed. 'Ar'ight. Ya know, I wish I could power up on yir hair right now.'

'You still have that lock, don't you?'

'Yeah, but it's juss not da same.'

'Well it'll have to do.' She probably meant it'll have to do for now, til he returns to Aristod.

'Hey?'

'What?'

'I love you.' (Pause) *'POWER UP, WIMP-WIMP!!!'* (Pause) 'Now you say it.'

'Power up.'

'No, in the voice.'

'Power up.'

He chuckled in the squirrel voice; she hung up.

One evening Vallano called his mother and, to her surprise, asked for the exact location of his father's grave. She explained as best as she could. Although Richard Vallano was buried in the cemetery next to their church, it was large and he was amid old relatives his son couldn't remember visiting. Nevertheless, his son now knew approximately where to find him. He just never went looking. He kinda wanted to, but he couldn't imagine what would happen there. The thought of him standing over his dead father scared him. What would he even say to him? It also scared him, and to greater extents, to think of visiting Pessi, but he knew he would. That was his best friend. They could talk all night long. He just hadn't got drunk enough yet.

Over the course of three days, Vallano (desperate to switch jobs) ended up funneling $20 to Ben, another summertime helper. The situation arose because, known for not keeping the same workers on the same job from start to finish, which caused communicative turmoil for the workers, Steve pulled Vallano away from Sandino by assigning him to work at Walmart with Teeny and Dent. Ben didn't mind switching (probably would've done it for free) because it also kept him with the crew he was most content with: his brother (Teeny) and the stupidest person alive (Dent). Still, Ben couldn't help but ask Vallano why he was so bent on not working at Walmart, to which Vallano dryly replied, 'Religious beliefs.' ☺

At another corporate job, union workers had hateful signs posted around the site letting everybody know that non-union workers were "stealing" jobs away. For the entire week, the union workers eyed Vallano and Sandino with contempt. At one point, words were exchanged, and, having a bad temper but not a union card or even a plumber's license, Sandino was close to knocking a union worker out with a large pipe wrench. But Vallano calmed him down by convincing him that they should just leave and spend the rest of the day at a bar. So Sandino took him to a dive joint in his old neighborhood in Monport. Before going in, Sandino asked if he had any "protection." Vallano didn't, but Sandino had a blade on him. The place was calm inside; kinda sad, though, when you have to watch your back while you're just trying to relax and have a mid-afternoon beer. Seemed like Vallano couldn't get away from violence, or the threat of violence, no matter where he went. Oh well! Safe from pipe wrenches and claw hammers, he drank on! For some reason, he always got drunk quicker—and the effects seemed heavier—whenever he drank during the day. But one clear and sober scenario kept running through his mind: He was envisioning himself telling all those union workers that his father had once been in the union, too, and somebody *did* take his job away, but it hadn't been because of someone like him. No, not someone like him or Sandino or even Glenn the racist...

Mid July
Sandino Camilleri was half-Sicilian, half-Okinawan. Like Vallano's mother, Sandino's mother had immigrated to America in her late teens, but she wasn't Sandino's Sicilian half. Sandino's parents met in the 50s when his father was stationed in Okinawa; after his military tenure ended, he brought his Okinawan girlfriend back to the States and married her. They raised Sandino and his sister in Monport. And although the Camilleris were a strict traditional family not strapped for cash, they lived in one of the roughest neighborhoods on the Eastside. But Sandino made it through to become a thirty-three-year-old father of a fifteen-year-old girl and a four-month-old boy, only concerned with their welfare. He'd grown up as a traditional (dark-skinned) skinhead worried about *other* things; this was back in the 80s when the area was becoming populated with racist skins, while traditional skins were moribund. He told Vallano that you had no choice in Monport: if you wanted protection, you either ran with the skins

or the blacks; in his high school, the jocks had no true unity, no true "muscle," and as a result, if they had the balls to run their mouth, they were beaten up, stabbed, or shot. Sometimes, the skins and the blacks would fight together against the jocks just for the sake of fighting, but more frequently and more violently, they fought against "outsiders." The skinhead and black movement in Monport wasn't wholly built around race or class warfare; it was predominately about territory. But Sandino didn't need to tell Vallano all this because he knew it growing up and ventured through Monport with his friends or visited family there. It was around the decline of the mills when Monport became a very territorial place where a turn down a wrong street could get you shot. On top of the hill in Verna, most territorial problems stemmed from shining one's pride, not protecting underground economics, and you would only end up in the hospital, instead of the morgue.

Although thirty-three with gray hairs sneaking into his shaved brown head, Sandino looked around Vallano's age. "Baby-faced" some would say. But if you ever said that to him, and he didn't know you, he wouldn't hesitate to knock you out no matter how big and bad you are. The notorious scraper stood around 5'4" with broad shoulders and cut (not big) but cut muscles; you could sense the Asian agility in him. But his skin! So Sicilian-brown! Could've been mistaken for half-black! (Glenn the racist never hesitated to call him a little monkey-looking nigger.) But the true color of Sandino's skin was tattoo. He didn't have "sleeves" like Jeremiah, for Sandino's work wasn't "colored in," but he did sport an array of singular images, most in the traditional style: the face of Christ on his right inner-bicep; a Japanese pinup on his right forearm; a generic mermaid on his left forearm; a brilliantly-shaded teal rope around his left wrist; a spider web on his right elbow; sailor stars here and there; even his daughter's name across his stomach. If it wasn't for his height and dominate pop-eyes—eyes as fathomable as a Margaret Keane caricature!—from a distance you would've thought Sandino was—well, Pessi. Even the same personality: laidback and smirky, but if you pushed the wrong button, you had better run because a bomb was about to explode. Didn't open up about serious issues unless it was one-on-one. Loved strictly old-school Punk, Oi!, and Hardcore; Social D was one of his favorite bands too! But what really had Vallano's head spinning: Sandino had a tattoo of a burning bottle with a banner across it that said Sick Boy: the name of a Social D song. But in Vallano's mind it rang reminiscent of Struck by the Fuck. So the thing about not wanting to work at Wal-mart wasn't just about Vallano's tongue-in-cheek "religious beliefs"; he just didn't want to be "pulled away" from Sandino because he felt like (almost *thought* that) he was working with Pessi. Of course he never said anything like that to Sandino. That's grounds for insanity! It was just comforting to have this strong intuitive feeling that they would've been best friends if Vallano had been born ten years earlier and raised in Monport, or if Sandino had been born ten years later and raised in Verna...

...Sandino and Vallano were doing copper work at an enormous two-story building set become a textile warehouse. They were on the first floor inside the men's bathroom, which was just a bunch of steel beams that you could walk in between; other rooms, though, were becoming closed off as the carpenters hung drywall. A lanky electrician with a goatee had just entered the bathroom to ask Sandino some questions about a matter in another room. Meanwhile, Vallano was down on his knees. He pulled over a piece of one-inch copper pipe. Angled it across the top of his work boot. Measured out thirty-eight and a half inches. Marked the measurement by slamming down in a husking motion the marking-tip on his copper-cutters. Then hooked the copper-cutters over the pipe. Slid it up a bit to align the wheel-blade with the measurement. Tightened the ball-grip on the bottom of the copper-cutters. Then gyrated the copper-cutters around and around and around and around and around...til the piece of pipe it hit the concrete. CHING! He loved the chime of accomplishment!

Break time! Sandino said that he would be over in a minute; he had to show the electrician some stuff in another room. In the construction world, where trades come together, and the confluence of goals from each trade runs the risk of conflicting with the overall goal, plumbers and electricians generally get along, while plumbers, especially the O'Malley crew, often clashed with carpenters. In Vallano's eyes, carpenters didn't even fit in with the rest of the construction workers. Not that a carpenter isn't working-class, but all they really do is measure, cut, and hang: the labor itself minimal. Whereas, a plumber's tasks are many, and at times, very physical, entailing knowledge of a variety of parts, tools, and machinery, as well as the application of tricky calculations. In his experience thus far, Vallano thought the carpenters tended to give off a pompous air, as if fellow alum Jesus Christ was strictly on their side. Vallano was always catching a carpenter walking around as if they were the almighty foreman. And the ones on this job fit the stereotype to a tee! Bob and Harry! And if you were there, you knew their names within minutes! Every time Bob the elder would yell out a measurement, it was like: 'Hey, Harry! I need, uhh, twelve dahn, four 'n' six-'n'-three-quarters out, Harry!' Then his young sidekick Harry would yell back: 'Ar'ight, Bob! Eh, Bob?!' – 'Yeah, Harry!' – 'I like you, Bob!' – 'Yir not so bad jirself, Harry!' It was like they had to be reacquainted every time a new piece of drywall needed cut! And just the way they said each other's name was so pompous and, colloquially speaking, so gay! (Jesus certainly wouldn't have approved, of this vanity!) And their humor was so lame! And Harry sung a lot! Vallano hated it so much! Stupid songs, awful voice! And Bob was always lurking behind him and Sandino! asking condescending questions! or throwing in his two-cents with regard to their personal conversations because Bob was older and thus thought himself wiser! not knowing he wasn't much older than Sandino! Vallano was just waiting for Bob to utter "baby face" so Sandino could shut him up! Somebody needed to knock these carpenters down a bloody peg or two! Vallano would even personally wash the hands of whoever did!

After grabbing his working-man's lunch box out of the van, Vallano walked back up to the front of the building. It was like a large porch because the second floor jutted out like a roof, and the air was blowing in freely from the parking lot since there weren't front walls or doors yet. In this area, off to the left, Vallano spotted two plastic lawn chairs and decided to take a seat. Then he pulled out his pudding, pealed the foil top back, and stuck his plastic spoon down into the rich vanilla. About three spoonfuls in, Bob (who was about ten years Christ's senior) came walking over with a lit cigarette hanging from his lip, yet still able to speak fast and rambly: 'Ose are my fuckin' chairs.'

A nonchalant pause. 'Ar'ight. Well I didn't know whose 'ey were.'

'Well der mine.'

'You on break or sum'n?'

'I'm goin' on it now so get up.'

'Okay, but ya don't gadda gidda fuckin' attitude about it.'

Bob promptly walked away, shaking his head. Vallano remained seated in Bob's throne, eating his pudding. Well, a few minutes later—(he'd now moved on to his Swiss cheese/American cheese sandwich)—Bob and his sidekick came back holding their working man's lunch boxes at the waist, ready to eat. Bob stepped forward; Harry sat down in the other lawn chair, which was straight across from Vallano, who was apparently sitting in the lawn chair Bob wanted to sit in.

'Didn't I juss tell ya deezer my fuckin' chairs?!'

'Cahm the fuck dahn; der fuckin' lawn chairs for Christ's sake.'

'Hey I didn't bring 'em from home juss so every fuckin' asshole here can sit on 'em.'

Asshole, eh? Vallano dropped his Swiss cheese/American cheese sandwich into his working-man's lunch box, closed the lid, picked it up with his right hand, stood up from the lawn chair, then reared back his left leg and kicked the lawn chair out towards the parking lot. Three munching masons sitting on a two-foot wall running along the sidewalk, froze at the sight, watching the chair do cartwheels passed them.

'I'm tellin' ya,' Bob began, 'ya bedder go get my chair right now.' He turned to his sidekick. 'You see dis liddle prick, Harry?'

Little prick, eh? Well, Vallano's vision instantly went red, and he would've punched Bob with his free hand or smashed him in the face with his working-man's lunch box right then and there if it wasn't for Steve O'Malley; amid the redness, Vallano could see that if he did take action it would come back on Steve and his business; plus make Jeremiah look bad, perhaps worsen Jeremiah's relations at home; and of course there was the chance Steve would throw Vallano out of his house. So despite all the inner stress, sore muscles, and mental provocation, he kept himself tamed.

'Go fuckin' get it now.'

'Ar'ight, *Bob.* I'm sorry, *Bob.* I'll go get it, *Bob.*'

With his working-man's lunch box swinging at his side, Vallano strolled straight passed the lawn chair...and down to the van, which was parked next to the curb out front. He opened up the passenger-side door, hopped up on the seat, rolled down the window, and continued eating his American cheese/Swiss cheese sandwich. Just as Bob was picking up the lawn chair, motherfucking Vallano under his breath, Sandino came walking out of the skeletal abyss. He was already smirking as if knew Vallano had something to do with it. He walked down to the van, opened up the driver-side door, and hopped up on the seat. Vallano began telling him the story. They were both laughing as they watched Bob and Harry sit on their plastic thrones.

Mid August

Vallano was now officially twenty-one, and as a result Robert Louis Albini died. (But some say the ghost of Albini still flies around the bars in LaSalle...*oooeeewwww!)* Being twenty-one hardly brought any change to his life besides an ounce less of paranoia. It certainly hadn't made him more bibulous because he already reached the apex. For the majority of the summer, he'd been following the same drunken schedule: Wake up at 6:30 a.m.; throw on his work jeans, work shirt, and work boots; drive to the shop; find out who he's working with; drive with 'em to the job site; work; take lunch around 12:00 p.m.—sometimes for two hours so he could drink at a bar; go back to work, feeling worn out til they called it quits, returning to the O'Malley's around 5 p.m.; then take a shower; eat; start writing, usually high, sometimes having a few drinks straight from the bottle; and he would write nonstop til bedtime around 11:00 p.m., unless he went to the bars, then it was a four-hour night of sleep which brought a suicidal 6:30 a.m. Sometimes, throughout these hours, he was leaving her sorrowful voice mails and text messages. Once in a while, she would return the text messages, saying things like "Im fine. Hows work? Hows ur mom?" – "R u drunk? Cant understand what u wrote" – "U need help." He could only return the last text message with: "I only need u".

But the weekends were fun and distracting. And now he had some extra money to throw around...

...He just threw down sixty beans on the bartop at Dis Co's. In exchange, the bartender handed him his debit card (needed to open a tab) and said she would be back with his change. But he said, 'Ahh, juss keep it, hun,' which meant a twenty-beans tip for her, and forty beans of alcohol in his gut; the ticket for the Hardcore show had only cost 1/5 of that! He hadn't been to a show in a while, and before getting drunk, it had felt so liberating to get out on the floor and release his self. So cathartic! Other outcasts dancing with him in the chaos! Dionysian in their aggression, yet seldom hurt because no one was out to hurt anyone, for they—straight-edgers and addicts, old-school or new-school—were all friends bonded by deeper things (theoretically), so numbed by the passion and energy (indeed). Yes, for a brief moment he slipped away from all the misery in the world, out amid hundreds of unknown sisters and brothers, swinging his arms around, throwing 'bows, stomping his legs around, even "pickin' up change." Once exhausted, he returned to the bar to watch the headliner. Once the drunkenness kicked in, he started dropping all his change.

He was now standing inside the caged bar, which was back behind the dance floor. Around him were Jeremiah, Dante, Eddie, Anson, Tim (an old friend), Teeny (from work), Morgan (used to work for O'Malley, also an old friend). Even sober Sandino was there but at the other end with his own crew. Having a family, Sandino rarely went out anymore; and seeing Sandino out made Vallano happy, especially since he was always trying to get him to hangout, for Sandino's punk heart still burned with youth.

'Let's go 'fore I fuckin' punchu,' slurred Vallano to Dante.

'We goin' out da the bars?' asked Eddie.

'No; I ain't got da money,' answered Dante. 'Besides, Anthony's havin' people over. So we can juss go over there. Free beer 'n' bitches.'

Even though Anthony Durkin recently got into Punk and Hardcore, he rarely went to the shows, even if Dante went, probably because the amoeba was so scared everyone there could see right through him, straight into the ephemerality and fakeness that sustained him.

'Ar'ight. I'll fuckin' go,' slurred Vallano. Then he yelled: 'I'm drivin'!'

Jeremiah laughed. 'Nah, yir one bir too drunk da drive.'

'No, I fuckin' drove here. 'N' it's *my* warhorse. 'N' I betcha nunna yinz even know *howda* fuckin' drive a warhorse, do you? Didn't think so. So fuck you; *I'm* drivin'.'

'Shotgun!' yelled Eddie.

'Shudup, you stupid motherfucker,' Vallano yelled. 'You know my rules: gadda fight for it. But I'll put my money on *you* 'cause I like *you*. You look like Wesley Snipes.' He put his arm around Eddie's neck and started squeezing hard; Eddie thought it was funny; he probably missed the youthful energy Vallano brought to the crew. And so Eddie was more than ready to vie for shotgun: one of the immature things that still riled him up; it used to be something he and Pessi would do, while Vallano watched with glee. One problem: Eddie had no competition tonight because Jeremiah and Dante—the other two riding with Vallano—weren't ones to push and shove for the front seat. So it was probably best for Eddie to support Jeremiah in not letting Vallano drive so *they*—Vallano and Eddie—could vie for shotgun.

Ten minutes later Vallano was starting to get really mad at Dante because he wouldn't stop talking to the bartender; Dante was under the impression that she liked him; Dante hadn't paid for his expensive tab of Guinness yet, so she was all over him, pretending to be buying into his blarney.

'Hey, April!' yelled Vallano; he knew her name because she'd been working at Dis Co's for years, and Vallano had been coming here for years.

'What, hun?'

'I like you 'n' 'at, buh Dante has herpes. *Yuuuck!* Right?'

Without waiting for her response, Vallano began zigzagging over to Sandino who was talking with his friends in 25 Ta Life, a band that had played earlier. Vallano told Sandino to go to Anthony's—told them *all* to go to Anthony's—but *all* declined. So he told Sandino that he was going to have Bob and Harry kick the shit out of him. Sandino told him to go burn some bras; at work, they would debate over *equality* because Sandino believed in the traditional role of women, and since Vallano didn't agree, Sandino called him a bra-burner. (Glenn the sexist never hesitated to call Vallano a little bra-burning faggot.) One time, Vallano told Sandino and Glenn that he was more like a bra-*dropper* because his charm and clarion call for equality is what drew the chicks in, made 'em drop their bras with ease, and kept 'em around in the long run if—key word—*if* he wanted to keep 'em around. Right...

...Outside, on the fourth level of a parking garage open to the orange and white lights spread across the hills of Pittsburgh, Vallano was ramming Eddie's head into the passenger-side window. (Without much of a fight, Vallano had given Jeremiah the keys.) Eddie had his arm wrapped around Vallano's waist, trying to reverse leverage, while stomping hard on Vallano's Docs. They hadn't even got the door open yet. Dante was in the backseat, driver's-side; months back, he enlisted in the army; Jeremiah thought Vallano already knew, so he never said anything, which is why Vallano didn't find out the news til earlier this night; when he asked why, Dante replied, 'I ain't tryin'ah be a fuckin' potato sacker da rest of my life'; Vallano told him that he wasn't a potato sacker; he was a *pallet driver;* nevertheless, Dante was ready to fight for freedom, including Vallano's freedom; he was looking forward to the next stage of training in two weeks, when he would be shipped out of state; *then* he could enjoy being far away from these nuts slamming each other's head into the window and stomping on each other's boots.

Jeremiah pushed the clutch and fired up the ol' warhorse. The radio was already blaring! Ears ringing, Jeremiah still heard Vallano yell, 'Lock da doors, Salley-O'-Malley!' Without breaking from the tussle, Vallano looked in through the window and yelled, 'Is it locked?!' – 'Yes!' So Vallano released Eddie. Jumped up on the bridge of the ol' warhorse's nose. Then climbed up on the saddle. Standing up, he raised both hands—then came flying off with a 'bow directed right at Eddie's head. Of course Eddie easily dodged it, but everyone was laughing besides Dante.

'Go 'head, Wesley. I don't even *want* shotgun. I wanna sit by Dante 'cause he's goin' bye-bye soon...Well—come on; openna fuckin' door! I won't hitcha, ya fuckin' pussy!'

Eddie opened the door, and Vallano shot straight into the backseat. Eddie sat down, shotgun secured. Jeremiah began backing the ol' warhorse out...and soon they were heading through dahntahn...then over a freshly-painted yellow bridge—Vallano was screaming, singing, and slapping the back of Eddie's head from one end to the other—and finally, getting off an exit that led into Fallwood, a southeast neighborhood about five miles from dahntahn, where Anthony lived...

...When they arrived, it was with many lessons learned: Eddie learned that sitting in shotgun, behind Vallano, requires staying turned around, facing the backseat; Jeremiah learned that manipulating the ol' warhorse is as frustrating as trying to get a Clydesdale to outrun a Quarter Horse; and Dante learned that it was time for his friends (*Vallano *cough*cough**) to grow up.

'Lemme da fuck out!' griped Vallano.

They began filing out. A few bodies were standing in Anthony's downward-sloped driveway, huddled around a shiny silver car, looking as if they were up to something. Two straight-haired girls were smoking cigarettes on the sidewalk. As soon as the one girl saw Jeremiah, she ran up and hugged him. Then Vallano heard Eddie say, 'Yo, wha' sup, Jenny Hustler?' to the other girl whose last name was Hossler. Instead of entering the large plain white-bricked house where everyone else was—and where Dante went without waiting for Da Hoolies—Vallano lit up a cigarette, butting in on Eddie's conversation with Jenny Hustler.

'Hey, Spagheddi, look: I wancha da go inside 'n' get Anthony da come out. But don't make it all suspicious, ya know. Tell 'em ya wanna show 'im sum'n.'

You could see on Eddie's face that he overstood Vallano's intentions. Still, Eddie asked, 'Wha' da fuck am I saposta be showin' 'im?—

Hey Jeremiah?!' Jeremiah was about to walk inside with the girl Vallano didn't know.

'Wha'?'

'Tell Durkin da come out. Tell 'im Jenny Hustler wansta talk do 'im.'

'Wha'?' remarked Jenny, pushing Eddie in a joking way. 'Why tell 'im 'at?'

'You'll see,' whispered Eddie.

A few minutes later, Anthony (who'd become a bit *chubby* but still had an unshaven face, owlish eyes, and an effeminate walk) came outside with Jeremiah and Dante, still attached to Dante's hip. The fear was already burning in his eyes as soon as he saw Vallano. But Vallano paid no mind to Anthony's presence by continuing to say whatever it was to Jenny that had her laughing and stroking his arm.

With a can of beer in his hands, Anthony walked up to Eddie and said what's up. He shook his hand and they exchanged friendly words. Then Anthony turned to Vallano:

'Wow, look who it is. Did you fall off the face of the earth? How's Aristod, man?'

Vallano shook his hand, sensing the fear in Durkin's voice and body language.

'It's ar'ight. Only got two semesters left. Juss back doin' some plumbin'...'

Just off the sidewalk, casually huddled in the grass, Dante and Jeremiah were now conversing with the two girls. Someone inside the house just turned the music up really loud. Anthony turned around—the front door was open a bit—and screamed for somebody to turn the music back down...but nobody did. He was about to walk back inside to do it himself—(turning the situation into an opportunity to "get away")—but Vallano quickly said, 'Yo, Anson do all yir new ink?' Anthony had a lot of tattoos now too.

'Yeah. He's doin' another one on my back next week. See you got more too.'

'Yeah, a few here 'n' 'ere, ya know. Hey, 'member Pess?'

'Huh?—' *BAM-BAM-BAM!!!* Anthony was dropped to the ground, twitching as Vallano started kicking his shielded ribs. *BAM!!!* Vallano was blindsided from the left; the punch turned him aside, almost knocking him to the ground but he kept himself up by using his hand as a pivot. When he turned back around it was to face Dante's fist coming right at him, connecting square on his chin. *BAM!!!* This time, Vallano *was* knocked to the ground. But he quickly got up and was in the first step of charging back when—*BAM!!!* Jeremiah smashed Dante. *BAM!!!* Eddie smashed Anthony downward as soon as he tried getting up. People were now rushing out of the house. Everyone was screaming! Bodies were everywhere! Vallano was looking for around *him*. Then—*BAM!!!* Another shot to Anthony's face. He was now bleeding from the mouth. As Vallano came back at him, Anthony stuck his hands out in front of him like "no! no! please get away! please!" but that kind of pathetic defense wasn't going to—*BAM!!!* Anthony was back on the ground. *BAM!!!* Vallano smashed somebody he didn't know in the face, then grabbed him from behind, around the neck, then slammed him to the ground. Since he didn't have time to waste on whoever that was, he got up, surveying the mêlée...til spotting Jeremiah and Dante. Jeremiah had Dante's body pressed down hard against the nose of the ol' warhorse, trying to keep him still with the weight of his entire body.

'I'm gonna kill 'at fuck!' yelled Dante.

Vallano walked towards them with a stone-cold glare; he didn't know Eddie was following behind; the rest of Anthony's fashionable friends stayed put in the yard, even the kid who Vallano randomly hit as was being held back by his friends. Jeremiah turned his head to see Vallano approaching with that stone-cold look in his eye.

'Stop, V!' yelled Jeremiah. 'It's over! Yinzer friends! It's done!'

'Fuck him!' spat Dante, struggling to break free.

'Cahm dahn, Dante! I'm not gonna let yinz fight!'

'Den why ja hit me?'

'Why ja hit V?'

''Cause he had no right da hit Anthony!'

Vallano bent his head down, looking right into Dante's sideway-pressed face.

'Fuck you, you sellout.'

'Lemme go, Jeremiah!' To Vallano: 'I'll fuckin' kill you, you liddle piece a shit!'

'Juss cahm dahn, Dante! Eddie, get V away from us. Now!'

Eddie didn't move; he didn't know what to do, who was whose friend anymore.

'Just let 'em go, Jeremiah. I don't give a fuck. He can beat me up. Won't change the fact he's a fuckin' sellout 'n' fucks Anthony in the ass. Fuckin' faggots.'

'Vallano!' shouted Anthony from the yard. 'Get the fuck oudda here right now or I'm cawin'ah cops.' Bleeding from the mouth, Anthony was surrounding by twenty of his friends.

Vallano turned around, smiling. In a cool, drunken tone: 'Dude, you sercly think I won't come back up 'ere 'n' beachir fuckin' head in again? 'N' yir friends ain't gonna do *shit*.' He looked them over collectively. 'I'll kill every wunna yinz motherfuckers.' He reached down into his boot and pulled out a switchblade.

'Come on, V; put dat shit away,' said Eddie in a cool tone.

He handed the blade over to Eddie. 'See, I don't need shit for yinz fuckin' faggot-ass pussies.' He stepped closer, into the yard. 'Come on; don't juss stand 'ere lookin' hard. I mean, 'ere's only three of us—'cause 'at faggot's obviously on yir side—'n' how many of yinz?'

Some girl screamed out, 'This is out of control! I'm callin' the cops!'

But Dante, with his face still pressed sideways against the ol' warhorse, screamed, 'No! Don't caw da fuckin' cops!'

Then Anthony said, 'Jackie, don't caw da cops.' He turned back to the broken Hoolies in the driveway. 'Yinz guys just leave, 'n' don't come back. It's over. No more fightin'. Everything's cool now, okay?'

Jeremiah into Dante's ear: 'I'm gonna letcha go, 'n' we're gonna leave, but if ya go after V, I'm gonna fuck you up. I mean, yir wunna my best friends, Dante, but I ain't gonna letcha touch 'im. Ar'ight?'

'Juss gih da fuck offa me.'

Jeremiah let him go. Dante rose up, looking murderous. Big Dante looked down on Little Vallano, while Giant Jeremiah kept his hand stuck out in between them.

'Ya know, Dante, I never did like you. We were only friends 'cause we grew up in the same neighborhood, but we ain't nuh'n alike. Took me years da figure that out.'

'Yeah, well I always thouchu were a liddle fuck, so it don't mean shit da me. Why dohnchu juss go back da cawidge. Yir the *rill* sellout.'

'Ar'ight,' interjected Eddie. 'Both yinz juss shudup. Yinzer drunk 'n' sayin' shit ya don't mean. Tamarra you'll be friends again, so juss let it drop.'

'Nah. I'll never be friends with him again,' said Vallano. He turned to Jeremiah: '*Mi nni futtu.*[6] (Saying this, he flung his hand up dismissively.) 'Let's juss get da fuck oudda here so he can go be with his *faggot* boyfriend.'

'Ya know wha'—' resumed Dante, 'you nee'dda grow the fuck up.'

'Ya know wha'—' rejoined V, '*si na testa ri minchia.*[7] So have fun gih'n yir *fuckin'* brains blown out—*you fuckin' faggot.*'

They lunged back at each other but Eddie and Jeremiah immediately grabbed and held 'em back, Eddie using all of his strength to pull Dante up into the yard.

"At's enough, V! Get in the fuckin' car! We're leavin'.' Under Jeremiah's command, Vallano walked around the front of the car and got shotgun without a fight...

...Later in the night, Vallano, Eddie, and Jeremiah were sitting on Eddie's front porch: a concrete slab with two lawn chairs. Eddie and Jeremiah were sitting in the chairs, Vallano down on the ledge of the concrete. Up to the right hung a light to the side of the door, highlighting the three friends drinking and conversing quietly. Vallano had puked a couple times but took a few painkillers then drank himself back into a state where, for thirty minutes straight, all he was saying was, 'I'm gonna have a black eye.' And Jeremiah or Eddie would say, 'You didn't even get hit in the eye, V.' And he would reply, 'Yeah, but my pinkie's broke.' (And it was. The top knuckle on his right pinkie was sticking up like a teepee, but he was too inebriated to feel the pain.) He would also lash out with: 'I hate Dante! Fuckin' hate 'im! Do yinz hate 'im *too?*' Then they would explain that they're all friends and everything will be all right tomorrow. That all cycled til out of nowhere Vallano said he was going to visit Pessi. He wanted to know where his grave was. Jeremiah said they would go tomorrow.

'No! Now! I wanna go now! All by myself! He's *my* best friend! Tell me or I'm gonna start screamin' loud as I can!'

'Shhhh. Come on, V; my parents 'n' sisters are sleepin'.'

'(Den tell me where my best friend is),' he whispered.

Eddie turned to Jeremiah. They bore the faces suburban parents give each other when their little twelve-year-old Alex wants to go out with his friends for the first time *without* parental supervision. Finally, Jeremiah said, 'Fine, V. I'll drive ya over.'

'Will ya lemme be alone with 'im?'

---

[6] [scn] Like saying, "I don't give a fuck."

[7] [scn] You're fuckin' stupid. [Literally, "You have a head of dicks."]

'Yeah. I'll wait inna car.'

'No! I wanna sleep 'ere!'

'*Shhhh.* You can't sleep 'ere. You'll get arrested.'

'(No, I won't),' he whispered. '(It's like four o'clock inna mornin'.)'

'No, it's only one-thirdy.'

'I don't give a fuck if it's a fuckin' million-thirdy! Juss show me where da fuck my best friend is 'n' lemme sleep 'ere!'

'*SHHHHH!*'

'(Juss lemme sleep 'ere. I'll come back tamarra. Promise...)'

...The graveyard was small. It was next to a small white church that the Pessinis never attended. The only lighting was a dull streetlight twenty yards away, and over four hundred million yards away, a waning crescent moon. After parking in the empty lot, Jeremiah gave the ol' warhorse a rest and began telling Vallano to keep it down outside because—Vallano heedlessly slung the stall gate, unconcerned with Jeremiah's warnings. Standing at the withers of the ol' warhorse, Vallano crossed his arms, bearing a sloppy, angered, impatient look. Passing through no cemetery gates, Jeremiah walked him towards the grave...up in the back corner, next to his mother. Vallano stood to the side of the headstone, looking down for a minute, flooded with befuddlement.

'Go home, Jeremiah. I wanna sleep here.'

'No. Juss do whacha gadda do. I'm gonna go wait inna car. But don't be long. It's late 'n' I'm tired as fuck.' After saying something to Pessi, Jeremiah walked back to the car...and sat in the front seat, watching, but out of earshot.

Meanwhile, Vallano had dropped to his knees, to the left of Pessi's head, placing Pessi's mother to Vallano's back.

'Hey, Pess. Look, who's here: it's me—V. You in Heaven? Hey, should I sit onna other side so I'm not in between you 'n' yir mum?' He rose up, stumbled around the backside of the headstone, and dropped to his knees on Pessi's right side. 'So I beat Anthony up tonight 'n' got into it with Dante too. I hate him. Hate everyone. Ya know, Dante thinks he's so cool now 'cause he joined the army. Wait, you know all 'iss? You in Heaven now? I wanna godda Heaven. Hey, can ya ask God da make Ivy come back da me 'n' I'll promise da be good. Hey, Pess? *Talk* da me. I won't tell anyone. See my new tats?' He went to take his shirt off—and fell over backwards. He began rolling around, fighting with his shirt...til he had it in his hands; he threw it back behind him. 'Look, Pess—I gotchir name inked across my tit,' he laughed. 'But don't fuckin' suck it 'cause I'm all oudda milk. Whoops, I prahblee shouldn't swear 'cuzza yir mum huh? Does she care?' He projected his voice over to Pessi's mother: 'Hey, Mrs. Pessini. Sorry for swearin' but me 'n' Pess are best friends. You 'member me: Vinny?—Vallano?—I lived dahn the block. 'Member I yoosta come over when I's liddle 'n' you'd always give me a Kool-aid popsicle? I loved dose things. Ya know, I always thought you 'n' Ma shoulda left 'ose assholes a long time ago. We coulda all gone somewhere far away, like Catania—'at's where Ma's at now.' He turned back to Pessi. 'Hey, Pess. Look at *this* tat.' He showed the plot his inner right forearm. The tattoo was a large red heart with one half heavily shaded with black to give it the traditional look. Behind the heart were crossed sledgehammers dripping blood from the edges of the heads. Across the chest of the heart, two banners waved closely together, tinted here and there with gold. In black italic lettering, the banners read *Forsan Miseros...Meliora Sequentur.* 'It's a Latin quote by Virgil. It says: "For dose in misery...perhaps bedder things will follow." Ya like it, Pess? It's my favorite one so far. Man, I'm priddy fucked up right now. I wanna godda sleep here but Jeremiah won't let me. Hey, Pess, ya prahblee don't wanna hear 'iss, but ya know wha' Teresa said...' He began explaining all that had happened; sometime in between, Jeremiah yelled out the window for him to come on. '...So don't worry; it's either 'at or it's over, ya know. I tolja, I'll never let it go. *Never.* No madder what *anyone* says. I swear, dey brainwashed Ivy 'n' made her turn against me. But I'll get her back; don't worry. Hey, Pess—where you think we go when we die? Juss kiddi—' (hiccup) 'kiddin'. Hey, Pess—is my widdle Razzu dere? He prahblee is, huh? Look, I wanchada tell everyone, all my friends 'n' my family 'n' Johnny Cash 'n' even Rick 'cause I—' (hiccup) 'I overstand now. But tell 'em all I said hello 'n' tell Razzu I said *POWER UP!!! HMHMHMH!!!*—' (hiccup) '—Don't fuckin' laugh at me, you smirky asshole. Or, or I'll kill you!!!' Vallano started rolling around on the ground, laughing and hiccupping...pounding his fist down on Pessi's chest because he couldn't catch his breath. 'Hey, Pess! You shoulda seen when I hit Anthony! I go, "Eh, you dumb amoebic whore! 'Member my best friend Pessi?!"' (Jeremiah just shut the door; he was now walking towards Vallano whose voice was echoing out into the street.) "N' he goes, "Huh?" 'N' I blasted that motherfucker so hard he dropped straight da the grahn!—TWITCHIN'!!! 'N' 'en I started kickin' his ribs 'n'—shiiit! Gadda go, Pess! (But I'll be back 'fore I go back da school, ar'ight?) I love you!'

Vallano was tearing up bones towards the darkness with an earthy smile. The boss was coming!...

...By running full speed ahead and slipping into the shadows, he managed to escape. He wasn't even sure if Jeremiah had pursued him very far, but he didn't want to chance it, so he ran for his life. Promptly after, Jeremiah called his cell. Vallano answered and said that he was going to visit Razzle. Jeremiah wanted to know where at. But wisely, drunken Vallano pleaded the 5th. He hung up then shut his cell off...

...After forty-five minutes of walking around without a shirt on, with his hands shoved down in his pockets in an attempt to make himself walk straighter, he was now staggering around the streets of Monport. Not many people to be seen. Only a few passing cars. Everything was closed besides a couple gas stations and a come-when-you're-drunk restaurant. Not hungry or needing gas, he continued heading blindly down an uneven sidewalk, the one next to the main drag (because he knew it well), but didn't want to be (because of cops). So at the next block, he turned right...went down a block where an alleyway lay straight ahead...cut through...and began staggering through residential streets...After another twenty minutes or so, he found himself in a dark ominous neighborhood. He couldn't recall ever having been here before. The street was lined with huddy two-story Section-8s: most were either red with white porches or dirty gold with brown porches, the "porch" being a ratty plank that ran, without division, from door-one down to door-ten. Here and there sat metal chairs and oddly shaped shadows that could've passed for porch furniture but very well could've been stuff for the garbagemen. Presently, he passed a building with a bike pit out front where tenants collectively locked up their transportation. Although this wasn't the way Vallano would've headed to Dellwood by car (or bike), he was pretty sure he was heading in the right direction to get to the pet cemetery above the river...

...As he walked deeper into this neighborhood, he felt increasingly sleepier. He didn't even have cigarettes or chew to keep him focused. One half of his brain was telling him to lie down on the sidewalk and go to sleep; the other half was saying Razzle wanted—*needed* a visit too. Luckily, Razzle kept him moving along by chewing up his brain, as well as flashing before his eyes Razzle's smoke-colored tail that used to comfort both whenever Vallano playfully tugged on it. That longing for tactility kept him moving along and along...til he came upon three black guys about to get into a metallic red beater parked along the curb.

'Yo, yinz guys know the pet cemetery in Dellwood?'

They looked at him as if he was out of his mind. This short visibly drunken kid around their age, coming right up to 'em without a shirt on, with lots of tattoos, asking 'em about a pet cemetery at 3:30 a.m.! The one on the driver's side leaned across the roof and folded his hands together. The other two, standing in front of Vallano on the sidewalk, glanced at each other. One said, 'Where ya from, liddle man?'

'*Liddle man?* Look, I'm juss tryin'ah go see my dog Razzle. Which way?'

The one standing by him who hadn't asked the question said, 'Kid's determined, ain't he?' with a look of comical surprise. 'Shit, didn't even have time da get dressed.'

'If yinz dunno, juss tell me. I ain't got time for fuckin' games.'

The comically-surprised one suddenly balked at him—but Vallano wasn't impressed. His friend stuck out his arm and told him to just chill. Then he said, 'Muss got a priddy big set of balls da be comin' 'round here in the dead of night by yirself.'

Vallano flashed a face of disgust. 'Wha', am I saposta be scared or sum'n 'cause yir black? I mean, I know 'iss is yir neighborhood 'n' all, but I'm juss askin' for directions: 'at's all.'

How are three young black males in the ghetto supposed to respond to that? He's talking about race in this situation? Somebody just shoot him and get it over with!

'Where ya from, liddle skin?' *Liddle* = short; *skin* = no shirt.

'Next door.'

'You live *here?*'

Vallano laughed because the more temperate one asking the questions had a high-pitched voice and a funny deliverance. 'No, I mean, next door as in Verna.'

'Oh okay. See, Mikey: kid's ar'ight.'

'I'm no stranger da Monport. Got family over on Belle Ave.'

'You in Arnik, liddle skin. Monport's over dere.' The temperate one pointed out into the darkness. Vallano hadn't realized he'd walked clear into Arnik, a small borough further south and westbound than Monport but still right along the river, and sunk deep in poverty—the whole place just drowning in poverty.

'Oh, Arnik. Well I'm still up onna hill in Verna. I'm juss all drunk 'n' wanna fine'ah pet cemetery in Dellwood. I know where idd is but I'm juss all drunk 'n' can't find it. How much longer dahn 'iss road is it?'

'Well first ya wanna turn around 'cause you walkin' inna wrong direction—'

'Bess caw a cab,' advised the driver.

'Why don'*jinz* juss gimme a ride—ya know, if yinz ain't in a rush da get anywhere or nuh'n. I'll even give ya twenty bucks. It's all I got. Yinz guys juss gadda promise not da kill me. But if ya do, ya gadda dump my body next da my dog Razzle—at da pet cemetery in Dellwood.'

They all thought that was funny. So they gave Little Skin a ride to the edge of Dellwood, and for only *ten* bucks because that's all Little Skin had. But he made up for short-changing 'em by knowing the underground rapper they were bumping: you could say they never saw *that* coming but it really impressed 'em. So let the new aphorism ring: 'Fearless respect, good humor, musical knowledge, misdirection pointed in the right direction, and a little cash, all goes a long way in the ghetto!' But jeez! he actually did that! Little Skin could've been shot and killed!...

...He staggered onto the hillside pet cemetery. Being close to the river, he felt the difference in the air. The ground was sodden. He suddenly heard the echoing roar of a tractor-trailer zooming by on the highway down below the hill. But he went straight to work, only worried with observing the headstones. The engravings were visible thanks to the collective light of the crescent moon up above, the reflection of the city lights in the river down below, and the actual lights of the city just off to his left. Yet his blurred vision and sleepiness were being counterproductive. He was walking down the rows, mostly filled with dogs, cats, and birds, taking a minute at each headstone to read it...then letting it register in his head as either *yes* or *move on*. He moved on...and on...and on...back and forth...back and forth...til he tripped and fell. He was now atop the grave of Cody, a tabby-colored Maine Coon that had weighed 17 LBS and lived from 1987-1999. He jerked forward a bit but didn't have the energy to get back up. One half of his brain was yelling at him to get up and find Razzle!; the other half was softly saying, *no, just go to sleep*. Yes, maybe a little catnap *would* do him good, *then* he could find Razzle, with a *clearer* mind. Yeeeeeees—NOOOOOOO! can't fall asleep! Gadda find Razzle *now!*—Nooooo, sleeeeeeep...His eyelids began closing heavily for seconds at a time...then springing back wide open with authority!...but – slooooowly – faaaaalling – baaaaaack – dooooown: cyclical caresses and jerks. In the head-bobbing process, he kept looking all around: *gray headstones (—)(—) black hill (—)(—) gray empty highway down below (—) (—) blackish-green river just beyond (—)(—) green-orange-white fluorescence dahntahn (—)(—) greenish-black river again (—)(—) orange lights all across South Side Slopes...*(he lies back into a full supine state)...*opaline crescent moon (—)(—) far off in the distance...opaline – crescent – moon...*blinkity-blink-blink—

MORE THAN JEW CAN CHEW

"Your hair in my mouth,
On my tongue, between my teeth,
If you only knew what it does to me,
If you only knew the feeling in the taste of your hair,
Your hair, your hair, oh your sweet beautiful hair,
When I die make sure they stuff my mouth with your hair,
Sounds silly but, baby, at least it's real and sincere..." [1]

...He was holding his breath as he walked down the fluorescent hall. The sweat of his palm was causing his suitcase to slip from his grip. If he only knew beforehand what was ahead of him! The Scholar at the front desk hadn't been able to figure out what Vallano was in store for because he just started working here and didn't know where the papers were since *most* students had checked in over the weekend, and here Vallano was showing up Sunday evening again!

'Cara should know. She's over in the rec room. I can go ask her.'

'No, 'at's ar'ight. I guess I'll juss see for myself. Thanks'o.' That's when Vallano went walking down the fluorescent hall, holding his breath, with slippy palms.

Before leaving for the summer, he'd put in a request not to have a roommate for his final year. Under REASON WHY, he'd boldly written: *My final two semesters are going to require constant studiousness. For this reason, I do not want to chance having a roommate who is inconsiderate and frequently parties. Furthermore, I have been a student here for four years, in the same room, so I think my seniority should count for something, considering some students are matriculated with single rooms already prepared for them.*

Well, it was time to find out if his mauvemailish request paid off. He set his suitcase down...slid the golden key into the lock, reading himself for yet another twist...the pangs of uncertainty were already sweeping over him in hot flashes!...but at this point in his life he could no longer push them away...so he pushed open the plain wooden door of room 122...to see that no one was inside except for—Jesus Christ...just kidding, ddikts ;)...he sighed and closed his eyes, thanking the Lord that he would be alone in his room for his last year...while, beneath the deep blacklining, the prayer that he wouldn't be alone forever outside these walls continued self-cyclically...

...After unpacking his things, he text-messaged Ivy to let her know he was back at school "so would u like to go get somethin to eat?" Twenty minutes later, his cell chirped. He sat down on his bed and read the long reply which came as three separate texts but was likely one long text coming from her end. In full it read: *No. U got 2 stop this ok? Im already worried cuz ur back now. I told my parents. They want me 2 get another tpo but i said no. Please dont make me get 1. Dont want u 2 get n trouble. I*

---

[1] Lyrics from "Mouthin' off Again" by Zippy Zane, from the album *Folk Ballads for and by the Happily Mentally Deranged*

dont live n Bennet anymore. My new place is unlisted. I dont hate u but also dont trust u. Dont take it 2 heart. Remember the bible says "this 2 shall pass" so youll be all right, SCREWY! Haha! Power up!

He set the phone down. So confused....*Screwy?* He isn't Screwy, is he? Had Ivy ever called him that before? He thought he'd only told her that Screwy is the name of one of his squirrel friends. And why was she being harsh?—then suddenly funny? A subtle hint that she actually wanted to be with him but also wanted to see how he would handle this? see whether or not he would go off his nut and thus prove if he's the kind of person she wants to be with? And *Power up!?* Had she taken a liking to that? Did she power up on her own now? Did she take her hair, put it inside her mouth, and then (in *her* version of *his* Screwy voice) say, '*POWER UP!!!*' while thinking of him and experiencing the most indescribable sensation in the world? And *this too shall pass?* [2] *Gam zeh ya'avor?!* Then why isn't this feeling of wanting to kiss her soft, pale, protuberant lips for the rest of his life passing?! Not even abating! And this feeling never would, he is certain, for he tasted (even feasted on) the Eternal Power of God in those soft, pale, protuberant lips...

...The following day—after the second day of fall classes—he took a drive to the orchard. He hadn't decided if he was up for a walk *inside*...but the prospect was instantly quelled anyway when he saw the FOR SALE was gone. He pulled into the driveway...looked around...drove up to the small house...looked around...drove back down...looked around...then turned back towards Aristod. It started coming up through him again. He was trying to push it back down. He was growing so hot. Things weren't looking right. He needed something to stop *it*. So he finally began asking the questions out loud. (He even turned the music down—committing a sin in the process—just so his voice could be heard.) He screamed, 'Ya know, what've I ever done so wrong?! I only want a few things in life, 'n' 'ey aren't superficial things like everyone else wants! I've stayed true to You! Yet those who haven't are the ones with all their stupid wishes fulfilled—never losin', always gainin'! Why don't You juss take my mother away too?! Wait! Ya kinda did, huh?! I mean, I guess I'm happy *she's* happy, 'n' I *did* push for it, but jeeze! It's like Murphy's Law rilly *does* gadda holda me! But, God, I can't deal with it anymore! It's too surreal! Too much for my head! Lately, I been havin' serious problems copin' with reality! I'm always feelin' so fuckin' displaced! It's like at any minute I'm gonna slip inda some irrevocable state of insanity! I mean, look at me! I'm drivin' 'n' screamin' through the roof! It's like I'm crazy but not crazy enough da not acknowledge it! Is 'iss sercly the life I gadda live da become an artist?! If so, I don't want it anymore! Pass the torture da someone else! You hear me?! I don't want THIS! You've taken

---

[2] Although "this too shall pass" isn't said in *The Bible*, it is associated with 2 Peter 3:10-11: "But the day of the Lord will come as a thief in the night; in which the heavens shall pass away with a great noise, and the elements shall melt with fervent heat, the earth shall also and the works that are therein shall be burned up. Seeing then that all these things shall be dissolved, what manner of persons ought ye to be in all holy conversations and godliness." *Gam zeh ya'avor* is Hebrew for "this too shall pass."

enough away from me! No, You've taken *everything* away from me! I mean, is my life some kinda blank tablet You wanna fill up with ironic jokes?!...I dunno, God; I'm sorry. You know I'm not questionin' You oudda hate or anything like 'at. I mean, You know how I am 'n' my reasoning for how I live 'n' think. I juss hope You overstand me on *deeper* level beyond these words. Either way, please—*please*, God, juss make Ivy come back. If not, juss take me too, 'n' make it soon, 'cause I refuse da live like 'iss. I'm sercly goin' crazy. I swear, You can take everything else away—*everything*—juss show me there's *some* kinda salvation here. Please, God; all I want is her...'

...Three days later, after tugging on the mnemonic cords of his memory, a spark of cleverness hit him: he remembered the name of the realtor who was selling Jack's property. So he called and asked if it had been sold...only to find out the owner had decided to take it off the market. And whom, according to the newspaper, had it been bequeathed to? *Abigail McArdle*, Jack's daughter who still lived in the area—the loyal daughter who, with her husband, had tried taking care of aging Jack, and although aging Jack didn't want that—he could still flex his muscles!—he knew in his heart that Abigail was *loyal blood.* So now Vallano wanted to call Abigail to find out what was going on. Had her father's ghost chewed her out for trying to sell his fruitful memoirs? If so, had she suddenly decided to move in herself? thereby taking away his and Ivy's orchard? What if she wanted to spend the rest of her life there?! He needed to know! He just wasn't sure if he wanted to express an interest in the place by feigning a businesslike air, or if he wanted to be even bolder and disclose who he was, that he knew Jack and the Pinedas, and was simply looking for permission to visit the orchard. But the new problem—(thanks to sexist traditions, as he now viewed it)—was: he wasn't sure *how* to get a hold of Abigail, given that her name wasn't in the phonebook as McArdle, and thus likely listed under her husband's surname—somewhere among the thousands of salsipotent surnames being splashed around by the alpha and flowing all the way out to the omega. You know, A to Z...

...On Friday—after the first week of fall classes—he went to Dr. Rosenbaum's office late in the afternoon to shoot the breeze. Besides, he had nothing else to do for the rest of the day (and night), and this would likely be his last human interaction until Monday's classes, unless he ordered pizza, then he could say thanks and bye to the deliverer. Funny: on the walk over, it finally hit him that, after four years down, Dr. Rosenbaum was his best friend at college! He hadn't made any other friends besides his brief and bitten time with Andrea the Vampire and his nonverbal friendship with Luke the Bear. (Side note: On Tuesday, Luke emailed Vallano's student-account, which included the line: "Just keeping in touch. ☺" Luke must've really loved that last pawy embrace.)

Anyway, Dr. Rosenbaum's office door was open. Vallano entered, shut the door, and quietly sat down. Dr. Rosenbaum was flipping through the book he was teaching this semester.

'Oh you're here. It just started yesterday. I kept jigglin' the handle but it wouldn't flush. It's back there.' Dr. Rosenbaum pointed back behind Vallano where the imaginary bathroom (and toilet) was.

'Funny thing is: I only set two toilets 'n' helped fix a broken one on a service-call. Plumbin's not whad it's cracked up da be.'

'Either is plumber's crack. Smoked it once and barely got high.'

Vallano vaddled. Felt good to hear the ol' wit. 'So how was yir summer vacation? Gitchirself a chick yet?'

'Yeah, but like the rest, they mostly go towards the bills.' (Vallano stared at Dr. Rosenbaum with that yeah-real-cute face.) 'Oh! *Chick*. Thought you said *check*. No, chicks aren't my thing.'

'You gay or sum'n?'

'Well *some* things in Life allow the dopamine to come oudda the chemical closet in me.'

'Great. So you spent da summer brushin' up on pun work.'

'Better than dealin' with all the other plumb[3] shit Life has to offer.'

'"N' another one! Wanna keep addin' ta the toll of killer puns?'

Vallano could tell Dr. Rosenbaum was trying to play off his last wordplay—but was all clogged up. So Dr. Rosenbaum switched up to the serious: 'How's Ivy belle?' (belle: bell: toll. How killer when added up!)

'Well we're in a liddle fight over stupid shit right now. Bounda happen after bein' together four years, ya know. But I think the summer apart did us good. Anyway, lass week I found out my friend back home's joinin'ah army. Said he don't wanna be a potato sacker da rest of his life.'

'*A potato sacker?*'

'Don't ask. It was akshly my first job too.'

'Well,' sighed Dr. Rosenbaum, relaxing back in his swivel chair, 'at least your friend can get a head off a life in the army.'

'Yeah, but, see, he dunno wha' da fuck he's doin'. Here, lemme tell ya about Dante. First, he's a few years older than me, 'n' he yoosta run with all 'eez, uhh, skinheads—non-racist skins, ya know. 'N' he yoosta be all about Hardcore 'n' Oi! music. *Hezza* one thit got me inda Punk Rock. 'N' *hezza* one thit brought all my friends together, a bunch of poor angry outcasts with nowhere da turn but a desire da turn *somewhere* 'cause we didn't fit in *anywhere*. I mean, even'o *I* was always nice da those who were nice da me, collectively we didn't like no one, 'n' no one liked us. I rilly looked up da him 'n' Jeremiah. (The kid I lived with over da summer). Dey were like big brothers da me, Pessi, 'n' Eddie. Almost mythical beings: deez big skinhead-types thit knew all the older kids in the neighborhood but were still willin'ah protect us younger punks.' He adjusted in his seat. 'I 'member 'iss one time, 'ere 'iss kid on my middle school football team. Tim Berkley. Everyone would *always* talk about how hezza toughest kid around; nobody fucks with him; blah blah blah. At the time, I's in 7th grade 'n' had blue hair, which got me slapped up by Rick. Anyway, this Berkley kid was in 8th grade 'n' about twice my size. One day he comes up da my locker 'n' says, "*You don't belong in this school. Go back da yir village, fuckin' Smurf.*" 'N' I mean, it's not like 'at was so painful or anything, but I's like *wha' da fuck did I ever do da this kid.* I dunno *why* but I didn't hit 'im or say a word; I juss walked away even'o I'd alriddy been in several fights 'n' he didn't intimidate me one bit. But after school, I go tell big high-schooler Dante about it—ya know, juss

---

[3] A double-sound pun on the word *dumb,* as well as a play on the literal shit plumbers have to deal with

da tell the story. Next day, Dante's outside my school waitin' for me. We get on Berkley's bus, get off his stop, 'n' Dante starts beatin'ah fuck out of 'im. 'N' 'en Berkley's older brother who's twenty-sum'n comes runnin' out. Dante knocks 'im square in the mouth. 'N' I'm juss standin' 'ere all stunned. So da younger Berkley runs inside 'n' comes back out with his mum. She sees what's goin' on, runs back inna house, cawzza cops—h' 'en comes out 'n' *tells* us she did. So I'm like, "Dante, let's go; she juss cawed da cops." But he looks up at me 'n' says, "No madder wha': *don't – fuckin' – leave.*" So I didn't. Cops come, pull 'im off Berkley's brother 'cause Dante refused da quit, 'n' the cops take 'im away in cuffs. Juss let me go 'cauze I played stupid, ya know. So next day I ask Dante why we didn't juss take off, 'n' he goes, "Look: if we woulda left, it woulda come back on *you* 'cause Tim knows you, not me. But den they woulda tried makin' you nark me out. See, V, I wanted ja da learn two things. One: you *never* hesitate da help yir friends. I know you coulda taken Tim yirself, bahcha came da *me*, 'n' I took care of it without questionin' ya or sayin', 'Hey, it ain't *my* problem. I ain't riskin' gih'n in trouble.' Now two: *never* let *anyone* or *anything* come in between you 'n' yir family, you 'n' yir friends, or you 'n' yir coworkers. Never let their tactics force you inda *their* way of life. *Never.* 'At's the skinhead way." 'N' kinda laughin', I say, "But, Dante, I'd woulda never told on ya anyway." He goes, "I know ya wouldnt've. But I's juss protectin' ya. Bottomline." 'N'—I dunno.' Vallano stopped for a moment. 'I honestly don't even know where I'm goin' with 'iss. I guess things change: 'at's all.'

    'Pining for the violent days of your youth?' Dr. Rosenbaum said sarcastically.

    'Yeah, kinda—felt a lot safer back 'en.'

    'Well as you already pointed out: we've come to learn all things deteriorate in time. But I don't know much about the intricacies of "the skinhead way." See, I grew up in an affluent suburb in Connecticut. And I only had one good friend—Josh Eisenberg. And, well, we didn't teach each other *shit*. My parents, however, taught me to be scared shit*less* of the skinheads down in New York, and they did all they could to soak the sentiment into my bones.'

    'Yeah, 'n' I overstand why. Hard explain' sum'n unner one word 'n' yet has two opposite meanings.'

    Dr. Rosenbaum didn't respond right away. Instead he examined the dark-featured hoodlum slouched on the other side of the desk. Looking back, Vallano thought Dr. Rosenbaum seemed to be aging right before his eyes. He couldn't tell if he was sad, confused, or proud. Finally, Dr. Rosenbaum, in a sincere gentle tone, said 'Vallano—you're like the curious-lookin' apple I spotted far from the tree. I went over, picked it up, took a bite—but realized I couldn't swallow all of it.'

    'Oh yeah? Bad apple?'

    'No, impenetrable core.'

    ...He was so busy his last fall semester that he quit his part-time job as a writing tutor. He had a good bit saved up from working over the summer, still had a bit left from his spring loans, and just received $1,700 more in loans. Plus, he was planning to be extra frugal til graduation, even if he never bought much anyway: some booze for the fridge, food for the gut, seeds for the weeds, chew for the lip, not as many cigarettes for the lungs since he only smoked whenever he drank now, some music for the ears, contact solution for fake tears, occasionally g(r)ass for the ol' warhorse, and of course he had to make monthly payments for his cell phone, insurance on the warhorse, and the minimal on four maxed out credit cards. So, yeah, he was good on cash. He could be his own boss for a while; that is, til the ends of those grace periods start biting him in the ass...

(Tick-TOCK! tick-TOCK! who ripped the hands right OFF the clock?!)

...Although the fall nights seemed long, looking back, fast away the old year passed, with school and reading and writing and driving around trying to see if he could find his *divine afflatus* [4] just so he could take a peek at what she looked like now. But not even a glimpse before the late December wind blew him back to the O'Malley residence for Christmas break. Talked to Ma a few times. Everything was good. Still hadn't heard anything from or about Milvio and Gennaro. How's Ivy? Pretty good. Just felt uncomfortable staying at her place for a month with her parents. They aren't like us, ya know...Yeah, when I graduate. No, you don't have to fly back to see me; I probably won't even go. Because it's not like high school...Yes, I plan to come live there. Her too. But she might not come right away. I just want to take a little break. And if I can't find a job, I'll have to go somewhere else. But I'm coming there first because I don't have anywhere else to go...I don't know, Ma; May; June. Somewhere around there...Merry Christmas to you too. You get my card? Yeah, I got yours. I bought her a bunch of things. I don't know; stupid stuff. You get anything for Christmas?

Off course, not of a word that in English. But to digress a bit, the second day back at the O'Malley residence, Vallano had, by chance, seen Kelly nude when she came out of the shower and walked freely into the hall, believing Vallano had gone with Jeremiah and Steve to a car show. Vallano wasn't sure if she went and told Steve about it, but Steve put him to work the next day, his only days off being weekends, New Year's, and of course to digress a bit, Christmas. Oi to the world!...

Spring semester, January 5 - April 30, 2004
...He lay on his bed, belly-down, fists inward, in motion. This fight began a very long time ago _____. [5] The violence of it would rip your stomach right out and stuff it back down your throat. It's completely unsafe on his bed. Classes? Sure. Almost like physical mishaps, missteps, then backtracks through The Studious Sway, pushing through today's fleeting images (incoming like the rapid pendulation of the devil's darning needle) just to get back to the war on the bed, the war with The World, (in the real)

---

[4] [lat] one who inspires an artist; a muse
[5] Who is the Postmodern Killer? – *Ooooo,* sorry, but close. – *What* is the Postmodern Killer? (NO! Refer to your stupid-ass shit then go fuck yourself. Gonna criticize? cry? perhaps explicate an analysis that makes you look smart and this stupid? Gonna get thousands of yes-men to back you up? – Where is nothing? WU!wu!WU!wu!WU!wu!WU!wu!WU!wu!

now wearing the false face that false he~~ar~~t doth know. (In the backstroking moment: not yet.) Overstanding things *dahn 'ere* can be tough...

...A yuppish man misshapen. The da forehead like a copter landing-spot. A mole on his cheek. No moling in his work; only rolling in your de~~ar~~th. An apocryphal fool descended from Godfrey through Henry VIII. HA! St. Paul the Effeminate: that's the way of the Renaissance, Mrs. ~~Art~~ Historian!; the dandy remnants, the blithe proof, in the fuscous churches of Pittsburgh. Alas, historical arrogance from a copper coping formulas, copying the labor of others, while coding the masses. (Refer to Kazantzakis, Baigent, Leigh, etc. etc.) $80 MILL shoved into his piggybank; it repeats every year. It's a fact that only causes so much hate. Thus, a punch of death for the arrogance, ignorance, and lies, hard and straight into the copter landing-spot. Now descend and genuflect. Inter underneath the bed. Kill all codes; don't ever try to crucify Christ again; you can't have His Throne; so may God remove and burn those gravity boots; can't have a star getting away from down here by flying into the sky; can't have this comedy discovered—this joke told. Amen...Oh win free of competition! For now. But one day *nothing* will go through you. *Nothing!* Dictate, discriminate: that only causes so much hate. There is a trend of misguidance in the audience. So may God send you to where fascists speak in all the lovely tongues of deception. Amen...An award show: bolt the doors: better off a ward. Wood burns. Strike a match, friends. Strike a match. Amen.

Forsan miseros meliora sequentur. For those in misery, perhaps better things will follow. Inked on his inner forearm. A landing spot for outer hope. Run back, Ivy; it's reserved just for you. The banners can be wiped clean just for you. Thank God this is "going to piece together""—piece *back* together—for there's "a reason for everything"—for this is all happening just like *this* because it "was meant to be." Yes, four-siders and foresighters: *la tristesse durera toujours* ☹ [VG + VV - V - G = $^2_2$^{2}] Decode some truth: language. "Nature is a language, can't you read?" God made Morrissey a great introspective lyricist but God was shunned by his shy charm—better than a witch's charm though! Witches live in he~~ar~~ts! Where does God live? He recently moved to South Park: three stones: a trinity ☺ What's that mean? Why does the word *fuck* still bother you? What about *fucking? Loving* someone makes you dirty. Let's listen in on a ditty from V to Screwy. It's a USO show *down 'ere* on his bed. (Keep in ear, the "r" in *Screwy* is so faint that it almost sounds like *Skew-ee*.)::::::☺:::::::☹

'...Screwy's so boodafool. Smells wike pizza! Screwy's so boodafool. *Criari la biddizza!...'* Spoken—> *'Hey, Screwy. Mommy's comin' home soon— but you don't even know whadda million times a billion is! Hmhmhmhmhm! – Mommy don't smell wike pizza, stupidhead! Mommy smells wike FWOWERS!...'*

True. But there's something else going on underneath it all, a scent of intuition for the outcome, but again, "false face must hide what the false he~~ar~~t doth know."[6] Of course all the sad and angry brilliance in the aforesaid language becomes negated under the indispensable supposition that Ivy will be there right by his side, her arm firmly locked around his forearm. If not, there's always a landing-spot in Heaven...

---

[6] Passage from *Macbeth*

April 26ᵗʰ, 2004

...It happened out of the blue. He was in his room studying at his escritoire when his cell phone rang. Once seeing that it was her number, he answered forthwith.

'Hello?'

'*Vinny?*' (Oh, how sad she sounds!)

'Yeah?'

'Are you busy?'

'Not rilly; juss studyin'. Why, what's up?'

'I dunno...School's almost done.'

'Yeah, sum'n I'm akshly *happy* about. Can't wait da gihdoudda here.'

'Where you goin'?'

'What's it madder? Thouchu hated me 'n' never wanted da talk da me again?'

'I dunno." Coronating her sadness, she crowned it with a puppy-dog sigh.

'Ya know, Ivy, once I leave, 'at's it. Iddle be done forever.'

'Vinny—I've been seein' someone for the past six months.'

Hearing the truth hurts. He closed his eyes. Seeing the truth hurts. Such sick visions passing before him. But once you see it eyes-closed, you need to replay it, and not just once but again and again so you can feel more and more pain til you feel it's equaled the seriousness of the matter. He momentarily hit pause so he could say, '*Who?*'

'Just someone that goes to school here.'

'Wow. *Wow...*' (She followed up with a short, trivial explanation of some kind, but all he could only hear were his wows.) Interjecting: 'Do you love 'im?'

'*Noooo.*'

'So why ja caw me? Da tell me this? You tryin'ah hurt me even *more?*'

'No, Vinny; I'm not tryin' to hurt you at all. I mean, I'm sure you've been with other girls, right?'

'Wrong. I tolja I would love you 'n' only you forever. 'N' I never broke 'at vow *when* we were together, 'n' I never *will,* no madder *what.* Now I'm gonna go—'

'No, wait!'

'What?'

'I wanna see you.'

'Nah, 'at's ar'ight. Juss like how you couldn't even look at me when ya believed Teresa's lies, I can never look at *you* again. Yir forever tainted in my eyes. *Fuck!* I can't take any more of 'iss fuckin' shit!' He removed the phone and, assailed by Pain, let out a primal scream. The blood was pouring from his eyes and spraying onto the walls. She was yelling on the phone, 'Vinny! Vinny!' Breathing in thick measures, with his top and bottom teeth at war, he put the phone back up to his ear.

'Vinny, I swear I never slept with him!'

'Wha'? You think I'm stupid or sum'n?'

'I seriously haven't. I told him I would never do that again til I'm married.'

'Don't believe 'at for a minute. But even so, you've done *other* things, 'n' 'at's sum'n I juss can't deal with.'

'Listen, Vinny: we haven't done *anything*. I swear.'

'You haven't *kissed* 'im?'

'Well, I mean, come on, Vinny—'

Another primal scream. He hung up the phone and immediately smashed his fist into the bloody concrete, rebreaking his pinkie finger. He pulled back and clutched his hand, while huffing back the rage in his mouth. He wanted to break his finger again (then break everything around him) but the phone rang again.

'What?!'

'Calm down! If you would've let me finish. Look, Vinny, I don't think I can be with him anymore; it doesn't feel right. Every time I'm with him, all I do is think about you. I've probably lost fifteen pounds since last time you saw me because I'm so stressed out I can't even eat. And everyone says you *gain* weight when you're stressed. I dunno what's wrong with me! I dunno *what* to do anymore!' She was on the verge of tears.

'So whaddaya sayin'? I mean, time's runnin' out rill fast, Ivy.'

'I know. But—but I'll be honest with you, Vinny: as much as I want to, I dunno if I could ever be with you again. Too many bad memories. I can never forget all the things you put me through—'

'Like wha'?'

'Like everything. And see, it's startin' again. I should've never called—'

'No, you shoulda cawed but before I left for the summer.'

'Why, did somethin' happen? Did you sleep with someone?'

'I already tolja: *no*. But lemme ask *you* sum'n: you still friends with her?'

'No. But she tries callin' me all the time to apologize. Besides, she moved in with her boyfriend. Somehow her aunt found out about her doin' heroin and told her dad, so he told her to get out because he didn't wanna be responsible for anything else that happens in his house.'

He vaddled sardonically. 'Oh yeah? So she was forced da move in with her massa?'

'Yeah—'

'What's his name again?'

'Why?'

'Juss wonderin' 'cause I forgot.'

'*Umm*, Jackson Price. We went to school with his brother.'

'Nuh'n like drugs 'n' local loyalty til the end, right?'

'Well she says she really does love him. And I can tell she means it.'

That enraged him anew but he suppressed the brunt of it. '*Rilly?* Well I thought she rilly loved *Pessi*. I mean, dohncha overstand yet: she's a junkie, 'n' junkies are nuh'n but desperate liars. Truss me, I grew up around thousands of 'em; I know their ways. 'N' what's worse is she's *Teresa Cazzata:* she lies about *everything;* she has an innate evil spirit inside her. I mean, you still believe wha' she tolja about the abortion 'n' 'at?'

A pause. 'Do you want me to be honest with you?'

Click!

She called right back.

'Vinny, we're not gonna get anywhere talkin' about her—'

'No, we're not gonna get anywhere long as you still believe her. Ya know, it's funny how you juss cast me away like I'm nuh'n, bahchu have empathy for her like she's sum'n. You think her comin'ah you first means *I'm* the one thit pushed her inda the fabricated bullshit she fehja. But, look, I gadda study. But keep an eye out for my book 'cause one day you'll see the mistakes *you* made. One day you'll see *the truth*. One d—'

'Friday.'

'*Wha'*?'

'I wanna see you Friday. I wanna go out to eat. Okay?'

'Thoucha had a liddle boyfriend.'

'Do you wanna go or not?'

'Fine,' he replied insouciantly; inside, the greatest sensation of relief washed over him. He was already thanking God. To be sure, the thought of this "boyfriend" of hers was burning mockingly within the cool relief, but he was still thanking God because the flame was still burning amorously inside *her: ahh, ssa focuzza rintra ri so cori!* [7]

'But, Vinny, you can't try anything: not even a kiss. And I'll meet you at your car and you can drive 'cause I can't take the chance bein' seen in my car.'

'By who?'

'By anyone.'

Exhale. 'Fine. So I assume you'll caw me Friday afternoon sometime 'n' 'en we can work out the details?'

'Okay, sounds good. But now I have to go get ready for work.'

'Hey?'

'What?'

'I love you, Wimp-Wimp. *POWER UP!!!...*You say it.'

'Power up.'

Click.

Let the celebration begin! After setting the phone down, he threw both hands up in the air and began dancing around the room! He was pumping his fist—although it was hurting so bad—but he was pumping his fist like, 'Yesssss! I *knew* everything would work out! FUCK YEAH!' He wanted to go out and dance in the hall! all over campus! down to LaSalle! up to Pittsburgh! letting his joy ring out! She was back! They were back! The greatest couple in the world! Nothing could ever break them! NOTHING! The moment continued to vibrate and resound and raise his heart to the ultimate apotheosis! which is why he sang and danced and thanked God the rest of the downy day and into the bright night, not having an iota of concern for his studies, for his whole heart was beating again!...

...And it only got better the next day. He just finished lunch and was exiting the commons when his cell rang. It was her! With his whole heart a-thumpin', he answered enthusiastically. She wanted to know what he was doing. He said not much, why. Thump-thump. She said that she was

---

[7] [scn] that dear little flame inside her heart

on her way to class but wanted to meet him real quick to give him something. He immediately thought that meant a kiss; just the way she said it. Either way, he was off and running to meet her in front of Bloy Hall where a horde of students were gathered around the Bloy Preacher. Although Vallano thought the guy was a nut, he hated the way everyone mocked him and said nasty things to him; Vallano could sense his misery, and how he was just a man who saw a world falling apart at the seams and was just explaining it the only way he knew how.

But look! Here she comes! The girl who requires a million words just to describe a strand of her hair! And her hair! Long, mocha, and curly again! She was smiling so coyly as she approached like a duck—no! like a runway model! And *his* smile—well, it engulfed his head like he was getting paid a billion-gastillion bucks just to smile that way!

Upon greeting, she grabbed his wrist and tugged him towards the side of the building, looking around as if paranoid.

'Where we goin'?'

'I can't take the chance of bein' seen. We have to make this quick.'

At the side of the bricked building, she was still surveying the area as she pulled her backpack around to her side and dug into a pouch. Then he almost fainted—almost collapsed straight to the ground because he just couldn't believe what was before his eyes, being held out for him to take!

'I was at the mall last night and came across him. Isn't he so cute?' (She handed him over; Vallano took him into his hands and froze.) 'Since I could never find a full-body suit, this will have to do.'

'*Screwy?*' he said confoundedly in the squirrel voice.

'Yes, it's Screwy. Now I have to go.'

'*Wook, Wimp-Wimp. It's Screwy Squirrel. Hmhmhmhmhm!*' He was holding widdle Screwy up for display; she was glancing around, looking very anxious. '*Screwy says yir da most booodafool girl inna whooole world. Now give Screwy a kiss!*'

'No.'

'*Screwy'll baaang youuuu.*'

'I really have to go, Vinny. I'll call you tomorrow.'

He moved into her—but she backed away. He said he that just wanted a hug and needed to power up real quick. So they hugged, her making sure it was a brief embrace. After Screwy pecked Ivy's cheek, Vallano grabbed a handful of that sinuous mocha hair and jammed it all into his mouth. '*POWER UP!!!*' But it could hardly be overstood because there was so much in his mouth...

...He began walking slowly back to his room, playing around with Screwy. He didn't even care if students walking passed saw that he was holding a little stuffed animal. In the voice, in his head, he kept saying things to the effect: '*Our very own Screwy, hmhmhmhmhm!*' Screwy had been conceived in an upright perched position. He stood five inches tall. He had little beady eyes of gloss black, little brown feet, and a big bushy tail that could be wagged. His tail ran from his bottom all the way to the top of his head. Besides his long cream belly, the rest of his coat was soft-brown with streaks of gold. Stitched into his hands, held up near his mouth, was an acorn the size of his head. Walking into his room, Vallano just couldn't get over that little acorn—couldn't get over the fact that he and Ivy had a little one to take care of now...

...Later on, he called her. After five minutes of normal conversation, he asked if she knew the name of Abigail's husband. She asked why. He said that he was just wondering because she decided not to sell the orchard. Then he asked if she knew that, and if she had been to the orchard lately. Yes, she knew about Abigail taking it off the market, and no she hadn't been there lately; she hadn't gone there since the last time they went together, over a year ago. He segued back to Abigail's husband's name. Ivy said that she didn't know. He asked her to find out. 'Why?' – "Cause I cawdda realtor, which is how I found out it wasn't up for sell anymore, 'n' she couldn't give out personal information. 'N' Abigail's name isn't in the phone book. But I wanna caw her juss da see if she'd ever consider sellin' it dahn the line 'cause, who knows, maybe I have a genuine interest in buyin' it. So I wanna let her know who I am now, know whadda mean.' Taking it as a joke, she said that he was crazy but would ask her dad in a bit and then text him the name. Hours later, the text came: *Brian Seaver.* The name churned and burned in his mind, as he and Screwy lay down for the night...

...And the next day—oh the next day. The plans were set: first, dinner at The Brooke, perhaps a movie, then who knew what would happen. But he was ready to find out! He even showed up early, waiting, in the breezy evening, by the ol' warhorse for her to come walking through the tunnel of greenness. He was spiffed up in clothes she'd bought him years ago, doused in trendy cologne she'd bought him years ago. Memories of *all these years* flooding into him with pleasant revival. No doubt, he was very, very, *very* nervous about what was in the back of the ol' warhorse, but more than ready to get the rest of his life underway. It was time to grow up, get a normal job, get married in the orthodox tradition, have a healthy family, and so on...

...And look! Here she comes! The girl he was going to spend more than a million years with! And her hair! Ahhhhhhhhhh! He watched it curl and flow all down her breasts...til she reached the ol' warhorse. His smile had engulfed his head again; he wasn't even able to say a word as he opened the door for her. He waited to make sure she was completely in and secure—ahhh! look at her smile lighting up the evening sky! He shut the door and walked around the front...and she already had the door open for him! Sweet memories swept him in, onto his seat, even shut the door.

'Wow, Ivy. You look so beautiful—like sercly, *wow!*'

'*Awww.* Thank y—Why you shakin'?'

He kinda laughed. 'I dunno; juss been so long, 'n' I'm all nervous, 'n' stressed out, but so excited 'n' overwhelmed, ya know.' Suddenly, she grabbed his right hand, examining the broken finger; the top knuckle still looked like a teepee. He'd been ignoring the pain and twitches, but now, through her soft vulnerary touch, he was healed.

'What happened? This looks really bad.'

'Happened when I's plumbin'. A water main fell on it.'

She didn't respond. She kept rotating his hand around in hers. Around and around: a slow perfect cycle. Meanwhile, he was watching her face: something was happening to it: tears beginning to drop? But why? Also overwhelmed with bliss?

'What's wrong, Wimp-Wimp? Why ya cryin'? I'll be ar'ight.'

'Vinny—I'm sorry.'

'For wha'?'

'*I just can't,*' she whispered.

'Can't wha'?' But his question was answered by the influx of sick feelings spaying into his insides. 'Can't wha'?' he asked again in a pathetic tone.

'This, Vinny.' She let his hand fall. 'I—I don't even know what to say. I should've never called you.' (She started balling.) 'I just thought—I dunno! I just missed you! But there's still somethin' inside me that says no! no! NO!'

'Come on, hun; juss cahm dahn.' (He was trying to stroke her head but she was pulling away.) 'Yir juss all nervous like me. It's been a while, so it's gonna feel a liddle strange at first, ya know. But we're gonna go eat 'n' in no time iddle feel like it did before—'

'No, it won't! I can't even touch you like that! I just did, and it wasn't right!'

'Whaddaya mean it wasn't right? What wasn't right?'

She went to open the door but he quickly reached across to prevent it. A struggle ensued. With her knee pressed into the door and body turned aside, she finally got it open and plunged herself out, as he attempted to pull her back in by snagging the back of her jeans pocket—tearing it. Slamming the door shut, she paid no mind. He threw his door open and began darting around the backend of the ol' warhorse. She was almost running across the parking lot. She had a good lead because he slipped rounding the corner and staggered a few steps. But the race was now on. He steadily had his eyes on her entering into the tunnel of greenness...then she disappeared...but he was quickly catching up, running in a full sprint...coming out only seconds apart. You could hear her sobbing. You could hear him saying, 'Stop! Juss wait a second!' Then—just before reaching the creamery—he snagged her from behind, throwing his arms around her shoulders and breasts...and as she tried unscrewing herself by twisting back and forth, he began sliding his body and circled grip down...and down...til locking it around her ankles.

'Get off!' she cried. 'Let go!'

(People were already huddled around, gazing.)

'No. You promised me we'd go out.'

'No, Vinny! I can't!'

'Why?'

'I'm sorry, but I can't! I should've never called you! I'm seriously so so sorry, Vinny. God, it's not right for me to be doin' this to you.'

'Then don't.'

Apparently talking to herself: 'I should've just listened to my parents and friends and just left it alone for good—'

'It's not about *them!* It's about us! *Us* 'n' *only* us!'

'Vinny, get off! You're hurtin' me! Please—people are watchin'!'

'I don't care! *Fuck* them! I love you, Ivy! I love you so fuckin' much!'

'I'm sorry, Vinny! I just—OW! Please stop! You're hurtin' me! Let goo-ahh!'

'No, I'll never let go! Never!'

Just then, a girl, an Aristod Scholar, accosts them: 'Hey, do you need me to call for help?'

'No!' answered Ivy in tears. 'I said NO! Just leave!'

But the girl didn't. To the one down on the ground using the circled grip, she said, 'Get off her now or else I'm gonna call security!'

'Fuck you, bitch!' he said with a trembling voice.

The girl jogged off. The crowd was growing, murmuring.

'Vinny, you're gonna get us in trouble! Let go!' She tried to step forward but his grip was so tight and compacted around her ankles that she fell over, down to the sidewalk. All of a sudden, three or four kids were trying to pull him off and away from her. It was only hurting her more. She was screaming. They were screaming. He was just holding on. Then came a campus security guard, mace already pulled.

'Ma'am, cover your eyes!'

'No! Don't touch him! Don't!'

'Is her hurting you?!'

'No! Just leave us alone! LEEEAVE!'

Of course the campus security guard couldn't just leave. Too much chaos, too much confusion, this scene too surreal. No one knew what to do. The campus security guard asked if she knew him. She said yes! just leave! don't touch him! The campus security guard must've took that as no real threat at hand because he put the mace away and with two other kids pried and pried til they pried his arms from her ankles. She stood up and told them to leave! to mind their own business! that they didn't know what they were doing! 'I SAID LEAVE US ALONE, YOU ASSHOLES!' So the two who helped free her walked off into the gazing, murmuring crowd. But the campus security guard stayed put. He needed to find out the details of the situation. Crying, Ivy could only force out how they were just playing around, and everyone took it to be something it wasn't. *Then why is he still on his knees with his face buried into the concrete?* the security guard must've been wondering. She told the one down on the ground that she was leaving: she was so embarrassed now because of *these* kids—pointing with anger at *those* kids—but she would call him later. But he knew she wasn't calling him later. He peaked up—enough to see the Walzy cuffs striding away. Then he rose up like a zombie. His vision—his *existence*—was so inexplicable, so burdened with pain, passion, and violence. The campus security guard said that he would walk him to wherever, and they could talk about whatever.

'*Fuck* you, you *fuck*,' spat Vallano in a trembling voice, jerking away, marching back towards the tunnel of greenness...

...He briefly stopped at the ol' warhorse to shut the stall gate. He looked into the back where on the floor, in a black bag, sat her present: the engagement ring he bought the night before, at the mall, perhaps at the same time she was buying him Screwy...

...When he entered his room, he turned the television on. Then he moved to the bed and laid down with his body compacted as if inside a coffin. He soon began slipping into a mindless state...but off in the distance he could still hear a news reporter talking about American troops being deployed to Iraq...then, in more local news, eight-year-old Lucinda West is steadily recovering from her seventh surgery. Lucinda was born with myelomeningocele, a rare form spina bifida which has left her paralyzed from the waist down. Today doctors performed a skin graft near her spine to help alleviate a burgeoning cyst. We asked Lucinda what she plans to do once she gets home, and here's what she had to say. 'I'm going to study real hard for my school's spelling-bee. I really want to win it for my mom, my dad, and my nurse...' Then, deeper inside himself, he heard, *'I'm so sorry, but I just can't. I should've never called you. I'm seriously so so sorry. God, it's not right for me to do this to you. I should've just listened to my parents and friends and just left it alone for good'*—then he saw, behind his eyes, Pessi smirking, just smirking—then he saw his father working in a steel mill, working harder than anyone else in the world—suddenly, his chest and eyes felt funny...his contacts seemed to be dissolving in the blur now overtaking his existence...he swiftly clutched his chest—bit down on his nether lip—started to gag involuntarily from his gut up to his throat, believing he was about to expectorate, but this phenomenon was shaking his insides too violently for that...so in a vigorous attempt to stop whatever it was, he tried to gag back, with force, the involuntary gags, working against them like an oar digging down into the waves of a storm—but he just couldn't stop himself from crying...yes, Vincent Ignazio Scandurra Vallano was crying for the first time since he was a little boy...so hard and copiously the foreign drops poured out...and it felt so good...all the pain of his life and the misery of the world had finally brought him one of the greatest feelings of release...but underneath the surface he realized what else the tears meant: confirmation of the washing aways waiting blindly in the imminence, for the heavy crying had just created a perforation for the subcutaneous beast to rip up through...all hope lost in a drop...but *for now*, it was just about crying and crying and crying...flooding the room all throughout the night...til the light of the sun began penetrating the curtains, whereupon he hid himself underneath the lion and finally fell asleep, holding Screwy tightly in his right hand, and the lock of her hair by the skin of his teeth...

(22) (WIMP-WIMP)

(WHAT WORDS)

(WHAT ACTIONS)

(WILL MAKE)

(YOU SEE)

(THAT I)

(WILL DO)

(EVERYTHING IMAGINABLE)

(TO PROVE)

(YOU ARE)

(FOREVER INSIDE)

(MY HE~~ART~~?)

(REMEMBER THAT)

(REMEMBER THIS)

(REMEMBER US)

(AS ONE)

(FOR NOTHING)

(CAN CHANGE)

(THE SACRIFICES)

(WE MADE)

(FOR LOVE.)

(I TRULY)

(APPRECIATE EVERYTHING)

(YOU DID)

(FOR ME.)

(JUST KNOW)

(I DID)

(ALL THIS)

(FOR YOU.)

OPTIMISM'S FREE FLIGHT

1) We tend seek solace in optimism because to face the darkness, we believe, is to fall to submission. And yet *not* to face a pessimistic circumstance (wherever it may exist, no matter the degree) is to keep one's self inside the coffin of fear.

2) Intrinsically, there is nothing optimistic about optimism.

3) Optimism itself *is* pessimism. This is so because optimism (in both its philosophical and lay forms) can't exist *unless* pessimism exists. [Note: Although obvious to the learned reader, the matter of optimism/pessimism doesn't concern *noumena,* but rather *phenomena,* since it requires circumstance coupled with human perception; coming before civilization, Nature *(noumena)* doesn't encompass circumstance, ethics such as right or wrong, or observations such as good things/bad things.]

4) Thus, in human reality, optimism is merely a reflection of a pessimistic circumstance. It's a perception connected to what is believed to be a *natural response* but is, in fact, the manipulation of one's sensibilities. Intrinsically, optimism has nothing to do with *action;* namely, *a policy for change.* And yet we have long believed that the pessimist is the one prone to be passive. False! Many times it's the opposite: the pessimist, due to the strong feelings of resistance against *the circumstance itself,* is more inclined to be *active* than the optimist. On the other hand, the optimist's "praxis"[1] tends to be found above all in the pipe dream, in the blind vision, in the material of the transcendental; everything else about optimism, *in the physical,* existing in the sensation of resistance against the notion of pessimism, not in the circumstance itself; that is, if optimism wants to set itself apart from the nature of pessimism, which is an effort done in vain insofar as it changes nothing here on earth, not to undermine its imagination and faith in Ultimate Justice.

5) To reiterate: pessimism is a realization from which sensibility naturally flows forth, and optimism (in its vain attempt to *appear* detached from pessimism and rooted in one's unadulterated sensibility) is actually a resistance against the pessimistic realization. This, of course, is *before* any modes of actions are considered, for it can be easily proven empirically that both the pessimist and the optimist can, once the circumstance has been planted, choose to be *active* or *inactive.* In other words, the optimist can have much hope, but have all their hope exist only in rhetoric. Whereas the pessimist can deem the circumstance, or the future of the circumstance, to

---

[1] Word used sarcastically here

be dismal, and yet, from that, feel more inclined to change it by employing whatever means the pessimist deems necessary, for the pessimist, by nature, will see the darkest aspects of the circumstance, but within that darkness, see the largest measure of workings at play, and thereby be driven into deeper counters. By this method, the pessimist is the one who develops the fibers of *true* optimism; that is, a philosophical overstanding stemming from the circumstance itself, then, removed from the philosophical shell, put on the back of Praxis for the sake of the here-and-now. (It seems that whenever one is a full-fledged optimist and rebukes the pessimist for being "too cynical" in their outlook, it's only because the optimist's "positive" energies have been manipulated to such an extreme degree; there's a determinate force of fear disguised as "rightness" preventing them from letting their self, so to speak, face *all* the darkness of a particular matter; they're still being held back by the fear of realization; and sometimes they're conscious of this fear but won't speak about it; and sometimes the truth of it is held within their subconscious, and thus they're not even aware how their thoughts and actions *are* hinged on fear. Nevertheless, there's a manipulative force making them believe that to face the darkness is to surrender.)

6) The truisms that state there's no *yin* without *yang,* or *love* without *hate,* are *not* equal with the matter of pessimism/optimism. The former sets are matters of reflection of their counterpart *outside* circumstance; namely, they, the former sets, under the assumption that they exist insofar as humans give them their existence, would have their essence *a priori.* [2] However, we, *a posteriori,*[3] tend to say that they are "opposites": a matter of dual-perception.[4] Nevertheless, the former sets remain contingent of each other. Whereas the existence of pessimism *always* comes before optimism, and therefore pessimism *can* exist outside of optimism, for if the proper circumstance is planted, pessimism is given natural birth from that alone, from which the lay sense of optimism only comes about by resistance and learned sensibilities.[5] In more flowery terms, optimism can only exist in a situation where pessimism has first sown its seeds of weeds, and thereby, if

---

[2] [lat] before examination [Used here to indicate society at the particular time a single life enters into it, not as stemming from Nature itself]

[3] [lat] after examination

[4] The first perception is the human creation of matters (e.g.: the root(s) from which good and evil springs forth). The second perception is the functions of a matter; that is, the creation of linguistic signifiers, which are then geared towards circumstances to establish differences based on normative rules of values (e.g.: *good* is the act of giving a poor person money; *evil* is the act of stealing money from anyone because stealing itself is evil.)

[5] Meant here as both manipulated and mimicked emotional responses. This paradox suggests they're not sensibilities but rather external designs "put into" one's brain, triggering basic sensory responses to circumstance, while subduing the deepest sensory responses (sensibilities): this is how emotions are manipulated, usually requiring graver circumstances than mental manipulation, for the brain and its rationalizations are utter manipulations from birth, *tabula rasa* not even lasting a second. [*Tabula rasa* is Latin for the mind before it receives impressions from experiences.]

not careful, optimism can be like a desire to grow roses from dandelion seeds; namely, it, optimism, in many minds, seems too quick to give up on *the physical* by embodying itself in "superearthly Hopes."

7) To expound: How can one ever be moved to be optimistic if things in a circumstance are *in the right*? And how can pessimism not be the *natural* result, the *first* reaction, in a circumstance where things are *in the wrong*? Whenever one sees a dismal thing, their first sensations are analogous to the nature of thing itself: the onlooker doesn't automatically see, feel, or ponder the positive side of it. (E.g.: on 9/11 when anyone with an ounce of sensibility fell down in misery with the buildings before attempting to shed positive light on the matter as well as how to "fix" it.) So again, a circumstance that is deemed to have slipped from a condition that is comfortable or "normal"—whether judged by the heart or the mind, the majority or the minority—begets pessimism, and from that, optimism comes about either to serve as resistance against the pessimism (the drive of fear, not wanting to face all that is)—or, if the fear is absent, optimism automatically becomes synonymous with pessimism, and thus destroying its lay sense, while leaving *action* or *nonaction* as an after-the-fact choice, essentially becoming part of *praxis* wherein *policy of change* opens up a whole new arena too extensive to go into here.

8) Thus, as *love* and *hate* are of the same matter, dependent of each other, so is *pessimism* and *the wrong*, with "optimism" originating as an act of resistance *in the physical* or as an embodiment of Hope in *ethereality,* signifying in its irony that things *in the physical* will always be wrong if "optimism" is to stay alive and prevail.

9) So what does all of this mean? That Hope *in praxis, within the earthly material of the future,* rests in the hope that "optimism" will soon die. In order for this to happen, religion or spirituality does *not* have to cease: this would only be counter-productive and detrimental to the imagination, the creative spirit, and the great mysteries of Life. Pandora's Box just needs to be reopened and reevaluated. The findings dealt with courageous hands and critical eyes, and not scientifically but artistically. Perhaps *then* what's at the bottom of the box will come out and shine over the entire world.[6]

10) So what does all of this *not* mean? That any wrong made right is everlasting; that any given wrong is unquestionably wrong; that any given right is unquestionably right; that all of this has meaning and value; that all of this is more than just nothing.

"Is the resolve to be so scientific about everything perhaps a kind of fear? An escape from, pessimism? A subtle last resort against—truth? And, morally speaking, a sort of cowardice and falseness? Amorally speaking, a ruse?" [7]

---

[6] When Pandora opens the box the second time, Hope comes out to heal the afflictions of humanity.
[7] From Nietzsche's "An Attempt at Self-Criticism" in the 1886 edition of *The Birth of Tragedy*

LIGHT AT THE END OF THE ORCHARD

"I walk through the arbor, down winding rows,
Where teal ivy climbs and red fruit glows,
And blue radiance floods the immortal sky,
Light or dark, doesn't matter,
When I think of her, I begin to cry,
For all the beauty around me
Begins to fade from the season of the squall,
So into the warmth of her he~~art~~, I try to crawl,
But winter comes and it's hard for me to feel
That when I kissed her lips, it was even real,
Because from the coldness of my breath
Spreads forth the whiteness of death,
And everything brittle snaps and falls,
Leaving me staring through wooden walls,
Stuck in a naked echo of the past,
But I know even this won't really last,
For all shall return again
In the blossom of a new season..." [1]

May 1: Vallano cuts Anson a check for $300: the peace in the box is on its way....*shhhhh*

May 2: After blocking the ID of his number, Vallano calls Brian Seaver. Brian answers. Vallano politely asks to speak with Abigail. He lets her know that he is Kip Mahoney from D.C. He has a friend who lives in LaSalle, and he, Kip Mahoney, is looking to move into the area because he fell in love with it while visiting. He'd driven by her place and seen it was for sell, but when he called he was told that it had been taken off the market. 'Yes. My husband and I decided to keep it. It was my father's before he passed.' (Kip expresses his sympathies for the unknown father.) 'May I ask how you got my number? Did Sharon' (the realtor) 'give it to you?' Kip tells her not exactly. He says that he doesn't want to get his source or Sharon in trouble but his source knows Sharon and got it for him. 'Oh, it's no biggie. So you looked around the place then?' Kip tells her that he drove up the driveway and thought it was such a quaint, serene place. He then asks how much land it included and what she was asking for it. 'Fifty acres. We were askin' $475,000, but we didn't even have one potential buyer. But it was like a sign I shouldn't have tried sellin' it in the first place.' Kip inquires about the future of the place. 'Well we're leavin' for Ireland for a month.' (Such a great thing to stay true to the roots!) 'Brian's cousin lives there, and he was gonna ask him if he wants the place, but chances are he'll decline because he's old and probably doesn't wanna move, especially not to another country. The rest of our family lives out of state. So we were thinkin' we might just fix the

---

[1] Lyrics from "Naked Echo of the Past" by Hea~~rt~~olins, from the album *In the Ashes of Our Wake*

house up and give it to one of our kids. My youngest son just found out that his wife is expecting, so maybe he'll want it in a year or so.' Kip makes a kind, flattering remark about her wanting to keep it in the family; meanwhile, he's doing internal calculations. 'Yeah, I'm sorry if I got your hopes up, Mr. Mahoney. See, I was just really upset after my father passed. My head was cloudy. Then I thought about it and realized he would've wanted us to keep it and pass it down.' Kip overstands. They exchange smalltalk before the conversation ends with Kip telling her to have a great time in Ireland, best wishes to the new grandchild on the way, and if she ever changes her mind she can contact him on his fake D.C. number.

May 3: Vallano calls Ma. Tells her that he won't be coming to Catania right away. He just landed a six-month paid internship at a magazine company in Toronto, which will help his career when he *does* come over. He can't pass up this once-in-a-lifetime opportunity. And, yes, Ivy's coming too. They'll be coming to Catania in a year. Ma is happy college did him good, and that he and Ivy are still coming.

May 4: It's a madhouse! The business of buying and selling shifts into full speed ahead! What was once a gradual process of minimizing the superficial goods has now turned into full-blown liquidation, eliminating nearly every superficial good while maximizing the necessities! There are several private one-on-one negotiations, but most of the business is conducted through pawnshops, online auctions, outside dumpsters, and grocery markets. Meanwhile, he does some calculations and records that he already has $3,115 (cash and bank combined), but will soon have a lot more, even though, according to his calculations, he'll only need about $1,000. Nevertheless, he agrees that he will put an additional $1,000 aside then put the rest in an envelope and leave it in front of whoever's door. After doing a few rough calculations, he records that he's over $85,000 in debt. He starts laughing so hard that he almost cries.

May 8: Vallano calls Eddie. Tells him about his paid internship in Toronto. He wants Eddie and Jeremiah to come down for his last weekend (the 15th and 16th). Eddie says that he wants to but it's up to Jeremiah because he still has no car. It's a perfect segue for Vallano to tell Eddie that he wants to sell his car because he's flying to Toronto, and his company is within walking distance from his apartment in Toronto. They make a verbal agreement of $50 for the ol' warhorse. Vallano informs Eddie that they will be able to transfer the title when he comes up, then Eddie can drive it back.
        Then Vallano calls Jeremiah and reiterates what he told Eddie. Jeremiah says that he will definitely come down. Jeremiah is happy college did him good, and that he isn't coming back to Verna; in other words, that Vallano "made it," "did it," "succeeded."

May 9: Mother's Day. He calls Ma first; she neither sees nor hears the tears running down his face. Then he calls Aunt Stella, for she has two daughters who are Vallano's cousins but older since Stella is his great aunt. He lets her know that he's moving to Toronto—(Ma already told her)—and so he's having his bills forwarded to her house until he gets settled in. He says that she won't be able to contact him on his cell phone because he's having it shut off in a few days and getting new service up there. He will call when that number is available. He then tells her to tell Uncle Alfonse: 'I get it: A god walks alone, a god walks alone—' – 'Whaddaya sayin'?! Yir not makin' any sense!' He repeats himself, but she still doesn't overstand his nonsense. So she puts Uncle Alfonse on the phone. Very slowly but very loudly, Vallano says, 'I get it, Uncle Alfonse! I overstand the nuances could mean everything! But it's either: "With God walk alone!" or "A god walks alone!"' Uncle Alfonse responds with 'Stellaaaa!' then hangs up the phone.

May 11: The peace in the box arrives....*shhhhh*

May 12: Vallano has the last meeting with Dr. Rosenbaum. He records it as "too inexplicable to be justified by a scene." He was on the verge of tears the entire time. He could sense that Dr. Rosenbaum knew by now that he was no longer with Ivy. And perhaps it was confirmed when Dr. Rosenbaum spoke his last words. Nothing too witty, ironic, complex, or sagacious. Just a summary of five years of lessons: '...Sometimes, Vallano, you don't have to let go things. You just have to let 'em be. Trust me: they'll always be there. Just don't look back in anger.' And Dr. Rosenbaum said those words to his back, for they were embraced in a long hug. It was a strange somber ending. But Dr. Rosenbaum was certain he wouldn't have to wait to read the papers to see that his gifted student, his best friend—his beloved *son?*—has become a name in the neon, for they would be keeping in touch in the interim. However, Vallano was certain he would soon be too far away for that, but perhaps *sometime* down the road their paths would converge again, just as long as he doesn't stop to look back in anger.

May 13: He takes the information from the phone book, and after his final final, spends the rest of the day taking that information and converting it into a map. Works out several crucial calculations.

May 14: He prints out everything he has written. Although condensed into a small font and single-spaced, it's still a very large stack. He takes it, along with a large collection of notes, to the orchard, and stores it inside the shed: so squirrelly.

May 15: Eddie and Jeremiah arrive at 7 p.m. They ask what happened to everything in his room; the only remaining things are a backpack and suitcase on the floor, with his cell phone on the desk, which, once calling Eddie and Jeremiah and finding out they were only thirty-minutes away, he'd called the phone company to have his service shut off. He tells 'em that he sold most of his possessions because he's buying everything new in Toronto. Eddie asks about his large CD collection. Vallano was momentarily stumped—but then informed Eddie that Aunt Stella came up a few days ago to haul back some of his clothes, books, and CDs, but—umm—inside his suitcase he has a small case with his favorite CDs for his stay in Toronto. At the moment, the suitcase contains a flashlight, a hat, a pair of clothes, a pair of sunglasses, a pair of scissors, a bottle of lotion, a can of shaving cream, electronic clippers, and a razor blade.

May 16: Aristod's class of 2004 graduates, and so does he, but he's out to eat with Eddie with Jeremiah. (He requested his degrees in English and Classics be sent to Aunt Stella's. He graduates with an overall GPA of 2.7: an average student.) After they finish eating, they go and transfer the title of the ol' warhorse. Then they walk around downtown, going here and there, before drinking the rest of the night away.

May 17: Eddie and Jeremiah leave in the morning. It wasn't a somber goodbye because they plan on reuniting before he leaves for Catania. Da Hoolies is but three, but three is for life! Afterward, he sits in his room...til Shawn from the front desk comes to his room and inspects it. All is good. Vallano drops the ol' golden key in Shawn's hand. Vallano takes once last look into the ol' room. Ahh! goodbye ol' prison! With his backpack on, suitcase in hand, and out-of-service cell phone in pocket, he heads outside to the dumpster. He takes the contents of the suitcase and transfers 'em into the backpack. Then he tosses the suitcase into the dumpster. He heads to the library and reads from *A Portrait of the Artist as a Young Man* til 8 p.m., at which time, he returns to Philemon through the back doors and goes to the bathroom on the top floor. He walks to the back enclave where the showers are. (Of course no one is in here.) He strips naked. From his backpack he pulls out a pair of scissors. He cuts the hair on his head as much as he can. He does the same to his chest and pubic hair. From his backpack he pulls out electronic clippers and plugs it in by the sink. He shaves the chopped hair on his head as much as he can. From his backpack he pulls out a can of shaving cream and razor. He carefully shaves off every single hair on his body including his eyebrows. It hurts. It takes over an hour. Then he showers and rubs lotion all over himself. Afterward, he puts on a pair of black boxer-briefs. Then a white long-sleeve shirt. A pair of baggy blue jeans. Black skater shoes. A black hat. And finally black sunglasses. After cleaning up and putting his things back in the backpack, he leaves the bathroom and heads down to the back door. (He takes the sunglasses off; it's dark out.) He walks downtown and calls a cab. The cab arrives in minutes. He gets in the backseat and asks to be taken to Suburban Estates. Although nighttime, he keeps his face in half-turn the entire drive. Once there, he directs the driver to drop him off at *that* blue trailer up on the left with the lights off and no car in the parking slot. He does. He pays the driver—tips him well—then thanks him. He begins walking towards the small front porch enclosed in plastic. When he sees the cab has left the trailer park, he picks up a handful of gravel from the narrow parking slot, carries the gravel to the porch, sets the pebbles down, pulls out the thick envelop from his backpack, sets it down in front of the door and covers it with the gravel, enough not to get blown away. Then he walks out to the main road. Cuts across. Clambers up a dirt bank. Onto a field. Then he walks deep into it but to a point where he still has a sense of where the road is. He continues back towards LaSalle at a regular pace...til the woods appear in front of him. From his backpack he retrieves a flashlight, turns it on, and begins navigating through the woods. Continues for twenty minutes...til the open field appears again, at which point he heads down to the road. Cuts across. Walks halfway up the driveway. Makes a right into the pathway through the thicket...and coming out, enters the orchard. He walks down to the shed, opens the door, and enters. There's a rope tied into the hole of the outside latch. From inside, he pulls the right door flush with the left door. Then he ties the rope several times around the leg of a metal shelf attached to the wall. He lights the wick of a kerosene lamp, lies down, and reads for a bit...He extinguishes the lamps and pulls his lion blanket over him for comfort, not warmth, while holding onto Screwy with his right hand, and the lock of her hair by the skin of his teeth. He shakes and cries...til falling asleep, many hours later...

May 18: No luck. Such a long painful walk.

May 19: No luck. Such a long painful walk. He realizes his best option would be to take a day off and try on May 21, Friday evening.

May 21: After waking up at 10 a.m., he makes breakfast: a can of beans, a side of salted spinach, two cookies, a multi-vitamin, with B-12 and Omega-3 supplements. While eating, he trembles, for he has an overpowering feeling that today is the day. He goes down to the creek and reshaves his body hair just in case there will be a case, even though he barely has stubble. Then he takes a quick bath in the cove: so cold that he decides to sponge from the bank. Back at the shed, he reorders things, trying to economize space. So much food and supplies! Thankfully it's a large shed, although to make room on the floor he had to drive the lawnmower out above the house where he parked it amid the thicket. After fiddling around with this and that, here and there, like a country boy, he decides it's time to get ready. He wants to arrive early and safely before dusk. He strips naked. Like twice before, he straps a holster for a plastic flashlight around his left leg, good and tight. Then he puts on a pair of blue jeans. A tight long-sleeve shirt, pure black. Then the torturous long tube socks! Five pairs, no shoes! He puts 'em on, pulling 'em up over the cuff of his jeans, kinda vaddling as he does. He stands up and exhales: completely bald, long-sleeve black shirt, blue jeans, authoritative gray tube socks. Before putting the black rubber gloves on, he smokes a couple cigarettes...then drops contact solution in his eyes. Once the rubber gloves are on, he grabs another pair, folds 'em up, and puts 'em inside his left pocket. Then he pulls out a small brown lunch bag, folds it up, and puts it inside his right pocket. Finally, the peace in the box: it's no longer in the box but on the piece. *Shhhhh.* (He's ready.)

The afternoon sun is bright. The air tepid. The ground grassy but hard. At 3 p.m. he begins walking down towards the creek, shaking, fighting off another anxiety attack. But just like the first two trips, he's pushed forward by the words of Praxis: 'Let your sorrow end! It is better for us all to avenge our friends! Not mourn them forever! Each of us will come to the end of his life on earth! He who can earn it should fight for the glory of his name! Fame after his death is the noblest of goals!'[2] But unlike Beowulf, Vallano is not seeking fame, for that would only fetter his wrists. He just wants his sorrow to end, as well as his close friends and friends in

---

[2] From *Beowulf,* a work from the Middle Ages based on what have long been considered Christian ethics [21, 1384-89]

spirit around the world to be avenged—and of course, he desperately wants her back. So he silently creeps along the winding creek, his wrists shaking freely in the light of day...

...An hour later, he reaches the crossing point. Although the creek is much wider and the current faster than where it runs through in the orchard, there is one narrow space where he can jump across without getting wet. And he does: he jumps over to the right side. He now has six feet of walkway between the creek to his left and the woods to his right. The sun is momentarily eclipsed by the precipice on the other side of the creek, which further down, comes to a point where the bank of creek goes directly into the hillside, meaning he wouldn't have been able to walk much further on that side anyway.

According to his calculations from the previous trips, he has about two more miles to tread, gradually turning northeast, before he has to cut across Downing Farms, a country road amid nowhere or nothing. From there, he'll have to go up and across the cornfield, then into the back of the other woods until coming upon the destination.

It's mostly soft sandy brush beneath him, but his heavily-socked feet hurt. He decides to take a fifteen-minute break. Since cigarettes and snuff aren't allowed on the trip, he lies on his back looking up at the sky, just breathing in the fresh air...but he isn't comfortable. The rubber gloves are bothersome like the socks. He wonders if he really needs to wear the gloves right now. It's reaffirmed that he must wear them *while motile:* to prevent cuts. But *for now* he doesn't need to wear 'em, so he takes 'em off and exposes his hands to the fresh spring air. He wiggles his fingers around: the thought of fast spiders passes through his mind. Still on his back, he feels more comfortable. Much peace in listening to the simple gurgle of the creek...he seems to be submerging in the water before him...so reflective...nostalgic...peaceful.........*another world,* he realizes in his tears, knowing his break is over. He stands up. Puts the gloves back on. Then sighs as he moves forward. And how grotesque and unreal this hairless creature looks moving through the tranquility of Nature! Even the birds up above seem to be stopping in mid-flight to look down upon this—this alopecic *thing!* But may nothing stop his motile hunt; and may his thoughts, from this time forth, be bloody or nothing worth, for *sa cœur a ses raisons que la raison ne connaît pas!...*[3]

...After safely crossing Downing Farms Road, and the vast corn field, he navigates through the back of the woods, which isn't very dense but has many pointy pines and dangerous woodblocks. He soon arrives in the vicinity. He moves silently towards the front edge of the woods where, in singular cuts, big country-style houses sit. Most are distanced from the main road (Killian) by long blacktop driveways, and are a bit obscured by the woods that run all the way to the bank of the road; but passing cars still have the ability to "peek in." He guesses it's around 7 p.m.: a bit early, but it

---

[3] Reference to "O, from this time forth, My thoughts be bloody, or nothing worth!" from *Hamlet* [IV,iv, 65-66]. *Sa coeur a ses raisons que la raison ne connaît point* is French for "his heart has its reasons that reason knows nothing of," non-verbatim but directly attributed to Blaise Pascal, a French mathematician and physicist turned Christian apologist.

will give him a promising time frame since he might catch them on their way out to socialize, as is customary on Friday nights. However, he realizes, if they *are* there, he'll still wait until they return. Can't have people *out there* expecting their arrival, growing worried if they should happen not to arrive.

Creeping along the edge of the woods, he sees that same blue tarp covering the neighbor's large oval pool in the backyard. Their backyard is about an acre and level. He assumes they, the Seymours, have kids, because there's a plastic jungle-gym beside the furnished patio. As he slowly passes by at a safe distance, transfixed on their backyard, RB comes to mind because there's a fountain rising from a manmade pond amid an "exotic scene." But it's not turned on. He remembers RB's frontyard fountain *was* turned on: rotating colors of the rainbow. Such a spoiled little brat! Why did she think she was so much better than him? She punched him right in the hallway! Her! A rich bitch from the other side where they have electronic fountains in their front yards! Besides, how distasteful! He's going to have a classical one: perhaps Doric like the Eros fountain in Catania: *a pinsata immuttali, i culura rû suli, a luna, l'acqua (scinnennu rê sciumi ie mari), tuttu cruru ie macari na l'univessu, alluciata nâ funtana*[4]*:* certainly no scientific taint! no technological colors!—no American enrichment! no American richness! RB, he imagines, ended up going to a big state university that promises both rich academics and rich social experiences. She drank and fucked and enjoyed a free ride on daddy's back. Now she's on her way to being something with "consultant" or "coordinator" in the title. (Too bad she wasn't smart enough to get into an elite school. Probably killed her parents who would've loved to boast of a 30K/year tuition.) Nevertheless, a consultant or coordinator can go far in the world; they can make a difference, consulting people on stuff and coordinating things for stuff. If he only could leave here and hunt down RB to prove to *her* how smart he is! *He* has *two* degrees from *Aristod!* And how he would love to go rub those degrees in the faces of every high school teacher who doubted him! And Ms. Charlton! HA! Fucking bitch! Look at him now! Right *there,* moving into his post, one of the greatest artists ever: VINCENT VALLANO! The poor boy from The Great Unwashed who bathed himself in *his* experiences and *your* education to become the man who shall never bend nor break in the face of adversity! never turn a blind eye from those in need! never refuse to break bread with the poor! never fold his arms to cold bodies! No! he shall let ALL in and NEVER – LET – GOOOOOOOOOO!...

...So it goes: time passes by slowly. It becomes so excruciating that he stands up several times and looks southbound, ready to retreat to the orchard. Each time, he fights himself, and he wins. He's now sitting atop a short, flaking log, which a week ago he positioned parallel with the wide blacktop driveway but in a way that the thick trunk of an oak protects him, as does the sky and his own darkness. He has taken the flashlight from his leg; it's beside him on the log; doesn't need it yet. The porch light is casting a yellowish haze around the front of the house, reaching as far as the hood of the white SUV over on the right side; the SUV he awaits is presently gone,

---

[4] [scn] the immortal idea, the colors of the sun, the moon, the rain (descending to the rivers and the seas), everything raw and pure in the universe, lit up in a fountain

and has been since arriving. As far as he can tell, all the lights *inside* the house are off. Back behind him, through the slotty woods that divide the neighbors, the light on the Seymours' garage shimmers at a safe distance. On the other side—straight in front of him—he can see through the woods numerous lights on inside the Peterson house; their house is angled in such a way that it seems to be turning towards *this* house. It makes him tremble. But it *is* late and dark, with a missing moon and thousands of trees that are watchguards on *his* side: they are God's gifts...

...It's near midnight when he sees a hunter-green SUV pulling up the driveway. It creeps in to the left of the white SUV...stopping ten yards ahead of his position. Crouched down, he pivots around, waiting. The ten yards between the edge of the woods and the driveway now seem a million miles. He's so locked into the stillness that he can't even tell that his heart is ripping through the black cloth. He begins taking as many crouched steps as he can before the driver door opens—then stops as the first leg swings across the threshold. Vallano rises from the crouch, and with great force, begins the dark debouchment: he's taking long solid steps northeast...brittle leaves are exploding like landmines! his soul has melted out and is glowing on his skin! but with adamance he parts through the combustion of flames. Just passed the front wheel, Jackson turns aside, then fully around. His mouth opens to say—*Phum. Phum.* His large body falls back against the fender. Spun around, he staggers a step towards the bumper. He slowly drops to his posterior...extending his thick legs out before him. He's moaning and gasping for breath. *Phum. Phum.* His left hand crosses over his chest where four holes are quickly leaking out the last of his life. Twenty seconds have passed from the first *phum* to the present. Since Vallano believes Jackson to be dead, or at least on his way, he begins darting towards Teresa. She has turned the corner of the SUV and is now making her way up the steps, heading for the front door, screaming for help.

'Stop right there, Teresa! One more step 'n' yir done!—I said *stop!*'

Yanking on the doorknob, she doesn't stop; she continues crying out hysterically. She needs let in, but the door is locked and not about to open by force or desperation. The key is on a keychain, lying on the ground next to Jackson. Despite the shock from the ambush, she's probably aware of this, yet she still cries for God to somehow help her.

'Teresa - *shudup* - turn around - now.'

Still pulling on the doorknob but now with half an effort, she turns her head over her boney shoulder to see the black-and-bald monster standing at the bottom of the steps, pointing her father's gun right at her.

'Look, Teresa, if you cooperate 'n' do whad I say quickly 'n' quietly, you'll be spared.' Keeping the gun pointed at her, he uses his other hand to pull out the extra pair of rubber gloves and the small brown paper bag. He sets 'em on the bottom step and backs away. 'Put doze gloves on. 'N' quit yir fuckin' cryin'. One more outburst 'n' 'at's it. I'm fuckin' seris: *move.*'

Trembling, she lets go of the doorknob. Wobbling (it looks like she doesn't know how to walk) she comes back towards him, descending the steps with buckling knees. She picks up the rubber gloves and tries sliding 'em on but they are flapping around furiously from her shaking. She's mumbling questions like *why are you doing this?* and requests like *please don't kill me, please.* He pays no mind.

'Okay. Now da bag. Pick it up 'n' breathe indo it. Iddle help you catch yir breath 'n' keep it unner control. Now when ya go over do 'im, 'n' if ya feel sick 'n' think yir gonna throw up, go inna bag. 'Cause if you throw up on the grahn, I'm gonna put holes all through you—'

She cries out but not too loud; nevertheless, it perfectly encapsulates the tremendous measure of horror within her reedy frame, almost as if it was just confirmed that she *is* going to die. Everything's happening so fast. Life and death. So fast, so fast.

'Pick up da bag 'n' breathe in it.'

She does. She puts the bag up to her mouth. The bag fills up, then quickly deflates. Back and forth: full, flat, full, flat. Whey-faced. Her bleary eyes are focused on Vallano. The tears are streaming down her milky skin...slowing a bit in the shallow part of her cheeks. Her hair has changed: dyed raven-black, pulled back in a ponytail, big glamorous bangs. How things are always changing. Full, flat. Full, flat.

'Sit dahn on the bottom step. You nee'dda pull yirself together 'cause we got some shit we gadda get done fast, 'n' more importantly, *correctly*.' (She sits down on the step, breathing into the bag, shaking like she's in an electric chair with the switch pulled.) 'First, were you expectin' anyone da come over?'

'Na-no-ah,' she answers into the deflated bag.

''Cause if ya are, tell me now 'n' we can get da fuck oudda here. 'Cause if anyone pulls up, *everyone's* goin' dahn, includin' *you.* So don't think ya can outsmart me 'n' save yirself; it's a whole different ballgame now. So again: are you *sure* nobody's saposta be comin' over?'

'Ye-yes. No one, no one should be ca-ca-, oh God, please don't kill—'

'Okay. Shudup 'n' listen. How much H is in the house?'

'I – I duno-noaah—'

'*Izzer* any in the house?'

'Ye-yes. I – I – think there is.'

'I dunno, Teresa; sounds like yir lyin'. I'd like da leave here with a bunch a H for us, so I hope yir not tryin'ah be difficult or devious. I mean, he'z still sellin' it, right?'

'*Mmhmm*,' she breathes affirmatively into the bag.

'You still do it?'

'*Mmhmm*.'

''At shit can rilly get a hold of ya, huh. But I'm akshly lookin' forwardda it. But anyway, herzza plan. Yir gonna walk over 'n' pick up the keys. Do not—I repeat, do *not* touch him in any way. He's dead now. Once ya got da keys, yir gonna walk back over. Go up da steps. Get dahn on yir hands 'n' knees in front of the door. Open it. Den slowly go in. I'll be right behind you. Once inside, yir gonna shut da porch light off. Den yir gonna crawl da wherever the H is. 'N' yir not gonna make any mess while we're inside. Then we're gonna come back outside 'n' go from 'ere. Now get up 'n' go get da keys—quickly. Remember: if ya feel sick, go inna bag. But if you don't look at 'im, you should be juss fine.'

Vallano stands off to the side, the side where he waited in the woods. Teresa stands up, shaking and breathing violently into the bag. Full, flat. Full, flat. She's being extremely hesitant moving forward until Vallano tells her to come on, let's go. She runs over to the body propped against the front wheel and retrieves the set of keys that has fallen from his hands. Vallano directs her back up the steps and down on her hands and knees. She's wearing high-soled flip-flops. Vallano foresees a potential problem, so he makes her remove 'em: set aside on the porch. He then asks if she'll be all right without the bag for a few minutes; in tears, she says she thinks. So she sets the bag aside, next to the flip-flops. And with rubber gloves on, she reaches upward with the key. Slides it in. Twists. Then pushes the quiet door open. She crawls across the threshold, moving like a malnourished dog. After cleaning off the bottom of his socks, Vallano remains at a safe distance behind her.

Once the porch light is turned off, he says, 'Okay. Where's the H?'

'Up – stairs,' she quavers. 'In the, the be-be-droom.'

'Well lead the way. 'N' don't stand up on the steps. *Crawl.*'

Down on the plush carpet, she maneuvers herself through a posh house full of blacks, whites, silvers, and incense...til coming upon the stairs. She starts a careful ascent but Vallano yells for her to move! move! He laughs at her pick-up and struggle. He's feeling more comfortable now. Naturally, though, he's still very anxious about fleeing the scene, even if Precalculations said things will remain unseen for at least a day, maybe the entire weekend; nevertheless, no one will be finding out tonight. Not a soul!

Upstairs, she moves down a shaded hallway as quickly as she can, and turns right into the master bedroom, which has a king size bed with red satin sheets—mirrors all over the wall—even on the ceiling above the bed. He's being watched by himself. He doesn't even recognize the grotesque image in the mirrors. To the side of the bed, on a nightstand, a clock says 12:04 a.m. Along the far wall, Teresa has crawled to a long dresser which also has a mirror attached to it: looks exactly like the one she had in her old bedroom, the one that once shone the eerie reflection of his best friend.

'I fuckin' said don't be tearin' shit apart! Move the clothes aside nice 'n'—ahh, there we go! Is it full?'

She opens a yellow cigar box. It's half-filled with bags of heroin. He directs her to shut it and slide it over to him. She does. He picks it up and directs her to fix the clothes then close the bottom drawer. Once done, she turns back to him like a huffing dog waiting command. He watches the tears drop to the ground, wondering if they could be detected—probably, with technology nowadays, but what would that even mean: *nothing*—for she lives and cries here every day.

'Oh shit. Almost forgot: got any clean needles? We need some clean needles.'

She reopens the bottom drawer and pulls out a Ziploc bag filled with medically-packaged needles.

'Toss it here. 'N' make sure 'at drawer's immaculate 'fore ya close it.'

She does as he says. He puts the packaged needles inside the cigar box. Then he steps to the side, near the bed, and directs her to crawl back downstairs and outside. Without touching anything (although he is gloved and glabrous) he inspects the dresser to make sure it's closed flush. Then he makes sure nothing superfluous is on the ground...

...Back outside, all is dark and quiet.

'Okay, Teresa. Putchir *sandals* back on...Okay, now lock da door 'n' take out da key...Pick 'at bag up juss in case ya need it 'cause I need ya da go back over 'n' drop da keys where ya got 'em from 'n'—'

'Vinny, you're not gonna kill me, right? When I put the keys back?' Back on her feet, Teresa seems calmer now, and very nice, like a polite little girl who's just really confused and curious.

'I tolja: as long as you don't fuck anything up or nuh'n weird happens. I'll explain everything as soon as we finish settin' things up.' He directs her to get goin', get goin', by waving the gun like a race flag. She's about to endeavor over to the body without using the bag but halfway there she puts the bags up to her mouth. Full, flat. Full, flat. She sets the keys back down in a manner best suited to her memory. Then she starts running back to the steps, in tears. Vinny allows her to run because he's at a safe distance, able to react if she should happen to act amiss. She sits down on the bottom step. Full, flat. Full, flat.

'Okay, now there's one last thing you gadda do.' He opens the box, takes a bag of heroin out, and carefully sets the box on the ground. 'Yir gonna go back over there with 'iss. 'N' I'm gonna be right behinja, guidin' ya through. You juss gadda tear a tiny hole in the bag. *Very carefully* so it don't spill out everywhere. Sprinkle *juss a liddle* on his left jean pocket, then make a liddle trail back towards the bumper, 'n' I'll show ya where da drop it. Oh! 'fore I even give ya this, I neeja da open all the doors. Izzer any shit inside?'

'No-ot that I-I know of.'

'Any stupid shit like jackets, papers, bags of whadever?'

'I dunno-ah,' she apologizes, her face burning with fear, stained with trails of yellowish tears. 'I'm sorry, Vinny. I really can't remember.'

'It's ar'ight. We'll find out. Dere's prahblee shit in the glove department. But juss throw anything ya see on the grahn 'n' seats, like yir robbin' it, ya know. 'N' 'member: I'm gonna be right behinja 'n' you don't have the keys anymore. So if ya try da lock yirself in, *I'll* use the keys, open up the door, 'n' kill you. Or bedder yet, I'll juss shoot ya through the windows 'fore ya can even move. Oh, 'n' where's your cell at?' Such acumen!

'It's over there, in my purse.' She points to the ground between the two SUVs where a small gold-trim black purse lies with nothing spilled out.

'We'll get it later. For now, let's get dis done so we can gihdoudda here.'

After placing the bag of heroin atop the cigar box, he stands out in the side yard, walking parallel with her down to the body. He suddenly decides to have her keep one hand behind her back at all times. So in that manner, she opens the driver door. She asks if she should open it fully because it might touch his (Jackson's) body. Vallano says no, just let the door fall back naturally but don't push it shut. Then Teresa opens the driver's-side back door, throws things around with one hand...walks around the back of the SUV...opens the other back door...then the other front door.

'Wait. Juss in case 'ere's a gun in the glove department, I wancha da lie on yir back across the seat with one arm behind yir back. Open it while lookin' straight up...'Ere ya go.' (He moves in closer and examines the glove department.) 'Okay. You can turn back over. *Nooo,* keep yir hand behin' jir back. Toss 'at shit everywhere...'

...They're back in the side yard, parallel with the body. Holding onto the paper bag for dear life, trying to stand still, Teresa stumbles a step back to the threshold of the driveway but remains facing Vallano.

'Stay up, soldier. Anyway, I'm sorry, Teresa, but I almost forgot: 'fore you sprinkle, you gadda reach indo his back pocket, pull out his wallet, 'n' take the credit cards 'n' money out 'cause we're gonna need it. Then dump everything else out like, like—well, you know wha' kinda picture I'm tryin'ah paint, so don't fuck it up. Now get to it.'

She just stares at him, right through him. 'Please, Vinny. I don't wanna go near him again. You have gloves on too. There'll be no traces—'

'Oh, I'm sorry, Teresa. I thought *I'm* the one with the gun.' He looks down at the gun as if for effect. 'Yes, I am. Now yir gonna go over there 'n' take his wallet out—don't fuckin' move' his ass, don't get any blood on ya— or I'm gonna fuckin' blow yir brains out. Now fuckin' move.'

She turns around. Quickly, she puts the bag up to her mouth. Full, flat. Full, flat. She slowly walks towards him, making sure she doesn't step in the blood, for trails of blood can be seen here and there thanks to the interior lights of the SUV; most of the blood, though, is soaked in his shirt. She's almost within reach now. Full, flat. Full, flat. As she struggles to make herself reach into his back pocket, it gives Vallano a chance to observe him: the thick soles of his shoes are tan; baggy blue jeans with oversized pockets; a dark red t-shirt; the splotches of blood on his chest simply look like wetness, as if he spilled a drink on himself; his big lips are lax; has that same scruffy beard as before but no hat: short curly hair; his head is lax, too, leaned towards the house; his eyes are semi open, looking at an indiscriminate spot in the woods; his arms are hanging down, right palm down, left palm up and a bit curled; looks like he's lost some weight: more fit: healthy chocolate skin: a handsome black man around thirty—

Full, flat. Full, flat. Tears, blood. Sweat, tears. Teresa has pulled out several cards and money, dropped some behind her on the ground. She's now shaking the leather wallet out. Business cards and pieces of paper falling into his lap. She drops the wallet beside him and begins running back towards the edge of the driveway until—

'Hey, come on; turn around 'n' pick 'at money 'n' dose cards up.'

She turns around. Tears, sweat. Blood, tears. Trying to pick up the money and cards as fast as she can. She pivots around like a shuttle run. Full, flat. Full, flat.

'Okay. Walk over da the box, put everything inside, 'n' bring 'at bag over. Hurry up 'cause we gadda get goin'.'

She runs up to the side of the steps...kneels down, grabs the bag, opens the box, throws the money and cards inside, closes the box, all very quickly, then runs back, leaving her breathing bag next to the box.

'Okay. Go back over, rip a tiny hole in the bag, 'n' sprinkle some by his left jean pocket. Den slowly trail it towards the back bumper but leave some empty spaces.'

'I dunno if I – if I can tear it with these gloves on.'

'The bag's plastic, Teresa: I'm sure iddle rip priddy easy.'

'But, but I don't wanna fuck it up 'cause, 'cause—'

'Cuzza dis?' He points the gun directly at her face, his finger wrapping around the trigger, then lowers it. 'Yeah, prahblee best not da fuck it up.'

She starts huffing again, sniffling, carefully ripping a tiny hole in the bag. He tells her to hold her rubber thumb over the hole as she walks back up to him in the same manner as before, but now with her free hand covering her nose and mouth, for she no longer has the breathing bag. She uses the other hand to sprinkle heroin on his jeans...then trails some towards the back bumper...leaving spaces as he sees fit.

'Back here.' He picks a random spot about five yards behind the SUV. 'Drop it.' She drops the bag; it puffs a bit. 'Okay. Good job, Teresa. Go back da the steps 'n' sit dahn. I think we're done. Does everything look good da you?'

'Mmhmm,' she replies in a whimper, walking back towards the house. She sits down on the bottom step. She hugs herself. She's shaking so violently. The midnight air has become a bit chilly. Vallano picks up the breathing bag and folds it up. He puts it in his left jeans pocket. He looks at the cigar box, trying to decide whether he wants to pick it up and hold it. He doesn't. He tells her to take the gloves off, fold 'em up, and toss 'em his way. She does. He puts the last item in the cigar box. A bit off to the side of the steps, he runs the entire scene of movements through his mind...things seems as planned. He moves in front of Teresa, five yards away. She looks him over, the hairless Vallano with a long-sleeve black shirt, blue jeans, and what appear to be socks on top of socks pulled up over the cuff of his jeans. She looks sad, confused, terrified. She's shaking so violently.

'Fffuck,' he moans to himself. A bad, bad thought. 'Extend yir legs out so I can see the bottom of yir flip-flops 'cause if you juss put blood on the steps—' He stops there.

Subserviently, so fearfully, she extends her shaking legs straight out. It's too dark to see the nuances of the soles but he doesn't want to go through the process of having her turn the porch light back on, or even worse, having to go through the agonizing duality of getting the flashlight in the woods. Besides, he suddenly realizes, whoever did this could've had her do anything. It's such a mystery! Means nothing, really!

'Well, looks fine as far as I can tell.' (So she withdraws her knees back into her chest, trying to hold herself together.) 'Anyway—betcha never saw this comin', huh?'

'No,' she whispers. 'Please don't kill me.'

'Oh, I'm not gonna kill you. I got plans for us. Me 'n' you are gonna escape da Sicily 'n' start a life together. I know a few people there. We'll get new identities 'n' whatnot. I mean, you would like da be with me, right?'

'Mmhmm.'

'Yeah, I knew you would. I still 'member 'at night ya tried gih'n on me. 'Azz a rill tough thing for meedda deal with, ya know. But I got through it. 'N' I also remember 'at one time on the phone you sayin' how me 'n' you shoulda been together, 'n' look: here we are, together. But before we move on, I neeja da confirm a few things dit've rilly been botherin' me. 'N' if I think yir lyin'—well, I'll shoocha. But don't be afraid da be honest with me 'cause I alriddy know the answers. I tolja: you can never outsmart me. Never. You didn't seem da believe me before, but whaddabout now?'

She looks up—sunken melancholy eyes—and says, 'Yes, I believe you.'

'Good. First, we never slept together, right?'

'Right. Never.'

'Which means the baby you murdered *waaaas?*'

The question (or perhaps the wording of the question) seems to catch her off guard. Her mouth opens but nothing comes out. He asks again, making sure she sees that the gun is being anxious in his hands, ready to dance, and he has the power to keep its legs tied or unfetter them.

'It was—*his.*' She looks passed Vallano towards the body.

'Oh rilly? So why ja murder yir baby? Wait, lemme guess. You couldn't have daddy comin' home to an oreo grandchild.'

'No, that's not it at all. I'm not racist. If I was I would've—' She stops.

'Woulda wha'? Never left Pessi for *him?*'

Her breaths (though restrained) are becoming heavy, probably because she realizes how entrapping his questions are becoming, while knowing deceptions can't be chanced; it's a whole different ballgame. 'Yeah, I guess. Me and Zach just weren't good together. But I honestly never wanted to hurt him. And it killed me when I found him. And I—'

'Slow dahn. Answer accordingly. Don't incriminate chirself. Now tell me, why would Pessi suddenly do that do himself? I mean, we all still seem da be at a loss for answers. But dohncha think it seemed kinda—I dunno— *suicidal?*'

'Mmhmm.'

'I agree. 'N' *what*, I wonder, coulda possibly pushed 'im da do it? Wait, lemme guess. He found out you were fuckin' around on 'im—'

'No, no. I wasn't. I swear, we weren't even together then. I swear to *gawd*, Vinny, we weren't. He—' She stops.

'He wha'?'

'He knew about the abortion.'

'Wha'?'

'Vinny, please don't kill me. I swear, I'll do whatever you want. I'll go tell Ivy the truth. I'll make her come back to you. I swear I will, and she'll believe me.'

He laughs...and laughs...and bends down and laughs some more. 'Oh, Teresa. It feels so good da laugh. 'At's the funniest thing I've heard all year. Look whad I juss did. I juss fuckin' killed somebody. 'N' you *akshly* think I'd letcha leave here 'n' "clear the problem up" with Ivy? You must think I'm rilly fuckin' stupid—'

'No, no, I don't. I'm just sayin' whatever you want, I'll do it.'

'Whad I *want* is for you da tell me how Pessi found out 'n' when.'

'The night before he died—I told him. But, but—please don't kill me, Vinny—I'm just bein' honest like you want me to.' (With the gun, he compassionately motions for her to continue.) 'I was really fucked up. So oudda my fa-king mind. We got into a fight and it just came out, but – but I told him that it was his because—well, I dunno why. I just couldn't think straight. But he already knew I was seein' someone else—'

'Wait. So yir sayin you were sleepin' with both of 'em?'

'Well, Zach only once in a while, just 'cause he was still around.'

'That don't make any sense. You juss said Pessi knew you were with Jackson, so I highly doubt he woulda kept fuckin' you. Pessi had dignity.'

'No, I didn't tell him *who* I was seein'. And I told him it was nothin' sexual; just seein' someone. And, and I just needed some time apart from him. So—'

'But it *was* sum'n sexual with *Jackson?*'

'Mmhmm.'

'So lemme get dis straight: You 'n' Pessi split. Den ya start fuckin' Jackson but the only thing ya tell Pessi is yir seein' some mystery person. Den ya get pregnant by Jackson. But how ja know it wasn't Pessi's if you were still fuckin' him?'

'Well by then I was already with Jackson for like five months. But when I took the pregnancy test me and Zach hadn't had sex in like two months. So I'm just sayin' *at first* me and Zach still had sex once in a while I was seein'—'

'Teresa, why you lyin'ah me. I'm—'

'No, I swear to gawd, I'm not lyin', Vinny. Please don't—'

'Den Pessi woulda known for a fact it wasn't his, not havin' slept with you in months.'

'No, see—I, I never told him when I was pregnant; I just told him when all was said and done, so he...'

'Go on. So he?'

'So he thought the abortion had happened like a month or so before it really did.'

'So yir sayin' Pessi thoucha got pregnant from the *last* time ya fucked—say, two months before he died—but the truth is, you'd juss found out you were pregnant by Jackson, went 'n' had an abortion, 'n' 'en told Pessi the night before he died?'

'Mmhmm.'

'So what's the rill reason for the abortion then?'

'I dunno; too young, scared, and although I *am* a piece a shit junkie, I'm at least responsible enough not to bring a child into—into *this.*'

He vaddled. '*Responsible?* No, that's *exactly* whachu weren't. With people thit do heavy drugs 'n' have sex, bein' *responsible* is bein' on birth control or usin' condoms. You were juss bein' stupid 'n' reckless. Wouldntcha agree?'

'Mmhmm.'

'Okay. So ya murder yir kid with Jackson. Den ya get "rill fucked up." Get indua fight with Pessi. 'N' blindly tell 'im you murdered *his* kid behind his back a month prior. Hmm...Well, Teresa, I think all you've said is true except one thing: I think ya told Pessi you murdered *our* kid—ya know, juss like ya told Ivy. 'N' I think you did this for one of two reasons: Either that night he tolja me 'n' him we're goin' back home for the weekend, 'n' it made ja mad 'cause you didn't wan' 'im da be around me, da be happy, da do his own thing—ya know, you wanted 'im da sit in 'at house 'n' juss be miserable—so ya told 'im about the abortion with the twist of the most vicious lie so he'd turn against me. *Or*—in the ironic opposite—you saw it as an easy way da get rid of 'im for good 'n' get 'im oudda yir house 'n' life, without 'im ever botherin' ya again, 'cause we both know he loved ju so much, 'n' so without bombs, it's takes longer da destroy things. Either way, him thinkin' it was *mine*—well, da me, *that's* wha' woulda pushed 'im over the brink: thinkin' his lifelong best friend had been fuckin' his girl behind his back, impregnated her, 'n' 'en tried da cover it up by gih'n an abortion. Now *that's* pain worthy of suicide.'

'No, I swear, Vinny, I didn't tell him it was—'

'Ya know, Teresa: I was fuckin' everything da that kid. I's the only one he rilly trusted—the only one he felt comfortable around...It's funny: me 'n' him were from the same fuckin' place, brought up on the same fuckin' shit, priddy much born inda the same fuckin' life. Yet *I'm* the one thit made it out "the right way." 'N' it's bothered me for so long. Why me? Why—oudda all my friends—why am *I* the one thit's literate? da one thit's gifted? da one thit gadda break? How'd I grow up doin' the same shit as 'ey did but I'm the one with the desire 'n' opportunity da rise above? Why not them? *Why?*' He paused, wanting to see if she had the answers, but sitting on the first step, looking down, she just lets a waterfall of tears quietly fall to the ground. 'Ya know, Teresa: my mother emigrated here when she'z still a kid. She's barely eighteen years older than me. She came here all she rilly knew houdda say is, *"'Ello. You ave work for me?'* Know what drew her here? She wantedda escape the poverty she grew up in. 'N' see, Teresa, before she left Sicily, she had son before me. I didn't even know til the day I left for cawidge. 'N' it fuckin' shocked me. I mean, I always thought of her as 'iss devout Roman Catholic; not some youthful exotic lover, ya know. It split the image I had of her. It split myself too. When she told me she had another son before me, I's juss—I dunno—I didn't feel like I's *me* anymore, ya know. But anyway, she gave da baby up da his father til she made enough money here da take care of 'im. But, see, things didn't go as planned. Not over there, 'n' certainly not here. She started to see The American Dream is a mirage. From across the sea it prahblee looked so promising—so beautiful. She came here thinkin' money juss flows through the fuckin' streets, 'n' all ya gadda do's go outside da get it. But she didn't know that, yeah, there might be alawda money here, but it only flows dahn certain streets. But once in a while the wind'll blow some bills dahn Poor Man's Lane, 'n' when *that* happens, someone runs outside, snatches it up rill quick, 'n' 'en shows everyone else with the greatest pride. Den everyone talks about it: *"The American Dream"*: see, it's true: *anyone* can make it. The hard work, the hustle, the determination: it *will* work out for anyone who tries; all ya have ta do is try. That's what my parents believed in, Teresa. 'N' my neighbors. 'N' their neighbors. But why don't we ever tell the truth: The American Dream is true—but The American Nightmare is far more common. See, Teresa, I'm wunna the lucky ones thit snatched up da bills thit got blown astray. Now I'm the one they wanna highlight. I'm saposta be a success story, the next rags-to-riches, the one who trumps all the sadness of my mother's story, my father's story, my neighbors' stories. But sum'n rilly went wrong 'iss time. I've seen too much. Know too much. 'N' I'm not gonna fuckin' cave like everyone else. See, Teresa,——————————————————————

——————————————————————
——————————————————————
——————————————————————
——————————————————————
——————————————————————.'

(Tears are now falling from his eyes.) 'Ya know, Teresa, I fuckin' hated my father so bad. He yoosta hit us. He was a drunk, a racist, uneducated—juss embodied everything I hate. But above all, I hated 'im so bad for the way I had da grow up. But still, that was *my* father. *My DAD* workin' in the still mill juss tryin'ah make it. But he didn't make it. Even if 'ey woulda never lost his job, he woulda *never* made it. Dohncha see, Teresa: it's all a lie. Everything's a fuckin' lie. Everything on the surface is a lie. All that shit like "work from the inside" is a lie; it's juss a mind-controlling tactic da keep people passive, 'n' 'at's why I can't be apart of it. I'll never sell my soul. *Never.* You may not believe me, but I *do* believe in God. But they say God's gonna send meedda Hell now. I'm gonna burn eternally. 'N' maybe they're right. Maybe I completely missed my target. But fuck, Teresa—you 'n' Jackson *did* take away da only two things I had left; 'n' I'm juss not so convinced izz part of "God's plan." So now—' (Wipes eyes. Breathes deep. Refocuses.) 'So why ja tell Ivy whacha did? 'At's sum'n I haven't been able da figure out. *Why?*'

'I dunno, Vinny,' she cried with her face still hung. 'I'm so sorry. I guess—I dunno—I guess I was just jealous 'cause I knew I'd never have what you two had, and it scared me and made me so bitter. And the drugs—I swear to gawd, Vinny, they just fucked my head up so much. Sometimes I don't even know what I'm doin', or where I am at, ya know?'

'Yeah—I know. But still, I'm gonna rilly miss her. She was the world da me. It won't bother ya thit I'm still gonna be in love with her while I'm with you, will it?'

'No. I understand. I really do. It's all my fault anyways.'

'No, don't say that, Teresa. Things are far too complex for it da be *all* yir fault. I only meant you 'n' Jackson were the physical, on-the-surface reason why I no longer have Ivy 'n' Pessi. I mean, I'm not stupid. I know how it is...Hey—look up at me. Come on; I wancha da look at me.'

Slowly, so fearfully, she looks up at him, her arms wrapped around her knees.

'Maybe we shouldn't do drugs. Maybe idd be best da gitcha cleaned up. Start a whole new life in Catania. How's that sound?'

'Yeah, I think that *would* be best. I've really been wantin' to get clean for a while. It's just so hard—'

'Hey?'

'What.'

'Yir a beautiful girl, ya know that. You rilly are. Very beautiful.'

'*Thank you,*' she whispers, fresh tears falling.

'Hey, smile for me. It's so weird: for some reason, in my mind, I can never seem da put a smile on yir face. So go ahead. I know it's rilly hard right now, but think of all the good things da come 'n' juss smile.'

She smiles for him: a flash of so much indescribable pain. She lowers her head back down.

'Well,' he sighs, looking around the encircling darkness. All is very quiet except the trees: they seem to be soughing. 'We should get goin'.'

'Okay.'

'Hey—'member Pess?'

'Hu—' *Phum.* Right through her mouth. *Phum. Phum.* Two into her chest. The side of her body hits the steps...then rolls to the ground...*Phum. Phum.*

...The trees are trying to eat him. Demon teeth are snapping at his heels, trying to tear through the socks. The flashlight is shining unsteadily on the predatory shadows about to snag him. Millions of death knells are thundering in the sky. He's running so fast. But doesn't want to be running so fast. It's just that (ten minutes into the woods) his creeping walk hadn't been feeling right. Something hit him. Perhaps externally, too, because the millions of things after him are trying to snag and devour him. Perhaps detain him. It's so dark. He's trying to run with his right hand holding the box tightly against his ribs, his left hand holding the flashlight out in front of him. He knows he shouldn't be running. There would be no reason to run if everything wasn't after him. Things are snagging him. Can't get snagged. He stops. Flashes the light all over him. Has he been torn into?—No. Does he still have everything on him?—Yes. But he desperately needs water. Needs to rest here for a minute but there's no water here. Needs to be somewhere else—someone else. Needs to die—and get it over with...

...Hours later, he's made it back to the orchard, in one piece. The flashlight is about dead. He falls to his knees in front of the shed, nearly dead. Needs water. Needs water. But can't move. Closes his eyes to see those atomic sparkles. They're rioting! Flying all over the place! There's a war behind his eyes! He reopens 'em. Either he needs to put new batteries in the flashlight, or Lucia[5] needs to appear and lead the way, because he still has things to get done, and quickly. Get up! Get up!...

...He's up in the field, to the left of the orchard, naked. He's rubbing his right hand back and forth over his skinned head. It's only making things worse. Where's his hair? He needs to burn those clothes. They're atop the pit he built a week ago. The pit is two logs connected together by a bunch of branches. Atop the branches sits prearranged tinder, which now includes the shirt, jeans, socks, gloves, and the paper bag. He needs to burn everything into nonexistence. Can a fire be seen from here? This late at night? It has to be past 4 a.m. This early in the morning? When does the sun rise? Must burn *now*. No one even knows yet. Must start a fire before anyone knows. Where's his hair? Pacing, pacing. Circling, rubbing. Talking to himself. Cahm dahn, cahm dahn. He drops to the ground, trying to get a grip on it. Get up! Get up! He gets up. Shaking violently. Bad images. Bad memories. Is it still present time? What's he doing here? He picks up the can of gasoline and douses the materials. Too much? Will this explode? Can't have noise. The rubber is going to reek. Will anybody be able to smell it? Or see the smoke? He tosses the match. FIRE! Burn! Burn! Burn! It's already smoking. He's pacing, rubbing, telling it to burn quicker! Hurry up! He's naked on the ground, trying to crawl to salvation. This isn't real life. Can't be. He's a murderer. No salvation. Burn! He's up. His heart is missing again.

---

[5] St. Lucia is the patron saint of blindness. She is also the patroness of Syracuse, Sicily. When her mother Eutychia is suffering from "bloody flux" (dysentery), St. Lucia remembers how St. Agatha (the patroness of Catania) had testified to a gospel in which a woman had been healed of the "bloody flux" by touching the hem of the coat of Christ. So St. Lucia convinces her mother to pray with her at St. Agatha's tomb; and she is healed. *Lucia* means "light," deriving from the Latin root *lux* which means "lucid."

It quit beating. No, it's beating too fast. Another heart attack! His father died of a heart attack. Massive heart attack from massive stress. He's massively stressed. He's going to die from a heart attack tonight! Or this morning! What time is it? He needs to die quickly or these materials need to burn quicker. Oh God! Oh God! It's thundering! God's mad! God saw what he did! God's coming! That's what thunder is! He can't deal with this anymore! He extinguishes the fire with a bucket of water. Are the clothes fully bur—come back tom—running back towards the orchard...everything and everybody is after him! Even God!...

...He's dressed comfortably, sitting underneath the shrouded apple tree. His back is against the trunk, which is barking and biting into his back. He's crying in stomach-thumping sobs, while Screwy rests in his lap, holding an acorn. Up above, the moon's missing and the sky's quiet. The darkness is lying over him like a blanket of exhaustion. It's about to rain. He tells Screwy to make everything all better, to make him sane again. He starts rubbing his face off. His hair's gone. He's telling God how sorry he is. He's crying. Life's over. What has he done? He starts repenting profusely but the voice of wrongness keeps interrupting and won't allow him to repent. Trying to collect himself, he squeezes his eyes shut and breathes. The war! The war! He reopens 'em. He reaches for it. A little in the spoon. A lighter underneath. A sucking needle. A prayer to never wake up again. A prayer that Hell awaits not. He looks at Screwy though a screen of tears. Screwy's holding an acorn. He smacks his arm. He puts the needle to his arm, clinching his teeth, believing his breaths are about to stop...

SNAP YOUR REVELATION

...the music stops when one ceases to believe...when the hero exposed as the coward they truly are turns away from the sinking ground of the metaphysical[1] and scampers back to terra firma, the *safe* grounds...Socrates, Descartes, Freud: all cowards...all doctors of the mind who never took the stand to step outside of time and into Time...all passive rationalists who thought their words alone were as good as gold...Socrates (the true sophist) proudly sat on his cell bench, self-righteously sipping hemlock...Descartes (the soul miscalculator) proudly sat on his desk chair, calmed by the certitude of his pineal gland...Freud (the closet sexist) proudly sat on his armchair, rationalizing the hysterical, never taking into account cultural constructs and the historical suffering of women...and like most other great thinkers and leaders, they never took the notion to stand up...cast the stethoscope aside...plunge deep into Soul...and listen to the primordial suffering that exists there...they never took a chance *there*...nor did they take a chance *here*...wipe away the illusion and you can still see them, and perhaps those in your world, frozen to the terra firma, each in their own time, each in their own way, always with a façade suggesting otherwise, making you think otherwise, making anyone who says otherwise today's insane pariah...HA! those insane pariahs!...laugh at them!...use your laughter to silence them!...HAHAHAHAHA!...

...and so the music turns inward, the beast outward...the bodies drop down, the needle pushes in...and another brilliant mind is destroyed, because they slain his heart...and—HA! HA! double ups History, as the complexity is simplified, mocked, and distorted...

...ahhh! but the day is young! and *you're* still alive! and *you're* still laughing! so who's too scared to come in and dance through his imagination?!— WARNING! WARNING! step back! it's not safe here! (safe here!) *gnôthi seauton?!* [2] NO! do not *know* thyself; *BE* THYSELF! it's not safe here! (safe here!) sinking down! (down!) all thoughts molded, supplemented, turned anew, treated brutally in a million and two extraneous ways...and now— they're GONE! it's not safe in here! (safe in here!) the crafty Hands of Time have torn apart your inventiveness! your History! your little insignificant life! can't escape this ether now! HAHAHAHAHA! your laughter is starting to ring out like madness! HAHAHAHAHA!...

...so warm warm warm, thinking thinking thinking—WHY?!—be realistic, demand the impossible! spit those sick thoughts out! YUCK! be not to be! touch a fragrance! smell a nerve! hear an eye! eye a voice! taste the tinges of being fucked and fucked over! experience an intuitive connection of

---

[1] General meaning for that which is beyond objective experience (the senses and the rational mind)
[2] [grc] Know thyself

energies! the things—these THINGS!—beyond the moment they can't transcend! on the page the he~~art~~ can't beat! emotions and sensations words can't depict! the rules of logic language follows! thought follows! tangible follows! but here—but HERE!—is *the ether*...like a breeze: you can feel it, and at times you can even see its effects, nevertheless, you can never see the breeze itself, so dry so warm so fast rush rush rush...

(The rain is falling in a pitter-patter. Through his eyes, everything is dimmed and refractive. He's slipping down beneath the trunk. Rush to safety. Rush.)

'...our whole modern world is entangled in the net of Alexandrian culture...it proposes as its ideal the *theoretical man* equipped with the greatest forces of knowledge and laboring in the service of science whose archetype and progenitor is Socrates...all our educational methods originally have this ideal in view: every other form of existence must struggle on laboriously beside it, as something tolerated, but not intended!'...not here, my feverish friend! it's all intended HERE! OPEN INVITATIONS TO PUT ~~ART~~ IN PRAXIS HERE! NO MORE MERETRICIOUS QUESTS OF SCIENCE AND LAW! THE PINS OF THE UNIVERSE ARE POPPING THE BALLOONS OF LOGIC! SYLLOGISMS! OBJECTIVITY! ALL SUBSTRATUMS!...*(he pukes)...PROBAE ESTI IN SEGETEM SUNT DETERIOREM DATAE FRUGES, TAMEN IPSAE SUAPTAE ENITENT?* [3]— IN WHAT GARDEN?!...*(he pukes again)*...INVADE THAT GARDEN MOTHERFUCKERS! WAR! SLAVERY! IGNORANCE! BLOOD FOR DEMOCRATIC CHAINS!...but wait—where's Christ to speak on the splendor of PEACE AND LOVE?! love thyself! love thy neighbor! love the Fabric of Nature which holds us in place! [4]...apple-tree boy has always been out of place...damn him...hey, who and where are *your* heroes?...are they fictionalized or just marginalized?...whatever, it's all the same...in the end, just like in the beginning, you only have yourself, chaotically placed within the balanced confines of Nature...and all who come along in between—the ones within your immediate senses—will vie for attention with yourself...and all who come along in between—the ones outside your immediate senses— will only become distractions and deceptions...and through it all, you will try to take it all in but will never get a grip on anything...*nothing*...iiiiiiit wiiiiill allllllllllllll goooooooooo a—

(—ahhh cooling down sunken ground emptied out slooooooooow is the world not safe nothing known known flashes of life wisps of deep deep music flashes drained...)

...and so knowing we are not the light of the world, we stick closely to our nooks where the small fires we kindle keep our bodies warm...in our homes

---

[3] [lat] A good seed, planted even in poor soil, will bear rich by its own nature. [Attributed to Lucius Accius in *Atreus*.]

[4] Allusion to St. Matthew 22:37-40 where Jesus says, "Thou shalt love the Lord thy God with all thy he~~art~~, and with all thy soul, and with all thy mind. This is the first and greatest commandment. And the second is like unto it, Thou shalt love thy neighbor as thyself. On these two commandments hang all the law and the prophets."

we keep the tip of our fires away from the belly of the bowls, and hoist the fire up on a candlestick, with the hope that it will be just enough to reach those intimately around us...but the more fiery souls feel as if they're creating fires larger than they actually are...fires still within the home yet they believe their fire alone is heating the nook and beyond...secretly, selfishly, they do so with the hope that *all* may see their good works[5]...that would be Vallano...but he's a dreamer...and for that, he now he sits alone under the apple tree, as raindrops sneak through the leaves and boughs, cooling his weary head...but never his heart!...that's his warring thought at the present moment: 'No! Never my heart! Iddle never change! Never!'...oh the blind passion of the youth!...it can make old invalids want to stand up and dance!...but in his defense, at one time or another, haven't we all felt that way in our little world?...but most of us—those who are "realistic" and have "matured"—learn to settle for snagging the dandelion dust in reach...only a few continue reaching up for the stars...either way, to be sure, throughout our lives, here and there, we all tend to experience such impassioned moments from which we make internal, sometimes vocal, promises that this—this very instance driving the heart mad—will neither be relinquished nor forgotten...and, yes, seemingly by our command, they *do* burn on, sometimes for weeks, for months—the greatest conflagrations can burn on for years!...til these impassioned moments of paragonic living— these fiery wisps of spirit weaving through us like ribbons of bliss whereby we come to feel truly alive—meet with the rain, and another, and another...and gradually all starts becoming blurry, unraveled, relinquished, and forgotten—diminutive remnants shrinking smaller and smaller in the nodding perception—like flickering embers dropping down slowly through the dawn sky...til falling into the ebb of a steady tide (the *plups* barely audible)...now moving away, towards the distant horizon...

...it's only a matter of time...so hold on to it, to pardon the cruel tripuns[6]...but all the same, mothers and fathers, sons and daughters, for Life is bound to be boundless and does whatever It wants...yes, that's Life: chaos, rhythm, and irony; in matters of perception, phenomena and noumena, the things we can and can't see, respectively...in sum, to all It is everything, even if to some, All is none...just like whether you're falling down like ice[7] or climbing like ivy, Life will still be on the run...

---

[5] Allusion to and play on St. Mathew 5:14-16
[6] The pun is threefold, the "cruelness" alluding either to its irony or the stark reality of human existence: 1) An allusion to the idiom "Hold on to what you got" when one is not physically embracing anything; namely love, and in the language here, but stated ironically, the remnants floating away in the ocean 2) An allusion to the saying "You can't take it with you" which originated from Paul's first letter Timothy: "For we have brought nothing into the world, and it is certain we can carry nothing out. And having food and raiment, let us be therewith content." [I Tim 6:7-8]; 3) "So hold on" as if one is on an adventurous (perhaps dangerous) ride.
[7] Hail

(...the pitter-patter of the rain has shifted into a full sprint towards the ground...he sighs...holds his arms closer to his chest...his head involuntarily drops in a nod...half-smile, half-frown on his face...vision in full-blur...he can't feel a thing besides a small prick of heat deep within his chest...this is the nature he presently sits in...)

...in the same respect that iron is the heaviest element produced exothermically through fusion, while the lightest through fission, and accordingly, within a star, these energetic phenomena inevitably cause it to burn and fade, it also seems inevitable that one day this peculiar character Vincent Vallano will find himself an old man living and dying, burning and fading, alone, far off in the country...that is, if he skirts and dupes any authorities who may seek him out in due time...but if a situation happens to arise, he will likely escape their crucifixions, for his linguistics, designs, and facades are quite impressive and tricky, like how a dead star once far away still shines so brightly for us...so then let us take Vincent Vallano to the countryside as the old man who got away from his youthful "experiments," "executions," and "whatnot"...

...one particular day in this hypothetical senescence, he happens to be sitting in a rocking chair, placed in the middle of an open gray porch, reading an old familiar book, when a rain begins to fall at dusk...instantly, it brings to mind all past rains, as if they were all the same, or continuations of the last having only been interrupted by the torrid affairs of Nature...blowing in with the misty breeze comes a wistful sensation impelling him to set the book aside...stand up...sigh deep...and again...and again...after shaking his head as if to break away from the state irking his bones, he hobbles to the edge of the porch...keeping his hunched body underneath the roof, he sticks his leathery hands out in the rain...he begins witnessing a million reflections of himself striking against his skin...but rolling off chaotically, imperceptibly, just too quickly to stare at them for more than a moment...it scares him, for he suddenly realizes for the millionth time that he doesn't know himself at all: these reflections are broken and fragmented, too symbolic of Life in the eye, too mocking of his own memoirs...but he still tries to clutch all the droplets anyway...but the rain only pours down harder...now more infinity is coming down all around him...splashing out every which way...each drop like a memory flung hither and yon...each drop like a part of his essence that had been stolen away so long ago...desperately he cups his hands together and lets it fill up...then he brings the flesh-cup of water up to his mouth...tilts it...letting whatever within roll down inside himself...but he can only taste a wisp of what once was, and at a degree less than the last rain because over the years the senses of his tongue have become stained from all the sour defeats, the ones that now taste so acidic, for, from the day he returned through the back of the woods to sit underneath the tree, he's lived out the rest of his life alone, being sustained by 'I'll never let it go'...and so, bitter and defeated, he drops his hands—the remnants drizzle to the ground: resuming their natural course—then he turns around...sits back down in his chair...and watches the rain continue to fall...idly looking out into the swirling mist— near blindness at this point in his life—he begins rocking back and forth to the rhythm of that same ol' hope that the great wind will eventually gust his way what he can't get a hold of on his own...all the things burning inside that once seemed so real...

...and perhaps there's a picture of this scene floating around somewhere...a fine picture, too, for it has the quality of a mirror...so phenomenally it reflects back the image...in it he's leaned over the edge of the gray porch...his old leathery hands stretched out into the air...his palms upward like a beggar's...and the rain is falling down freely into the flesh-cup...but the fresh rain, just like his old weathered body, has been frozen by the *SNAP!!!*...and there, in that little frame of time, in the way just explained, contains the ironic truth, for it moves along...everything else forever lost in the glare of the flash.

AND BURY THIS APART FROM ME

May 23: I know I'm not crazy. If I can write these words, comprehend these words, say that I'm not crazy, then no matter what, I'm not. Still, I'm not sure if I really heard sirens last night, or saw a helicopter flying nearby, watching through the cracks of the shed door. I'm obviously not going outside for a while. Right now it's 7:12 p.m. I bought a wristwatch. It's a bit crowded in here but I have everything I need to last a few months, although I plan on making my escape sooner than later. God, I'm still shaking and having panic attacks one after another. I'm so afraid to go outside and that fear only makes me want to go outside and run for my life. I'm trying so hard to concentrate on these words: keeping focused is key. I know it's all in my head...Oh man, it's ten minutes after that last line because I just ran outside. Had a really bad panic attack. Went down to the creek and splashed myself with water. Then paced around in circles, rubbing my head. Feel a lot better now. Two things I can't believe: 1) I've actually estivated to the orchard, and 2) I'm still sane. I think I am; therefore, I know I am. It sucks. Feels like I'm stuck in the middle. Perhaps it would be better to just be insane and not know it, than to be thinking about insanity...It's 1 a.m. I can't sleep. I have a kerosene lamp on. I bought enough kerosene to last a lifetime. Stacked against the back wall is canned food, instant foods, breadcrumbs, Nutella, bags of chips, vitamins, juices, processed milk, and all this other shit. Jack stored gardening tools in here. I'm going to need the shovel to make a garbage pit in the woods. I have garbage bags too. That way it won't get messy or smelly. There's two long metal shelves on each side of the shed. Except for the lamp, I threw away most of the stuff and put my stuff on them. I have clothes and soaps to wash them in the creek. I really think I have all the essentials, and enough to last a while. I even bought five bottles of Nero d'Avola and Aglianico: it's all in a box stacked in the back corner. I have an ounce of weed. But I wasn't sure what to do about my nicotine habit. The way I saw it: if I continued chewing then I would've had to buy so many rolls, and you're supposed to keep them refrigerated. I guess the same goes with smokes but I decided to start smoking again. I bought ten cartons. But I have to smoke in moderation because I can't leave here to buy anything. Where am I going to go? I couldn't figure it out before. I figured the cops might check in on me, and if they would've seen I immediately flew somewhere, then that would be suspicious. I wanted to go to Catania, and still do. But again, any immediate traces of travel might do me end, even though graduating college *would* be a good alibi. Still, if they ever come after me, I think I did things so smoothly that they wouldn't have the evidence to do anything. I think it looked so like a heroin jack. Perhaps they will link it back to Pessi and just assume there's been some dirty business going on in the underground. Besides, how could they ever link it to me? I already opened up all the bags and scattered them in the creek. I burned the bags and needles yesterday. Then again, Jackson did say that shit about "knowing" the police. Well, where I'm from the police don't give a fuck. If he'd been intimidating them, then they're probably glad he's dead. But if they had been making side-cash off him, then they might be more curious. But I doubt it. Well, I kind of hope they were doing corrupt shit because that will be more incentive for them to just close the case and move on. Plus, there's no traces to lead them here, about eight miles away from the scene, in the middle of nowhere. The only way I get found is if Abigail shows up. But according to Brian Seaver's address in the phonebook, they live 30 miles away. And according to her, she's going to Ireland for a month and she's in no rush to do anything here. Well, maybe with the house, but it would just be bad luck for her to take a nostalgic trip in the orchard. I think for once Time is finally on my side...Okay, now I'm worried. It's 20 minutes later. I just realized Ivy's going to be so distraught. What if she unknowingly narks me out? Would she say bad things about me? Possibly speak of violent intentions? Tell them all the stories within our little circle? My odd questions about the orchard and Abigail's last name? I might be fucked. Maybe I should hide somewhere else for a while. But where? I have so much shit in this shed. If they would open it up things would look so suspicious. Could I just say I graduated and I'm homeless? No matter what, they would still need *physical evidence at the crime scene* to prosecute me. But if that should happen, would it be best for me to chance it? No way! I can't stand the thought of prison. I wouldn't last a day. No, they'll never take me away. Never. Which is why I'm just going to chance staying here. I have a lot of things to work out with God, but therein lies my faith, have to hope God will see me through this. Until then, I'm going to keep this gun right by me because they'll never take me away...I don't know how to write in *this* manner. I'm just sitting here on my blankets and pillows. I just got high but I'm still so fucking sore. I can barely move my legs. I'm wearing a black shirt, gray fleece pants, socks, and skater shoes tied up tight. In front of me, the kerosene lamp burns. (It smells funny.) The gun is next to me with a new clip in it. I took the extension and silencer off. (Probably should send that shit to the bottom of the creek. Perhaps they can tell when bullets have passed through a silencer? So if I don't have one, that's even less evidence. But fuck, they will still know it's Teresa's dad's! Fuck!!!) Anyway, yeah, I'm going insane in my sanity. And I have a black pen in my hand. This notebook is on my lap. Screwy's underneath it between my legs. My legs are crossed. I'm crying so hard. I'm so confused. What the fuck happened? I started a diary?...

May 28: There's been no sign of anyone. I feel a bit safer. But this past week has been pure hell. I honestly don't know how I haven't gone out of my mind and *stayed there.* I keep getting sucked back into this surreal reality. I'm guessing they've been found by now. Ivy's probably been questioned. No matter what she said, there was obviously no mention of the orchard. And why would she? If anything, she thinks I'm in Catania, while everyone else thinks Toronto. But I wonder if she will come here just to reminisce. Funny thing is, if she found me, I would still trust her. I don't know if she would ever take me back, but I don't think she would tell on me. That last time when she stuck up for me by the creamery when I was pulling on her leg—it seemed to say something. But I just don't overstand. What's she so afraid of? She knows I love her so much. She knows deep-down I'm a good person. I just seem otherwise because I'm really hurt.

June 1: I can't fucking bathe in the creek! It's so cold! I decided I'll just have to sponge it. I'll heat up some water in the pot and just sponge it. But I hate making fires! I mean, I have a fire pit up in the field, and I can't see any houses or roads from there. It's just endless fields and woods and mountains off in the distance. And looking back towards LaSalle, I can't see shit. Even at night, I can't see any lights unless I walk way back into this one part of the field, then I can see what appears to be the lights in the towers of Old Main. Over on the far side of the orchard, it's nothing but woods. But from the field—I guess looking down at the orchard it would be due north—but there's a bunch of small neighborhoods like Suburban Estates, and further up just a bunch of houses that sit off the main road. I think they would be the ones who might be able to see smoke in the air. But I don't think the smoke would be able to be seen at night. Even though the fire itself seems so ominous to me, I know they can't see the flames. But who knows? I *could* get by without fire. But it's nice to bathe in warm water. Plus, I need warm water to make a few things like my pasta and instant oatmeal.

June 3: Well, I guess it's time to move on. Suffer the surreal as best as I can. "Life will go on." And since I still have life, it must move on however it may. I'm going to figure out how to get out of here safely. Best to let things *out there* cool down anyway. Until then, I'm going to pass the time by taking walks, reflecting on Nature while deep in it, and trying to survive as Primitive Man. I also brought seven books with me: a Norton anthology (the first book I bought for Dr. Rosenbaum's class, which has over 2,000 pgs. of classic lit); *A Portrait of the Artist as a Young Man; Thus Spake Zarathustra; The Prophet; War and Peace; The Kingdom of God Is within You* (my newfound connection with Christ); and my old-school *Bible* (the former barrier between me and God). But of course I'm going to spend most of my time finishing *my* book. I brought plenty of paper, a dictionary, and a folder filled with passages, quotes, and anything else I thought might be of use. Oh shit, I just realized I didn't print out any lyrics for future chapters. Luckily I know a lot of songs off by heart. I'm definitely going to use "Naked Echo of the Past" at some point. Such a beautiful song! Well, I'm going to get started. Try to "catch up to myself." Funny thing is, I've been thinking about all that's happened, and now I can't help but wonder if I've been writing the book about my life, or has the book been writing my life for me.

June 05: It's 2:10 a.m. I just had a horrible nightmare. So vivid and sensational: I could feel every jerk in every nerve, every mental sting, every affliction within my soul. All these people were chasing after me because of my book. They wanted to kill me. I was running away and suffering from haematodrosis. The blood was just gushing from my pours, but everyone was running through it with no problem. Then it skips ahead to me here in the shed. I could've sworn I was awake and actually paralyzed in real life. I was trying to scream out for help because somehow I could still see everyone coming after me. There were two mes: the one running with haematodrosis, and the one paralyzed here in the shed. When I was finally able to speak, I screamed, "Help, Dad! Help!" Then I actually woke up, but I still felt stricken with paralysis. Now I'm slowly coming to terms with reality. I don't know what to do. There's no peace anywhere....

June 13: I'm so fucking sick. Think it's the flu. I have aspirin and medicine but it's not doing shit. What's it been? A week now? I don't think I've ever been sick longer than a week except when I was seven and had bronchitis. I even tried getting drunk on wine just to subdue the rubbery pain but that only made it worse: warm wine! yuck! I think I might be dying. If I am, I need to get this book done first, but I can't even think straight right now. I need a fucking fan in here. Poor little Screwy is sick too...

June 18: I'm sitting on the ledge of the shed, writing by the light of a potent moon. It's so beautiful out. Me and Screwy just got back from our midnight walk. We went down to the creek and walked all along it, feeding rocks to the water. I love that gulping sound and watching those things that skate across the surface of the water. (I wonder what those things are called?) Screwy doesn't like the dragon flies. But I would like to get some to come live with us because, despite the insect repellant I coat myself in, the mosquitoes are eating me alive. I probably have AIDS now. Anyway, there's a red and blue haze out tonight. A full moon too. It's beautiful because the moon is sitting perfectly inside the red haze with the blue haze spread out below. I long for poetic nights like this. It's funny though, we kept walking towards the moon (and this started around 9) but I was trying to see if we could somehow get closer to the moon, like stand right underneath it, but it's impossible. Despite the strong magnetic energy that made me feel like I *was* getting closer, it just kept moving away or something. Oh well. Maybe I was walking wrong. I just can't wait until the next crescent moon. Hopefully one where the bottom part of the moon is lighted, as opposed to the sides. Then I'll get to see part of her eyes in that sharp cusp. So to speak, a lash of memory *(nu gighiu ri guaiu dulurusuni)* [1] sure to smite my heart...I'm still sitting outside the door, looking up at the sky. I've always adored how a hazy sky looks so close. I always try reaching up to tear a little piece out. If I ever get a piece, I'm going to chew on it to see if it has the power up effect, although I know (just like every other time I've tried) I'll just be reaching up to what seems close but is actually far away...Yep, I just tried, and like the light of a star, it's a false reflection, of a true memory. Or the Real that's simply intangible. Well, me and Screwy are going to take our pillow, blanket, and a box of wine and go sleep down by the creek. May the devil's darning needle be piercing tonight!

June 25: Ehh, today's her birthday. Strange how I don't even have a picture of her to reminisce. Only pictures I have are the ones Ma sent of my family in Catania. I never did like pictures anyway. All the ones Ivy forced me to take, she kept. The ones I had on my cell I deleted a while back not thinking it would ever mean anything since I could always just look up at her. Now I can't even call her, although I wouldn't anyway. Well, maybe I would. I wonder if it's a happy birthday for her. I hope so. She's free from all the

---

[1] [scn] an eyelash of woe so painful

bodies of pain that once surrounded her. Speaking of bodies: I still have a piece of hers: the lock. I'm chewing on it right now. I do every day, especially at night and when I'm writing. I can still smell her—still *feel* her. So luxurious and epicurean. Thick, dark, ophidian, seven inches of perfumed mocha heaven. I think I could live off this forever. *POWER UP, WIMP-WIMP!!! Screwy says HAPPY BIRFDAY—'n' ya don't even know, HMHMHMHMHM!!!* Anyway, today me and Screwy have to go wash up...

July 1: My hair is finally growing back. I've made a vow to *never* shave again. I forgot how *The Bible* says we're not to shave the sides of our heads or trim our beards (Leviticus 19:27). Or how we're not to eat the meat of animals that "divideth not the hoof," such as rabbits, pigs, and camels. Nor are we to eat animals of the sea without fins and scales, such as lobsters, crabs, oysters, and clams. The 11th chapter of Leviticus specifically names all the animals we're not supposed to eat but do anyway. Guess we of the biblical breed just pick and choose what we see as fit (or say "that was for the Jews"), and condemn others who haven't picked and chosen the same, of course all in the name of *The Bible*, just not all of it...

July 2: I think I'm fucked. I've been on the backside of this shed for hours now but who knows. My shoes are tied up tight and I got the gun right here. The shoes or the gun: depends on who emerges. I can't believe I'm documenting this like I'm some kind of journalist caught in foreign crossfire! But maybe I'm just being paranoid? Maybe I *didn't* hear anything?...No, I *positive* I heard something this time. I was walking by the arbor and heard something in the thicket. It wasn't a scurrying animal either because it was constant and flat like footsteps. But I didn't hear a car. Could I even hear a car running from the driveway? I mean, why would someone walk into the orchard, or partially in, then nothing? I could (and still can) see if anyone would walk even to the front edge of the trees. I could definitely hear them. Maybe Abigail is back from Ireland? This is about the time she would be returning. Maybe she stopped at the house and what I heard was on the *other* side of the thicket? Yeah, that has to be it because by now the police would've showed up. At least I would think...It's an hour later. I'm hungry. Evening is approaching. I haven't ate since breakfast and I wanted to make a *hot* meal. I'm not going to just in case there's a case. But I think I'm safe now. Thank God. Maybe it was Ivy? Maybe she knows? Maybe she will come back in a bit, or maybe tomorrow? Maybe she was just shocked by the realization but once it settles in she'll come back? Who knows what would happen then? I guess I hope it *was* her. Better her than someone else. Perhaps best if it was just a deer? No, best if it was her. I would take the chance. What do I have to lose at this point anyway?...

July 4: Right.

July 9: ...and it rained last night. Me and Screwy just got back from refilling the bucket. On the way down to the creek we spotted a deer eating apples up in the orchard. It was so big, an 8-point. It had a silver shimmer to it. I was so absorbed. The way it ate was so graceful. It would pick up an apple and kind of sling its head to the side: I guess to get a better grip on it. I thought maybe I could pet it, like it could sense the peace I had with it, but it ran off as soon as it heard me. Then! at the creek, we spotted a raccoon over on the other side by the woods! It was soooo fat! It *didn't* run away! Screwy didn't like it! But I did! I would've went over and played with it if I didn't feel like getting wet. I was beating on the bucket, playing some made-up song, and it didn't even care! It's eyes were so awesome! Eyes as unfathomable and brilliant as were Hawthorne's! *With* Dean's Shadow! I think Pessi is here with me in spirit! He'll protect me! He's MY saint! St. Pessini disguised as a raccoon!...

July 12: I've been so paranoid since I heard that noise but I shouldn't be. Nothing's happened: proof in itself. Even though I consider myself safe here—(deep-down I know this, or at least I need to convince myself I know this)—there's still a cloud of fear hanging over me. Deep Down *versus* Over Me: what a—well, what a something! I'm trying to find some peace inside, trying to find a rational way to move ahead. Move beyond. Just get the fuck out of here! Meanwhile, it's like having an authoritative shadow right behind me, at all times, keeping me locked inside this box, moving from here to there, on the lookout. This place used to be so peaceful...

July 16: Lately I've been longing to walk around the orchard with great poets. Let's see: Shakespeare, Blake, Goethe, Byron, Shelley, Coleridge, Wordsworth, Keats, Yeats, and to make the circle an even thirteen, Wilde, Clare, and Gibran. I don't know why I still long for the impossible! What would we even say to each other? What would be the thing that would consume our time together? Them and I: we would look different, talk different, act different, think different, but feel so much the same. Well, I guess I just answered my question. I think I would be really good friends with Byron, Shelley, and Wilde. I can see me showing off by using improv wordplay to make fun of Wordsworth. Angered, he would run to Yeats and act all mature. Me, Byron, Shelley, and Wilde would probably end up creating an enclave by the end of the day: The Cool Coup Crew. Coo-coo. Coo-coo.

July 20: I seriously need to get out of here. Someone's bound to show up. I'm about halfway through my stock. I have the money to get *somewhere.* But where IS *somewhere?* I want to leave the country. I *need to* leave the country. I want to go to Catania so bad. (I was just looking at the pictures, balling my eyes out!) But besides my fear of stepping foot out of here and seeing what's actually going on, there's *something else* holding me back...It's that thing out there. I don't want to be a part of it. I just can't. No. But I can't stay here forever either...Haha. I just fucking realized I forgot my birthday! I'm 23 now! Five years gone! 23! I wanted to be close to marriage! I wanted to be a father soon! My little Quorra! That's all I can think about: that I'll never be a father, that I'll never have this amazing daughter who jumps on top of me and says, "Power up, Daddy! Power up!" I can see her! She's running all around the orchard! Chasing butterflies! Her long curly hair is decorated with glitter and forget-me-nots! Every silky strand and wild whorl flowing in cadence like a Venezuelan cascade! Angel Falls! Get up, hunny! She giggles, and it sounds like an Aeolian harp plucked by the wind!

Chi a nica dia![2] Oh God! she won't stop playing in my mystical matrix! But my little Quorra is an eternal quarry because she won't ever come into my arms and let me hold her even though I'm her Daddy!...

August 2: Ecclesiastes 1:17-18: "And I gave my heart to know wisdom, and to know madness and folly: I perceived that this also is vexation of the spirit. For in much wisdom is much grief: and he that increaseth knowledge increaseth sorrow." Amen to that...God, I'm seriously ready now. I know (and have long known) that I'm a great sinner. You know my reasons for every choice I've made, from the kindest to the cruelest things. As You also know, in my eyes, it's all been for the same. So I put my faith in You, not through the hand of man, but through Our disjoined hearts. Our connection lies in intuition, and through that, I have faith that the actions of man are all the same in the end, and it's through intuition where Your Word is truly read and overstood. Please, God, don't let them mock me. Please let me share a laugh with You. Let me cry away my sorrow and sins before You. Then let me cry in joy with Quorra. Let us dance with You, God, while Our little angel Quorra sings Us a song about Screwy and Razzu chasing each other's tails...

August 10: ...And I remember during my one summer class (a philosophy course) there was this beautiful girl —. Only seventeen but taking college credits while in high school. Her mother is a renowned —, and her father is a published —. Anyway, this girl blew my mind physically (such amazing lips), intellectually (the brightest person I've ever known around my age), and spiritually—well, I don't know what to say in that respect because she seemed to be a humanist. But still, she was so intriguing and did funny things inside me: I felt all these crazy energies. I never wrote her into the book, although we talked a lot, and even hungout a couple times, just me and her. Many reasons I kept her name out of my mouth. But I think she (by her own means) will be well known one day. She was like a female version of Dr. Rosenbaum, but less humorous while more directly philosophical. She would always say how she wasn't as well read as me, yet her supposed naïveté was so brilliant. I remember her saying, "Did you know that what seems cryptic always seems holy? and infatuation is attractive beyond anything else (because we create divinity through it) and so we worship the cryptic?"...

September 3: Well, I guess I finally "caught up to myself." Estivate and ye shall create—an ending. I didn't know how far to take it, but I ended it with me underneath the tree after I shot up. Then I painted a surreal picture of the future. Looking back, I think at the time I was hoping *everything* would've ended right there underneath the tree. Anyway, yeah, I guess my wonderful work is done! But since it's about my life I don't think it can ever have a consummated ending until I have an ending. But then who would write the ending for me? Don't really care right now. I'm just so fed up with writing! A rough calculation says with the time that has passed (three years), and the printed and handwritten pages here (total of 1,208), it

---

[2] [scn] What a little goddess!

roughly comes to a page a day. Doesn't seem like much of a day's work, but it's actually a ton with all the crafting involved. I even tried reading the so-called finished version straight through twice but I keep changing things. I want to try once more, this time with nothing in my hand, then see how I feel. But that's for another day because I'm so sick of it all. So drained. Anyway, even though I said the written word of Memory is nevertheless fiction, what's wrong with some blatant fiction in the mix? I mean, the thing with Luke and me returning at the same time to see the painting up on the wall? Although I was seriously out of my mind that weekend, and I still don't know what happened because I did think it happened, and it was Sunday, Luke didn't return until 4 or 5. I don't know if the reader would pick up on that. You would have to figure, Luke would be going to church back home, hanging out with family, perhaps go out to lunch, before driving back to college. Oh well, I'm leaving it like that. I'm not sure what I would call what I did to Father Carr, but he doesn't read Latin Scripture all the time; implicitly, from the *Vulgate.* I think the Latin Rite quit using the *Vulgate* in the 1500s. I guess it's satirical. Same with him looking like a turtle. Put two and two together: being a turtle + using an ancient book = symbolic of being slow to catch up on the times, so to speak, in a shell. Oh well. All in good fun. I like Father Carr. He's a nice man. We even share the same favorite biblical quote: "It is easier for camels to pass through the eye of a needle than rich men to enter the kingdom of God." I know he wouldn't like my book but who cares. I don't think many would. Hell, I really don't. Although I'm in a strange good mood, the book is nothing but a big pile of pain to me. I'm just glad it's finally off my back. Well, I'm going to go make my new dessert: mushed apple with cinnamon, cashews, and Nutella. Screwy loves apples! But he won't ever put that damn acorn down! *HMHMHMHMHM!!!*

September 5: I've finally come up with a title after changing it a million times. First it was *The Torture of the Artist as a Young Man,* but then I figured that would make my work sound like a satire, or worse, a self-indulgent pity party. Then I was thinking *The Shape of Literature to Come* as homage to *The Shape of Punk to Come* by Refused, one the best and innovative albums ever. But I decided it would be best to reflect deeper and give my work its own distinction: *Catapult Soul.* It can be interpreted in several ways but I won't spell them out. All I'll say is that it came to me as an image, this surreal, symbolic, three-second reel of what really happened...

...If I were to offer advice on writing it would be to never write extensively about a part of your life that you're still living out, especially when there exists the "catching up to yourself" element, because you will never catch up you to yourself. (Although fictional, even *Humbert* wrote about his craziness *after the fact.*) But in *my* process, you fall apart *in the chase*, from which you repeatedly experience sensations of the worst break-up in the world: dissociation, depersonalization. I believe writing an intricate book only intensified the sundry factors that have culminated in what I call *dissociative psychosis.* Yes, I believe, in a way, I'm psychotic, and was long before my artistic endeavor (when it was in its nascent form). That's the thing with this kind of psychosis: as opposed to standard psychosis in which you lack the rational capacity "to know," you're so aware of the dissociation. It's an over-awareness of your me's everywhere. (I can still see and feel them everywhere.) Out-of-body, you're also overaware of your constant estrangement in the present and ahh! I just lack the psychological touch! I'm laughing right now. Psychotic laughter? I guess, but not really: I'm too aware of the comedy. Dissociative psychosis, hahahahaha...

September 8: Looking back and feeling what I feel right now, I can only say there's no such thing as loveD, for through all this chaos and change, indecision and pain, confusion and deception, abandonment and betrayal, I still love her the same. Not more, not less: no such thing; just the same. And I truly believe I had all the power in the world to change the fate that has befallen me. But I also know I couldn't have made compromises between Art and Ivy. I really couldn't: the feelings were too strong each way, and both three-lettered trinities wanted the same thing from me: ME. Sure, I could've chosen to sacrifice the one I didn't—but lo! the causality paradox! To be able to go back and change it all? But then I wouldn't have all these lovely pages lying here to mock me in my loneliness and torture...This is funny: I just realized—wow, has my head actually been *this* foggy?—anyway, what I once thought would bring me and her a few small freedoms would now, with its ending, only bring me incrimination and cost me my life. Haha, I can't believe I'm this stupid! Even if I should happen to take a chance *out there,* I could never sell the book as is. It would kill me to make so many alterations. _Every thing_ needs to be there: _every sentence_ is a piece of the puzzle; _every word_ is a part of its image. Taking out certain pieces would essentially make the puzzle a broken image and thus unavailing, even though it already is because words can only go so far and say so much! My book is literally worthless! Over a thousand days fucking lost! Even this diary is incrimination of the insanity! It's "madness to keep this journal but it gives me a strange thrill to do so; and only a loving" peruser "could decipher my microscopic script." Furthermore, I don't think I can burn or drown these or those words because I have an instinctive drive to spell out my life in full, and the consequence of blank pages would ultimately be the negation of my existence...

September 8: A geyser is like the opposite of a waterfall, but I've never seen a geyser in person.

September 11: ...and so I wonder if me and eighteen of my friends would've rammed airplanes into those buildings, if they, in response, would've bombed Pennsylvania...

September 12: Ran out of beans. Looked around and apparently Jack didn't plant a reserve stalk for me to climb out of here.

September 14: So bored. Still going through musical withdrawal. Miss my music so much. Still can't believe I brought all my CDs. I just couldn't let go of them. Miss watching comedies too. *Really* miss lying in bed with her late at night, eating calzones and watching classic movies or PBS: listening to relaxing music and traveling to beautiful remote places filled with peace, culture, sometimes simplicity. Although I said I'm done writing for a while, I have nothing else better to do. Seems I can't just relax and enjoy Nature. I've been writing all different kinds of poetry. All of it sucks. I'm just not what I thought I was or could become, not even while immersed in a Romantic's paradise! I've also been writing quotes. I guess my quotes are decent. Some are pretty funny, on the surface, but most just show the bitterness I can't let go of *out there.* Here's my last 22: 1) What's *love* if not the thing you'll do anything and everything to get back once lost? What's *hate* if not the thing you'll do anything and everything to get rid of once found? 2) Individuality or Unity? I say there's room for both. 3) Live free, die happy. Live un-free, die happy. 4) I'll take a redrum with a rellik please. 5) Don't hate me 'cause I'm booed a fool! 6) I write my own quotes. Except this one. I obviously stole this from somebody really clever. 7) True friends: only a few have them, but only a few will admit that they don't. 8) I'm broken-minded too. 9) If you ever run out of ideas, try walking instead. 10) If you don't like what's going on behind your back, turn around. 11) A government full of Democrats would rather have you be a Republican, and a government full of Republicans would rather have you be a Democratic, than have you oppose both. 12) You might not be able to stomach it, but as long as you can mind it, your heart will be all right. 13) Dreams do come true, in dreams. 14) It's there, in the air, colored by the breath of my soul. – But what is it? – My memory in tears. 15) Some people put up a peace sign with one hand. Some put up the middle finger instead. I use two hands and put up both. 16) The Dynasty must die nasty. 17) How is it the War on Drugs has used up so much ammo but fired nothing but blanks? 18) Everyone tries to wish for more wishes; I just wish mine would come true. 19) We can all make birds fly away. 20) I want to be remembered by those who never knew me, and forgotten by those who thought they did. 21) As much as it hurts, I would rather miss someone than hit someone. 22) Strange where you'll find your peace of mind: wherever you find the missing piece of your heart.

September 15: Can't get this "poem" right. Supposed to be a poetic summary of my life but it sucks. So amateurish, incomplete, and filled with gaps. But I'm done with it. This is the last quarter of it, regarding the future:

...It might be a lie, it might be hope, but I'm in Messina now, looking about thirty-five years old. I'm a respected revolutionary and a decent writer (or so I've been told). But after writing that first book, and getting off the hook, I learned what's truly important to hold. Her! I'm so glad she took me back! Without her, I would've completely flown off the tracks. I remember back in the States—and this is funny—she goes, "Who could've killed them? and where have *you* been?" – "*Me?*" I tease. "Well, hey, you left, so I was out killing time by sending bellas to their knees!" Suddenly she flies at me and sticks her tongue down my throat. Then we have a good ol' conversation about God's Mysterious Ways before getting on the boat. Oh, Ma? She's doing just fine. We go down to Catania so she can see her granddaughter from time to time. Yep, my little Quorra: only five and already fluent in two languages. All day long she sings and dances and has a laugh that's so heartwarming and contagious. I swear I wouldn't trade one moment with her for another. Whenever I power up on her black curly hair, she giggles and says, "Never let little brother!" There is no little brother yet; Mommy's just been filling her head with wishes. Then just as quick as lightening strikes, Mommy collapses while doing the dishes. *Strange?* We both exercise and we both eat healthy, so why was *she* just diagnosed with a deadly disease? *Two months to live? Two months to say goodbye?* But were supposed to be together forever; that is, til the day we die. "It's just my time," she says with a smile on her face, "and so I want you to move on." "No!" I cry, my mind so far gone. "No one can ever take your place!" – "Aww, you're too sweet. Will you power up on my hair?" Ignoring her request, I say, "What about Quorra? Don't you even care? She's gonna grow up without a mother! Or a brother named Zach! She's going to spend her life blaming God and Society for the things she'll always lack!" – "What do you want me to do? It's just the way it is. So will you please come lie next to me and fulfill my final wish?" And so I do; I shove a healthy lock deep inside my mouth. *"POWER UP!!!"* (Which one of us really needs help?) But how we laugh and kiss and of course reminisce. Then comes the *flash*...

...."Why can't Mommy move anymore?" Quorra asks candidly. "Because Mommy had to go to Heaven," I reply with her body pressed against me. "Will we ever see her again?" she asks, her face growing sadder with every second that goes by. After I bounce her upward in my arms, I say, "Sure: every time you close your eyes." So she closes her eyes and suddenly smiles. When she opens them (so artless her face), she cries, "Daddy, you're silly; I can't see Mommy with my eyes closed!" "Oh, hun," I begin, my face so hard to hold, "one day you will and well before you're old." "Promise?" she asks quickly. "Promise," I reply strongly, assuring her with Daddy's same ol' smile. Then we turned around. And as Fear drove my tongue, Force drives our legs back down the aisle...

...Driving to the airport, it's just me and her. A heavy rain has just begun to fall. Everything before us is swirling into a blur. I have no idea the roads I'm taking. The music on the radio goes silent. Even Quorra seems to be fading. I head down one way...soon I'm heading back. I pause—then go—pause—then go: forward my mind wants to head, but my heart pines for the past! We drive around the city...the town...then the woods. Occasionally I run my hands through her hair; I would kiss her if I could. She says she doesn't like this new place, then asks to go back to the big plane. I tell her, "But this is where Mommy and Daddy grew up," and whisper to myself, "*I can't really tell if things have changed...*" Finally the rain settles, conforming to a rhythmic drizzle. I believe Quorra has fallen asleep now, for her head hangs down flaccidly in the middle. The hours seem to be passing by as if each is turning twice. And since I'm still confused, I think about waking up Quorra, for any direction would be nice. Perhaps she senses this because she suddenly takes hold of my free hand. (It feels good to know someone's always there even when things don't go as planned.) Then my little muse looks out the window and says, "Look at the moon, Daddy! It's so big tonight!" And so I look up at that big moon and its scintillating light—then my eyes focus on another familiar sight. I'm instantly connected together with it—my essence—like Irony and Life. Yes, the orchard: that's where these roads have brought me, like it's all been one straight road to the end. But as soon as I focus on the orchard, Quorra says, "Daddy, is it time to go home yet?" I touch her hair and say, "*There, there.*" Forever and Ever. Amen.

September 16: I was out walking around earlier, feeling so bored and lonely. I walked down along the creek and found a little pathway off to the left where I could climb up the cliff. So I did. Just a bunch of woods and stuff at the top. But walking around I spotted (up ahead) a bird on the ground. It had sleek gray feathers with a fluffy white chest spotted posthumously with red where another bird was pecking away at it. You know, eating it. Such sanguinary primitiveness: kind of made me sick. But funny thing is, the miniature feast of hearts (its two avian lovers together til death do they not part—yet bound to pick apart the void!) only made me feel lonelier. Made me realize that even *loneliness* comes from an inherent intuition that love exists, and that there's an absence of it.

September 17: I just ran out of contact solution. I woke up (contacts still in as usual) and went to dump solution in my eyes because they were so dry and my vision so clouded, and the last drop came splashing down. Now I'm out. I need solution for many things. I took my contacts out and put on these glasses from who knows when; I think they were last updated in 11th grade. Now I *really* can't see where I'm going. I was thinking about just walking out, finding the closest phone, and calling one of my friends to come pick me up. I would have to tell them what's been going. But I could trust them with my life; that is, I could trust Jeremiah and Eddie with my life. But Anson's the one who would know how to get me out of the country on the low...I don't know. I'm growing so weak and apathetic. On one hand, I have a burning desire to get out of here and start a new life somewhere far away. On the other, I think how unrealistic that sounds. This coming from someone who's in *this* situation. HA! My life HAS become a real-life myth! Brings to mind Daedalus and Icarus. They actually found a way to escape *their* labyrinth. Unfortunately, I don't have feathers or wax to make wings. Funny how fucking Daedalus could make it to Sicily but I can't, and I have the option of taking a plane! Ahh, poor Ma. I would be such a disgrace to her. I could never explain to her why Ivy isn't with me and why I'll never be happy. But maybe I could still get by on one of the Ionian Islands? I'm such a dork: I actually know the names of the Eptanese: Zakynthos, Corfu, Lefkada, Kefalonia, Kythira, Ithaki! All right off the coast of Greece! So far away! I would even settle for living down in Latin America. Maybe on a Caribbean island. I can see myself in Dominica. Waterfalls there. You can jump off some. That would be awesome. I can see myself crying (submerged in the deepest cry) while watching the way of exotic animals. Maybe Saint Vincent and the Grenadines would accept me out of love for the name. I think they even speak English there. Or Saint Lucia. Maybe there I could see my way through this. Maybe—well, maybe I don't know. Maybe I should've been something else in this crazy world. I'm good with voices. Could've done voices for cartoons. Kept myself young. Could've taught lit and prevented the next revolutionary from going overboard. (I know Dr. Rosenbaum tried with me, not because he disliked my visions of a better world, but because he sensed what kind of fate would be before me.) Or I could've studied law and been a lawyer: "go where the real money is." Or I could've been a consulting-coordinator and coordinated things while consulting stuff. This jack could've found his niche in many trades, instead of doing this, being this, in this...Fuck, it's getting cold out. I'm trying to keep myself warm by visualizing my prospects. Memories are so cold. But visions are so warm. I can vividly see me and Quorra here in the orchard...

September 26: Right now I'm underneath the ol' apple tree. It's 6:30 p.m. Getting dark out. A slight breeze blowing. Everything is calm besides some damn bird I can't spot. It keeps squawking. The leaves are beginning to drop: Nature's ironic sign that it's time to start bundling up because it's going to be getting real cold. I have hoodies, long johns, and my lion blanket. Who knows how that will hold up? The bigger problem seems to be food: I'm almost out. I mean, what am I going to do: survive off apples, grapes, nuts, berries, and fish? (Ahh, my tears are already staining the page. I'm fucking ruining this page. Hold on.) Yeah, so I've been crying for the last half an hour. Since I came back from my walk. I took a real long walk today. To a place I've never been. I started off going along the creek. When I got to the point where I crossed over before, I crossed but kept going straight. It was amazing. The creek kept getting wider and wider. The woods nearing an end. I could see a field up ahead. Out across: a barn, a house, a road running left-right. Probably a whole new town on the *other* side. But I didn't go any further because in the creek was the most amazing thing: waterfalls! Yes, this part of the creek had *three* waterfalls! Just drops of a foot or so but they were surprisingly loud. The water was roaring. It's all I could hear. And the path opened up to a kind of beach on both sides. Basically all sand. So spongy and mossy. It barely left footprints. There were a couple fire pits around the area. But the creek! The waterfalls! These huge rocks! The one rock that caused the first waterfall looked like a huge bronze eagle submerged underwater with its wings spread from bank to bank, probably twenty yards wide, the water just crashing over the aquiline rock. It looked like the eagle was coming up to the surface, just about to break free. The sun was brilliantly shining down on the water, casting yellow and silvers gleams everywhere, rocking out rhythmically, interminably, as new ones formed, *na sfunnacata rì calancuni lustri, quacchi aggentu, quacchi giannu, quacchi iancu...cc'èrunu culura tantu ca i mè senzi nun î putèvunu abbrazzari.*[3] On the other side, down a little further, was a rock island jutting upward. So huge! It had different levels to it! The water coming off the second waterfall was repeatedly crashing into it, splitting the water into a Y, sneaking around each side of the rock island. There were so many other rocks in the most extraordinary shapes and colors! In some areas you could leap from one to the next. But the biggest rock was right on the edge of my shore, half planted in the sand, half submerged in the water. Just this rough jagged rock taller than me. Probably weighed five tons. I climbed to the top like I was an explorer who just discovered new land, thousands of acres, beautiful and pure. Down below I could see schools of minnows. I wanted to go out into the water to lie on a rock right in the middle and relax. So I climbed down and began jumping rocks (at one point, almost falling in)

---

[3] [scn] a multitude of shiny ripples, some silver, some yellow, some white...more colors than my senses could handle

until I was out in the middle of the creek. I laid down on a big flat bronze rock. The water wasn't really splashing up but it was wet. I didn't care. I just laid back and closed my eyes. Back behind me: the gurgling sound of the second waterfall. I could even differentiate it from the louder roars of the eagle rock that was back another ten yards. The water was streaming passed me. Indescribable sounds and sensations. Actually nodded off. When I woke up, I turned over, facing the eagle (or towards the orchard). I was wading my hand in the water. I could see the fish. I started crying so hard. Looking all around me. The waterfalls: just like my tears: how it flushed over the curl: like my cheeks. The real rapid parts of the creek here and there so white and bubbly. But all was becoming a blur. The sound just engulfed me. I was gone. For a while. But I had to come back sometime, which is why I'm here underneath this ol' apple tree, still crying so heavily, as it can be seen: the furrowed stains, the scrawl of letters. Oh well...

...All right. I'm back. I went and got a couple poems I've been working on. Of course I had to get Screwy, the lock, the gun, and smokes. I'm just going to work on these poems for a while then who knows what. Screwy says he's cold. I told him I'll make him a hoodie if he hands over the acorn. No deal. Haha. Ehh, even Screwy knows we can't stay here forever. But we don't want to go back *out there* ever again. Screwy's like me: he doesn't like the thought of being trapped. Sorry, Screwy. At least—hold on. All right. Damn the wind is blowing like a motherfucker! Just making it colder. Reminds me of my old house. I remember how my room was on the "weather side." That's what Rick called it. I used to complain because it was real hot in the summer and real cold in the winter. He would say it's because my room is on the "weather side." Like the wind *only* blew in that direction. I believed it when I was little, not knowing all sides are weather sides. I think? But the house was poorly built. The windows sucked. Bad cocking and whatnot. God, that place was such a hellhole! It just sits atop the ground. Nothing underneath but the frame and pipes! I know because there was a hole right next to the bathtub, up by the spigot. I don't know how it got there, but if you pealed the carpet back you could reach down and touch dirt. There were holes all over the place. Even in the ceiling. Well, not really holes there but certain places were rotted out: all orange, brown, cracked, and lumpy. Whenever it rained, me and Ma would get out the "rain pots" and set them up to catch the rain. Haha, I remember exactly were each one went too: right when you walk in the front door, one by the back door, one by the cabinets that would leak down on the counter, and one right in front of the toilet. Rain pots! Haha, I would give anything to be back in that hellhole setting up rain pots! But back then it was just one of those things I was so embarrassed about. One more thing that made me hate my father even more. I never got that man. Like how he would never allow us to turn the thermostat above 70˚. I guess partly a money issue. Besides, people used to tell me that the weather in Heaven is always perfect—at 70˚! But I swear our thermostat was broke: 70˚ was really 60˚. We even had a winter where we had to heat the house with the oven for a month because the gas bill got too far behind. Oh well. I know he didn't want that and it deeply shamed him. But there were still so many other intolerable things he did. Like him hitting Ma and whatever he did to Razzle. No matter what, I still think, "Murderer." Like father like—I won't even write it. Oh the past to the present. It might still be so surreal and scary but I've truly made peace with God. I guess underneath all this misery there's a small sense of peace because they kind of took away my soulmate and best friend. But just like my father, it wasn't really them but rather something deeper, underneath the surface, and I'm afraid I didn't even scratch it...

...I've learned that words can never describe how much I miss her, or prove that I could never be happy without her. But so many people would be quick to give me their fast-remedies for heartbreak and strong lines for fish in the sea. Ahh! how sick that would make me! But what can I do about it now? Oh well....*Mmmmm.* I can't stop chewing on her hair. Tastes so good. So much life in it. It IS Life. I swear it is! Fuck any aesthetic philosophy or psychological disorder (or order) that might be behind it! It's just fucking hair! But it's HERS! And I love it so much! So spiritual and powerful! My lustrous common gold! The stitching of virtue in my soul! The strand that's held me together throughout my loneliness! I'll never let it go! I might not be able to stop crying—and, yes, it's tears of sorrow and self-pity—but this hair makes me so happy, no matter what. Although it's not hope, it IS my salvation. Yes! Just like Dostoyevsky said, "You're told a lot about your education, but some beautiful, sacred memory, preserved since childhood, is perhaps the best education of all. If a man carries many such memories into life with him, he is saved for the rest of his days. And even if only one good memory is left in our hearts, it may also be the instrument of our salvation one day." And I have the most beautiful, scared memory twined into this lock! The instrument of my salvation! *Heeeeey Prooooooust! Guuuuuess whaaaaat?* I've come upon my material object, but too bad I had an inkling! So—a long time! always! Ivy's hair in my mouth! (Something, something.) I AM drinking deep the wine of memory! (I'm sure Baudelaire won't care that I too love hair, and changed his words.) Ah Brown, Brown Ivy, Brown Ivy, I am looped in the loops of your hair! Yep...Now sigh, sigh, sigh. What else is there to do anymore? Be critical and penetrative? So strategic and strong-willed? I no longer care to. I'll just chew on a thought and write about it. Chew on this lock and cry about it. Laugh and rhyme. Just fruitlessly pass the time. Until I accidentally choke to death on the lock, or the paper runs out. Yep, I'm locked in here, for life. I'm not running off to anywhere, ever. But who cares? I still have a box of wine and an eternal lock of hair, barring it doesn't get suicidal on me and run off to a salon!...

...Okay, back. Just watching a plane pass through the evening stars up in that sweet multihued sky. Getting a little drunk now and (hold on: need to readjust). *Hmmm.* This is pretty strange: I'm lying down (with my head resting on my arm, which is spread out on the ground) and I'm looking down through the darkening field without my contacts in or glasses on, but I think I can actually see the ends of the weeping willows. Reminds me of a time I went wandering...and look! I can still see our shadows playing underneath the weeping willow and holding hands as we walk back up to here. We *are* here. Here we are! Now I overstand what he meant: I really don't have to let her go. I just have to let her be. I just have to let us be. Look, Screwy. Isn't it so beautiful?

* * *

That was the last passage in the diary. The entirety of ninety-two passages omitted. Separate from the diary are two pages previously withheld: the first and last page of the large stack. Both hand-written. The first page reads *Catapult Soul* by Vincent Vallano, for Wimp-Wimp. The last page as follows:

I lie down on the roots of insanity,
Screaming for my soul to be free,
As your tears drop from the apple tree,
I squeeze my way into eternity.

"Sternitur infelix alieno vulnere, coelumque, adspicit et moriens ducles reminiseitur...pomarium."[4]

* * *

On November 8, 2004, Abigail McArdle's husband Brian Seaver found him lying underneath the apple tree. He ran back out and called the police, and subsequently he was taken away. Various pieces of paper, including those of the diary, were strewn throughout the orchard. Atop his chest were leaves that had fallen from above. Beneath the leaves, his hand was held over his heart. The lock was in the grass but still resting against his neck, presumably having slipped from his mouth. Screwy was sitting down in the apple cubbyhole, presumably placed there intentionally. Although he kept his heart pure, his mind apparently couldn't take it anymore. On November 8, 2004, Vincent Ignazio Scandurra Vallano was found dead from a self-inflicted gunshot to the head. They say it happened a week prior. I didn't find out until the evening after they found him when two policemen showed up with Screwy, the lock, and a pile of papers addressed to me: these were the only things around him. They said that Vinny had put the papers inside a plastic bag and placed a large rock on top to keep them from getting wet or blown away. At the time, the police were unaware of the answers that lie behind the cover. The two who came to my house—neither of whom Vinny had ever encountered—are friends of the family. They live in my neighborhood and have known me since I was little. The one is the father of my fiancé, Eli. I suppose he gave me the papers instead of considering it potential evidence because he felt it was something personal that belonged only to me. After being questioned about everything, I was told that the gun was Teresa's dad's. I just didn't know that he was in the

---

[4] [lat] He falls, unhappy, by a wound intended for another, looks up to the skies, and dying, remembers the sweet orchard.

orchard all along. For some reason, I had a feeling that he went to Catania after graduation; he was always saying that he wanted go there and see his family and finally take a "real vacation" before starting his career. Anyway, the police told me that it was now an open-and-shut case, but if I ever came across anything relevant in the thousands of papers to let them know. Although our math had never been certain, he did it about a month after what would've been our fifth anniversary. It's possible that he did it intentionally on November 2nd, All Souls' Day, an important holiday in Sicily. It's based on the Roman Catholic doctrine that states there are "souls of the faithful" still suffering in purgatory because at death they hadn't been cleansed or atoned for past transgressions. This means these souls in purgatory can't attain the Beatific Vision but might be able to through prayer, the sacrifice of Mass, and the celebrations on All Souls' Day. Vinny told me that on this day his mother used to bake a cake with funny skulls on it and cinnamon cookies shaped like bones called *ossa di morti*. And the night before, she would leave a present and candy by his bed. But in spirit of the tradition, deceased relatives are the ones who leave these things. I remember him saying that the presents are called *murticeddi,* which means "dear little dead ones." This year he never received his *murticeddu,* but he did become one.

The police found lots of other papers in the shed and scattered throughout the orchard. Many were poems. One was his last poem to me, which is for my eyes only. One was a poem written in Sicilian and addressed to his mother; apparently it was about how to "mend her broken wings" and join the other angels in the Kingdom of God. He wrote a long, erratic, unfinished letter to his father. They also found a loose paper expressing his "dying wish" in which Vinny talked about how he might die of starvation. This paper seems to side with argument that he had gone insane at some point. His handwriting is different than the papers of the book and diary. Plus, a lot of it doesn't make sense. He wrote a good bit on his failures as "the artist who was destined to change the world, and now the world won't let me back in. They exiled me and want me to die in exile." It ends with a desperate plea that if he should happen to die before he can get out, he wants his body to be dropped naked and freely into the Ionian Sea. Of course that wasn't allowed. So his mother and I decided to bury him in Verna, by Pessi. Although he had distanced himself from nearly everybody as the years went by, a lot of people showed up to his funeral, which was nine months prior to writing this. So many unknown faces kept telling me how much they loved Vinny, how he was "one of a kind," "so funny," "so smart," "so true." As I stood there in shock, I listened to them telling each other all these stupid stories. It didn't make any sense. Everyone seemed to have these narrow (and wrong) perceptions of who he was. They all thought *their* memories of him were him in whole, and it only made me cry harder. Then, at the gathering, I met Anson, and from him the beginning of this story was finally revealed, one Vinny never came to know about. And I mean "the beginning of this story" as in what really allowed us all to meet. First, Anson isn't Anson. He is the only one Vinny renamed; just like I thought it best to rename "Eli" and "Jackson." Funny how three small-role characters—one on Vinny's side, one on mine, and one on Teresa's—ended up being the only ones with protected identities. Anyway, I'm able to explain some of this since Teresa and Anson have different last names. (Sorry, this is on my laptop and I'm stumped. I just don't want anyone to take this as Anson being some criminal at-large.) But whenever Teresa would visit family in Pittsburgh, she would hangout with Anson. Then she would bring back drugs for herself until she befriended Jackson when she was sixteen. Yes, unbeknownst to Vinny, Jackson and Teresa go way back. At some point, Jackson wanted Teresa to see if Anson would hook him up with large quantities of marijuana. Anson agreed. So Jackson would drive up to Pittsburgh once a month, then come back and sell to it "middlemen" who pushed it to students and other locals. Then Anson said Jackson asked if he could get heroin. Anson didn't sell it but knew someone who did. And well, as you can see, what started off as two distant cousins culminated in a drug connection between a big city and a small town/private college. I'm sure there are other stories that have resulted from that, but the one that solidified *my* circle, and *this* story, was Vinny applying to Aristod, trying to "get away," while his friend had already and unknowingly began the circle that would bring it all back together years later when that same friend (again unknowingly) would help Vinny erase that circle *(shhhhh)*. But see, ladies and gentlemen, the only person Vinny erased was himself. He never killed Teresa and Jackson. They are still alive and were never even approached by him. The last part of his book that's "real" seems to be him leaving Aristod to live in the orchard. After that it's either a mixture of myth and reality, or he went insane early on and truly believed he killed them. It's really anyone's call. Personally, I believe he set out to do what he said he did but backed out because of moral reasons. After that, he started driving himself crazy over how to end the book—to come up with "the perfect ending"—so he decided to write the ending as he envisioned it or wanted it to be. Under this premise, an artistic genius existed and preceded any state of insanity. I know that he was, in fact, mentally tortured and had been long before we met. It's just a matter of when the torture finally pushed him to the brink. In other words, when did he lose full rational capacity: the day he left college? the day he supposedly went to Jackson's through the woods? or maybe it came gradually as he continued out his days in the orchard while keeping a diary? or right after the last passage? or maybe it suddenly happened right before he killed himself? Nobody will ever know, and perhaps deep down he knew this, like his heart felt it coming and it pushed him to finish his work as he did. Again, this would mean a touch of genius existed along with the insanity. However, if you want to side with the argument that what happened with the end of the work and his life was purely driven by psychosis and delusion, I can tell you that all the prerequisites are there. Also, Vinny had several medical conditions besides panic attacks that he never mentioned. First, he was a synesthete. He would often tell me how he could taste colors and see colors in and around shapes, numbers, and words. No, it's not linked to psychosis but it's still neurological. Second, he started suffering from another neurological disorder about five months before we broke up: hypnic jerks. It was awful. He would keep jerking up right before falling asleep. At first, he thought it was sleep apnea so he took a polysomnogram but it came back negative. His sleep doctor ended up prescribing him Valium. It didn't help much. On a good night he would jerk up only four or five times. On a bad night it was endless. He said they felt so weird and not like the typical "falling sensation" as others described them in online forums. It got to the point where he said he was so afraid to go to sleep because he thought he was going to die or that he simply didn't feel like battling it. As a result, he didn't sleep much, although he never really did to begin with.[5] Finally, the things he said about his dissociation and feeling "fragmented" are true. It could very well be that he came to a point where he could no longer distinguish reality from fiction. Certain forms of dissociation have strong isolationist qualities, which would make sense of his desire to retreat then remain alone in the orchard. If anything, this would be the most genuine "medical evidence" that suggests he had slipped into insanity, and therefore the end of his book wasn't a "conscious literary effort" on his part but rather an intense delusion. The only other evidence that I can think of that would support true insanity is that his struggles with Art and Life, for they were as true as he wrote them, finally overtook him. But again, the question of *When?* remains.

Since his death, I've had several lengthy discussions with Dr. Rosenbaum to try to fill in the missing pieces. He, too, has a different perception of who Vinny was, although like Pessi and I, he got to see the same loving and sensitive side of Vinny that many others didn't. He has already read the manuscript three times and said that he is going to do everything in his power to see that it becomes part of the literary cannon. He said that he considers it "one of the most courageous and sincere works ever penned," "an unbelievable accomplishment for someone his age," "ultimately unpretentious, for it remains coherent and readable, yet so layered that it will take several generations of critics to fully understand its significance." When I asked Dr. Rosenbaum about the ending, he said that he believes Vinny probably *did* contemplate killing Teresa and Jackson. He said that, looking back on their discussions, one of Vinny's biggest conflicts was whether to "take charge like Nietzsche's Übermensch or be passive and turn the other cheek like Christ." On a similar note, Dr. Rosenbaum said that Vinny often praised Tolstoy for clearly pointing out the contradictions in the *Bible,* namely an eye-for-an-eye vs. non-resistance to evil by force, the Nicene Creed vs. the Sermon on the Mount, and thus illustrating the stark difference between the teachings of the Church and the teachings of Christ. Dr. Rosenbaum went on to say that he believes Vinny ultimately did what he felt was right in his heart: followed Christ and turned the other cheek. He said that Vinny was alluding to this when he mentioned in the diary that he brought "*The Kingdom of God is within You* (my newfound connection with Christ) and my old-school *Bible* (the former barrier between me and God)," which what you see in parentheses is what Vinny had written in the margin with arrows pointing to the original text. Dr. Rosenbaum also believes that Vinny started the diary for the typical reason: to keep a daily log, but then Vinny realized the irony in it, given that he had joked about the aspiring writer who ends up becoming a slaving diary-keeper. And so according to Dr. Rosenbaum, Vinny "creatively and ironically stitched the diary into what would become the end of his novel.

---

[5] Surprisingly they found no traces of drugs in his body. Not even his sleep medication. Therefore, any drugs that he may have taken to the orchard were either consumed early on or washed away at some point.

After having read the diary closely, it looks like some of it was real, as in it shows what he was actually doing, feeling, and thinking, and some of it (namely the murder snippets) was intentionally forged in order to make his last chapters appear authentic until explained otherwise to the reader. I believe it was his genius shining through one last time, not to exclude the fact that it subtly (and perhaps consciously on his part) keeps his work in line with *A Portrait of an Artist as a Young Man* where it suddenly ends with Dedalus writing a few diary passages." But it's still debatable whether Vinny truly intended the diary to be a formal part of *Catapult Soul* since it was left untitled.[6] Dr. Rosenbaum also pointed out that there's a rhythmic flow to the chapter titles, and not only do they play on things within the chapters, but they also tell an abstract story if you read them straight down. For this reason, Dr. Rosenbaum gave the diary a fitting ironic title, making *Catapult Soul* an even 30 chapters. When I told him that I was asked to write the "final ending," he slightly smiled and said, "Well then I guess it will end with the greatest irony of all." What he was referring to is that, in a way, this book tore Vinny and I apart, and when I saw it beginning to happen, I resented him for starting it, and yet I'm the one who's finishing it. The last thing Dr. Rosenbaum wanted to contribute is that he is indeed of the same opinion as I am in that Vinny ultimately made the right moral decision and remained (or became) a true Christian, finished the book on his own accord and to his liking, and only afterwards slipped into a full-blown state of insanity due to any of the reasons listed above.[7]

   I really don't know what else to say. His mother is back in Sicily. The few times I've tried talking to her on the phone, she sounded so vacant. She wasn't even crying. She would just mumble things in Sicilian. Her English wasn't the clearest either. Without trying to sound disrespectful, I would tell her that I can't understand her. She would suck in a breath as if preparing to speak clearly then say things like, "Yes, Ivy dear, it's not *your* fault," or "Don't worry; Vinny is with God now. *Mmhmm, mmhmm.*" Such is the shock and confusion here in LaSalle. Two tragic deaths in four years. I guess for people from big cities, two homicides in four years seems petty. But since LaSalle has long been known as a crime-free community, it's remained the talk of the town and college. It honestly feels like *everyone* knows who I am now and they all hate me. I'm sure many do or will. But I'm changing my name, since it really is Ivy Pineda, and Eli and I are moving away. I have an internship working with animals. And I promise if I ever come across any

---

[6] Despite being heavily marked with random notes and symbols, the word "art" was not altered anywhere in the diary. Dr. Rosenbaum suggests that Vinny underscored everywhere "art" appears in the work the first time he read it simply for the fun of discovery. Then Vinny struckthrough it during the second read out of frustration. Hence, art.

[7] In her critique "When Reality Ruins Fiction," Dr. Chalipa Niknam of Cornell University criticized Dr. Rosenbaum and Ivy for "romanticizing and moralizing" Vincent's end within the work itself, stating that it was selfish to "allow their delusions and coddling of Vincent to sweeten the taste for the reader, instead of letting the natural bleakness—the existential aura that Vincent couldn't seem to escape—speak for itself." (http://www.chalipaniknam.com/lc, 2007) –Ed.

sick or injured squirrels, I'll take care of them to the best of my ability. I'll power them up. God, it may seem like Vinny exaggerated all the things about the squirrels, but I truly think he wanted to be one. I know if I had bought him that full-body squirrel suit he would've worn it *everywhere.*

There are other things that I can fill you in on about Vincent Vallano. One thing, he was very compassionate and generous. He spent many weekends and holidays doing community service, especially things dealing with sick children, abused animals, and the poor. He refused to celebrate Thanksgiving because he claimed it's the same thing as celebrating "the rape, slaughter, robbery, and deception suffered by Native Americans." He also donated money to various charities, even though it was money from school loans. He was an avid Pittsburgh Steelers and Penguins fan. (We went to about ten games together.) His favorite athlete was Joe Sakic. His favorite coach was Joe Paterno. In the "dying wish" letter, he said that he would do anything to die to listening to "Vincent" by Don McLean because "it's so beautifully sad. Obviously written about Van Gogh, but technically he only says 'Vincent,' so I'd like to believe he was prophesying my life, instead of recounting Van Gogh's. Either way, I can just will myself hear it over and over in my head, right? I'm already sitting in the setting." Although he loved folk songs like "Vincent," he lived and breathed Punk Rock. But he often expressed his discontent with the current Punk Rock culture, saying that in many cases it has become the thing it claims to hate. On this matter, I don't know enough to go into detail because, to be honest, many times it simply didn't interest me. Anyway, he watched a lot of old and foreign films and seemed to enjoy them more at night when he would sit up in bed and twirl my hair until I fell asleep. His all-time favorite movie was *La Vita E Bella.* And yes, he read more books in one year than you'll read in your lifetime. For someone who struggled to understand the essence of Time, he sure knew how to economize it, except for when it came to me.

Now, I'm not sure if it had been an on-going thing or a last-minute thing but Vinny had thoroughly organized his notes on his works, which included a detailed list of everything that had been rejected by magazines, literary agents, and publishers. It started when he was sixteen. In the end, he had seven short stories rejected 49 times; fifteen poems rejected 225 times; sample chapters from *Catapult Soul* rejected 22 times; and his query letter for *Catapult Soul* rejected 50 times. Not one person had ever expressed any interest in his works. The letters and e-mails he saved pretty much all say the same thing: "Not for us. But best of luck." Neither Dr. Rosenbaum nor I knew that he had attempted publication before going to the orchard. With regard to *Catapult Soul,* I believe he struggled to show how sharp he actually was in conversation. By that, I mean his dialogue, in my opinion, doesn't even come close to showing how witty he was in person, as opposed to him as a writer where he might have "overdone" things here and there and insisted upon himself and his work. Perhaps that sprung from a subconscious desire to compensate for what he couldn't show through dialogue? I'm not really sure. Sounds kind of Freudian, and I hate Freud. Oh yes, don't think I don't have literary interests too. Anyway, in a typical conversation Vinny was very sarcastic, in such a dry way, and would play off what people said like a game of racquetball. I honestly don't think there's anybody who could have outwitted him or been quicker to make someone laugh over the stupidest off-the-wall things. He could even make what would sound lame coming from someone else sound charming, hilarious, clever, etc. etc. I can't stress enough the natural command he had on language and expression. But nobody besides me, Pessi, and Dr. Rosenbaum really saw anything past his comedic façade. With that said, he still kept many things to himself, and these things, as I learned, he could only reveal to Art.

So I guess you're wondering how and why *I* ended up here on the page? Well, after several stories about Vinny aired on the news in Pittsburgh, I was contacted by a literary agent. She wanted to read the first three chapters of his book. I sent them but not before receiving legal advice; I wasn't sure who actually owned *Catapult Soul*, and I was told that I do or legally would once his mother and I go over some matters. After sorting things out, the agent called back and said that she wanted to read the entire manuscript. I had the entire thing copied then mailed it. A month later, she wanted to represent *Catapult Soul.* She said that with everything surrounding it, it's sure to be bought by a major publisher, possibly become a bestseller, maybe even a movie.[8] At first, I was a bit skeptical because Vinny wrote that, after finding out how things "really work," he wanted to self-publish *Catapult Soul* or find an independent publisher that would allow him to keep control. But she assured me that the work will be honored by those he would've wanted to read it, and that his words will be kept pure, only editing "the obvious." Then she asked if I cared to write a short ending that filled the reader in on what exactly happened. But since knowing "exactly" what happened is impossible, I just took this approach. Besides, through his eyes, nearly everything he said *is* true. After reading the book, I now believe he never slept with Teresa. I really do. And not because of that last fictionalized scene where he had Teresa confess (as if it was his way of letting me know the truth when all was said and done), but because I think I *made* myself believe it happened. Perhaps *I* was the one who was really scared of the future, of "growing up," even if I was the one who had pushed for it. Either way, I'm now left with a million what-ifs to haunt me for the rest of my life. I honestly don't know what else to say. I don't have the words or energy to explain "my side" or tell "my story," and I doubt I ever will. After reflecting on everything—the words of his book and my memories of "the real"—I'm just left with this strange feeling crawling all through me, making me wonder if I have anything at all.

At the present moment, *Catapult Soul* is in the pre-printing process. Who really knows what will happen? Maybe Vincent Vallano *will* become a famous writer posthumously. And maybe as a result, more people will start waking up to the things going on around us. Maybe if we "overstand" things aren't always as they seem, we will finally rise up and take a stand. Like Vinny once said to me in a random debate: "This ain't about politics; this is about life, and it's simple: divide *any* heart and it *will* stop beating."

Yep.

---

[8] Close friend and former colleague, Dr. Holland of New York University has been consulting with Dr. Rosenbaum on a screenplay.

Well, ladies and gentlemen, this concludes the story of an artist who started something that resulted in his end, but maybe this will also be the start of something new. I'm not sure if Vinny would want me to point out that it seemed like Chapter 0 had little to do with the story that followed, but here it is repeated: "History, lie of our lives, mire of our loins. Our sins, our souls." I believe he was using the Lolitan parody as a way of saying it's always a few who benefit from everybody else's sacrifice while we're made to believe, and remain ignorant enough to believe, it's the other way around. Then again, I could be way off. Either way, no matter how well *Catapult Soul* sells, I plan to send 20% of the profits to his mother; 20% to Arba Sicula to help preserve the Sicilian language and culture; 20% to Eddie and Jeremiah; 20% to a charity that helps the sick and poor; and if I ever have a girl, her middlename will be Quorra and the other 20% will go towards her education. I think this appropriation would've made Vinny really happy. Seems to cover everybody he considered family, from his blood, to his best friends, to the robbed and forgotten, to his imaginative hope up ahead—*her.* I swear to God I never knew he was dying to start a family—dying to bring alive some imaginary little girl named Quorra. Seems Dr. Rosenbaum said it best: he had an impenetrable core ♡

4292297

Made in the USA
Lexington, KY
12 January 2010